W9-DGB-239

LIFE
A USER'S MANUAL

LIFE
A USER'S MANUAL

Georges Perec

Translated by David Bellos

David R. Godine, Publisher
Boston

First published in English in 1987 by
DAVID R. GODINE, PUBLISHER, INC.
Horticultural Hall
300 Massachusetts Avenue
Boston, Massachusetts 02115

Originally published in French in 1978 by Hachette

Assistance for the translation of this volume was given by the French Ministry of Culture.

Library of Congress Cataloging-in-Publication Data
Pérec, Georges, 1936–1982.
Life, a user's manual.
Translation of: La vie, mode d'emploi.
Includes index.
I. Title.
PQ2676.E67V513 1987 843'.914 87-8782
ISBN 0-87923-700-7

Second printing, March 1988
Printed in the United States of America

This book was set in Galliard. Designed by Matthew Carter and introduced in 1978 by the Mergenthaler Linotype Company, Galliard is based on a type made by Robert Granjon in the sixteenth century, and is the first of its genre to be designed exclusively for phototypesetting. A type of solid weight, Galliard possesses the authentic sparkle that is lacking in the current Garamonds. The italic is particularly felicitous and reaches back to the feeling of the chancery style, from which Claude Garamond in his italic had departed.
The book was designed by Peter Carr.

to the memory of
RAYMOND QUENEAU

Contents

PART TWO

PART THREE

PART FOUR

PART FIVE

PART SIX

Friendship, history, and literature have supplied me with some of the characters of this book. All other resemblances to living persons or to people having lived in reality or fiction can only be coincidental.

G. P.

Look with all your eyes, look

(Jules Verne, *Michael Strogoff*)

Preamble

The eye follows the paths that have
been laid down for it in the work
(Paul Klee, *Pädagogisches Skizzenbuch*)

To begin with, the art of jigsaw puzzles seems of little substance, easily exhausted, wholly dealt with by a basic introduction to Gestalt: the perceived object – we may be dealing with a perceptual act, the acquisition of a skill, a physiological system, or, as in the present case, a wooden jigsaw puzzle – is not a sum of elements to be distinguished from each other and analysed discretely, but a pattern, that is to say a form, a structure: the element's existence does not precede the existence of the whole, it comes neither before nor after it, for the parts do not determine the pattern, but the pattern determines the parts: knowledge of the pattern and of its laws, of the set and its structure, could not possibly be derived from discrete knowledge of the elements that compose it. That means that you can look at a piece of a puzzle for three whole days, you can believe that you know all there is to know about its colouring and shape, and be no further on than when you started. The only thing that counts is the ability to link this piece to other pieces, and in that sense the art of the jigsaw puzzle has something in common with the art of go. The pieces are readable, take on a sense, only when assembled; in isolation, a puzzle piece means nothing – just an impossible question, an opaque challenge. But as soon as you have succeeded, after minutes of trial and error, or after a prodigious half-second flash of inspiration, in fitting it into one of its neighbours, the piece disappears, ceases to exist as a piece. The intense difficulty preceding this link-up – which the English word *puzzle* indicates so well – not only loses its *raison d'être*, it seems never to have had any reason, so obvious does the solution appear. The two pieces so miraculously conjoined are henceforth one, which in its turn will be a source of error, hesitation, dismay, and expectation.

The role of the puzzle-maker is hard to define. In most cases – and in particular in all cardboard jigsaws – the puzzles are machine-made, and the lines of cutting are entirely arbitrary: a blanking die, set up once and for all, cuts the sheets of cardboard along identical lines every time. But such jigsaws are eschewed by the true puzzle-lover, not just because they are made of cardboard instead of wood, nor because the solutions are printed on the boxes they come in, but because this type of cut destroys the specific nature of jigsaw puzzles. Contrary to a widely and firmly held belief, it does not really matter whether the initial image is easy (or something taken to be easy – a genre scene in the style of Vermeer, for example, or a colour photograph of an Austrian castle) or difficult (a Jackson Pollock, a Pissarro, or the poor paradox of a blank puzzle). It's not the subject of the picture, or the painter's technique, which makes a puzzle more or less difficult, but the greater or lesser subtlety of the way it has been cut; and an arbitrary cutting pattern will necessarily produce an arbitrary degree of difficulty, ranging from the extreme of easiness – for edge pieces, patches of light, well-defined objects, lines, transitions – to the tiresome awkwardness of all the other pieces (cloudless skies, sand, meadow, ploughed land, shaded areas, etc.).

Pieces in puzzles of this kind come in classes of which the best-known are

the little chaps

the double crosses

and the crossbars

and once the edges have been put together, the detail pieces put in place – the very light, almost whitish yellow fringe on the carpet on the table holding a lectern with an open book, the rich edging of the mirror, the lute, the woman's red dress – and the bulk of the background pieces parcelled out according to their shade of grey, brown, white, or sky blue, then solving the puzzle consists simply of trying all the plausible combinations one by one.

The art of jigsaw puzzling begins with wooden puzzles cut by hand, whose maker undertakes to ask himself all the questions the player will have to solve, and, instead of allowing chance to cover his tracks, aims to replace it with cunning, trickery, and subterfuge. All the elements occurring in the image to be reassembled – this armchair covered in gold brocade, that three-pointed black hat with its rather ruined black plume, or that silver-braided bright yellow livery – serve by design as points of departure for trails that lead to false information. The organised, coherent, structured signifying space of the picture is cut up not only into inert, formless elements containing little information or signifying power, but also into falsified elements, carrying false information; two fragments of cornice made to fit each other perfectly when they belong in fact to two quite separate sections of the ceiling, the belt buckle of a uniform which turns out *in extremis* to be a metal clasp holding the chandelier, several almost identically cut pieces belonging, for one part, to a dwarf orange tree placed on a mantelpiece and, for the other part, to its scarcely attenuated reflection in a mirror, are classic examples of the types of traps puzzle-lovers come across.

From this, one can make a deduction which is quite certainly the ultimate truth of jigsaw puzzles: despite appearances, puzzling is not a solitary game: every move the puzzler makes, the puzzle-maker has made before; every piece the puzzler picks up, and picks up again, and studies and strokes, every combination he tries, and tries a second time, every blunder and every insight, each hope and each discouragement have all been designed, calculated, and decided by the other.

PART ONE

CHAPTER ONE

On the Stairs, 1

Yes, it could begin this way, right here, just like that, in a rather slow and ponderous way, in this neutral place that belongs to all and to none, where people pass by almost without seeing each other, where the life of the building regularly and distantly resounds. What happens behind the flats' heavy doors can most often be perceived only through those fragmented echoes, those splinters, remnants, shadows, those first moves or incidents or accidents that happen in what are called the "common areas", soft little sounds damped by the red woollen carpet, embryos of communal life which never go further than the landing. The inhabitants of a single building live a few inches from each other, they are separated by a mere partition wall, they share the same spaces repeated along each corridor, they perform the same movements at the same times, turning on a tap, flushing the water closet, switching on a light, laying the table, a few dozen simultaneous existences repeated from storey to storey, from building to building, from street to street. They entrench themselves in their domestic dwelling space – since that is what it is called – and they would prefer nothing to emerge from it; but the little that they do let out – the dog on a lead, the child off to fetch the bread, someone brought back, someone sent away – comes out by way of the landing. For all that passes, passes by the stairs, and all that comes, comes by the stairs: letters, announcements of births, marriages, and deaths, furniture brought in or taken out by removers, the doctor called in an emergency, the traveller returning from a long voyage. It's because of that that the staircase remains an anonymous, cold, and almost hostile place. In old buildings there used to be stone steps, wrought-iron handrails, sculptures, lamp-holders, sometimes a bench to allow old folk to rest between floors. In modern buildings there are lifts with walls covered in would-be obscene graffiti, and so-called "emergency" staircases in unrendered concrete, dirty and echoing. In this block of flats, where there is an old lift almost always out of order, the staircase is an old-fashioned place of questionable cleanliness, which declines in terms of middle-class respectability as it rises from floor to floor: two thicknesses of carpet as far as the third floor, thereafter only one, and none at all for the two attic floors.

Yes, it will begin here: between the third and fourth storey at 11 Rue Simon-Crubellier. A woman of about forty is climbing the stairs; she is wearing a long imitation-leather raincoat and on her head a kind of felt hat shaped like a sugar-loaf, something like what one imagines a goblin's hat to be, divided into red and grey squares. A big dun canvas hold-all, a case of the sort commonly called overnight bags, hangs on her right shoulder. A small cambric handkerchief is knotted through one of the chromed metal rings which attach the bag to its strap. Three motifs, which look as if they had been printed with a stencil, are regularly repeated over the whole fabric of the bag: a large pendulum clock, a round loaf cut through the middle, and a kind of copper receptacle without handles.

The woman is looking at a plan held in her left hand. It's just a sheet of paper, whose still visible creases attest to its having been folded in four, fixed by a paperclip to a thick cyclostyled volume – the terms of co-ownership relating to the flat this woman is about to visit. On the sheet there are in fact not one but three sketch-plans: the first, at the top right-hand corner, shows where the building is, roughly halfway along Rue Simon-Crubellier, which cuts at an angle across the quadrilateral formed by Rue Médéric, Rue Jadin, Rue de Chazelles, and Rue Léon Jost, in the Plaine Monceau district of the XVIIth *arrondissement* of Paris; the second, at the top left-hand corner, is a vertical cross-section of the building giving a diagrammatic picture of the layout of the flats and the names of some of the residents: Madame Nochère, concierge; Madame de Beaumont, second floor right; Bartlebooth, third floor left; Rémi Rorschach, television producer, fourth floor left; Dr Dinteville, sixth floor left, as well as the empty flat, sixth floor right, occupied by Gaspard Winckler, craftsman, until his death; the third plan, in the lower half of the sheet, is of Winckler's flat: three rooms facing the street, kitchen and bathroom on the courtyard side, and a boxroom without natural light.

The woman carries in her right hand a bulky set of keys, no doubt the keys of all the flats she has inspected that day; some are fixed to novelty key-rings: a miniature bottle of Marie Brizard *apéritif*, a golf tee and a wasp, a double-six domino, and a plastic octagonal token in which is set a tuberose flower.

It is almost two years since Gaspard Winckler died. He had no child. He was not known to have any surviving family. Bartlebooth entrusted a notary with the task of finding any heirs he might have. His only sister, Madame Anne Voltimand, died in 1942. His nephew, Grégoire Voltimand, had been killed on the Garigliano in May 1944, at the breakthrough on the Gustav line. The notary took many months to unearth a third cousin of Winckler's called Antoine Rameau, who worked for a manufacturer of knockdown divans. The taxes on the inheritance, added to the legal costs of the search for heirs, turned out to be so high that Antoine Rameau had to auction off everything. It is already a few months since the furniture was dispersed at the Sale Rooms, and a few weeks since the flat was bought by a property agency.

The woman climbing the stairs is not the director of the property agency, but his assistant; she doesn't deal with the commercial side, nor with customer relations, but only with the technical problems. From the property angle, the deal is a good one, the area is decent, the façade is of ashlar, the staircase is OK despite the agedness of the lift, and the woman is now coming to inspect in greater detail the condition of the flat itself, to draw up a more detailed plan of the accommodation with, for instance, thicker lines to distinguish structural walls from partitions and arrowheaded semicircles to show which way the doors open, and to decide on the work needed, to make a preliminary costing for complete refurbishment: the partition wall between the toilet and the boxroom to be knocked down, allowing the installation of a bathroom with a slipper-bath and WC; the kitchen tiles to be renewed; a wall-mounted gas-fired boiler (giving both central heating and hot water) to replace the old coal-fired boiler; the woodblock floor with its zigzag moulding to be lifted and replaced by a layer of cement, a felt underlay, and a fitted carpet.

Not much is left of these three small rooms in which Gaspard Winckler lived and worked for nearly forty years. His few pieces of furniture, his small workbench, his jigsaw, his minute files have gone. On the bedroom wall, opposite his bed, beside the window, that square picture he loved so much is no longer: it showed an antechamber with three men in it. Two were standing, pale and fat, dressed in frock-coats and wearing top hats which seemed screwed to their heads. The third, similarly dressed in black, was sitting by the door in the attitude of a man expecting visitors, slowly putting a pair of tight-fitting new gloves on over his fingers.

The woman is going up the stairs. Soon, the old flat will become a charming pied-à-terre, two recept. + bedr., all mod. cons., open outlook, quiet. Gaspard Winckler is dead, but the long and meticulous, patiently laid plot of his revenge is not finished yet.

CHAPTER TWO

Beaumont, 1

Madame de Beaumont's drawing room is almost entirely filled by a concert grand, on the stand of which sits the closed score of a famous American melody, *Gertrude of Wyoming*, by Arthur Stanley Jefferson. An old man with his head covered with an orange nylon scarf sits in front of the piano, preparing to tune it.

In the left-hand corner of the room there is a large modern armchair made of a huge hemisphere of steel-ringed Plexiglass on a chromed metal base. Beside it an octagonal block of marble serves as a low table; a steel cigarette lighter stands on it, as does a cylindrical pot-holder from which there emerges a dwarf oak tree, one of those Japanese bonsai plants whose growth has been so controlled, arrested, and altered that they show all the symptoms of maturity and even of old age almost without having grown at all, and about which growers say that their perfection depends less on the material care given to them than on the concentrated quality of meditation devoted to them.

Lying directly on the light-coloured woodblock floor, slightly to the front of the armchair, is a wooden jigsaw puzzle of which virtually all the edges have been assembled. In the lower right-hand third of the jigsaw some additional pieces have been put in place: they depict the oval face of a sleeping girl, whose blonde hair is wound in plaits around her head and held over her forehead by a double band of plaited cloth; she leans her cheek on her cupped right hand as if in her dream she were listening to something.

To the left of the puzzle, a decorated tray carries a coffee jug, a cup and saucer, and a silver-plated sugarbowl. The scene painted on the tray is partly masked by these objects, but two details can be made out nonetheless: on the right, a boy in embroidered trousers leans over a river bank; in the centre, a carp out of water twists on a line; the fisherman and the other characters remain invisible.

In front of the puzzle and the tray, several books, exercise books, and folders are spread out on the floor. The title of one of them is visible: *Safety Regulations in Mines and Quarries*. One of the folders is open at a page partly covered with equations written out in a small, fine hand:

If $f \in$ Hom (υ, μ) (resp. $g \in$ Hom (ξ, υ)) is a homogeneous morphism whose degree is the matrix α (resp. β), $f0g$ is homogeneous and its degree is the product matrix $\alpha\beta$.

Let $\alpha = (\alpha_{ij})$, $1 \leqslant i \leqslant m$, $1 \leqslant j \leqslant n$ and $\beta = (\beta_{ke})$, $1 \leqslant k \leqslant n$, $1 \leqslant l \leqslant p$ ($|\xi| = p$) be the given matrices. Suppose that $f = (f_1, \ldots, f_m)$, $g = (g_1, \ldots, g_n)$, and let $h : \pi \to \xi$ be a morphism, ($h = (h_1, \ldots, h_p)$). Finally let $a = (a_1, \ldots, a_p)$ be an element of A^p. For each index i between 1 and m ($|\mu| = m$) we compute the morphism

$$x_i = f_i 0 g\, 0\, (a_1 h_1, \ldots, a_p h_p).$$

First we get

$$x_i = f_i\, 0\, (a_1^{\beta_{11}} \ldots \ldots a_p^{\beta_{1p}}\, g_1, \ldots, a_1^{\beta_{i1}} \ldots \ldots a_p^{\beta_{ip}}\, g_i$$

then

$$x_i = a_1^{\alpha_{i1}\beta_{11} + \ldots + \alpha_{ij}\beta_{j1} + \ldots + \alpha_{in}\beta_{n1}} \ldots \ldots a_j^{\alpha_{i1}\beta_{ij} \ldots + \alpha_{in}\beta_{nj}} \cdot a_p^{\alpha_{i1}\beta_{1p} + \ldots} \; f_i 0 g 0 h.$$

Thus $f0g$ satisfies the homogeneity condition of degree $\alpha\beta$([1.2.2]).

*   *   *

The room's walls are painted in white gloss. Several framed posters are hanging on them. One of them depicts four greedy-looking monks sitting at table around a Camembert cheese on the label of which four greedy-looking monks – the very same – are again at table around, etc. The scene is repeated distinctly four times over.

Fernand de Beaumont was an archaeologist as ambitious as Schliemann. He tried to find the traces of the legendary city called Lebtit by the Arabs and which was supposed to have been their capital in Spain. Nobody disputed the existence of such a city, but most specialists, be they Arabists or Hispanists, agreed that it should be identified either as Ceuta, on African territory opposite Gibraltar, or as Jaén, in Andalusia, at the foot of the Sierra de Magina. Beaumont wouldn't agree to these identifications, on the grounds that none of the excavations made at Ceuta and at Jaén had displayed some of the features attributed to Lebtit by the literature. Stories told in particular of a strong castle "with leafed gates meant neither for going in nor for going out but only to be kept locked. Whenever a king died and another took the high throne after him, he set with his own hands a new lock to the gate, until these locks numbered twenty-four – one for each of the kings." There were seven rooms in the castle. The seventh was "so long that the ablest archer shooting from the threshold could not get his arrow to fix in the end wall". In the first, there were "perfect figures" representing Arabs "mounted on their swift horses and camels, with turbans hanging down their shoulders and scimitars dangling from their belts and bearing long lances in their right hands".

Beaumont belonged to that school of medievalists which described itself as "materialist" and which prompted a professor of the history of religion, for example, to go through the accounts of the Vatican chancery with the sole aim of proving that in the first half of the twelfth century the consumption of parchment, lead, and sigillary ribbon so far exceeded the amount justified by the number of officially declared and registered bulls that even allowing for possible meltings and probable muddles one had to conclude that a relatively large number of bulls (and we are talking about bulls, not briefs, since only bulls were sealed with lead, briefs being sealed with wax) had been kept confidential if not clandestine. Whence the thesis, justly famous in its time, on *Secret Bulls and the Question of the Antipopes*, which shed new light on the relations between Innocent II, Anaclete II, and Victor IV.

In a roughly similar manner Beaumont showed that if you took as a yardstick not Sultan Selim's 1798 world record of 888 metres but the good though not outstanding performance of the English bowmen at Crécy, the seventh room in the castle at Lebtit could not have been less than two hundred yards long and, taking account of the angle of projection, could scarcely have had less than thirty yards' ceiling height. Neither the excavations at Ceuta nor those at Jaén nor any others had uncovered a room of the requisite dimensions, which allowed Beaumont to state that "if the legend of this city has its origins in some real fortress, then it is not any one of those whose remains we know of to date".

Beyond this purely negative argument, another fragment of the legend of Lebtit seemed destined to give Beaumont a hint of the citadel's site. On the unreachable end wall of the archers' room, so the legend went, the following sentence was carved: "If ever a King opens the door of this castle, his warriors will turn to stone like the warriors of the first room, and his enemies shall lay his kingdom to waste". Beaumont saw this metaphor as a translation of the upheavals which shook the *Reyes de taifas* and provoked the *Reconquista*. More exactly, in his view, the legend of Lebtit described what he called the "Cantabrian débâcle of the Moors", that is to say, the battle of Covadonga in the course of which Pelage defeated the emir Alkhamah before having himself crowned King of Asturias on the battlefield. And with an enthusiasm that brought him the admiration of even his sharpest critics, Fernand de Beaumont decided that it was at Oviedo, in the heart of the Asturias, where the remains of the legendary fortress were to be found.

The origins of Oviedo were obscure. Some believed it was a monastery built by two monks to escape from the Moors; others saw it as a Visigoth citadel; still others held it to be a Hispano-Roman oppidum sometimes called Lucus asturum, sometimes Ovetum; and finally there were those who said that it was Pelage himself (called Don Pelayo by the Spaniards, who believed him to have been King Rodriguez's old lance-bearer at Jerez, and Belaï al-Roumi by the

Arabs since he was supposed to be of Roman extraction) who had founded the city. So many contradictory hypotheses served to support Beaumont's argument: he took Oviedo to be the fabled Lebtit, the most northerly of the Moorish strongholds in Spain and by that token the symbol of their domination over the peninsula. Its loss would have signalled the end of Islamic hegemony over Western Europe, and it would have been to assert this defeat that the victorious Pelage settled there.

Excavations began in 1930 and lasted more than five years. In the final year Beaumont was visited by Bartlebooth, who had come to nearby Gijon, also an ancient capital of the Asturian kings, to paint the first of his seascapes.

A few months later, Beaumont returned to France. He drew up a 78-page technical report on the conduct of the excavations, in which, in particular, he proposed a system for exploiting the results based on the Dewey Decimal Classification, and which is still regarded as a model of its kind. Then, on 12 November 1935, he committed suicide.

CHAPTER THREE

Third Floor Right, 1

This will be a drawing room, almost bare, with polished floorboards. The walls will be covered with metal panels.

Four men squat in the middle of the room, virtually sitting on their heels, with knees wide apart, elbows resting on knees, their hands together with middle fingers hooked and the other fingers stretched out. Three of the men will be in a row, facing the fourth. All will be bare-chested and barefoot, wearing only black silk trousers printed with a repeated design representing an elephant. A metal ring set with a circular obsidian will be worn by each on the ring finger of the right hand.

* * *

The room's only furniture is a Louis XIII armchair with whorled legs and studded leather arms and back. A long black sock is hooked over one of the arms.

The man facing the others is Japanese. His name is Ashikage Yoshimitsu. He belongs to a sect founded in 1960 in Manila by a deep-sea fisherman, a post-office employee, and a butcher's mate. The Japanese name of the sect is "Shira Nami", which means "The White Wave"; in French it is called "Les Trois Hommes Libres", or "The Three Free Men".

In the three years following the founding of the sect, each of these "three free men" managed to convert three others. The nine men of the second generation initiated twenty-seven over the next three years. The sixth level, in 1975, numbered seven hundred and twenty-nine members, including Ashikage Yoshimitsu, who was given the task, along with some other members, of spreading the new faith in the West. Initiation into the sect of The Three Free Men is long, hard, and very expensive, but it does not seem that Yoshimitsu had much difficulty in finding three converts rich enough to set aside the time and the money obligatorily required for such an enterprise.

The novices are at the very first stage of initiation and have to overcome preliminary trials in which they must absorb themselves in the contemplation of a perfectly trivial mental or material object to such a degree as to become oblivious to all feeling, even to extreme pain: to this end, the squatting tyros' heels are not resting directly on the floor, but on large metal dice with particularly sharp edges held in balance with one side touching the floor and the opposite side touching the heel: the slightest tautening of the foot makes the dice tumble instantly, causing the prompt and irreversible expulsion not only of the inadequate pupil but also of his two companions; the slightest relaxation of the position causes the edge of the dice to cut into the flesh, with an ensuing pain which quickly becomes unbearable. The three men have to stay in this disagreeable position for six hours; two minutes' break is allowed every three quarters of an hour, but recourse to this concession more than three times per session is frowned upon.

As for the object of meditation, each has a different one. The first novice, who has the exclusive sales rights in France for the products of a Swedish manufacturer of hanging files, has to solve a puzzle presented to him in the form of a small square of white card on which the following question has been finely handwritten in violet ink:

Who loved to eat her fill alongside Aymon?

above which a bow has been drawn around the figure 6.

The second pupil is German, the owner of a baby-wear factory in Stuttgart. He has in front of him, placed on a steel cube, a piece of flotsam of a shape quite closely resembling a ginseng root.

The third – who is French, and a star singer – faces a voluminous treatise on the culinary arts, the sort of book that usually goes on sale in the Christmas season. The book is placed on a music stand. It is open at an illustration of a reception given in 1890 by Lord Radnor in the drawing rooms of Longford Castle.

Printed on the left-hand page in a frame of *art-nouveau* colophons and garland decorations is a recipe for

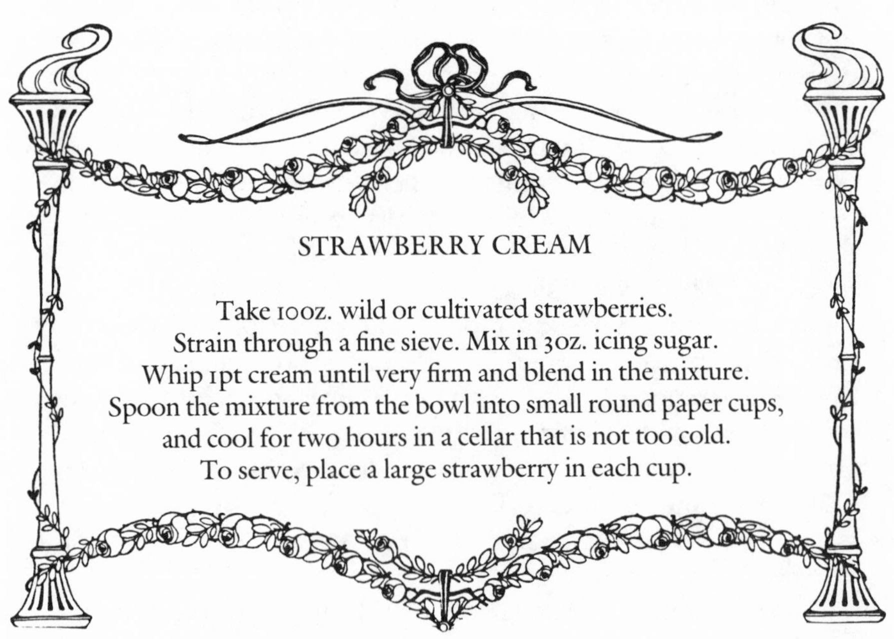

STRAWBERRY CREAM

Take 10oz. wild or cultivated strawberries.
Strain through a fine sieve. Mix in 3oz. icing sugar.
Whip 1pt cream until very firm and blend in the mixture.
Spoon the mixture from the bowl into small round paper cups,
and cool for two hours in a cellar that is not too cold.
To serve, place a large strawberry in each cup.

Yoshimitsu himself is sitting on his heels, but without the encumbrance of dice. Between the palms of his hands he holds a small bottle of orange juice. From it a straw sticks out, connected to several other straws in a line, in such a way as to reach as far as his mouth.

Smautf has calculated that in 1978 there would be two thousand one hundred and eighty-seven new members of the sect of The Three Free Men, and, assuming none of the older disciples dies, a total of three thousand two hundred and seventy-seven keepers of the faith. Then things would go much faster: by 2017, the nineteenth generation would run to more than a thousand million people. In 2020, the entire planet, and well beyond, would have been converted.

Nobody lives on the third floor right. The owner is a certain Monsieur Foureau, who is said to live on an estate at Chavignolles, between Caen and Falaise, in a farm of thirty-eight hectares, with a sort of manor house. Some years ago, a television drama was filmed there, under the title *The Sixteenth Edge of This Cube*; Rémi Rorschach took part in the shooting but never met this owner.

Nobody ever seems to have seen him. There is no name on the door on the landing, nor on the list fixed on the glass pane of the concierge's office door. The blinds are always drawn.

CHAPTER FOUR

Marquiseaux, 1

An empty drawing room on the fourth floor right.

On the floor there is a woven sisal mat, its strands entwined in such a way as to form star-shaped designs.

On the wall, an imitation of Jouy cretonne wallpaper depicts big sailing ships, Portuguese four-masters, armed with cannon and culverins, making ready to put into a harbour; the main jibs and spanker sails billow in the wind; sailors have climbed up the ropes to clew the others.

There are four paintings on the walls.

The first is a still life that despite its modern manner is strongly reminiscent of those compositions constructed on the theme of the five senses which were so common throughout Europe from the end of the Renaissance to the eighteenth century: on a table, there is an ashtray with a lighted Havana, a book of which the title and subtitle can be seen – *The Unfinished Symphony: A Novel* – though the name of the author is hidden, a bottle of rum, a cup-and-ball, and, in a shallow bowl, a pile of dried fruit, walnuts, almonds, apricot halves, prunes, etc.

The second depicts a street on the edge of a city, at night, alongside wasteland. To the right, a metal pylon with crossbars supporting at each point of intersection a large, lighted electric lamp. To the left, a constellation of stars reproduces precisely the inverse image of the pylon (base in the sky, apex towards the ground). The sky is covered in a flower pattern (dark blue on a lighter background) identical to the shapes made by frost on glass.

The third is of a legendary beast, the tarand, first described by Gelon the Sarmatian:

> A tarand is an animal as big as a bullock, having a head like a stag, or a little bigger, two stately horns with large branches, cloven feet, hair long like that of a furred Muscovite, I mean a bear, and a skin almost as hard as steel armour. The Scythian said that there are but few tarands to be found in Scythia, because it varieth its colour according to the diversity of the places where it grazes and abides, and represents the colour of the grass, plants, trees, shrubs, flowers, meadows, rocks, and generally of all things near which it comes. It hath this in common with the sea-pulp, or polypus, with the thoes, with the wolves of India, and with the chameleon; which is a kind of lizard so wonderful, that Democritus hath written a whole book of its figure, and anatomy, as also of its virtue and property in magic. This I can confirm, that I have seen it change its colour, not only at the approach of things that have a colour, but by its own voluntary impulse, according to its fear or other affections: as for example, upon a green carpet, I have certainly seen it become green; but having remained there some time,

it turned yellow, blue, tanned and purple, in course, in the same manner as you see a turkey-cock's comb change colour according to its passions. But what we find most surprising in this tarand is, that not only its face and skin, but also its hair could take whatever colour was about it.

The fourth picture is a black-and-white reproduction of a painting by Forbes called *A Rat Behind the Arras*. This painting was inspired by a true story which took place at Newcastle-upon-Tyne during the winter of 1858.

Old Lady Forthright had a collection of watches and clockwork toys of which she was very proud; the jewel in this crown was a minute watch set in a fragile alabaster egg. She had entrusted the keeping of her collection to her oldest servant. He was a coachman who had been in her service for more than sixty years and who had been madly in love with her ever since he had first had the privilege of driving her. He had transferred his silent passion to his mistress's collection, and, since he was particularly clever with his hands, he maintained it with ferocious care, and spent his days and his nights keeping these delicate mechanisms in good order, or restoring them, for some of the pieces were more than two centuries old.

The finest items of the collection were kept in a small room used only for that purpose. Some were locked away in glass-fronted cases, but most were hung on the wall and protected from dust by a thin muslin curtain. The coachman slept in an adjacent boxroom because a few months previously a solitary scientist had settled not far from the castle, in a laboratory where, like Martin Magron and Vella in Turin, he was studying the contradictory effects of strychnine and curare on rats: whereas the old lady and her coachman were convinced that he was a brigand drawn to the area by greed alone and was plotting some diabolical stratagem for getting hold of these precious jewels.

One night the old coachman was woken by tiny mewings that seemed to come from the collection room. He imagined that the demon scientist had trained one of his rats and taught it to fetch the watches. He got up, took a hammer from the toolbag he never let out of his sight, went into the room, approached the curtain as silently as he could, and hit hard at the place where the noise seemed to be coming from. Alas, it was not a rat, but only that magnificent watch set in its alabaster egg; its works had got a little out of adjustment, and had given it an almost imperceptible squeak. Lady Forthright, woken in a start by the hammer-blow, ran thereupon to the room, where she found the old servant dumbfounded, open-mouthed, holding in one hand the hammer and in the other the broken jewel. Without giving him time to explain what had happened, she called her other servants and had her coachman locked away as a raving lunatic. She died two years later. The old coachman learnt of her death, managed to escape from his far-distant asylum, returned to the castle, and hanged himself in the very room where the drama had taken place.

In this early work over which the influence of Bonnat still hangs heavily, Forbes has made very free use of the original story. He shows the room with its clock-covered walls. The old coachman is dressed in a uniform of white leather; he has climbed onto an elaborately shaped, dark-red lacquered Chinese chair. He is hanging a long silk scarf onto one of the ceiling rafters. Old Lady Forthright stands at the doorway; she is looking at her servant with an expression of great anger; in her right hand she is holding, with outstretched arm, a silver chain at the end of which hangs a shard of the alabaster egg.

There are several collectors in this building, and they are often more maniacal than the characters in the painting. Valène himself kept the postcards Smautf sent him from each place they stopped off at. He had one such from Newcastle-upon-Tyne, in fact, and another from the Australian Newcastle, in New South Wales.

CHAPTER FIVE

Foulerot, 1

On the fifth floor, right-hand side, right at the end: right below where Gaspard Winckler had his workroom. Valène remembered the parcels he received every fortnight for twenty years: even at the height of war they had kept coming regularly, and every one identical, absolutely identical; obviously, the postage stamps varied, allowing the concierge, who wasn't yet Madame Nochère, but Madame Claveau, to ask if she could have them for her son Michel; but apart from the stamps there was nothing to distinguish one parcel from another: it was the same kraft paper, the same string, the same wax seal, the same address label; it made you think that before leaving, Bartlebooth must have asked Smautf to work out in advance how much tissue paper, kraft paper, string, and sealing wax would be needed for all five hundred parcels! He probably hadn't needed to ask, Smautf would have understood without prompting! It's not as if they had been short of trunks.

Here, on the fifth floor right, the room is empty. It is a bathroom, painted a dull orange colour. On the rim of the bath, a large oyster shell lined with mother-of-pearl – for it had once contained a pearl – now holds a piece of soap and a pumice stone. Above the washbasin there is an octagonal mirror in a veined marble surround. Between the bath and the basin, a Scottish cashmere cardigan and a skirt with braces have been thrown onto a folding chair.

The door at the end is open and gives onto a long corridor. A girl of barely eighteen comes towards the bathroom. She is naked. In her right hand she holds an egg, which she will use for washing her hair, and in her left hand she carries issue No. 40 of *Les Lettres Nouvelles* (July–August 1956), a review containing, alongside a note by Jacques Lederer on *Le Journal d'un prêtre* by Paul Jury (Gallimard), a short story by Luigi Pirandello, dating from 1913, entitled *In the Abyss*, and telling the tale of how Romeo Daddi went mad.

CHAPTER SIX

Servants' Quarters, 1

It's a maid's room on the seventh floor, to the left of the one right at the end of the corridor where the old painter Valène lives. The room is attached to the large flat on the first floor right, the one where Madame de Beaumont, the archaeologist's widow, lives with her two granddaughters, Anne and Béatrice Breidel. Béatrice, the younger, is seventeen. A clever child, outstanding at school, she is studying for the entrance examination to the girls' section of the Ecole Normale Supérieure at Sèvres. She has obtained the permission of her strict grandmother to use this independent room to study, but not to live in.

There are hexagonal red tiles on the floor, and the walls are papered with a design depicting various shrubs. Despite the tiny size of the flatlet, Béatrice has invited five of her classmates in. She is seated at her work-desk on a high-backed chair, which stands on feet carved in the shape of sheep bones. She is wearing a skirt with braces and a red top with slightly puffed cuffs; on her right wrist she wears a silver bangle and holds between the thumb and index finger of her left hand a long cigarette, which she is watching burn away.

One of her friends, dressed in a long white linen coat, is standing by the door and seems to be carefully studying a map of the Paris underground. The other four, uniformly dressed in jeans and striped shirts, are seated on the floor, around a tea-set on a tray, placed beside a lamp of which the base is a small barrel, of the sort Saint Bernard dogs are generally supposed to carry. One of the girls pours tea. Another opens a box of cheese packed in small cubes. The third is reading a novel by Thomas Hardy, on the cover of which can be seen a bearded character sitting in a rowing boat in the middle of a stream and fishing with rod and line, whilst on the bank a knight in armour appears to be hailing him. The fourth, with an air of profound indifference, is looking at an engraving depicting a bishop leaning over a table on which you can see one of those games called *solitaire*. It is made of a wooden board, trapezoidal in shape, much like a racket-press, in which twenty-five holes have been drilled so as to form a lozenge, deep enough to take the pieces which are in this case good-sized pearls, placed to the right of the board on a little black silk cushion. The engraving, which manifestly copies the famous painting by Bosch known as *The Conjuror*, in the Municipal Gallery at Saint-Germain-en-Laye, has a humorous – though not, apparently, very illuminating – title, handwritten in Gothic lettering:

He that with his soup will drink
When he is dead shall see no wink

The suicide of Fernand de Beaumont left his widow Véra with a daughter of six, Elizabeth, who had never seen her father, kept far from Paris by his Cantabrian excavations; nor had she seen much more of her mother, who had pursued her career as a singer in the Old World and in the New practically uninterrupted by her brief marriage to the archaeologist.

Born in Russia at the turn of the century, Véra Orlova – that is the name by which music-lovers still know her – fled in the spring of 1918 and settled first in Vienna, where she was Schoenberg's pupil at the *Verein für musikalische Privataufführung*. She followed Schoenberg to Amsterdam, but their ways parted when he returned to Berlin and she came to Paris to give a series of recitals at the Salle Erard. Despite the sometimes sarcastic and sometimes tempestuous hostility of audiences clearly unfamiliar with the technique of *Sprechgesang*, and supported only by a small band of aficionados, she managed to insert into her programmes, mostly composed of operatic arias, *lieder* by Schumann and Hugo Wolf, and songs by Mussorgsky, some of the vocal pieces of the Vienna School, which she thus introduced to Parisians. It was at a reception given by Count Orfanik, at whose request she had come to sing Angelica's last aria in Arconati's *Orlando* –

Innamorata, mio cuore tremante
Voglio morire

– that she met the man who would become her husband. But she was in demand, everywhere, more and more insistently, and was dragged off on triumphant tours which sometimes lasted a full year, and hardly lived at all with Fernand de Beaumont, who, for his part, only ever left his study in order to check his speculative hypotheses in the field.

Born in 1929, Elizabeth was therefore brought up by her paternal grandmother, the old Countess de Beaumont, and saw her mother for scarcely a few weeks each year when the singer consented to resist her impresario's ever-increasing demands and came to take a rest at the Beaumont castle at Lédignan. It was only towards the end of the war, when Elizabeth had just turned fifteen, that her mother, who had now given up concerts and touring to devote herself to teaching singing, brought her to Paris to live with her. But the girl soon rejected the guardianship of a woman who, when deprived of the glitter of boxes and gala performances, of the bunches of roses thrown at the end of her recitals, turned shrewish and domineering. She ran away one year later. Her mother would never see her again, and all the enquiries she made to track her down came to nought. It was only in September 1959 that Véra Orlova learnt, at the same time, what her daughter's life had been, and how she died. Elizabeth had married a Belgian bricklayer, François Breidel, two years earlier. They lived in the Ardennes, at Chaumont-Porcien. They had two little girls, Anne, who was one year old, and Béatrice, who was a newborn baby. On Monday 14 September, a neighbour, hearing crying in the house, tried to break in. Unable to do so, she went to fetch the gamekeeper. They shouted, but the only reply they could get was the ever more strident crying of the babies; then, with the help of some other villagers, they broke down the back door and rushed to the parents' bedroom, where they found them, lying naked in bed, their throats slit, swimming in blood.

Véra de Beaumont heard the news that same evening. Her wailing scream echoed through the whole building. Next morning, after being driven through the night by Bartlebooth's chauffeur, Kléber, who when he was told of the business by the concierge spontaneously offered his services, she arrived at Chaumont-Porcien, and left almost straightaway with the two children.

CHAPTER SEVEN

Servants' Quarters, 2
Morellet

Morellet had a room in the eaves, on the eighth floor. On his door could still be seen the number 17, in green paint.

After plying diverse trades which he enjoyed reciting in an accelerating list – bench hand, music hall singer, baggage handler, sailor, riding instructor, variety artist, musical conductor, ham stripper, saint, clown, a soldier for five minutes, verger in a spiritualist church, and even a walk-on in one of the first Laurel and Hardy shorts – Morellet, at the age of twenty-nine, had become a technician in the chemistry lab at the Ecole Polytechnique, and would no doubt have remained so until retirement if, like so many others', his path had not been crossed one day by Bartlebooth.

When he returned from his travels, in December nineteen fifty-four, Bartlebooth sought a process which would allow him, once he had reassembled his puzzles, to recover the original seascapes; to do that, first the pieces of wood would need to be stuck back together, then a means of eliminating all the traces of the cutting lines would have to be found, as well as a way of restoring the original surface texture of the paper. If the two glued layers were then separated with a razor, the watercolour would be returned intact, just as it had been on the day, twenty years before, when Bartlebooth had painted it. It was a difficult problem, for though there were on the market even in those days various resins and synthetic glazes used by toyshops for puzzles in window displays, they left the cutting lines far too visible.

As was his custom, Bartlebooth wanted the person who would help him in this search to live in the same building, or as near as possible. That is how, through his faithful Smautf, whose room was on the same floor as the lab technician's, he met Morellet. Morellet had none of the theoretical knowledge required to solve such a problem, but he referred Bartlebooth to his head of department, a chemist of German origin named Kusser, who claimed to be a distant descendant of the composer

> KUSSER or COUSSER (Johann Sigismond), German composer of Hungarian extraction (Pozsony, 1660–Dublin, 1727). He collaborated with Lully during his stay in France (1674–1682). Music-master at various princely courts in Germany, conductor in Hamburg, where he wrote and performed several operas: *Erindo* (1693), *Porus* (1694), *Pyramus and Thisbe* (1694), *Scipio Africanus* (1695), *Jason* (1697). In 1710 he was appointed master of music at Dublin Cathedral and remained there until his death. He was one of the founders of the Hamburg opera, where he introduced the "French overture", and was a precursor of Handel in the field of oratorio. Six of his overtures and various other compositions have survived.

After many fruitless trials using all kinds of animal and vegetable glues and various synthetic acrylics, Kusser tackled the problem from a different angle. Grasping that he had to find a substance capable of bonding the fibres of the paper without affecting the coloured pigmentation which it supported, he fortunately recalled a technique he had seen used, in his youth, by certain Italian medal makers: they would coat the inside of the die with a very fine layer of powdered alabaster, which allowed them to strike almost perfectly smooth coins and eliminated virtually all trimming and finishing work. In pursuing this line of research, Kusser discovered a type of gypsum that turned out to be satisfactory. Reduced to an almost impalpably fine powder and mixed with a gelatinous colloid, injected at a given temperature under high pressure through a microsyringe which could be manipulated in such a way as to follow precisely the complex shapes of the cutting lines Winckler had originally made, the gypsum reagglutinated the threads of the paper and restored its prior structure. The fine powder became perfectly translucid as it cooled and had no visible effect on the colour of the painting.

The process was simple and required only patience and care. Appropriate instruments were specially built and installed in Morellet's room; handsomely remunerated by Bartlebooth, Morellet let his job at the Ecole Polytechnique slip more and more, and he devoted himself to the wealthy amateur.

In truth, Morellet didn't have much to do. Every fortnight Smautf brought him up the puzzle which, despite its difficulty, Bartlebooth had, once again, succeeded in reassembling. Morellet inserted it into a metal frame and put it under a special press which gave an imprint of the cutting lines. With this imprint he used an electrolytic process to make an open-work stencil, a piece of rigid, fantastical metal lace which faithfully reproduced all the delineations of the puzzle on which this matrix was then delicately and accurately overlaid. After preparing his gypsum suspension and heating it to the required temperature, Morellet filled his microsyringe and fixed it on an articulated arm so that the needle-point, no more than a few microns thick, was located precisely above the open lines of the stencil. The remainder of the operation was automatic, since the ejection of the gypsum and the movement of the syringe were controlled by an electronic device using an X-Y table, giving a slow but even deposit of the substance.

The last part of the operation did not concern the lab technician: the puzzle, rebonded into a watercolour stuck to a thin sheet of poplar, was taken to the restorer Guyomard, who detached the sheet of Whatman paper by means of a blade and disposed of all traces of glue on the reverse side, two tricky but routine operations for this expert who had made his name famous by lifting frescoes covered by several layers of plaster and paint, and by cutting in half, through its thickness, a sheet of paper on which Hans Bellmer had drawn on recto and verso sides.

All in all, what Morellet had to do, once a fortnight, was simply to make ready and supervise a series of manipulations which, including cleaning and tidying away, took a little less than a day.

This enforced idleness had unhappy consequences. Relieved of all financial cares, but bitten by the research bug, Morellet took advantage of his free time to devote himself, in his flat, to the sort of physical and chemical experiments of which his long years as a technician seemed to have left him particularly frustrated.

In all the local cafés he gave out his visiting card, which described him as "Head of Practical Services at the Ecole Pyrotechnique", and he offered his services generously; he obtained innumerable orders for superactive hair and carpet shampoos, stain-removers, energy-saving devices, cigarette filters, martingales for 421, cough potions, and other miracle products.

One evening in February 1960, whilst he was heating a pressure cooker full of a mixture of rosin and diterpene carbide destined to produce a lemon-flavoured toothpaste, the apparatus exploded. Morellet's left hand was torn to shreds, and he lost three fingers.

This accident cost him his job – preparing the metal grid required some minimal dexterity – and all he had to live on was a part-pension meanly paid by the Ecole Polytechnique, and a small pension from Bartlebooth. But his vocation for research did not abate; on the contrary, it grew sharper. Though severely lectured by Smautf, by Winckler, and by Valène, he persevered with experiments which turned out for the most part to be ineffective, but harmless, save for a certain Madame Schwann who lost all her hair after washing it in the special dye Morellet had made for her exclusive use; two or three times, though, these manipulations ended in explosions, more spectacular than dangerous, and in minor fires which were quickly brought under control.

These incidents filled two people with glee: his neighbours on the right, the Plassaert couple, young traders in printed cotton goods, who had ingeniously converted three maids' rooms into a pied-à-terre (in so far as a dwelling situated right under the eaves may be referred to as a foot on the ground), and who were reckoning on Morellet's room for further expansion. After each explosion they made a complaint, and took a petition around the building demanding the eviction of the former technician. The room belonged to the building manager, who, when the property had gone into co-ownership, had bought up almost all of the two top floors in his own name. For several years, the manager held back from putting the old man out on the street, for he had many friends in the building – to begin with, Madame Nochère herself, who regarded Monsieur Morellet as a true scientist, a brain, a possessor of secrets, and who had a personal stake in the little disasters which now and again struck the top floor of the building, not so much because of the tips she sometimes got on these occasions as for the epical, sentimental, and mysterious accounts she could give of them to the whole *quartier*.

Then, a few months ago, there were two accidents in the same week. The first cut off the lights in the building for a few minutes; the second broke six windowpanes. But the Plassaerts won their case this time, and Morellet was locked away.

In the painting the room is as it is today; the printed-cotton trader has bought it from the manager and has started to have work done on it. On the walls there is a dull, old-fashioned light-chestnut paint, and on the floor a coconut-fibre carpet worn down almost everywhere to the backing. The neighbour has already put two pieces of furniture in place: a low table, made of a pane of smoked glass set on a polyhedron of hexagonal cross-section, and a Renaissance chest. Placed on the table is a box of Münster, the lid of which depicts a unicorn, an almost empty sachet of caraway seeds, and a knife.

Three workmen are now leaving the room. They have already begun the work needed to unite the two dwellings. They have stuck on the bottom wall, by the door, a large tracing-paper plan showing the intended location of the radiator, the routing of the pipework and electrical wires, and the section of partition wall to be knocked down.

One of the workmen is wearing big gloves like those used by electrical cable-layers. The second has an embroidered suede waistcoat with fringes. The third is reading a letter.

CHAPTER EIGHT

Winckler, 1

Now we are in the room Gaspard Winckler called the lounge. Of the three rooms in his flat, it is the one nearest the stairs, the furthest to the left from where we are standing.

It is a rather small, almost square room whose door gives straight onto the landing. The walls are covered in hessian, once blue, now returned to an almost colourless condition except in the places where the furniture and the pictures have protected it from the light.

There weren't many pieces of furniture in the lounge. It's a room which Winckler didn't live in very much. He worked all day in the third room, the one where he had set up his equipment. He didn't eat at home anymore; he had never learnt to cook and hated it. Since 1943, he preferred to take even his breakfast at Riri's, the bar on the corner of Rue Jadin and Rue de Chazelles. It's only when he had guests whom he didn't know very well that he entertained them in his lounge. He had a round table with extension flaps that he couldn't have used very often, six straw-seated chairs, and a chest that he had carved himself with designs illustrating the principal scenes of *The Mysterious Island:* the landing of the balloon that had got away from Richmond, the miraculous finding of Cyrus Smith, the last match rescued from Gedeon Spilett's waistcoat pocket, the discovery of the trunk, down to Ayrton's and Nemo's heartrending confessions, which end these adventures and connect them magnificently to *The Children of Captain Grant* and *Twenty Thousand Leagues Under The Sea*. It took a long time to see this chest, to really see it. From a distance it looked like any old rustic-Breton-Renaissance box. It was only when you got closer, almost fingering the incrustation, that you discovered what these minute scenes showed, and realised how much patience, meticulousness, and even genius had gone into their carving. Valène had known Winckler since 1932, but it was only in the early 1960s that he had noticed that it wasn't any ordinary sideboard and that it was worth looking at more closely. It was the period when Winckler had begun to make rings and Valène had brought along the girl who ran the cosmetics shop in Rue Logelbach and who wanted to set up a knickknack display in her shop for the Christmas season. All three sat down at the round table on which Winckler had spread his rings, there must have been about thirty at the time, all lined up, on black satin cushions in presentation boxes. Winckler had apologised for the poor light from the ceiling fixture, then opened his chest and got out three small glasses and a decanter of 1938 brandy; he drank very rarely, but every year Bartlebooth sent him several bottles of vintage wines and spirits which Winckler generously redistributed around the building and the *quartier*, keeping only one or two for himself. Valène was sitting next to the chest, and while the cosmetics girl took the rings gingerly one by one, he sipped his brandy and looked at the carvings. What amazed him before he was even clearly aware of it was that where he had expected to find stags' heads, garlands, foliations, or puffy-cheeked cherubs, he was discovering miniature characters, the sea, the horizon, and the whole island, not yet named Lincoln, in the same way as the spacewrecked travellers, dismayed and challenged at the same time, had first seen it, when they had reached the highest peak. He asked Winckler if it was he who had carved the chest, and Winckler said yes; when he was younger, he added, but gave no further details.

Everything has gone now, of course: the chest, chairs, table, ceiling lamp, the three framed reproductions. Valène can only recall one of them with any accuracy: it portrayed *The Great Parade of the Military Tattoo*; Winckler had come across it in a Christmas issue of *L'Illustration*; years later, in fact only a few months ago, Valène learnt as he flicked through the *Petit Robert* dictionary that it was by Israël Silvestre.

It went just like that, from one day to the next: the removal men came, the distant cousin auctioned the lot, not at Drouot but at Levallois; when they heard, it was too late, or else they – Smautf, Morellet, or Valène – would have tried, maybe, to get there and buy a thing Winckler had particularly held to – not the chest, they'd never have found room for it, but maybe that engraving, or the one that hung in the bedroom and showed the three men in evening dress, or some of his tools or picture books. They spoke about it to each other and said to themselves that maybe after all it was better they hadn't gone, that the only person who should have was Bartlebooth, but that neither Valène nor Smautf nor Morellet would have made so bold as to mention it to him.

Now in the little lounge what is left is what remains when there's nothing left: flies, for instance, or advertising bumph slipped under the door by students, proclaiming the benefits of a new toothpaste or offering twenty-five centimes' reduction to every buyer of three packets of washing powder, or old issues of *Le Jouet Français*, the review he took all his life and to which his subscription didn't run out until a few months after his death, or those things without meaning that lie around on floors and in cupboard corners, you never know how they got there nor why they stayed: three faded flowers of the field; bendy sticks with probably calcinated threads etiolating at each end, an empty Coke bottle, a cake box, opened, still keeping its false raffia string and its legend "Aux Délices de Louis XV, Pastrycooks and Candymakers since 1742" forming a fine oval shape surrounded by a garland and flanked by four puffy-cheeked *putti*, or behind the door to the landing a kind of cast-iron coatstand, with a mirror cracked roughly Y-shaped into three unequal surface portions, and in the edge of which there is still stuck a postcard showing an incontrovertibly Japanese woman athlete holding a flaming torch at arm's length.

Twenty years ago, in 1956, Winckler completed as planned the last of the puzzles Bartlebooth had ordered. There is every reason to suppose that the contract he had signed with the multimillionaire contained a clause stipulating explicitly that he would never make any other puzzles, but in any case it's likely he didn't want to.

He began to make little wooden toys, cubes for children, very simple ones with designs on them copied from his albums of popular Epinal prints, which he coloured in with tinted inks.

It was not until later that he started to make rings: he took small stones – agate, cornelian, Ptyxes, Rhine pebbles, sunstones – and mounted them on delicate rings made of minutely plaited silver threads. One day he explained to Valène that they were also a kind of puzzle, one of the most difficult there is: in Turkey they are called "Devil's Rings": they are made of seven, or eleven, or seventeen gold or silver circles chain-linked to each other, and whose complex interweaving produces a closed, compact, and perfectly regular coil. In the cafés of Ankara, streetsellers accost foreigners, and show them the ring assembled, and then flick the linked coils apart; they usually have a simplified design with only five circles that they entwine in a few invisible moves and then open out again, leaving the tourist to struggle in vain with it for a few long moments until an associate – most often one of the café waiters – agrees to fit the ring together with a few careless turns of his hand or gives away the knack, something like once over, once under, then turn it all inside out when there's only one coil left disengaged.

What was admirable in Winckler's rings was that the coil, once entwined, although perfectly regular, left a minute circular space in which was set a semi-precious stone; once inserted and tightened with two minute tweaks of a pincer, it closed the ring for ever. "It's only for me," he said one day to Valène, "that they're diabolical. Bartlebooth himself would approve." It was the only time Valène heard Winckler utter the Englishman's name.

He took ten years to make five score of the rings. Each required several weeks' work. To begin with, he tried to sell them through local jewellers. Then he began to lose interest in them; he gave some on sale or return to the cosmeticist's shop; he lent some others to Madame Marcia, the antique dealer whose shop and flat were on the ground floor of the building. Then he began to give them away. He gave some to Madame Riri and her daughters, to Madame Nochère, to Martine, to Madame Orlowska and her two neighbours, to the two Breidel girls, to Caroline Echard, to Isabelle Gratiolet and to Véronique Altamont, and even, in the end, to people who didn't live in the building and whom he hardly knew.

Some time later he found at the flea market at Saint-Ouen a set of small convex mirrors and he began to make what are called "witches' mirrors" by inserting them into infinitely crafted wooden mouldings.

He was prodigiously clever with his hands and kept all his life quite exceptional gifts of accuracy, control, and eye, but it seems that from that time on he didn't want to work very much at all. He finicked over each frame for days on end, cutting, fretsawing endlessly away until it was an almost immaterial piece of wooden lace in whose centre the small polished mirror looked like a metallic glance, an icy eye, wide open, full of irony and malice. The contrast between the unreal corona, as elaborate as a Gothic stained-glass window, and the harsh grey light of the mirror created a feeling of unease, as if this quantitatively and qualitatively disproportionate surround was only there to emphasise the maleficent power of convexity which seemed to want to concentrate all available space into a single point. The people he showed them to didn't like them. They would take one in their hand and then put it down quickly, almost awkwardly. They wanted to ask him why he spent so much time on them. He never tried to sell them and never gave any as a present to anybody; he didn't hang them on his wall at home; as soon as he finished one, he put it away stored flat in a cupboard and began to make another.

These were virtually his last works. When he had run out of his stock of mirrors, he made a few more baubles, little toys that Madame Nochère would beg him to make for one or another of her innumerable great-nephews or for one of the children in the building or the block who had just caught whooping cough or measles or mumps. He always began by saying no, then ended up making an exception for a two-dimensional bunny rabbit made of wood with ears that flapped, or a cardboard puppet or a rag doll or a little landscape with a handle which when turned made you see first a rowing boat, then a sailing boat, then a swan-shaped punt pulling a water-skier.

Then, four years ago, two years before he died, he stopped altogether, carefully packed his tools away, and dismantled his workbench.

At first, he still enjoyed going out. He would go to the park at Monceau for a walk, or would go down Rue de Courcelles and Avenue Franklin-Roosevelt as far as the Marigny gardens, at the bottom of the Champs-Elysées. He would sit on a bench, legs together, his chin resting on the handle of his walking stick, which he gripped with both hands, and he would stay like that for an hour or two, without moving, looking straight ahead at the children playing in the sand or at the old blue-and-orange-canvas-covered roundabout with its horses and their stylised manes and its two gondolas decorated with an orange-coloured sun, or at the swings or the little Punch and Judy stall.

Soon his excursions became less frequent. One day he asked Valène if he would be kind enough to come to the cinema with him. They went to the Film Theatre at the Palais de Chaillot one afternoon to see *Green Pastures*, an ugly, feeble rehash of *Uncle Tom's Cabin*. On leaving, Valène asked him why he'd wanted to see this film; he replied that it was only because of the title, because of that word "pastures", and that if he'd known that it was going to be what they'd just seen, he would never have come.

After that he only went out to have his meals at Riri's. He would come at about eleven in the morning. He would sit down at a little round table, between the counter and the terrace, and Madame Riri or one of her daughters would bring a big bowl of chocolate and two fine slices of bread and butter. That wasn't his breakfast but his lunch, it was his favourite food, the only thing he ate with real pleasure. Then he would read the papers, all the papers that Riri took – *The Auvergne Messenger*, *The Soft Drink Echo* – as well as those left by the morning's customers: *L'Aurore*, *Le Parisien Libéré*, or, less often, *Le Figaro*, *L'Humanité*, or *Libération*. He didn't skim through them but read them through conscientiously, line by line, without making any heartfelt or perspicacious or indignant comments, but in a calm and settled manner, without taking his eyes off the page, not noticing the midday cannon which filled the café with the hubbub of fruit machines and jukeboxes, glasses, plates, the noises of voices and of chairs being pushed back. At two o'clock, when the effervescence of lunch subsided and Madame Riri went upstairs for a rest and the two girls did the washing-up in the tiny working quarters at the back of the café and Monsieur Riri drowsed over his accounts, Winckler was still there, in between the sports page and the used-car mart. Sometimes he stayed at his table all afternoon, but usually he went back up to his flat at around three o'clock and came down again at six: that was the great moment of his day, the time for his game of backgammon with Morellet. Both played heatedly, excitedly, breaking out into exclamations, swearwords, and tempers, which were not surprising in Morellet but seemed quite incomprehensible in

Winckler – a man whose calmness verged on apathy, whose patience, sweetness, and resignation were imperturbable, whom no one had ever seen angry; such a man could, when for example it was Morellet's go and he threw a double five, thus enabling him to get his leading man to a blot and back in one go (he persisted in calling it his "jockey" in the name of an allegedly rigorous etymology he had found in some dubious source like Vermot's Almanach or the *Reader's Digest* "Enlarge Your Vocabulary" column), such a man, then, was able to seize the board with both hands and send it flying, calling Morellet a cheat and unleashing a quarrel which the café's customers sometimes took ages to sort out. Usually, though, it all calmed down pretty quickly so that the game could begin again before they shared, in freshly made-up amity, the veal cutlet with pasta shells or the liver with creamed potatoes that Madame Riri cooked especially for them. But several times one or other went out slamming the door behind him, thus depriving himself of backgammon and of dinner.

In his last year he didn't go out at all. Smautf became accustomed to taking him up his meals twice a day, and seeing to his cleaning and washing. Morellet, Valène, or Madame Nochère did all the bits of shopping he needed. He stayed all day in his pyjama trousers and a sleeveless red cotton vest over which he would pull, when he was cold, a kind of indoor jacket of soft flannel and a polka-dot scarf. Valène called on him in the afternoon several times. He found him sitting at his table looking at the hotel labels that Smautf had added for him to each of the watercolours he'd despatched: Hotel Hilo Honolulu, Villa Carmona Granada, Hotel Theba Algeciras, Hotel Peninsula Gibraltar, Hotel Nazareth Galilee, London, Hotel Cosmo, s.s. *Ile de France*, Regis Hotel Canada, Hotel Mexico DF, Hotel Astor New York, the Town House Los Angeles, s.s. *Pennsylvania*, Hotel Mirador Acapulco, Compaña Mexicana de Aviación, etc. He wanted, so he said, to sort the labels into order, but it was very difficult: of course, there was chronological order, but he found it poor, even poorer than alphabetical order. He had tried by continents, then by country, but that didn't satisfy him. What he would have liked would be to link each label to the next, but each time in respect of something else: for example, they could have some detail in common, a mountain or volcano, an illuminated bay, some particular flower, the same red and gold edging, the beaming face of a groom, or the same dimensions, or the same typeface, or similar slogans ("Pearl of the Ocean", "Diamond of the Coast"), or a relationship based not on similarity but on opposition or a fragile, almost arbitrary association: a minute village by an Italian lake followed by the skyscrapers of Manhattan, skiers followed by swimmers, fireworks by candlelit dinner, railway by aeroplane, baccarat table by chemin de fer, etc. It's not just hard, Winckler added, above all it's useless: if you leave the labels unsorted and take two at random, you can be sure they'll have at least three things in common.

After a few weeks he put the labels back in the shoebox where he kept them and tidied the box away in the back of his cupboard. He didn't start on anything special again. He stayed all day in his bedroom, sitting in his armchair by the window, looking down onto the street, or maybe not even looking, just staring at nothing. On his bedside table there was a radio that was permanently on at low volume; no one ever really knew if he could hear it, although one day he did stop Madame Nochère from switching it off, saying that he listened to the hit parade every night.

Valène had his bedroom immediately above Winckler's workroom, and for nearly forty years his days had been accompanied by the thin noise of the craftsman's tiny files, the almost inaudible throb of his jigsaw, the creaking of his floorboards, the whistling of his kettle when he boiled water, not for making tea but for some glue or glaze he needed for his puzzles. Now, since he had dismantled his bench and packed away his tools, he never went into the room. He never told anybody how he spent his days and nights. People only knew that he hardly slept anymore. When Valène came to see him, he entertained him in his bedroom; he offered him his armchair and sat on the edge of the bed. They didn't talk much. Once he said he was born at La Ferté-Milon, on the Ourcq Canal. Another time, with sudden warmth, he told Valène about the man who had taught him his work.

He was called Monsieur Gouttman and he made religious artefacts which he sold himself in churches and procurators' offices: crosses, medals, and rosaries of every size, candelabra for oratories, portable altars, artificial jewellery, bouquets, sacred hearts in blue cardboard, red-bearded Saint Josephs, china calvaries. Gouttman took him on as an apprentice when he had just turned twelve. He took him away to live with him in a sort of hut at the back end of Charny, in the Department of Meuse, installed him in the bunker he used as a workshop, and, with amazing patience, since he was otherwise a bad-tempered man, undertook to teach him what he could do. It took several years, since he could do everything. But Gouttman, despite his innumerable talents, was not a very good businessman. When he'd sold out his stock, he went to town and ran through all his money in two or three days. He came back home and began again at modelling, weaving, plaiting, threading, embroidering, sewing, moulding, colouring, glazing, cutting, fitting, until he'd built up his stock in trade again, and again set off on the highways to sell his wares. One day he never came back. Winckler later learnt that he had died of cold, by the roadside, in the Argonne forest, between Les Islettes and Clermont.

That day Valène asked Winckler how he'd come to Paris and how he'd met Bartlebooth. But Winckler replied only that it was because he was young.

CHAPTER NINE

Servants' Quarters, 3

This is the room where the painter Hutting houses his two servants, Joseph and Ethel.

Joseph Nieto is the chauffeur and odd-job man. He's a Paraguayan of about forty who used to be a quartermaster in the merchant navy.

Ethel Rogers, a Dutch woman of twenty-six, serves as cook and laundress.

The room is almost entirely filled by a big Empire bed with posts topped by carefully polished brass spheres. Ethel Rogers is getting dressed, half-hidden by a rice-paper screen decorated with floral motifs, over which a cashmere-style shawl has been thrown. Nieto, dressed in an embroidered white shirt and broad-belted black trousers, is stretched out on the bed; in his left hand, held up to his eyes, he has a letter with a diamond-shaped stamp bearing the image of Simon Bolivar, and in his right hand, the middle finger adorned with a heavy signet ring, he holds an ignited cigarette lighter, as if he is preparing to burn the letter he has just received.

Between the bed and the door, there is a small sideboard made of fruit-tree wood, on which a bottle of Black and White whisky stands, identifiable by the two dogs on the label, as well as a plate containing an assortment of salted biscuits.

The room is painted light green. The floor is covered with a carpet of yellow and pink squares. A dressing table, and a single straw chair, with a well-thumbed book on it: *French Through Reading. Intermediate Level. Second Year*, complete the furnishing.

Above the bed they have pinned a reproduction entitled *Arminius and Sigimer*: it depicts two grey-cloaked, bull-necked giants with Herculean biceps and red faces sprouting thick moustaches and bushy sideburns.

On the main door a postcard has been fixed with drawing pins: it shows a monumental sculpture by Hutting – *Beasts of the Night* – adorning the main courtyard of the Prefecture at Pontarlier: entwined lumps of slag dimly suggestive, overall, of some prehistoric animal.

The bottle of whisky and the salted biscuits are a present, or more precisely a tip which Madame Altamont has sent up to them in advance. Hutting has close ties with the Altamonts, and the painter has lent them his servants, who will serve this evening as extras at the annual reception they are holding, in their big flat on the second floor left, beneath Bartlebooth's. It happens the same way each year, and the Altamonts return the favour for the often lavish parties which the painter gives, every quarter, in his studio.

FOR FURTHER INFORMATION:

BOSSEUR, J.	*Les Sculptures de Franz Hutting*. Paris, Galerie Maillard, 1965
JACQUET, B.	*Hutting: vor Angst hüten*. Forum, 1967, 7
HUTTING, F.	*Manifeste du Mineral Art*. Brussels, Galerie 9 + 3, 1968
HUTTING, F.	*Of Stones and Men*. Urbana Museum of Fine Arts, 1970

Nahum, E. "Towards a planetary consciousness: Grillner, Hagiwara, Hutting", in S. Gogolak (ed.), *An Anthology of Neo-Creative Painting*. Los Angeles, Markham and Coolidge, 1974

Nahum, E. *Haze over Being. An Essay on Franz Hutting's painting*. Paris, XYZ, 1974

Xertigny, A. de *Hutting portraitiste*. New Art Review, Montreal, 1975, 3

CHAPTER TEN

Servants' Quarters, 4

On the top floor, a tiny little room, occupied by a sixteen-year-old girl, Jane Sutton, who works as an au pair for the Rorschachs.

The girl is standing by the window. Her face is lit up with joy as she reads a letter – or maybe, even, rereads it for the twentieth time – whilst chewing the crust end of a French loaf. There is a cage hanging in the window; it holds a bird with grey plumage, with a metal ring on its foot.

The bed is very narrow: actually it's a foam mattress laid on three wooden cubes which serve as drawers, and covered with a patchwork quilt. Fixed to the wall above the bed is a cork board, about two feet by three, on which are pinned several bits of paper – instructions for the use of an electric toaster, a laundry ticket, a calendar, an *Alliance Française* timetable, and three photographs showing the girl – two or three years younger – in school plays put on at Greenhill, near Harrow, where, some sixty-five years previously, Bartlebooth, following in the footsteps of Byron, Sir Robert Peel, Sheridan, Spencer, John Percival, Lord Palmerston, and dozens of other equally eminent men, had been educated.

On the first photo Jane Sutton appears as a page, dressed in red brocade breeches with gold piping, light-red hose, a white shirt, and a short, collarless doublet, red in colour, with slightly puffed sleeves and edged with a yellow silk fringe.

On the second, she is Princess Beryl, kneeling at the bedside of her grandfather, King Utherpandragon (*"When King Utherpandragon felt the sickness of death coming upon him, he had the princess brought to his side . . ."*).

The third snapshot shows fourteen girls in a row. Jane is the fourth from the left (an X over her head shows which she is, otherwise it would be hard to recognise her). It is the last scene from Yorick's *Count of Gleichen*:

The Count of Gleichen was taken prisoner in a battle against the Saracens, and condemned to slavery. As he was employed in the gardens of the harem, the Sultan's daughter espied him. She judged him to be a man of quality, was inspired with love for him, and offered to assist in his escape if he would marry her. He gave the reply that he was married already; which caused not the slightest scruple to the princess, accustomed as she was to the plurality of wives. They soon agreed on't, set sail, and landed at Venice. The Count went to Rome, and told Pope Gregory IX his tale in every particular. On the Count's promise to convert the Saracen, the Pope gave him a dispensation to keep both his wives.

His first wife was so overcome with joy at her husband's return, no matter what conditions were attach'd to it, that she acquiesced to everything, and demonstrated the full extent of her gratitude to her benefactress. History recounts that the Saracen had no children, and loved those of her rival as their mother did. What pity 'tis, that she did not bring into the world a being that resembled her!

At Gleichen can be seen the bed in which these three rare individuals slept together. They were buried in the same grave, at the Benedictine monastery at Saint Petersburg; and the Count, who survived both his wives, ordered that their tomb, which was later to be his own also, should bear this epitaph, which he composed:

"Here lie two rival wives who loved each other as sisters, and loved me in equal measure. One of them abandoned Mahomet to follow her husband, and the other threw herself into the arms of the rival who brought him back to her. United by ties of love and marriage, we had but one nuptial bed throughout our lives; and the same stone covereth us all after death." An oak and two limes, as is proper, were planted beside the grave.

* * *

The only other piece of furniture in the room is a narrow low table filling the available space between the bed and the window, on which stands a gramophone – a tiny model, known as a disc-muncher – plus a quarter-full bottle of Pepsi-Cola, a set of playing cards, a potted cactus complemented by some multicoloured gravel, a little plastic bridge, and a minute parasol.

There are some records piled up on the low table. One of them, out of its sleeve, stands almost vertical against the edge of the bed: it's a jazz record – *Gerry Mulligan: Far East Tour* – and the sleeve depicts the temples of Angkor Wat in morning haze.

A macintosh and a long cashmere scarf hang on a coathook fixed to the door.

A fourth photograph, of large square format, is stuck with drawing pins on the right-hand wall, not far from where the girl is standing; it depicts a large drawing room at Versailles with a wood-block floor, without any furniture except a huge, carved armchair in Second Empire style, to the right of which, with one hand on the top of the chair-back and the other on his hip, with his chin jutting forward, there stands a very short man dressed as a musketeer.

CHAPTER ELEVEN

Hutting's Studio, 1

In the left-hand corner of the two top floors of the building, Hutting the painter has knocked eight maids' rooms, a stretch of corridor, and the corresponding roof-space into a huge studio, with a raised gallery running round three sides of it giving access to several bedrooms. Around the open spiral stairs leading to the gallery he has made a sort of lounge, where he likes to rest between working sessions, and where during the day he receives friends and clients, separated from the main part of the studio by an L-shaped piece of furniture, a two-sided bookcase, vaguely Chinese in style, that is to say lacquered black with imitation mother-of-pearl and beaten brass inlays; it is tall, broad, and long – more than seven feet along the larger arm, about five feet along the shorter. Lined up on top of this bookcase are various casts, an old Marianne from some town hall, large vases, three fine alabaster pyramids, whilst the five layers of shelving bow under the weight of a heap of knickknacks, curios, and gadgets: kitsch objects from a 1930s Inventors' Exhibition: a potato-peeler, a device for stirring mayonnaise with a little cylinder that releases the oil drop by drop, a tool for fine-slicing hard-boiled eggs and another for making butter whorls, a terrifyingly complicated monkey wrench no doubt intended to be merely the ultimate in corkscrews; ready-mades of surrealist inspiration – a silver-coated stick loaf – and of the pop-art age: a bottle of 7-Up; dried flowers under glass in little romantic or rococo settings made of painted cardboard and cloth, charming *trompe-l'oeil* works in which every detail is minutely reproduced, from a lace doily on a table no more than an inch high to a zigzag parquet floor of which each woodblock is no more than one tenth of an inch long; a whole collection of old postcards showing Pompeii at the turn of the century: Der Triumphbogen des Nero (Arco di Nerone, Arc de Néron, Nero's Arch), la Casa dei Vetti (*"one of the best examples of a noble Roman villa, the fine paintings and marble decorations have been preserved in the peristyle, which was decorated with greenery . . ."*), Casa di Cavio Rufio, Vico di Lupanare, etc. The finest pieces of the collections are dainty musical boxes; one of them, allegedly antique, is a small church with bells which play the famous *Smanie implacabili che m'agitate* from *Così fan tutte* when you gently lift the bell-tower; another is a tiny, valuable pendulum clock whose movement powers a little ballerina in a tutu.

In the rectangle defined by the L-shaped structure each arm of which ends on an opening that can be closed by a leather drape, Hutting has placed a low sofa, a few poufs, and a drinks trolley equipped with bottles, glasses, and an ice bucket from the famous Beirut nightclub *The Star*: it portrays a short, fat, seated monk holding a goblet in his right hand; he is dressed in a long grey robe tied with a cord; his head and shoulders are enclosed in a black hood which forms the bucket's lid.

The wall on the left, facing the longer arm of the L, is hung with cork paper. On the track fixed about nine feet up, several metal hangers run, and on them the painter has hung a score of his canvases, mostly small ones: they almost all belong to one of the painter's earlier styles, the one he refers to himself as his "*haze period*" and which gained him his notoriety: they are, generally, minutely executed copies of well-known paintings – *Mona Lisa*, *The Angelus*, *The Retreat from Russia*, *Le Déjeuner sur l'herbe*, *The Anatomy Lesson*, etc. – over which he has then painted a more or less heavy haze, producing a greyish blur beneath which you can only just make out the silhouette of his celebrated originals. The private viewing of his Paris exhibition at Gallery 22 in 1960 was complemented by artificial fog, made even denser by the crowds of cigar- and cigarette-smokers amongst the guests, to the great joy of the gossip-columnists. It was an instant success. One or two critics carped, for example Beyssandre from Switzerland, who wrote: "Hutting's greys hark back less to Malevich's *White on White* than to bad jokes by vulgar comedians about black men in unlit tunnels." But most of them enthused over what one called his *romantic meteorology*, which, he said, placed Hutting on a par with his famous quasi-namesake, Huffing, the New York pioneer of *Arte brutta*. Astutely advised, Hutting kept nearly half his canvases himself and will consent to parting with them only on exorbitant terms.

There are three people in this little lounge. One is a woman, fortyish; she is coming down the gallery stairs; she is wearing black leather dungarees and holds in her hand an intricately carved oriental dagger, which she is cleaning with a piece of chamois leather. Tradition has it that this is the dagger used by the fanatic Suleiman el-Halebi in the assassination of General Jean-Baptiste Kléber, at Cairo on 14 June 1800, when this strategist of genius, who had been left on station by Bonaparte after the semi-success of the Egyptian Campaign, had just replied to Admiral Keith's ultimatum by winning victory at the Battle of Heliopolis.

The two other occupants are seated on poufs. They are a couple in their sixties. The woman is wearing a patchwork skirt reaching down to her knees, and wide fishnet stockings; she stubs out her lipstick-stained cigarette in a cut-glass ashtray shaped something like a starfish; the man is dressed in a dark suit with red pinstripes, a pale-blue shirt with matching tie, and breast-pocket handkerchief in blue with red stripes; pepper-and-salt hair cut short and brushed up;

tortoiseshell spectacles. On his knees he has a booklet bound in red, entitled *Internal Revenue Legislation*.

The young woman in the leather dungarees is Hutting's secretary. The man and woman are Austrian clients. They have come especially from Salzburg to negotiate the purchase of one of Hutting's most highly rated *hazes*, the one which began as nothing less than *The Turkish Bath*, supplied by the Hutting process with a superabundance of steamy vapour. From afar, the canvas looks curiously like Turner's watercolour *Harbour near Tintagel*, which, at the time he was giving him lessons, Valène showed to Bartlebooth as the most accomplished example of what can be achieved in watercolours, and which the Englishman went to copy exactly, on site, in Cornwall.

Although he is not often in his Paris flat, dividing his time between his New York "loft", his château in the Dordogne, and a country *mas* near Nice, Hutting has returned for the Altamonts' reception. At the moment he is at work in one of the upper rooms, where, of course, it is strictly forbidden to disturb him.

CHAPTER TWELVE

Réol, 1

For a very long time the small two-roomed flat on the fifth floor left was occupied by a single lady, Madame Hourcade. Before the war she worked in a cardboard factory making casings for art books in strong card covered in silk, leather, or suedette and with cold-hammered lettering, storage folders, advertising display folders, office sundries – file boxes in red or Empire-green cloth bindings with thin gold edging – and novelty boxes with stencilled decorations, for gloves, cigarettes, chocolates, and fruit jellies. It was of course from her that Bartlebooth, a few months before his departure in nineteen thirty-four, ordered the boxes in which Winckler would pack his puzzles after he had made each one: five hundred absolutely identical boxes, twenty centimetres long, twelve centimetres wide, and eight deep, in black cardboard, with a black ribbon for tying them closed and which Winckler would seal with wax, and with no labelling other than an oval sticker bearing the initials P.B. followed by a number.

During the war the factory could no longer manage to obtain raw materials of adequate quality and had to close. Madame Hourcade survived with difficulty until she had the luck to find a position in a large hardware store on Avenue des Ternes. It seems she enjoyed the work, for she stayed on after the Liberation, even when the factory reopened and offered to take her back.

She retired in the early seventies and settled in the little house she owned near Montargis. There she leads a quiet and peaceful life and, once a year, returns the good wishes sent her by Mademoiselle Crespi.

The people who have succeeded her in the flat are called Réol. At the time they were a young couple with a little boy of three. A few months after moving they posted on the glass pane of the concierge's door an announcement of their marriage. Madame Nochère made a collection around the building to buy them a present, but gathered no more than 41 francs!

The Réols will be in the dining room and just finishing dinner. On the table there will be a bottle of pasteurised beer, the remains of a sponge cake with the knife still in it, a cut-glass fruit bowl containing what are called "the four beggarmen", that is to say an assortment of dried fruits, prunes, almonds, walnuts and hazelnuts, sultanas, raisins, figs, and dates.

The young woman stands on tiptoe beside a Louis XIII-style dresser, her arms outstretched to reach from the top shelf an earthenware plate decorated with a romantic landscape: wide fields surrounded by wooden fences and broken by dark spinneys of pine and little streams spilling over into lakes, and, in the distance, a tall narrow barnhouse with a balcony and a flattened roof on which a stork has landed.

The man is wearing a polka-dot pullover. He holds a fob watch in his left hand which he looks at whilst with his right hand he resets the hands of a large Early American carriage clock on which a group of

Negro Minstrels is carved: a dozen musicians wearing top hats, cutaway jackets, and big bow ties, playing various wind instruments, banjos, and a shuffleboard.

The walls are hung with hessian. There aren't any pictures, or reproductions, not even a standard post-office calendar. The child – now aged eight – is on all fours on a very thin straw mat. He wears a kind of red leather cap. He's playing with a small whistling top bearing a bird design drawn in such a way that as the top slows down it looks as though the birds are flapping their wings. Beside him, in a strip comic, you can see a tall mop-haired young man with a blue-and-white-striped sweater jumping onto a donkey. In the bubble coming from the donkey's mouth – for it's a talking donkey – are the words: "If you want to play donkey you must be an ass".

CHAPTER THIRTEEN

Rorschach, 1

The entrance hall of the Rorschachs' large duplex. The room is empty. The walls are in white gloss, the floor is laid with grey flagstones. One piece of furniture, in the centre: a huge Empire desk, with a set of drawers fitted in the backpiece, separated by wooden pillars making an arch over the middle, in which a clock is set, with a design carved in it representing a naked woman beside a little waterfall. On the desktop two objects are displayed: a bunch of grapes, each fruit being a delicate sphere of blown glass, and a bronze statuette of a painter, standing in front of a full-size easel, leaning back from the waist, tipping back his head; he has a long drooping moustache, and curly hair down to his shoulders. He wears a full doublet and holds a palette in one hand and a long-handled brush in the other.

On the wall at the end, a large pen-and-ink drawing depicts Rémi Rorschach himself. He's an old man, tall and wizened, with a birdlike profile.

Rémi Rorschach's life, as narrated in a volume of memoirs

ghosted for him with indulgence by a writer specialising in that kind of service, is a painful combination of courage and error. He began his career at the end of the 1914–18 war in a Marseilles music hall doing impressions of Max Linder and other American comedians. A tall, thin man with melancholy, heartbroken gestures and expressions which could indeed remind you of Keaton, Lloyd, or Laurel, Rorschach might have made a name for himself if he hadn't been a few years before his time. The fashion was for soldier comedians and whilst the crowds flocked to Fernandel, Gabin, and Préjean, soon to be made famous by films, "Harry Kobinz" – that was the name he'd taken – mouldered in miserable poverty and found it harder and harder to get his act taken on. What with the war just over, the recent national unity government, and the "sky-blue" conservative victory at the elections, he got the idea of founding a group specialising in rousing brass flourishes, military tunes from Tipperary, square dances, and a kitbag of similar Armentières. A photo from that period shows him with his band – "Albert Greenfield and his Jolly Rogers" – wearing a cocky look, a fake kepi tilted to one side, a broad-frogged combat jacket, and impeccably tight puttees. It was an instant success, but lasted only a few weeks. The invasion of the paso doble, the foxtrot, the beguine, and other exotic dances from North, South, and Central America and elsewhere closed to him the doors of dance halls and nightspots, and his valiant efforts to adapt ("Barry Jefferson and His Hot Pepper Seven", "Paco Domingo and the Three Caballeros", "Fedor Kowalski and His Magyar Minstrels", "Alberto Sforzi and His Gondoliers") all failed in succession. In fact, he recalls on this point, only names and headgear changed: the act stayed virtually the same, as they were happy enough to make slight changes of tempo, to swap a guitar for a balalaika, a banjo, or a mandolin, and to utter the appropriate "*Baby*", "*Olé*", "*Tovarich*", "*mio amore*", or "*corazón*", occasionally, with meaning.

Shortly after this, dejected, his mind made up to abandon the performing arts, but not wishing to leave the world of show business, Rorschach became the manager of an acrobat, a trapeze artist who had rapidly become a celebrity because of two features: the first was that he was very young – Rorschach met him when he was not yet twelve – and the second was his talent for staying on his trapeze for hours at a stretch. Crowds flocked to the music halls and circuses where he was on, not only to see him do his act, but to watch him napping, washing, dressing, or drinking a cup of chocolate on the narrow bar of his trapeze, ninety or a hundred feet from the ground.

At the start the partnership flourished, and all the major cities of Europe, North Africa, and the Middle East applauded the amazing feats of the young man. But as he grew older, the trapeze artist became more and more demanding. At first purely out of a desire to improve but subsequently from the tyranny of habit as well, he so organised his life that, for as long as he was working in one establishment, he spent his whole time, day and night, on his trapeze. His very modest needs were all met by relays of servants who kept watch below and who raised and lowered everything required up above in specially constructed containers. His way of life occasioned no particular difficulties as far as those around him were concerned, except that, during the other acts on the programme, it was slightly disturbing that he stayed aloft – the fact could not be concealed – and that the audience, though it usually remained calm, let its gaze stray in his direction. The management forgave him this, however, because he was an outstanding and irreplaceable artist. Also, of course, they appreciated that he did not live like that out of mischief and that it was in fact the only way he could keep himself in constant form and maintain his act at the level of perfection.

The problem was harder to manage when his seasons ended and the trapeze artist had to travel to another town. His manager saw to it that he was spared any unnecessary prolongation of his sufferings: for trips in towns they used racing cars, dashing, if possible at night or in the very early morning, through the deserted streets at top speed, though of course still too slowly for the languishing trapeze artist; in trains, they took a whole compartment, where, adopting a pathetic but at least partial substitute for his normal way of life, he spent the journey up in the luggage rack; in the next theatre on their tour the trapeze was in place long before the acrobat's arrival and all the doors between them and the auditorium were wide open and all the corridors clear, so that he could be back up on high without losing a second. "Seeing him set foot on the rope-ladder," Rorschach wrote, "and climb back up to his eyrie with the speed of lightning, were the happiest moments of my life."

* * *

The day came, alas, when the artist refused to come down from his trapeze. He had just done his last performance at the Grand Theatre at Leghorn and was due to leave that evening by car for Tarbes. Despite Rorschach's and the music hall manager's pleadings, increasingly hysterical appeals from the other members of the troupe, from the musicians, the entire staff, the technicians, and from the crowds who had begun to leave but had stopped and returned on hearing all this noise, the acrobat, in a fit of pride, cut the rope he could have come down by and began to perform, at ever-faster pace, an uninterrupted succession of grand circles. This supreme performance lasted two hours and caused fifty-three spectators to pass out. The police had to be brought in. In spite of Rorschach's warnings, the policemen brought a long fire-ladder and began to climb up. They didn't even get halfway: the trapeze artist opened his grip, and, with a long scream, describing a perfect parabola, he crashed to the ground.

After paying compensation to the theatre owners who had been trying to get the acrobat for months, Rorschach had some capital left, and he decided to invest it in an export-import business. He bought a stock of sewing machines and shipped them to Aden in the hope of trading them for perfumes and spices. He was persuaded to adopt a different course by a trader he became acquainted with on the crossing, who was lugging various copper instruments and utensils, from valve rods to spiral condensing tubes, from pearl-sieves to frying pans and fish kettles. The spice market, so this businessman explained, and more generally everything to do with trade between Europe and the Middle East, was tightly controlled by Anglo-Arabian syndicates which, in order to keep their monopolies, did not flinch from even physically eliminating their most minor rivals. On the other hand, business between Arabia and black Africa was much less supervised and offered opportunities for profitable deals. In particular, the trade in cowrie shells: as is well known, these shells are used as currency by many people in Africa and India. But it is not widely known – and that's where there was money to be made – that there are several different kinds of cowries, with different values for different tribes. Thus Red Sea cowries (*Cypraea turdus*) are very highly valued in the Comoro Islands, where they can easily be exchanged for Indian cowries (*Cypraea caput serpentis*) at a very favourable rate of fifteen caput serpentis for one turdus. Now not far away, in Dar-es-Salaam, the rate for caput serpentis is constantly going up, and deals are often struck there at one caput serpentis for three *Cypraea moneta*. This last kind of cowrie is commonly called the coin-cowrie: as you would expect from its name, it is negotiable almost everywhere, but in West Africa, in Cameroon and especially in Gabon, it is so highly valued that some tribes pay for it with its own weight in gold. With all expenses offset, you could aim to multiply your stake tenfold. The operation was entirely safe but needed time. Rorschach didn't feel he had the makings of a great traveller and was not too keen, but the trader's certainty was sufficiently impressive to make him accept unhesitatingly the offer of partnership that was put to him when they landed at Aden.

The transactions proceeded exactly as the trader had foreseen. In Aden they exchanged their shipments of copper and sewing machines for forty cases of Cypraea turdus without any difficulty. They left the Comoros with eight hundred cases of caput serpentis, the only problem having been to get the wood for the said cases. In Dar-es-Salaam they chartered a caravan of two hundred and fifty camels to cross Tanganyika with their one thousand nine hundred and forty cases of coin-cowries, reached the great Congo river, and made their descent nearly to the estuary in four hundred and seventy-five days, of which two hundred and twenty-one had been spent on water, one hundred and thirty-seven in rail transshipment, twenty-four in portered transshipment, and ninety-three days in waiting, resting, enforced idleness, palavers, administrative hassles, and diverse incidents and nuisances, which nonetheless constituted, all in all, a remarkable achievement.

It was a little over two and a half years since they had landed at Aden. What they didn't know – and how in God's name could they have known! – was that, at the very time they got to Aden, another Frenchman, called Schlendrian, was leaving Cameroon after flooding it with coin-cowries obtained in Zanzibar; he had brought about an irreversible depreciation of the currency throughout Western and Central Africa. Rorschach's and his partner's cowries had not just become unnegotiable, they had become a dangerous liability: the

French colonial administration reckoned, quite rightly, that putting seven hundred million shells in circulation – more than thirty per cent of the global mass of cowries used for trade in the whole of French West Africa – would provoke an unprecedented economic catastrophe (the mere rumour sent the prices of colonial goods into a seesaw, an upset viewed by some economists as a prime factor in the causes of the Wall Street crash): the cowries were therefore impounded; Rorschach and his companion were courteously, but firmly, requested to catch the first steamer leaving for France.

Rorschach would have done anything to take his revenge on Schlendrian, but he never managed to track him down. All he managed to learn was that in the war of 1870 there had indeed been a General Schlendrian. But he'd died long before and didn't seem to have left any descendants.

Exactly how Rorschach got through the following years remains obscure. In his memoirs he is very discreet on this point. In the early 1930s he wrote a novel largely based on his African adventure. The novel appeared in 1932, under the title *African Gold*, published by Les Editions du Tonneau. The one critic who reviewed it compared it to *Journey to the End of the Night*, which had appeared at about the same time.

The novel was not much read, but it allowed Rorschach to get into literary society. A few months later he founded a review which he entitled, rather bizarrely, *Prejudices*, thereby wishing no doubt to signify that the review had none. It appeared at a rhythm of four issues a year up until the war. It published several pieces by some authors who subsequently established themselves. Though Rorschach is very close with precise details on this point, it seems probable that it was a vanity-publishing enterprise. In any case, of all his pre-war projects it is the only one he does not describe as a total failure.

Some say that he spent his war with the Free French Army, and that he was entrusted with several missions of a diplomatic nature. Others assert, to the contrary, that he collaborated with the Axis powers and that after the war he had to flee to Spain. What's certain is that he returned to France, rich and flourishing, and even married, in the early sixties. It was at a time when, as he recalls jokingly, all you had to do to be a producer was to set up in one of the innumerable empty offices in the *Maison de la Radio*, and he began to work for television. It was also at this time that he bought from Olivier Gratiolet the last two apartments in the building still owned by him, apart from the little flat he lived in himself. Rorschach had them knocked into a single, prestigious duplex which was photographed many times for *La Maison Française, Maison et Jardin, Forum, Art et Architecture Aujourd'hui*, and other specialist reviews.

Valène can still remember the first time he saw him. It was one of those days when (so as not to cause a surprise) the lift was out of order. He had come out of his flat and was on his way downstairs to see Winckler, and passed in front of the newcomer's door. It was wide open. Workmen were coming and going, and in the lobby Rorschach was scratching his head as he listened to the advice of his interior designer. At that time he'd gone for the American look, with floral shirts, neckerchiefs, and wristbands. Later he went in for the weary lion look, the old loner who's seen it all, happier with desert Bedouins than in the drawing rooms of Paris: canvas rubbers, leather jerkins, grey linen shirts.

Today he is an ill old man, forced to spend most of his time in nursing homes or in long-drawn-out convalescence. His misanthropy remains as proverbial as ever, but has a diminishing field for expression.

BIBLIOGRAPHY

RORSCHACH, R.	*Memories of a Struggler*. Paris, Gallimard, 1974.
RORSCHACH, R.	*African Gold*. Paris, Ed. du Tonneau, 1932.
Gen. A. COSTELLO	"Could the Schlendrian Offensive have saved Sedan?", *Army Hist. Review*, 7, 1907.
LANDES, D.	"The Cauri System and African Banking", *Harvard J. Econ.*, 48, 1965.
ZGHAL, A.	"Les Systèmes d'échanges interafricains. Mythes et réalités", *Zeitschrift für Ethnol.*, 194, 1971.

CHAPTER FOURTEEN

Dinteville, 1

Dr Dinteville's consulting room: an examining couch, a metal desk, almost bare, with only a telephone, an anglepoise lamp, a prescription pad, a matt-finished steel pen in the groove of a marble inkstand; a small yellow leather divan, above which hangs a large reproduction of a Vasarely, two broad and sprouting succulents rising out of plaited raffia pot-holders, one on each side of the window; a set of freestanding shelves, the top shelf supporting a number of instruments, a stethoscope, a chrome-plated cotton-wool dispenser, a small bottle of medicinal alcohol; and along the whole right-hand wall, shining metal panels concealing various pieces of medical apparatus and the cupboards where the doctor keeps his instruments, his records, and his pharmaceutical stores.

Dr Dinteville sits at his table writing a prescription with a look of complete indifference. He is a man of about forty, almost bald, with an egg-shaped head. His patient is an old woman. She is about to get down from the examining couch where she has been lying, and is adjusting the brooch which holds her blouse together: a metal lozenge inscribed with a stylised fish.

A third person is seated on the divan; he is a man of mature years, wearing a leather jacket and a wide check scarf with fringed edging.

The Dintevilles are descended from a Post Master knighted by Louis XIII for the help he gave Luynes and Vitry at the time of Concini's murder. Cadignan has left us this striking portrait of a character who seems to have been an uncommonly rough old trooper:

> D'Inteville was of middling stature, neither too big nor too small, and his nose was somewhat aquiline, the shape of a razor handle. At that time he was thirty-five or thereabouts, and about as fit for gilding as a lead dagger. He was a very proper-looking fellow, but for the fact that he was a bit of a lecher and naturally subject to a malady that was called

> at that time "the lack of money, pain incomparable!" However he had sixty-three ways of finding it at a pinch, the commonest and most honest of which was by means of cunningly perpetrated larceny. He was a mischievous rogue, a cheat, a boozer, a roysterer, and a vagabond if there ever was one in Paris, but otherwise the best fellow in the world; and he was always preparing some trick against the sergeants and the watch.

His descendants were generally less wild and gave France a dozen or score of bishops and cardinals, as well as various other remarkable characters, of whom the following are particularly worthy of note:

Gilbert de Dinteville (1774–1796): a fervent Republican, he enlisted at the age of seventeen and rose to be a colonel in three years. He led his battalion in the attack on Montenotte. This heroic gesture cost him his life but ensured the successful outcome of the battle.

Emmanuel de Dinteville (1810–1849): a friend of Liszt and Chopin, known particularly as the composer of a waltz, fittingly entitled *The Spinning Top*.

François de Dinteville (1814–1867): came top in the final examination at the Ecole Polytechnique at the age of seventeen, spurned the brilliant career he could have had in engineering or in industry, and devoted himself to research. In 1840 he believed he had discovered the secret of making diamonds from coal. On the basis of what he dubbed "crystal duplication theory", he succeeded in making a carbon-saturated solution crystallise by cooling. The Academy of Sciences, to which he submitted his samples, declared his experiment interesting, but inconclusive, since the diamonds obtained were dull, brittle, easily scored by a fingernail, and sometimes even friable. This refutation didn't deter Dinteville from patenting his method, nor from publishing, between 1840 and his death, thirty-four original articles and technical reports on the subject. Ernest Renan mentions his case in one of his chronicles (*Miscellany*, 47, *passim*): *"Had Dinteville truly manufactured diamond, he would thereby no doubt have pandered, in some measure, to that crude materialism which must now be reckoned with evermore by any man who makes so bold as to concern himself with the business of humanity; to souls aspiring to the ideal, he would have given nary a molecule of that exquisite spirituality upon which we have lived so long, and do still."*

Laurelle de Dinteville (1842–1861) was one of the unfortunate victims and probably the cause of one of the most horrible news stories of the Second Empire. During a reception given by the Duke of Crécy-Couvé, whom she was to have married a few weeks later, the young lady drank a toast to her future in-laws, emptying her champagne glass in a single draught, and then flung the glass in the air. Fate determined that she should be standing immediately beneath a gigantic chandelier, which came from the famous workshop of Baucis at Murano. The chandelier snapped and caused the deaths of eight people, including Laurelle and the Duke's father, old Marshal Crécy-Couvé, who'd had three horses shot under him during the Russian Campaign. Foul play could not be suspected. François de Dinteville, Laurelle's uncle, who was present at the reception, put forward the theory of "pendular amplification produced by the conflicting vibratory frequencies of the crystal glass and the chandelier" but no one took this explanation seriously.

CHAPTER FIFTEEN

Servants' Quarters, 5
Smautf

Under the eaves, between Hutting's studio and Jane Sutton's room, the room of Mortimer Smautf, Bartlebooth's aged butler.

The room is empty. With eyes half-closed, with its front legs tucked in a sphynx-like posture, a white-furred cat drowses on the orange bedspread. Beside the bed, on a small bedside table, lie a cut-glass ashtray of triangular shape, with the word "Guinness" engraved on it, and a detective story entitled *The Seven Crimes of Azincourt*.

Smautf has been in Bartlebooth's service for more than fifty years. Although he calls himself a butler, his services have been more those of gentleman's gentleman or secretary; or, to be even more precise, both at the same time: in fact, he was above all his master's travelling companion, his factotum, and if not his Sancho Panza at least his Passepartout (for there was indeed a touch of Phineas Fogg in Bartlebooth), in turns porter, clothes valet, barber, driver, guide, treasurer, travel agent, and umbrella holder.

Bartlebooth's, and therefore Smautf's, travels lasted twenty years, from 1935 to 1954, and took them in a sometimes fanciful way all around the world. From 1930 Smautf began to prepare for the journey, getting hold of all the papers necessary for obtaining visas, reading up on the formalities currently used in the different countries they would pass through, opening properly funded accounts in various appropriate places, collecting guidebooks, maps, timetables and fares lists, booking hotel rooms and steamer tickets. Bartlebooth's idea was to go and paint five hundred seascapes in five hundred different ports. The ports were chosen more or less at random by Bartlebooth, who thumbed through atlases, geography books, travellers' tales, and tourist brochures and ticked off the places that appealed to him. Smautf then studied how to get there and find accommodation.

The first port, in the first fortnight of January 1935, was Gijon, in the Bay of Biscay, not far from where the unfortunate Beaumont was carrying on trying to find the last remains of an improbable Arab capital of Spain. The last was Brouwershaven, in Zeeland, at the estuary of the Scheldt, in the second fortnight of December nineteen fifty-four. In between, there had been the little harbour of Muckanaghederdauhaulia, not far from Costelloe, in Ireland's Camus Bay, and the even tinier port of U in the Caroline Islands; there were Baltic ports and Latvian ports, Chinese ports and Malagasy ports, Chilean ports and Texan ports; tiny harbours of two fishing boats and three nets, huge ports with several miles of breakwaters, with docks and quaysides, with hundreds of fixed and travelling cranes; ports cloaked in fog, sweltering ports, and ports locked in ice; deserted harbours, silted harbours, yachting harbours, with artificial beaches, transplanted palms and grand hotels and gaming halls fronting the waterside; infernal dockyards building liberty ships by the thousand; ports devastated by bombing; quiet ports where naked girls sprayed each other beside the sampans; ports for canoes and ports for gondolas; naval harbours, creeks, dry-dock basins, roads, cambers, channels, moles; piles of barrels, rope, and sponges; heaps of redwood trees, mountains of fertiliser, phosphates, and minerals; cages crawling with lobsters and crabs; stalls of gurnard, brill, lasher, bream, whiting, mackerel, skate, tuna fish, cuttlefish, and lampreys; ports stinking of soap or chlorine; ports tossed by storms and deserted ports crushed by heat; battleships repaired in the dark by thousands of blow lamps; festive liners surrounded by fire-tenders pumping jets of water in the air amidst a hubbub of hooting sirens and ringing bells.

Bartlebooth allowed two weeks for each port, inclusive of travelling time, which usually gave him five or six days on site. The first two days he spent walking on the sea front, looking at boats, chatting with the fishermen if they spoke one of Bartlebooth's five languages – English, French, Spanish, Arabic, and Portuguese – and sometimes going to sea with them. On the third day he would choose his place, and sketch a few drafts which he tore up straight away. On the penultimate day he would paint his watercolour, usually towards the end of the morning, unless he sought or expected some special effect – sunrise, sunset, the build-up to a storm, drizzle, high or low tide, a flight of birds, fishing boats leaving, a ship arriving, women washing clothes, etc. He painted extremely fast, and never corrected himself. Scarcely was the watercolour dry than he tore the sheet of Whatman paper from the pad and gave it to Smautf. (Smautf was free to wander as he pleased for the rest of the time, to visit the souks, temples, brothels, and dives, but he had to be there when Bartlebooth was painting and to stand behind him holding steady the large parasol which protected the painter and his fragile easel from rain, sun, and wind.) Smautf wrapped the seascape in tissue paper, slipped it into a stiffened envelope, and packed the parcel in kraft paper with string and sealing wax. That same evening, or at the latest next day, if there were no post office nearby, the parcel was dispatched to:

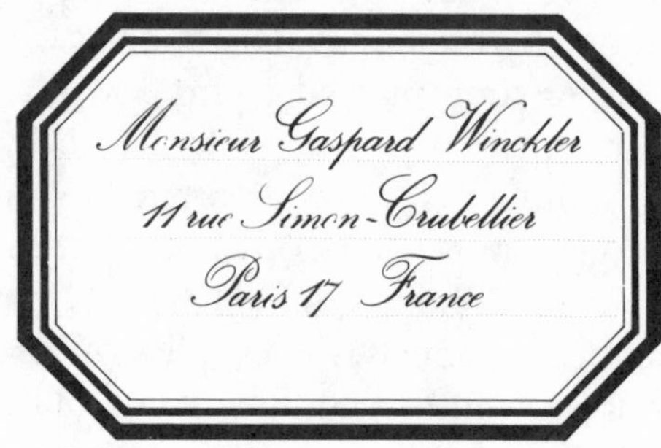

Monsieur Gaspard Winckler
11 rue Simon-Crubellier
Paris 17 France

The site was identified with great care and entered by Smautf in an *ad hoc* register. The next day Bartlebooth would call on the British Consul if there was one thereabouts, or on some other local notable. The day after, they departed. The length of the leg of voyage sometimes modified this timetable slightly, but in general it was scrupulously adhered to.

They didn't proceed necessarily to the nearest port on their itinerary. Depending on the most convenient means of travel, they would perchance come back on their tracks or make fairly large detours. For example, they went by rail from Bombay to Masulipatnam, then crossed the Bay of Bengal to the Andaman Islands, went back to Madras, whence they reached Ceylon, and set off again towards Malacca, Borneo, and the Celebes. Instead of going thence directly to Puerto Princesa on Palawan Island, they went first to Mindanao, then Luzon, and up to Taiwan before coming back down to Palawan.

Nonetheless it is fair to say that in practice they explored the continents one after another. After visiting large parts of Europe from 1935 to 1937, they moved on to Africa and toured it clockwise from 1938 to 1942; from there they reached South America (1943–1944), Central America (1945), North America (1946–1948) and finally Asia (1949–1951). In 1952 they covered Oceania, in 1953 the Indian Ocean and the Red Sea. In the last year they crossed Turkey and the Black Sea, crossed into the USSR, and went up as far as Dudinka, beyond the Arctic Circle, at the mouth of the Yenisei, crossed the Kara and the Barents Seas on a whaler and, from North Cape, came down the Scandinavian fjords before ending their long circular tour at Brouwershaven.

Historical and political circumstances – the Second World War and all the regional conflicts before and after 1939 and 1945: Abyssinia, Spain, India, Korea, Palestine, Madagascar, Guatemala, North Africa, Cyprus, Indonesia, Indochina, etc. – had virtually no influence on their travels, except that they had to wait a few days in Hong Kong for a visa for Canton, and a bomb exploded in their hotel when they were at Port Said. It had a small charge and their trunks hardly suffered at all.

Bartlebooth returned from his travels almost empty-handed: he had only gone in order to paint his five hundred watercolours, and had dispatched them to Winckler as each one was done. Smautf, for his part, had built up three collections – of postage stamps, for Madame Claveau's son, of hotel stickers, for Winckler, and of postcards, for Valène – and brought back three objects which are now in his room.

The first is a magnificent sea chest of soft coral (*gummiferous pterocarpous*, he likes to specify) with brass fittings. He found it at a ship chandler's at St John's, Newfoundland, and entrusted it to a trawler which brought it back to France.

The second is a carved curio, a basalt statue of the tricephalous Mother-Goddess, about fifteen inches high. Smautf obtained it in the Seychelles in exchange for another sculpture, similarly tricephalous, but of an entirely different design: it was a crucifix on which three wooden figurines had been fastened by means of a single thick bolt: a black child, a tall old man, and a life-size dove, once white. That object he'd found in the souk at Agadir, and the man who sold it to him explained that they were the movable figures of the Trinity, and that each took yearly turns "on top" of the others. The Son was then foremost, the Holy Ghost (almost out of sight) against the cross. It was a cumbersome object, but apt to fascinate Smautf's particular cast of mind for a long while. Thus he bought it without haggling and lugged it around with him from 1939 to 1953. The day after he got to the Seychelles, he went into a bar: the first thing he saw was the statue of the Mother-Goddess, standing on the counter between a beat-up cocktail shaker and a glass full of little flags and champagne mixers shaped like miniature shepherds' staves. His stupefaction was such that he returned forthwith to his hotel, came back with the crucifix, and engaged the Malay barman in a long conversation in pidgin concerning the statistical near-impossibility of coming across two statues with three heads twice in fourteen years, at the end of which conversation the barman and Smautf swore undying friendship cemented by the exchange of their works of art.

The third object is a large engraving, a kind of primitive woodcut. Smautf found it at Bergen in the last year of their peregrinations. It depicts a child receiving a book as a prize from an old dominie. The child is seven or eight years old, wearing a sky-blue jacket, short trousers, and polished slip-on shoes; a laurel wreath crowns his head; he is climbing the three steps of a parquet-floored platform adorned with succulents. The old man wears an academic gown. He has a long grey beard and steel-framed spectacles. In his right hand he holds a ruler of boxwood and in his left a large folio volume in a red binding on which can be read *Erindringer frå en Reise i Skotland* (it was the account, Smautf learnt, of the Danish pastor Plenge's journey to Scotland in the summer of 1859). Near the schoolmaster there is a table covered in a green cloth with other volumes placed on it, as well as a globe and an open, oblong musical score. A narrow engraved brass plate attached to the print's wooden frame gives its title, apparently unrelated to the represented scene: *Laborynthus*.

Smautf would like to have been this prize-winning good schoolboy. His regret at having had no schooling has turned over the years into an unhealthy passion for addition, subtraction, multiplication, and division. Right at the start of their travels, he had seen a prodigious mental arithmetician performing at a music hall in London, and over the twenty years of his world tour, by dint of reading and rereading a well-thumbed treatise on mathematical and arithmetical diversions which he'd picked up at a secondhand bookshop at Inverness, he took up arithmetic; on his return he was capable of extracting square and cube roots of nine-digit numbers with relative speed. When that began to get a bit too easy for him, he was seized by a fever for factorials: 1 ! = 1; 2 ! = 2; 3 ! = 6; 4 ! = 24; 5 ! = 120; 6 ! = 720; 7 ! = 5,040; 8 ! = 40,320; 9 ! = 362,880; 10 ! = 3,628,800; 11 ! = 39,916,800; 12 ! = 479,001,600; [. . .]; 22 ! = 1,124,000,727,777,607,680,000, that is to say more than a billion times seven hundred and seventy-seven billions.

So far Smautf has got up to 76! but he can no longer find paper of sufficient width, and even if he could no table would be big enough to lay it out on. He has less and less confidence in himself, which means that he is for ever doing his sums over again. A few years ago Morellet tried to discourage him by telling him that the number written $9^{(9^9)}$, that is, nine to the power of nine to the ninth, which is the largest number you can write using only three figures, would have, if written out in full, three hundred and sixty-nine million digits, which at the rate of one second per digit would keep you busy for eleven years just in writing it, and at the rate of four digits per inch would be one thousand one hundred and fifty-four and one eighth miles long! But that hasn't deterred Smautf from filling backs of envelopes, notebook margins, and butcher's wrappers with columns and columns of numbers.

Smautf is now nearly eighty. Bartlebooth offered him retirement long ago, but Smautf has always refused. To tell the truth, he doesn't have much to do anymore. In the morning he prepares Bartlebooth's clothes and helps him dress. Until five years ago, he shaved him – with a cut-throat that had belonged to Bartlebooth's great-great-grandfather – but his sight has dimmed a lot and his hand shakes a little, so he was replaced by a lad sent up every morning by Monsieur Pois, the hairdresser on Rue de Prony.

Bartlebooth no longer ever goes out, he scarcely leaves his study all day. Smautf stays in the next room with the other servants, who don't have much more work than he does and spend their time playing cards and talking of times past.

Smautf stays for long periods each day in his bedroom. He tries to make some little progress with his arithmetic; for relaxation he does crosswords, reads detective stories which Madame Orlowska lends him, and spends hours stroking the white cat, which purrs whilst massaging the old man's knee with its claws.

The white cat doesn't belong to Smautf but to the whole floor. At times it goes to live in Jane Sutton's room or at Madame Orlowska's, or goes down to Isabelle Gratiolet or Mademoiselle Crespi. Three or four years ago it came in from the roof. It had a large wound on its neck. People noticed that its eyes were different colours, one was as blue as Chinese porcelain, the other was gold. A little later, people realised that it was completely deaf.

CHAPTER SIXTEEN

Servants' Quarters, 6
Mademoiselle Crespi

Old Mademoiselle Crespi is in her room on the seventh floor, between Gratiolet's flat and Hutting's maid's room.

She is lying in bed, beneath a grey woollen blanket. She has a dream: an undertaker, eyes gleaming with hatred, stands opposite her in the doorway; in his half-raised right hand he proffers a pointed, black-edged card. His left hand supports a round cushion on which two medals lie, one of which is the Stalingrad Hero's Cross.

Below him, beyond the doorway, lies an Alpine scene: a lake, a frozen and snow-covered round, bordered with trees; the mountains seem to slope directly down to its further shore, while beyond there again show unfamiliar peaks, all in full snow, overtopping each other against the blue sky. In the foreground, three young people are climbing a path which leads to a cemetery, in the middle of which a column surmounted by an onyx basin rises from a clump of oleander and aucuba trees.

CHAPTER SEVENTEEN

On the Stairs, 2

On the stairs the furtive shadows pass of all those who were there one day.

He remembered Marguerite, and Paul Hébert and Laetizia, and Emilio, and the saddler, and Marcel Appenzzell (with two *z*'s, unlike the canton or the cheese); he remembered Grégoire Simpson, and the mysterious American girl, and the not at all nice Madame Araña; he remembered the man in yellow shoes with a pink in his buttonhole and his malachite-handled stick who came every day for ten years to see Dr Dinteville; he remembered Monsieur Jérôme, the history teacher whose *Dictionary of the Spanish Church in the Seventeenth Century* had been turned down by 46 publishers; he remembered the young student who lived for a few months in the room now occupied by Jane Sutton and who had been kicked out of a vegetarian restaurant where he worked in the evenings after being caught pouring a big bottle of beef extract into the pot of simmering vegetable soup; he remembered Troyan, the secondhand book dealer whose shop was in Rue Lepic and who found one day in a pile of detective novels three letters from Victor Hugo to Henri Samuel, his Belgian publisher, about the publication of *Les Châtiments*; he remembered Berloux, the air-raid warden, a fumbling cretin in a grey smock and a beret, who lived two houses up the road and who, one morning in 1941, in virtue of God knows what ARP regulation, had had put in the hallway and in the back yard, where the rubbish bins were kept, barrels of sand which never had any use at all; he remembered the time when Judge Danglars gave grand receptions for his Appeal Court colleagues: on these occasions, two Republican Guards in full regalia would stand sentry at the door of the building, the porch would be decorated with big pots of aspidistra and philodendron, and a cloakroom was set up to the left of the lift: it was a long tube mounted on casters and fitted with coat hangers which the concierge draped as required with minks, sables, breitschwanzes, astrakhans, and big cloaks with otter-skin collars. On those days

Madame Claveau wore her black, lace-collared dress and sat on a Regency chair (hired from the same caterers as the coat hangers and the indoor plants) beside a marble-topped sideboard on which she put her box of tokens, a square metal box decorated with little cupids armed with bows and arrows, a yellow ashtray praising the virtues of Cusenier Bleach (white or green), and a saucer equipped in advance with five-franc coins.

He had lived in the building longer than anyone else. He had been there longer than Gratiolet, whose family had formerly owned the whole house, but who only came to live here during the war, a few years before inheriting what was left, four or five flats which he'd got rid of one by one, keeping in the end only his own little two-roomed dwelling on the seventh floor; longer than Madame Marquiseaux, whose parents had already had the flat and who was practically born there when he had lived there for almost thirty years already; longer than old Mademoiselle Crespi, than old Madame Moreau, than the Beaumonts, the Marcias, and the Altamonts. Longer even than Bartlebooth; he remembered very precisely the day in nineteen twenty-nine when the young man – for he was a young man at the time, he wasn't yet thirty – told him at the end of his daily water-colour lesson: "I say, it seems that the big flat on the third floor is vacant. I think I'll buy it. I'll waste less time coming to see you."

And he had bought it, that same day, without arguing over the price, of course.

At this time Valène had lived there for ten years already. He had rented his room one day in October nineteen nineteen when he came up from his native town of Etampes, which he'd practically never left before, to enrol at the Fine Art School. He was just nineteen. It was supposed to be a temporary lodging provided by a friend of the family, to tide him over. Later he would marry and become famous, or return to Etampes. He didn't wed or go back to Etampes. Fame didn't come after fifteen years, he acquired at best a modest reputation: some steady customers, some work as an illustrator of collections of folk tales, some teaching allowed him to live relatively comfortably, to paint without hurrying, to travel a little. Even later, when the opportunity arose of finding a larger flat or even a real studio, he realised he was too attached to his room, to his house, to his street, to leave them.

There were of course people he knew almost nothing about, whom he wasn't even sure of having identified properly, people he passed from time to time on the stairs and of whom he wasn't certain whether they lived in the building or only had friends there; there were people he couldn't manage to remember anymore, others of whom only a single derisory image remained: Madame Appenzzell's lorgnette, the cork figurines that Monsieur Troquet used to get into bottles and sell on the Champs-Elysées on Sundays, the blue enamel coffee pot always kept hot on a corner of Madame Fresnel's cooker.

He tried to resuscitate those imperceptible details which over the course of fifty-five years had woven the life of this house and which the years had unpicked one by one: the impeccably polished linoleum floors on which you were only allowed to walk in felt undershoes, the oiled canvas tablecloths with red and green stripes on which mother and daughter shelled peas; the dishstands that clipped together, the white porcelain counterpoise light that you could flick back up with one finger at the end of dinner; evenings by the wireless set, with the man in a flannel jacket, the woman in a flowery apron, and the slumbering cat rolled up in a ball by the fireplace; children in clogs going down for the milk with dented cans; the big old wood-stoves of which you would collect up the ashes in spread-out sheets of old newspaper . . .

Where were they now, the Van Houten cocoa tins, the Banania cartons with the laughing infantryman, the turned-wood boxes of Madeleine biscuits from Commercy? Where were they gone, the larders you used to have beneath the window-ledge, the packets of Saponite, that good old washing powder with its famous Madame Don't-Mind-If-I-Do, the boxes of thermogene wool with the fire-spitting devil drawn by Cappiello, and the sachets of good Dr Gustin's lithium tablets?

The years had flowed past, the removal men had brought down pianos and trunks, rolled carpets and boxes of crockery, standard lamps and fish tanks, birdcages, hundred-year-old clocks, soot-blackened cookers, tables with their flaps, the six chairs, the ice-makers, the large family portraits.

The stairs, for him, were, on each floor, a memory, an emotion, something ancient and impalpable, something palpitating somewhere in the guttering flame of his memory: a gesture, a noise, a flicker, a young woman singing operatic arias to her own piano accompaniment, the clumsy clickety-clack of a typewriter, the clinging smell of cresyl disinfectant, a noise of people, a shout, a hubbub, a rustling of silks and furs, a plaintive miaow behind a closed door, knocks on partition walls, hackneyed tangos on hissing gramophones, or, on the sixth floor right, the persistent droning hum of Gaspard Winckler's jigsaw, to which, three floors lower, on the third floor left, there was now by way of response only a continuing, and intolerable, silence.

CHAPTER EIGHTEEN

Rorschach, 2

Rorschach's dining room, to the right of the large entrance hall. It's empty. The room is rectangular, about fifteen feet long by twelve feet wide. On the floor: a thick ash-grey carpet.

On the left-hand wall, painted matt green, hangs a steel-rimmed glass display case containing 54 antique coins all bearing the image of Sergius Sulpicius Galba, the praetor who had thirty thousand Lusitanians killed in a single day, but saved his own neck by presenting his children with emotion to the tribunal.

On the back wall, which is done in white gloss paint like the entrance hall, a large watercolour has been put, over a low sideboard; entitled *The Rake's Progress* and signed U. N. Owen, it depicts a little railway station in open country. On the left, a railwayman stands leaning against a high desk which serves as a ticket office. He looks about fifty, with his receding hairline, round face, and bushy moustache. He is wearing a waistcoat. He is pretending to look something up in a timetable whilst in fact completing his transcription onto a small rectangular piece of paper of a recipe for mint cake he's found in an almanac half-hidden by the timetable. In front of him, on the opposite side of the desk, a bespectacled customer whose face expresses a phenomenal degree of exasperation files his fingernails whilst waiting for his ticket: to the right a third character in short sleeves, wearing broad, flower-embroidered braces, is rolling a big drum out of the station. Fields of alfalfa, where cows are grazing, stretch out all around.

On the right-hand wall, which is painted a slightly darker green than the left-hand wall, hang nine plates decorated with representations of:

- a priest giving ashes to a believer
- a man putting a coin into a barrel-shaped savings box
- a woman sitting in the corner of a railway carriage, with her arm in a sling
- two men in clogs, in snowy weather, stamping the ground to warm their feet
- a lawyer pleading a case, looking vehement
- a man in a smoking jacket about to drink a cup of chocolate
- a violinist playing, with a mute attached to his instrument
- a man in a nightgown, holding a candlestick, looking at a spider, symbolising hope, on the wall
- a man holding out his visiting card to another man. Both look aggressive, suggesting a duel.

In the middle of the room there is a modern-style round table in citronwood, surrounded by eight chairs upholstered in raised velvet. In the middle of the table there is a silver statuette about ten inches high. It represents a naked, helmeted man on the back of an ox, holding a pyx in his left hand.

The watercolour, the statuette, the antique coins, and the plates, according to Rémi Rorschach, are evidence of his "untiring efforts as a producer". The statuette, a classic caricatural representation of the minor arcanum called the Knight of Cups, is supposed to have been unearthed during work on that "drama" entitled *The Sixteenth Edge of This Cube* which we have already had occasion to mention, and which does indeed deal with a murky tale of seeing into the future; the plates are supposed to have been painted specially as background images for the credits of a serial in which the same actor was to have played in succession the roles of a priest, a banker, a woman, a peasant, a lawyer, a good-food-guide writer, a virtuoso, a gullible ironmonger, and an obdurate archduke; the ancient coins – claimed to be genuine – were said to have been given by a collector and admirer of a series of programmes on the Twelve Caesars, though this Sergius Sulpicius Galba has no connection whatever with the Servius Sulpicius Galba whose reign, one and a half centuries later, lasted seven months, between Nero and Othon, before he was slaughtered on the Campus Martius by his own troops, having refused them the *donativum*.

As for the watercolour, it is, allegedly, simply one of the models for the set of an Anglo-French adaptation in modern dress of Stravinsky's opera.

It's hard to be sure how much truth there is in these explanations. Of the four programmes, two were never made: namely, the nine-part serial, turned down by each of the actors approached – Belmondo, Bouise, Bourvil, Cuvelier, Haller, Hirsch, and Maréchal – after they'd read the script; and the updated *Rake's Progress*, considered too expensive by the BBC. The series on the Twelve Caesars was made for the schools' broadcasting service, with which Rorschach was, apparently, unconnected, and similarly *The Sixteenth Edge of This Cube* seems to have been produced by one of those service companies to which French television so often has recourse.

In fact Rorschach's television career was conducted exclusively in office-work. Under the vague title of "Project Controller to the Managing Director" or "Test and Research Resources Reorganisation Officer", his sole function consisted of daily attendance at pre-meetings, joint meetings, study workshops, management boards, interdisciplinary discussion meetings, general meetings, plenary meetings, reading-panel meetings, and other working parties which, at this level of the hierarchy, make up the main business of life in the French broadcasting organisation, alongside phone calls, conversations in the corridor, business lunches, rush screenings, and trips abroad. There's no reason not to think he might have put forth the idea of an Anglo-French opera at one of these sessions, or of a history serial based on Suetonius, but it's more likely he spent his time drawing up or extrapolating from audience surveys, trimming budgets, drafting reports on the utilisation rates of editing studios, dictating memos, and going from meeting room to conference suite, taking care to be at all times indispensable in at least two places at once so that scarcely had he sat down than he would be called to the phone, and have to leave, unavoidably.

Such multifarious activities satisfied Rorschach's vanity, his taste for power, his talent for plotting and haggling, but they gave no nourishment to his nostalgic desire to be "creative": in fifteen years, he managed nonetheless to put his name to two productions, both educational serials for export: the first, *Doudoune et Mambo*, was on French-language teaching for black Africa; the second – *Anamous et Pamplenas* – used exactly the same scenario, but it aimed "to introduce the pupils of overseas colleges run by the Alliance Française to the beauty and harmony of Greek civilisation".

In the early seventies, Rorschach got wind of Bartlebooth's enterprise. At the time, though Bartlebooth had been back for fifteen years, no one really knew the whole story. Those who could have known something about it said little or nothing; others were aware that Madame Hourcade, for instance, had supplied him with boxes, or that he'd had a funny sort of machine set up in Morellet's room, or, to take another example, that he'd travelled right around the world for twenty years with his servant and that over the twenty years Winckler had received about two parcels a month from all over the world. But no one really knew how these pieces fitted together, and, what's more, nobody really tried to find out. And Bartlebooth, though he wasn't unaware that the little secrets which cloaked his existence were the subject of contradictory and often incoherent theories around the building, didn't ever dream that anyone could come one day and upset his plans.

But Rorschach got keen, and what he heard in fragments about those twenty years of circumnavigation, about the paintings cut in pieces, reassembled, and reseparated, etc., as well as all Winckler's and Morellet's stories, gave him the idea of a huge programme in which nothing less than the whole story would be re-enacted.

Bartlebooth said no, obviously. He let Rorschach in for a quarter of an hour and had him shown out. Rorschach persisted, interrogating Smautf and the other servants, grilling Morellet who buried him in increasingly incomprehensible heaps of mumbo jumbo, harassing Winckler who stayed obstinately silent, going out as far as Montargis to talk (pointlessly, for him) to Madame Hourcade, and falling back on Madame Nochère, who didn't know much but didn't mind elaborating.

Since there was no law forbidding him to tell a story of a man who did watercolours and jigsaw puzzles, Rorschach decided to go over Bartlebooth's head, and submitted to Programme Control a proposal for something in between *Great Works at Risk* and *Great Battles of the Past*.

Rorschach was too influential in television for his proposal to be turned down. He wasn't quite influential enough for it to be acted on speedily. Three years later, when Rorschach became so ill as to be forced, in the space of a few weeks, to terminate virtually all professional activity, none of the networks had yet given final approval and the scenario was still incomplete.

Without wishing to anticipate events, it might be useful to point out that Rorschach's initiative had serious consequences for Bartlebooth. It was by hearing of these televisual misadventures that Beyssandre got wind, last year, of Bartlebooth's story. And, oddly enough, it was to Rorschach that Bartlebooth came for the name of a director to film the final stage of his enterprise. However, that got him nowhere, except a step deeper into the web of contradictions which he'd known for many years would tie him inexorably tighter.

CHAPTER NINETEEN

Altamont, I

On the second floor, at the Altamonts', preparations are underway for the traditional annual reception. There will be a buffet in each of the five rooms of the flat facing the street. In this room, normally the small drawing room – the room nearest the main entrance hall, and leading onto a smoking-room-cum-library, a large drawing room, a boudoir, and a dining room – the carpets have been rolled up, revealing a valuable cloisonné floor. Almost all the furniture has been removed; they have left only eight chairs, made of lacquered wood with scenes from the Boxer Uprising painted on the backs.

There are no paintings on the walls, because the walls and doors are themselves the decor: they have been hung with painted wallpaper, providing a lavish panorama (a number of *trompe-l'oeil* effects suggest that we are dealing with a copy specially made for this room, probably based on older drawings) showing life in India as it was popularly imagined in the second half of the nineteenth century: first, a luxuriant jungle peopled with wide-eyed monkeys, then a clearing beside a marigot in which three elephants disport themselves at spraying each other; further on, in front of straw huts on stilts, women in yellow, sky-blue, and sea-green saris and men in loincloths dry tea leaves and ginger roots, whilst others, at wooden stalls, decorate large squares of silk with blocks which they dip in pots of vegetable dyes; and finally, on the right-hand edge, a classic tiger-hunting scene: between two rows of sepoys, two deep, shaking rattles and banging cymbals, strides a richly bedecked elephant, with a fringed and tasselled rectangular banner embossed with a red winged horse on his forehead; a howdah rises up behind the mahout squatting between the pachyderm's ears, bearing a red-haired European with sideburns and a pith helmet, and a maharajah wearing a jewel-studded costume and an immaculate turban decorated with a long plume held in place by an enormous diamond; in front of them, at the jungle's edge, half-emerging from the undergrowth, with its stomach to the ground, the big cat prepares to pounce.

In the centre of the left-hand wall, there's a huge pink marble fireplace surmounted by a large mirror; on the mantel, a tall crystal vase, of rectangular cross-section, filled with everlasting flowers, and a turn-of-the-century savings box: it has the form of a full-length, grinning, somehow twisted Negro, dressed in a flowing tartan oilskin cape, mostly red, with white gloves, steel-rimmed spectacles, and a top hat decorated with the stars and stripes and emblazoned with the number "75" in blue and red figures. His left hand is outstretched, his right hand grips the knob of a walking stick. When you put a coin into the outstretched palm, the arm rises and the coin is inexorably swallowed: by way of thanks, the clockwork man shakes his legs half a dozen times, in a fairly good imitation of the jitterbug.

A trestle table draped in a white tablecloth fills the whole back wall. The dishes which will provide the buffet are not yet in place, except for five reassembled scarlet lobster shells, laid out radially on a large silver platter.

The only living being in the scene is a black-trousered, white-coated servant: seated on a stool between the buffet and the door leading to the entrance hall, he has his back leaning against the wall, and his legs outstretched and apart; a man of thirty or so, with a round, red face; he is reading with an air of utter boredom the publisher's blurb on a novel, the cover of which depicts an almost naked woman lying in a hammock, with a long cigarette holder between her lips, and casually pointing a mother-of-pearl-butted revolver at the reader:

> "*The Mousetrap*" is Paul Winther's latest novel. Readers will enjoy catching up once again with the author's favourite character, the hero of *Roll over Clover*, *The Scotch Are Gunning*, *The Waterproof Man*, and many other blue-chip classics of today's and tomorrow's crime-fiction lists. This time, Captain Horty is destined to grapple with a dangerous psychopath wreaking murder in a Baltic port.

CHAPTER TWENTY

Moreau, 1

A bedroom in the big apartment on the first floor. The carpet is tobacco-brown; the walls are decorated with light-grey hessian panels.

There are three people in the room. One is an old lady, Madame Moreau, who owns the flat. She is lying in a large Empire bed under a bedspread embroidered with blue flowers.

Standing in front of the bed, Madame Moreau's childhood friend Madame Trévins, wearing a macintosh and a silk scarf, takes a postcard she's just received from her handbag and shows it to the old lady: the card depicts a monkey wearing a cap at the wheel of a truck.

A pink phylactery unfurls over the image, bearing the caption: *Souvenir de Saint-Mouezy-sur-Eon*.

On the bedside table, to the right of the bed, there is a reading lamp with a yellow silk shade, a cup of coffee, a box of Breton shortbread *sablé* biscuits on the lid of which you can see a peasant tilling his fields, a phial of perfume whose perfectly hemispherical base recalls the shape of the inkwells of old, a saucer containing a few dried figs, a piece of cooked Edam cheese, and a metal lozenge with moonstone stud-nails set at each corner framing a photograph of a forty-year-old man in a fur-collared jacket sitting in the open at a rustic table groaning under a weight of victuals: a sirloin, plates of tripe and black pudding, a fricassé chicken, sweet cider, stewed-fruit pie, and plums in brandy.

On the second shelf of the bedside table there is a pile of books. The one on top is called *The Love Life of the Stuarts* and its film-wrapped jacket shows a man in Louis XIII attire – wig, plumed hat, broad lace bands – with a wench of visibly ample bosom on his knee, and raising an enormous carved tankard to his lips: it's a compilation of doubtful authenticity which gloatingly details the alleged debauchery and corruption of Charles I: one of those unattributed works sold under sealed wrappers labelled "For Adults Only" on quayside stalls by the Seine and in railway station halls.

The third person, sitting on the left, set back a little from the bed, is a nurse, carelessly thumbing through an illustrated magazine. On its cover you can see a crooner in a grey-blue silver-spangled fancy-dress tuxedo, with sweat streaming down his face as he kneels, legs and arms open wide, in front of a wildly excited audience.

At 83 years of age, Madame Moreau is the building's senior inhabitant. She moved in around 1960, when the growth of her business made her leave her little village of Saint-Mouezy-sur-Eon (Department of Indre) in order to do justice to the obligations she had as the head of the company. Having inherited a small timber-working firm mainly supplying turned wood to furniture dealers in the Saint-Antoine district of Paris, she soon turned out to be a remarkable businesswoman. When in the early 1950s the furniture trade collapsed, leaving only unreliable and unprofitable outlets for turned wood – pillars for staircase and balcony railings, standard lamp uprights, altar columns, spinning tops, cup-and-ball games, and yoyos – she boldly switched the firm to manufacturing, servicing, and retailing household tools, as she foresaw that the rising cost of services would inevitably lead to a booming market for do-it-yourself equipment. Her hunch was confirmed far beyond her expectations, and the business flourished, soon reaching nationwide size and even beginning to pose a direct threat to its powerful German, British, and Swiss competitors, who soon got round to offering her lucrative contracts of association.

Today she is a helpless cripple; though a widow since nineteen forty – her husband, an officer in the Reserves, died on 6 June at the Battle of the Somme – though childless, though friendless apart from her old classmate Madame Trévins, whom she has brought in to help her, the old lady carries on running with a rod of iron, from her bed, a prosperous company with a catalogue covering virtually the entire range of home decorating and outfitting appliances, and even touching on other associated branches:

WALLPAPERING KIT. Includes 6′ folding yardstick; scissors; roller; hammer; 6′ metal rule; electrician's screwdriver; trimmers; knife; brush; plumbline; pliers; paint knife; handle; all in a portable plastic case, lgth. 2′, wdth. 4′, hght. 4″. Weight 6lbs. Fully guaranteed 1 yr.

WALLPAPERING STAPLE GUN. For 4, 6, 8, 10, 12 & 14mm staples. Supplied in a portable metal kitcase containing 1 box staples of each size, 6 boxes in all, contents totalling approx. 7,000 staples. Instruction leaflet included. Accessories available: bending knife, adapter (TV, telephone, electric wire). Destapler, cloth-cutter, magnetic wedge. Fully guaranteed 1 yr.

HOME DECORATOR'S KIT. Includes: 2-gallon plastic bucket; driptray; polyamid roller handle, wdth. 175mm; foam roller; mohair roller for gloss work; round-tip **PURE BRISTLE** brush 25mm dia × 60mm lgth.; 4 **PURE BRISTLE** flat brushes, 60, 45, 25 & 15mm × 17, 15, 10 & 7mm thick. Top quality. Lengths 55, 45, 38 & 33mm. Fully guaranteed 1 yr.

ELECTRICAL AIRLESS PAINT SPRAYER. Heavy duty sprayer gun complete with viscosimeter, extra nozzle for heavy duty paints, flexible extension nozzle, injection nozzle for rustproofing cars, etc. Spraying pressure 2,300 p.s.i. Container capacity 1 pt. Fully guaranteed 1 yr.

PORTABLE SCAFFOLD. Comprising 5′ wide ladder frame on casters; 5′ wide ladder frame on feet; two 2′ bars; platform,

4′6″ × 2′, with safety rail, support bar and crossbars, floor height adjustable from 18″ to 8′ at 1″ intervals. Base area 6′ × 2′. Safety lock. Weight 80lbs. Fully guaranteed 1 yr.

3-WAY TOP FLIGHT LADDER. Made from aluminium. Converts to extending ladder, household steps or offset ladder on stairs. Special lift and lock safety action in all positions. Highest usable tread when in step position, 4′6½″. Max. tread height 8′9½″. Weight 48lbs. Accessories: block, rod rail, detachable feet. Fully guaranteed 1 yr.

WM700 DELUXE "WORKMATE". Dual working heights 23″ and 30¼″. Extra large 8½″ deep rear vice-jaws. Large vice pegs for improved grip. Comprehensive vice-jaw marking for precision jobs. Folds flat for storage. Weight 125lbs. Fully guaranteed 1 yr.

D142 HAMMER DRILL. 220v, 250w, with Electronic diode. No-load speed to 1,400/3,000 r.p.m., hammer action 14,000/35,200 strokes p.m. Drills steel to 10mm, concrete to 12mm, wood to 20mm. Supplied with 10mm chuck, 3 yards flex, neck strap, calibrated depth gauge; chuck key. Weight 5lbs. Accessories: universal adapter, grip handle, side grip, top grip, clasp, twin chuck, stand, side guide, small template, small, medium and large routing stands, percussion attachment, circular saw, fretsaw, ribbon saw, sanding/polishing disc, soft disc, sander, orbital sander, abrasive coated sander, plane, jigsaw, plunging router, paraguide, all-purpose sharpener, brushes, hedge-trimmer, agitator, compressor, spray-gun, extension lead, grinder, vice. Supplied with a set of 13 high-speed steel drill bits dia. 4, 5, 6, and 8mm, and a set of chrome vanadium drill bits dia. 4, 5, 6 and 8mm, one 8mm plunge bit, one 10mm plunge bit, chisel bit, plane blades, wood turning bit, adapter for standing plane, spin adapter. Fully guaranteed 1 yr.

150 PIECE TOOL KIT. Contains 23 piece ½″ square drive socket set; 61 piece ¼″ and ⅜″ square drive socket and tool set; 5 AF and 5 metric O/E spanners; 5 AF and 5 metric spanners; BA spanners; 6 screwdrivers; 5 piece punch and chisel set; combination pliers; multigrip pliers; ball pein hammer; 8 AF and 8 metric Allen keys; 1 each AF and metric gauges; junior hacksaw; wire brush, spark plug spanner; magneto file; spark plug drills. All in a 5-tray tool box. Fully guaranteed 1 yr.

THIRTY PIECE TOOL ROLL. Includes 5 metric ring spanners 6–17mm; 5 metric O/E spanners 8–17mm; 7 double-ended socket spanners 4–10mm; 1 multigrip wrench; 4 screwdrivers; 6″ pliers; spark plug spanner; wire brush; hammer; set of 8 BA spanners; torch; plastic oilcan and duster. All folds into a neat and attractive carrying case with handle. Fully guaranteed 1 yr.

ELEVEN PIECE COMBINATION SPANNER SET. Alloy steel in attractive individually pouched wallet. Sizes 8–24mm. Fully guaranteed 1 yr.

38 PIECE TAP AND DIE SET. Contains 17 each taps and dies – AF, metric and ⅛″ BSP plus 5 accessories in presentation/storage case. Fully guaranteed 1 yr.

38 PIECE DRILL SET. Contains 19 high-speed twist drills 3⁄64″–½″, 7 wood boring bits 5⁄32″–½″, 8 masonry drills 5⁄32″–⅜″, 3 extra long masonry drills 7⁄16″–9⁄16″, and 1 × 12mm countersink bit.

MASONRY KIT. Contains 1 metal spirit level, with 3 chambers × 50mm; 10″ round-end trowel; 9″ square-end trowel; 8″ diamond trowel; masonry chisel; bricklayer's peg; stiff metal brush. Fully guaranteed 1 yr.

HOME ELECTRICIAN'S KIT. Set comprises wire cutter and stripper, insulated radio pliers, various fuses and fuse wire, mains tester, screwdriver and 3 rolls of insulating tape. Contained in PVC wallet. Continuity tester requires 1 × R65 battery. Fully guaranteed (except battery) 1 yr.

TWENTY-TWO PIECE WOODWORKING KIT. Comprises handsaw; tenon saw; carpenter's hammer; pliers; tweezers; 3 wood chisels, 8, 10 and 15mm; rabbet; 2 screwdrivers. Fully guaranteed 1 yr.

PLUMBER'S KIT. A metal tool box 16″ × 9″ × 5″ containing: blowlamp set with automatic ignition (requires cartridge) with plumber's extra-fine flame burner, 5 all-metal solder sticks, 1 × 250mm chrome-vanadium wrench, 1 pipe-cutter for apertures from 0 to 30mm, 1 pipe-grip 0/25mm, 1 plumbing-in tap set. Fully guaranteed 1 yr.

MOTOR MECHANIC'S TOOL KIT. Comprises: folding crossbar spanner; windscreen scraper; set of 9 socket spanners 4/4; set of 6 flat spanners from 6 × 7 to 16 × 17mm; eight-blade feeler gauge; pocket lamp with battery; oilcan; insulated combination pliers; all-purpose pliers; chrome Allen key; spark plug brushes; set of 4 screwdrivers; chrome-plated hammer; spark plug spanner with cranking handle; file for contact points; set of magneto spanners; zinc-coated pin-drift; soft duster; grease gun; foot pump; hazard warning triangle; fire extinguisher; hydraulic jack; pressure gauge 0/3 bars; battery acid tester; antifreeze gauge; revolving handlamp with white lens and detachable red lens. Fully guaranteed 1 yr.

FIRST AID KIT. Contains peroxide flask with 10 calibrations; surgical spirit flask; 2 large adhesive plasters; 4 small adhesive plasters; 1 splinter tweezers; a pair of scissors; bottle of tincture of iodine; 6 absorbent lint dressings, 2 rolls of lint, 2 rolls of crepe; tourniquet; tape measure; chrome metal torch with battery and bulb; marking chalk; five packs of disinfectant swabs; one pack of face fresheners; a tube of safety pins; an empty tube for pills; five absorbent cotton swabs; 3 pairs of plastic disposable gloves; **A RUBBER MOUTH-TO-MOUTH RESUSCITATION TUBE** with instruction leaflet. Fully guaranteed 1 yr.

24 PIECE "GREEN IVY" PICNIC SET. Luxury model for six place settings, comprising one polyethylene bucket with dish lid, 1 salad bowl with clip-on lid, 6 flat plates; 6 soup plates; hermetic foodbox; jug; egg-box; 6 goblets, 6 cups, 6 cutlery settings (knife, fork, soup spoon). With **FREE** salt and pepper shakers. Dimensions 42 × 31 × 24cm. Total weight 10lbs. Fully guaranteed 1 yr.

CLIMBING FRAME. 11′, 8 bars with fittings. Tubular steel, stove-enamelled gloss finish in green. Main beam dia. 80mm, internal verticals dia. 40mm, external verticals dia. 35mm. Lgth. 12′, wdth. 8′, max. displacement 19′. Fixtures attached by patent bolt device. Attachments: 2 swings, 1 trapeze with polypropylene ropes, dia. 12mm; hemp climbing rope dia. 22mm; polypropylene rope ladder dia. 12mm. Other accessories by special order: knotted rope, set of rings, single/double balancelle. Supplied with full assembly instructions and fixing pins. Fully guaranteed 1 yr.

BUSINESS FOLDER. "Leather-look" vinyl with metal corners. Comprising two document pockets, A4 pad and pen. Size 12½″ × 9¾″. Fully guaranteed 1 yr.

CHAPTER TWENTY-ONE

In the Boiler Room, 1

A man is lying flat on his stomach on the top of the boiler which provides heat to the whole building. He is about forty; he doesn't look like a workman, but more like an engineer or gas-board inspector; he's not wearing working clothes, but a lounge suit, a spotted tie, and a sky-blue tergal shirt. He has protected his head by knotting over it a red handkerchief, looking vaguely like a cardinal's zucchetto. With a small piece of chamois leather he wipes a little cylindrical part having a ribbed tube to one side and a spring-loaded flap to the other. Beside him, on a piece of newspaper on which some of the headlines, insets, and excerpts can be read

General Shalako, who cleaned up the Vézelize pocket, has just died in Chicago.

The Worried Hulk by John Whitmer (Scarecrow Publishing Co.) has been awarded the Liter-

Who destroyed my people's peace and the country's government which is why

THE BAND of the 2nd N. African Regiment will perform this afternoon at the Garden

lie other parts: bolts, screws, washers and clamps, rivets, spindles, and some tools. On the front of the boiler there is a round nameplate bearing the inscription RICHARDT & SECHER above a stylised diamond.

The central heating is a relatively recent installation. Whilst the Gratiolets remained majority owners in the co-ownership they were forcefully opposed to what they considered to be an unnecessary expense, since they heated their flat, like almost all Parisians at that time, by wood- or coal-burning stoves or open fireplaces. It was only in the early sixties, when Olivier Gratiolet sold Rorschach virtually all his remaining shares, that the works were approved and carried out, at the same time, as it happened, as a complete renewal of the roof and a costly stone-cleaning exercise required by a recent law (for which André Malraux would be remembered), all of which – and on top of it there was the wholesale interior conversion of Rorschach's duplex, and of Madame Moreau's apartment – transformed the entire building for nearly a year into a dirty, noisy building site.

The Gratiolets' story begins more or less like the tale of Puss-in-Boots but ends much less happily: neither the one who had almost everything nor those who got almost nothing ended up with much. Juste Gratiolet had grown rich in the wood supply and sales business – he invented, in particular, a grooving machine still used in many floorboard factories – and when he died, in 1917, his four surviving children shared his fortune in the manner stipulated in their father's will. The estate consisted of a block of flats – the one we have been dealing with from the start – farmland in Berry given over one part to cereal crops, one part to cattle, and one part to forestry, a hefty slice of shares in the Upper Boubandjida Mining Co. (Cameroon), and four large canvases by the Breton landscape and animal painter Le Meriadech', who was very highly rated at that time. As a result, the eldest, Emile, got the building, Gérard inherited the farm, Ferdinand got the shares, and Hélène, the only daughter, had the paintings.

Straightaway, Hélène, who some years earlier had married her dancing teacher – a man by the name of Antoine Brodin – tried to dispute the legacy, but counsel's opinion was not favourable. It was pointed out to her, in the first place, that by leaving her with works of art her father had acted first and foremost with a view to relieving her of the burdens and responsibilities which the management of a block of flats, an agricultural estate, or a portfolio of African shares would have put upon her, and moreover, in the second place, that it would be difficult if not impossible to demonstrate that the division had been inequitable, since four canvases by a painter at the height of his fame were worth at least as much as a parcel of shares in a mine that had not even begun to produce and maybe never would.

Hélène sold the paintings for 60,000 francs, an exorbitant sum for the period if you think of the discredit Le Meriadech' fell into a few years later (and from which he is nowadays coming back into notice). With this little nest egg she and her husband emigrated to the United States. They became professional gamblers, organised clandestine dice games sometimes lasting a whole week or more on night trains and in village bars. On 11 September 1935, at dawn, Antoine Brodin was murdered; three rowdies he'd refused to let into his gaming hall two days before took him off to a deserted quarry at Jemima Creek, thirty miles from Pensacola (Fla), and beat him to death with sticks. Hélène returned to France a few weeks later. Her nephew François, who had inherited the building on the death of Emile one year before, allowed her to use a two-roomed flat on the sixth floor, next to Dr Dinteville's. There she lived, a sobered, fearful, retiring woman, until her death in nineteen forty-seven.

For the seventeen years of his ownership, Emile managed the building carefully and competently, and undertook various pieces of modernisation, in particular putting in a lift in 1925. But the feeling which he had of being sole beneficiary of the inheritance, and of having done wrong by his brothers and sister by his insistence on respecting his father's last wishes, led him to feel responsible for them, so much so that he wanted to run their affairs for them. Such scruples sowed the seed of the eldest's undoing.

Gérard, the second son, managed his farm business more or less adequately. But Ferdinand, the third, ran into serious trouble. The Upper Boubandjida Mining Co. (Cameroon), of which he'd become a relatively major shareholder, had been set up some ten years before with the aim of prospecting for and then extracting the rich deposits of tin discovered by three Dutch geologists attached to the Zwindeyn Mission. There had been several preliminary expeditions in succession, reporting back with discouraging results: some confirmed the presence of substantial veins of cassiterite but expressed concern about mining conditions and especially transport; others claimed that the ore was too poor to warrant extraction, since the cost price would necessarily be too high; yet others maintained that the samples that had been taken contained no trace of tin, but on the other hand actually held abundant quantities of bauxite, iron, manganese, copper, gold, diamonds, and phosphates.

Though mostly pessimistic, these contradictory surveys in no way deterred the Company from trading its shares actively on the Stock Exchange and increasing its capital annually by a new issue. In 1920, the Upper Boubandjida Mining Co. (Cameroon) had amassed nearly twenty million francs subscribed by seven thousand five hundred shareholders, and on its Board of Directors sat three former ministers of state, eight bankers, and eleven industrialists. That year, at an initially riotous but in the end enthusiastic shareholders' meeting, the decision was reached unanimously to call a halt to these useless preliminaries and to go ahead immediately with mining the ore, whatever it was.

Ferdinand was a trained civil engineer and managed to get appointed site controller. On 8 May 1923, he reached Garoua and undertook the ascent of the upper reaches of the Boubandjida as far as the high plateaux of Adamawa with five hundred locally recruited hands, eleven and a half tons of equipment, and twenty-seven management staff of European origin.

Building the foundations and cutting the drifts turned out to be difficult; work was delayed by rain, which fell every day, causing the river to burst its banks in an irregular and unpredictable way, but on average with sufficient force on each occasion to wash out everything that had been cut or embanked so far.

After two years Ferdinand Gratiolet caught the fevers and had to be repatriated. He was inwardly convinced that mining the tin of the Upper Boubandjida would never be economically viable. On the other hand, he'd seen in the lands he'd crossed great quantities of

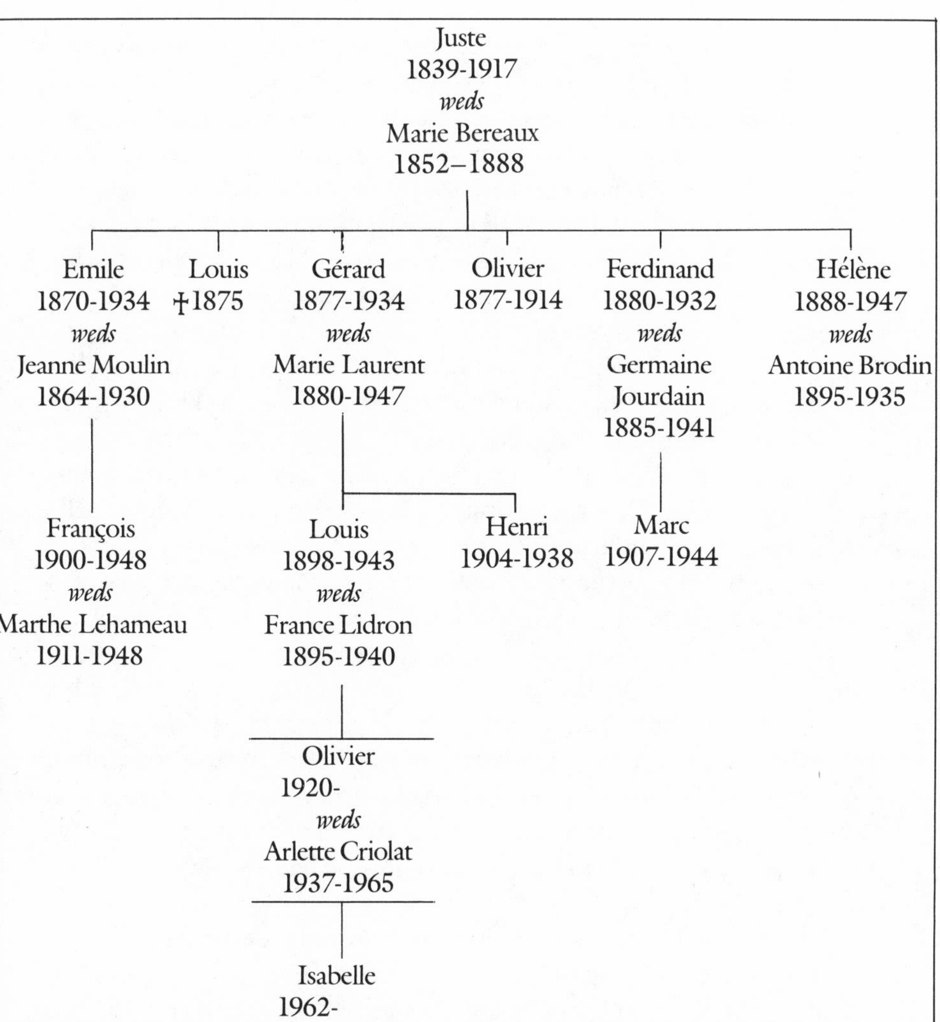

animals of all species and varieties, and that gave him the idea of going into the skin and fur trade. Scarcely out of convalescence, he sold his shares and set up a company for the import of animal skins, furs, horns, and exotic carapaces, which quickly specialised in furnishings: at that time the fashion was for fur bedside rugs, for cane furniture upholstered in zorille, antelope, giraffe, leopard, or zebra hide: a small deal dresser with buffalo-hide decorations sold easily for 1,200 francs, and a Tortosi vanity set in a trionix shell had been auctioned up to 38,295 francs at the Drouot Sales Room!

The business took off in 1926. From 1927, world prices for leathers and skins began falling headlong over the next six years. Ferdinand refused to believe in the crisis and carried on building up stocks. By the end of 1928 his entire capital was frozen in virtually non-negotiable goods, and he could not meet his freight and storage charges. To avoid a bankruptcy which would cheat his creditors, Emile put his brother afloat again by selling off two of the flats in his apartment house, including the one Bartlebooth moved into. But that didn't do much good.

In April 1931, when it was becoming clearer and clearer that Ferdinand, the owner of some forty thousand animal skins that had cost three or four times the price he could now get for them, was as unable to provide for their upkeep and security as he was unable to meet any of his other commitments, the warehouse at La Rochelle where his goods were in store was burnt to the ground.

The insurance companies refused to pay and publicly accused Ferdinand of criminal arson. Ferdinand fled, leaving his wife, his son (who had just passed his philosophy *agrégation* with first-class marks) and the still-smoking ruin of his business. A year later his family heard that he had met his death in Argentina.

But the insurance companies continued to persecute his widow. Her two brothers-in-law, Emile and Gérard, sacrificed themselves to come to her aid, the former selling seventeen of the thirty dwellings he still owned, the latter cashing in almost half of his agricultural estate.

Emile and Gérard both died in 1934; Emile first, of pneumonia, in March; Gérard second, in September, of a brain haemorrhage. They left their children a shaky legacy which the following years would continue to gnaw away.

END OF PART ONE

PART TWO

CHAPTER TWENTY-TWO

Entrance Hall, 1

The entrance hall is relatively spacious, and almost perfectly square. At the rear, on the left, there is a door to the cellar; in the middle, the lift cage; on its wrought-iron door, a notice

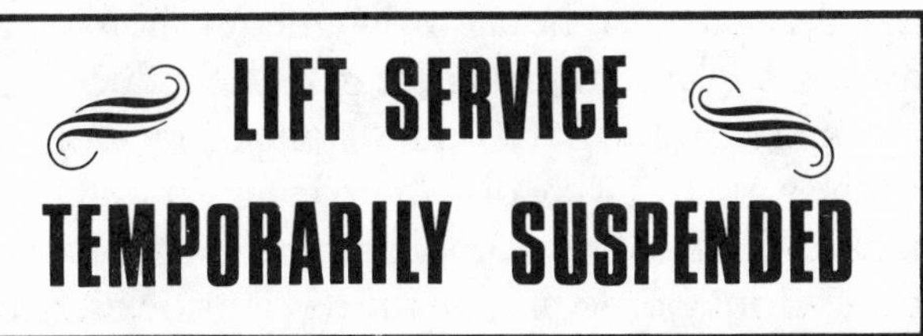

has been hung; on the right, the first flight of the stairs. The walls are painted in light green gloss, the floor is laid with a very tightly knotted cord carpet. On the left-hand wall, the glass-panel door of the concierge's office, draped with little lace curtains.

A woman is standing in front of the office, reading the list of the building's occupants; she is wearing a capacious brown linen overcoat done up with a large fish-shaped brooch set with alabandite stones. A blood-red canvas bag is slung over her shoulder, in the manner of a bandolier, and in her right hand there is a sepia-tint photograph of a man in a black cloak. He has sideburns and pince-nez; he is standing beside a brass-and-mahogany revolving bookcase in Second Empire style, on the top of which there is a paste-glass vase filled with arum lilies. His top hat, gloves, and stick are laid beside him on a shell-encrusted kneehole desk.

This man – James Sherwood – was the victim of one of the most celebrated swindles of all time: in eighteen ninety-six, a pair of tricksters of genius sold him the vase in which Joseph of Arimathæa gathered the blood of Christ. The woman – an American novelist by the name of Ursula Sobieski – has spent three years unravelling this shady deal for her next book, and her research has finally brought her to visit this block of flats today, for some piece of information to end her investigations.

Born in Ulverston (Lancashire) in 1833, James Sherwood went overseas very young and became a druggist in Boston. In the early eighteen seventies he invented a ginger-based recipe for lung pastilles. In less than five years, these cough sweets became famous: they were vaunted by a celebrated slogan, "*Sherwoods Put You in the Mood*", and illustrated on hexagonal vignettes showing a knight in armour driving his lance through the ghost of influenza personified as a grumpy old man lying flat on his stomach in a fog-enshrouded landscape: the vignettes were distributed in great numbers throughout America and painted on school blotters, on the backs of matchboxes, on soft-drink bottlecaps, on the reverse side of cheesebox lids, and on thousands of little toys and classroom baubles given away free to people who purchased a tin of *Sherwoods* at specified periods: pen-stands, exercise books, wooden cubes, little jigsaws, small goldpans (exclusively for Californian customers), photos of leading music hall stars with forged autographs.

The colossal fortune which came with such prodigious popularity did not suffice, unfortunately, to cure the druggist of his affliction: he was kept in a virtually chronic state of lethargy and exhaustion by ineradicable neurasthenia. But at least the fortune allowed him to indulge just about the only activity which helped him forget his troubles: collecting *unica*.

In the jargon of the rare book, antique, and curio trade, an *unicum*, as its name implies, is an object which is the only one of its kind. This rather vague definition covers several classes of object; it can mean things of which only one example was ever made, such as the octobass, a monstrous double-bass for two musicians, one at the top of a ladder doing the fingering, the other on a mere stool drawing the bow, or the Legouix-Vavassor Alsatia, which won the Amsterdam Grand Prix in 1913 but was never marketed owing to the war; or it can mean animal species of which only one member is known to exist, like the tendrac *Dasogale fontoynanti*, the sole specimen of which was caught in Madagascar and is now in the

Natural History Museum in Paris, like the butterfly *Troides allottei* bought by a collector in 1966 for 1,500,000 francs, or like the *Monachus tropicalis*, the white-backed seal whose existence is known only by a photograph taken in 1962, in Yucatan; or it can mean objects of which only one example now remains, as is the case for several postage stamps, books, engravings, and sound-recordings; or, finally, it can mean objects rendered unique by this or that detail of their history: the pen with which the Treaty of Versailles was initialled and signed, the bread basket into which the head of Louis XVI or Danton rolled, the stub of the piece of chalk Einstein used at his memorable 1905 lecture, the first milligram of pure radium isolated by the Curies in 1898, the Ems Telegram, the boxing gloves Dempsey wore to defeat Carpentier on 21 July 1921, Tarzan's first underpants, Rita Hayworth's glove in *Gilda*, are all classic instances of this last category of *unica*, the most common but also the most slippery class, when you think that any object whatsoever can always be identified uniquely, and that in Japan there is a factory mass-producing Napoleon's hat, or Napoleon hats.

Scepticism and passion are the two traits of *unica*-lovers. Scepticism will lead them to amass an excess of evidence of the genuineness and – especially – of the uniqueness of the sought-after object; passion will lead them into sometimes boundless gullibility. It was with these two traits in mind that the confidence tricksters succeeded in stripping Sherwood of a third of his fortune.

One day in 1896, an Italian workman called Longhi, hired a fortnight earlier to repaint the railings around his estate, came up to the druggist as he was giving his three greyhounds their daily walks, and explained in rather approximate English that three months earlier, he, the workman, had rented a room to a compatriot, a certain Guido Mandetta, who claimed to be a history student; this Guido had gone without warning, leaving behind only an old trunk full of books and papers. Longhi said he'd like to get his money back by selling the books, but was afraid of being swindled, and asked if Sherwood would like to help him. Sherwood didn't see much to interest him in history textbooks and lecture notes and was about to say no, when Longhi added that the books were mainly old, and in Latin.

Sherwood's curiosity was awakened, and it was not disappointed. Longhi took him back to his house, a big wooden barn, brimful with bambini and masses of mammas, and took him into the little room under the roof where Mandetta had lived; scarcely had he opened the trunk than Sherwood shuddered with surprise and joy: in the midst of a heap of notebooks, loose leaves, pads, newspaper cuttings, and dog-eared books, he discovered an ancient Quarli, one of those sumptuous books with wooden boards and painted edges which the Quarlis printed in Venice between 1530 and 1570 and which have almost entirely disappeared from sight.

Sherwood studied the volume carefully: it was in very poor condition, but there was no doubt that it was genuine. The druggist didn't hesitate: he pulled two hundred-dollar bills from his billfold and handed them to Longhi; he cut short the Italian uttering jumbled thanks, had the trunk carried over to his house, and began to explore its contents systematically, and as time went on and his discoveries became clearer, his feeling of intense excitement became more and more overwhelming.

The Quarli itself was valuable not just in bibliographic terms. It was the celebrated *Vita brevis Helenae* by Arnaud de Chemillé, in which the author, after retracing the main episodes in the life of the mother of Constantine the Great, vividly describes the building of the Church of the Holy Sepulchre and the circumstances of the discovery of the True Cross. Inserted into a kind of pocket sewn onto the vellum endpaper were five manuscript sheets, of much later date than the volume but nonetheless very old, probably late eighteenth century: they contained a painstaking, highly detailed compilation enumerating in unending columns of tiny and now almost indecipherable handwriting the locations and specifications of the Relics of the Passion: the fragments of the Holy Cross at St Peter's, Rome, at St Sophia, at Worms, at Clairvaux, at Chapelle-Lauzin, at the Hospice of the Incurables at Baugé, at St Thomas's, Birmingham, etc.; the Nails at the Abbey of Saint-Denis, at Naples Cathedral, at S Felice at Syracuse, at SS Apostoli in Venice, at the Church of Saint-Sernin, Toulouse; the spear with which Longinus pierced the Lord's breast at S Paolo fuori le Mura, at S Giovanni in Laterano, at Nuremberg, and at the Sainte-Chapelle in Paris; the chalice, in Jerusalem; the Three Dice used by the soldiers to gamble for Christ's

Tunic, at Sofia Cathedral; the Sponge Soaked in Vinegar and Gall at S Giovanni in Laterano, at S Maria-di-Trastevero, at S Maria Maggiora, at Saint Mark's, at S Silvestro-in-capite, and at the Sainte-Chapelle in Paris; the Thorns of the Crown at St Taurin's, Evreux, Châteaumeillant, Orléans, Beaugency, and at Notre-Dame in Rheims, at Abbeville, Saint-Benoît-sur-Loire, Vézelay, Palermo, Colmar, Montauban, Vienna, and Padua; St Lawrence's Vase at S Lorenzo in Genoa, Veronica's Veil (the *vera icon*) at S Silvestro in Rome; the Holy Shroud, in Rome, Jerusalem, Turin, Cadouin in the Périgord, Carcassonne, Mainz, Parma, Prague, Bayonne, York, Paris, Ayrshire, etc.

The remaining items were no less interesting. Guido Mandetta had collected a whole scientific and historical file on the Relics of Golgotha and most particularly on the most highly treasured of all, the vase Joseph of Arimathæa was said to have used to gather the blood springing from Christ's wounds: a set of articles by J. P. Shaw, formerly professor of history at Columbia University, New York, reviewed the various legends circulating about the Holy Vase and attempted to identify the elements of reality on which they might be rationally based. Professor Shaw's analysis was not very hopeful: the tradition that Joseph himself had taken the Vase to England and founded the monastery at Glastonbury to house it in merely rested, according to his demonstration, on a (late?) Christian contamination of the Grail legend; the *Sacro Catino* at Genoa Cathedral was an emerald goblet, allegedly discovered by Crusaders at Caesarea in 1102, and it was not obvious how Joseph of Arimathæa could have got hold of it; the two-handled Golden Vase kept at the Church of the Holy Sepulchre in Jerusalem, which Bede (who had never seen it) said had contained the Saviour's Blood, was obviously just an ordinary chalice, mistakenly identified through a scribal error, "contained" having been copied instead of "consecrated". As for the fourth legend, which said that Gonderic's Burgundians, allied at Aetius's instigation to the Saxons, the Alani, the Francs, and the Visigoths in order to halt Attila the Hun, reached the Catalaunian Fields bearing in front of them – as was customary for the period – their propitiatory relics, including the Holy Vase left to them by the Aryan missionaries who had converted them and which Clovis would take from them thirty years later at Soissons, Professor Shaw rejected this as the least plausible of all, for never would Arianists, who did not recognise the Transubstantiality of Jesus, have thought of worshipping or making others worship his relics.

Nonetheless, Professor Shaw concluded, in the context of the intense movement between the Christian West and Constantinople lasting from the beginning of the fourth to the end of the thirteenth centuries, and of which the Crusades formed but a tiny chapter, it was not inconceivable that the True Vase could have been preserved, in so far as it had been, from the day after the Burial, an object of the greatest veneration.

When he'd finished going through all of Mandetta's material exhaustively – even though most of the documents remained undecipherable – Sherwood was convinced that the Italian had tracked down the Holy Vase. He put an army of detectives on his trail, but they came up with nothing, since Longhi hadn't even been able to give a correct description of the man. He then decided to turn to Professor Shaw for advice. He found his address in the latest edition of *Who's Who in America* and wrote to him. A reply arrived one month later: Professor Shaw had just returned from a voyage; kept busy by final examinations, he could not come to Boston but would willingly see Sherwood at his place in New York.

The interview therefore took place at J. P. Shaw's New York home on 15 June 1896. Sherwood had barely mentioned his discovery of the Quarli when Shaw interrupted him:

"It's the *Vita brevis Helenae*, isn't it?"

"That's right, but . . ."

"There's a pocket, on the rear endpaper, containing a list of all the Relics of Golgotha?"

"Indeed there is, but . . ."

"Well, my dear fellow, I'm delighted to make your acquaintance at last! That's my copy you've found! As far as I know there aren't any others. It was stolen from me two years ago."

The professor rose, hunted through a filing cabinet, and returned with a few crumpled sheets in his hand.

"Look, here's the announcement I had put in specialist journals and sent to every library in the country:

STOLEN *on 6 April 1893 from the house of Professor J. P. SHAW in New York, N.Y., United States of America, an extremely rare copy of* **VITA BREVIS HELENAE** *by Arnaud de Chemillé. Venice, Quarli, 1549, 171 num.pp., 11 unnum.pp. Badly damaged wooden pressboards. Vellum endpapers. Painted edges. Two of three hasps intact. Numerous mss. annotations in margins.* ***INSET OF 5 MANUSCRIPT SHEETS BY J. B. ROUSSEAU***

Sherwood had to return to Shaw the book he thought he'd got so cheaply. He turned down the two hundred dollars' compensation which Shaw offered. In return he asked the historian to help him exploit Mandetta's copious file of information. Now it was the Professor's turn to refuse: he was entirely absorbed in his work at the University, and above all he did not believe that he would learn anything from Mandetta's papers: he had been studying the history of the relics for twenty years, and he didn't think anything of the slightest importance had escaped him.

Sherwood insisted, and in the end offered the Professor such a fabulous sum of money that he got him to consent. A month later, when the examination season was over, Shaw settled in Boston and began to sift through the innumerable piles of notes, articles, and press cuttings left by Mandetta.

The inventory of the Relics of Golgotha had been made in 1718 by Jean-Baptiste Rousseau, who, after being expelled from France as a result of the murky affair of the Café Laurent couplets, had taken service as secretary to Prince Eugene of Savoy. The previous year this Prince, fighting under the colours of Austria, had recaptured Belgrade from the Turks. This victory, coming after several others, put an end for a while to the long-drawn-out conflict setting Venice and the Hapsburgs against the Ottoman Empire; peace was signed on 21 July 1718 at Passarowitz, with Britain and Holland acting as mediators. It was on the occasion of the peace treaty that Sultan Ahmed III, hoping to curry favour with Prince Eugene, sent him a whole collection of major relics originating in a hiding place in one of the walls of St Sophia. The fact of this dispatch is known from a letter from Maurice de Saxe – who'd put himself under the Prince's orders to learn the profession of arms, which he actually already knew better than anyone – to his wife, the Countess of Loben: ". . . *a blade of the Holy Spear, the Crown of Thorns, the thongs and rods of the Flagellation, the paltry Cloak and Reed of the Passion, the Holy Nails, the Very Holy Vase, the Sindon, and the Very Holy Veil*".

No one knew what had become of these relics. No church of the Austro-Hungarian Empire or elsewhere ever prided itself in having any of them amongst its treasures. The cult of relics, which had flourished throughout the Middle Ages and the Renaissance, had then begun to weaken considerably, and it is reasonable to assume that it was in order to deride them that Prince Eugene had asked Jean-Baptiste Rousseau to catalogue all those relics that were still worshipped.

However, less than fifty years later, the Very Holy Vase cropped up again: in a letter in Italian, dated 1765, the polemicist Beccaria told his protector Charles-Joseph de Firmian that he had visited the famous collection of antiquities left on his death in 1727 by the philologist Pitiscus to the College of St Jerome in Utrecht, of which he had been rector, and mentioned in particular "*one sigillated earthenware vase which was said to be the one from the Calvary*".

Professor Shaw did of course know Jean-Baptiste Rousseau's catalogue, of which the original was inset in his Quarli, and Maurice de Saxe's letter. But he didn't know Beccaria's letter: it made him jump for joy, for the description "sigillated earthenware vase" was, finally, support for the theory he'd always held, but never dared to publish: the Vase in which Joseph of Arimathæa had gathered the Blood of Christ, on the evening of the Passion, had no reason to be made of gold, brass, or bronze, even less cause to be carved from a single emerald stone, but was, quite plainly, earthenware: an ordinary piece of pottery Joseph had bought at the market before going to wash the Wounds of his Saviour. In his enthusiasm Shaw wanted to edit and publish Beccaria's letter, and Sherwood had all the trouble in the world to persuade him not to, promising him he would have the material for an even more sensational article when they found the Vase!

But first they had to discover the origin of the Utrecht vase. Most of the items in Pitiscus's collection came from the huge holdings of

Christina of Sweden, in whose retinue the philologist had spent many years, but the two catalogues which listed them, Havercamp's *Nummophylacium reginae Christinae* and the *Musoeum Odescalcum*, didn't mention a vase – fortunately enough, for Queen Christina's collections had been assembled long before Ahmed III had dispatched the Holy Relics to Prince Eugene. Therefore it had to be a later acquisition. In so far as Prince Eugene had not distributed the Relics to churches, and hadn't kept them – they didn't appear in the descriptions of his own collections, which were known – it was not unreasonable to think he had given them as gifts to his followers, or at least to those of his followers, of which there were many, who had a lively interest in archaeology, and that he did so at the very time he received them, that is to say during the negotiations for the Peace of Passarowitz. Shaw checked out this crucial detail and discovered that the secretary to the Dutch Delegation was none other than the writer Justus Van Effen, who was not only a pupil but a godson of Pitiscus; that made it obvious that it was Van Effen who had asked for, and been given, the vase, for his godfather, not because it was a devotional object – the Dutch were Reformed and thus profoundly hostile to the cult of relics – but as a museum piece.

Letters flowed thick and fast between Shaw and several Dutch professors, curators, and Head Archivists. Most of them could not provide satisfactory information. Only one, a certain Jakob Van Deeckt, a librarian at the Rotterdam Local Archives, could enlighten them on the history of the Pitiscus Collection.

In 1795, on the founding of the Batavian Republic, the College of St Jerome was closed and turned into a barracks. Most of the books and collections were at that point put into "safekeeping". In 1814, the former College became the seat of the new Military Academy of the Kingdom of the Netherlands. Its collection, together with those of several other public and private institutions, including the old Artistic and Scientific Society of Utrecht, constituted the founding endowment of the Museum van Oudheden (Museum of Antiquities). But the catalogue of this museum, though it had several entries for sigillated earthenware vases of the Roman period, specified that the objects were all remains found at Vechten, near Utrecht, the site of a Roman camp.

This attribution, however, was controversial, and several scholars reckoned there could have been a confusion when the first catalogue was made. Professor Berzelius, of Lund University, had examined the pottery and demonstrated that attention to the seals, imprints, and inscriptions confirmed that one of them, inventory no. BC 1182, was without doubt much earlier than the others and probably could not have been found at the Vechten excavation, since the camp, as everyone knew, was a late Roman settlement. These results had been summarised in German in an article in *Antigvarisk Tidsskrift* (Copenhagen), 1855, vol. 22, of which Jakob Van Deeckt attached an offprint to his letter: it contained annotated reproductions of several drawings of the vase in question. But, added Jakob Van Deeckt, by way of conclusion, four or five years previously, that very vase BC 1182 had been stolen. The librarian couldn't remember exactly how it had been stolen, but no doubt those in charge of the Museum van Oudheden would give him the precise details.

With Sherwood panting, Shaw wrote to the Museum's Curator. A reply came in the form of a long letter accompanied by cuttings from the *Nieuwe Courant*. The robbery had happened on the night of 4 August 1891. The museum, situated in Hoogeland Park, had been substantially refurbished the previous year, and not all the rooms had been reopened to the public. A student from the Fine Art School, by the name of Theo Van Schallaert, had obtained permission to copy some antiques, and was at work in one of these rooms, which, since they were not open, had no guard on duty. On the evening of 3 August he managed to get himself locked in the museum, and let himself out simply by breaking a windowpane and sliding down a drainpipe, bearing the precious Vase. Searches made the next day at his dwelling proved the deed had been premeditated, but all the efforts made to track him down were in vain. The matter was not yet covered by the statute of limitations and the Curator ended his letter by requesting in his turn any information which might lead to the arrest of the thief and to recovery of the antique vase.

For Sherwood there was not a shadow of doubt that this vase was the Very Holy Vase and that Mandetta the history student and Theo Van Schallaert the fine-art student were one and the same person. But how could he find him? Mandetta had disappeared a full six months ago, and the detectives hired by Sherwood were still searching for him fruitlessly on both sides of the Atlantic.

It was then that a sublime coincidence occurred. Longhi, the Italian workman who'd been landlord to the fraudulent Mandetta-Van Schallaert, called on Sherwood. He had been working at New Bedford, and, three days before, he'd seen the student coming out of the Hotel Xiphias. He'd crossed the pavement to speak to him, but the man had got into a buggy and driven off at a gallop.

The very next day Sherwood and Shaw were at the Xiphias. Speedy enquiries identified Mandetta as the person who had checked in under the name of Jim Brown. He hadn't left the hotel and he was even at that moment in his room. Shaw introduced himself, and Jim Brown-Mandetta-Van Schallaert raised no objection to seeing him with Sherwood and giving some explanations.

When he was a student in Utrecht he'd discovered in a second-hand bookshop an unbound copy of the *Correspondence* of Beccaria, whom he knew of course as the author of the famous treatise *On Crimes and Their Punishment*, which had revolutionised penal law. He had bought the work and taken it home, where, yawning a little and despite his rather summary command of Italian, he had read through until he came upon the letter narrating the visit to the Pitiscus Collection. Now, his great-grandfather had been a pupil at the College of St Jerome. Fascinated by this succession of coincidences, Schallaert decided to track down the Calvary Vase, and, having found it, decided to steal it. The plan came off, and at the time when the museum guards were discovering the theft, he was already on board a scheduled steamer on the Amsterdam–New York line.

Of course, he reckoned on selling the vase, but the first antique dealer he offered it to laughed in his face, demanding better authentication than a vague lawyer's letter and some catalogue snippets. Well, even if it really was the one Berzelius described, and most certainly the one Beccaria had seen, the prior provenance of the vase remained problematic. In the course of his research Schallaert had heard of Professor Shaw – you are, he told him, a leading light in the Old World as in the New, which made the Professor blush – and after conscientiously reading up everything to be found in libraries and discreetly mingling in the Professor's lectures and seminars, he let himself into his home during a party celebrating his appointment to the Headship of the Department of Ancient History, and purloined the Quarli. Thus, although he had started from a different point, he, like Shaw and Sherwood, had managed to reconstitute the history of the Vase. So, with the evidence to support his claim, he began a tour of the United States, beginning in the South, where he'd heard it said he would find wealthy customers. Indeed, a New Orleans bookseller had introduced him to a fabulously wealthy cotton planter who had offered him $250,000, and he'd come back to New Bedford to fetch the Vase.

"I'll offer double", Sherwood said simply.

"Impossible, I've given my word."

"For another two hundred and fifty thousand dollars you could break it."

"Out of the question!"

"I'll make it a million!"

Schallaert seemed to waver.

"How do I know you've got a million dollars? You haven't got it in your pocket!"

"No, but I can get the cash together by tomorrow evening."

"How do I know you won't have me arrested before then?"

"And how do I know you'll really give me the vase?"

Shaw interrupted and proposed the following arrangement. Once the authenticity of the Vase had been proved, Sherwood and Schallaert together would deposit it in a bank safe. They would meet again a day later, Sherwood would give the million dollars to Schallaert, and they would proceed to open the safe.

Schallaert found the idea ingenious, but refused to use a bank, and stipulated a secure and neutral meeting place. Once again Shaw came to their help: he knew the President of Harvard University, Michael Stefensson, and knew he had a safe in his office. Why not ask him to handle this delicate exchange operation? He would be asked to be discreet and anyway there was not even any reason why he should know what would be in the bags to be exchanged. Sherwood and Schallaert accepted. Shaw rang Stefensson on the telephone and got him to agree.

"Don't do anything you might regret!" Schallaert then said,

suddenly. He took a small pistol from his pocket, stepped backwards to the rear of the room, and added, "The vase is under the bed. Look but take care!"

Shaw pulled a little suitcase out from under the bed and opened it. Inside, protected by thick wadding, was the Very Holy Vase. It looked exactly like Berzelius's drawings of vase BC 1182, and the inscription was clearly marked in red ink inside the base.

That very evening they reached Harvard, where Stefensson awaited them. The four men went into the President's office, and he opened the safe and placed the case in it.

Next evening the four men met again. Stefensson opened his safe, took out the case, and gave it to Sherwood. The latter handed Schallaert a travelling bag. Schallaert checked the contents quickly – two hundred and fifty bundles of two hundred twenty-dollar bills – then greeted the three men with a little nod of his head and was gone. "Gentlemen," said Shaw, "I think we've earned ourselves a glass of champagne."

It was getting late and after a few glasses Shaw and Sherwood gratefully accepted the President's offer of hospitality. But when Sherwood woke in the morning he found the house entirely deserted. The case was on a low table by his bedside, and the Vase was in the case. The rest of the residence, which he'd seen the previous night full of servants, amply lit, richly furnished with *objets d'art* of all kinds, turned out to be a suite of empty dance halls and lounges, and the President's office was merely a sparsely furnished little room, probably a cloakroom, entirely devoid of books, safe, and pictures. Sherwood later learnt that he had been received in one of those halls which the many alumni associations – Phi Beta Rho, Tau Kappa Pi, etc. – hire for their annual dinners, and that it had been booked two days earlier by a certain Arthur King, on behalf of a supposed *Galahad Society*, of which, of course, no trace could be found anywhere.

He called Michael Stefensson and in the end got a voice on the line that he'd never heard before, and certainly not last night. President Stefensson did, in fact, know Professor Shaw by name, and he was rather surprised that he was already back from directing his excavations in Egypt.

* * *

The massed mammas and the bountiful bambini at Longhi's house, like the servants at Stefensson's residence, were hired walk-ons. Longhi and Stefensson were accomplices with specified roles, but knowing only very vaguely the inside story of the coup that Schallaert and Shaw, whose true identities remain unknown, had stage-managed from start to finish. Schallaert, a talented forger, had fabricated Beccaria's letter, Berzelius's article, and the cuttings from the *Nieuwe Courant*. From Rotterdam and Utrecht he'd sent the forged letters of Jakob Van Deeckt and the Curator of the Museum van Oudheden, before coming back to New Bedford for the final scene and denouement of the plot. The other items, that is to say Shaw's articles, the *Vita brevis Helenae*, Jean-Baptiste Rousseau's catalogue, and the letter from Maurice de Saxe, were authentic, unless the latter two items were forgeries from some much older swindle: the imposter Shaw had found these documents – and that was where it had all started – in the library of the Professor whose absolutely aboveboard tenant he had been since the latter's departure for the land of the Pharaohs. As for the vase, it was a slightly dissimulated gugglet of sorts, bought at a souk at Nabeul (Tunisia).

James Sherwood is Bartlebooth's great-uncle, his maternal grandfather's brother or, equally, his mother's uncle. When he died, four years after this affair, in 1900 – the year of Bartlebooth's birth – the remainder of his huge fortune came to his sole heiress, his niece Priscilla, who had married a London businessman, Jonathan Bartlebooth, eighteen months previously. The estates, the greyhounds, horses, and collections were disposed of in Boston, and the "Roman vase with descriptions by Berzelius" went for two thousand dollars all the same: but Priscilla brought some pieces of furniture to England, amongst them a mahogany study set in the purest English Colonial style, comprising a desk, a filing cabinet, an easy chair, a revolving and rocking chair, three straight-backed chairs, and the revolving bookcase beside which Sherwood had been photographed.

This bookcase, like the other furniture and some other items from the same source, including one of the *unica* so passionately sought after by the druggist – the very first cylinder phonograph built by

John Kruesi to Edison's design – is now in Bartlebooth's apartment. Ursula Sobieski hopes she will be able to examine them and find in them the document that would allow her to conclude her lengthy investigations.

As she pieced the affair together and studied the accounts of it made by some of the actors (the "real" Professors Shaw and Stefensson, and Sherwood's private secretary, to whose diary the novelist had had access), Ursula Sobieski often came to wonder whether Sherwood hadn't guessed from the start that he was being mystified: whether he had paid up not for the vase but for the staging, allowing himself to be hooked by the bait, responding to the programme scripted by the so-called Shaw with an appropriate combination of gullibility, doubt, and enthusiasm, and finding such play-acting a more powerful palliative for his melancholy than the search for a real treasure would have been. This is a tempting theory and would fit Sherwood's character quite well, but Ursula Sobieski hasn't yet managed to find solid evidence for it. All there is to vindicate her theory is the fact that James Sherwood doesn't appear to have minded at all about losing a million dollars, a fact perhaps explained by a news item dated two years after the end of the affair: in 1898, in Argentina, a syndicate of forgers was arrested whilst attempting to pass off huge quantities of twenty-dollar bills.

CHAPTER TWENTY-THREE

Moreau, 2

Madame Moreau hated Paris.

In 1940, after her husband's death, she took over the factory. It was a very small family business which he had inherited after the 1914–18 war and which he'd run in relaxed prosperity with three cheerful woodworkers at his side whilst she kept the books in big, black-cloth-bound registers with ruled paper and pages she had numbered in violet ink. The rest of the time she led an almost peasant-like existence, busy with the backyard chickens and the kitchen garden, making jams and pâtés.

She'd have done better to sell up and go back to the farm where she'd been born. Rabbits and chickens, some tomato plants, and a couple of beds for lettuces and cabbages – what more did she need? She would have sat by her fireside amongst her placid cats, listening to the clock ticking, to the rain falling on the zinc drainpipes, and the seven-o'clock bus passing by in the far distance; she'd have carried on warming her bed with a warming pan before getting into it, warming her face in the sun on her stone bench, cutting recipes out of *La Nouvelle République* and sticking them into her big kitchen book.

Instead of that, she had developed, transmogrified, metamorphosed her little business. She didn't understand why she'd done so. She had told herself it was out of fidelity to her husband's memory, but he would not have recognised what had become of his old workroom with its smells and shavings: two thousand people, millers, turners, fitters, mechanics, installers, electricians, testers, draftsmen, roughers-out, model-makers, painters, warehousemen, treatment specialists, packers, drivers, delivery men, foremen, engineers, secretaries, publicity writers, commercial agents, and sales reps, making and marketing every year more than forty million tools of all kinds and calibres.

She was tenacious and tough. She rose at five, went to bed at eleven, dealt with all her business in exemplary fashion, punctually, precisely, firmly. She was authoritarian and paternalistic, trusted nothing and nobody save her own intuitions and her own mind; she wiped out all her competitors and took a share of the market larger than anyone had predicted, as if she were mistress of both supply and demand, as if she knew instinctively, on launching each new product, where the real opportunities lay.

Up until the last few years, until age and illness virtually confined her to her bed, she had divided herself tirelessly between her factories in Paris and Romainville, her offices in Avenue de la Grande Armée, and this luxury flat which was so unlike her. She inspected the shopfloors at a gallop, terrorised accountants and typists, insulted suppliers who didn't keep delivery dates, and chaired Board Meetings energetically and inflexibly, making all heads bow when she opened her mouth.

She hated it all. Whenever she could tear herself away, even for only a few hours, she went to Saint-Mouezy. But her parents' old farm had gone to ruin. Weeds grew wild in the orchard and vegetable garden; the fruit trees no longer produced. Damp was eating the walls, unsticking the wallpaper, warping the doorframes.

Madame Trévins would help her to light a fire in the fireplace, open the windows, and air the mattresses. She who had four gardeners at Pantin to tend the lawns, flowerbeds, bushes, and hedges surrounding the works couldn't even manage to find a local man to keep an eye on the garden. Saint-Mouezy, which used to be a sizable little market town, was now a mere juxtaposition of houses restored as second homes, empty all week and chock-full on Saturdays and Sundays with townsfolk who, as they brandished their Moreau hand-drills, their Moreau circular saws, their Moreau portable work-benches, their Moreau all-purpose ladders, laid bare old beams and old stone, hung coachlamps, and rallied to the attack on barns and cartstalls.

Then she would come back to Paris, don her Chanel two-pieces, and for her wealthy foreign customers would give lavish dinners served in crockery designed especially for her by the greatest of Italian designers.

She was neither a miser nor a spendthrift, but simply indifferent to money. In order to become the businesswoman she'd decided to be, she accepted without any apparent effort a radical transformation of her habits, of her wardrobe, of her style of life.

The conversion of her flat was carried out with this aim in mind. She kept just one room for herself, her bedroom, had it completely sound-proofed, and brought up from the farm a high, deep Empire bed and the wing chair in which her father had listened to the wireless. All the rest she entrusted to an interior designer whom she briefed in four sentences: it was to be the Paris residence of the head of a company; a spacious, luxurious, opulent, high-class, and even lavish interior; designed to make a good impression on Bavarian industrialists, Swiss bankers, Japanese buyers, and Italian engineers, as well as on university professors, junior trade and industry ministers of state, and mail-order business managers. She gave him no other advice, expressed no specific wishes, and laid down no budget limit. He would have to do everything and would answer for everything: the choice of glassware, the lighting, kitchen appliances, knickknacks, table linen, colour schemes, door furniture, curtains, curtain linings, etc.

The designer, Henry Fleury, did more than just carry out his brief. He realised what a unique opportunity he'd been given to effect his masterwork: usually, kitting out a space for living always ends up being a sometimes tricky compromise between the contractor's ideas and the often self-contradictory demands of his client, but here, with this prestigious decoration of an initially anonymous space, he could give an unmediated and true image of his gifts, an exemplary demonstration of his theories of interior architecture: the reshaping of spatial volumes, the theatrical redistribution of light, and the mixture of styles.

The room we are now in – a smoking room-cum-library – is fairly representative of his work. It was originally a rectangular space, twenty feet by twelve. Fleury began by making it into an oval room with eight dark, carved wooden panels on the walls: he went to Spain to get them; apparently they come from the Prado. In between the panels he placed tall brass-inlaid Brazilian rosewood bookcases, bearing on their shelves a great number of books all bound in the same tan-brown leather, mostly artbooks, in alphabetical order. Huge, chestnut-brown button-leathered sofas are placed beneath the shelves and fit the curves precisely. Between the sofas stand dainty kingwood low tables, whilst in the middle of the room there looms a heavy, four-leafed, centre-pillar table heaped with newspapers and reviews. The woodblock floor is almost entirely masked by a dark red woollen carpet with triangular motifs in an even darker red. In front of one of the bookcases there is a set of library steps, in oak with brass fittings, which allows access to the upper shelves, and one of the risers of which is studded all over with gold coins.

In several places, the bookshelves have been made into glass-fronted display cases. That is how some old calendars, almanacs, and Second Empire diaries are shown off in the first case, on the left, together with some small posters, including Cassandre's *Normandy* and Paul Colin's *Grand Prix of the Arc de Triomphe*; in the second display case – the only reminder of the activities of the mistress of the house – there are a few old tools: three planes, two adzes, a twibill, six cold chisels, two files, three hammers, three gimlets, two augers, all bearing the monogram of the Suez Canal Company and all used during the cutting of the canal, as well as a magnificent Sheffield *Multum in parvo* looking like an ordinary pocketknife (wider, of course) but containing not just blades of various sizes but a screwdriver, a corkscrew, pincers, pen nibs, nailfiles, and punches; in the third case, various objects which had belonged to Flourens, the physiologist, and in particular the skeleton, red through and through, of the young pig whose mother the scientist had fed for the last 84 days of her pregnancy on food mixed with madder to prove experimentally the direct relationship of mother and foetus; and in the fourth case, a doll's house, parallelepipedal, three feet high, two feet nine inches wide, and two feet deep, dating from the late nineteenth century and representing a typical English cottage down to the smallest detail: 1 drawing room with bay windows (2 lancets), thermometer affixed, 1 sitting room, 4 bedrooms, 2 servants' rooms, tiled kitchen with close range and scullery, lounge hall fitted with linen wallpresses, fumed oak sectional bookcase containing the *Encyclopaedia Britannica* and the *New Century Dictionary*, transverse obsolete medieval and oriental weapons, dinner gong, alabaster lamp, bowl pendant, vulcanite automatic telephone receiver with adjacent directory, hand-tufted Axminster carpet with cream ground and trellis border, loo table with pillar-and-claw legs, hearth with massive firebrasses and ormolu mantel chronometer clock, guaranteed timekeeper with cathedral chime, barometer with hygrographic chart, comfortable lounge settees and corner fitments, upholstered in ruby plush with good springing and sunk centre, three-banner Japanese screen and pyramidically prismatic central chandelier lustre, a bentwood perch with its tame parrot, and hundreds of everyday objects, baubles, crockery, clothes, all reproduced almost microscopically with manic accuracy: stools, lithos, cheap champagne bottles, capes on coat hangers, socks and stockings drying in the scullery, and even two minute copper pot-holders, tinier than thimbles, with greenery sprouting from them; and lastly, in the fifth set of bookcases, on raked stands, there are several open musical scores, amongst them the title page of Haydn's Symphony No. 70 in D as printed in London by William Forster in 1782:

A favorite

OVERTURE

in all its parts

Composed by

GIUSEPPE HAYDEN

of Vienna

and PUBLISHED by his

AUTHORITY. Pr: 2 6

LONDON

Printed for and Sold by W. FORSTER Violin and Violoncello Maker
to his Royal Highness the Duke of Cumberland, the Corner of Dukes
Court St. Martins Lane.

Where may be had the new Works of the following Authors

Cambini's Quartettos Op: 3d - - - - - - - - - -	10.6
Baumgarten's Do. Op: 3d - - - - - - - - - - -	10.6
Bach's Double Orchestre Overtures with three Single Do. - - -	1.1.0
Wynne's Trios - - - - - - - - - - - - - - -	7.6
Bach's Harpsichord Concertos - - - - - - - - - - -	12.0
also the above Overture for the Harpsichord adapted by C.F. Baumgarten -	8.0

Madame Moreau has never told Fleury what she thinks of his work. She will only acknowledge that it is effective, and that she is grateful for his choice of objects, each one of which can easily give rise to a pleasant conversation before dinner. The miniature house is the delight of Japanese guests; the Haydn score allows academics to shine, and the old tools usually set junior trade and industry ministers off onto well-turned phrases on the manual skills and handicrafts of France that live on and of which Madame Moreau is the indefatigable guardian. It is of course Flourens's red piglet skeleton which is the most successful, and people have frequently offered large sums for it. As for the gold coins studded into one of the stair risers, Madame Moreau has been forced to replace them with imitations after realising that unknown hands have tried, and sometimes managed, to unnail them.

Madame Trévins and the nurse have taken tea in this room before joining Madame Moreau in her bedroom. On one of the little low tables there is a round elm-bur tray with three cups, a teapot, a water jug, and a saucer in which a few crackers remain. On the sofa beside it, a newspaper has been folded in such a way as to leave only the crossword visible: the grid is almost entirely blank: only 1 Across, ASTONISHED, and the first part of 3 Down, ONION, have been found.

The two house cats, Pip and La Minouche, are asleep on the carpet, paws stretched out and relaxed, the muscles in their napes quite loose, in the position associated with what is called *paradoxical* sleep, which is generally thought to correspond to the state of dreaming.

Beside them, a little milk jug lies broken in several pieces. One guesses that once Madame Trévins and the nurse left the room, one of the cats – was it Pip? was it La Minouche? or did they join forces for this guilty deed? – knocked it over with a sudden pawstroke, but to no avail, as the carpet instantly drank up the precious liquid. The stains are still visible, indicating that this scene took place just a few minutes ago.

CHAPTER TWENTY-FOUR

Marcia, 1

The back room of Madame Marcia's antique shop.

Madame Marcia, her husband, and her son live in a three-roomed flat on the ground floor right. Her shop is also on the ground floor, on the left, between the concierge's office and the servants' entrance. Madame Marcia has never made any real distinction between the furniture she has for sale and the furniture she has to live in, and she is therefore busy for much of the time with carrying furniture, chandeliers, lamps, crockery, and miscellaneous objects between the flat, the shop, the back room, and the cellar. Such swaps, occurring as a consequence of opportunities to sell or buy something (in the latter case, in order to make room for it) just as much as on impulse, or a sudden whim, or a change of mood for or against some object, are not performed in random order, and do not exhaust all twelve possible permutations which could be made between the four locations, as is made clear in figure 1; they strictly follow the schema in figure 2: when Madame Marcia buys something, she puts it in her domestic space, either in the flat or the cellar; the said object may thence proceed to the back room of the shop, and from the back room into the shop itself; from the shop front it may return to (or arrive at, if it began in the cellar) Madame Marcia's flat. What is ruled out is for an item to return to the cellar, or to get into the front shop without having been in the back room, or to go in reverse from the front shop to the back room, or from the back room to the flat, or, lastly, to move directly from the cellar to the flat.

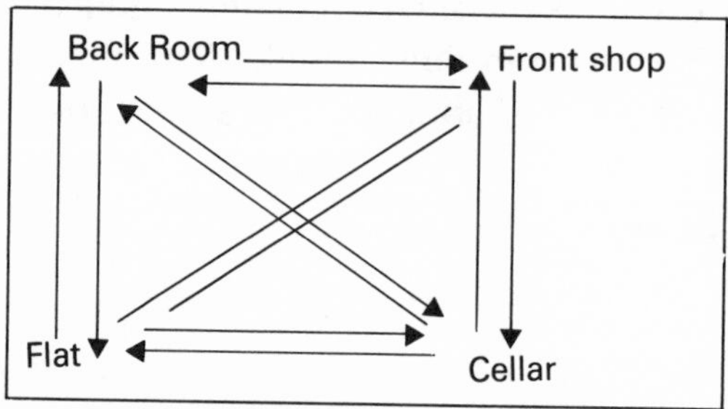

Figure 1

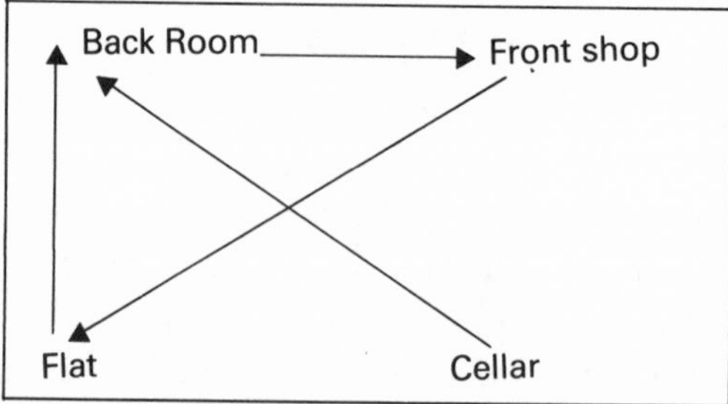

Figure 2

The back room is dark and narrow, with a lino floor, and cluttered to the point of inextricability with objects of every shape and size. The jumble is such that an exhaustive list of contents is impossible, and we shall have to be satisfied with a description of the pieces protruding from this heteroclite heap with a degree of visibility.

Against the left-hand wall, beside the door leading from the back room to the front shop, the door whose opening creates just about the only empty space in the room, there is a large Louis XVI roll-top desk, rather coarsely made; the top is open, revealing a green leather writing pad on which a partly unrolled *emaki* (painted scroll) has been put: it depicts a famous scene from Japanese literature: Prince Genji has got into the palace of the governor Yo No Kami, where, from behind an arras where he has hidden, he watches the governor's wife, the beautiful Utsusemi, with whom he is passionately in love, playing go with her friend Nokiba No Ogi.

Further along the wall are six wooden chairs painted willow green, supporting rolls of printed cretonne wallpaper. The roll on top depicts a pastoral scene in which a peasant tilling his field alternates with a shepherd leaning on his crook, with his hat tilted back and his dog on a lead, with his sheep scattered all around him, and who raises his eyes to the sky.

Yet further along, past the pile of military paraphernalia – weapons, shields, drums, shakos, pointed helmets, knapsacks, belt buckles, frogged wool-cloth hussars' jackets, leather goods, in the middle of which you can see more distinctly a set of those stubby and slightly curved infantrymen's swords which the French call *briquets* – there is an S-shaped mahogany sofa upholstered in flower-patterned cloth, which was given in 1892, so they say, to the singer Grisi by a Russian prince.

Then, taking up the whole right-hand corner, heaped in shaky piles, there are the books: dark-red folio volumes, bound sets of *La Semaine théâtrale*, a fine copy of the *Dictionnaire de Trévoux* in two volumes, and a whole set of *fin-de-siècle* books in green and gold board covers, including works signed by Gyp, Edgar Wallace, Octave Mirbeau, Félicien Champsaur, Max and Alex Fisher, Henri Lavedan, as well as the extremely rare *Revenge of the Triangle* by Florence Ballard, which is held to be one of the most surprising precursors of science fiction.

Then, in disorder, on shelves, on little bedside tables, low tables, dressing tables, church stools, card tables, and benches, are dozens and hundreds of knickknacks: snuff boxes, make-up boxes, medicine boxes, and boxes for keeping beauty-spots in; silver-plated metal trays, candleholders, chandeliers, and torches, desk sets, inkpots, horn-handled magnifying glasses, phials, oil jugs, vases, chessboards, mirrors, small frames, Dorothy bags, sets of sticks: whilst in the middle of the room there rises up a monumental butcher's stall on which there stands a beer mug with a carved silver lid and these three naturalist's curios: a huge trap-door spider; an object purporting to be a fossilised dodo's egg mounted on a marble cube; and a large ammonite.

Many chandeliers – Dutch, Venetian, Chinese – hang from the ceiling. The walls are almost completely covered in paintings, engravings, and miscellaneous reproductions. In the penumbra of this room most of the pictures are but a vague blur with, here and there, a signature – Pellerin – standing out, or a title engraved on a plate on the bottom of the frame – *Ambition*, *A Day at the Races*, *La Première Ascension du Mont-Cervin* – or a detail: a Chinese peasant pulling a cart, a kneeling youth being knighted by his suzerain. No more than five pictures permit more precise description.

The first is a portrait of a woman, entitled *The Venetian Woman*. She is wearing a dress of flaming-red velvet with a jewelled belt, and her broad sleeve, lined with ermine, reveals her bare arm, which touches the balustrade of a staircase going up behind her. On her left, a tall column rises to the top of the canvas, where it joins a curving mass of architecture. Below, clumps of orange trees, almost black in colour, are dimly visible, framing a blue sky streaked with white clouds. On the carpeted balustrade there is a silver dish containing a bunch of flowers, an amber rosary, and a casket of old, yellowish ivory, overflowing with golden sequins; some of these sequins have fallen on the floor and lie scattered in a series of shining drops, so as to lead the eye towards the tip of her foot – for she is posing on the last step but one, in a natural attitude and full in the light.

The second is a pornographic engraving entitled *The Servants*: a fifteen-year-old boy wearing a kitchen-hand's cap braces himself against a table, with his trousers round his ankles, as a fat cook buggers him; on a bench in front of the table a liveried valet has unbuttoned his flies and exhibits his erect penis as a serving girl lifts her skirts with both hands and lowers herself onto him. Sitting at the other end of the table in front of a copious dish of macaroni is a fifth character, an old man dressed all in black, who watches the scene with manifest indifference.

The third is a pastoral scene: a rectangular meadow, on a slope, with thick, green grass and a great many yellow flowers (apparently, common dandelions). At the top of the meadow is a chalet, and at the front door there are two women chatting busily, a peasant woman with a headscarf, and a nanny. Three children are playing on the grass, two little boys and a girl, gathering the yellow flowers and making bouquets of them.

The fourth is a caricature by Blanchard, entitled *When Hens Grow Teeth . . .* It shows General Boulanger and the member of parliament Charles Floquet shaking hands.

The fifth and last is a watercolour under the title of *The Handkerchief*, which illustrates a classic scene of Parisian life: in the Rue de Rivoli a fashionable young lady drops her handkerchief and a young man in morning dress – narrow moustache, monocle, patent-leather shoes, a pink in his buttonhole, etc. – rushes to pick it up.

CHAPTER TWENTY-FIVE

Altamont, 2

The Altamonts' dining room, like all the other street-facing rooms in the flat, has been specially set up for the great reception that will be held there shortly.

It is an octagonal room, the four diagonal wall-sections of which hide a great number of cupboards. The floor is laid with glazed red hexagonal tiles, the walls are lined with cork paper. At the rear, there is the door to the kitchens, where three white shapes are bustling. To the right, double doors open wide onto the reception rooms. On the left, along the wall, four barrels of wine are set on wooden X-bar stands. In the middle, beneath a chandelier with an opaline bowl hanging on three gilded cast-iron chains, stands a table made out of a cylindrical block of lava from Pompeii, on which sits a six-sided smoked-glass table laden with little saucers, decorated in Chinese style, holding various snacks: fillets of marinated fish, shrimps, olives, cashew nuts, smoked sprats, stuffed vine leaves, canapés topped with salmon, asparagus tips, slices of egg, tomato, red tongue, anchovies, as well as miniature quiches, dwarf pizzas, and cheese sticks.

An evening paper has been spread beneath the barrels, no doubt for fear the wine might drip. On one of the pages you can see a crossword puzzle, the same as the one Madame Moreau's nurse had; on this one, though the grid has not been filled in completely, progress has nonetheless been made.

A	S	T	O	N	I	S	H	E	D
P	O	■	N				■		
A	L		I				■		
R	I	S	O	T	T	O			
T	L		N	■	■				
M	O								
E	Q								
N	U						■		
T	Y	■					■		
S	S	N	O	R	M	A	N	D	Y

Before the war, long before the Altamonts made a dining room out of it, this was the room where Marcel Appenzzell came to live for his short time in Paris.

* * *

Trained in the school of Malinowski, Marcel Appenzzell wanted to take his master's teaching to its logical conclusion, and resolved to share the life of the tribe he would study so completely as to merge himself into it. In 1932, when he was twenty-three, he left, alone, for Sumatra. Laden with minimal baggage as free as he could make it of the instruments, weapons, and utensils of Western civilisation and consisting largely of traditional gifts – tobacco, rice, tea, necklaces – he hired a Malay guide called Soelli and began the ascent by canoe of the River Alritam, the black river. On the first days they passed some rubber tappers, and some men floating huge tropical-wood tree trunks downstream. After that they were completely alone.

The aim of their expedition was a mysterious people whom the Malays called the Anadalams, or Orang-Kubus, or just Kubus. Orang-Kubus means "they who defend themselves", and Anadalams means "the Sons of the Interior". Whilst almost all of Sumatra's population is settled near the coastline, the Kubus live in the heart of the island, in one of the most inhospitable regions of the world, a tropical forest full of leech-infested swamps. But many legends, documents, and remains seem to indicate that the Kubus were once masters of the island, before being conquered by invaders from Java and going into the heart of the jungle in search of their last retreat.

One year earlier Soelli had managed to establish contact with a Kubu tribe in a village built not far from the river. He reached it with Appenzzell after three weeks on the river and on foot. But the village – five huts on stilts – was deserted. Appenzzell managed to persuade Soelli to carry on upriver. They found no other village, and after eight days Soelli decided to go back down to the coast. Appenzzell insisted on staying and in the end gave Soelli the canoe and almost all the equipment before plunging, almost empty-handed, into the forest.

Soelli informed the Dutch authorities when he reached the coast. Several search parties were set up, but they found nothing.

Appenzzell reappeared five years and eleven months later. A team of mineral surveyors travelling in a motor launch found him on the banks of the Musi, more than four hundred miles from his starting point. He weighed four and a half stone and was dressed only in a kind of trousers made of dozens of bits of cloth sewn together and held up by yellow braces that looked intact but had lost all their elasticity. He was brought back to Palembang and, after a short stay in the hospital, repatriated, not to Vienna, where he had been born, but to Paris, where his mother had settled in the meanwhile.

The return journey lasted a month and gave him a chance to recover. At the start an invalid, barely able to move or feed himself, he had virtually lost the use of words and uttered only inarticulate grunts or, during the bouts of fever which gripped him every three to five days, long delirious strings; but bit by bit he recovered most of his physical and mental abilities, learnt again how to sit in a chair, how to use a knife and a fork, how to do his hair and how to shave (after the ship's barber had rid him of nine-tenths of his hair and the whole of his beard), to wear a shirt, a detachable collar, a tie, and even – though this was certainly the hardest, for his feet resembled deeply fissured lumps of horn – how to put on shoes. When he landed at Marseilles his mother, who had come to meet him, was able to recognise him without too much trouble after all.

Before his departure Appenzzell had been an assistant professor of ethnography at Graz (Steiermark). He was Jewish; the Anschluss had been proclaimed a few months earlier and it led to the application of a *numerus clausus* in all Austrian universities. Even his salary, which they'd carried on paying throughout his years of fieldwork, was frozen. Through the good offices of Malinowski, to whom he wrote, he met Marcel Mauss, who allowed him to give a course at the Institute of Ethnology in Paris on the Anadalams' way of life.

Marcel Appenzzell brought no articles, no documents, no notes, nothing at all, back from those 71 months, and he virtually refused to talk about them, on the pretext that he needed to keep his memories, impressions, and analyses whole and entire for his first lecture. He gave himself six months to sort his material out. To start with, he worked quickly, with pleasure, almost with ardour. But soon he began to slow down, to hesitate, to cross things out. When his mother came into his room she found him, most often, not at his desk but sitting straight-backed on the edge of his bed, hands on his knees, staring sightlessly at a wasp worrying a windowpane, or gazing as if he were trying to find some lost thread in the fringed grey-brown linen towel with its double black-brown border hanging on a nail behind the door.

A few days before his first lecture – the title, *The Anadalams of Sumatra. A Preliminary Approach*, had been announced in various papers and journals, but Appenzzell hadn't yet handed in to the Institute office the forty-line abstract for *The Year's Work in Sociology* – the young ethnologist burnt all he had written, put a few things in a suitcase, and left, leaving a laconic note for his mother informing her he was going back to Sumatra and did not feel he had the right to divulge anything at all concerning the Orang-Kubus.

A slim notebook partly filled in with mostly incomprehensible notes had escaped the burning. Some students at the Institute of Ethnology struggled to decipher it and, with the help of the few letters Appenzzell had sent Malinowski and others, alongside information from Sumatra and the accounts of people to whom Appenzzell had, exceptionally, let slip some detail of his adventures, they managed to piece together the main outline of what had happened to him and to rough out a crude picture of the mysterious "Sons of the Interior".

After a march of many days Appenzzell had finally found a Kubu village, a dozen huts on stilts set in a circle around the edge of a small clearing. The village had looked deserted at first glance, then he'd noticed several old men, lying on mats under the awnings of their huts, looking at him. He'd gone forward, greeted them with the Malayan gesture of stroking their fingers before placing his right hand on his heart, and put a gift-offering in front of each – a little bag of tea or tobacco. But they didn't answer, didn't nod their heads, didn't touch the gifts.

A little later dogs began to bark and the village filled with men, women, and children. The men were armed with spears, but were not threatening. Nobody looked at him, nobody seemed to notice he was there.

Appenzzell spent several days in the village without succeeding in making contact with its laconic inhabitants. He exhausted his small supply of tea and tobacco to no effect; no Kubu – not even a child – ever took a single one of these little bags which the daily storm made useless by each evening. The best he could do was to watch how the Kubus lived and to begin to commit what he saw to writing.

His main observation, as he described it briefly to Malinowski, confirms that the Orang-Kubus are indeed the descendants of a developed civilisation which was expelled from its lands and plunged into the forest, where it regressed. Thus the Kubus had steel tips on their spears and silver rings on their fingers, though they had lost all knowledge of metalworking. As for their language, it was quite close to the coastal tongues, and Appenzzell could understand it without major difficulty. What struck him especially was that they used a very restricted vocabulary, no larger than a few dozen words, and he wondered if the Kubus, in the image of their distant neighbours the Papuans, didn't voluntarily impoverish their vocabulary, deleting words each time a death occurred in the village. One consequence of this demise was that the same word came to refer to an ever-increasing number of objects. Thus the Malay word for "hunting", *Pekee*, meant indifferently to hunt, to walk, to carry, spear, gazelle, antelope, peccary, *my'am* – a type of very hot spice used lavishly in meat dishes – as well as forest, tomorrow, dawn, etc. Similarly *Sinuya*, a word which Appenzzell put alongside the Malay *usi*, "banana", and *nuya*, "coconut", meant to eat, meal, soup, gourd, spatula, plait, evening, house, pot, fire, silex (the Kubus made fire by rubbing two flints), fibula, comb, hair, *hoja'* (a hair-dye made from coconut milk mixed with various soils and plants), etc. Of all the characteristics of the Kubus, these linguistic habits are the best known, because Appenzzell described them in detail in a long letter to the Swedish philologist Hambo Taskerson, whom he'd known in Vienna, and who was working at that time in Copenhagen, with Hjelmslev and Brøndal. He pointed out in an aside that these characteristics could perfectly well apply to a Western carpenter using tools with precise names – gauge, tonguing plane, moulding plane, jointer, mortise, jack plane, rabbet, etc. – but asking his apprentice to pass them to him by saying just: "Gimme the thingummy".

On the fourth day, when Appenzzell woke in the morning, the village had been abandoned. The shacks were empty. The whole population had gone; men, women, children, dogs, even the old men who normally didn't budge from their mats had all gone and taken their meagre stock of yams, their three goats, their *sinuya* and their *pekee*.

Appenzzell took more than two months to catch up with them. This time their shacks had been hurriedly built beside a stagnant, mosquito-infested pool. The Kubus didn't speak or respond to his advances any more than they had the first time; one day, he saw two men trying to raise a great tree trunk felled by lightning, and went up to lend them a hand; but he'd hardly touched the tree before the two men dropped it and moved away. Next day, the village was once again deserted.

For nearly five years, Appenzzell pursued them obstinately. Each time he barely caught up with them before they moved on again, plunging into more and more uninhabitable areas, rebuilding their villages ever more shakily. For a long time Appenzzell pondered on the function of this migratory behaviour. The Kubus were not nomadic, and since they did not grow crops on burn-baited land, they had no reason to move on so frequently; nor could it be accounted for by hunting or gathering requirements. Was it a religious ritual, or something to do with initiation rites, or magic connected with life or death? There was nothing to support any of these theories; Kubu rituals, if they existed, were impenetrably discreet, and there was nothing that seemed to connect these departures which were for Appenzzell, each time, quite unforeseeable.

However, the truth, the cruel and obvious truth, finally dawned. It is admirably summarised at the end of the letter Appenzzell wrote to his mother from Rangoon about five months after leaving:

> However irksome are the discomfitures which a man who has given himself body and soul to the profession of ethnography may encounter in his attempt to grasp the deeper nature of Man in concrete terms – or, in other words, to apprehend the minimal sociality defining the human condition by conquering the heteroclite evidence of diverse cultures – and although an ethnographer may not aspire to more than the discovery of relative truths (since it is vain to hope to reach any final truth), the worst difficulty I have had to encounter was not at all

> of that kind: I wanted to go to the absolute limit of the primitive; had I not got all I wanted in these graceful Natives whom no one had seen before me, who would perhaps not be seen again after me? At the end of an exhilarating search, I had my savages, I asked for nothing more than to be one of them, to share their days, their pains, their rituals. Alas! they didn't want to have me, they were not prepared to teach me their customs and beliefs! They had no use whatever for the gifts I laid beside them, no use at all for the help I thought I could give! It was because of me that they abandoned their villages and it was only to discourage me, to convince me there was no point in my persevering, that they chose increasingly inhospitable sites, imposing ever more terrible living conditions on themselves to show me they would rather face tigers and volcanoes, swamps, suffocating fog, elephants, poisonous spiders, than men. I think I know a good deal about physical suffering. But this is worst of all, to feel your soul dying. . . .

Marcel Appenzzell wrote no further letter. The search his mother undertook in order to find him was fruitless. Very soon war came and put a stop to it. Madame Appenzzell obstinately stayed on in Paris even after her name had appeared on a list of Jews not wearing the yellow star, published in the weekly *Au Pilori.* One evening the hand of a sympathiser slipped a note under her door warning her that she would be arrested next day at dawn. She succeeded in getting to Le Mans that night and from there crossed into the free zone and joined the Resistance. She was killed in June 1944 near Vassieux-en-Vercors.

The Altamonts – Madame Altamont is Madame Appenzzell's second cousin – took over the flat in the early nineteen fifties. They were then a young couple. Today, she is forty-five and he is fifty-five. They have a daughter of seventeen, Véronique, who paints watercolours and plays the piano. Monsieur Altamont is an international expert, virtually always away from Paris, and it even seems that this great reception is being held on the occasion of his annual return.

CHAPTER TWENTY-SIX

Bartlebooth, 1

An antechamber, in Bartlebooth's flat.

It's an almost empty room, furnished with but a few straw-seated chairs, a pair of three-legged stools with red, fringed flat cushions, and a long, straight-backed bench-seat in greenish imitation-leather upholstery of the sort you used to see in railway-station waiting rooms.

The walls are painted white, the floor is laid with a thick plastic covering. On a large cork square fixed to the rear wall, several postcards have been pinned: the battlefield of the Pyramids, the fish market at Dumyât, the old whalers' quay at Nantucket, the *Promenade des Anglais* at Nice, the Hudson's Bay Company building at Winnipeg, sunset at Cape Cod, the Bronze Pavilion in the Summer Palace in Peking, a reproduction of a drawing showing Pisanello offering four gold medals on a cushioned tray to Lionel d'Este, as well as an announcement edged in black:

Your presence is requested at the burial of

GASPARD WINCKLER

who passed away on 29 October 1973, in Paris
in his 63rd year

The funeral will take place on 3 November 1973
and will leave the Bichat Hospital Morgue,
170 Boulevard Ney, Paris 17, at 10 a.m.

NO FLOWERS OR WREATHS

Bartlebooth's three servants stay in this antechamber, awaiting their master's problematical summonses on the bell. Smautf is standing near the window with one arm in the air, whilst Hélène, the maid, is restitching the seam that has come undone in the armpit of the right-hand sleeve of his jacket. Kléber, the chauffeur, sits on one of the chairs. He is not wearing his livery, but broad-belted cord trousers and a white woollen polo-neck sweater. He has just laid out on the green leather bench-seat a pack of fifty-two playing cards, face up, in four rows, and he is about to play a game of patience in which you first remove the four aces and then sort the pack into its four colour-suites by using the spaces made by the removal of the aces. Beside the cards lies an open book: it is an American novel by George Bretzlee, entitled *The Wanderers:* its action takes place in New York jazz circles in the early nineteen fifties.

Smautf, as we know, has been Bartlebooth's servant for fifty years. Kléber was hired as chauffeur in 1955 when Bartlebooth and Smautf returned from their world tour, at the same time as Madame Adèle was engaged as cook, Simone as the kitchen maid, Léonard as the wine steward-cum-butler, Germaine as the laundress, as well as an odd-job man, Louis, and a footman, Thomas. In those days Bartlebooth went out a lot, and also liked to entertain, giving very well-thought-of dinner parties; he would also invite distant relatives to stay, as well as people whose acquaintance he had made in the course of his travels.

From nineteen sixty on, his lavishness began to decline, and staff leaving were not replaced. It is only three years since Smautf engaged Hélène, after Madame Adèle took her retirement. Hélène, who is only just thirty, copes with everything, laundry, meals, cleaning, with Kléber, who hardly has occasion to use the car these days, lending a hand for heavy jobs.

Bartlebooth has not entertained for many years, and these last two years he has scarcely ever left the flat. Most of the time he shuts himself up in his study, having once and for all forbidden anyone to disturb him unless he calls. Sometimes forty-eight hours go by without his giving any sign of life: he sleeps in his clothes in great-uncle Sherwood's easy chair, and lives on nibbles of crispbread and gingernut biscuits. Only exceptionally does he now take his meals in his large, austere, Empire dining room. When he does consent to do so, Smautf dons his old coat-tails and, trying to keep his hand from shaking, serves him his boiled egg, his small helping of poached haddock, and his cup of verbena tea, which to Hélène's despair are the only foods he has, these many months, agreed to ingest.

Valène took many years to grasp exactly what Bartlebooth was after. The first time he came to see him, in January nineteen twenty-five, all Bartlebooth said was that he wanted to learn all there was to know about painting watercolours, and he wanted a lesson a day for ten years. The frequency and the duration of these private lessons startled Valène, who was perfectly content if he landed eighteen lessons a quarter. But Bartlebooth seemed determined to devote as much time as was necessary to his apprenticeship, and he seemed to have no money worries. Fifty years later, Valène sometimes reflected that, anyway, those ten years hadn't been such a waste, seeing how Bartlebooth displayed at the start a complete lack of natural talent.

Not only did Bartlebooth know nothing about the delicate art of watercolours, he'd never even held a paintbrush and scarcely ever tried a crayon. For the first year, therefore, Valène began by teaching him how to draw, and had him do copies in charcoal, in pencil, in red chalk, of models on squared grids, had him do positioning sketches, and exercises in crosshatched sketches highlighted with chalk, and exercises in shading, and exercises in perspective. Next he made him work with Indian ink and sepia wash, forced him to practise complicated calligraphy, and showed him how to make his brush strokes thicker and thinner so as to establish different values and obtain a range of tones.

In two years Bartlebooth learnt to master these initial skills. The rest, Valène assured him, was just a matter of material and experience. They began to do open-air work, at first in the Monceau Gardens, on the banks of the Seine, and in the Bois de Boulogne, then further afield in the Paris region. Every day at two, Bartlebooth's chauffeur – not yet Kléber, but Fawcett, who had served Priscilla, Bartlebooth's mother – called for Valène; in the capacious black-and-white Chenard & Walker limousine, the painter would find his pupil dressed sensibly in golfing breeches, spats, check cap, and woollen sweater. They would go to the Forest of Fontainebleau, to Senlis, to Enghien, to Versailles, to Saint-Germain, or to the Chevreuse valley. There they would set up their three-legged camp stools (known as "Pinchart stools") side by side, and their parasol with its jointed pole and ground spike, and their fragile articulated easel. With manic precision, so obsessively meticulous as to be almost clumsy with it, Bartlebooth would first hold his sheet of Whatman paper (already damped on the reverse side) up to the light, so he could check by the watermark that he had got it the right way round, then he would take drawing pins and fix it onto his board of cross-grained ash, and then he would open his zinc palette with its enamelled inside surfaces spotlessly cleaned after the previous day's session, and would arrange on it, in ritual sequence, thirteen little cups of paint – ivory black, coloured sepia, burnt sienna, yellow ochre, Indian yellow, chrome yellow, vermilion, madder gloss, Veronese green, olive green, ultramarine, cobalt, Prussian blue, as well as a few drops of Madame Maubois's zinc white – then he would set out his water, his sponges, and his crayons, check that his brushes were properly mounted in their handles, perfectly tipped, not too thick in the middle, had no stray, loose hairs, and then he would get down to it, first sketching in softly in crayon the volumes, the horizon, the foreground, the vanishing lines, before trying to fix in all their unforeseeable, split-second splendour the ephemeral metamorphoses of a cloud, or a breeze rippling the surface of a pond, or a sunset over the Ile-de-France, a flock of starlings ascending, a shepherd bringing in his sheep, moonrise over a dormant village, a road lined with poplars, a dog halting at a thicket, and so on.

Most of the time Valène would shake his head and with a few curt phrases – your sky's too heavy, that's out of balance, you've missed the effect, not enough contrast, you haven't got the atmosphere, there's no gradation, the layout is banal – alternating with ringings and crossings-out nonchalantly scrawled over the watercolour, he would mercilessly destroy the work of Bartlebooth, who, without a word, would tear the sheet from his ashwood board, affix a fresh piece, and start all over again.

Outside this laconic tuition, Bartlebooth and Valène hardly spoke to each other. Although they were exactly the same age, Bartlebooth seemed entirely uninterested in Valène, and Valène, though intrigued by his employer's eccentricity, usually didn't dare question him straight out. Nonetheless, several times, during the return journeys to Paris, he did ask him why he was so obstinately determined to learn to paint watercolours. Bartlebooth's usual reply was:

"Why not?"

"Because," Valène retorted one day, "most of my pupils, in your shoes, would have given up long ago."

"Am I that bad?" Bartlebooth asked.

"In ten years you can get anywhere, and you will get there; but why do you want to master an art for which you have absolutely no spontaneous inclination?"

"It's not watercolours I'm interested in, but what I plan to do with them."

"And what is that?"

"Why, to make puzzles, of course," was Bartlebooth's unhesitating reply. That day Valène began to grasp more precisely what was in Bartlebooth's mind. But only after getting to know Smautf and then Gaspard Winckler could he gauge the full extent of the Englishman's ambition.

Let us imagine a man whose wealth is equalled only by his indifference to what wealth generally brings, a man of exceptional arrogance who wishes to fix, to describe, and to exhaust not the whole world – merely to state such an ambition is enough to invalidate it – but a constituted fragment of the world: in the face of the inextricable incoherence of things, he will set out to execute a (necessarily limited) programme right the way through, in all its irreducible, intact entirety.

In other words, Bartlebooth resolved one day that his whole life would be organised around a single project, an arbitrarily constrained programme with no purpose outside its own completion.

The idea occurred to him when he was twenty. At first it was only a vague idea, a question looming – *what should I do?* – with an answer taking shape: *nothing*. Money, power, art, women did not interest Bartlebooth. Nor did science, nor even gambling. There were only neckties and horses that just about did, or, to put it another way, beneath these futile illustrations (but thousands of people do order their lives effectively around their ties, and far greater numbers do so around their weekend horse-riding) there stirred, dimly, a certain idea of perfection.

It grew over the following months and came to rest on three guiding principles.

The first was moral: the plan should not have to do with an exploit or record, it would be neither a peak to scale nor an ocean floor to reach. What Bartlebooth would do would not be heroic, or spectacular; it would be something simple and discreet, difficult of course but not impossibly so, controlled from start to finish and conversely controlling every detail of the life of the man engaged upon it.

The second was logical: all recourse to chance would be ruled out, and the project would make time and space serve as the abstract coordinates plotting the ineluctable recursion of identical events occurring inexorably in their allotted places, on their allotted dates.

The third was aesthetic: the plan would be useless, since gratuitousness was the sole guarantor of its rigour, and would destroy itself as it proceeded; its perfection would be circular: a series of events which when concatenated nullify each other: starting from nothing, passing through precise operations on finished objects, Bartlebooth would end up with nothing.

Thus a concrete programme was designed, which can be stated succinctly as follows.

For ten years, from 1925 to 1935, Bartlebooth would acquire the art of painting watercolours.

For twenty years, from 1935 to 1955, he would travel the world, painting, at a rate of one watercolour each fortnight, five hundred seascapes of identical format (royal, 65cm × 50cm) depicting seaports. When each view was done, he would dispatch it to a specialist craftsman (Gaspard Winckler), who would glue it to a thin wooden backing board and cut it into a jigsaw puzzle of seven hundred and fifty pieces.

For twenty years, from 1955 to 1975, Bartlebooth, on his return to France, would reassemble the jigsaw puzzles in order, at a rate, once again, of one puzzle a fortnight. As each puzzle was finished, the seascape would be "retexturised" so that it could be removed from its backing, returned to the place where it had been painted – twenty years before – and dipped in a detergent solution whence would emerge a clean and unmarked sheet of Whatman paper.

Thus no trace would remain of an operation which would have been, throughout a period of fifty years, the sole motivation and unique activity of its author.

CHAPTER TWENTY-SEVEN

Rorschach, 3

It suggests some kind of petrified memory, like a Magritte painting in which stone may have come to life or life been turned to stone, some kind of image indelibly fixed for all time. The man is sitting down; his moustache droops, his arms are crossed on the table top, his thick neck emerges from a collarless shirt. The woman stands behind him, with her left arm on his shoulder, her hair pulled back, in a black skirt and flowered blouse. Hand in hand, the twins stand in front of the table, in sailor suits with short trousers, with the armbands worn for confirmation on their sleeves and their socks falling down around their ankles. On the oilcloth table-covering stands a blue-enamel coffee pot and a photograph of grandfather in an oval frame. On the mantelpiece, bluish clumps of rosemary sprout from two flowerpots that have conical bases and are decorated with black-and-white chevrons. Between them, under an oblong glass bell, appears a bridal wreath with artificial orange blossoms (pellets of cotton dipped in wax), a beaded armature, and ornamental garlands, birds, and bits of mirror.

In the fifties, long before Gratiolet sold Rorschach the two superimposed apartments that would become his duplex, an Italian family called Grifalconi lived for a while on the fourth floor to the left of the stairs. Emilio Grifalconi was a cabinet-maker from Verona. His speciality was repairing antiques, and he had come to Paris to restore the furnishings in Château de la Muette. He was married to a young woman fifteen years his junior; her name was Laetizia; three years before, she had borne him twins.

The building, the block, and the neighbourhood were captivated by Laetizia's severe, almost sombre beauty. Every afternoon, in the Monceau Gardens, she used to walk her children in a double perambulator built especially for twins. No doubt it was during such an outing that she met one of the men most troubled by her beauty. His name was Paul Hébert. (He also lived in the building, on the fifth floor to the right.) He had been arrested on 7 October 1943, when he was barely eighteen, in the big roundup on Boulevard Saint-Germain that followed the assassination of Captain Dittersdorf and Lieutenants Nebel and Knödelwurst. Paul Hébert was sent to Buchenwald. He was liberated in forty-five. After spending seven years in a sanatorium in the Grisons, he had only recently returned to France and found a job teaching physics and chemistry at Collège Chaptal, an independent school. Naturally, his students at once nicknamed him pH.

Their affair – not intentionally platonic, but probably limited by circumstance to furtive hand-holding and an occasional embrace – had been going on for four years when, in the autumn of 1955, pH was transferred to Mazamet. His doctors had insisted he be moved to a dry climate near the mountains.

For several months he wrote letters to Laetizia begging her to join him; each time she refused. By chance a draft of one of her replies was found by her husband:

> I am depressed, troubled, a mass of nerves. I feel the way I did two years ago, horribly on edge. Everything wounds me, tears me to pieces. Your last two letters made my heart beat almost to bursting.

They move me so, when I unfold them and the scent of your writing paper rises to my nostrils and the fragrance of your caressing words penetrates me to the heart. Spare me; you make me giddy with your love! We must convince ourselves, however, that we cannot live together. We must resign ourselves to a flatter, more pallid existence. I wish that you would accustom yourself to this; I want the thought of me to comfort you, not consume you; to console you, not drive you to despair. What can we do, darling? It must be so. We cannot continue with these convulsions of the soul. The despondency that follows is a kind of death. Work, think of other things. You have so much intelligence: use a little of it to become more serene. I am at the end of my strength. I had plenty of courage for myself: but for two! My role is to sustain everyone, and I am exhausted. Don't distress me with your outbursts, which make me curse myself, without seeing any remedy. . . .

Emilio naturally could not know for whom this unfinished draft was intended. He so trusted Laetizia that he thought at first that she must have copied a passage out of some novelette; and Laetizia could have made him believe this, had she so wanted. But if, during those long years, she had been able to leave the truth unspoken, she was incapable now of disguising it. When Emilio questioned her, she confessed with appalling calm that her dearest wish had been to live with Hébert, and that she had decided against doing so only for his sake and the twins'.

Grifalconi let her go. He did not commit suicide or become an alcoholic but instead devoted all his attention to the care of the twins. Each morning before going to work he took them to school, and in the evening he brought them home. He did the shopping, he cooked for them and washed them. He cut up their meat, helped with their homework, read them bedtime stories, took them on Saturday afternoons to Avenue des Ternes to buy them shoes, duffel-coats, and jumpers. He made sure they went to Sunday school and were confirmed.

In 1959, at the termination of his contract with the Ministry of Cultural Affairs (the agency overseeing the work at Château de la Muette), Grifalconi returned with his children to Verona. A few weeks earlier, he called on Valène to commission a picture. He wanted the painter to portray him in the company of his wife and their two children. The four of them would be in the dining room. He would be seated; she would be standing behind him in her black skirt and flowered blouse, her left hand resting on his left shoulder in a gesture of serene trust; the twins would be wearing their handsome sailor suits and their confirmation armbands. A photograph of his grandfather, who had visited the Pyramids, would be set on the table; and on the mantel Laetizia's bridal wreath would appear between the two pots of rosemary she so loved.

Instead of a painting, Valène executed a coloured pen-and-ink drawing. With Emilio and the twins posing for him, making use for Laetizia of several photographs that were none too new, he lavished the greatest care on all the details the cabinet-maker requested of him – the little blue and purple flowers on Laetizia's blouse, his forebear's spats and pith helmet, the laborious gilding of the bridal wreath, the damask folds of the twins' armbands.

Emilio was so pleased with Valène that he insisted not only on paying him but on presenting him with two objects that were incomparably dear to him. He brought the painter to his apartment and laid an oblong case of green leather on the table. Having turned on a ceiling spotlight to illuminate the case, he opened it. A weapon rested on the brilliant red lining, its smooth handle of ash, its bill-shaped flat blade of gold. "Do you know what this is?" he asked. Valène raised his eyebrows to express his perplexity. "It's a golden billhook – the kind the Gallic druids used for harvesting mistletoe." Valène looked at Grifalconi incredulously, but the cabinet-maker seemed sure of himself. "I made the handle, of course, but the blade is original. It was discovered in a tomb near Aix-en-Provence. It's said to be typical Salian workmanship." Valène examined the blade more closely. Seven minute engravings were delicately chased on one of its sides, but he was unable to make out what they represented, even with the aid of a powerful magnifying glass. All he could see was that in several of them there apparently figured a woman with very long hair.

The second object was even stranger. When Grifalconi extracted it from its padded case, Valène thought at first that it was a large cluster of coral. Grifalconi shook his head. In one of the attics in Château de la Muette he had found the remains of a table. Its oval top, wonderfully inlaid with mother-of-pearl, was exceptionally well preserved; but its base, a massive, spindle-shaped column of grained wood, turned out to be completely worm-eaten. The worms had done their work in covert, subterranean fashion, creating innumerable ducts and microscopic channels now filled with pulverised wood. No sign of this insidious labour showed on the surface. Grifalconi saw that the only way of preserving the original base – hollowed out as it was, it could no longer support the weight of the top – was to reinforce it from within; so once he had completely emptied the canals of their wood dust by suction, he set about injecting them with an almost liquid mixture of lead, alum, and asbestos fibre. The operation was successful; but it quickly became apparent that, even thus strengthened, the base was too weak, and Grifalconi had to resign himself to replacing it. It was after he had done this that he thought of dissolving what was left of the original wood so as to disclose the fabulous arborescence within, this exact record of the worms' life inside the wooden mass: a static, mineral accumulation of all the movements that had constituted their blind existence, their undeviating single-mindedness, their obstinate itineraries; the faithful materialisation of all they had eaten and digested as they forced from their dense surroundings the invisible elements needed for their survival, the explicit, visible, immeasurably disturbing image of the endless progressions that had reduced the hardest of woods to an impalpable network of crumbling galleries.

Grifalconi went back to Verona. Once or twice Valène sent him one of the linoleum prints he made for his friends as New Year's greetings; they went unacknowledged. In 1972 one of the twins, Vittorio, now professor of botanical taxonomy at the University of Padua, informed him that his father had died as a result of an attack of trichinosis. All he said about the other twin was that he was living in South America and was in good health.

* * *

Several months after the Grifalconis' departure, Gratiolet sold the apartment they had occupied to Rémi Rorschach. It is now the lower floor of a duplex. The dining room has become a living room. The mantel on which Emilio Grifalconi placed his wife's bridal wreath and the two pots of rosemary has been modernised: its surface is now of burnished steel. The floor is covered with a profusion of wool rugs of exotic design heaped on top of one another. The only other furnishings are three so-called director's chairs in unbleached linen (scarcely more than modified camping chairs). Examples of American gadgetry are strewn around the place, among them an electronic Feedbackgammon, whose players have only to roll their dice and push the numerically corresponding buttons: the counters, circles that light up on the translucent surface, are shifted by microchips built into the board and programmed to follow optimal strategies. (Since each player thus disposes in turn of the best possible offence/defence, the most common outcome of the game is a reciprocal jamming amounting to a draw.)

After tortuous legal proceedings involving impounding and seizure, Paul Hébert's apartment was finally reclaimed by the building manager, who has since rented it. It is at present occupied by Geneviève Foulerot and her little boy.

Laetizia never came back, nor was she heard from again. It was thanks to young Riri, who ran into him by chance in 1970, that something at least was learned about Paul Hébert.

Young Riri is now almost twenty-five; his real name is Valentin, Valentin Collot. He is the youngest of three children born to Henri Collot, who runs the *café-tabac* at the corner of Rue Jadin and Rue de Chazelles. Henri has always been called Riri by everyone, and his wife Lucienne has been called Madame Riri, and their two daughters Martine and Isabelle the little Riris, and Valentin Young Riri – except by Monsieur Jérôme, the retired history teacher, who opted for Riri the Younger after first trying to introduce the title Riri II, an undertaking in which no one supported him, not even Morellet, usually so sympathetic to such initiatives.

Young Riri had for one miserable year been pH's pupil at Collège Chaptal; he still shuddered at the memory of joules, coulombs, ergs, dynes, ohms, and farads, and of "acid plus base yields salt plus water". He spent the period of his military service in the town of Bar-le-Duc. One Saturday afternoon, as he was wandering through its streets in the state of intractable boredom known only to conscripts, he spied his former teacher. Behind a stand outside a supermarket, dressed as a Norman peasant (blue smock, red-checked scarf, and cap), Paul Hébert was proposing to passers-by his assortment of country sausages, bottled cider, Breton biscuits, and bread guaranteed to have been baked in wood-fired ovens. Approaching the stand, Young Riri bought a few slices of garlic sausage and wondered if he would work up the courage to accost his old teacher. When Paul Hébert gave him his change, their eyes met for a fraction of a second. Young Riri saw that the other man knew he had been recognised and was imploring him to go away.

CHAPTER TWENTY-EIGHT

On the Stairs, 3

It was here, on the stairs, it must have been a good three years ago, that he met him for the last time; on the stairs, on the fifth-floor landing, opposite the door of the flat where the unfortunate Hébert had lived. The lift was out of order once again and Valène, painfully climbing back up, crossed the path of Bartlebooth, who, perhaps, had been to see Winckler. He was wearing his usual grey worsted trousers, a check jacket, and one of those lisle-thread shirts of which he was so fond. He greeted him in passing with a very brief nod of the head. He hadn't changed much; his back was bent, but he walked without a stick; his face had got a little thinner, his eyes had gone almost white: that's what struck Valène the most, his gaze which did not manage to meet his own, as if Bartlebooth had sought to look behind his head, had wanted to pierce his head to reach beyond it the neutral asylum of the stairwell with its *trompe-l'oeil* decorations mimicking old marbling and its staff skirting board made to resemble wood panelling. There was in that avoiding look something more violent than a void, something that was not merely pride or hatred, but almost panic, something like a mad hope, like an appeal for help, like a signal of distress.

Bartlebooth had been back for seventeen years, for seventeen years he had been chained to his desk, seventeen years ferociously recomposing one by one the five hundred seascapes which Gaspard Winckler had cut into seven hundred and fifty pieces each. He had already reconstituted more than four hundred of them! At the beginning he went fast, he worked with pleasure, resuscitating with a kind of ardour the scenes he had painted twenty years earlier, watching with childlike glee as Morellet delicately filled in the tiniest gaps left in the completed jigsaw puzzles. Then as the years wore on it seemed as though the puzzles got more and more complicated, more and more difficult to solve. Though his technique, his practice, his intuition, and his methods had become extremely subtle, and though he usually anticipated the traps Winckler had laid, he was no longer always able to find the appropriate answer: in vain would he spend hours on each puzzle, sitting for whole days in this swivelling and rocking chair that had belonged to his Bostonian great-uncle, for he found it harder and harder to finish his puzzles in the time he had laid down for himself.

For Smautf, who used to see them covered over by a black cloth on the big square table when he brought his master tea (which the latter most often forgot to drink), an apple (which he nibbled a little before letting it brown in the wastepaper basket), or mail which he only opened now as an exception, the puzzles remained attached to wisps of memory – smells of seaweed, the sounds of waves crashing along high embankments, distant names: Majunga, Diégo-Suarez, Comoro, Seychelles, Socotra, Moka, Hodeida . . . For Bartlebooth, they were now only bizarre playing-pieces in an interminable game, of which he had ended up forgetting the rules, who his opponent was, and what the stake was, and the bet: little wooden bits whose capricious contours fed his nightmares, the sole material substance of a lonely and bloody-minded replay, the inert, inept, and merciless components of an aimless quest. Majunga was neither a town nor a port, it was not a heavy sky, a strip of lagoon, a horizon dog-toothed by warehouses and cement works, it was only seven hundred and fifty variations on grey, incomprehensible splinters of a bottomless enigma, the sole images of a void which no memory, no expectation would ever come to fill, the only props of his self-defeating illusions.

Gaspard Winckler had died a few weeks after this meeting, and Bartlebooth had virtually stopped going out. From time to time Smautf would give Valène news of the absurd voyage that twenty years on the Englishman was pursuing in the silence of his padded study: "We've left Crete" – Smautf identified himself with Bartlebooth quite often, and spoke of him in the first person plural (it is true they had made all these journeys together) – "we're approaching the Cyclades: Zafora, Anafi, Milo, Paros, Naxos, that won't be plain sailing!"

Sometimes Valène had the feeling that time had been stopped, suspended, frozen around he didn't know what expectation. The very idea of the picture he planned to do and whose laid-out, broken-up images had begun to haunt every second of his life, furnishing his dreams, squeezing his memories, the very idea of this shattered building laying bare the cracks of its past, the crumbling of its present, this unordered amassing of stories grandiose and trivial, frivolous and pathetic, gave him the impression of a grotesque mausoleum raised in the memory of companions petrified in terminal postures as insignificant in their solemnity as they were in their ordinariness, as if he had wanted both to warn of and to delay these slow or quick deaths which seemed to be engulfing the entire building storey by storey: Monsieur Marcia, Madame Moreau, Madame de Beaumont, Bartlebooth, Rorschach, Mademoiselle Crespi, Madame Albin, Smautf. And himself, of course, Valène himself, the longest inhabitant of the house.

And sometimes a feeling of unbearable sadness ran through him: he would think of the others, of all those who had already gone, all those whom life or death had swallowed up: Madame Hourcade, in her little house near Montargis, Morellet at Verrières-le-Buisson, Madame Fresnel and her son in New Caledonia, and Winckler, and

Marguerite, and the Danglars, and the Claveaus, and Hélène Brodin with her frightened little smile, and Monsieur Jérôme, and the old lady with the little dog whose name he'd forgotten, the old lady's name, that is, for the little dog (actually it was a bitch) he remembered very well indeed, it was called Dodéca and since it frequently did its business on the landing, the concierge – Madame Claveau – never called it anything but Dodefecate. The old lady lived in the fourth floor left, beside the Grifalconis, and she could often be seen walking up or down the stairs dressed only in her undies. Her son wanted to be a priest. Years later, after the war, Valène met him in Rue des Pyramides trying to sell pornographic novelettes to tourists about to see Paris aboard a double-decker bus, and he told him an endless story about gold-smuggling in the USSR.

Once again his head began to whirl with the sad round of removers and undertakers, property agents and their customers, plumbers, electricians, painters, decorators, tilers, and carpet-layers: he began to think of the tranquil life of things, of crockery chests full of wood shavings, of cartons of books, of the harsh light of bare bulbs swinging on their wires, of the slow installation of furniture and objects, of the slow adaptation of the body to space, that whole sum of minute, nonexistent, untellable events – choosing a lamp-stand, a reproduction, a knickknack, placing a tall rectangular mirror between two doors, putting a Japanese garden in front of a window, lining cupboard shelves with a flower-printed fabric – all those infinitesimal gestures in which the life of a flat is always most faithfully encapsulated, and which will be upset from time to time by the sudden – unforeseen or ineluctable, tragic or benign, ephemeral or definitive – fractures of an ahistorical daily grind: one day the young Marquiseaux girl will run off with the Réol boy, one day Madame Orlowska will leave again for no apparent reason, for no real reason either; one day Madame Altamont will fire a revolver at Monsieur Altamont and the blood will spurt onto the glazed hexagonal tiles of their octagonal dining room: one day the police will come to arrest Joseph Nieto and will find hidden in one of the brass spheres on his large Empire bedstead in his bedroom the famous diamond stolen long ago from Prince Luigi Voudzoï.

* * *

One day, above all, the whole house will disappear, the street and the *quartier* will die. That will take time to happen. To begin with, it will seem like a legend or a barely plausible rumour: someone will have heard something about a possible extension of the Monceau Gardens, or a plan for a big hotel, or a direct link from the Elysée palace to Roissy airport using the line of Avenue de Courcelles to get to the ring road. Then the rumours will harden; the names of the developers will become known, as will the precise nature of their plans, illustrated in expensive, four-colour-printed fold-outs:

> . . . As part of the enlargement and modernisation of the accommodation housing the main Post Office of the XVIIth arrondissement included in the Seventh Five-Year Plan and made inevitable by the substantial expansion of this public service in the last two decades, it has now become possible and desirable to implement a total restructuring of the surrounding area . . .

and then

> . . . The result of teamwork between government agencies and private ventures, this vast multipurpose development, sensitive to the ecological balance of its environment, but with designed capacity for the social and cultural facilities which are indispensable humanising factors in contemporary life, will thus come at the right time to replace an urban fabric that reached saturation point several years ago . . .

and finally

> . . . A few minutes from Etoile-Charles-de-Gaulle (Express Metro) and the Saint-Lazare railway station, scarcely a few yards from the bosky groves of the Monceau Gardens, HORIZON 84 offers you on three million square metres' floorspace the THREE THOUSAND FIVE HUNDRED finest offices in Paris: triple-thick carpet, thermophonic insulation by floating floortiles, non-skid surfaces, power-controlled partitions, telex, CCTV, computer terminals, conference rooms with simultaneous

> interpreting facilities, office canteens, snack bars, swimming pool, clubhouse . . . HORIZON 84 also means SEVEN HUNDRED apartments from bijou miniflats to five-roomed residences, fully serviced – from electronic porterage to pre-programmable cookers, and TWENTY-TWO reception suites – three hundred square metres of drawing rooms and balconies; and there's also a shopping centre totalling FORTY-SEVEN shops and service outlets, and you'll have TWELVE THOUSAND underground car parking spaces, ONE THOUSAND ONE HUNDRED AND SEVENTY-FIVE square metres of landscaped grounds, TWO THOUSAND FIVE HUNDRED installed telephone lines, an AM-FM relay station, TWELVE tennis courts, SEVEN cinemas, and the most modern hotel complex in Europe! HORIZON 84, 84 YEARS OF EXPERIENCE SERVING TOMORROW'S REAL ESTATE!

But before these cubes of glass, steel, and concrete rise up from the ground, there will be the long palaver of sales and takeovers, of compensation, exchanges, rehousing, and evictions. One by one the shops will close and stay empty, one by one the windows of vacated flats will be bricked up and the floors lifted to discourage squatters and tramps. The street will be no more than a string of blank facades – *bleak walls, vacant eye-like windows* – alternating with poster-patched palisades and nostalgic graffiti.

Who, on seeing a Parisian apartment house, has never thought of it as indestructible? A bomb, a fire, an earthquake could certainly bring it down, but what else? In the eyes of an individual, of a family, or even a dynasty, a town, street, or house seems unchangeable, untouchable by time, by the ups and downs of human life, to such an extent that we believe we can compare and contrast the fragility of our condition to the invulnerability of stone. But the same fever which around eighteen fifty brought these buildings out of the ground from Batignolles to Clichy, from Ménilmontant to Butte-aux-Cailles, from Balard to Pré Saint-Gervais, will henceforth strive for their destruction.

The demolition men will come and their heavy hammers will smash the stucco and the tiles, will punch through the partitions, twist the ironwork, displace the beams and rafters, rip out the breeze blocks and the stone: grotesque images of a building torn down, reduced to piles of raw materials which scrapmerchants in thick gloves will come to quarrel over: lead from the plumbing, marble from the mantelpieces, wood from the structure and the floors, the doors and the skirting boards, brass and cast iron from handles and taps, large mirrors and the gilt of their frames, basin stones, bathtubs, the wrought iron of the stair rail . . .

The tireless bulldozers of the site-levellers will come to shovel off the rest: tons and tons of scree and dust.

CHAPTER TWENTY-NINE

Third Floor Right, 2

The main drawing room in the flat on the third floor right could well display all the classic signs of the morning after a party.

It is a huge room with light-coloured woodwork, revealing its finely laid parquet floor as the carpets have been either rolled up or pushed back. The whole rear wall is taken up by a Regency-style bookcase, the middle part of which is in fact a door painted in *trompe l'oeil*. Through this half-opened door can be seen a long corridor down which a girl of maybe sixteen is walking, holding a glass of milk in her right hand.

In the drawing room another girl – maybe it's for her that the restoring glassful is meant – lies asleep on a grey suede sofa: buried beneath the cushions, half covered by a black, flower-and-leaf-embroidered shawl, she seems to be wearing only a nylon jerkin which is clearly several sizes too big for her.

On the floor, everywhere, the remains of the party: several odd shoes, a long white sock, a pair of tights, a top hat, a false nose, cardboard plates in piles, or crumpled, or lying singly, laden with left-overs – tops of radishes, heads of sardines, slightly gnawed lumps of bread, chicken bones, cheese rinds, crimped paper boats that have been used for *petits fours* and chocolates, cigarette butts, paper napkins, cardboard cups; on a low table, various empty bottles and an almost entire pat of butter in which several cigarettes have been neatly crushed; in other places, a whole assortment of small triangular trays with various morsels still in them: green olives, roast nuts, salty biscuits, prawn crackers; further on, where there is just a little more open space, a barrel of Côtes-du-Rhône on its own stand, beneath which floorcloths, a few yards of kitchen towel that has capriciously loosed itself from its dispenser, and a whole collection of glasses and cups, some of them still half-full, are spread; coffee cups lie about, here and there, as do lumps of sugar, liqueur glasses, forks, knives, a cake-slice, coffee spoons, beer cans, Coca-Cola bottles, almost untouched bottles of gin, port, Armagnac, Marie-Brizard, Cointreau, *crème de banane*, hairpins, innumerable receptacles used as ashtrays and overflowing with carbonised matchsticks, cigarette ash, pipe ash, butts with and without lipstick stain, date stones, walnut, almond, and peanut shells, apple cores, orange and tangerine peel; in various places lie large plates piled with the remains of diverse dishes: rolled ham in now running jelly, slices of roast beef garnished with gherkins, half a cold hake decorated with sprigs of parsley, tomato quarters, whorls of mayonnaise and crinkle-cut slices of lemon; other shapes have found sanctuary in sometimes implausible locations: balancing on a radiator there is a big Japanese lacquered-wood salad bowl with a bit of rice salad left in it (olives, anchovy fillets, hard-boiled eggs, capers, strips of green pepper, shrimps); under the sofa, a silver dish on which untouched drumsticks lie alongside bare and half-bare chicken bones; a bowl of gooey mayonnaise sits in an armchair; under a bronze paperweight depicting Scopas's *Ares Resting*, a saucerful of radishes; dried-out cucumbers, aubergines, and mangoes and a remnant of a lettuce gone sour perch near the top of the bookcase, above a six-volume edition of Mirabeau's salacious stories, and the remains of an elaborate party cake – a huge meringue in the shape of a squirrel – are precariously wedged between two folds in one of the carpets.

Innumerable records, with and without their sleeves, are spread around the room, mostly dance records, but with a few surprising variations included, such as: *The Marches and Fanfares of the 2nd*

Armoured Division, *The Ploughman and His Children, told in Cockney by Pierre Devaux*, *An Evening in Paris with Tom Lehrer*, *May '68 at the Sorbonne*, *La Tempesta di Mare, concerto in* E^b *major, op. 8, No. 5, by Antonio Vivaldi, performed on the synthesiser by Léonie Prouillot*; and absolutely everywhere dismembered cartons, hurriedly opened packaging, pieces of string, and gold-painted ribbon with curly spiral ends, showing that the party was given to celebrate the birthday of one or the other of the two girls, and that her friends have done her proud: amongst other things, and not counting the comestible solids and liquids brought as gifts by some of the guests, she received as presents: a small musical-box device which we can safely presume plays *Happy Birthday To You*; an ink drawing by Thorwaldsson depicting a Norwegian groom in his wedding outfit: short jacket with close-set silver buttons, starched shirt with straight corolla, waistcoat with silk-braided border, tight trousers brought in at the knee in bunches of woolly tassels, a soft hat, yellowish boots, and at his waist, in its leather sheath, his *Dolknif* or Scandinavian knife, which the true Norseman always carries; a tiny box of English watercolours – from which we may deduce that the girl enjoys painting; an old-fashioned poster showing a barman with mischievous eyes holding a long clay pipe and pouring himself a glass of Hulstkamp geneva (which he's already raised to his lips on a smaller poster behind him, incorrectly mirroring the larger one in which it's set), whilst crowds prepare to invade the tavern with three men – one in a straw boater, one in a felt hat, one in a top hat – jostling at the door; another drawing, by a certain William Falsten, an American cartoonist of the early years of this century, entitled *The Punishment*, showing a boy lying in bed thinking of the wonderful cake his family is sharing – this mental image being realised in a cloud-bubble above his head – and which he has not been allowed to taste, owing to some silly behaviour; and lastly, presents from jokers with a mildly morbid sense of humour, various trick items including a flick-knife that springs open at the slightest touch, and a frightful imitation of a big black spider.

We can deduce from the general appearance of the room that the party was lavish, perhaps even grandiose, but that it did not turn riotous: there are a few spilt glasses, a few scorch-marks made by cigarettes on cushions and carpets, quite a few grease and wine stains, but no really irreparable damage has been done, except for one torn parchment lampshade, one pot of strong mustard spilt on Yvette Horner's golden disc, and a bottle of vodka broken in a plantpot containing a fragile papyrus, which will surely not recover.

CHAPTER THIRTY

Marquiseaux, 2

It is a bathroom. The floor and the walls are laid with glazed ochre-yellow hexagonal tiles. A man and a woman are kneeling in the bath, which is half-full of water. They are both about thirty years old. The man has placed his hands on the woman's waist, and he is licking her left breast whilst she, with slightly arched back, clasps her companion's sex organ in her right hand and caresses her own with her left. A third character is present at this scene: a young cat, black with bronze flecks and a white spot under the neck, is stretched out on the rim of the bath and seems to express utter astonishment in his yellow-green gaze. He wears a plaited leather collar bearing the regulation nameplate – *Petit Pouce* – with his RSPCA registration number, and the telephone number of his owners, Philippe and Caroline Marquiseaux; not their Paris number, since it would be most unlikely for Petit Pouce ever to go out of the flat and get lost in Paris, but the number of their country house: Jouy-en-Josas (Yvelines) 50.

Caroline Marquiseaux is the Echards' daughter and has taken over their flat. In 1966, when she had just turned twenty, she married Philippe Marquiseaux, whom she'd met a few months earlier at the Sorbonne, where both of them were history students. Marquiseaux was from Compiègne and lived in Paris in a minute room in Rue Cujas. The newly-weds thus moved into the room in which Caroline had grown up, whilst her parents kept their bedroom and the lounge-dining room. Within a few weeks, all four found such cohabitation unbearable.

The first skirmishes broke out over the bathroom: Philippe, Madame Echard would howl in her sourest voice, preferably when the windows were wide open so that the whole building could hear properly, Philippe spends hours in the WC and purposely leaves the lavatory pan in a mess for others to clean up after him; the Echards, Philippe riposted, quite intentionally forgot their false teeth in toothmugs he and Caroline were supposed to use. Monsieur Echard would intervene as peacemaker and succeeded in preventing such conflicts from escalating beyond verbal insults and offensive allusions, and a bearable status quo was established on the basis of some gestures of good will on both sides and some agreed measures to facilitate shared domesticity: a timetable for the use of sanitary facilities, rigid separation of space, elaborate differentiation of towels, face cloths, and bathroom accessories.

But if Monsieur Echard – a retired librarian with a bee in his bonnet about collecting evidence that Hitler was still alive – was bonhomie itself, his wife was an untamed shrew whose endless recriminations at mealtimes caused hostilities to be re-engaged: every evening the old woman harangued her son-in-law, on a different, made-up pretext almost every time: he would be late, or he would come to table without washing his hands, he hadn't earned what was on his plate but that wouldn't stop him being particular, my word no, he really ought to help Caroline now and again to lay the table or wash the dishes, etc. Usually Philippe bore this incessant nagging with phlegm, and sometimes even tried to joke about it; for example, one evening he brought his mother-in-law a present, a cactus, "as it so suits your character, mother dear", but one Sunday, towards the end of lunch, for which she had made the dish he most detested – French toast – and which she was trying to force him to eat, he lost control of himself, seized the cake-slice from his mother-in-law's grasp and with it banged her head a few times. Then he packed his cases calmly and went back to Compiègne.

Caroline persuaded him to come back: if he stayed at Compiègne he would jeopardise not just his marriage but also his studies and his chance of competing for a Teaching Scholarship which, if he did land one, would allow them to have their own flat the very next year.

Philippe allowed himself to be talked round, and Madame Echard, yielding to her husband's and daughter's intercessions, also agreed to tolerate for a while longer the presence of her son-in-law under her own roof. But soon her natural nastiness reasserted itself, and a hail of harangues and prohibitions rained down on the young couple: no using the bathroom after eight in the morning, no going in the kitchen except to do the washing up, no using the telephone, no visitors, no coming in after ten in the evening, no listening to the radio, etc.

Caroline and Philippe bore these rigorous conditions heroically. In truth they didn't have any option: the miserly allowance Philippe got from his father – a wealthy trader who disapproved of his son's marriage – and the few pennies Caroline's father secretly slipped into her hand added up to barely enough to pay for their daily travel to the Latin Quarter and for meal tickets in the student cafeteria: sitting on a café *terrasse*, going to the cinema, buying a copy of *Le Monde* were, in those days, almost luxurious events for the two of them, and in order to buy Caroline a woollen overcoat which a very cold February rendered indispensable, Philippe had to decide to sell the only really precious object he'd ever owned to an antique dealer in Rue de Lille: it was a XVIIth-century mandola on the belly of which were etched the silhouettes of Harlequin and Columbine in domino costumes.

This hard life lasted nearly two years. According to her mood, Madame Echard was by turns sympathetic, going so far as to ask her daughter if she would like a cup of tea, and bad-tempered, laying injury upon annoyance, for example switching off the hot water precisely at the moment Philippe went to shave, or turning up the volume on her television to maximum from morning to night on the days the two young ones were studying at home for an oral examination, or having combination padlocks fitted to all the cupboards on the pretext that her stocks of sugar, dry biscuits, and toilet paper were being plundered systematically.

The conclusion of these hard years of apprenticeship was as sudden as it was unexpected. One day Madame Echard choked on a fish bone; Monsieur Echard, who'd been waiting for that day for ten years, retired to a tiny shack he had put up near Arles; a month later Monsieur Marquiseaux killed himself in a car accident and left his son a comfortable inheritance. Philippe hadn't got his scholarship, but he'd completed his first degree and was planning to do research for a doctorate – *Wetland Allotments and Arable Farming in Picardy Under Louis XV* – but gave it up gladly and with two friends founded an advertising agency which is now a flourishing business, specialising in selling not detergents but music hall stars: The Trapezes, James Charity, Arthur Rainbow, "Hortense", *The Beast*, Heptaedra Illimited – to mention only some – are amongst the best runners from his stable.

CHAPTER THIRTY-ONE

Beaumont, 3

Madame de Beaumont is in her bedroom, sitting in her Louis XV-style bed, propped up by four pillows in finely embroidered slips. She is an old woman of seventy-five with a lined face, snowy white hair, and grey eyes. She is wearing a white silk bedjacket and on her left ring finger has a ring whose stone is a topaz cut into a lozenge. A folio artbook, entitled *Ars vanitatis*, lies open on her lap at a full-page reproduction of one of the celebrated *Vanities* of the Strasbourg school: a skull set amongst attributes symbolising the five senses, not at all the canonical symbols in this instance, but easily recognisable: taste is represented not by a fattened goose or a fresh-killed hare, but by a ham hanging from a rafter, and a fine white porcelain tea-urn takes the place of the standard glass of wine; touch is figured by dice and by an alabaster pyramid topped with a diamond-shaped cut-glass stopper; hearing by a small finger-stopped (not valve-stopped) trumpet of the sort used for sounding flourishes; sight, which is also, in the symbolic system of these kinds of pictures, the perception of inexorable time, is figured by the skull itself and, in dramatic contrast, by a wall-clock in a fretwork case; and lastly, smell is suggested not by the traditional bunches of roses or pinks, but by a succulent, a sort of dwarf anthurium whose biannual inflorescences give off a strong smell of myrrh.

An inspector from Rethel was given the task of elucidating the events that had led to the double murder at Chaumont-Porcien. He took barely a week to complete his investigation, and succeeded only in deepening the mystery surrounding this murky business. It was established that the murderer had not broken into the Breidels' bungalow, but had probably entered by the back door, which was almost never locked, even at night, and that he had left in the same way, locking the door behind him. The murder weapon was a razor or, to be more precise, a scalpel with a replaceable blade, which the murderer had no doubt brought with him and in any case taken away, since there was no trace of it in the house; nor were there any fingerprints or other clues. The crime had taken place in the night of the Sunday; the exact time could not be ascertained. Nobody had heard a thing. No shout, no noise. It was very probable that François and Elizabeth were killed in their sleep so quickly that they didn't have time to resist: the murderer slit their throats with such dexterity that one of the first police hypotheses was that the criminal must have been either a professional killer, or a meat butcher, or a surgeon.

Obviously, all these points proved that the crime had been carefully premeditated. But nobody, at Chaumont-Porcien or anywhere else, could imagine why anyone would have wanted to murder somebody like François Breidel or his wife. They had settled in the village a little more than a year before; it wasn't known exactly where they came from; maybe from the South, but nobody knew for certain and it seemed that before settling down they had led a rather nomadic life. The interrogations of the Breidel parents, at Arlon, and of Véra de Beaumont, produced no new information: like Madame de Beaumont, the Breidel parents had lost touch with their child many years earlier. Appeals for information, with photographs of the two victims, were posted widely in France and abroad, but they too led to nothing.

For a few weeks the public paid enthusiastic attention to this mystery, which was taken up by dozens of amateur Maigrets and journalists scraping around for a story. The double crime was turned into a far-flung twist of the Bazooka affair, with some commentators claiming Breidel had been one of Kovacs's strong-arm men; the story was mixed up with the FLN by some, with the *Main Rouge* anarchists by others, and also with the right-wing Rexists, and even with an obscure story of pretenders to the throne of France, since amongst Elizabeth's alleged ancestors there was a certain Sosthène de Beaumont who was none other than a legitimatised bastard son of the Duc de Berry. Then, as the investigation began to peter out, the police and the gossip-columnists, the armchair Holmeses and the inquisitive onlookers began to tire of the business. Without a shred of plausible evidence, the coroner's verdict was that the crime had been "committed by a tramp or lunatic, such as are still too often to be found in suburban areas and on the outskirts of our villages".

Outraged by a judgement which told her nothing of what she felt she had a right to know about her daughter's fate, Madame de Beaumont asked her lawyer, Léon Salini, whose liking for criminal cases was well known to her, to reopen the investigation.

For many months Véra de Beaumont had almost no news at all from Salini. From time to time she received laconic postcards informing her that he had not given up hope and was pursuing his enquiries in Hamburg, Brussels, Marseilles, Venice, etc. Finally on 7 May 1960 Salini came back to see her: "Everyone," he said, "from the police on, has grasped that the Breidels were murdered for something they did or for something that happened in the past. But up to now no one has been able to uncover any clue at all which would direct their enquiries in one direction rather than another. The life of the Breidel couple seems to have been absolutely uneventful, in spite of the itching feet they seem to have had in the first year of their marriage. They met in June 1957 at Bagnols-sur-Cèze and married six weeks later; he was working at Marcoule, she had recently been hired as a waitress in the restaurant where he took his evening meal. His life as a bachelor also left no gaps for mysteries. At Arlon, the small town he had taken his leave from four years earlier, he was thought of as a good workman, a foreman in the making, potentially good enough to set up his own small business; to find work he had to translate himself to Germany, to the Saar actually, and went to Neuweiler, a small village near Saarbrücken; then he went to Château d'Oex in Switzerland, and from there to Marcoule, where he was working on a villa being built for one of the engineers at the reactor site. In none of these places did anything sufficiently serious happen to him that might motivate his murder five years later. Apparently the only incident he was involved in was a brawl with soldiers after a dance.

"Things are completely different for Elizabeth. From the moment she left you in 1946 until her arrival at Bagnols-sur-Cèze in 1957, her life is a blank, a complete unknown blank, except for the fact that she introduced herself to the restaurant manageress under the name of Elizabeth Ledinant. The official investigation established those facts anyway, and the police tried desperately to find out what Elizabeth might have been up to over those eleven years. They hunted through hundreds and hundreds of files. But they found nothing.

"So I reopened the investigation with nothing to go on. My working hypothesis, or more precisely my initial scenario, was this: many years before her marriage Elizabeth had committed some heinous fault and was forced to flee and hide. The fact that she finally got married shows that she thought she was at last completely free of the man or woman whose vengeance she had had reason to fear. But two years later, nonetheless, that vengeance strikes her down.

"Overall my reasoning was coherent; but the gaps had to be filled in. I conjectured that if the problem were to be soluble, then the heinous fault must have left at least one extant trace, and I decided to comb systematically all the daily newspapers from 1946 to 1957. It's a tiresome task, but in no sense an impossible one. I hired five students to work at the Bibliothèque Nationale listing all the articles and fillers dealing – explicitly or implicitly – with a woman between fifteen and thirty years of age. For every news story that fitted this criterion, I conducted further investigations. Thus I examined several hundred cases corresponding to stage one of my scenario; for example, a certain Emile D., driving a royal-blue Mercedes with a young blonde in the passenger seat, ran over and killed an Australian camper trying to hitch a lift between Parentis and Mimizan; or again, during a brawl in a Montpellier bar, a prostitute using the name of Véra slashed the face of a man called Lucien Campen, alias Monsieur Lulu, with broken bottle-glass; that story appealed to me, especially because of the name Véra, which would have illuminated your daughter's personality in a quite disturbing way. But unfortunately for me, Monsieur Lulu turned out to be in prison, and Véra alive and well and running a haberdashery at Palinsac. As for the first story, that one also came up short: Emile D. had been arrested, convicted, and given a heavy fine and a three months' suspended prison sentence; the identity of his travelling companion had been kept out of the papers in order to avoid a scandal, as she was the lawful wife of a cabinet minister in office at the time.

"None of the cases I had to examine withstood these complementary checks. I was on the verge of giving up the whole affair when one of the students I had hired pointed out that the event we were hunting for could well have happened abroad! The prospect of having to go through the lost pets of the whole planet did not exactly fill us with joy, but we buckled down to it nonetheless. If your daughter had fled to the States I think I would have lost hope sooner, but this time luck was with us: in the Exeter *Express and Echo* of Monday the fourteenth of June 1953 we read this heartbreaking story: Ewa Ericsson, the wife of a Swedish diplomat posted to London, was spending her holiday with her five-year-old son in a villa she had rented for a month at Sticklehaven, in Devon. Her husband, Sven Ericsson, had had to stay behind in London for the Coronation celebrations and was due to join her on Sunday the thirteenth of June, after attending the great reception given on the evening of the twelfth by the royal couple for more than two thousand guests. Ewa's health was not strong, and before leaving London she had taken on an au pair of French origin whose task was to look after the child, since a local charlady would take care of the cleaning and do the cooking. When Sven Ericsson arrived on the Sunday evening, he saw a horrible sight: his son, bloated like a kipper, was floating in the bath, and Ewa was lying on the bathroom tiles with her wrists slashed; they had died at least forty-eight hours earlier, that is to say on the Friday evening. The facts were accounted for in this way: told to bath the little boy whilst Ewa took a rest, the au pair girl, intentionally or unintentionally, allows him to drown. Realising the inexorable consequences of her act, she decides to run away immediately. A little later Ewa discovers her child's corpse and, mad with grief, not knowing how to live on without her son, takes her own life. The absence of the charlady, who was only due to come again on the Monday morning, prevented these events being discovered before Sven Ericsson's arrival and also gave the au pair girl forty-eight hours' head start.

"Sven Ericsson had only ever seen the girl for a few minutes. Ewa had put small ads in various places: the YWCA, the Danish Cultural Centre, the Lycée français de Londres, the Goethe-Institut, the Swiss Centre, the Dante Alighieri Foundation, American Express, etc., and had taken on the first girl to turn up, a young Frenchwoman of about twenty, a student with nursing qualifications, tall, blonde, with pale eyes. She was called Véronique Lambert; her passport had been stolen a month before, but she showed Madame Ericsson a copy of the declaration of loss made out at the French consulate. The charlady's statement contained little further detail; she clearly didn't like the way the French girl dressed and behaved, and had spoken as little as possible to her, but she was nonetheless able to state that she had a beauty spot beneath her right eyelid, that there was a picture of a Chinese junk on her perfume bottle, and that she had a slight stutter. This description was circulated throughout Britain and France to no avail.

"I didn't find it difficult," Salini continued, "to establish with certainty that Véronique Lambert was indeed Elizabeth de Beaumont and that her murderer was Sven Ericsson, because when I went to Sticklehaven a fortnight ago to try to find the charlady so as to show her a photograph of your daughter, the first thing I learnt was that Sven Ericsson – *who, ever since the tragedy, had carried on renting the villa year in, year out, without ever using it* – had returned there and taken his own life, on the seventeenth of September preceding, only three days after the double murder at Chaumont-Porcien. But if this suicide on the very site of the first tragedy proved the identity of Elizabeth's murderer beyond doubt, the main point still remained unclear: how had the Swedish diplomat succeeded in tracking down the girl who had caused the deaths of his son and his wife six years before? I was vaguely hoping that he'd left a letter explaining his act, but the police were adamant: there was no letter near the corpse, nor anywhere else.

"But my hunch had been correct: when I finally got to question Mrs Weeds, the charlady, I asked her if she had ever heard of an Elizabeth de Beaumont who had been murdered at Chaumont-Porcien. She rose and fetched a letter which she handed to me.

"'Mr Ericsson,' she said, 'told me that if anyone came one day to speak to me about the French girl and her dying in the Ardennes, I should give him this letter.'

"'And if I hadn't come?'

"'I was to wait, and after six years, to send it to the address marked on it.'

"Here is the letter," Salini continued. "It was intended for you. Your name and address are on the envelope."

Motionless, stiff, and silent, Véra de Beaumont took the pages from Salini's hand, unfolded them, and began to read:

Exeter, the sixteenth of September 1959.

Madam,

One day, sooner or later, whether you find it by looking for it or having it looked for, or whether it reaches you by mail in six years' time – that's how long it has taken me to slake my vengeance – you will have this letter in your hands and you will finally know why and how I killed your daughter.

A little over six years ago, your daughter, who used the name of Véronique Lambert, was engaged as an au pair by my wife, who was not very well and wanted someone to take care of our son Erik who had just turned five. On Friday 11 June 1953, for reasons I still do not understand, Véronique, either on purpose or by accident, allowed our son to drown. Incapable of assuming her own responsibility for this criminal act, she fled, probably within the following sixty minutes. A little later my wife discovered the corpse of our son, became insane, and slit her wrists with a pair of scissors. I was in London at that moment, and I did not see them until the Sunday evening. I swore then to devote my life, my fortune, and my mind to taking my revenge.

I had only seen your daughter for a few seconds when she arrived at Paddington to catch the train with my wife and our son, and when I learnt that the name she was using was fake, I despaired of ever tracking her down.

During the debilitating sleepless nights which began to afflict me then and have never since left me in peace, I recalled two anodine details that my wife had told me when mentioning the interview she had had with your daughter before giving her the job: my wife, learning that the girl was French, spoke of

Arles and Avignon, where we had stayed several times, and your daughter said she had been brought up in that area; and when my wife complimented her on her English, she said she had already spent two years in Britain and was studying archaeology.

Mrs Weeds, the charlady who worked in the house my wife had rented, and who will be the guardian of this last letter until it reaches your hands, was of even greater help to me: it was she who told me your daughter had a beauty spot beneath her right eyelid, that she used a perfume called "Sampang", and that she stuttered. It was with her, too, that I searched the villa from top to bottom looking for any clues that the false Véronique Lambert might have left. To my discomfiture, she had not stolen any jewels or things, but only the kitchen purse my wife had got ready for Mrs Weeds to do the shopping, containing three pounds eleven shillings and sevenpence. On the other hand she hadn't been able to take all her own things and she had left, in particular, the linen of hers that was in the wash that week: various cheap underclothes, two handkerchiefs, a rather loud print neckerchief, and, especially, a white blouse embroidered with the initials E. B. The blouse could have been borrowed or stolen but I hung on to those initials as a possible clue; I also found various objects of hers scattered around the house – in particular, in the lounge she had not dared go into before fleeing in case she woke my wife, who was sleeping in the room next to it, the first volume of Henri Troyat's serial novel *Les Semailles et les Moissons*, which had been published a few months earlier in France. The label inside revealed that this copy came from Rolandi's Bookshop, 20 Berners Street, a bookshop specialising in lending out foreign books.

I took the book back to Rolandi's. There I learnt that Véronique Lambert had a borrower's ticket: she was a student at the Institute of Archaeology, a branch of the British Museum, and lived in a Bed-and-Breakfast at 79 Keppel Street, just behind the Museum.

Breaking into her room was a waste of time: she had left when my wife took her on as an au pair. Neither the landlady nor the lodgers could tell me anything. I had more luck at the Institute of Archaeology: not only was there a photograph in her registration file, but I was able to meet some of her classmates, and amongst them there was a boy with whom she'd gone out a couple of times; he provided me with a key piece of information: a few months earlier, he had invited her to see *Dido and Aeneas* at Covent Garden. "I hate opera," she had told him, and added, "It's not surprising, my mother was a singer!"

I hired several private detective agencies to trace, in France or elsewhere, a young woman aged between twenty and thirty, tall, blonde, with pale eyes, a slight mark beneath her right eyelid, and a mild stammer; the information card also mentioned that she perhaps used "Sampang" perfume, was perhaps using the name of Véronique Lambert, that her real initials could be E. B., that she grew up in the south of France, had stayed in England, spoke good English, had been a student, and was interested in archaeology, and, lastly, that her mother was, or had been, a singer.

This last clue was the decisive one: reference to the biographies – in *Who's Who* and other specialist listings – of all women singers whose name began with B produced nothing, but when we checked all those who had a daughter between 1912 and 1935 your name came up together with about seventy-five others: Véra Orlova, born at Rostov in 1900, married the French archaeologist Fernand de Beaumont in 1926; one daughter, Elizabeth Natasha Victorine Marie, born 1929. Enquiries quickly revealed that Elizabeth had been brought up by her grandmother at Lédignan, Department of Gard, and had run away from you on 3 March 1945 at the age of sixteen. I then grasped that it was in order to evade your pursuit that she had concealed her true identity, but that also meant, alas, that the trail I had found stopped short, since neither you nor your mother-in-law, despite all the appeals you had put out on the radio and in the papers, had had any news of her for seven years.

We were already in 1954; it had taken nearly a year to find out whom I was going to kill: it took another three for me to find her.

For those three years, and this is something I want you to know, I supported teams of detectives who worked shifts to watch you twenty-four hours a day and to shadow both of you, whenever you went out in Paris, and whenever Countess de Beaumont went out in Lédignan, in the ever less probable case that your daughter might try to see you again or to take refuge with her grandmother. Their surveillance was completely useless, but I didn't want to leave any stone unturned. Everything that had even the slightest chance of putting me on a trail was tried out systematically: that was why I financed a huge market survey on "exotic" perfumes in general and "Sampang" perfume in particular; why I obtained the names of all persons having borrowed one or more volumes of *Les Semailles et les Moissons* from a public library; why all plastic surgeons in France received a personal letter enquiring whether they had had occasion since 1953 to conduct an operation to excise a naevus located under the right eyelid of a young woman aged about twenty-five; why I went round all the speech pathologists and elocution teachers looking for a tall blonde who'd been cured of a mild stammer; and why, lastly, I set up several entirely bogus archaeological expeditions devised uniquely to allow me to recruit through classified advertisements a "young woman with excellent English for N.

American field study carrying out archaeological excavations nr Pyrenees".

I put a lot of hope into this last trap. It bagged nothing. There were crowds of candidates each time, but Elizabeth didn't show up. By the end of 1956 I was still fumbling and had spent more than three-quarters of my fortune; I had sold all my securities, all my land, all my properties. All I had left was my collection of paintings and my wife's jewels. I began to dispose of them one by one so as to keep on paying the army of investigators I had marching on the steps of your daughter.

The death of your mother-in-law, the Countess de Beaumont, reawakened my hopes in early 1957, for I knew how attached your daughter was to her; but she no more came to the funeral at Lédignan than you did, and it was a complete waste of effort to have the cemetery watched for several weeks in case she was determined, as I imagined she might be, to put flowers on the grave.

These successive failures became increasingly exasperating, but I would not give up. I could not admit that Elizabeth might be dead, as if I had become the only person competent to dispose of her life and death, and I wanted to go on believing she was in France: I had found out in the end how she had managed to get out of England without leaving any record of embarkation: on 12 June 1953, the day after the crime, she took a boat from Torquay to the Channel Islands: by erasing the first letter of her name on the declaration of loss of her passport, she had managed to register under the name of Véronique Ambert, and her embarkation card, filed under A, had eluded the search made by the harbour police. This belated discovery didn't get me any further, but it gave me a basis for my belief that she was still hiding in France.

That year I began, I think, to lose my reason. I began to explain things to myself like this: I am looking for Elizabeth de Beaumont, that is to say a tall, blonde, pale-eyed young woman with good English, brought up in the Gard, etc. Now Elizabeth de Beaumont knows I am looking for her, thus she is hiding, and in this case hiding means removing as many as she can of the distinguishing features by which she knows I know her; therefore I should be looking not for a tall, blonde, etc. Elizabeth, but for an anti-Elizabeth, and I started getting suspicious about short, swarthy women jabbering Spanish.

On another occasion I awoke covered in sweat. I had just dreamt the obvious solution to my nightmare. Standing beside a huge blackboard covered in equations, a mathematician was concluding his demonstration, in front of a turbulent audience, that the celebrated "Monte Carlo theorem" was generalisable; that meant not just that a roulette player placing his stake on a random number had just as much chance of winning as a martingale player systematically doubling his stake on the same number on each loss in order to recoup eventually, but that I had as much if not more chance of finding Elizabeth by going to Rumpelmeyer's for tea next day at sixteen hours eighteen minutes precisely than by having four hundred and thirteen detectives looking for her.

I was weak enough to give way to the dream. At 16 hours 18 minutes I went into the teashop. A tall redhead left as I entered. I had her followed, uselessly of course. Later on I told my dream to one of the investigators who was working for me: he said quite seriously that I had only made a mistake of interpretation: the number of detectives should have made me suspicious: 413 was obviously the inverse of 314, that is to say of the number π: something would have happened at 18 hours 16 minutes.

So then I began to appeal to the exhausting resources of the irrational. If your mysterious and beautiful American neighbour had still been there, you can be sure I would have had recourse to her disturbing services; instead, I went in for turning tables, I wore rings encrusted with particular stones, I had magnets and hanged men's fingernails and tiny bottles of herbs, seeds, and coloured stones sewn into the hems of my clothes; I consulted wizards and water diviners, fortune tellers and crystal-ball gazers and soothsayers of all sorts; they threw dice, or burnt a photograph of your daughter in a white porcelain plate and examined the ash, they rubbed their left arms with fresh verbena leaves, put hyenas' gallstones under their tongues, spread flour on the floor, made unending anagrams of your daughter's names and pseudonyms, or replaced the letters of her name with figures in an attempt to reach 253, examined candle flames through vases filled with water, threw salt into fire and listened to the crackling, or jasmine seed or laurel branches to watch the smoke, poured the white of an egg laid by a black hen into a cup of water, or dropped in lead, or molten wax, and watched the shapes that were made; they had sheep's shoulder blades grilled on hot coals, hung sieves on wire and rotated them, examined carp roes, asses' brains, and circles of grain pecked by a rooster.

On the eleventh of July 1957 there was a *coup de théâtre*: one of the men stationed at Lédignan to continue the watch despite the death of Countess de Beaumont rang me to say that Elizabeth had written to the town hall to request a copy of her birth certificate. She had given a hotel address in Orange.

Logic – if in these circumstances one may still talk of logic – demanded I should grasp this opportunity to end this inextricable affair. All I needed to do was to take from its green leather sheath the weapon which, some three years earlier, I had decided would be the instrument of my revenge: a bone-handled field surgeon's scalpel, similar in appearance to a razor but infinitely sharper, which I had learned to handle with unrivalled dexterity, and to burst in at Orange. But instead I heard myself ordering my men simply to tail your daughter and not to relax their surveillance. They missed her at Orange in any case – the hotel didn't exist; she had gone to the post office saying she had made a mistake and the postman dealing with mail returned to sender had fished out the letter from Lédignan town hall and handed it to her – but they caught up with her, a few weeks later, at Valence. That is where she got married, with two of François Breidel's workmates acting as witnesses.

She left Valence that same evening with her husband. They had certainly guessed they were being followed, and for more than a year they tried to evade me; they did everything they could, laying all sorts of false trails, decoys, and simulations, dropping misleading clues, holing up in sordid lodging houses, and accepting squalid jobs in order to survive: night porterage, bottle washing, grape picking, cess-pit cleaning. But week by week, the four detectives whose services I could still afford to use tightened the net. More than twenty times I had the opportunity of killing your daughter with impunity. But each time, on one pretext or another, I let the opportunity slip: it was as if my long pursuit had led me to forget the oath in the name of which I had undertaken it: the easier it became to assuage my vengeance, the more I drew back from doing so.

On 8 August 1958, I received a letter from your daughter:

> *Sir,*
>
> *I have always known you would use every effort to find me. At the moment your son died, I knew it would be no use begging you or your wife for a gesture of mercy or pity. News of your wife's suicide reached me a few days later and convinced me you would spend the rest of your life hunting me down.*
>
> *What was to begin with only an intuition and an apprehension was confirmed over the following months; I was aware you knew almost nothing about me, but I was sure you would use every available means to exploit to the full the meagre details you possessed; on the day when in a street in Cholet a researcher offered me a sample of the perfume I'd used that year in England, I guessed instinctively that it was a trap; a few months later a small ad asking for a young woman with good English to accompany a team of archaeologists told me you knew more about me than I thought. From then on my life became a long nightmare. I felt I was being watched by everybody, everywhere, always, I began to suspect everybody, waiters*

who spoke to me, check-out girls who gave me change, customers at the butcher's who shouted at me for not waiting my turn; I was being followed, tracked down, observed by taxi drivers, policemen, pseudo-drunks slumped on park benches, chestnut sellers, lottery-ticket sellers, newsboys. One night, at the end of my tether, in the waiting room at Brive station, I began to hit a man who was staring at me. I was arrested, taken to the police station, and but for a quasi-miracle I would have been sectioned in a psychiatric ward: a young couple who had witnessed the scene offered to take charge of me: they lived in the Cévennes, in a deserted village whose ruined houses they were rebuilding. I lived there for nearly two years. We were alone, three humans, a score of goats and chickens. We had no newspapers and no radio.

With time my fears evaporated. I convinced myself you had given up, or died. In June 1957 I returned to live among men. Shortly after, I met François. When he asked me to marry him, I told him my whole story and he had little difficulty persuading me that my sense of guilt had made me imagine that incessant surveillance.

I regained my confidence bit by bit, sufficiently to risk asking the town hall for a copy of my birth certificate, since I needed it to get married. It was, I guess, one of the mistakes which you, in your lair, had been waiting for me to make.

Since then we have lived continually on the run. For a year I believed I could get away from you. I know now that I cannot. You will always have luck and money on your side; it is pointless believing I will ever succeed in getting through the holes in the net you have cast, just as it is illusory to hope that you will ever cease to pursue me. You have the power to kill me, and you believe you have the right to do so, but you won't make me run any further: together with my husband François, and Anne, to whom I have just given birth, I shall live from now on, without shifting, in Chaumont-Porcien, in the Ardennes. I await you with serenity.

For more than a year I made myself give no sign of life; I sacked all the detectives and investigators I had hired; I closeted myself in my flat, hardly went out, lived on ginger crackers and tea bags, using alcohol, tobacco, and maxiton tablets to maintain myself in a sort of pulsating fever which gave way at times to bouts of complete torpor. The certain knowledge that Elizabeth was waiting for me, went to bed each night thinking she might never awake, kissed her daughter each morning almost surprised to be still alive, the feeling that this reprieve was for her a new torture every day, was sometimes like being inebriated with revenge, a sensation of evil, omnipotent, ubiquitous exaltation, and sometimes it threw me into a boundless depression. For weeks on end, day and night, unable to sleep for more than a few minutes at a stretch, I paced the corridors and rooms of my flat chortling, or sobbing, seeing myself suddenly in front of her, rolling on the floor, begging her pardon.

Last Friday, 11 September, Elizabeth got her second letter to me:

> *Sir,*
>
> *I am writing from the Rethel maternity clinic, where I have just delivered my second daughter, Béatrice. Anne, my first, has just had her first birthday. Come, I beg you, it's now or never that you must come.*

I killed her two days later. In killing her I understood that death delivered her just as, the day after tomorrow, it will deliver me. The meagre remnants of my fortune, deposited with my lawyers, will be shared, in accordance with my last instructions, between your two granddaughters when they come of age.

Madame de Beaumont, even if she had been overcome on learning of her daughter's death, read without a shiver to the end of this story, by whose sadness she seemed no more touched than she had been some twenty-five years before by her husband's suicide. This apparent indifference to death is perhaps explained by her own history: one morning in April nineteen eighteen, when the Orlov family, scattered to the four corners of Holy Russia by the Revolution, had miraculously succeeded in uniting almost intact, a detachment of Red Guards took their villa by storm. Véra saw her grandfather, old Sergei Ilarionovich Orlov, whom Alexander III had appointed Minister Plenipotentiary to Persia, her father, Colonel Orlov, the officer commanding the famous battalion of Krasnodar Lancers and nicknamed the "Butcher of Kuban" by Trotsky, and her five brothers, the youngest only just eleven years old, shot dead before her eyes. She and her mother managed to escape, protected by a thick fog that lasted three days. After a nightmare of 79 days' forced march, they got at last to Crimea, then occupied by Denikin's commandos, and thence via Romania to Austria.

CHAPTER THIRTY-TWO

Marcia, 2

Madame Marcia is in her bedroom. She is a woman of sixty or so, tough, broad, and bony. Half-undressed, wearing a white lace-edged nylon slip, a girdle, and stockings, and with her hair in curlers, she is sitting in a modern-made moulded wooden armchair upholstered in black leather. In her right hand she is holding a large barrel-shaped glass jar full of pickled gherkins and is trying to get hold of one between the index and medius fingers of her left hand. At her side there is a low table overloaded with papers, books, and miscellaneous objects: a prospectus printed in the style of a family announcement, advertising the marriage of Delmont and Co. (interior design, decor, *objets d'art*) and the House of Artifoni (flower arrangers, designers of decorative gardens, greenhouses, balconies, flowerbeds, and potted plants); an invitation from the Franco-Polish Cultural Association to an Andrzej Wajda Festival; an invitation to a private viewing of an exhibition of Silberselber's paintings: the work reproduced on the card is a watercolour entitled *Japanese Garden, IV*, of which the lower third is taken up by a set of perfectly parallel dotted lines and the upper two-thirds by a realistic representation of a heavy, storm-laden sky; a novel, probably a detective story, called *Clocks and Clouds*, on the cover of which you can see, against a background of a backgammon board, a pair of handcuffs, a small alabaster figurine copying Watteau's *L'Indifférent*, a pistol, a saucer full of a no doubt sugary liquid since several bees are buzzing over it, and a six-sided tin token in which the number 90 has been cut by stamping; a postcard bearing the legend *Choza de Indios, Beni, Bolivia*, exhibiting a group of savage women in striped loincloths, squatted, blinking, suckling, frowning, sleeping, amid a swarm of infants, outside some primitive shanties of osier; a photograph, certainly depicting Madame Marcia herself, but at least forty years younger: the picture shows a frail young girl dressed in a spotted sleeveless jacket and a bonnet; she is driving a cardboard motor car – one of those painted panels with various cutouts for heads used by fairground photographers – and is accompanied by two young men in pin-striped white jackets and boaters.

The furnishing of the flat boldly combines the ultramodern – the armchair, the Japanese wallpaper, three floorlamps looking like large luminescent pebbles – with curios of different periods: two display cases full of Coptic cloth and papyri, above which two gloomy landscapes by a seventeenth-century artist from Alsace, with the outlines of towns and burning fires in the background, are placed on either side of and show off a plate covered in hieroglyphs; a rare set of so-called "highwayman's" glasses, widely used by nineteenth-century innkeepers in major ports with the aim of reducing brawls between sailors: on the outside they appear properly cylindrical, but they are tapered on the inside like sewing thimbles, the intended imperfection being skilfully masked by uneven bubbles blown into the glass; parallel rings engraved from top to bottom show how much can be drunk for such and such a price; and lastly a sumptuous bed, a Muscovite fantasy alleged to have been offered to Napoleon I for the night he spent at the Petrovsky Palace, but which he certainly declined in favour of his customary camp bed: it's an imposing piece, all its surfaces inlaid with tiny lozenge-shaped marquetry of sixteen different woods and shells, creating a mythical picture: a world of roseate forms and entwined garlands from the midst of which arises, Botticelli-like, a nymph clad only in her own hair.

CHAPTER THIRTY-THREE

Basement, 1

Cellars.

The Altamonts' cellar, clean, tidy, and neat: from floor to ceiling, shelving and pigeonholes labelled in large, legible letters. A place for every thing, and every thing in its place; nothing has been left out: stocks and provisions to withstand a siege, to survive a crisis, to see through a war.

The left-hand wall is allocated to food provisions. First, basic ingredients: wheat flour, semolina, corn flour, potato starch, tapioca, oat flakes, sugar lumps, granulated sugar, castor sugar, salt, olives, capers, condiments, large jars of mustard and gherkins, cans of cooking oil, packets of dried herbs, packets of peppercorns, cloves, freeze-dried mushrooms, and small tins of sliced truffle; wine vinegar and pickling vinegar; chopped almonds, peeled green walnuts, vacuum-packed hazelnuts and peanuts, biscuits, aperitifs, sweets, bars of cooking chocolate, bars of dessert chocolate, honey, jam, tinned milk, powdered milk, powdered eggs, yeast, pre-cooked puddings, tea, coffee, cocoa, herb tea, stock cubes, tomato concentrate, nutmeg, bird pepper, vanilla pods, spices and flavourings, breadcrumbs, crispbread, sultanas, candied fruits, angelica; then come tinned foods: tinned fish, tuna chunks, sardines in oil, rolled anchovies, mackerel in white-wine sauce, pilchards in tomato sauce, hake Spanish style, smoked sprats, lumpfish roe, smoked cods' roe; tinned vegetables: garden peas, asparagus tips, button mushrooms, baby runner beans, spinach, artichoke hearts, mange-tout peas, salsify, diced vegetable salad; as well as sachets of dried vegetables, split peas, lentils, broad beans, green beans, bags of rice, of pasta products, macaroni, vermicelli, pasta shells, spaghetti, crisps, mashed-potato flakes, and packets of soup powders; tinned fruit: apricot halves, pears in syrup, cherries, peaches, plums, packs of figs, boxes of dates, dried bananas, prunes; preserved meats and pre-cooked meals: corned beef, ham, *terrine* and *rillette* pâtés, chopped liver, liver pâté, boned meat in aspic, ox muzzle, sauerkraut, *cassoulet*, sausage and lentil stew, ravioli, lamb with potatoes and turnips, *ratatouille niçoise*, couscous, chicken with boletus and Bayonne ham, paella, and traditional veal *blanquette*.

The rear end wall and the larger part of the right-hand wall are reserved for bottles, stacked on their sides in plastic-coated wire racks in an apparently canonical order: first come the so-called table wines, then the Beaujolais, Côtes-du-Rhône, and that year's white wine from the Loire, then the wines to be drunk young, Cahors, Bourgueil, Chinon, Bergerac; then the real wine cellar, the grand *cave* controlled by a wine list in which every bottle is entered by geographical origin, name of grower, name of supplier, vintage, date of entry, optimal maturity date, and, where relevant, date of leaving: Alsace wines: Riesling, Traminer, Pinot noir, Tokay; red Bordeaux: Médoc vineyards: Château-de-l'Abbaye-Skinner, Château-Lynch-Bages, Château-Palmer, Château-Brane-Cantenac, Château-Gruau-Larose; Graves vineyards: Château-Lagarde-Martillac, Château-Larrivet-Haut-Brion; Saint-Emilion vineyards: Château-La-Tour-Beau-Site, Château-Canon, Château-La-Gaffelière, Château-Trottevieille; Pomerol vineyards: Château-Taillefer; white Bordeaux: Sauternes vineyards: Château-Sigalas-Rabaud, Château-Caillou, Château-Nairac; Graves vineyards: Château-Chevalier, Château-Malartic-Lagravière; red Burgundy wines: Côtes de Nuits vineyards: Chambolle-Musigny, Charmes-Chambertin, Bonnes-Mares, Romanée-Saint-Vivant, La Tâche, Richebourg; Côtes de Beaune vineyards: Pernand-Vergelesse, Aloxe-Corton, Santenay Gravières, Beaune Grèves "Vignes-de-l'enfant-Jésus", Volnay Caillerets; white Burgundy wines: Beaune Clos-des-Mouches, Corton Charlemagne; Côtes-du-Rhône wines: Côte-Rôtie, Crozes-Hermitage, Cornas, Tavel, Châteauneuf-du-Pape; Côtes-de-Provence wines: Bandol, Cassis; wines from the Mâcon and Dijon areas, ordinary wines from the Champagne vineyards – Vertus Bouzy, Crémant – and various Languedoc wines, wines from Béarn, from the region of Saumur, from Touraine, and wines from abroad: Fechy, Pully, Sidi-Brahim, Château-Maffe-Hughes, Dorset wine, Rhine and Mosel wines, Asti, Koudiat, Hochmornag, Egri Bikavér, etc.; and last of all come a few cases of champagnes, aperitifs, and various spirits – whisky, gin, kirsch, calvados, cognac, Grand-Marnier, Bénédictine, and, up on the shelving again, various cartons containing miscellaneous non-alcoholic beverages, effervescent and still, mineral waters, beer, fruit juices.

To the far right, finally, between the wall and the door – a thick wooden palisade with iron braces, and two large padlocks for closing it – comes the maintenance, cleansing, and miscellaneous supplies section: stacks of floorcloths, cartons of washing powder, detergents, descaling liquid, bleach products for unblocking wastepipes, supplies of ammonia bleach, sponges, products for polishing floors, cleaning windows, shining brass, untarnishing silver, for brightening glassware, floortiles, and linoleum, broomheads, Hoover bags, candles, spare matches, piles of electric batteries, coffee filters, soluble aspirin with added vitamin C, candle bulbs for chandeliers, razor blades, cheap Eau de Cologne in litre bottles, soap, shampoo, cottonwool, cottonbuds, emery nailfiles, ink cartridges, beeswax, paint pots, dressings for minor cuts, insecticides, firelighters, dustbin liners, flints for cigarette lighters, and kitchen paper towel rolls.

Cellars.

The Gratiolets' cellar. Here generations have heaped up rubbish unsorted and unordered by anyone. Three fathoms deep it lies, under the watchful eye of a fat ginger-striped cat crouching high up on the other side of the skylight, tracking through the wire netting the inaccessible but nonetheless just perceptible scuttling of a mouse.

The eye, becoming slowly accustomed to the dark, could end up making out beneath the layer of fine grey dust heteroclite remains coming from each of the Gratiolets: the base and posts of an Empire bed, hickorywood skis having lost their spring long ago, a pith helmet that was of purest white once upon a time, tennis racquets held in heavy trapezoidal presses, an old Underwood typewriter of the celebrated *Four Million* model, which was held to be, in its time, and owing to its automatic tabulator, one of the most sophisticated objects ever made, and on which François Gratiolet began to type his invoices when he decided he had to modernise his accounting systems; an old *Nouveau Petit Larousse Illustré* beginning with a half-page 71 – ASP *sbs* (Grk *aspis*). Colloquial for viper. *Fig. Asp-tongue* perpetrator of calumnies – and ending with page 1530: MAROLLES-LES-BRAULTS (Dept of Sarthe, Mamers County); pop. 2,000 (vill. 950); an old cast-iron coatstand still holding up a raw-wool cloak patched with pieces of different colours and even different materials: the overcoat worn by Pte Gratiolet, Olivier, taken prisoner at Arras on 20 May 1940, released as early as May 1942 thanks to the efforts of his uncle Marc (Marc, the son of Ferdinand, was not Olivier's uncle but his father Louis's second cousin, but Olivier called him "my uncle" just as he said "uncle" to his father's other cousin, François); an old cardboard globe, with quite a few holes; piles and piles of incomplete runs of papers: *L'Illustration*, *Point de Vue*, *Radar*, *Détective*, *Réalités*, *Images du Monde*, *Comédia*; on a cover of *Paris-Match*, Pierre Boulez, wearing a tuxedo, waves his baton at the première of *Wozzeck* at the Paris Opera; on a cover of *Historia* two adolescents can be seen, one in the uniform of a colonel in the Hussars – white kerseymere trousers, midnight-blue dolman with pearl-grey frogging, tasselled shako – and the other in a black cloak and lace cravat and cuffs, rushing into each other's arms, above the following legend: *Did Louis XVII secretly meet Napoleon II at Fiume on 8 August 1808? The most amazing mystery of French history finally solved!* A hatbox full of curling photographs, of yellowed or sepia-tinted snapshots you can never remember of what, or taken by whom: three men on a country lane; that dark man of graceful carriage, with curling black moustaches, wearing light-coloured check trousers, is surely Juste Gratiolet, Olivier's great-grandfather, the first proprietor of the block of flats, with friends of his, who might be the Bereaux, Jacques and Emile, whose sister Marie he married; and those other two, standing in front of the War Memorial in Beirut, both with empty right sleeves and rows of medals on their chests, are Bernard Lehameau, a cousin of Marthe, François's wife, and his old friend Colonel Augustus B. Clifford, for whom he worked as interpreter at Allied Forces General HQ at Péronne, where, like the colonel, he lost his right arm when the said GHQ was bombed by Richthofen, the "Red Baron", on 19 May 1917; and the other one, the obviously short-sighted man reading a book on a raked lectern, is Gérard, Olivier's grandfather.

Beside it there is a square tin containing piles of seashells and pebbles collected by Olivier Gratiolet at Gatseau, on the Isle of

Oléron, on 3 September 1934, the day his grandfather died, as well as a set of popular Epinal woodblock prints, wrapped in a rubber band, of the kind you used to get at school as a prize for a given number of merit marks: the one on top shows a meeting between the Czar of Russia and the President of France. This takes place on a ship. All about, as far as can be seen, are many other ships, the smoke from their funnels vanishing in the bright sky. Both Czar and President have rushed towards each other with long strides and are clasping one another by the hand. Behind the President stand two men. By comparison with the gay faces of the Czar and President, the faces of their attendants are very solemn, the eyes of each group focused on their master. Lower down – the scene evidently takes place on a top deck – stand long lines of saluting sailors cut off by the margin.

CHAPTER THIRTY-FOUR

On the Stairs, 4

Gilbert Berger hops down the stairs. He has almost got to the first-floor landing. In his right hand he is holding an orange plastic dustbin out of which poke two out-of-date directories, an empty bottle of *Arabelle* maple syrup, and various vegetable peelings. He is a lad of fifteen with a mop of blond, almost white, hair. He is wearing a check linen shirt and broad black braces embroidered with a design representing sprigs of lily-of-the-valley. He has on his left ring finger a tin ring of the sort generally found as free gifts with chemical-flavoured bubble gum in those blue wrappers labelled *To Give Is a Joy, To Receive a Pleasure* and which have come to replace standard gift packs, and which you can get for a franc from the vending machines outside stationers' and haberdashers' shops. The oval inset of the ring imitates the shape of a cameo with an embossed head attempting to represent a long-haired youth distantly reminiscent of an Italian Renaissance portrait.

Gilbert Berger is called Gilbert despite the ugly sound of the reduplicated "ber" syllable because his parents were both fans of

Gilbert Bécaud and met at a concert the singer gave in 1956 at *The Empire*, in the course of which 87 seats were smashed. The Bergers live on the fourth floor left, beside the Rorschachs, beneath the Réols, and over Bartlebooth, in a flat of two rooms and a kitchen where once lived the lady who went out on the landing in her smalls and had a little dog called Dodéca.

Gilbert is in the fourth form. In his class, the French teacher makes the pupils produce a wall-sheet newspaper. Each pupil or group of pupils is responsible for one page or column, and produces copy which the whole class, meeting each week as an editorial committee for two hours, discusses and sometimes even rejects. There are political and trade-union columns, sports pages, strip cartoons, school news, classified advertisements, local news, space fillers, advertising (usually from parents with businesses near the school), and several games and hobbies columns (tips for hanging wallpaper, making your own backgammon board, getting your picture-framing right, etc.). Together with two classmates, Claude Coutant and Philippe Hémon, Gilbert has taken on the job of writing a serial. The story is called *The Prick of Mystery*, and they have got to the fifth episode.

In the first episode, *For the Love of Constance*, a famous actor, François Gormas, asks the painter Lucero, who has just won a major Academy prize, to do a portrait of him in the scene which made him famous, where, playing d'Artagnan, he duels with Rochefort for the love of pretty young Constance Bonacieux. Though he thinks Gormas is a conceited, third-rate ham unworthy of his palette, Lucero accepts, hoping, it must be said, for a princely fee. On the appointed day, Gormas comes to Lucero's spacious studio, dons his costume, and poses with a foil in his hand; but the model booked some days earlier to do Rochefort hasn't come. Gormas sends for a certain Félicien Michard, the son of his concierge, working as a floor-scrubber for the count of Châteauneuf, to act as a last-minute stand-in. End of the first episode.

Second episode: *Rochefort's Lunge*. So the first sitting can now begin. The two opponents take up their positions, Gormas pretending to parry in a clever delayed move Michard's fearsome secret lunge which is supposed to pierce his jugular. That's when a bee flies into the studio and begins to buzz around Gormas, who suddenly puts his hand to the back of his neck and collapses. Fortunately a doctor lives in the building, and Michard runs to fetch him; the doctor arrives a few minutes later, diagnoses paralytic shock from a bee-sting touching the rachidian bulb, and takes the actor into hospital as an emergency. End of the second episode.

Third episode: *The Poison That Kills*. Gormas dies on his way to hospital. The doctor, surprised at the speed of the effect of the sting, refuses to sign the death certificate. The autopsy shows in fact that the bee had nothing to do with it: Gormas was poisoned by a microscopic quantity of topazine from the tip of Michard's foil. This substance, a derivative of the curare used by Amerindian hunters, who call it *Silent Death*, has a curious property: it is effective only on individuals having recently been infected with viral hepatitis. As it happens, Gormas had indeed recently recovered from an illness of this kind. Given this new element, which seems to indicate premeditated murder, a detective, Chief Inspector Winchester, is put in charge of the investigation. End of the third episode.

Fourth episode: *To Ségesvar in Confidence*. Chief Inspector Winchester informs his assistant Ségesvar of the points that the case raises in his mind:

> *firstly*, the murderer must be close to the actor since he knew that the latter had recently had viral hepatitis;
> *secondly*, he must have been able to obtain
> item one, the poison, and especially
> item two, the bee, since the case occurred in December, and there are no bees in December;
> *thirdly*, he must have had access to Michard's foil. Now this foil, like Gormas's, was lent to Lucero by his art dealer, Gromeck, whose wife was known to have been the actor's mistress. That makes six suspects in all, each with a motive:

1. the painter Lucero, galled at having to do the portrait of a man he despises; moreover, the scandal which the case could not fail to arouse could be very advantageous to him commercially;
2. Michard: in days gone by Madame Gormas, the mother, used

to invite young Félicien to spend holidays with her son; since then, the poor lad has been continually humiliated by the actor, who exploits him shamelessly;

3. the count of Châteauneuf, a bee-keeper, is known to harbour a mortal hatred for the Gormas family, since Gatien Gormas, president of the Beaugency Public Safety Committee, had Eudes de Châteauneuf sent to the guillotine in 1793.

4. the art dealer Gromeck, both out of jealousy and for publicity;

5. Lisa Gromeck, who never forgave Gormas his having rejected her for the Italian actress Angelina di Castelfranco;

6. and finally Gormas himself; a successful actor, but an incompetent and unlucky impresario, he is in fact completely insolvent and has been unable to get the agreement needed from his bank to finance his latest spectacular: a suicide disguised as a murder is the only way he can get out with dignity and at the same time (because of a substantial life-insurance policy) leave his children with an inheritance commensurate with their ambitions. End of the fourth episode.

This is where the serial has got to, and it's not too difficult to identify some of its immediate sources: an article on curare in *Science et Vie*, another on outbreaks of hepatitis in *France-Soir*, the adventures of Inspector Bougret and his faithful assistant Charolles in Gotlib's *Odds and Endpiece*, various news items on the regular financial scandals in the French film world, a quick reading of *Le Cid*, a detective story by Agatha Christie called *Death in the Clouds*, a Danny Kaye film called *Knock on Wood* in English and *A Touch of Madness* in France. The first four episodes were most warmly received by the whole class. But the fifth one poses awkward problems for the authors. In the sixth and last episode, it will be discovered that the culprit is in fact the doctor living in the building where Lucero has his studio. It is true that Gormas is on the verge of bankruptcy. A murder bid from which he could miraculously escape unharmed would guarantee enough publicity to relaunch his latest film, on which shooting had been stopped after eight days. So with the doctor, Dr Borbeille, as an accomplice – for he is none other than Gormas's foster brother – he had thought up this convoluted plot. But Jean-Paul Gormas, the actor's son, loves Isabelle, the doctor's daughter. Gormas is fiercely opposed to the marriage which the doctor, on the other hand, looks on favourably. That is why he takes advantage of the journey to the hospital, when he is alone with Gormas in the rear of the ambulance, to poison him with an injection of topazine, since he is certain that Michard's foil will be held guilty. But Chief Inspector Winchester will learn when interrogating the model whom Félicien Michard stood in for at short notice that he had in fact been paid to call off his booking, and from this revelation he will take the entire machine to pieces. Despite a few last-minute revelations which break one of the golden rules of detective fiction, this solution and its final peripeteia constitute a perfectly acceptable denouement. But before getting there, the three young authors have to rule out all the other suspects, and they are not too sure how to go about it. Philippe Hémon has suggested that as in *Murder on the Orient Express* they should all be guilty, but the other two have turned the idea down vehemently.

CHAPTER THIRTY-FIVE

The Concierge's Office

Until nineteen fifty-six the concierge of the building was Madame Claveau. She was a woman of middle height, with grey hair and a narrow mouth, and always wore a tobacco-coloured headscarf and (except on evenings when there was a reception and she was in charge of the cloakroom) a black pinafore with small blue flowers. She watched over the cleanliness of her building with as much care as if she had owned it. She had married a delivery man working for the Nicolas Wine Co. who travelled Paris from end to end on his tricycle, his cap slanted jauntily over one ear, a fag-end stuck out of the side of his mouth, and who was sometimes to be seen, at the close of his day, swapping his beige leather jerkin, all crisscrossed with cracks, for a quilted jacket left him by Danglars, and lending his wife a hand with polishing the brass on the lift cage or doing the big mirror in the entrance hall with whiting whilst whistling the latest hit all the while: *Paris Romance*, *Ramona*, or *First Meeting*. They had a son, named Michel, and it was for him that Madame Claveau asked Winckler for the stamps from the parcels that Smautf sent him twice a month. Michel killed himself in a motorbike accident at the age of nineteen, in 1955, and no doubt his premature death had something to do with his parents' departure the following year. They retired to the Jura. Morellet claimed for a long while that they had opened a café which ran down straight away because old man Claveau drank his stock in trade instead of selling it, but no news ever came to confirm or deny this rumour.

Their place was taken by Madame Nochère. She was then twenty-five. She had just lost her husband, a regular staff sergeant, fifteen years her elder. He died in Algiers, not in a bomb outrage, but from gastroenteritis induced by an excessive consumption of little bits of gum, not chewing gum, which could not have had such grave consequences, but India-rubber gum. Henri Nochère was in fact assistant to the deputy director of 95 Section, that is to say the "Statistics" office of the Projections and Planning Division of the Personnel Service attached to the General Headquarters of the Xth Military District. His work had been quite quiet up to 1954–1955, but from the first call-ups of conscript soldiers it worried him increasingly and Henri Nochère, in order to calm his nerves and to cope with his heavy workload, began to suck his pencils and chew his erasers as he started over for the *n*th time his endless adding up. Such nutritional practices, harmless when kept within reasonable bounds, can be dangerous if abused, for the minute fragments of involuntarily ingested rubber may cause ulceration and lesions of the intestinal membrane which are all the more serious for remaining imperceptible for a considerable period of time, for which reason it is not possible to make a correct diagnosis sufficiently early on. Sent to hospital for "digestive disorders", Nochère died before the doctors really had any idea what he was ill with. In fact, his case would probably have remained a medical mystery if, in the same quarter and probably for the same reasons, Warrant Officer Olivetti, at the Oran inducting centre, and Lance Sergeant Dasiweel, at the Constantine Transit Centre, had not died in almost identical circumstances. That is where the term "The Three Sergeants' Syndrome" comes from, an utter misnomer with respect to military hierarchy, but with enough appeal to the imagination to carry on being used for this type of affliction.

Today Madame Nochère is forty-four. She is a tiny, rather plump, voluble, and obliging woman. She doesn't correspond in the slightest to the usual image of a concierge: she neither yells nor mumbles, does not deliver hoarse-throated harangues against house pets, does not shoo off doorstep salesmen (which is, moreover, something that several co-owners and tenants might well reproach her for), she is neither servile nor money-grubbing, does not leave her television set switched on all day, and does not rage against people emptying dustbins in the morning or on Sundays or growing flowers in pots on their balconies. She is not mean or petty in any sense, and the only thing that could be held against her is that she is a little too much of a gossip, even a little overbearing, always wanting to know the story of this one and that, always ready to feel sorry for someone, to help, to find a way out. Everyone in the building has had occasion to appreciate her kindness and at one time or another has set off with a mind at rest knowing that the goldfish would be properly fed, the dogs walked, the flowers watered, the meters read.

Only one person in the building really hates Madame Nochère: and that is Madame Altamont, because of something that happened one summer. Madame Altamont was leaving for a holiday. With her characteristic concern for propriety and orderliness, she emptied her refrigerator and gave the left-overs to the concierge: two ounces of butter, a pound of fresh green beans, two lemons, half a pot of redcurrant jam, a dab of fresh cream, a few cherries, a spot of milk, a few bits of cheese, various herbs, and three Bulgarian-flavour yoghurts. For reasons that were never entirely clear, but were probably connected with her husband's long absences, Madame Altamont was unable to leave at the planned time, and had to stay on twenty-four hours longer at home; so she went back to see Madame Nochère and explained in an admittedly rather embarrassed tone of voice that she had nothing to eat in the flat and that she'd like to take back the fresh green beans she had given her earlier that day. "Well, it's just that I've topped them already," Madame Nochère said, "and they're cooking now." "I can't help that!" Madame Altamont replied.

Madame Nochère herself took up the cooked beans to Madame Altamont, as well as the other foodstuffs she had left. Next morning, Madame Altamont, leaving properly this time, again took her leftovers down to Madame Nochère. But the concierge refused them politely.

The story – told here for once without any exaggeration – rapidly spread around the building and the *quartier*. Since then Madame Altamont hasn't missed a single co-owners' meeting, and each time, on one pretext or another, she asks for Madame Nochère to be replaced by a new concierge. She is supported by the manager and Plassaert, the printed-cotton trader, who haven't forgiven Madame Nochère for taking Morellet's side, but the majority regularly refuses to put the item on the agenda.

Madame Nochère is in her office; she is getting off a stool after changing the fuses controlling one of the entrance-hall lamps. The office is a room about twelve square yards in area, painted light green, floored in red hexagonal tiles. It is divided into two by a louvred wooden partition. On the other side of the partition, the barely visible "living" side includes a bed with a lace bedspread, a sink with a small wall-mounted water-heater, a marble-topped washstand, a two-ring cooker on a tiny rustic sideboard, and several shelves full of boxes and suitcases. On this side of the screen, in the office proper, there is a table with three green plants on it – the puny and discoloured bougainvillea is the concierge's, the two others are much more flourishing rubber plants belonging to the owners of the first floor right, the Louvets, who are away and have left them to be looked after – and the afternoon mail, in the midst of which Madame Moreau's magazine, *Jours de France*, is particularly noticeable, its cover showing Gina Lollobrigida, Gérard Philipe, and René Clair arm in arm on the Croisette with the caption "Twenty years ago *Belles de Nuit* triumphed at Cannes". Madame Nochère's dog, a fat, sly little ratter answering to the name of Rolypoly, is lying under another small kidney-shaped table on which the concierge has set her place for lunch: one flat plate, one soup plate, a knife, spoon, and fork, and a stem glass, next to a dozen eggs in their corrugated cardboard eggbox and three mint and verbena tea sachets decorated with a picture of girls from Nice in straw hats. Against the partition there stands an upright piano, the piano on which Madame Nochère's daughter Martine, nowadays finishing medical school, hammered out for ten years *The Turkish March*, *Für Elise*, *Children's Corner*, and *Le Petit Ane* by Paul Dukas; it's now been shut up for good at last and supports a potted geranium, a sky-blue cloche hat, a TV set, and a Moses basket in which Geneviève Foulerot's baby soundly sleeps: Geneviève is the tenant of the fifth floor right and hands her baby over to the concierge every day at seven a.m., collecting it only at eight p.m. after she's got home, had a bath, and changed.

Against the rear wall, above the table with the green plants, is a wooden board with numbered pegs most of which support sets of keys, a printed notice with instructions for the use of the central-heating safety device, a colour photograph, no doubt cut out of a catalogue, of a ring with a huge solitaire, and a square-shaped piece of embroidery on canvas, with a quite startling design compared to the hunting scenes and fancy-dress balls on the Grand Canal you usually find; it depicts a parade in front of a great circus tent: to the right, two tumblers, one of whom is huge, a Falstaff two yards tall with a barrel-sized head and shoulders to match, a chest like a blacksmith's bellows, legs as thick as twelve-year-old staddles, arms like push-rods and hands like crocodile shears, and is holding aloft at arm's length the other, a slim, small lad of twenty whose weight in pounds would not number a quarter of what the other weighs in kilograms; in the middle, a group of dwarves performing various somersaults around their queen, a dog-faced dwarf dressed in a crinoline; and lastly, on the left, a lion tamer, a shabby little man with a black shade over one eye, wearing a black coat, but a beautiful sombrero with long gay tassels down the back.

CHAPTER THIRTY-SIX

On the Stairs, 5

On the landing of the second floor. The Altamonts' door, framed by two dwarf orange trees emerging from hexagonal marble plant pot-holders, is open. Through it exits an old family friend, who obviously arrived too early for the reception.

He is a German industrialist called Hermann Fugger, who made a fortune in the early postwar years selling camping equipment, and has since moved into one-piece floor coverings and wallpaper. He is wearing a double-breasted suit, whose sobriety is overcompensated for by a mauve scarf with pink polka dots. He carries under his arm a Dublin daily – *The Free Man* – on which the following headline can be read:

NEWBORN STAR WINS PIN BALL CONTEST

and also a small display box advertising a travel agency:

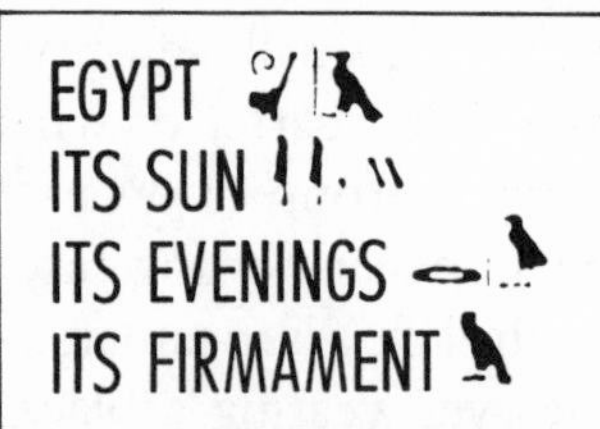

Hermann Fugger has in fact arrived very early on purpose: an amateur cook, he spends his time regretting that business does not permit him to be at his stove more often, dreaming of the ever less likely day when he will be able to devote himself entirely to the culinary arts, and he was planning to cook his own recipe this evening for leg of wild boar in beer, whose knuckle end, he claims, is the most delectable thing on earth, but the Altamonts angrily refuse.

CHAPTER THIRTY-SEVEN

Louvet, 1

The Louvets' flat on the first floor right. An executive's living room. Walls hung with yellow leather; a sunken grate in a hexagonal fireplace, and a made-up fire on the point of flaming; an integrated suite of audio-visual equipment: stereo, tapedeck, TV, slide projector; sofa and matching armchairs in buttoned natural leather. Purple, cinammon, and toast-coloured hues; a low table tiled with small brownish hexagonal tiles, supporting a dish-bowl containing a set of poker dice, several darning eggs, a miniature bottle of angostura bitters, and a champagne cork that is actually a lighter; a pack of matches advertising the San Francisco club it comes from, *Diamond's*; a naval officer's desk, with a modern imported Italian lamp, a slender skeleton of black metal which can be made to hold almost any position; an alcove hung with red curtains and a bed buried under tiny multicoloured cushions; on the rear wall, a large watercolour depicting musicians playing antique instruments.

The Louvets are away. They travel a lot, on business and for pleasure. Louvet looks – perhaps a bit too much – like the image people have of him, and which he shares: English fashions, Viennese moustache. Madame Louvet is a very stylish woman, coming on forty, who likes to wear culottes, yellow check waistcoats, leather belts, and chunky tortoiseshell bracelets.

There is a photograph showing them on a bear hunt in the Andes, in the Macondo area; they are posing with another couple who can only be described as exercises in the same style: all four wear khaki combat jackets full of pockets and pouches. In the foreground, Louvet half-squats with one knee on the ground and a gun in his hand; behind him his wife is seated on a deckchair; behind the deckchair the other couple are standing.

A fifth person, no doubt the guide whose job it was to go with them, stands a little to the side: a tall man with close-cropped hair, looking like an American GI; dressed in camouflage fatigues, he seems totally rapt in reading a cheap detective novel with an illustrated jacket, entitled *El Crimén piramidal*.

CHAPTER THIRTY-EIGHT

Lift Machinery, 1

The lift is out of order, as usual. It has never worked really well. On the night of the fourteenth to the fifteenth of July 1925, barely a few weeks after it was installed, it got stuck for seven hours. There were four people in it, which allowed the insurance to refuse to pay for the repair, since it was designed for three people or two hundred kilograms. The four victims were Madame Albin, then called Flora Champigny, Raymond Albin, her fiancé, then doing his military service, Monsieur Jérôme, who was then a young history teacher, and Serge Valène. They had gone to Montmartre to see the firework display and had walked back by way of Pigalle, Clichy, and Batignolles, stopping at most of the bars for a glass of dry white wine or a drop of well-chilled rosé. They were therefore rather more than merry when the event occurred, around four in the morning, between the fourth and fifth floors. After the first moment of panic, they called the concierge: it wasn't yet Madame Claveau, but an old Spanish woman who'd been there ever since the early days of the building; she was called Madame Araña and really looked like her name, as she was dry, dark, and hunched. She came, dressed in an orange dressing gown with green branch motifs and a sort of cotton sock serving as a nightcap, ordered them to be quiet, and warned them not to expect to be rescued for several hours.

Left alone in the grey light of dawn, the four young folk, for they were all young then, made a list of their assets. Flora Champigny had scraps of roast hazelnut in the bottom of her handbag, and they shared them, but regretted it immediately as it increased their thirst.

Valène had a lighter and Monsieur Jérôme had some cigarettes; they lit a few, but obviously they'd have preferred a drink. Raymond Albin suggested they pass the time with a game of *belote* and got a greasy pack of cards out of his pocket, but saw straightaway that the jack of clubs was missing. They decided to substitute for the lost jack a piece of card-sized paper on which they were going to draw a face both ways up, a club (♧), a capital J, and even the jack's name. "Baltard!" said Valène. "No! Ogier!" said Monsieur Jérôme. "No! Lancelot!" said Raymond Albin. They argued in whispers for a while, then agreed they really didn't have to name the jack. Then they tried to find a piece of paper. Monsieur Jérôme proposed one of his visiting cards, but it wasn't the right size. The best they found was the back of an envelope that Valène had got the previous evening from Bartlebooth to tell him that owing to Bastille Day he would not be able to come tomorrow for his daily watercolour lesson (he had already told him that orally a few hours earlier, at the end of his last session, but the letter no doubt demonstrated one of the characteristic traits of Bartlebooth's behaviour, or perhaps simply provided an opportunity to use the letterhead he had just had printed on a magnificent *hazy* vellum paper, almost bronze in colour, with his monogram in modern style inscribed in a lozenge). Obviously Valène had a pencil in his pocket, and when they had managed to use Flora Champigny's nail scissors to cut out a correct-sized piece of envelope more or less neatly, he dashed off a very presentable jack of clubs with a few strokes, which provoked his three companions into whistles of admiration for the good likeness (Raymond Albin), for the speed of execution (Monsieur Jérôme), and for the intrinsic beauty of the drawing (Flora Champigny).

But they then ran into another problem because, brilliant as it was, the substitute jack was too easy to distinguish from the other cards, which in itself was not reprehensible except in *belote* where the jack does in fact play an important role. The only solution, Monsieur Jérôme then said, was to use an otherwise ordinary card, say the seven of clubs, as the jack of clubs, and to draw a seven of clubs on another piece of envelope. "You should have said so in the first place," grumbled Valène. And in fact there wasn't enough envelope left. What's more, Flora Champigny, tired no doubt from waiting to be taught to play *belote*, had gone to sleep, and her fiancé had ended up following her example. Valène and Monsieur Jérôme thought for a while of playing two-handed, but neither was very keen, and they soon gave up the idea. Thirst and hunger more than weariness gnawed at them; they began to tell each other of the best meals they'd ever had, then to swap recipes, a domain in which Monsieur Jérôme turned out to be unbeatable. He hadn't quite finished listing the ingredients needed to make eel pâté, according to a recipe going back (he said) to the Middle Ages, before it was Valène's turn to drop off. Monsieur Jérôme, who must have drunk more than any of the others, and wanted to carry on having fun, tried for a few minutes to wake him. He couldn't, and to pass the time he began to hum some of the hits of the day, then, getting into his stride, began to improvise freely on a tune which in his mind must have been the closing theme of *L'Enfant et les Sortilèges*, of which he had seen the Paris premiere a few weeks before at the Théâtre des Champs-Elysées.

His merry vociferation soon roused from their beds, then from their respective flats, the occupants of the fourth and fifth floors: Madame Hébert, Madame Hourcade, grandfather Echard with his cheeks in lather, Gervaise (Monsieur Colomb's housekeeper) in a zenana-cloth bedjacket, lace bonnet, and bobbled slippers, and finally, with his moustache bristling, Emile Gratiolet himself, the landlord, who lived at the time on the fifth floor left in one of the two flats Rorschach would knock into one thirty-five years later.

Emile Gratiolet was not exactly an accommodating man. In other circumstances he would certainly have evicted the four trouble-makers on the spot. Was it the spirit of Bastille Day that moved him to clemency? Or Raymond Albin's trooper's uniform? Or the delicious flush on Flora Champigny's cheeks? Whatever the cause, the upshot was that he pulled the lever allowing the lift doors to be opened from the outside, helped the four merrymakers to clamber out of the narrow cage, and sent them to bed without even threatening to sue or fine them.

CHAPTER THIRTY-NINE

Marcia, 3

Léon Marcia, the curio dealer's husband, is in his bedroom. He is a thin, puny, sick old man, with an almost grey face and bony hands. He is sitting in a black leather armchair, dressed in pyjama trousers and a collarless shirt, an orange check scarf thrown over his skinny shoulders, faded felt slippers on his sockless feet, and a sort of flannel thing vaguely like a Phrygian bonnet on his skull.

This burnt-out, blank-eyed, slow-moving man is still considered even now by most valuers and art dealers to be the world authority in areas as diverse as Prussian and Austro-Hungarian coins and medals, Ts'ing ceramics, French Renaissance prints, antique musical instruments, and Iranian and Persian Gulf prayer mats. He made his reputation in the early 1930s when in a series of articles published in *The Journal of the Warburg and Courtauld Institute* he showed that the set of small engravings attributed to Léon Gaultier and sold at Sotheby's in 1899 under the name of *The Nine Muses* in fact depicted Shakespeare's nine greatest female roles – Cressida, Desdemona, Juliet, Lady Macbeth, Ophelia, Portia, Rosalind, Titania, and Viola – and was the work of Jeanne de Chénany, an attribution which caused a sensation because at that time no works were known by this artist, who had been identified solely by her monogram and by a biography written by Humbert and published in his *Brief History of the Origins and Progress of Engraving, Woodcuts, and Intaglio* (Berlin, 1752, in-8°), which claimed – though unfortunately without quoting any sources – that she had worked in Brussels and Aachen from 1647 to 1662.

Léon Marcia – and this is what is certainly the most surprising thing – is completely self-taught. He left school at nine. At twenty he hardly knew how to read, and the only thing he did read regularly was a sporting daily called *Lucky Strike*; at that time he was working for a motor mechanic on Avenue de la Grande Armée who built racing cars, which not only never won, but almost always crashed. Thus it was not long before the garage closed down for good, and, with a small gratuity in his pocket, Marcia spent a few months resting; he lived in a cheap hotel, the Hôtel de l'Aveyron, rose at seven, drank a hot strong coffee at the bar whilst leafing through *Lucky Strike*, and went back up to his room (the bed had meanwhile been made up) where he lay back for a nap, but not before spreading the paper over the end of the bed so as not to dirty the eiderdown with his shoes.

Marcia, a man of very modest needs, could have lived like that for many years, but he fell ill the following winter: the doctors diagnosed tubercular pleurisy and strongly recommended mountain air: since he clearly could not afford a long stay in a sanatorium as a patient, Marcia solved the problem by getting a job as a room waiter in the most luxurious of them all, the Pfisterhof at Ascona, in the Ticino. It was there that in order to fill the long hours of compulsory resting, which he forced himself to observe once his work was done, he began to read, and grew to enjoy reading everything he could lay his hands on, borrowing book upon book from the wealthy international clientele – the owners of and heirs to corned-beef kingdoms, rubber empires, or tempered-steel syndicates – staying at the sanatorium. The first book he read was a novel, *Silbermann*, by Jacques de Lacretelle, which had won the Prix Fémina the previous autumn; the second was a critical edition with facing-page translation of Coleridge's *Kubla Khan*:

In Xanadu did Kubla Khan
A stately pleasure-dome decree . . .

In four years Léon Marcia read a good thousand volumes and learned six languages: English, German, Italian, Spanish, Russian, and Portuguese, which he mastered in eleven days, not with the help of Camoëns's *Lusiades* through which Paganel thought he was learning Spanish, but with the fourth and last volume of Diego Barbosa-Machado's *Bibliotheca Lusitana*, which he'd found, without the rest of the set, on the penny shelf of a Lugano bookshop.

The more he learnt, the more he wanted to find out. His enthusiasm seemed to have no practical limit, and was as boundless as his ability to absorb knowledge. He only needed to read something once to remember it for good, and he consumed treatises on Greek grammar, histories of Poland, epic poems in twenty-five songs, and instruction manuals on fencing and horticulture with as much speed, as much appetite, and as much intelligence as popular novels and encyclopaedic dictionaries, although admittedly he did have a marked predilection for the latter.

In nineteen twenty-seven, a group of residents at the Pfisterhof, on the initiative of Herr Pfister himself, subscribed to a fund to provide Marcia with an income for ten years to allow him to devote himself entirely to whatever studies he wished to pursue. Marcia, who was then thirty, spent a whole term hesitating between courses given by Ehrenfels, Spengler, Hilbert, and Wittgenstein, then, since he'd been to listen to Panofsky lecturing on Greek statuary, discovered that his true vocation was art history and left forthwith for London to enrol at the Courtauld Institute. Three years later he made his spectacular entry into the art world in the way we have seen.

His health remained delicate and made him housebound nearly all his life. He lived in hotels for a long time, first in London, then in Washington and New York; he scarcely travelled except to check this or that detail in a library or an art gallery, and he gave his increasingly sought-after opinions from his bed or his armchair. It was he who demonstrated, amongst other things, that the *Hadriana* at Atri (better known by their nickname of *Hadrian's Angels*) were forged, and he who established the authoritative chronology of Samuel Cooper's miniatures at the Frick Collection: it was this latter work which provided the occasion where he met the woman he was to marry: Clara Lichtenfeld, the daughter of Polish-Jewish immigrants to the United States, who was on a course at the museum. Though she was fifteen years his junior, they married a few weeks later and decided to live in France. Their son David was born in 1946, shortly after they arrived in Paris and moved into 11 Rue Simon-Crubellier, where Madame Marcia set up her antique shop in premises formerly used by a saddler. Oddly, her husband always refused to take any interest in it.

Léon Marcia – like some other occupants of the building – has not left his room for many weeks; all he eats any more is milk, *petit-*

beurre, and raisin biscuits; he listens to the radio, reads or pretends to read old art reviews; there is one such on his lap, the *American Journal of Fine Arts*, and two others by his feet, a Yugoslav review, *Umetnost*, and *The Burlington Magazine*; on the cover of the *American Journal* there is a reproduction of a splendid, flamboyant, green, red, golden, and inky blue ancient American *estampe* – a locomotive with a gigantic smokestack, great baroque lamps, and a tremendous cow-catcher, hauling its mauve coaches through the stormy prairie night and mixing a lot of spark-studded black smoke with the furry thunder clouds. On the cover of *Umetnost*, hiding *Burlington Magazine* almost completely, there is a photograph of a work by the Hungarian sculptor Meglepett Egér: rectangular metal plates fixed to each other in such a way as to form an eleven-sided solid object.

Usually Léon Marcia is silent and still, plunged in recollections: one of which, surfacing from the depths of his prodigious memory, has been obsessing him for several days: it is a memory of a lecture which Jean Richepin, shortly before he died, went to give at the sanatorium; the subject was the Legend of Napoleon. Richepin recounted that in his youth the tomb of Napoleon had been opened once a year, and the embalmed face was displayed to disabled soldiers filing past in procession; the face was bloated and greenish, more a spectacle of terror than of admiration, which is why they later stopped opening the tomb. But nevertheless Richepin saw the face from the arms of his great-uncle, who had served in Africa and for whose sake the Commandant opened the tomb.

CHAPTER FORTY

Beaumont, 4

A bathroom floored with large, square, cream-coloured tiles. On the walls, flower-printed washable wallpaper. No item of decoration complements the purely sanitary furniture and fittings, apart from a small round table with a moulded cast-iron centre pillar on whose veined marble top, lipped with a vaguely Empire-style rim, stands an ultraviolet lamp of brutally modernistic ugliness.

On a turned-wood clothes-stand hangs a green satin dressing gown with a cat silhouette and the symbol designating *spades* at cards embroidered on its back. Béatrice Breidel alleges that this indoor gown which her grandmother still occasionally uses was the match robe of an American boxer called Cat Spade, whom her grandmother must have met on one of her US tours and who had been her lover. Anne Breidel does not agree at all with this version. It is the case that in the nineteen thirties there was a black boxer called Cat Spade. His career was very short. In nineteen twenty-nine he won the Combined Forces Tournament, left the army to go professional, and was beaten successively by Gene Tunney, Jack Delaney, and Jack Dempsey, even though this last was on the way out. So he went back into the army. It's not likely he moved in the same circles as Véra Orlova, and even if they had met, a white Russian with rigid prejudices would never have given herself to a black, even if he was a gorgeous heavyweight. Anne Breidel's explanation is different but also based on the many anecdotes of her forebear's love life: the dressing gown, she claims, was indeed a present from one of her lovers, a history professor at Carson College, New York, called Arnold Flexner, the author of a significant thesis on *The Voyages of Tavernier and Chardin and the Image of Persia in Europe from Scudéry to Montesquieu*, and, under various pseudonyms – Marty Rowlands, Kex Camelot, Trim Jinemewicz, James W. London, Harvey Elliott – of detective stories laced with quite explicitly sexy, not to say pornographic, interludes: *Murders at Pigalle*, *Hot Nights in Ankara*, etc. They met, so the story went, at Cincinnati (Ohio), where Véra Orlova had been engaged to sing Blondine in *Die Entführung aus dem Serail*. Quite apart from their sexual suggestiveness, which Anne Breidel mentions only in passing, the cat and the spade allude directly, in her view, to Flexner's most famous novel, *The Seventh Crack Shot of Saratoga*, the story of a pickpocket working the racecourse, nicknamed "The Cat" because of his quick, light touch, who gets mixed up against his will in a police investigation which he solves with flair and cunning.

Madame de Beaumont is unaware of these two explanations; for her part, she has never made the slightest comment on the origin of her dressing gown.

On the rim of the bath, designed to be wide enough to serve as a shelf, there are some bottles, a sky-blue dimpled rubber bathcap, a purse-shaped toilet bag made of a spongy pink substance with a plaited string closing, and a shiny parallelepipedic metal box, with a long slit opening on the top side, out of which emerges, in part, a Kleenex.

Anne Breidel lies prone on the floor by the bath, on a green bath towel. She is wearing a white buckram nightdress pulled halfway up her back; on her stretchmarked buttocks there lies an electrical thermal massage vibrator, about fifteen inches in diameter, covered in a red plastic material.

Whilst Béatrice, her sister, younger by one year, is tall and slim, Anne is chubby and puffed with fat. As she is constantly preoccupied by her weight, she imposes Draconian diets on herself but never has the strength to keep them up to the end, inflicts on herself treatments of every variety, from mud baths to sweating suits, from saunas followed by twig-beating to anorexic pills, from acupuncture to homeopathy, and from medicine balls, home trainers, forced marches, foot treading, chest expanders, parallel bars, and other exhausting exercises to every kind of massage possible: hair-glove massage, dried-squash massage, boxwood rolling-pin massage, massage with special soap, pumice stone, alum powder, gentian, ginseng, cucumber milk, and coarse salt. The one she is going through now has a particular advantage over all the others: it allows her to get on with other things at the same time; specifically, she uses these daily seventy-minute sessions during which the vibrator cushion will bring its alleged benefit successively to her shoulders, her back, her hips, her buttocks, her thighs, and her stomach to tot up her dietary performance: she has in front of her a little brochure entitled *Complete Table of Energy Values of Customary Foods*, in which the foods whose names are printed in special characters are obviously those to avoid, and she compares the figures it gives – chicory 20, quince 70, haddock 80, *sirloin* 220, *raisins* 290, *coconut* 620 – with those of the foods she took the previous day and of which she has noted the precise quantities in a diary obviously kept for this purpose alone:

Tea, no sugar, no milk	0
One pineapple juice	66
One yoghurt	60
3 rye biscuits	60
Grated carrots	45
Lamb cutlets (two)	192
Courgettes	35
Goat cheese, fresh	190
Quinces	70
Fish soup (without bread or garlic mayonnaise)	180
Fresh sardines	240
Cress and lime salad	66
Saint-nectaire	400
Blueberry sorbet	110
TOTAL	1,714

Despite the Saint-Nectaire, this analysis would be absolutely reasonable if it did not sin grievously by omission; to be sure, Anne has scrupulously entered all she ate at breakfast, lunch, and dinner, but she has taken no account at all of the forty or fifty furtive raids she made between meals on the fridge and the larder to try to calm her insatiable appetite. Her grandmother, her sister, and Madame Lafuente, the cleaning lady who's looked after them for more than twenty years, have tried everything to stop her, even going so far as to empty the fridge every evening and shut all edibles in a padlocked cupboard; but it was pointless: deprived of snacks, Anne Breidel flew into indescribable tantrums and went out to a café or to friends to appease her irrepressible bulimia. As it happens, the worst thing is not that Anne eats between meals, which many dieticians even believe to be quite beneficial, but that whilst she is irreproachably strict about her diet at table, forcing it moreover on her grandmother and sister as well, once she has left the dining room she turns amazingly slack: though she will not tolerate on the dinner table bread or butter or even supposedly neutral foods like olives, shrimps, mustard, or salsify, she wakes up at night to go and wolf down quite shamelessly ***oat flakes*** (350), ***slices of bread and butter*** (900), ***bars of***

chocolate (600), ***stuffed brioches*** (360), ***Auvergne blue cheese*** (320), ***walnuts*** (600), ***rillette pâté*** (600), ***Gruyère cheese*** (380), or ***tuna in oil*** (300). In fact she is practically continuously nibbling something or other, and whilst she is now doing her self-consoling sum with her right hand, with her left hand she is gnawing a chicken leg.

Anne Breidel is only eighteen. She is as clever at school as her younger sister. But where Béatrice shines at languages – she won first place in the nationwide *Concours général* for Greek – and aims to do ancient history and maybe even archaeology, Anne is a scientist: she graduated at sixteen, and has just come seventh at her first attempt at the entrance examination for the Ecole Centrale.

In 1967, at the age of nine, Anne discovered her vocation to be an engineer. That year, a Panamanian tanker, the *Silver Glen of Alva*, capsized off Tierra del Fuego with one hundred and four crew on board. Her distress signals were poorly received due to storms raging over the South Atlantic and the Weddell Sea, and her position could not be pinpointed. For two weeks, Argentinian coastguards and Chilean civil-defence teams, with help from ships sailing in the waters, searched tirelessly around all the myriad islets off Cape Horn and Nassau Bay.

Every evening, with increasing excitement, Anne read the news of the search; bad weather hampered it considerably, and, with every week that passed, the chances of finding survivors diminished. When all hope had been abandoned, the national dailies paid their respects to the unselfish men of the rescue teams, who had done the impossible in dreadful conditions to help any survivors there might have been; but several journalists claimed with some justification that the real cause of the disaster was not the bad weather but the absence in Tierra del Fuego, and more generally on all the seven seas, of receiving aerials of sufficient power to pick up Maydays in all atmospheric conditions from vessels in distress.

It was after she had read these articles, and cut them out, and stuck them into a special scrapbook, which she later used as the basis for a talk she gave in class (she was then in the first form), that Anne Breidel decided she would build the biggest radio beacon in the world, an aerial eight hundred yards high which would be called

Breidel's Tower and which would be capable of picking up any message broadcast within a radius of five thousand miles.

Up until she was about fourteen years of age, Anne spent most of her spare time drawing plans of her tower, calculating its weight and wind resistance, checking its coverage, working out its optimal siting – Tristan da Cunha, the Crozet Islands, the Bounty Islands, São Paolo Island, Isla Margarita, and, finally, Prince Edward Islands, south of Madagascar – and inventing detailed accounts of all the miraculous rescues it would make possible. Her taste for the physical and mathematical sciences grew out of this mythical image of a fusiform mast piercing the freezing fog of the Indian Ocean.

Her two last years of school, studying hard for competitive college entrance examinations, and the growth of satellite telecommunications finally got the better of her project. All that is left of it now is a newspaper photograph of her at the age of twelve, posing in front of a model she had spent six months making, an airy metal construction made out of 2,715 steel pickup needles held together by microscopic dots of glue, two yards high, as delicate as lace, as graceful as a ballerina, and bearing at its apex 366 minute parabolic receiving dishes.

CHAPTER FORTY-ONE

Marquiseaux, 3

By knocking the Echard parents' old bedroom and the little dining room into one, and incorporating into the new room the corresponding and now redundant portion of the hall as well as a broom cupboard, Philippe and Caroline Marquiseaux have created a quite spacious area which they have turned into a meeting room for their agency: it is not at all like an office, but a room inspired by the latest techniques of brainstorming and group dynamics, what Americans call an "Informal Creative Room", abbreviated to ICR, familiarly, *I see her*; for their part, the Marquiseaux call it their bawlroom, their cogitorium, or, even better, considering the kind of music they are responsible for promoting, their popshop: it is where they decide on the grand strategy of each campaign, the details of which will be settled later in the offices their agency occupies on the seventeenth floor of one of the skyscrapers at La Défense.

The walls and ceiling are papered in white vinyl; the floor is covered in a foam-rubber carpet identical to those used by the practitioners of some of the martial arts; nothing on the walls; almost no furniture: a low sideboard painted in white gloss with bottles of V-8, 7-Up, and root beer on it; an octagonal, "zen"-style jardiniere full of coloured sand in thin stripes, whence emerge a few solitary pebbles; and a host of cushions, of every colour and shape.

Four objects fill most of the space: the first is a bronze gong about as big as the one used on the credits of films produced by Rank, that is to say more than man-size; it comes not from the Far East but from Algiers: it is alleged to have been used to rally the prisoners in the sadly celebrated Barbary jail where Cervantes, Régnard, and St Vincent-de-Paul were incarcerated; in any case, an inscription in Arabic

بِسْمِ ٱللهِ ٱلرَّحْمٰنِ ٱلرَّحِيمِ

the very same one, the *al-Fâtiha*, which begins every one of the one hundred and fourteen surahs of the Koran: "In the name of kind and merciful God", is engraved in the middle of it.

The second is a shiny chrome-plated "Elvis Presley"-type juke-box; the third is an electric pinball machine of a particular model known as *Flashing Bulbs*: its back and board have no studs or springs or counters: only mirrors pierced by innumerable little holes behind each one of which is a bulb connected to an electronic flash device; the movement of the steel ball, which can be neither seen nor heard, sets off flashing lights of such intensity that in a darkened room an observer three yards away from the machine can easily read print as small as that in a dictionary; for anyone standing right in front of it or just beside the pinball table, and even if protective spectacles are worn, the effect is "psychedelic" to such a degree that one hippie poet spoke with reference to it of *astral copulation*. Production of this machine was stopped after it had been acknowledged as the cause of six cases of blindness; it has become very difficult to get hold of one, because some fans grow accustomed to these miniature flashes as to a drug, and surround themselves with three or four machines which they play simultaneously.

The fourth object is an electric organ, incorrectly referred to as a synthesiser, flanked by two spherical loudspeakers.

The Marquiseaux, absorbed in their aquatic caresses, have not yet come into this room, where they are awaited by two friends who are both also clients.

One of them, a young man in a denim suit, barefoot, slumped on the cushions, lighting a cigarette with a Zippo lighter, is a Swedish musician called Svend Grundtvig. A disciple of Falkenhausen and Hazefeld, a believer in post-Webernian music, the composer of constructions as scholarly as they are secretive, the most famous of which, *Crossed Words*, presents a score curiously similar to a crossword, with the across and down lines corresponding to sequences of chords and the blacked-out boxes serving as rests, Svend Grundtvig is nonetheless keen to tackle more popular kinds of music and has just written an oratorio, *Proud Angels*, with a libretto based on the story of the fall of the angels. This evening's meeting will look at ways of promoting it prior to its first performance at the Tabarka Festival.

The other is the famous "Hortense", a much more curious individual. She is a woman of about thirty, with a hard face and anxious eyes; she is squatting by the electric organ and is playing it to herself, with the headphones on. She too is barefoot – it must be a house rule to take your shoes off before entering this room – and is wearing long, khaki silk bloomers tied beneath the knee and at the waist by white laces decorated with paste-diamond tabs, and a short jacket, more a sort of bolero, made of a multitude of small pieces of fur.

Up until 1973, "Hortense" – it has become customary to write her name in quotation marks – was a man called Sam Horton. He played the guitar and wrote for *The Wasps*, a small New York group. His first song, *Come in, Little Nemo*, stayed in the Top 50 in *Variety* for three weeks, but the ones that followed – *Susquehanna Mammy*, *Slumbering Wabash*, *Mississippi Sunset*, *Dismal Swamp*, *I'm Homesick for Being*

Homesick – did not live up to expectations, despite their very nineteen-fortyish charm. So the group vegetated and watched anxiously as bookings got thinner and recording-company managers passed on messages that they were in a meeting, until, in early 1973, Sam Horton read by chance, in a magazine he was thumbing through in his dentist's waiting room, an article on that Indian Army officer who became a respectable lady. What caught Sam Horton's interest was not so much that a man had been able to change sex, but that the story recounting this unusual experience had been a bestseller. Yielding to the misleading temptation of analogical reasoning, Sam Horton convinced himself that a pop group composed of transsexuals would necessarily top the charts. Obviously he didn't manage to convince his four partners, but the idea went on bothering him. It certainly corresponded to a need of his beyond mere publicity, for he set off alone for Morocco, where he underwent the necessary surgery and endocrine treatment in a specialist clinic.

When "Hortense" returned to the States, *The Wasps* had in the meanwhile taken on a new guitarist and seemed to be making a go of it, and they refused to take him back; fourteen publishers sent him back his manuscript, "merely a copy", they said, "of a recent hit". It was the start of several months of roughing it, when s/he had to work mornings as a cleaner in travel agencies to survive.

From the depths of misery – to use the terms of the potted biography printed on the back of the sleeves of the discs she cut – "Hortense" began to write songs again, and since no one else wanted to sing them, she began to perform them herself: her rough and wobbly voice indisputably brought that *new sound* which the trade is always after, and the songs themselves fitted the anxious expectation of an increasingly agitated audience, for whom "Hortense" quickly became the incomparable symbol of the fragility of all things: *Lime Blossom Lady*, a nostalgic ballad of a herbalist's shop demolished to make way for a pizzeria, won her in a few days the first of her 59 Golden Discs.

By getting the exclusive European and North African rights for this timid and unstable creature, Philippe Marquiseaux has certainly pulled off the best deal in his as yet brief career; not because of "Hortense" herself, who, with her unending escapades, her breaches of contract, suicide attempts, depressions, court cases, sex parties and orgies, her convalescences and miscellaneous manias, costs him at least as much as he earns out of her, but because all those who aspire to making their name in music hall are now determined to belong to the same agency as "Hortense".

CHAPTER FORTY-TWO

On the Stairs, 6

Two men meet on the fourth-floor landing, both over fifty, both with square-framed glasses, both dressed in the same black suit, trousers, jacket, waistcoat, a little oversized, shod in black shoes, black tie on white shirt with an untapered collar, black bowler hat. But the one seen from behind has a printed cashmere-type scarf, whilst the other has a pink scarf with violet stripes.

They are two doorstep salesmen. The first is selling a *New Key to Your Dreams*, allegedly based on the Teachings of a Yaqui sorcerer collected at the end of the seventeenth century by an English traveller named Henry Barrett, but actually composed a few weeks earlier by a botany student at Madrid University. Apart from the anachronisms without which this key to dreams would obviously unlock nothing at all, and the ornamentations with which the Spaniard's imagination had sought to embellish this tiresome enumeration by emphasising its chronological and geographical exoticism, several of the suggested associations turn out to be surprisingly rich:

BEAR = CLOCK
WIG = ARMCHAIR
HERRING = CLIFF
HAMMER = DESERT
SNOW = HAT
MOON = SHOE
FOG = ASH
COPPER = TELEPHONE
HAM = SINGLE PERSON

The second door-to-door man is selling a newspaper called *The Watchtower!*, the organ of Jehovah's Witnesses. In each issue there are some longer articles – "What is Human Happiness?", "The 67 Truths of the Bible", "Was Beethoven Really Deaf?", "The Magic and the Mystery of Cats", "Learn to Love the Prickly Pear" – and some pieces of general news: "Do Before you Die!", "Did Life Begin by Chance?", "Fewer Marriages in Switzerland" and a few old saws of the likes of *Statura justa et aequa sint pondere*. Secretly slipped in between the pages are advertisements for articles of hygiene, offering mailing under plain wrappers.

CHAPTER FORTY-THREE

Foulerot, 2

A room on the fifth floor right. It was Paul Hébert's room, until his arrest, a student's room with a woollen carpet spotted with cigarette burns, greenish wallpaper, and a cosy-corner covered with striped cloth.

The perpetrators of the outrage on Boulevard Saint-Germain on the seventh of October 1943, which cost three German officers their lives, were arrested the same day towards evening. They were two former serving Army officers who belonged to a "Davout Action Group", and it soon became apparent that they were its only members; their gesture was intended to restore their lost Dignity to the French: they were arrested as they were preparing to hand out a leaflet beginning: "That splendid sturdy fellow the Boche soldier is strong and healthy and thinks only of the greatness of his country, *Deutschland über alles!* Whereas we are hopelessly sunk in dilettantism!"

All those picked up in the raids made within sixty minutes of the explosion were released the following afternoon after identity checks, except for five students whose situations were not regular and about whom the authorities required further information. Paul Hébert was one of them: his papers were in order, but the inspector who interrogated him was surprised that he had been picked up at the Odéon crossroads at three p.m. on a Thursday when he should have been at the Civil Engineering College, 152 Avenue de Wagram, studying for the entrance examination to the Ecole Supérieure de Chimie. The thing in itself was not important, but the explanations Paul Hébert gave were not at all convincing.

The grandson of a druggist with a shop at 48 Rue de Madrid, Paul Hébert took abundant advantage of his doting and generous grandfather by relieving him of phials of paregoric elixir which he traded for forty to fifty francs each to the young addicts of the Latin Quarter; he had made his monthly delivery that day and was on his way to the Champs-Elysées to spend the five hundred francs he'd just made when he was arrested. But instead of flatly saying that he'd skipped class to go to the cinema to see *Pontcarral, Colonel d'Empire* or *It Happened at the Inn*, he launched into ever more contorted justifications, starting with the story that he had had to go to Gibert's bookshop to buy a copy of Polishovsky & Spaniardel's *Course in Organic Chemistry*, a weighty tome of 856 pages published two years previously by Masson. "So where is it, then, this book?" the inspector asked. "Gibert's didn't have it," Hébert claimed. The inspector, who, at this stage of the enquiry, no doubt only wanted a bit of fun, sent a man to Gibert's who obviously came back a few minutes later with the aforementioned *Course*. "Sure, but it was too expensive for me," Hébert mumbled, tying his own noose.

In so far as the perpetrators of the outrage had just been arrested, the inspector was no longer trying to find "Terrorists" at any price. But out of ordinary conscientiousness, he had Hébert searched, found the five hundred francs, and, thinking he had hit upon a band of black marketeers, ordered a full search of his flat.

In the boxroom adjacent to Hébert's room, in the midst of piles of old shoes, stocks of mint and verbena tea, dented copper electrical footwarmers, ice skates, loose-strung racquets, odd issues of magazines, illustrated novels, old clothes, and bits of string, they found a grey macintosh, and in the pocket of this macintosh they found a cardboard box, not very deep, about fifteen centimetres by ten, on which was written:

The only reliable
inkeraser

KANSELL

Sold by Hely's Ltd

85 Dame Street, Brussels

Inside the box was a green silk handkerchief, probably cut from a parachute, a diary full of sibylline notes such as "Stand up", "Lozenge engraving", "X-27", "Gault-de-Perche" etc., which when deciphered after much trouble provided no conclusive evidence; a fragment of a map of Jutland, scale of 1:160,000, based on J. H. Mansa's cartography; an unused envelope containing a sheet of paper folded in four: at the top left of the sheet there was a printed letterhead

Anton

Tailor & Shirt-Maker

16 bis, avenue de Messine
Paris 8e

EURope 21-45

above a silhouette of a lion which in heraldic terms would be described as *passant* or *passant gardant*. On the remainder of the sheet was a carefully drawn plan in violet ink of Le Havre town centre, from the Grand-Quai to Place Gambetta: an X in red marked the position of *Les Armes de la Ville*, a hotel just about on the corner of Rue d'Estimauville and Rue Frédéric-Sauvage.

Now it was in this hotel, which the Germans had requisitioned, that just over three months previously, on 23 June, Ordnance General Pferdleichter had been assassinated: he was one of the senior members of the Todt Organisation, and had supervised the fortification of the Jutland coastline, where he had had moreover two miraculous escapes from assassination attempts; and he had just been entrusted by Hitler with the supervision of Operation *Parsifal*, an operation similar to the *Cyclops* project, which had been begun one year before in the Dunkirk area. Its purpose was to build, about fifteen miles behind the main Atlantic Defence Wall, in the area between Goderville and Saint-Romain-du-Colbosc, a set of three remote control bases and eight underground silos from which V2s and multistage rockets capable of reaching the United States could be launched.

Pferdleichter was killed by a bullet at a quarter to ten – German time – in the main lounge of his hotel, whilst playing a game of chess with one of his executive officers, a Japanese engineer called Ushida. The marksman had taken up position in the attic of an uninhabited house just opposite the hotel, and took advantage of the fact that the lounge windows were wide open; despite having a particularly difficult angle of departure, he needed only one shot to wound Pferdleichter fatally, severing his carotid artery. Because of this it was assumed that the assassin was a crack marksman, and this was confirmed the next day by the discovery, in the bushes in the public gardens in the Town Hall square, of the weapon he had used, an Italian-made .22 sports rifle.

The investigation followed several tracks which all led nowhere: the registered owner of the gun, a certain Monsieur Gressin, from Aigues-Mortes, could not be found; as for the owner of the house where the marksman had hidden, he turned out to be a colonial civil servant in post at Nouméa.

The items produced by the search of Paul Hébert's flat gave new life to the affair. But Paul Hébert had never seen that macintosh nor, *a fortiori*, the box and its contents; the Gestapo tortured him in vain, without learning anything from him.

Despite his youth, Paul Hébert lived alone in the flat. He was looked after by an uncle whom he saw barely more than once a week and by his grandfather, the druggist. His mother had died when he was ten, and his father, Joseph Hébert, a rolling stock inspector on the State Railways, was virtually never in Paris. The Germans' suspicions were directed towards the father, from whom Paul Hébert had had no news for more than two months. It became quickly apparent that he had also stopped working, but all attempts to find him failed. There was no Hely's Ltd in Brussels, any more than there was a tailor called Anton at number 16 bis of the Avenue de Messine, which was a fictitious number in any case, as fictitious as the telephone number which, they later realised, corresponded simply to the time of the murder. After a few months, the German authorities took the view that Joseph Hébert had either been killed already or had succeeded in getting to England, so they closed the file and sent his son to Buchenwald. After the torture he had been undergoing every day, it was almost a liberation for him.

Today, a young girl of seventeen, Geneviève Foulerot, lives in the flat with her son, who is just a year old. Paul Hébert's old bedroom has become the baby's room, a room that is almost empty except for a few pieces of children's furniture: a white wickerwork crib on a folding stand, a changing table, a rectangular playpen with rims padded for safety.

The walls are bare. Only one photograph is pinned to the door. It depicts Geneviève, her face beaming with joy, holding her baby with her arms outstretched; she is wearing a tartan two-piece swimsuit and is posing beside a portable swimming pool of which the outside metal wall is decorated with large, stylised flowers.

This photograph comes from a mail-order catalogue for which Geneviève works as one of six permanent models. In it she can be seen paddling a studio canoe in an orange plastic inflatable lifejacket, or sitting in a tubular steel garden chair in yellow-and-blue-striped canvas beside a blue-roofed tent, wearing a green bathing robe and accompanied by a man in a pink bathing robe, or in a lace-necked nightdress holding small dumbbells, and in a host of working clothes of all kinds: in blouses for nurses, sales girls, infant teachers, in tracksuits for gym teachers, in waitresses' aprons, butcheresses' pinafores, dungarees, jumpsuits, jackets, pilot-coats, etc.

Besides earning a living in this unglamorous way, Geneviève Foulerot is studying drama and has already appeared in several films and serials. She will perhaps soon be the female lead in a television drama adapted from a Pirandello story which she is preparing to read, at the other end of the flat, in her bath: her madonna-like face, her large clear eyes, her long black hair got her selected from amongst the thirty who were auditioned to play Gabriella Vanzi, the woman whose glance, direct and depraved at the same time, drove Romeo Daddi mad.

CHAPTER FORTY-FOUR

Winckler, 2

To begin with, the art of jigsaw puzzles seems of little substance, easily exhausted, wholly dealt with by a basic introduction to Gestalt: the perceived object – we may be dealing with a perceptual act, the acquisition of a skill, a physiological system, or, as in the present case, a wooden jigsaw puzzle – is not a sum of elements to be distinguished from each other and analysed discretely, but a pattern, that is to say a form, a structure: the element's existence does not precede the existence of the whole, it comes neither before nor after it, for the parts do not determine the pattern, but the pattern determines the parts: knowledge of the pattern and of its laws, of the set and its structure, could not possibly be derived from discrete knowledge of the elements that compose it. That means that you can look at a piece of a puzzle for three whole days, you can believe that you know all there is to know about its colouring and shape, and be no further on than when you started. The only thing that counts is the ability to link this piece to other pieces, and in that sense the art of the jigsaw puzzle has something in common with the art of go. The pieces are readable, take on a sense, only when assembled; in isolation, a puzzle piece means nothing – just an impossible question, an opaque challenge. But as soon as you have succeeded, after minutes of trial and error, or after a prodigious half-second flash of inspiration, in fitting it into one of its neighbours, the piece disappears, ceases to exist as a piece. The intense difficulty preceding this link-up – which the English word *puzzle* indicates so well – not only loses its *raison d'être*, it seems never to have had any reason, so obvious does the solution appear. The two pieces so miraculously conjoined are henceforth one, which in its turn will be a source of error, hesitation, dismay, and expectation.

The role of the puzzle-maker is hard to define. In most cases – and in particular in all cardboard jigsaws – the puzzles are machine-made, and the lines of cutting are entirely arbitrary: a blanking die, set up once and for all, cuts the sheets of cardboard along identical lines every time. But such jigsaws are eschewed by the true puzzle-lover, not just because they are made of cardboard instead of wood, nor because the solutions are printed on the boxes they come in, but because this type of cut destroys the specific nature of jigsaw puzzles. Contrary to a widely and firmly held belief, it does not actually matter whether the initial image is easy (or something taken to be easy – a genre scene in the style of Vermeer, for example, or a colour photograph of an Austrian castle) or difficult (a Jackson Pollock, a Pissarro, or the poor paradox of a blank puzzle). It's not the subject of the picture, or the painter's technique, which makes a puzzle more or less difficult, but the greater or lesser subtlety of the way it has been cut; and an arbitrary cutting pattern will necessarily produce an arbitrary degree of difficulty, ranging from the extreme of easiness – for edge pieces, patches of light, well-defined objects, lines, transitions – to the tiresome awkwardness of all the other pieces (cloudless skies, sand, meadow, ploughed land, shaded areas, etc.).

Pieces in puzzles of this kind come in classes of which the best-known are the little chaps

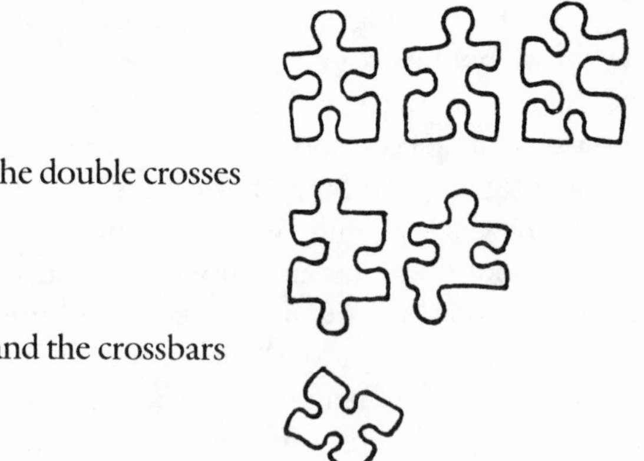

the double crosses

and the crossbars

and once the edges have been put together, the detail pieces put in place – the very light, almost whitish yellow fringe on the carpet on the table holding a lectern with an open book, the rich edging of the mirror, the lute, the woman's red dress – and the bulk of the background pieces parcelled out according to their shade of grey, brown, white, or sky blue, then solving the puzzle consists simply of trying all the plausible combinations one by one.

The art of jigsaw puzzling begins with wooden puzzles cut by hand, whose maker undertakes to ask himself all the questions the player will have to solve, and, instead of allowing chance to cover his tracks, aims to replace it with cunning, trickery, and subterfuge. All the elements occurring in the image to be reassembled – this armchair covered in gold brocade, that three-pointed black hat with its rather ruined black plume, or that silver-braided bright yellow livery – serve by design as points of departure for trails that lead to false information. The organised, coherent, structured signifying space of the picture is cut up not only into inert, formless elements containing little information or signifying power, but also into falsified elements, carrying false information; two fragments of cornice made to fit each other perfectly when they belong in fact to two quite separate sections of the ceiling, the belt buckle of a uniform which turns out *in extremis* to be a metal clasp holding the chandelier, several almost identically cut pieces belonging, for one part, to a dwarf orange tree placed on a mantelpiece and, for the other part, to its scarcely attenuated reflection in a mirror, are classic examples of the types of traps puzzle-lovers come across.

From this, one can make a deduction which is quite certainly the ultimate truth of jigsaw puzzles: despite appearances, puzzling is not a solitary game: every move the puzzler makes, the puzzle-maker has made before; every piece the puzzler picks up, and picks up again, and studies and strokes, every combination he tries, and tries a second time, every blunder and every insight, each hope and each discouragement have all been designed, calculated, and decided by the other.

To find his puzzle-maker, Bartlebooth put advertisements in *Le Jouet Français* and in *Toy Trader*, asking applicants to submit a sample, fourteen centimetres by nine, cut into two hundred pieces. He got twelve responses; most were obvious and unappealing, of the *Meeting at the Field of the Cloth of Gold* kind, or an *Evening in an English Cottage* in all its purportedly authentic detail: an aged Lady So-and-So in a black silk dress with a hexagonal quartz brooch, a butler bringing coffee on a tray, Regency furniture and the portrait of the ancestor (a gentleman with short side whiskers, wearing a red jacket of the period of the last horse-drawn stagecoaches, dressed in white jodhpurs, top boots, and a grey top hat, holding a switch in his hand), a patchwork rug over the hearth, issues of *The Times* laid out on the small table by the wall, a large Chinese carpet with a sky-blue ground, a retired general (recognisable as such by his cropped grey hair, his short white moustache, his ruddy skin, and his row of decorations) beside the window, looking at the barometer with a supercilious air, a young man standing at the fireplace engrossed in *Punch*, etc. Another design, which simply showed a magnificent peacock in his pride, Bartlebooth liked enough to summon its inventor – a Russian émigré prince living rather poorly at Le Raincy – but he looked too old for Bartlebooth's plans.

Gaspard Winckler's puzzle matched exactly what Bartlebooth had wanted. Winckler had made it from an image in the style of popular Epinal prints, signed with the initials M. W. and entitled *The Last Expedition in Search of Franklin*. For the first few hours of his attempt to solve it, Bartlebooth believed that it consisted only of variations on white; in fact, the main body of the picture showed a ship, the *Fox*, trapped in pack ice: standing by the ice-covered tiller, swaddled in light-grey furs from which their deathly pale faces could barely be distinguished, two men, Captain M'Clintoch, leader of the expedition, and his Inupik interpreter, Carl Petersen, point towards a group of Eskimos emerging from a swirling fog covering the whole horizon, and coming towards them on dog-drawn sledges; in the four corners of the picture, four insets showed, respectively: the death of Sir John Franklin, succumbing to exhaustion in the arms of his two surgeons, Peddie and Stanley, on 11 June 1847; the expedition's two ships, the *Erebus*, under Fitz-James, and the *Terror*, captained by Crozier; and the discovery by Lieutenant Hobson, the *Fox*'s first mate, on 6 May 1859, on King William Island, of the cairn containing the last message left by the five hundred survivors on 25

April 1848 before they abandoned their ships crushed by the pack ice and attempted to get back to Hudson's Bay by sledge or on foot.

Gaspard Winckler had just arrived in Paris at that time. He was barely twenty-two. Nothing has ever leaked out about the contract he made with Bartlebooth, but a few months later he and his wife Marguerite moved into Rue Simon-Crubellier. She was a miniaturist: it was she who had painted the gouache Winckler had used for his trial puzzle.

For nearly two years Winckler had almost nothing to do apart from equipping his workroom (he had the door padded and the walls lined with cork), ordering his instruments, preparing his materials, carrying out trials. Then, in the last days of 1934, Bartlebooth and Smautf set off, and three weeks later Winckler received the first watercolour from Spain. Thenceforth they followed without interruption for twenty years at a rhythm of two per month. None was ever lost, even at the height of the war, when sometimes a second secretary at the Swedish Embassy would bring them round himself.

On the first day Winckler would place the watercolour on an easel near the window and would look at it without touching it. On the second day, he would glue it to a backing board (poplar plywood) of slightly larger dimensions. He used a special glue, of a rather pretty blue hue, which he made up himself, and he would insert between the Whatman art paper and the wood a blank sheet of fine paper intended to make the later reseparation of the reconstituted watercolour from the plywood easier, and which would serve as a border to the future puzzle. Then he coated the whole surface with a protective glaze which he put on with a wide flat brush shaped like a fishtail. Then for three or four days he would study the watercolour under a magnifying glass, or, putting it back on the easel, he would sit opposite it for hours on end, getting up now and again to go and examine a detail more closely, or padding around it like a panther in its cage.

The first week would be spent uniquely in such anxious and minute observation. Then everything began to happen very quickly: Winckler would put an extremely thin piece of tracing paper on the watercolour and would draw the puzzle's cutting lines in one sweep of the hand. The rest was only a technical business, a slow and dainty procedure demanding scrupulous care and craft but requiring no further inventiveness. From the tracing paper, the craftsman would make a kind of mould – prefiguring the open-work grid Morellet would use twenty years later to reconstitute the watercolour – which allowed him to control efficiently the movement of his swan-necked jigsaw. Filing each piece with glasspaper, then with chamois leather, and a few final fiddlesome tasks filled the last days of each fortnight. The puzzle would be stored in one of Madame Hourcade's black boxes with their grey ribbons; a rectangular label, showing the time and place of the watercolour's painting

★ FORT-DAUPHIN (MADAGASCAR) 12 JUNE 1940 ★

or

★ PORT SAID (EGYPT) 31 DECEMBER 1953 ★

was glued inside, beneath the lid, and the box, numbered and sealed, would go off to join the other puzzles in a safe-deposit box at the Société Générale; the next day or shortly thereafter another watercolour would arrive in the post.

Gaspard Winckler did not like to be watched working. Marguerite never went into his workshop, where he could shut himself off for days on end, and when Valène came to see him the craftsman always found a pretext for stopping and hiding his work. He never said, "You are disturbing me", but rather something along the lines of "Ah, how convenient you came, I was just going to stop", or he would begin to do the housework, opening the window to air the room, dusting his bench with a linen cloth, or emptying his ashtray, a huge pearl-oyster shell in which apple cores were piled high amongst the long stubs of yellow-paper Gitane cigarettes which he never relit.

CHAPTER FORTY-FIVE

Plassaert, 1

The Plassaerts' flat consists of three rooms under the eaves on the top floor. A fourth room, the one that Morellet occupied until he was interned, is in process of conversion.

The room we are now in is a bedroom with a woodblock floor; there is a divan that can be turned into a bed and a folding table of the sort used for bridge, the two items so placed that, given the smallness of the room, the divan-bed cannot be folded out unless the table is folded up, and vice versa. On the walls there is a light-blue wallpaper with a regularly spaced pattern of four-pointed stars; on the table, a game of dominoes is set out alongside a porcelain ashtray in the shape of a ferocious-looking bulldog head with a studded collar, and a bouquet of pretty-by-night in a parallelepipedal vase made of that special substance called azure stone or lapis lazuli and which owes its colour to an oxide of cobalt.

Lying flat out in the divan, dressed in a brown pullover and black short trousers, with espadrilles on his feet, is a twelve-year-old boy, Rémi, the Plassaerts' son; he is sorting his collection of promotional blotters; for the most part they are medical prospectuses, distributed in specialist journals such as *Medical Press*, *The Medical Gazette*, *The Medical Tribune*, *Medical Weekly*, *Hospital Weekly*, *The Doctor's Week*, *The Doctor's Journal*, *The Doctor's Daily*, *The Family Practitioner*, *Aescalupe*, *Caduceus*, etc. – with which Dr Dinteville is regularly inundated and which he sends down without even opening to Madame Nochère, who gives them to students making wastepaper collections, but not before taking the trouble to share out the blotters between the children in the building: Isabelle Gratiolet and Rémi Plassaert are the main beneficiaries of this operation, since Gilbert Berger collects stamps and is not interested in blotters; Mahmoud, Madame Orlowska's son, and Octave Réol are still a bit too young; as for the other girls in the house, they are already too grown up for this kind of thing.

* * *

Using criteria known only unto himself, Rémi Plassaert has sorted his blotters into eight piles topped respectively by:

- – a singing toreador (*Diamond Enamel* toothpaste)
- – a seventeenth-century Oriental rug from a Transylvanian basilica (*Kalium-Sedaph*, a soluble propionate of potassium)
- – *The Fox and the Stork* [sic], a print by Jean-Baptiste Oudry (Marquaise Stationery, Stencils, Reprographics)
- – a sheet entirely covered in gold ink (*Sargenor*, for physical and mental fatigue, insomnia. Sarget Laboratories)
- – a toucan (*Ramphastos vitellinus*) (Gévéor series of *Animals of the World*)
- – a few gold coins (Courlandish and Toruń rixdollars) shown head-side, enlarged (Gémier Laboratories)
- – the huge open maw of a hippopotamus (Bristol Laboratories *Diclocil* [dicloxacillin])
- – *The Four Musketeers of Tennis* (*Cochet, Borotra, Lacoste, and Brugnon*) (Aspro series of *Great Champions of the Past*)

In front of these eight piles the oldest of these blotters lies on its own; it is the one which started the whole collection off; it was produced by Ricqlès – *the mint with bite that makes you feel all right* – and reproduces a very pretty drawing by Henry Gerbault illustrating the children's nursery song *Papa les p'tits bateaux*: the "papa" is a little boy in a grey cloak with a black collar and equipped with top hat, eye glasses, gloves, walking stick, blue trousers, and white spats; the child is a baby in a big red hat, a large lace neck-ruff, a red-belted jacket, and beige spats; in his left hand he holds a hoop, in his right hand a stick with which he points to a little circular pond on which three toy boats sail; a sparrow sits on the rim of the pond; another one flutters inside the rectangle in which the rhyme is printed.

The Plassaerts found this blotter behind the radiator when they took possession of the room.

The previous occupant was Troyan, the secondhand bookseller with a shop in Rue Lepic. In his attic room there had indeed been a radiator, and also a bed, a sort of pallet with a completely faded flower-printed cotton bedspread, a straw-seated chair, and a wash-stand with a chipped pitcher and a bowl and glass that didn't match, and on which you were more likely to find the remains of a pork chop or an opened bottle of wine than a towel or a sponge or a piece of soap. But most of the space was taken up by heaps of books and miscellaneous things piled up to the ceiling, in which anyone brave enough to rummage could well make interesting discoveries: Olivier Gratiolet found a stiff cardboard panel, perhaps for use by opticians, on which was printed in large letters

YOU ARE REQUESTED TO CLOSE THE EYES

and

YOU ARE REQUESTED TO CLOSE AN EYE

Monsieur Troquet came across a print depicting a prince in armour, riding a winged horse, couching his lance against a monster with a lion's head and mane, a goat's body, and a snake's tail; Monsieur Cinoc unearthed an old postcard portraying a Mormon missionary named William Hitch, a man of tall stature and very dark complexion, with a black moustache, black stockings, black silk hat, black waistcoat, black trousers, white tie, and dog-skin gloves; and Madame Albin discovered a sheet of parchment on which the music and words of a German hymn were printed

Mensch willtu Leben seliglich
Und bei Gott bliben ewiglich
Sollt du halten die zehen Gebot
Die uns gebent unser Gott

which Monsieur Jérôme told her was a choral song by Luther published at Wittenberg in 1524 in Johann Walther's famous *Geystliches Gesangbüchlein*.

It was Monsieur Jérôme, in fact, who made the finest discovery: at the bottom of a big carton full of old typewriter ribbons and mouse droppings, he found all folded and lined but otherwise almost intact a large canvas-backed map entitled

ADMINISTRATIVE HISTORIQUE ET ROUTIÈRE

Les Chemins de Fer et leurs Stations, les Routes Nationales,
Les Rivieres navigables, les Canaux, et les Etablissements d'Eaux Thermales et Minérale.
Les Cours d'Appel, Evêchés et Archevêchés
La Traversee des Bateaux à Vapeur sur la Méditerranée et l'Océan.

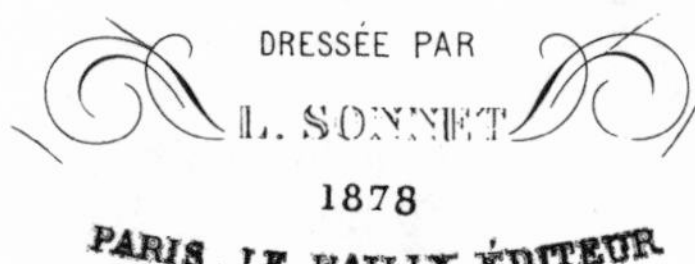

Rue Cardinale 6.

The centre of the map showed France, with a plan of the Paris area and a map of Corsica in two inset panels; beneath it, the legend and four scales measured respectively against kilometres, geographical miles [sic], English miles, and German *Meilen*. In the four corners of the sheet were maps of the French colonies: top left, Guadeloupe and Martinique; top right, Algeria; bottom left, quite damaged, Senegal and New Caledonia with its dependencies; bottom right, French Cochinchina and La Réunion. Along the top of the sheet, a row of coats of arms of twenty cities and twenty portraits of famous men born in them: Marseilles (Thiers), Dijon (Bossuet), Rouen (Géricault), Ajaccio (Napoleon I), Grenoble (Bayard), Bordeaux (Montesquieu), Pau (Henri IV), Albi (La Pérouse), Chartres (Marceau), Besançon (Victor Hugo), Paris (Béranger), Mâcon (Lamartine), Dunkirk (Jean Bart), Montpellier (Cambacérès), Bourges (Jacques Coeur), Caen (Auber), Agen (Bernard Palissy),

Clermont-Ferrand (Vercingétorix), La Ferté-Milon (Racine), and Lyons (Jacquard). On the right- and left-hand edges, twenty-four small insets, twelve of them depicting towns, eight showing scenes from French history, and four showing regional dress: on the left: Paris, Rouen, Nancy, Laon, Bordeaux, and Lille; local costumes from Auvergne, Arles, and Nîmes, and those of Normans and Bretons; and the siege of Paris (1871); Daguerre discovering photography (1840); the Capture of Algiers (1830): Denis Papin discovering the motive power of steam (1681); on the right: Lyons, Marseilles, Caen, Nantes, Montpellier, Rennes; local costumes from Rochefort, La Rochelle, and Mâcon, and those of Lorraine, the Vosges, and Annecy; and the Defence of Châteaudun (1870); Montgolfier inventing hot-air balloons (1783), the Storming of the Bastille (1789) and Parmentier presenting Louis XVI with a bouquet of potato flowers (1780).

Troyan had enlisted in the International Brigade and spent almost the whole of the war as a prisoner in the camp at Lurs, from which he succeeded in escaping at the end of 1943 to join the maquis. He returned to Paris in 1944, and, after a few months of intense political activity, became a secondhand book dealer. His shop in Rue Lepic was in fact just a barely converted entrance porch to a building. He sold mostly one-franc books and obscure reviews of undressed girls – with titles like *Sensations*, *Paris by Night*, *Pin-Up* – for gulping schoolboys. Three or four times more interesting items passed through his hands: Victor Hugo's three letters, for example, but also an 1872 edition of *Bradshaw's Continental Railway Steam Transit and General Guide*, or the *Memoirs* of Falckenskiold, preceded by an account of his campaigns in the Russian Army against the Turks in 1769 and followed by considerations on the military situation of Denmark and a note by Secrétan.

END OF PART TWO

PART THREE

CHAPTER FORTY-SIX

Servants' Quarters, 7
Monsieur Jérôme

A room on the seventh floor which is virtually uninhabited; like many other maid's rooms it belongs to the building manager, who has kept it for his own use primarily and secondarily for lending to friends from the provinces spending a few days in Paris for this or that International Exhibition or Fair. He has furnished it in an utterly impersonal style; panels of hessian on the walls, twin beds separated by a Louis XV-style bedside table with an orange plastic promotional ashtray on the eight sides of which are written, in alternation, four times each, the two words COCA and COLA, and by way of a bedside light, one of those clip-on lamp fixtures of which the bulb is adorned with a little painted metal cone-shaped cowl serving as a shade; a worn floor-rug, a mirrored wardrobe with miscellaneous coat hangers from various hotels, cubic poufs covered in synthetic fur, and a low table with three puny legs ending in gilt metal ferrules and a kidney-shaped coloured formica top, supporting an issue of *Jours de France* with a cover embellished by a close-up of the singer Claude François, smiling.

It was to this room that Monsieur Jérôme returned, towards the end of the 1950s, to live and die.

Monsieur Jérôme had not always been the bitter and burnt-out old man that he was in the last ten years of his life. In October 1924, when he moved into Rue Simon-Crubellier for the first time – not into this maid's room but into the flat Gaspard Winckler would occupy after him – he was a young history teacher with the highest qualifications earned at the prestigious Ecole Normale Supérieure, sure of himself, full of enthusiasm and ideas. Slim and elegant, fond of American-style white starched collars over pin-striped shirts, he enjoyed the good life, took pleasure in fine food, had a penchant for Havanas and cocktails, went to English bars, mixed in fashionable circles, and held advanced opinions which he propounded with just the right balance of condescension and casualness so as to make his listener feel humiliated for not knowing about them and at the same time flattered at having them explained to him.

For some years he taught at the Lycée Pasteur at Neuilly; then he won a scholarship from the Thiers Foundation to work on his doctoral thesis. He chose for his subject *The Spice Road*, and analysed with a not entirely humourless subtlety the economic evolution of exchanges between the West and the Far East, setting it in the context of Western culinary habits of the relevant periods. Since he wanted to show that the introduction into Europe of those small dried pimentos called "bird pepper" corresponded to a real transformation in the way game was prepared for cooking, at his examination he did not hesitate to make the three old professors who constituted the board of examiners taste the marinades he had made up himself.

He passed, obviously, with the examiners' commendation, and a little while after, on his appointment as Cultural Attaché in Lahore, left Paris.

On two or three occasions Valène heard people speak of him. At the time of the *Front populaire*, his name appeared several times beneath manifestoes and appeals put out by the Anti-Fascist Intellectuals' Vigilance Committee. Another time, on a visit to France, he gave a lecture at the Guimet Museum on *Caste Systems in the Punjab and Their Sociocultural Consequences.* A little later he published a long article on Gandhi in *Vendredi*.

He came back to Rue Simon-Crubellier in 1957 or 1958. He was unrecognisable, done in, worn out, done for. He didn't ask for his old flat back, but only a maid's room if there was one free. He was no longer a teacher or a Cultural Attaché; he was working in the library of the Institute for the History of Religions. An "aged scholar" whom he had, apparently, met on a train, was paying him one hundred and fifty francs a month to make a card index of the Spanish clergy. In five years he had made out seven thousand four hundred and sixty-two biographies of churchmen in office in the reigns of Phillip III (1598–1621), Phillip IV (1621–1665) and Charles II (1665–1700), and had sorted them under twenty-seven different headings (by a marvellous coincidence, he would add with a grin, 27 is precisely the number used, in the universal decimal classification system – better known as Dewey Decimal – for the general history of the Christian Church).

Meanwhile, the "aged scholar" had died. Monsieur Jérôme tried in vain to interest the Ministry of Education, the National Centre for Scientific Research (CNRS), the VIth section of the Ecole Pratique des Hautes Etudes, the Collège de France, as well as some fifteen other public and private bodies, in the history of the Spanish Church in the seventeenth century – more turbulent than you might think – and tried also, but equally unsuccessfully, to find a publisher. After receiving his forty-sixth absolute and categorical refusal, Monsieur Jérôme took his manuscript – more than twelve hundred pages of incredibly close-spaced handwriting – and went to burn it in the courtyard of the Sorbonne, which incidentally cost him a night in a police station.

These brushes with publishers were not, however, entirely useless. A little later, one of them offered him translation work from English. It concerned children's books, the kind of little books called "primers" in English-speaking countries and in which you still quite often find things like

Icky licky micky sticky!
I'm a tiny tiny thing
Ever flying in the spring
Round and round a ring-a-ring
Long ago I was a king
Now I do this kind of thing
On the wing, on the wing!
Bing!

and they obviously had to be adapted in translation so as to fit the everyday characteristics of French life.

This was the wherewithal which allowed Monsieur Jérôme to eke out an existence until his death. It didn't take much work, and he spent most of his time in his bedroom, stretched out on an old bottle-green moleskin settee, wearing the same machine-patterned pullover or a greyish flannel undervest, with his head leaning on the only thing he had brought back from his Hindu years: a patch –

scarcely bigger than a pocket handkerchief – of a once sumptuous cloth, with a purple field, embroidered with silver thread.

All around him the floor would be strewn with detective novels and Kleenex (he had a constantly dripping nose); he consumed easily two or three detective novels a day and prided himself on having read and being able to remember all one hundred and eighty-three titles in the *Fingerprint* series and at least two hundred titles in the *Mask* collection. He liked only detective stories with a mystery to solve, the good old pre-war English and American detective novels with locked rooms and perfect alibis, with a slight preference for mildly incongruous titles: *The Ploughman Killer*, or *The Corpse Will Play for You on the Piano*, or *The Agnate Will Be Angry*.

He read extremely fast – a habit and a technique he had kept from the Ecole Normale – but never for a long stretch. He would stop often, stay lying down doing nothing, and close his eyes. He would push his thick tortoiseshell spectacles up over his balding forehead; he would put the detective novel at the foot of the settee after marking his page with a postcard depicting a globe whose turned-wood stand made it look like a spinning top. It was one of the first known globes, the one which Johannes Schoener, a cartographer who was a friend of Copernicus, had made at Bamberg in 1520, and which was kept at the Library in Nuremberg.

He never told anyone what had happened to him. He practically never talked about his travels. One day, Monsieur Riri asked him what was the most amazing thing he had seen in his life: he replied, a Maharajah sitting at a table all incrusted with ivory, dining with his three lieutenants. No one said anything, and the three fierce men of war seemed, in front of their leader, like little children. Another time, without anyone asking him anything at all, he said that the most beautiful, the most dazzling thing he had seen in the world was a ceiling divided into octagonal sections, decorated in gold and silver, and more exquisitely worked than any jewel.

CHAPTER FORTY-SEVEN

Dinteville, 2

Dr Dinteville's waiting room. A quite spacious room, rectangular, with a herringbone woodblock floor and leather-padded doors. Against the rear wall, a large sofa upholstered in blue velvet; more or less everywhere, armchairs, lyre-back chairs, nesting tables with various magazines and periodicals spread out on them: on the cover of one of them can be seen a photograph of Franco on his deathbed watched over by four kneeling monks who look as though they have come straight out of a painting by La Tour; against the right-hand wall, a leather-padded writing desk on which stands a Napoleon III papier mâché pen-stand with small tortoiseshell inlays and fine gilt arabesques and, under its glass dome, a dead burnished clock with its hands stopped at ten minutes to two.

There are two people in the waiting room. One is an extremely thin old man, a retired teacher of French who still gives tuition by correspondence, and who whilst waiting his turn is correcting a pile of scripts with a pencil sharpened to a fine point. On the script he is about to examine, the essay title can be read:

> In Hell, Raskolnikov meets Meursault ("The Outsider"). Imagine a dialogue between them using material from both novels.

The other person is not sick: he is a telephone salesman whom Dr Dinteville has summoned at the end of his day to show him the new models of telephone answering machines. He is leafing through one of the publications strewn over the side-table next to which he is sitting: a horticulturalist's catalogue with a cover depicting the garden of the Suzaku temple at Kyoto.

There are several pictures on the walls. One of them in particular attracts attention, less for its pseudo "naïve" manner than for its size – almost ten feet by six – and its subject: it shows in minute, almost laborious detail the inside of a café: in the centre, leaning his elbow on the bar, a bespectacled young man bites into a ham sandwich (with butter and a lot of mustard) whilst drinking half a pint of beer. Behind him stands a pinball machine representing a tawdry Spain – or Mexico – with a woman fanning herself betwen the four counters. The same bespectacled young man – the technique was abundantly used in medieval painting – is also busy at the pinball machine, and victoriously so, since his counter shows a score of 67,000 and only 20,000 points are needed to win a free game. Four children stand like a row of onions beside the machine, with their eyes at the height of the ball, and watch his exploits with jubilation: three lads with mottled jumpers and berets, looking just like the traditional image of the Paris urchin, and a girl wearing round her neck a string of plaited black thread on which hangs a single red ball, holding a peach in her left hand. In the foreground, just behind the café window on which large white letters spell out backwards

two men are playing tarot: one of them is putting down the card showing a man armed with a stick, carrying a knapsack, and followed by a dog, the character called the Fool, that is to say the Joker. To the left, behind the counter, the proprietor, an obese man in shirtsleeves with check braces, is looking guardedly at a poster which a timid-looking girl is probaby asking him to put in the window: at the top, it depicts a long metallic horn, very pointed, pierced with several holes; in the centre, it announces the world premiere in the Church of Saint Saturnin at Champigny on Saturday, 19 December 1960 at 8:45 p.m. of *Malakhitès*, opus 35, for fifteen brasses, voice, and percussion, by Morris Schmetterling, to be performed by the *New Brass Ensemble of Michigan State University at East Lansing*, conducted by the composer. At the very bottom, it shows a map of Champigny-sur-Marne with directions from various Paris exits – Porte de Vincennes, Porte de Picpus, Porte de Bercy.

Dr Dinteville is the *quartier*'s general practitioner. He holds his surgery every morning and evening and spends all afternoons on home calls to his patients. People don't like him much, thinking he lacks warmth, but they appreciate his efficiency and punctuality and stay with him.

For a long time the doctor has nourished a secret passion: he would like to leave his name to a cooking recipe: he wavers between "Crab Salad à la Dinteville", "Crab Salad Dinteville" or, more enigmatically, "Dinteville Salad".

> *For six servings: three live crabs – or three maias (spider crabs) or six small* tourteau *crabs; half a pound of pasta shells; a small Stilton cheese; 2 oz. butter; a small glass of cognac; a tablespoon of horseradish sauce; a few drops of Worcester sauce; fresh mint leaves; three dill seeds. For the court-bouillon: sea salt, peppercorns, 1 onion. For the mayonnaise: one egg yolk, strong mustard, salt, pepper, olive oil, vinegar, paprika, a teaspoon of tomato double-concentrate.*
>
> 1 Using a large pot three-quarters full of cold water, make a court-bouillon with sea salt, 5 white peppercorns, 1 peeled onion sliced in two. Boil for 10 minutes. Leave to cool. Immerse the shellfish in the lukewarm court-bouillon. Bring back to boil, lower heat, cover, and simmer for 15 minutes. Take out the shellfish and leave to cool.
>
> 2 Bring the court-bouillon back to the boil. Sprinkle the pasta shells into it. Stir and boil for 7 minutes. The pasta must stay firm. Drain the pasta shells, rinse quickly in cold water, and put to the side with a drop of olive oil to prevent sticking.
>
> 3 Mix in a mortar with a pestle or wooden spatula the Stilton, moistened with a little of the cognac and Worcester sauce, with the butter and horseradish sauce. Pound well to obtain a creamy but not too liquid consistency.

4 Detach the legs and claws of the cooled shellfish. Empty the flesh out of them into a large bowl. Crack the shells, remove the central cartilage, drain, empty out the flesh and soft parts. Chop into large pieces and add the crushed dill seeds and the mint leaves chopped very fine.

5 Make a very stiff mayonnaise. Colour it with the paprika and tomato double-concentrate.

6 Place the pasta shells in a large salad bowl and stir in *very gently* the chopped shellfish, the Stilton, and the mayonnaise. Decorate as desired with chiffonade of lettuce, radishes, prawn, cucumber, tomatoes, hard-boiled eggs, olives, orange quarters, etc. Serve *very* cool.

CHAPTER FORTY-EIGHT

Servants' Quarters, 8
Madame Albin

An attic room under the eaves in between Morellet's old room and that of Madame Orlowska. It is deserted, inhabited only by a goldfish in its spherical bowl. The tenant, Madame Albin, though she is seriously ill, has gone, as she goes every day, to pray on her husband's grave.

Like Monsieur Jérôme, Madame Albin returned to live in Rue Simon-Crubellier after a long absence. Shortly after her marriage, not to the soldier Raymond Albin, her first fiancé, whom she let a few weeks after the lift incident, but to a typographer named René Albin, unrelated to the other except by homonym, she left France for Damascus where her husband had found work at a major printing press. Their aim was to earn enough money as quickly as possible so as to be able to return to France and set themselves up on their own account.

The French Protectorate aided their ambitions or, more exactly, speeded up their progress, through a system of interest-free loans, designed to develop investment in the colonies, which allowed them to establish a small factory producing schoolbooks and which quickly grew to a substantial size. When the war broke out, the Albins reckoned it was wiser to stay in Syria, where their publishing business was increasingly prosperous, and in 1945, as they were getting ready to sell up and return to France with their fortune made, assured of a more than comfortable income, anti-French riots erupted which together with the stern measures taken against them reduced all their efforts to naught overnight: their publishing house had become a symbol of the French presence in Syria and was burnt down by the Nationalists; a few days later, Franco-British troops shelled the city and destroyed the luxury hotel the Albins had built and into which they had put more than three-quarters of their fortune.

René Albin died of a cardiac arrest on the night of the shelling. Flora herself was repatriated in 1946. She brought her husband's remains back with her and had him buried at Juvisy. Thanks to the concierge, Madame Claveau, with whom she had kept in touch, she managed to get her old room back.

Then began for Madame Albin an endless rigmarole of court cases which she lost one after another and which swallowed up the few million old francs she had left, her jewels, her silver, and her carpets: she lost versus the French Republic, she lost versus the Crown of the British Empire, she lost versus the Republic of Syria, she lost versus the City of Damascus, she lost versus all the insurance and reinsurance companies she took to court. All she obtained was a civilian war-victim's pension and, as the printing works she had founded with her husband had been nationalised, a compensation payment converted into an annuity: that gives her a net monthly income after tax of four hundred and eighty francs, or precisely 16 francs a day.

Madame Albin is one of those tall, dry, and bony women who look as though they have come out of Germaine Acremant's *Those Ladies in Green Hats*. She goes to the cemetery every day: she leaves her flat around two o'clock, takes the number 84 bus from Courcelles, gets off it at Orsay station, then catches the train to Juvisy-sur-Orge, and gets back to Rue Simon-Crubellier around six-thirty or seven o'clock; she spends the rest of her time shut in her room.

She keeps her room impeccably tidy: the small floortiles are meticulously polished, and she asks visitors to walk on shoe-slippers made of sackcloth; her two armchairs have nylon dustcovers.

* * *

On her table, her mantelpiece, and her two low tables there are objects wrapped in old pages from the only paper she enjoys reading, *France-Dimanche*. It is a great honour to be permitted to see these objects; she never unwraps them all at once, and rarely shows more than two or three of them to any single person. Valène, for example, was allowed to admire a purplewood chess set with inlaid mother-of-pearl, and a *rebab*, or two-string Arab violin, reputed to date from the sixteenth century; to Mademoiselle Crespi she showed – without explaining where it came from or its connections with her life in Syria – a Chinese erotic print depicting a supine woman being pleasured by six little wrinkle-faced gnomes; Jane Sutton, whom she does not like because she is English, was allowed to see only four postcards similarly without any apparent relevance to Madame Albin's biography: a cockfight in Borneo; Samoyeds bundled in furs, driving sledges drawn by reindeer through the snowy wastes of Siberia; a young Moroccan woman, in a costume of striped silk, with trappings in the shape of chains, bracelets, and rings, her swelling breasts half bared, with dilated nostrils, the eyes full of animal life, the features in play as she shows her white teeth in a laugh; and a Greek peasant wearing a kind of big beret, a red shirt, and a grey jacket, pushing a hand-plough. But to Madame Orlowska, who, like her, had lived in the Muslim world, she showed the most precious things she possessed: an open-work copper lamp with little oval cutouts in the shape of legendary flowers, from the Ummayad mosque where Saladin is buried, and a hand-coloured photograph of the grand hotel she had built: a big square courtyard, surrounded on three sides by buildings painted white with broad horizontal stripes of red, green, blue, and black; an enormous clump of oleander with all its flowers in full bloom, red blotches on green; on the coloured marble paving in the centre of the courtyard, there gambols a small, black-eyed, dainty-hoofed gazelle.

Madame Albin is beginning to lose her memory and maybe also her reason; people along the corridor began to realise when she started knocking on their doors in the evenings to warn them of unseen threats which she called the *black shirts* or sometimes *harkis* or even on occasions the *OAS*; another time she began to unwrap one of her packages to show its contents to Smautf and Smautf noticed she had wrapped up a small carton of orange juice as if it had been one of her precious mementos. One morning a few months ago she forgot to put in her false teeth, which she leaves overnight in a glass of water; she has not worn them again since then; the prosthesis lies in its glass on the bedside table, covered in a kind of aquatic moss whence minute yellow flowers occasionally emerge.

CHAPTER FORTY-NINE

On the Stairs, 7

At the very top of the stairs.

On the right, the door of the flat that Gaspard Winckler lived in; on the left, the lift shaft; at the end, the glazed door giving onto the small staircase leading to the servants' quarters. A broken pane has been replaced by a page of *Détective* on which can be read: "Five Minors Took Turns to Satisfy the Campsite Manageress", above a photograph of the said manageress, a woman of about fifty, wearing a flowery hat and a white overcoat beneath which she may well be supposed stark naked.

To begin with, the two attic floors were occupied only by servants. They weren't allowed to use the main staircase; they had to come in and go out by the servants' door at the left-hand side of the building and use the servants' stairs which on each floor gave onto kitchens or pantries and on the top two floors onto two long corridors leading to their attic rooms. The glazed door at the top of the main stairs was to be used only on the very exceptional occasions when a master or a mistress might need to go into one of his or her servant's rooms, for instance to "inspect his (or her) belongings", that is to say to check that he or she wasn't carrying off a silver teaspoon or a pair of candlesticks on being dismissed, or to take up to old Victoire on her deathbed a cup of herb tea or the last rites.

At the end of the 1914 war, this sacrosanct rule which neither masters nor servants would have dreamt of transgressing began to bend, largely because the maids' rooms and attics were less and less exclusively reserved for the use of servants. The example was set by Monsieur Hardy, an olive-oil merchant from Marseilles, who lived on the second floor left, in the apartment later to be occupied by the Appenzzells and then the Altamonts. He rented one of his servants' rooms to Henri Fresnel: Henri Fresnel was in some sense a serving man, since he was chef at the restaurant Monsieur Hardy had just opened in Paris to show off the freshness and quality of his produce (*The Famous Bouillabaisse*, 99 Rue de Richelieu, next to the *Restaurant du Grand U*, at that time a celebrated gathering place of politicians and journalists), but he – Monsieur Fresnel – didn't serve in the building, and it was therefore with a perfectly clear conscience that he used the glazed door of the masters' staircase to come down. The second was Valène: Monsieur Colomb, a queer old fish, publisher of specialised almanacs (*The Race-Goer's Almanac*, *The Coin-Collector's Almanac*, *The Music-Lover's Almanac*, *The Oyster-Breeder's* . . ., etc.), father of Rodolphe, the trapeze artist currently in vogue at the Nouveau-Cirque, and a distant friend of Valène's parents, rented him his servant's room for a few francs, often paid back by way of an order for work for one of his almanacs; he had no use for the room since Gervaise, his housekeeper, had slept for ages in one of the rooms in his flat on the third floor right, beneath the Echards. And then when some years later this glazed door that was only supposed to be used in exceptional circumstances was opened daily by the young Bartlebooth on his way up to his watercolour lesson with Valène, it became apparent that it was no longer possible to judge membership of social class by a person's position with respect to this glazed door, just as in the preceding generation it had become similarly impossible to establish class membership on notions even as deep-rooted as those of ground floor, mezzanine, and noble storey.

Today, out of twenty rooms originally set aside for the serving classes on the street side of the building, and initially numbered in green stencil-painted digits from 11 to 30 (the twenty other numbers from 1 to 10 and 31 to 40 belonging to the rooms on the courtyard side, on the other side of the corridor), there are no more than two actually lived in by servants working in the building: room No. 13, which is Smautf's, and No. 26, where the Paraguayo-Dutch couple who work for Hutting sleep; one could stretch a point and add No. 14, Jane Sutton's room, since she pays the rent by doing two hours' daily housework for the Rorschachs (which actually comes out at a rather exorbitant rent for such a small room), and, at the very limit, No. 15, lived in by Madame Orlowska, who sometimes also does some cleaning, but not usually in the building, except, on rare occasions, for the Louvets and the Marquiseaux, when her Polish and Arabic piecework for the *Bulletin signalétique du CNRS* isn't enough for her and her little boy to live on. The other maids' rooms and attics no longer even belong necessarily to the owners of flats in the building: the manager has bought back several of them and rents them out as "flatlets" after putting in plumbing; several people have put two or more of the rooms together, starting with Olivier Gratiolet, the heir of the former owners of the building, and – in contravention of the terms of the co-ownership agreement, through loopholes in the law and by bribery – some have even annexed parts of the "service areas", like Hutting, who appropriated the old corridor when he converted his big studio.

The servants' stairs are now hardly used at all, except by some delivery men and suppliers, and by workmen working on the building. The lift – when it is in order – is freely used by all. But the glazed door remains a subtle and fearfully persistent mark of a difference. Even if there are people upstairs much richer than those downstairs, that does not prevent it being the case that from the point of view of downstairs people those upstairs are somehow inferior: as it happens, if they are not servants, then they are paupers, children (*young people*), or artists for whom life must necessarily be inscribed within these tiny rooms where there is space only for a bed, a cupboard, and a stack of shelves for jars of jam with which to eke out the days before the next pay cheque. It is of course quite normal that Hutting, a painter with an international reputation, should be much richer than the Altamonts, and it is moreover quite clear that the Altamonts are flattered to be hosts to Hutting or to be his guests at his château in the Dordogne or at his farmhouse at Gattières, but the Altamonts will never miss an opportunity of recalling that in the seventeenth century painters, writers, and musicians were only valets with a specialism, just like perfumers, hairdressers, dressmakers, and restaurateurs still were in the nineteenth century, who today are destined to reach fame as well as fortune; although one can see how dressmakers or restaurateurs could become businessmen, even industrialists, by their own efforts, an artist, on the other hand, could never cease to be dependent on middle-class need.

This vision of things, magnificently set out in 1879 in Edmond About's *Worker's ABC*, where he calculates without a hint of irony that when Mademoiselle Patti (1843–1919) goes to sing in a financier's drawing room she produces, on opening her mouth, the equivalent of forty tons of cast iron at fifty francs per thousand kilos, this vision of things is obviously not shared with equal intensity by all the inhabitants of the building. For some it is a pretext for recriminations and enviousness, displays of jealousy and scorn; for others, it belongs to folklore and is of no real consequence. But for both groups of people, and for both the upstairs and the downstairs dwellers, it functions ultimately as a basic fact of life: the Louvets, for instance, say that the Plassaerts have "converted the maids' rooms, but made their flat quite nice all the same"; the Plassaerts for their part feel obliged to stress that their three little attic rooms are "really cute" and to add that they got them for a song and to insinuate that *they* don't lower their backsides onto reproduction Louis XV antiques like that old Moreau woman (which is, as it happens, entirely false). In much the same way Hutting will often say apologetically that he'd grown weary of the great barn of a luxury flat that he had had at the Porte d'Orléans and that he'd been dreaming of a small and peaceful studio in a quiet neighbourhood; on the other hand, the manager refers to Morellet as "Morellet" but to Cinoc and Winckler as "Monsieur Cinoc" and "Monsieur Winckler", and if it should happen that Madame Marquiseaux gets into the lift at the same time as Madame Orlowska, she will make some tiny and perhaps unconscious gesture signifying that it is her lift, of which she condescends to share the usufruct for a short moment with someone who on arriving on the sixth floor will still have two flights to climb on foot.

On two occasions the upstairs and the downstairs folk have entered into open conflict: the first time was when Olivier Gratiolet asked the Co-owners' Association meeting to approve an extension of the stair carpet to the seventh and eighth floors, beyond the glazed door. He had the support of the manager, for whom a carpet on the stairs meant an extra one hundred francs per month per room. But the majority of the co-owners, whilst they deemed the operation permissible, demanded that its costs be borne solely by the owners of the two top floors, not by the whole association of co-owners. That would not have been worth it to the manager, who would have had to pay for the carpet almost on his own, so he took steps to have the idea buried.

The second time, it was about mail delivery. The present concierge, Madame Nochère, though she may be the salt of the earth, has class prejudices, and the separation marked by the glazed door is no mere fiction for her: she delivers mail to people living below the door, but the others have to collect at her office: those were the instructions given by Juste Gratiolet to Madame Araña, handed on by Madame Araña to Madame Claveau, who passed them down to Madame Nochère. Hutting, and even more virulently the Plassaerts, demanded the repeal of this discriminatory and dishonourable measure, and the Co-owners' Association was obliged to yield to them so as not to appear to ratify a practice inherited from the nineteenth century. But Madame Nochère refused point blank, and when the manager gave her formal notice to deliver mail to all floors without distinction, she produced a medical certificate, signed by none other than Dr Dinteville, certifying that the condition of her legs did not permit her to climb the stairs on foot. Madame Nochère's principal motivation in this affair was hatred for the Plassaerts and for Hutting; for she delivers the mail even when there is no lift working (which is fairly often) and few days pass without her visiting Madame Orlowska, Valène, or Mademoiselle Crespi, and she takes advantage of the opportunity to bring them up their mail.

That obviously has little practical consequence except for the concierge herself, who knows once and for all that she shouldn't rely on much of a Christmas box from Hutting or the Plassaerts. It is one of those breaches around which the life of a building is structured, a source of tiny tensions, of micro-conflicts, allusions, implications, skirmishes: it is one of the sometimes bitter controversies which rock the Co-owners' Association meetings, such as the argument over Madame Réol's flowerpots, over David Marcia's motorcycle (did he or did he not have the right to park it in the lean-to adjoining the dustbin area? Today the answer is no longer important, but in the attempts to find it, a good half-dozen legal experts were called in, for completely wasted fees), or, again, over the disastrous musical habits of the crackpot who lived on the second floor right to the rear of the courtyard and who felt deprived, at certain unspecifiable periods and for an unforeseeable length of time, unless he listened thirty-seven times in a row, preferably between the hours of midnight and three a.m., to *Heili Heilo*, *Lili Marlene*, and other jewels of Hitlerian music.

There are even subtler, almost unguessable fractures: for instance, the older versus the newer inhabitants, where the rules governing distribution belong to the realm of the imponderable: Rorschach, who bought his flat in 1960, is an "elder", whereas Berger, who arrived less than a year later, is a "newer"; Berger, moreover, moved in straight away, whilst Rorschach spent a year and a half refurbishing his flat; or the Altamont side versus the Beaumont side; or people's attitudes during the last war: of the four still living in the building today who were then of an age to take part, only one had an active commitment to the Resistance – Olivier Gratiolet, who ran a clandestine printing press in his cellar and for almost a year kept under his bed a dismantled American submachine gun which he'd transported there, in pieces, in a shopping basket. Véra de Beaumont, on the other hand, willingly adopted pro-German attitudes and appeared several times in public with impeccable, high-ranking Prussians; the two others, Valène and Mademoiselle Crespi, seemed not to take sides.

All that makes a pretty tranquil history, with dramas over dog-dirt and dustbin tragedies, the Bergers' dawn radio and coffee grinder waking Madame Réol too early, Hutting still complaining about Gratiolet's doorbell, or Léon Marcia's sleepless nights which the Louvets find hard to bear: for hours and hours the old man paces up and down in his bedroom, then goes to the kitchen to get a glass of milk from the fridge, or to the bathroom to rinse his face, or switches on the radio, at low volume but still too loud for his neighbours, to listen to crackling broadcasts from the other end of the world.

In the whole history of the building there have been few serious events, apart from the little accidents consequent upon Morellet's experiments and, much earlier on, around Christmas 1925, the fire in

Madame Danglars' dressing room, which is today the room where Bartlebooth does his puzzles.

The Danglars were dining out; there was no one in the room, but a fire, lit by the servants, was burning in the fireplace. The blaze was explained by a spark flying over the rectangular, painted metal fireguard in the front of the fireplace and landing in a vase standing on a low coffee table: unfortunately, the vase held magnificent artificial flowers which caught fire immediately: the flames spread to the fitted carpet and the cretonne with which the walls were papered, and which depicted a classical rustic scene: a gambolling faun, one hand on his hip and the other bent prettily behind his head, sheep grazing with a black ewe in their midst, a mower-girl cutting grass with a sickle.

Everything went up in flames, and especially Madame Danglars's most valuable jewel: one of Carl Fabergé's 49 Easter eggs, an egg of rock crystal containing a bush of roses; when the egg was opened, the roses formed into a circle at the centre of which there appeared a group of songbirds.

All that was recovered was a pearl bracelet that Monsieur Danglars had given his wife as a birthday present. He had bought it at the sale of a descendant of Madame de La Fayette, to whom it was given by Henrietta of England. The case it was kept in had stood up to the fire without damage, with the pearls completely black inside it.

Half of the Danglars' flat was destroyed; the rest of the building did not suffer.

Sometimes Valène dreamt of cataclysms and tempests, of whirlwinds that would carry the whole house off like a wisp of straw and display the infinite marvels of the solar system to its shipwrecked inhabitants; or that an unseen crack would run through the building from top to bottom, like a shiver, and with a long, deep, snapping sound it would open in two and be slowly swallowed up in an indescribable yawning chasm; then hordes would overrun it, bleary-eyed monsters, giant insects with steel mandibles, blind termites, great white worms with insatiable mouths: the wood would crumble, the stone would turn to sand, the cupboards would collapse under their own weight, all would return to dust.

But no. Only these shabby squabbles over buckets and tubs,

over matches and sinks. And behind that ever-closed door the morbid gloom of that slow revenge, that ponderous business of two senile monomaniacs churning over their feigned histories and their wretched traps and snares.

CHAPTER FIFTY

Foulerot, 3

Geneviève Foulerot's bedroom, or rather her bedroom-to-be.

The room has just been repainted. The ceiling has been decorated in matt white, the walls in ivory-white gloss, the quartered wood-block floor in black gloss. A bare bulb on a wire has been partly covered by a makeshift shade consisting of a big piece of red blotting paper rolled into a cone.

The room is entirely devoid of furniture. A picture of large dimensions has not yet been hung up and stands against the right-hand wall, where it is partly reflected in the dark mirror of the floor.

The picture itself represents a room. On the windowsill there is a bowl of goldfish next to a pot of mignonette. Through the open window a rural landscape can be seen: the soft-blue sky, rounded like a dome, rests along the horizon on the jagged outline of the woods; in the foreground, at the roadside, a little girl, barefoot in the dust, lets a cow graze. Further in the distance, a painter in a blue smock is working at the foot of an oak, with his paintbox on his knee. In the background there shimmers a lake on the shores of which a misty city rises, with houses all verandas one above the other, and high streets whose railed parapets look out over the water.

This side of the window, a little to the left, a man in a fancy-dress uniform – white trousers, chintz jacket overloaded with épaulettes, stripes, sabretaches, and frogging, a big black cape, boots with spurs – sits at a rustic writing desk – an old junior school desk with a hole for an inkwell and a slightly raked top – on which stand a jug of water, a stem glass of the sort known as *flûtes*, and a candlestick whose pedestal is an admirable iron egg set in silver. The man has just received a letter and reads it with an expression of utter dismay on his face.

Just to the left of the window there is a telephone fixed to the wall and, still further left, a picture: it represents a seashore landscape with, in the foreground, a partridge perched on a branch of a wizened tree whose twisted, knobbly trunk springs out of a pile of boulders which open out onto a foaming inlet. In the far distance, out to sea, a boat with a three-cornered sail.

To the right of the window there is a large gilt mirror which is supposed to reflect a scene allegedly taking place behind the back of the seated character. Three people, all also in disguise, a woman and two men, are standing. The woman wears an austere long dress in grey wool and a Quaker's headgear and holds a jar of pickles under her arm; one of the men, an anxious-looking forty-year-old, is dressed in a medieval Fool's costume with a doublet divided into narrow-pointed triangles of alternating red and yellow, a bauble, and a cap with bells; the other man, an insipid youngster with thinning yellow hair and a baby face, is disguised, precisely, as a fat infant, with rubberised pants bulging over a nappy, short white socks, patent-leather bootees, and a bib; he is sucking a celluloid coral of the kind babies are for ever sticking in their mouths, and in his hand he holds a giant feeding bottle with marked levels alluding in colloquial or vulgar terms to the sexual exploits and fiascos which are supposed to correspond to the amount of alcohol absorbed: *C'mon baby*, *Get right on and you'll see the sights*, *The Bridge over the River Kwai*, *Money back if not satisfied*, *Come again*, *Rock-a-bye baby*, *Lights out*, etc.

The painter of this picture was Geneviève's agnate grandfather, Louis Foulerot, better known as an interior designer than as an artist. He was the only member of the Foulerot family not to disown the girl when she decided to keep and raise her child and ran away from home. Louis Foulerot agreed to meet the costs of doing up his granddaughter's flat, and it seems he has done her proud; the structural work is finished, the kitchen and bathroom are ready, painting and finishing are in progress.

His painting was inspired by a detective story – *The Murder of the*

Goldfish – the reading of which gave him such pleasure as to make him think of using it as the subject of a picture which would bring almost all the elements of the mystery together into a single scene.

The action is set in an area quite reminiscent of the Italian lakes, not far from an imaginary city which the author named Valdrada. The narrator is a painter. Whilst he is working in the countryside, a young shepherdess comes up to him. She has heard a loud scream coming from the luxurious villa recently rented to a hugely rich Swiss diamond-trader called Oswald Zeitgeber. In the company of the girl, the painter lets himself into the house and finds the victim: the jeweller, wearing a fancy-dress uniform, lies struck down, blasted to death by an electric shock, next to the telephone. A footstool has been placed in the centre of the room, and a rope tied into a slipknot hangs from the chandelier. The goldfish in the bowl are dead.

Detective Inspector Waldemar, who conveniently takes the painter-narrator as his confidant, is in charge of the investigation. He searches every room in the villa thoroughly, and has many forensic tests done in the lab. The most revealing clues are all inside the school desk: found in it are, item a, a live tarantula; item b, the classified advertisement about the rental of the villa; item c, the programme of a fancy-dress ball held on the evening of the crime, with the singer Mickey Malleville in person as a special attraction; and item d, an envelope containing a blank sheet on which the following cutting from an African daily has been simply glued:

> BAMAKO (APA). *16 June.* A mass grave containing the bones of at least 49 human corpses has been discovered near Fouïdra. First reports suggest that the bodies were buried 30 years ago. An enquiry is taking place.

Three people had called on Oswald Zeitgeber that day. They had all arrived more or less at the same time – the painter saw them drop in one after the other at intervals of a few minutes – and left together. All three were in fancy dress for the ball. They were quickly identified and questioned separately.

The first person to have come was the Quaker lady. She is called Madame Quaston. She claims she came to offer her services as charlady, but nobody can prove it. Moreover, the investigation soon discovers that her daughter had been Madame Zeitgeber's maid and had drowned in circumstances that remained obscure.

The second caller was the man wearing the Fool's suit. His name is Jarrier; he owns the villa. He came, he says, to see if his tenant had settled in and to get his signature on the inventory of furniture and fittings. Madame Quaston had been present at the interview and can confirm his statement; she adds that scarcely had he arrived than Jarrier nearly came a cropper on the newly polished parquet floor, but had caught himself on the windowsill, spilling half the contents of the goldfish bowl onto a rug placed near the wall-mounted telephone.

The third visitor was the big baby: he is the singer Mickey Malleville. He confesses straightaway that he is none other than Oswald Zeitgeber's son-in-law, and that he had come to borrow money from him. Jarrier and Madame Quaston both confirm that when the singer came in, the jeweller almost immediately asked them to leave the two of them alone. A little later he called them back in, apologised for not accompanying them to the ball, but promised to come along later when he had dealt with some urgent telephone calls. The painter saw the three disguises pass by again and even when, he says, he saw them from the front walking side by side across the whole width of the little lane, he could not avoid having an unpleasant impression. About an hour later the shepherdess heard the scream.

The cause of death is easily established: there was a long metal plate beneath the rug: when he used the telephone, Zeitgeber caused a short circuit, which was what killed him. Only Jarrier could have fitted the plate, and it becomes immediately obvious that it was so as to cause an electrocution that he had arranged to soak the rug with water on entering the room; then two more details of even greater significance are discovered: first, that it was Jarrier who had given Zeitgeber his fancy dress for the ball, and the steel tips and spurs on the boots and all the metallic decorations of the jacket were also intended to facilitate the conduction of an electric current; second, and most important, that Jarrier had adapted the telephone fixture so that the fatal short could only occur if the victim, identified by his very disguise – Zeitgeber in his superconductive suit – dialled a particular number: that of the surgery where Jarrier's wife worked!

Confronted with these damning pieces of evidence, Jarrier confesses almost straight away: a pathologically jealous man, he had noticed that Oswald Zeitgeber – whose philandering was notorious throughout the area – was chasing after his wife. Wanting to resolve his suspicions, he designed a homicidal device which would not be triggered unless the jeweller was truly guilty, that is to say unless he telephoned the surgery.

Even if the motive was manifestly imaginary – Madame Jarrier weighs twenty stone, and anyone "chasing after" her would catch up with her without much effort – the murder was nonetheless premeditated by Jarrier: he is charged, arrested, and held in custody. But that clearly doesn't satisfy the detective or the reader: the death of the goldfish, the hangman's noose, the tarantula, the envelope with its African cutting remain unexplained, as does Waldemar's latest discovery: a long pin, like a hatpin but without a head, found buried in the pot of mignonette. As for the forensic tests, they produce two results: first, the fish were poisoned by a fast-acting substance called fibrotoxin; second, on the tip of the pin there are traces of a much slower poison, hydantergotine.

After various subplots have been worked out, and after various false trails have been followed and abandoned – suspicions being entertained respectively as to the possible guilt of Madame Jarrier, Madame Zeitgeber, the painter, the shepherd girl, and one of the organisers of the fancy-dress ball – the perverse and polymorphous solution of this indulgent brainteaser is finally found, and it allows Detective Inspector Waldemar, at one of those gatherings at the scene of the crime, with all the surviving actors present, and without which a detective novel would not be a detective novel, to reconstruct the whole affair with brilliance: obviously all three are guilty, and each was acting on a different motive.

Madame Quaston – whose daughter, pursued by the old lecher, had to jump into a lake to save her honour – had introduced herself to the diamond-trader claiming she was a clairvoyant, and set about reading the lines in his hand: she took advantage of this to prick him with her pin, smeared with a poison which she knew would take some time to have an effect. Then she hid the pin in the mignonette and put the tarantula, concealed so far in the lid of her pickle jar, in the desk: she knew that a tarantula sting provokes reactions similar to the effects of her poison, and though she was aware that the subterfuge would be unmasked eventually she thought, rather naïvely, that it would mislead the investigators for long enough to allow her to escape scot-free.

Mickey Malleville, for his part, the victim's son-in-law, a failed singer riddled with debt, unable to foot the extravagant bills run up by the jeweller's daughter – a scatterbrain accustomed to yachts, breitschwanzes and caviar – knew that his father-in-law's death alone could save him from his ever more inextricable plight: he had nonchalantly poured into the water jug the contents of a small phial of fibrotoxin hidden in the teat of his giant bottle.

But the real bottom of this business, the story's ultimate twist, its terminal turn, its final revelation and closing fall, was something entirely different: the letter Oswald Zeitgeber was reading sealed his own death warrant: the mass grave recently unearthed in Africa was all that was left of an insurgent village whose entire population he had had killed and which he had razed to the ground before pillaging a fabulous elephant graveyard. From this crime committed in cold blood came his colossal fortune. The man who sent him the letter had been on his trail for twenty years, restlessly seeking evidence of Zeitgeber's guilt: now he had the evidence, and the news would be out next day in all the Swiss papers. Zeitgeber had that confirmed to him on the telephone by his associates who had been accomplices in the old business and who, like him, had received the letter: none saw any way out of the scandal except death.

So Zeitgeber went to get a stool and a rope to hang himself. But first, maybe with a superstitious feeling that he had to do one good deed before dying, he saw that the goldfish did not have enough water and emptied the jug of water into the bowl which Jarrier had spilt on purpose when he came. Then he set up his rope. But the first symptoms of hydantergotine poisoning (nausea, cold sweat, stomach cramp, palpitations) were already upon him and, bent double by the pain, he called the lady doctor – not because he was remotely in love with her (in fact he had his eye rather more on the barefoot shepherdess) but to ask for help.

Does a man about to commit suicide worry that much about stomach pains? The novelist was aware of the question and added a postscript where he specified that hydantergotine produces alongside its toxic effects a pseudohallucinatory psychic state, in which the jeweller's reactions would not be unimaginable.

THE FIFTY-FIRST CHAPTER

Valène (Servants' Quarters, 9)

He would be in the painting himself, in the manner of those Renaissance painters who reserved for themselves a tiny place in the midst of the crowd of vassals, soldiers, bishops, or burghers; not a central place, not a significant or privileged place at a chosen intersection, along a particular axis, in this or that illuminating perspective, in the line of any deeply meaningful gaze which could give rise to a reinterpretation of the whole painting, but an apparently inoffensive place, as if it had been done just like that, in passing, a little accidentally, because the idea had arisen without his knowing why, as if he had not wanted it to be too noticeable, as if it were only supposed to be a signature to be read by initiates, something like a mark which the commissioning buyer would only just tolerate the painter signing his work with, something to be known only to a few and forgotten straightaway: as soon as the painter died, it would become an anecdote to be handed down from generation to generation, from studio to studio, a legend people would no longer believe in until, one day, proof of its truth would be found, thanks to a chance cross-reference, or by comparing the picture with preparatory sketches unearthed in the attic of a gallery, or even in a completely haphazard fashion, just as when reading a book you come across sentences you have read before somewhere else: and maybe people would realise then what had always been a bit special about that little figure, not just the greater care taken with the facial detail, but a greater blankness, or a certain way he tips his head imperceptibly to one side, something that might resemble understanding, a certain gentleness, joy tinged perhaps with nostalgia.

*　　*　　*

He would be in the painting himself, in his bedroom, almost at the top on the right, like an attentive little spider weaving his shimmering web, standing, beside his painting, with his palette in his hand, with his long grey smock all stained with paint, and his violet scarf.

He would be standing beside his almost finished painting, and he would be precisely in the process of painting himself, sketching in with the tip of his brush the minute silhouette of a painter in a long grey smock and a violet scarf, with his palette in his hand, painting the infinitesimal figurine of a painter painting, once again one of these nested reflections he would have wanted to pursue to infinite depths, as if his eyes and his hand had unlimited magnifying power.

He would paint himself painting, and already you would be able to see the ladles and knives, the serving spoons and door handles, the books and newspapers, the rugs, jugs, firedogs, umbrella stands, dishstands, radios, bedside lamps, telephones, mirrors, toothbrushes, washing lines, playing cards, cigarette stubs in ashtrays, family photographs in insect-repellent frames, flowers in vases, radiator shelves, potato mashers, floor protectors, bunches of keys in saucers of small change, sorbet makers, catboxes, racks of mineral water, cradles, kettles, alarm clocks, Pigeon lamps, and universal spanners. And Dr Dinteville's two plaited raffia pot-holders, Cinoc's four calendars, Berger's Tonkinese landscape, Gaspard Winckler's carved chest, Madame Orlowska's lectern, the Tunisian babouches Béatrice Breidel brought back for Mademoiselle Crespi, the manager's kidney table, Madame Marcia's mechanical toy and her son David's map of Namur, Anne Breidel's pages of equations, the spice box belonging to Madame Marcia's cook, Dinteville's Admiral Nelson, the Altamonts' Chinese chairs and their precious tapestry depicting amorous old folk, Nieto's lighter, Jane Sutton's macintosh, Smautf's sea chest, the Plassaerts' starry wallpaper, Geneviève Foulerot's mother-of-pearl oyster shell, Cinoc's printed bedspread with its large triangular leaves and the Réols' synthetic leather bed – *doeskin style, master saddler finish, strap and chrome-plated buckle* – Gratiolet's theorbo, the curious coffee boxes in Bartlebooth's dining room and the shadowless light of his scialytic lamp, the Louvets' exotic carpet and the Marquiseaux', the mail on the concierge's table,

Olivia Rorschach's big cut-glass chandelier, Madame Albin's carefully wrapped objects, the antique stone lion found by Hutting at Thuburbo Majus, and all around the long procession of his characters with their stories, their pasts, their legends:

1 The Coronation at Covadonga of Alkhamah's victor, Don Pelage

2 The Russian singer and Schönberg living in Holland as exiles

3 The deaf cat on the top floor with one blue & one yellow eye

4 Barrels of sand being filled by order of the fumbling cretin

5 The miserly old woman marking all her expenses in a notebook

6 The puzzlemaker's backgammon game giving him his bad tempers

7 The concierge watering potted plants for residents when away

8 The parents naming their son Gilbert after Bécaud their idol

9 A bigamous count's wife accepting his Turkish female rescuer

10 The businesswoman, regretting that she had to leave the land

11 The boy taking down the bins dreaming how to write his novel

12 The Australian round-the-worlder and her well-dressed nephew

13 The anthropologist, failing to locate the ever-evasive tribe

14 The cook's refusal of an oven with the self-cleansing device

15 1% sacrificed to art by the MD of a world-wide hotel company

16 The nurse casually leafing through a shiny new photomagazine

17 The poet who went on a pilgrimage shipwrecked at Arkhangelsk

18 The impatient Italian violinplayer who riled his miniaturist

19 The fat, sausage-eating couple keeping their wireless set on

20 The one-armed officer after the bombardment of General H.-Q.

21 The daughter's sad reveries, at the side of her father's bed

22 Austrian customers getting just *the* steamiest "Turkish Bath"

23 The Paraguayan odd-job man, getting ready to ignite a letter

24 The billionaire sporting knickerbockers to practice painting

25 The Woods & Water Dept. official opens a sanctuary for birds

26 The widow with her souvenirs wrapped in old weekly magazines

27 An international thief taken to be a high-ranking magistrate
28 Robinson Crusoe leading a very decent life style on his isle
29 The domino-playing rodent who feasted on dried-out Edam rind
30 The suffering "word-snuffer" messing around in old bookshops

31 The black-clad investigator selling the latest key to dreams
32 The man in vegetable oils opening a fish restaurant in Paris
33 The famous old soldier killed by a loose Venetian chandelier
34 The injured cyclist who then married his pace-maker's sister
35 The cook whose master ingested only eggs and poached haddock
36 The newly-weds taking credit over 2 yrs to have a luxury bed
37 The art dealer's deserted wife, left for an Italian Angelina
38 The childhood friend reading the biographies of her 5 nieces
39 The gentleman who inserted into bottles figures made of cork
40 An archaeologist researching the Arab kings' Spanish capital

41 The Pole living quietly in the Oise now his clowning is over
42 The hag who cut the hot water to stop her son-in-law shaving
43 A Dutchman who knew any No. could be but the sum of K primes
44 Robert Scipion devising his supremely clever cross-word clue
45 The scientist learning to lip-read the deaf-mute's equations
46 The Albanian terrorist serenading his love, an American star
47 The Stuttgarter businessman wanting to roast his leg of boar
48 Dodéca's owner's son preferring the porn trade to priesthood
49 A barman speaking pidgin in order to swap his mother-goddess
50 The boy seeing in his dream the cake he had not been allowed

51 7 actors each refusing the role after they'd seen the script
52 A deserter from US forces in Korea allowing his squad to die
53 The superstar who started out as a sex-changed guitar-player
54 A redheaded white man enjoying a rich maharajah's tiger hunt
55 A liberal grandfather moved to creation by a detective story
56 The expert penman copying *suras* from the Koran in the casbah
57 Angelica's aria from Arconati's *Orlando* requested by Orfanik
58 The actor plotting suicide with the help of a foster brother

59 Her arm held high a Japanese athlete bears the Olympic torch
60 Embattled Aetius stopping the Huns on the Catalaunian Fields

61 Selim's arrow hitting the end wall of a room 888 metres long
62 The staff sergeant deceasing because of his rubber-gum binge
63 The mate of the *Fox* alighting on Fitz-James's final messages
64 The student staying in a room for six months without budging
65 The producer's wife off yet again on a trip around the globe
66 The central-heating engineer making sure the fueljet ignites
67 The executive who entertained all his workmates very grandly
68 The boy sorting medical blotters he'd been collecting avidly
69 The actor-cook hired by an American lady who was hugely rich
70 The former croupier who turned into a shy, retiring old lady

71 The technician trying a new experiment, and losing 3 fingers
72 The young lady living in the Ardennes with a Belgian builder
73 The Dr's ancestor nearly solving the synthetic gem conundrum
74 The ravishing American magician and Mephisto agreeing a deal
75 The curio dealer's son in red leather on his Guzzi motorbike
76 The principal destroying the secrets of the German scientist
77 The historian, turned down 46 times, burning his 1200-pp. MS
78 A Jap who turned a quartz watch Co into a gigantic syndicate
79 The Swedish diplomat trying madly to avenge his son and wife
80 The delayed voyager begging to have her green beans returned

81 The star seeking admission by meditating a recipe for afters
82 The lady who was interested in hoarding clockwork mechanisms
83 The magician guessing answers with digits selected at random
84 The Russian prince presenting a mahogany sofa shaped in an S
85 The superfluous driver playing cardgames to use up his hours
86 A medic, hoping to make a mark on gastronomy with crab salad
87 An optimistic engineer liquidating his exotic hides business

88 The Japanese sage initiating in great anguish Three Free Men
89 A selftaught old man again going over his sanatorium stories
90 A relative twice removed, obliged to auction his inheritance

91 Customs & Excise men unpacking the raging princess's samovar
92 The trader in Indian cotton goods doing up a flat on the 8th
93 French-style overtures brought to the Hamburg Opera by a Hun
94 Marguerite, restoring things seen through a magnifying glass
95 The puzzlemaker with his ginger cat taking the name of Chéri
96 The nightclub waiter, legging up on stage to start a cabaret
97 The rich amateur leaving his musical collection to a library
98 A housing and estate agency woman looking at that empty flat
99 The lady doing the Englishman's black cardboard puzzle boxes
100 The critic committing 4 crimes for 1 of Percival's seascapes

101 The Praetor ordering 30000 Lusitanians to be killed in a day
102 A student in a long coat staring at a map of the Paris metro
103 The building manager, trying to solve his cash-flow problems
104 The girl studying the craftsman's rings to sell in her store
105 Nationalists fighting the Damascene publisher who was French
106 A little girl gnawing at the edges of her shortbread cookies
107 The maid, imagining she'd seen the evil eye in an undertaker
108 A painstaking scientist examining rats' reactions to poisons
109 The pranking student who put beef stock in vegetarians' soup
110 A workman gazing at his letter, as he leaves with two others

111 The aged gentleman's gentleman recomputing his *n*th factorial
112 The staggered priest offering help to a Frenchman lost in NY
113 The druggist spending his fortune on the Holy Vase of Joseph
114 The jigsaw glue being perfected by a head of a chemistry lab
115 That gent in a black cloak donning new, tight-fitting gloves
116 Old Guyomard cutting Bellmer's sheet in 2 through the middle
117 Original fine champagne proffered to Colbert by Dom Pérignon
118 A gay waltz being written by an old friend of Liszt & Chopin

119 Agreeably drowsy after lunch, M. Riri sitting at his counter
120 Gallant Amerigo learning a continent was to be named America

121 Mark Twain reading his obituary long before he'd intended to
122 The woman polishing a dagger that was Kléber's murder weapon
123 The college endowed by its ex-rector, an expert in philology
124 The single mother reading Pirandello's story of Daddi, Romeo
125 The historian who used pseudonyms to publish rubbishy novels
126 The librarian collecting proof that Hitler continues to live
127 A blind man tuning a Russian prima donna's grand piano-forte
128 A decorator making the most of the young pig's crimson bones
129 The agent trading cowries believing he'd make millions at it
130 The disappointed customer who in dyeing her hair lost it all

131 The assistant librarian using red pencil to ring opera crits
132 The lovelorn coachman who thought he'd heard a rodent mewing
133 The kitchen-lads bringing up hot tasty snacks for a grand do
134 The nurse's milk jug spilt on the carpet by two naughty cats
135 A Tommy and his bride-to-be stuck between floors in the lift
136 The bookdealer who found three of Victor Hugo's original MSS
137 The English "au pair" reading an epistle from her boy-friend
138 The ordnance general who was shot in the lounge of his hotel
139 The doctor whom loaded fire-arms forced to carry out surgery
140 Safari-buffs with their native guide - posing for the camera

141 The French prof, getting pupils' vacation assignments marked
142 A beautiful Polish woman and her wee son dreaming of Tunisia
143 The judge's spouse whose pearls had cooked black in the fire
144 The cyclist struggling for recognition for his 1-hour record
145 A conscript startled on seeing his old physics schoolteacher
146 The ex-landlord dreaming of a "hero" of the traditional kind
147 A conductor rehearsing his band for 9 weeks, again and again
148 A gifted numerate, aspiring to construct a massive radiomast

149 Antipodean fans giving their idol a present of 71 white mice
150 The Spanish ex-concierge not too keen to unjam the lift door

151 Listening to an enormous phonogram, a smoker of an 89c cigar
152 A choreographer, returning to torment the loveless ballerina
153 The man who delivered wine on a trike doing the hall mirrors
154 An obviously *pornographic* old man waiting at the school gate
155 The botanist hoping an ivory Epiphyllum would carry his name
156 The so-called Russian who solved every brainteaser published
157 The infant Mozart, performing for Louis and Marie-Antoinette
158 A sword-swallower who on medication threw up a load of nails
159 A man who made religious articles dying of cold in the woods
160 Blind horses, deep down in the mine, hauling railway waggons

161 A urologist musing on the arguments of Galen and Asclepiades
162 A handsome pilot looking for the castle at Corbenic on a map
163 The carpenter's workman warming his hands at a woodchip fire
164 Visitors to the Orient trying to solve the magic ring puzzle
165 A ballet maestro beaten to death in the U.S.A. by 3 hoodlums
166 A princess, who said prayers at her regal granddad's bedside
167 The tenant (for 6 wks) insisting on full checks on all pipes
168 A manager who managed to be away for four months in the year
169 A lady who owned a curio shop fishing for a malosol cucumber
170 The man who saw his own death warrant in a newspaper cutting

171 The emperor thinking of the "Eagle" to attack the Royal Navy
172 Famous works improved by a celebrated artist's layer of haze
173 Eugene of Savoy having a list made of the relics of Golgotha
174 In a polka-dot dress, a woman who knitted beside the seaside
175 The Tommies enjoying girls' gym practices on a Pacific beach
176 Gedeon Spilett locating the last match in his trouser pocket
177 A young trapeze artist refusing to climb down from his perch
178 Woodworms' hollow honeycombs solidified by an Italian artist
179 Lonely Valène putting every bit of the block onto his canvas

CHAPTER FIFTY-TWO

Plassaert, 2

One of the rooms in the Plassaerts' flat: the first one they moved into, a little over thirteen years ago, a year before their child was born. A few years later Troyan died, and they bought his attic from the manager. Then they bought the room at the bottom of the corridor from the Marquiseaux: it was occupied by an old man called Troquet who eked out a living by collecting empty glass bottles; he would reclaim the deposit on them but kept some for himself, into which he would fit little figures made of cork representing drinkers, boxers, sailors, Maurice Chevalier, General de Gaulle, etc., which he would sell to Sunday strollers on the Champs-Elysées. The Plassaerts immediately started proceedings to obtain an eviction order because Troquet didn't pay his rent regularly, and, as Troquet was halfway to being a tramp, they won easily.

In the first of the two bedrooms there had once lived for two years a curious young man by the name of Grégoire Simpson. He was a history student. He worked for a time as assistant sub-librarian at the Bibliothèque de l'Opéra. His work was far from fascinating: a wealthy amateur, Henri Astrat, had bequeathed to the library a collection of documents he had spent forty years of his life assembling. He was passionately keen on opera and had practically not missed a single first night since nineteen ten, thinking nothing of crossing the Channel or even the Atlantic a couple of times to hear Fürtwangler conducting the *Ring*, Tebaldi singing Desdemona, or Callas playing Norma.

For each performance Astrat made up a file of press reviews, together with the programme – fulsomely autographed by the conductor and performers – and, depending on the nature of the occasion, various items from the costumes and sets: violet braces worn by Mario del Monaco in the role of Rodolfo (*La Bohème*, Covent Garden, Neapolitan Opera, 1946), Victor de Sabata's baton, the score of *Lohengrin* annotated by Heinz Tietjen for his historic production in Berlin in 1929, the models for the set designed by Emil Preetorius for the same production, the false marble mask which Karl Böhm had Haig Clifford wear for the part of the Commendatore in the production of *Don Giovanni* he put on at the Urbino *Maggio musicale*, etc.

Henri Astrat's bequest came with an income attached to it intended to subsidise the continuation of this specialist archive, the only one of its kind in the world. The Bibliothèque de l'Opéra was therefore able to establish an Astrat Collection consisting of three exhibition and reading rooms, watched over by two guards, and two offices occupied respectively by the curator and a sub-librarian, together with a part-time assistant sub-librarian. The curator – a professor of art history specialising in Renaissance *fêtes* – received people entitled to consult the archive – researchers, theatre critics, theatre historians, musicologists, directors, designers, musicians, costumiers, actors, etc. – and organised exhibitions (Homage to the Met, One Hundred Years of *La Traviata*, etc.); the sub-librarian read almost all Paris dailies and a significant number of weeklies, magazines, reviews, and miscellaneous periodicals, ringing in red pencil all articles dealing with opera in general ("Will the Opéra be closed?", "Plans for the Opéra", "Where the Opéra is at", "The ghost of the Opéra: myth and reality", etc.) or with a particular opera; the part-time assistant sub-librarian cut out the red-ringed articles and put them loose into "provisional clips" (PC) held together by elastic; after an interval of variable length, but generally never longer than six weeks, the press cuttings (also abbreviated to PC) were got out of the PCs, stuck on sheets (21cm × 27cm) of white paper, and inscribed in red ink, at the top, from left to right, with: title of work in upper case with double underlining; genre (opera, light opera, opera-bouffe, dramatic oratorio, vaudeville, operetta, etc.); name of composer; name of conductor; name of producer; place of performance in upper case with single underlining; and date of first public performance; the cuttings thus mounted were then returned to their clips but instead of being held together by elastic they were now tied with flax laces, which made them "Buffer Files" (BF) to be kept in a glass-fronted cupboard in the office of the sub-librarian and part-time assistant sub-librarian (SL2PT); after a few weeks, when it had long been clear that no further articles would be published on the relevant performance, the BF would be transferred to one of the big wire-mesh-fronted cupboards in the exhibition and reading rooms where it finally became a "Shelved File" (SF) of the same status as the rest of the Astrat Collection, viz. "available for consultation on the premises to holders of full reader's cards or a special authorisation issued by the Curator i/c the Collection" (Summary of Statutes, article XVIII, §3, clause *c*).

Unfortunately this part-time job was not renewed. An auditor brought in to discover the cause of the inexplicable deficits incurred each year by libraries in general and by the Bibliothèque de l'Opéra in particular opined in his report that two guards for three rooms were too many, and that one hundred and seventy-five francs and eighteen centimes a month for cutting articles out of newspapers was one hundred and seventy-five francs and eighteen centimes wasted, since a single guard with nothing to do but guard could just as easily guard whilst cutting cuttings. The sub-librarian, a shy lady of fifty with sad eyes and a hearing aid, tried to explain that such comings and goings of PCs and BFs between her office and the exhibition and reading rooms would be a constant source of bother likely to do great harm to the SFs – which turned out to be the case – but the curator, only too happy to keep his own job at least, fully shared the auditor's opinion and, "determined to staunch the chronic financial haemorrhage" of his department, resolved 1) that there would be henceforth one guard only, 2) that there would be henceforth no part-time assistant sub-librarian (SL2PT), 3) that the exhibition and reading rooms would be open to the public henceforth on only three afternoons a week, 4) that the sub-librarian would cut out the articles she considered "most important" herself, and give the remainder to the guard to cut out, and, lastly, 5) that as an economy measure, cuttings would be stuck henceforth on recto and verso sides of the sheets.

Grégoire Simpson completed the academic year by finding various temporary jobs: he showed flats for sale to potential buyers, inviting them to climb on kitchen stools so they could see for themselves that by craning the neck only a little they had a view of the Sacré-Cœur, he had a go at doorstep selling, hawking "artbooks" up staircases, as well as ghastly encyclopaedias prefaced by senescent celebrities, "unlabelled" handbags which were just bad copies of mediocre originals, "young people's" magazines of the *Do You Like Students?* kind, and doilies embroidered in orphanages and mats plaited by the blind. And Morellet, his neighbour, who had just had the accident which robbed him of three fingers, entrusted him with finding customers in the *quartier* for his soaps, his air-fresheners, his fly-killer discs, and his hair and carpet shampoos.

The following year Grégoire Simpson won a scholarship which came to not very much but was at least enough to live on without his being absolutely obliged to find work. But instead of studying hard and completing his degree, he fell into a sort of neurasthenia, a strange lethargy from which nothing, it seemed, could arouse him. Those who had occasion to meet him at this time had the feeling he was in a state of weightlessness, in a kind of sensorial void, a condition of total indifference: indifferent to the weather, to the time of day, to the information which the external world continued to address to him but which he seemed ever less inclined to receive: he began to lead a drab kind of life, wearing the same clothes every day, dining every day at the same hot-dog stall, standing at the counter, eating the same meal: a full-course menu, that is to say steak and French fries, a large glass of red wine, and a coffee, reading *Le Monde* line by line every evening in the back of a café, spending whole days playing patience or washing three of his four pairs of socks or one of his three shirts in a pink plastic bowl.

Then came the period of his long walks around Paris. He let himself wander, going wherever the whim took him, plunging into the five-o'clock bustle of office workers. He trailed along shopfronts, went into all the art galleries, walked slowly through the arcades in the IXth *arrondissement*, stopping at every store. He stared with equal attention at rustic washstands in furniture stores, bedheads and springs in mattress-makers' windows, artificial wreaths in undertakers' shopfronts, curtain rails in haberdasheries, "erotic" playing cards with macromammaried pin-ups in novelty stores (*Mann sprich deutsche*, *English speaken*), the yellowing photographs advertising Art Studios: a moon-faced urchin in a vulgarly-cut sailor suit, an ugly boy in a cricket cap, a pug-nosed youth, a rather repellent bulldog type of man by a brand-new car; in a pork-butcher's, Chartres Cathedral in lard; the humorous visiting cards in a joke-shop window display

Adolf Hitler

German Lieder

Frank F Herder

Sausagemaker

Mr and Mrs FLIESS
of Wool (Dorset)
are happy to announce
the birth of their son
SEAN

MADELEINE PROUST
" Souvenirs "

DR IVOR PAZ-TOMACEK
Gastro-enterologist

MD, DM

the faded visiting cards and letterhead- and announcement-style models in typesetters' windows

LE PANNEAU METALLISE
S.A.R.L. AU CAPITAL DE
6 810 000 F

Marcel-Emile Burnachs, S.A.
"Tout pour les Tapis"

ASSOCIATION
DES ANCIENS ELEVES
DU COLLEGE GEOFFROY SAINT-HILAIRE

Sometimes he invented ridiculous constraints for himself, such as listing all the Russian restaurants in the XVIIth *arrondissement* or working out an itinerary which would pass by each one without ever crossing over its own track, but usually he chose a trivial target – the one hundred and forty-seventh bench, the eight thousand two hundred and thirty-seventh step – and he would spend several hours sitting on the green slats of the bench with its cast-iron lion-paw ferrules somewhere near Denfert-Rochereau or Château-Landon, or stand stock still like a statue in front of a shopfitter's shop showing not only wasp-waisted dummies and display trays displaying only themselves, but also a whole range of advertising streamers, stickers, and shop signs

SALE

Discontinued Styles

BARGAIN ITEM

NEW STOCK

Our Very Latest Creation

EXCLUSIVE

which he would stare at for minutes at a stretch as if he were still endlessly ruminating the logical paradox inherent in these kinds of shop windows.

Later, he began to stay in his room, losing little by little all sense of time. One day his alarm clock stopped at a quarter past five, and he did not bother to wind it up again; sometimes his light stayed on all night; sometimes a day, two days, three days, and even a whole week would go by without his leaving his room except to go to the toilet at the end of the corridor. Sometimes he went out at ten p.m. and returned the next morning, unaltered, showing no apparent sign of his sleepless night; he went to see films in filthy cinemas on the Grands Boulevards that stank of disinfectant; he haunted all-night cafés, playing pinball for hours on end or gazing, bleary-eyed, across his filter coffee at merry revellers, gloomy boozers, fat butchers, sailors, and tarts.

For the last six months he virtually stopped going out altogether. From time to time he would be seen at the baker's in Rue Léon-Jost (which almost everyone still called Rue Roussel at that time); he would put a twenty-centime coin on the glass pane of the counter, and if the baker-woman raised a questioning eye at him – which happened a few times at the start – he merely indicated by a nod of his head the stick loaves stacked in their wicker baskets and made a kind of scissor gesture with his left hand, meaning he wanted only half a loaf.

He no longer spoke to anyone, and when spoken to replied only with a sort of low grunt which discouraged any attempt at conversation. From time to time he could be seen opening his door a crack to make sure there was no one at the top on the landing before going to fill his pink plastic bowl.

One day Troyan, his neighbour on the right, coming home around two in the morning, saw that the light was still on in the student's room; he knocked, got no reply, knocked again, waited a moment, pushed open the door, which was not properly shut, and found Grégoire Simpson curled up like a sleeping child on his bed but with his eyes wide open, smoking a cigarette clasped between his medius and ring fingers, using a slipper for an ashtray. He didn't raise his head when Troyan entered, he didn't answer when the bookseller asked him if he felt ill, if he wanted a glass of water, if he needed anything, and it was only when the other man touched his shoulder gently, as if to make sure he wasn't dead, that he swung himself round all at once to face the wall and whispered: "Fuck off".

A few days later he disappeared completely and no one ever knew what became of him. The general opinion in the building was that he had committed suicide, and some people even stated that he had done it by jumping under a train from the Pont Cardinet. But nobody ever came up with the evidence.

After a month, the manager, who owned the room, had it sealed by bailiffs; after the second month had passed he had the premises certified vacant by legal officers and threw away the few paltry belongings found there: a narrow bench barely long enough to be used as a bed, a pink plastic bowl, a few dirty shirts and socks, piles of old newspapers, a set of fifty-two stained, greasy, torn playing cards, an alarm clock stopped at five fifteen, a metal stem with a ribbed bolt at one end and a spring-loaded flap at the other, a reproduction of a quattrocento portrait of a man with a face both vigorous and fat and a tiny scar above his upper lip, a portable record player in a grenadine pegamoid case, a fan heater, blower type, *Congo* model, and a few dozen books including Raymond Aron, *Eighteen Lectures on Industrial Society*, dropped at page 112, and volume VII of Fliche and Martin's monumental *History of the Church*, borrowed sixteen months previously from the Teachers' Institute Library.

Despite the sound of his name, Grégoire Simpson was not in the least English. He came from Thonon-les-Bains. One day, well before his fatal hibernation had gripped him, he had told Morellet how as a little boy he had played drum major with the *Matagassiers* on mid-Lent Sunday. His mother, a dressmaker, made the traditional costume herself: the red-and-white-squared trousers, the loose blue blouse, the white cotton bonnet with a tassel; and his father had bought him, in a fine circular box decorated with arabesques, the cardboard mask which looked like a cat's head. As proud as Punch and as grave as a judge, he ran through the streets of the old town along with the procession, from the Place du Château to the Porte des Allinges, and from the Porte de Rives to Rue Saint-Sébastien, before going up into the high town, to the Belvederes, to stuff himself with juniper-roast ham and to slake his thirst with great gulps of Ripaille, that white wine as light as glacier water, as dry as gunflint.

CHAPTER FIFTY-THREE

Winckler, 3

The third room in Gaspard Winckler's flat.

It was there that the picture used to be, opposite the bed, beside the window, the square picture which the puzzle-maker liked so much and which showed three men in black, in an antechamber; it wasn't a painting, but a retouched photograph, cut from *La Petite Illustration* or *La Semaine Théâtrale*. It depicted Act III, scene 1, of *Lost Ambitions*, a sombre melodrama by a mediocre imitator of Henry Bernstein called Paulin-Alfort, and showed the two seconds of the hero (played by Max Corneille) coming to fetch him at his home half an hour before the duel in which he would meet his death.

Marguerite had found the photograph at the bottom of a box of secondhand books of the kind you could still find at the time under the arches of the Théâtre de l'Odéon: she had stuck it onto canvas, mounted it, coloured it, framed it, and given it to Gaspard as a present on their moving into Rue Simon-Crubellier.

Of all the rooms in the building, this is the one Valène remembered best, this quiet and rather heavy bedroom with its high, dark, wooden skirting board, its bed covered with a mauve quilted bedspread, its turned-wood shelf-stacks collapsing under the weight of unsorted books, and, in front of the window, the table where Marguerite used to work.

He remembered her peering through a magnifying glass at the delicate arabesques on one of those gilded cardboard Venetian boxes with their embossed scallops, or preparing her paints on a minute ivory palette.

She was pretty, to a modest degree: a pale skin dotted with freckles, slightly hollowed cheeks, grey-blue eyes.

She was a miniaturist. She did not often paint original subjects: she preferred to copy or to base her work on pre-existing material; for example, she drew the design of the sample puzzle Winckler had cut for Bartlebooth from prints published in *Le Journal des Voyages*. She could reproduce miraculously even the tiniest, almost imperceptible details of the minuscule scenes depicted on the inside lids of fob watches and snuff boxes and the cover-pages of Lilliputian prayer books; and she could also restore snuff boxes, fans, candy boxes, and medallions. Her customers were private collectors, curio dealers, ceramics manufacturers wanting to issue copies of prestigious dinner sets (Napoleon's return from Egypt, Malmaison), jewellers who would ask her to paint (from a photograph of often doubtful authenticity) the portrait of the loved one on the back of a pendant intended to contain a single wisp of hair, and specialist booksellers for whom she would retouch romantic vignettes or the illuminations of hour-books.

Her meticulousness, her carefulness, and her cleverness were extraordinary. Into a frame measuring four centimetres long by three wide, she could get a whole landscape with a pale-blue sky dotted with white clouds, a horizon of softly undulating hills with vine-covered slopes, a château, two roads at the junction of which there galloped a rider dressed in red on a bay horse, a cemetery with two gravediggers carrying spades, a cypress, two olive trees, a river flanked by poplars with three fishermen sitting by the bank and, in a punt, two little characters dressed in white.

Or on the flat part of the enamelled face of a signet ring she could restore a mysterious landscape where beneath a dawn sky, among pale flowers at the edge of a frozen lake, a donkey sniffed the roots of a tree; on the trunk a grey lantern was nailed; in the branches an empty nest was perched.

Paradoxically for such a precise and measured woman, Marguerite was irresistibly attracted to jumble. Her table was an eternal glory-hole, always stacked with great amounts of useless equipment, piled high with heteroclite objects, invaded by a tide of muddle which she had to stem each time before she set to work: letters, glasses, bottles, labels, quill-stands, matchboxes, cups, tubes, scissors, notebooks, medicines, banknotes, small change, compasses, photographs, press cuttings, stamps; and loose leaves, pages pulled out of writing pads or diaries, letter scales, a brass-rimmed weaver's glass, the heavy cut-glass inkstand, quill boxes, the green and black box of one hundred Republic quills number 705 by Gilbert and Blanzy-Poure and the beige and brown box of one hundred and forty-four rounded quills number 394 by Baignol and Farjon, the horn-handled paperknife, rubbers, boxes of drawing pins and paperclips, nailfiles and emerised cardboard, and the everlasting flower in its Kirby Beard soliflor, and the packet of *Athletic* cigarettes with the sprinter in the blue-and-white-striped vest sporting a red number 39 tag crossing the finishing line far ahead of the others, and the keys linked together on a little chain, the yellow wooden ruler, the tin marked CURIOUSLY STRONG ALTOIDS PEPPERMINT OIL, the blue china pot with all its crayons, the onyx paperweight, the little hemispherical bowls, somewhat similar to those used as eye-baths (or for cooking snails), in which she mixed her colours, and the silver-plated assay-dish whose two sections were always filled with salted pistachios on the one side and violet sweets on the other.

Only a cat could move amongst these piles without setting off a landslide, and, as it happened, Gaspard and Marguerite did have a cat, a big red tom they had first called Leroux, then Gaston, then Chéri Bibi, then, in a final aphetism, Ribibi, who liked nothing better than walking amongst all these things without disturbing them in the slightest, ending up squatting quite comfortably in them, unless he settled on his mistress's neck, letting his paws hang lazily down on either side.

Marguerite told Valène one day how she had met Gaspard Winckler. It was on a November morning in 1930 in Marseilles, in a café in Rue Bleue, not far from the arsenal and Saint-Charles barracks. Outside, a thin cold drizzle was falling. She was wearing a grey suit and a black oilskin, fastened at the waist by a broad belt. She was nineteen, had just returned to France, and, standing at the counter, was drinking a black coffee whilst reading the small ads in the *Dernières Nouvelles de Marseille*. The café owner, a man named La Brigue but as unlike the character from the plays of Courteline as could be imagined, was eyeing with suspicion a soldier who, he seemed to have assumed in advance, would not have the wherewithal to pay for his *café au lait* and buttered bread.

It was Gaspard Winckler, and the café owner wasn't very wide of the mark: the death of Monsieur Gouttman had left his apprentice in a difficult situation; scarcely nineteen years of age, a master of many skills but without a real trade, Winckler had virtually no experience of professional life and had neither a home nor a friend nor a family: for when he was expelled from Charny by the owner of the house Gouttman rented and went back to La Ferté-Milon, it was to discover that his father had died at Verdun, his mother had remarried an insurance agent and was now living in Cairo, and his sister Anne, one year his junior, had just married a certain Cyrille Voltimand, a tiler from the XIXth *arrondissement* of Paris. And that's how one day in March nineteen twenty-nine Gaspard Winckler arrived on foot in the capital, which he was seeing for the first time in his life. He traipsed dutifully up and down the streets of the XIXth *arrondissement* and whenever he met a tiler he asked politely after a Cyrille Voltimand whom he supposed to be his brother-in-law. But he didn't find him and ended up enlisting.

He spent the next eighteen months at a fortalice between Bou-Jeloud and Bab-Fetouh, not far from the Spanish zone of Morocco, where he had almost nothing to do other than to carve over-elaborate skittles for three quarters of the garrison, a job no worse than another and which had the merit of keeping his hand in.

He had returned from Africa the previous day. He had gambled on the crossing and had been stripped of almost his entire gratuity. Marguerite was also jobless, but nonetheless managed to pay for his coffee and buttered bread.

They married a few days later and went up to Paris. The first weeks were hard, but the two of them were lucky enough to find work fairly quickly: Gaspard at a toyshop overwhelmed by the Christmas rush, and Marguerite, a little later, with a collector of antique musical instruments who asked her to decorate, from contemporary documents, a wonderful spinet that was supposed to have belonged to Champion de Chambonnières, and the lid of which had had to be reconstructed. In the midst of a wealth of foliage, garlands, and tracery imitating marquetry, Marguerite painted in two circles, each three centimetres in diameter, two portraits: a young man with a rather weak face, at a three-quarters angle, with a powdered wig, black jacket, yellow waistcoat, white lace cravat, standing, with his elbow leaning on a marble mantelpiece, in front of a half-drawn, salmon-pink curtain partly revealing a window through which could be seen a railing; and a young woman, beautiful and plump, with large brown eyes and crimson cheeks, a powdered wig with a pink ribbon and a rose, and a white muslin shawl that opened wide at the front.

Valène met the Wincklers a few days after they had moved in to Rue Simon-Crubellier, at Bartlebooth's flat, where all three had been invited to dine. He felt himself attracted straight away to this soft and smiling woman who looked upon the world through such limpid eyes. He liked the movements she made to push her hair back; he liked the firm but graceful way she would steady herself by leaning on her left elbow before sketching in with the tip of her hair-thin brush a microscopic green shadow in an eye.

She almost never spoke to him about her family, childhood, travels. Just once she told him she had seen in a dream the house in the country where she had spent all her adolescent summers: it was a big white barn overgrown with clematis, with an attic she was frightened of, and a little cart drawn by a donkey answering to the sweet name of Boniface.

Often, when Winckler shut himself in his workroom, they would go for a walk together. They went to the park at Monceau, or followed the track of the inner circle railway along Boulevard Pereire, or went to see exhibitions in the centre of town, in Boulevard Haussmann, Avenue de Messine, or Rue du Faubourg Saint-Honoré. Sometimes Bartlebooth took all three to visit the Loire châteaux or invited them to stay at Deauville for a few days. Once, even, in the summer of 1937, when he was coasting on board his yacht *Halcyon* off the Adriatic shores, he summoned them to spend two months with him between Trieste and Corfu, having them discover the pink palaces of Pirano, the grand hotels of Portoroz, Diocletian's ruins at Spalato, the myriad Dalmatian islands, Ragusa, which had become Dubrovnik a few years before, and the wild contours of the Boka-Kotorska and Montenegro.

It was during this unforgettable journey that one evening, facing the crenellated walls of Rovigno, Valène declared to the young woman that he loved her, and obtained in reply only an ineffable smile.

Many times he dreamt of eloping with her or fleeing from her, but they stayed where they were, near yet far, in the warmth and in the despair of an insuperable friendship.

She died in November 1943 whilst giving birth to a stillborn child.

For the entire winter, Gaspard Winckler stayed seated at the table where she used to work, holding in his hands, one by one, all the objects she had touched, she had looked at, she had loved, the vitrified pebble with its white, beige, and orange grooves, the little jade unicorn saved from a valuable chess set, and the Florentine brooch he had given her as a present because it had on it, in minute mosaics, three Paris daisies, or marguerites.

Then one day he threw away everything that was on the table, and burnt the table; he took Ribibi to the vet in Rue Alfred-de-Vigny and had him put to sleep; he threw away the books and the turned-wood shelf-stack, the mauve quilted bedspread, the low-backed, black-leather-seated English armchair in which she sat, everything which had her trace, bore her mark, and he kept in the room only the bed and, opposite the bed, that melancholy picture of the three men dressed in black.

Then he went back to his workroom, where eleven watercolours, still untouched in their envelopes bearing Argentinian and Chilean stamps, were waiting to be turned into puzzles.

The bedroom is today a room grey with dust and sadness, an empty, dirty room with faded wallpaper; through the open door that gives onto the broken-down bathroom, you can see a rust-stained, scale-incrusted sink on whose chipped rim a half-drunk bottle of orange pop has spent the last two years going green.

CHAPTER FIFTY-FOUR

Plassaert, 3

Adèle and Jean Plassaert are sitting side by side at their desk, a grey metal structure fitted with hanging file drawers. The worktop is cluttered with open ledgers, their long columns covered in meticulous handwriting. Light comes from an old petrol lamp with a cast-iron stand and two green globes. To one side, a bottle of whisky: *McAnguish's Caledonian Panacea*, with a label depicting a jovial wench giving a dram to a moustachioed grenadier in a bearskin hat.

Jean Plassaert is a short and rather fat man; he is wearing a multicoloured Hawaiian party shirt, and a tie consisting of a bootlace with shiny ends held in a plaited leather woggle. In front of him he has a whitewood box copiously provided with stickers, postage stamps, rubber stamps, red wax seals, and from it he has taken five *art-déco* silver and paste-glass brooches representing five stylised female athletes: a swimmer doing the crawl amidst a wreath of ripples, a skier schussing downhill, a gymnast in a tutu juggling lighted torches, a golfer with raised mashie, and a diver performing a perfect swan. He has laid four of them side by side on his blotting pad and is showing the fifth – the diver – to his wife.

Adèle is a woman of about forty, small, dry, thin-lipped. She is wearing a fur-collared red velvet two-piece suit. In order to look at the brooch which her husband is showing her, she has raised her eyes from the book she has been studying: a bulky guide to Egypt, open at a double-page reproduction of an extract from one of the earliest known dictionaries of Egyptology, F. Rablé's *Libvre mangificque dez Merveyes que pouvent estre vuyes es La Egipte* (Lyons, 1560):

> HIEROGLYPHICKS: Holie inscriptions. Were thus ycleped the lettres of the clerkes of Auntient Egypte made on divers images of trees, grasses, animals, fisshes, briddes, & tools by nature and office of whiche was shewn their designationes.
>
> OBELISKS: Longe and heighe stone bodkins, brode at the foot and tapering to a poinct at yr hede. To be seen at Rome, about the Church of Seint Peter, is one swich intire, and manie others also. Upon those that be aboute an stronde, they weren wont to licht a leming fire the Seylors to avaunce in stormie weather, and weren cleped obeliskolychnies.
>
> PYRAMIDS: Tall and square biltings of stone or brickes, brode at the foot and poincted at the top, in the shap of a flame of fire. Manie are to be seen above the Nil, by Cayre.
>
> CATADUPES of the Nil: a place in the Ethiops' land whereon the Nil falleth from high mountaines in swich horribile noise that men of those parts are almost alle deaf as is wryt by Claude Galen. The noise is herd more an thrie days off,

which is as much as from Paris to Tours.
See Ptol., Cicero in *Som. Scipionis*; Plinius, *lib.* 6, *cap* 9, and Strabo.

The Plassaerts, traders in Indian cotton goods and other exotic merchandise, are organised, efficient, and, in their own words, "professional".

Their first contact with the Far East, about twenty years ago, coincided with their first meeting. That year the Employees' Association of the bank where they were both on placement (he at the Aubervilliers branch, she at Montrouge) organised a trip to Outer Mongolia. The country itself held little interest for them, Ulan Bator Hoto being just a big village with a few official buildings of typically Stalinist design, and the Gobi desert having nothing much to show for itself apart from its horses and a few grinning Mongols with protruding cheekbones and fur hats, but the stop-overs they made in Iran on the outward journey and in Afghanistan on the return filled them with excitement. They shared a taste for travel and for fixing deals; they both possessed a certain kind of unconventional inventiveness, a developed sense of alternative life styles, and considerable resourcefulness; all of which prompted them to pack in the cash counter, where in truth nothing very exalting awaited them, and to set up in the antiques business. With a patched-up truck and a float of a few thousand francs, they started to clear cellars and attics, touring country fairs and on Sunday mornings selling at the then not very popular flea market at Vanves slightly dented hunting horns, mostly incomplete encyclopaedias, silver forks, some flaking, and decorated plates (*A Bad Joke*: a man asleep in a garden, another man stealing up on him, pouring a liquid into his ear; or, on another one, in the middle of a thicket in which the faces of two grinning scamps are hidden, an angry gamekeeper: *Where have those two scoundrels got to?*; or another, showing a very young sailor-suited sword-swallower, with the caption: *One Swallow doesn't make a Mummer*).

Competition was fierce, and though they had flair, they lacked experience; on several occasions they got landed with job lots containing nothing saleable, and the only good deals they pulled off were with stocks of old clothing, RAF jackets, American-style button-down shirts, Swiss moccasins, T-shirts, Davy Crockett headgear, and blue jeans, thanks to which they managed to survive through those years even if they didn't expand.

In the early sixties, not long before they moved into Rue Simon-Crubellier, they came across a most curious character, in a pizzeria in Rue des Ciseaux: a neurasthenic lawyer, of Dutch origin, settled in Indonesia, who had spent many years as the Djakarta agent for several trading companies before setting up his own export-import business. With his remarkable knowledge of all the craft products made in Southeast Asia, having no equal when it came to evading customs controls, or short-circuiting insurance companies and handling agents, or avoiding taxes, he packed three rusty freighters to the gunwales, all year round, with Malaysian seashells, Philippine handkerchiefs, Formosan kimonos, Indian shirts, Nepalese jackets, Afghan furs, Sinhalese lacquers, Macao barometers, Hong Kong toys, and a hundred other kinds of goods from dozens of different places, which he redistributed around Germany with a mark-up of between two and three hundred per cent.

He liked the Plassaerts and decided to give them a commission. For seven francs he would sell them shirts which had cost him three, and which they would resell at seventeen, twenty-one, twenty-five, or thirty francs according to the case. They started off in a tiny cobbler's stall near Place Saint-André-des-Arts. Today they have three stores in Paris, two others in Lille and Cannes, and plan to open a dozen more on a permanent or seasonal basis in spas, on the Atlantic coast, and in winter sports resorts. Meanwhile, they have succeeded in tripling – and soon they will have quadrupled – the floor area of their Parisian apartment and have entirely refurbished a country house near Bernay.

Their business acumen is the perfect complement to their Indonesian associate's commercial talents: not only do they go over there to find local products that can be marketed easily in France, but they also have European knickknacks and jewellery manufactured there on modern-style or *art-déco* patterns: in the Celebes, at Macassar, they have found a craftsman, whom they describe unreservedly as a genius, and who, with his dozen workers, can supply on demand and for a few centimes per item clips, rings, brooches, novelty buttons, lighters, smoker's sets, pens, false eyelashes, yoyos, spectacle frames, combs, cigarette holders, inkwells, letter openers, and a whole heap of trinkets, gewgaws, and baubles in Bakelite, celluloid, galalith, and other plastic materials which you could swear were at least half a century old and which he supplies with 'pre-aged patina' and even sometimes with fake repair marks.

Though they still go in for the laid-back style, offering coffee to customers and calling employees by their first names, their rapid expansion is beginning to create difficult problems for them, in stock control, accounting, profitability, and personnel; they are being forced to attempt to diversify their range of products, to sub-contract a portion of their business to major stores or to mail-order warehouses, and to look elsewhere for new materials, new items, and new ideas; they have begun to make contacts in South America and black Africa, and they have already signed up an Egyptian trader for the supply of fabrics, imitation Coptic jewellery, and small painted furniture for which they have secured the exclusive rights for Western Europe.

The Plassaerts' dominant character trait is meanness – methodical, organised meanness, on which they even pride themselves from time to time: for instance, they boast that in their flat and in their shops they never have any fresh flowers – highly perishable goods – but display instead arrangements of everlasting flowers, reeds, Alpine sea holly, and honesty, enhanced by a few peacock feathers. Their meanness is constant and unremitting: not only does it prompt them to eliminate the superfluous – the only overheads allowed are supposed to be productive overheads contributing to prestige required for professional purposes and therefore able to be accounted as investments – but also inspires them to commit acts of unspeakable stinginess, such as pouring Belgian whisky into bottles bearing expensive labels when they have guests, or systematically scrounging sugar lumps from cafés for their own sugar bowl, or asking in the same cafés for the *Entertainment Guide* which they then leave by their own cash desk for their customers to use, or paring a few pennies off their shopping by haggling over every item and buying loss leaders most of the time.

With an exactness that leaves nothing to chance, in the same way as in the nineteenth century the mistress of the house went through her cook's account book and didn't hesitate to demand two pennies back on the turbot, Adèle Plassaert enters every day in a school exercise book the stark figures of her daily outgoings:

bread	0. 90
paperclips	0. 40
2 artichokes	1. 12
ham	3. 15
petits-suisses	1. 20
wine	2. 15
hairdresser	16. 00
tip	1. 50
stockings	3. 10
repair to coffee grinder	15. 00
washing powder	2. 70
razor blades	4. 00
light bulb	2. 60
plums	1. 80
coffee	3. 00
chicory	1. 80
TOTAL	59. 42

Behind them, on the off-white-painted wall with pale-yellow gloss mouldings, hang sixteen little rectangular drawings in a style reminiscent of *fin-de-siècle* caricatures. They represent the classical "Paris Streetsellers", with captions giving their traditional cries:

THE SEAFOOD-SELLER

"Cockles and mussels, alive, alive-o!"

THE RAG AND BONE MAN

"Any old rags, any old iron
Any any any old iron"

THE SNAIL LADY

"I've got snails, juicy snails
A shilling a dozen, fresh snails"

THE FISH WOMAN

"Prawns, lovely prawns, alive-o!
Skate, nice fresh skate"

THE COOPER

"Barrels, barrels!"

THE OLD-CLOTHES MAN

"Old clothes, any old clothes
Old . . . clothes"

THE GRINDER AND HIS STONE

"Knives, scissors, razors!"

THE COSTERMONGER

"Tender and green artichokes
Tender and young
Ar . . . tichokes"

THE TINKER

"Tan, ran, tan, tan, ran, tan
For pots and cans, oh! I'm your man
I'll mend them all with a tink, tink, tink
And never leave a chink, chink, chink"

THE WAFFLE LADY

"Enjoy yourselves, ladies
Here's a treat!"

THE ORANGE LADY

"Valencia oranges, lovely ripe oranges!"

THE DOG-CLIPPER

"I clips dogs
And cuts yer cats
Tails an' ears an' all"

THE VEGETABLE-SELLER

"Lettuce, cos lettuce, not to hawk
Lovely cos lettuce out for a walk"

THE CHEESE MAN

"Good cream cheese, fresh cheese!"

THE SAW-SETTER

"Here comes the saw-setter
Any saws to set?"

THE GLAZIER

"Glazier, gla-zier
Any broken panes
Here comes the gla-zier!"

CHAPTER FIFTY-FIVE

Servants' Quarters, 10

Henri Fresnel, the chef, came to live in this room in June nineteen nineteen. He was a sad-hearted Southerner aged about twenty-five, short, dry, with a thick black moustache. He had quite stylish ways of doing fish and shellfish dishes, and also vegetable starters: raw artichokes in pepper and salt, cucumber in dill, courgettes with turmeric, cold ratatouille flavoured with mint, radishes in cream and chervil, capsicum with basil, plum tomatoes in Provençal thyme. By way of homage to his long-dead namesake (the inventor of the optical lens, or *lentille*) he had also invented a recipe for lentils cooked in cider and served cold with a sprinkling of olive oil and saffron on toasted circular slices of the kind of bread used for the dish known as *pan bagnat*.

In nineteen twenty-four this man of few words married the daughter of the sales director of a sizable cooked-meats supplier at Pithiviers specialising in the celebrated lark *pâté* which gives the town one part of its renown, the remainder deriving from its famous almond cake. Bolstered by the reputation his cuisine had acquired, and correctly reckoning that Monsieur Hardy, far too concerned with promoting his olive oil and casks of anchovies to the exclusion of all else, would not give him the means to build on it, Henri Fresnel decided to go it alone, and with the help of his young bride Alice – who put her dowry into it – he opened his own restaurant in Rue des Mathurins, near the Madeleine. They called it *La Belle Alouette*. Fresnel manned the hotplates, Alice managed the dining room: they stayed open late at night, to attract the actors, journalists, night birds, and high-lifers who thronged the area, and their reasonable prices combined with the very high quality of their cuisine soon meant that they had to turn customers away, and the light-coloured wood panelling of their small dining room soon began to sport autographed snapshots of music hall stars, leading actors, and boxing champions.

Everything went swimmingly, and the Fresnels were soon planning for the future, thinking of having a baby and of leaving their cramped flatlet. But one morning in nineteen twenty-nine, when Alice was six months pregnant, Henri disappeared, leaving his wife a laconic note explaining that he was dying of boredom in his kitchen and was off to make his long-cherished dream come true: to be an actor!

Alice Fresnel reacted to this news with surprising calm: the very same day she hired a chef, and with uncommon energy she took over the running of the business, letting go only for the time it took to deliver a chubby-cheeked baby boy whom she baptised Ghislain and put out to a wet-nurse straight away. As for her husband, she made no effort to find him.

She saw him again forty years later. In the meantime, the restaurant had gone downhill and been sold; Ghislain had grown up and gone into the army, and Alice lived on in her room on the income from her savings, poaching a turbot on the side-plate of her enamelled cooker, or simmering a stew or a *blanquette* or a hotpot which filled the servants' staircase with delicious smells, and with which she provided feasts for some of her neighbours.

Henri Fresnel had given it all up not for an actress – as Alice had always believed – but really for acting. Like one of those Strolling Players of Molière's time, who came in the pouring rain to the gates of a dilapidated castle and sought shelter from a ragged squire who would join the errant band next morning, Henri had set off on the road with four companions in misfortune who had failed drama school and despaired of ever getting a part: two twins, Isidore and Lucas, a pair of strong, tall men from the Jura who did swashbucklers and young male leads, a girl hailing from Toulon who played the innocent, and a distinctly butch contralto who was in fact the youngest member of the troupe. Isidore and Lucas drove the two trucks that had been converted into caravans and set up the stage, Henri did the cooking, the accounts, and the directing, fresh-faced Lucette designed, made, and above all darned the costumes, and buxom Charlotte did everything else: washing up, cleaning the caravans, shopping, combing and ironing needed at the last minute, etc. They had two painted canvas sets: one depicted a palace with a perspective effect and did indiscriminately for Racine, Molière, Labiche, Feydeau, Coward, and Courteline; the other, rescued from a church guild, showed a Bethlehem nativity scene: the addition of two plywood trees and a few artificial flowers turned it into the Enchanted Forest where the troupe played its greatest success, *The Force of Destiny*, a post-romantic drama with no connection whatsoever with Verdi, a play which had made the fortunes of the Boulevard theatres and of six generations of repertory managers: the Queen (Lucette) comes across a cruel brigand (Isidore) hanging in the sun from an instrument of torture. She takes pity on him, goes up to him, brings him water, notices he is a handsome and likable young man. She frees him under cover of darkness and tells him to flee disguised as a tramp and to await her arrival in the royal coach in the depths of the woods. But at that point a magnificent Amazon (Charlotte, in a gilt-painted cardboard helmet) leading an army (Lucas and Fresnel) arraigns her:

> – O Queen of the Night, the man you have freed belongs unto me: Prepare yourself to fight; the war against the armies of light will last in the midst of the trees of the forest till dawn!
> (*Exeunt omnes*. Lights down. Silence. Thunder. Trumpets sound.)

And then the two Queens reappear on stage wearing plumed helmets, jewel-incrusted armour, and gauntlets, holding long lances and cardboard shields decorated respectively with a flaming sun and a crescent moon on a starry background, and riding two legendary beasts, one a relative of the dragon (Fresnel), the other cognate to the camel (Isidore and Lucas), with coats cut and sewn by a Hungarian tailor in Avenue du Maine.

With only a handful of other paltry props – an X-shaped stool for a throne, an old mattress and three cushions, a black-painted score cupboard, door and window openings made of old orange boxes which a piece of patched green baize could turn into that desk with its silver-gilt rims, piled high with books and papers, at which a contemplative cardinal – who is not Richelieu but his ghost Mazarin (Fresnel) – decides to have brought out of the Bastille an aged prisoner who is none other than Rochefort (Isidore) and entrusts this mission to a lieutenant of the Black Musketeers who is none other than D'Artagnan (Lucas) – and with costumes altered a thousand times, repaired and resurrected with bits of wire, Sellotape, and safety pins, with two rusty spotlights they took turns to operate and which failed fifty per cent of the time, they produced historical dramas, comedies of manners, the classics, bourgeois tragedies, modern melodramas, vaudevilles, farces, Punch-and-Judy shows, hasty adaptations of sentimental novels like *Les Misérables* or *Pinocchio* – in which Fresnel played Jiminy Cricket in an old tuxedo purportedly painted to depict the body of a cicada, and with two clockwork springs sticking out of corks glued to his forehead, representing the antennae.

They played in school yards and playgrounds, in village squares at unlikely locations in the heart of the Cévennes or the hills of Provence, pulling off nightly prodigious feats of imagination and improvisation, swapping six roles and twelve costumes in a single play, before an audience of ten adults drowsing in their Sunday best and fifteen youngsters with galoshes on their feet, berets on their heads, and warm knitted scarves around their necks, who nudged and spluttered when they saw the leading lady's pink knickers through the rents in her skirt.

Rain interrupted their plays, the trucks wouldn't start, a bottle of cooking oil got spilled a few minutes before Monsieur Jourdain was due to go on in the only remotely presentable seventeenth-century costume they possessed – a sky-blue velvet jacket with a flower-embroidered doublet and lace cuffs – and obscene abscesses sprouted on the heroines' bosoms, but they did not lose heart for three years. Then, in the space of a few days, everything fell apart: Lucas and Isidore ran off in the middle of the night with one of the trucks and the week's takings, which, for once, had not been disastrous; two days later Lucette got herself abducted by a scurrilous surveyor who had been chasing her to no avail for the previous three months. Charlotte and Fresnel stuck together for another fortnight, attempting to perform their repertoire of plays two-handed and yielding to the fallacious illusion that they would be able to rebuild their troupe once they reached a large town. They ended up at Lyons and separated by mutual agreement. Charlotte went back to her Swiss banking family, for whom acting was a sin; Fresnel joined a troupe of tumblers leaving for Spain: a snake-man permanently dressed in a thin scaly leotard who contorted his way under a burning panel twelve inches off the ground, and a couple of female dwarves (one of whom was actually a man) who did a Siamese-twin act with banjo, castanets, and ditties. As for Fresnel, he became Mister Mephisto the Magician, the soothsayer and healer acclaimed by all the crowned heads of Europe. Wearing a red tuxedo with a pink in his buttonhole, with a top hat on his head and a diamond-topped walking stick in his hand, he would put on a slight Russian accent and take a full set of Tarot cards out of a tall, narrow, lidless, old-leather box, and lay out eight of them on a table in a rectangle; using an ivory spatula, he would sprinkle them with a blue powder which was nothing more than ground galena but which he called Galen's Dust and to which he granted certain organo-therapeutic properties effecting cures for all past, present, and future afflictions, but especially recommended for the extraction of teeth, migraines and cephalalgias, menstrual pain, arthritis, arthrosis, neuralgia, cramps, convulsions, colic and kidney stones, and such other ills as he might select as appropriate to the place, the time of year, and the specific audience addressed.

They took two years to cross Spain, went over to Morocco, then down to Mauritania and as far as Senegal. Around nineteen thirty-seven they took a boat to Brazil, reached Venezuela, then Nicaragua, then Honduras, and that was how in the end Henri Fresnel found himself in New York, NY, United States of America, on his own, one morning in nineteen forty, with seventeen cents in his pocket, sitting on a bench opposite St Mark's-in-the-Bowery, in front of a stone plaque, placed diagonally by the wooden porch, attesting that this church, dating from 1799, was one of the 28 buildings in America built before 1800. He went to ask for help from the priest of the parish who – maybe touched by Fresnel's accent – agreed to listen to him. The cleric nodded his head in sadness as he learnt that Fresnel had been a charlatan, an illusionist, and an actor, but as soon as he discovered that the man had run a restaurant in Paris and had had a clientele including Mistinguett, Maurice Chevalier, Serge Lifar, Tom Lane the jockey, Nungesser, and Picasso, he broke into a broad smile and as he reached for the telephone assured the Frenchman that his troubles were over.

It was thus that after eleven years of wandering Henri Fresnel became cook to an eccentric and super-rich American woman, Grace Twinker. Grace Twinker, then aged seventy, was none other than the famous *Twinkie*, the very same who started at sixteen in a burlesque show dressed as the recently inaugurated Statue of Liberty and who became at the turn of the century one of the most legendary Queens of Broadway, before marrying five billionaires in succession who all had the good sense to die shortly after their weddings and leave Twinkie all their money.

Twinkie was extravagantly generous and supported choreographers and dancers, writers, librettists, set designers, etc., whom she had hired to write a musical based on her own fabulous biography: her triumph as Lady Godiva in the streets of New York, her marriage to Prince Guéménolé, her stormy affair with Mayor Groncz, her arrival in a Duesenberg at East Knoyle airfield for the meeting at which the Argentinian flyer, Carlos Kravchik, who was madly in love with her, jumped from his biplane after a suite of eleven dead-leaf dives and the most impressive zoom climb ever seen, her purchase of the monastery of the Brothers of Mercy at Granbin, near Pont-Audemer, which she had transported stone by stone to Connecticut and presented to Highpool University, which used it for its library, her giant crystal bath shaped like a champagne glass, which she filled with said (Californian) beverage, her eight Siamese cats with navy-blue eyes watched over day and night by two vets and four nurses, her lavish and extravagant contributions (which the beneficiaries, it was frequently reported, would have rather not had) to Harding's and Coolidge's and Hoover's campaigns, the famous telegram – *Shut up, you singing buoy!* – she sent to Caruso a few minutes before his first appearance at the Metropolitan Opera, all these episodes were supposed to appear in an "All-American" show beside which the wildest *Follies* of the period would pale into provincial insignificance.

Grace Slaughter – the surname of her fifth husband, a manufacturer of pharmaceutical toners and "prophylactic" products, recently deceased due to a ruptured peritoneum – was sharply chauvinistic and would allow no more than two exceptions to her all-American views, exceptions with which her first spouse, Astolphe de Guéménolé-Longtgermain, no doubt had something to do: cooking had to be done by French nationals of male gender, laundry and ironing by British subjects of female gender (and absolutely not by Chinese). That allowed Henri Fresnel to be hired without having to hide his original citizenship, which is what had to be done by the director (Hungarian), the set designer (Russian), the choreographer

(Lithuanian), the dancers (Italian, Greek, Egyptian), the scriptwriter (English), the librettist (Austrian), and the composer, a Finn of Bulgarian descent with a large dash of Romanian.

The attack on Pearl Harbor and the entry of the United States into the war at the end of 1941 put an end to these grandiose plans, which in any case did not satisfy Twinkie as she thought that every version inadequately emphasised the galvanising part she had played in the life of the nation. Though in total disagreement with the Roosevelt administration, Twinkie decided to devote herself to the war effort by sending all American soldiers serving in the Battle for the Pacific packets of samples of consumer products made by firms she controlled directly or indirectly. The packets were wrapped in a nylon sleeve depicting the American flag; they contained a toothbrush, a tube of toothpaste, three soluble effervescent tablets recommended for neuralgia, stomach pains, and heartburn, a piece of soap, three doses of shampoo, a bottle of pop, a ball-point pen, four packs of chewing gum, a set of razor blades, a plastic card case designed to hold a photograph – as an example, Twinkie had had her own put in, showing her at the launch of MTB *Remember the Alamo* – a small medallion cut to the shape of the soldier's home state (foreign-born military received a medallion cut to the shape of the USA), and a pair of socks. The executive committee of the "Godmothers of America at War" which the Pentagon had made responsible for checking the contents of these gift packs, had had samples of "prophylactic" products withdrawn and strongly disapproved of any being sent to individuals.

Grace Twinker died in nineteen fifty-one, from complications arising from a little-known disease of the pancreas. She left all her servants more than comfortable incomes. Henry Fresnel – he had adopted the English spelling of his first name – used his money to open a restaurant which he dubbed *Le Capitaine Fracasse* in memory of his years as a travelling player, published a book boastfully titled *Mastering the French Art of Cookery*, and founded a school of cooking which rapidly flourished. That didn't stop him from satisfying his deepest passion. Thanks to all the show-business personalities who had tasted his cooking at Twinkie's and who soon found their way to his restaurant, he became producer, technical adviser, and the main actor in a TV series called *I Am the Cookie* (Higher Ham Zee Cool

Key, in Fresnel's inimitable Marseilles accent, which had stood up successfully to so many years of exile). The broadcasts, which ended each time with Fresnel presenting one of his own original recipes, were so popular that analogous acting parts as a likable Frenchman were offered to him on several occasions, and thus did he finally fulfil his vocation.

He retired from business in 1970 at the age of seventy-six and decided to go back to see Paris, which he had left more than forty years before.

He was undoubtedly surprised to discover that his wife was still living in the little room in Rue Simon-Crubellier. He went to see her, told her all he had lived through, the nights in barns, the rutted roads, the messes of rain-sodden potatoes in pork fat, the slit-eyed Touaregs seeing right through every one of his sleights of hand, the heat and the hunger in Mexico, the wonderland soirées of the aged American lady for whom he made set pieces out of which, at the right moment, troupes of girls with ostrich plumes would prance.

She listened to him silently. When he had finished, after he had nervously offered to give her some of the money he had amassed in the course of his peregrinations, she said only that none of all that, his story or his money, was of any interest to her, and she showed him the door without even asking for his address in Miami.

There is every reason to believe that she had only stayed on in this room to await her husband's return, however brief and disappointing the meeting might be, for within a few months she sold up and went to live with her son, a serving officer stationed at Nouméa. A year later, Mademoiselle Crespi received a letter from her; it described her life out there, in the Antipodes, a sad existence where she was used for household chores and for looking after her daughter-in-law's children, sleeping in a room with no running water, reduced to washing in the kitchen.

Today the room is occupied by a man of about thirty: he is on his bed, stark naked, prone, amidst five inflatable dolls, lying full length on top of one of them and cuddling two others in his arms, apparently experiencing an unparalleled orgasm on these precarious simulacra.

The rest of the room is more bare: blank walls, a sea-green lino on the floor, strewn with odd pieces of clothing. A chair, a table with an oilcloth covering, the signs of a meal – a can, shrimps in a saucer – and an evening newspaper lying open at a monster crossword puzzle.

CHAPTER FIFTY-SIX

On the Stairs, 8

On the sixth floor, in front of Dr Dinteville's door. A patient is waiting for the door to open; he's a man of about fifty, with a military bearing of the up-country bruiser variety, wearing cropped hair, a grey suit, a printed silk tie pinned by a tiny diamond, and a heavy gold stopwatch. Under his left arm he carries a morning daily on which can be seen advertisements for stockings, for the forthcoming premiere of a Gate Flanders film, *Love, Maracas and Salami*, with Faye Dolores and Sunny Philips, and a banner headline – *The Princess of Faucigny-Lucinge is back!* – above a photograph of the princess, sitting in an *art-nouveau* armchair with a furious look on her face while five customs officials extract with the utmost care, out of the recesses of a crate, stamped all over with international markings, a solid silver samovar and a large mirror.

Beside the doormat stands an umbrella-holder: a tall plaster cylinder made to look like a classical pillar. To the right, a bundle of newspapers tied with string and intended for the students who periodically come to the building to make a collection of wastepaper. Even after the concierge has extracted all the illustrated blotters, which she gives away, Dr Dinteville remains one of the best suppliers. The paper on the top of the pile is not a medical publication, but a journal of linguistics with the following table of contents to be seen:

Bulletin de l'Institut de Linguistique de Louvain

98e année — 1973 — Fasc. 3-4

CHAPTER FIFTY-SEVEN

Madame Orlowska (Servants' Quarters, II)

Elzbieta Orlowska, the Polish Beauty – as everyone in the *quartier* calls her – is a tall, stern, and majestic woman of thirty with a head of long, thick blonde hair most often done up in a bun, dark-blue eyes, a very pale complexion, and a fleshy neck on round and almost plump shoulders. She is standing in her bedroom, almost in the middle of the room, with one arm in the air, as she wipes a brass lighting fixture with open-work branches resembling a scaled-down copy of a Dutch domestic chandelier.

The room is tiny and tidy. On the left, against the partition wall, is a bed – a narrow pallet graced with a few cushions, and with fitted drawers underneath; then a whitewood table with a portable typewriter and various papers on it, then another table, an even smaller one, made of metal, collapsible, holding a gas camping cooker and several kitchen utensils.

Against the right-hand wall stands a cot and a stool. Another stool by the pallet-bed, filling the tiny space between it and the door, serves as a bedside table: on it, a lamp with a whorled pedestal huddles against an octagonal white porcelain ashtray, a small carved-wood cigarette box in the shape of a barrel, a voluminous essay entitled *The Arabian Knights. New Visions of Islamic Feudalism in the Beginnings of the Hegira*, by a certain Charles Nunneley, and a detective story by Lawrence Wargrave, *The Magistrate Is the Murderer*: X kills A in such a way that the law, which knows he did it, cannot convict him. The examining magistrate kills B in such a way that X is suspected, arrested, tried, found guilty, and executed without his being able to do anything to prove his innocence.

The floor covering is dark-red linoleum. The walls, fitted with shelving on which clothes, books, crockery, etc. are stacked, are painted light beige. They are enlivened a little by two posters in very bright colours pinned to the right-hand wall between the cot and the door: the first is a portrait of a clown with a ping-pong-ball nose, a wisp of carrot-red hair, a chequerboard costume, a huge polka-dot bow tie, and long, very flat shoes. The second depicts six men standing in a row: one of them has a full beard, black, another has a heavy ring on his finger, another has a red belt, another has trousers rent at the knees, another has only one eye open, and the last of them bares his teeth.

When asked what is the meaning of this poster, Elzbieta Orlowska replies that it illustrates a popular Polish nursery rhyme told to children to get them to sleep:

– I met six men, says the mother.
– What were they like? asks the child.
– The first has a black beard, says the mother.
– Why? asks the child.
– Because he doesn't know how to shave, silly! says the mother.
– And the second one? asks the child.
– The second wears a ring, says the mother.
– Why? asks the child.
– Because he's married, silly! says the mother.
– And the third one? asks the child.
– The third has a belt round his waist, says the mother.
– Why? asks the child.
– Because otherwise his trousers would fall down, silly! says the mother.
– And the fourth one? asks the child.
– The fourth has torn his trousers, says the mother.
– Why? asks the child.
– Because he ran too fast, silly! says the mother.
– And the fifth one? asks the child.
– The fifth has only one eye open, says the mother.
– Why? asks the child.
– Because he's nearly asleep, just like you, my little one, says the mother ever so softly.
– And the last one? the child asks in a whisper.
– The last one is baring his teeth, says the mother
all in one breath.

Now the child mustn't ask anything at all, for if he should make the mistake of saying:

– Why?
– Because he's coming to eat you up if you don't go to sleep, silly! the mother will say in a booming voice.

Elzbieta Orlowska was eleven when she first came to France. It was a summer camp at Parçay-les-Pins in Maine-et-Loire. The camp was run by the Foreign Ministry and catered for the children of staff of the Ministry and of embassies abroad. Little Elzbieta went to the camp because her father was a concierge at the French Embassy in Warsaw. The camp was designed to be international, but it so happens that French youngsters were in a large majority that year, and the few foreign children that were there felt quite at sea. One of them was a Tunisian boy by the first name of Boubaker. His father, an orthodox Muslim who lived in almost total isolation from French culture, would never have dreamt of sending his son to France, but his uncle, an archivist in the French Foreign Ministry on the Quai d'Orsay, had insisted on bringing the boy over, as he was convinced it was the best way to acquaint his nephew with a language and a civilisation which the next generation of Tunisians, henceforth self-governing, could not afford not to know.

Elzbieta and Boubaker quickly became inseparable. They kept apart from the others and did not join in their games, but walked together holding hands by their little fingers, smiled at each other, and told each other long stories in their respective tongues which the other listened to, enchanted, without understanding a word. The other children didn't like them, played cruel tricks on them, hid dead field mice in their bunks, but the adults who came to spend a day with their offspring went into ecstasy over the young pair, a chubby little girl with blonde locks and bisque skin, and a slim, curly-headed boy as lithe as a liana, with sallow skin, jet-black hair, and huge eyes brimming with angelic sweetness. On the last day of camp they pricked their thumbs and mixed their blood, swearing eternal love.

They did not see each other again for the next ten years, but wrote twice a week to each other in increasingly amorous terms. Elzbieta soon managed to persuade her parents to let her learn French and

Arabic because she would be going to live in Tunisia with her husband Boubaker. Things were more difficult for him, and for months he strove to convince his father, who had always terrified him, that he had not the slightest wish to be disrespectful, that he would remain faithful to the traditions of Islam and to the teachings of the Koran, and that just because he was going to marry a Westerner did not mean he would dress in European clothes or live in a French town.

The toughest problem was to obtain all the authorisations needed for Elzbieta to come to Tunisia. It took more than eighteen months of administrative hassles on both Tunisian and Polish sides. There was a treaty of co-operation between Poland and Tunisia, which allowed for Tunisian students to go to Poland to study engineering, and for Polish dentists, agronomists, and vets to work in Tunisia for the Ministries of Health and Agriculture. But Elzbieta was neither a dentist nor an agronomist nor a vet, and for a whole year every application she submitted for a visa, whatever explanation she added to it, was sent back with a note saying: "Does not correspond to criteria laid down in treaty referred to above." What Elzbieta had to do in the end, through a singularly contorted sequence of steps, was to bypass the official channels and tell her story to an Under-Secretary of State so that, barely six months later, she was finally appointed to a post as translator/interpreter at the Polish Consulate in Tunis – with the administration finally taking account of the fact that she had degrees in Arabic and French.

She landed at Tunis-Carthage airport on the first of June nineteen sixty-six. There was a glaring sun. She was radiant with happiness, with liberty, with love. She looked for her fiancé amongst the crowd of Tunisians waving expansively to passengers from the balcony, but could not see him. They had sent each other photographs many times, showing him playing football, or in swimming trunks on Salammbo's beach, or wearing a djellaba and embroidered babouches beside his father, a head shorter than he was, showing her skiing at Zakopane, or vaulting a horse. She was sure she would recognise him, but nonetheless held back for an instant when she did set eyes on him: he was in the arrivals hall, just behind the immigration desk, and the first thing she said to him was:

– But you haven't grown at all!

When they had met, at Parçay-les-Pins, they were the same height; but whereas he had grown only another eight or ten inches, she had put on at least twenty: she was five foot ten and he was not quite five foot two; she was a sunflower in midsummer, he was dry and shrivelled like an old lemon left on the kitchen shelf.

The first thing Boubaker did was to take her to see his father. He was a public scribe and calligrapher. He worked in a minute hut in the medina; he sold satchels, key-pouches, and pencils, but his customers mostly came to have him write in their names on degree and diploma certificates, or to copy out holy sayings on parchments they would frame. Elzbieta first set eyes on him sitting cross-legged with a plank on his lap, wearing spectacles with lenses as thick as bottle-glass, sharpening his quill with a ponderous air. He was a short, thin man with very drawn features, a greenish complexion, shifty eyes, and a hideous smile, ill at ease and taciturn with women. In two years he barely spoke three words to his daughter-in-law.

The first year was the worst; Elzbieta and Boubaker spent it in the father's house, in the Arab quarter. They had their own room, which was a space just large enough for their bed, but without any light, separated from the brothers-in-law's bedrooms by flimsy partitions through which she felt that she was being not only overheard, but watched. They were not even able to eat together; he ate with his father and elder brothers; she had to wait on them silently and return to the kitchen with the women and children, where her mother-in-law smothered her with kisses and caresses and sweets as well as distressing her with lamentations on the shape of her belly and her buttocks and almost obscene questions on the kind of love-making her husband provided or requested.

The second year, after she had borne a son, who was named Mahmoud, she rebelled and took Boubaker off in her rebellion. They rented a three-roomed flat at 15, Rue de Turquie, in the European quarter, three cold, high-ceilinged rooms with frightful furniture. Once or twice they were invited round by some of Boubaker's European colleagues; once or twice she gave dull dinner parties for wishy-washy foreign-aid volunteers; the rest of the time she had to argue for weeks to go out together to a restaurant; every time, he sought an excuse for staying at home or for going out alone.

He was persistently and inquisitively jealous: every evening, on coming home from the Consulate, she had to tell him every detail of her day and list all the men she had seen, state how long they had been in her office, what they had said, what she had answered, where she had lunched, and why she spent so long on the telephone to this girlfriend or that, etc. And when they did happen to walk together in the street, and men turned their heads as the blonde beauty went by, as soon as they got home Boubaker would give her terrible rows, as if she were to blame for the blondeness of her hair, for the whiteness of her skin, for the azure of her eyes. She felt he would have liked to imprison her, to remove her for ever from the sight of other people, to keep her for his own eyes only, for his silent and feverish admiration alone.

It took her two years to get the full measure of the gap between the dreams they had cherished for a decade and the mean reality of her future life. She began to hate her husband, transferred to her son all the love she had felt, and decided to run away with him. With the complicity of some of her compatriots she managed to leave Tunisia clandestinely, on board a Lithuanian ship which landed her at Naples whence she reached France overland.

Fate determined that her arrival in Paris coincided with the height of the student revolt in May '68. In that great wave of intoxication and joy she had a fleeting and passionate affair with a young American folk singer, who left Paris on the night the police reoccupied the Odéon theatre. Shortly after that she found this room: it had belonged to Germaine, Bartlebooth's seamstress, who retired that year and who was not replaced.

For the first months she hid, fearing Boubaker might break in one day and reclaim his son. Later she learnt that he had given in to his father's exhortations and been married by a matchmaker to a widowed mother of four, and had gone back to live in the medina.

She began a simple and almost monkish existence, centred entirely on her son. To earn a living she found a job in an export-import business trading with Arab companies and for which she translated users' manuals, administrative regulations, and technical specifications. But the business soon went bankrupt and since then she has lived on short-term contracts from the CNRS research council, for whose *Bulletin signalétique* she abstracts articles in Arabic and Polish, and makes up the pittance they pay her by doing housework.

She was straightaway the darling of the whole building. Even Bartlebooth, her landlord, whose indifference to everything going on in the building had always seemed to everyone to be a fact of life, took a shine to her. Several times, before his morbid passion had condemned him to ever stricter solitude, he invited her to dinner. Once – and this is something he had never done for anyone, and would never do again – he showed her the puzzle he was reassembling that fortnight: it was a fishing port on Vancouver Island, a place called Hammertown, all white with snow, with a few low houses and some fishermen in fur-lined jackets hauling a long, pale hull along the shore.

Apart from the friends she has made in the apartment house, Elzbieta knows almost no one in Paris. She has lost touch with Poland and doesn't mix with Poles in exile. Only one visits her regularly, a rather old man with empty eyes, a walking stick, and an eternal white flannel scarf. This man, who seems past caring about anything, was, she says, the most popular clown in Warsaw before the war, and it is he who is portrayed on the poster on her wall. She met him three years ago in Anna de Noailles Square, where she was watching her son play in the sand pit. He sat down on the same bench, and she noticed he was reading a Polish edition of Gérard de Nerval's *Les Filles du feu – Sylwia i inne opowiadania*. They became friends. He comes for dinner twice a month at her flat. As he has not a single tooth left, she feeds him on hot milk and custard.

He doesn't live in Paris, but in a small village called Nivillers, in the Department of Oise, near Beauvais, in a one-storey house, long and low, with windows made of small panes of coloured glass. That is where Mahmoud, who is now nine years old, has just gone for his holidays.

CHAPTER FIFTY-EIGHT

Gratiolet, 1

The penultimate descendant of the building's original owner lives with his daughter on the seventh floor, in two former maid's rooms converted into a small but comfortable dwelling.

Olivier Gratiolet sits reading at a collapsible table covered with a green cloth. His daughter Isabelle, aged thirteen, is kneeling on the parquet floor: she is building a house of cards as fragile as it is ambitious. Opposite them, on a television screen which neither is watching, a female announcer, set against a hideous science-fiction background – shiny metal panels adorned with jingoistic insignia – and sheathed in something intended to suggest a space suit, points out the evening's programmes written on a signboard whose hexagonal outline is supposed to represent the bounds of the French Republic: at eight thirty, *Yellow Thread*, a detective fantasy by Stewart Venter: at the beginning of the century, a bold jewel-thief takes refuge on a timber-raft floating down the Yellow River, and at ten o'clock, *This Golden Serp in the Field of Stars*, a chamber opera by Philoxanthe Schapska, adapted from Victor Hugo's *Booz endormi*, world premiere inaugurating the Besançon Festival.

The book Olivier Gratiolet is reading is a history of anatomy, an outsize volume open flat on the table at a full-page reproduction of a plate by Zorzi da Castelfranco, a disciple of Mondino di Luzzi, with the description on the facing page which François Béroalde de Verville made of it a century and a half later in his *Tableau des riches inventions couvertes du voile des feintes amoureuses qui sont représentées dans l'Hypnerotomachia Poliphili*:

> The corpse has not been reduced to a skeleton but the remaining flesh is impregnated with soil which forms a dry and, as it were, cardboard-like magma. nonetheless in some places bones are partially extant: sternum, collarbones, kneecaps, tibias. overall complexion is yellow brown on the front side, the back side is blackish and dark grey, humid and full of worms. head leaning to left shoulder, skull covered in white hair impregnated with soil and fragments of winding sheet. eyebrows

hairless; the lower jaw presents two teeth, yellow and semi-transparent. brain and cephalic fluid occupy approximately two thirds of the skull cavity but it is no longer possible to identify the various organs comprising the encephalum. dura mater is extant as a membrane of bluish colour; as if it were in almost a normal condition. there is no spine marrow left. cervical vertebrae are visible though partly covered by a thin ochre layer. the saponified soft internal parts of the larynx can be found at the level of the sixth vertebrum. the two sides of the chest seem empty except for containing a little soil and some small flies. they are blackish, smoky and carbonised. the abdomen is collapsed, covered in soil and chrysalids; the abdominal organs have shrunk and are not identifiable; the genital organs are destroyed to the point that sex cannot be established. the upper limbs have been placed on the sides of the body in such a way as to put arms and forearms and hands together. The left hand seems whole, grey mixed with brown. The right hand is darker and several of its bones have already separated. lower limbs are apparently intact. the short bones are no spongier than in normal state but are drier on the inside.

Olivier owes his first name to his grandfather Gérard's twin brother who was killed on 26 September 1914 at Perthes-lèz-Hurlus, in the Champagne region, in rearguard action following the first Battle of the Marne.

Of the four Gratiolet children, Gérard was the one who inherited the farms in Berry; he sold off almost half of them, just as his brother Emile sold off the building bit by bit, in attempting to rescue his other brother Ferdinand and, a little later, Ferdinand's widow. Gérard had two sons, the younger of whom, Henri, remained a bachelor. On his father's death in 1934 he took over the farm. He tried to modernise his equipment and his methods, mortgaged himself to buy machinery, and on his death in 1938 – he died from a horse-kick – left so many debts that his elder brother Louis, Olivier's father, preferred simply to refuse the inheritance rather than lumber himself with a business which would take years to become profitable.

Louis had been to college at Vierzon and at Tours and had entered the Woods & Water Department. As soon as war broke out, and although he was only twenty-one, he was put in charge of the Saint-Trojan nature reserve on the Isle of Oléron, one of the first such projects in France, in which, as on the Sept-Iles archipelago off

Perros-Guirec where a reserve had been established in 1912, every possible measure was to be taken to protect and preserve local fauna and flora. Louis thus settled on Oléron, where he married France Lidron, the daughter of a craftsman blacksmith, a bizarre old character who had begun to swamp the island with consistently hideous wrought-iron railings and decorative gilded bronze, and whose fortunes never flagged thereafter. Olivier was born in 1920 and grew up on beaches that were in those days usually deserted, and went to board at the Rochefort Lycée when he was ten. He hated boarding and he hated school, and spent all week at the back of the class in deepest gloom, dreaming of riding his horse on Sunday. He had to repeat fourth year and failed his school certificate four times before his father gave up trying to get him through and resigned himself to seeing his son get a job as a stable lad at a breeder's near Saint-Jean-d'Angély. He liked the work and might have made his way in it, but less than two years later war broke out: Olivier was called up, taken prisoner at Arras in May 1940, and sent to a stalag at Hof, in Franconia. He spent two years there. On 18 April 1942, Marc, the son of Ferdinand, who had passed the *agrégation* in philosophy in the same year that his father went bankrupt and absconded, and who had since then worked in branches of the France–Germany Committee, was appointed to the staff of Fernand de Brinon, the new Secretary of State in the second Laval administration of Vichy France. Louis wrote to him asking for his help, and one month later obtained without difficulty the release of Marc's uncle's son from captivity.

Olivier settled in Paris. François, his father's other cousin, who, together with his wife Marthe, still owned about half the flats in the building and was manager of the co-ownership association, got him a three-roomed flat, underneath the one he lived in himself (the one where the Grifalconis would live in years to come). Olivier spent the rest of the war years there, going down to the cellar to listen to *Des Français parlent aux Français* on the BBC and producing and distributing, with the help of Marthe and François, a news sheet for several resistance groups, a kind of daily letter giving news from London and coded messages.

Olivier's father Louis died in 1943, of brucellosis. The following year Marc was assassinated in obscure circumstances. Hélène Brodin, the last of Juste's children, died in 1947. When Marthe and François perished in the fire at the Rueil Palace cinema, Olivier became the last surviving Gratiolet.

A
GENEALOGICAL TREE
OF THE GRATIOLET FAMILY
CAN BE FOUND ON P.77

Olivier took his role of landlord and trustee very seriously, but a few years later war once again pursued him: called up again and sent to Algeria in 1956, a landmine exploded under him and his leg had to be amputated above the knee. At the military hospital at Chambéry, where he was treated, he fell in love with his nurse, Arlette Criolat, and, although she was ten years his junior, married her. They went to live with the young woman's father, who was a horse trader: Olivier took over his accounting and found once again his old vocation.

His convalescence was long and costly. He was given an experimental prototype of an entire artificial limb, a veritable anatomophysiological model of a leg, incorporating all the latest developments in muscular neurophysiology and fitted with servo systems allowing self-reciprocating contractions and extensions. After many months of practice, Olivier succeeded in mastering his contraption sufficiently to walk without a stick and even, on one occasion, with tears in his eyes, to ride a horse.

Even if he was forced to sell off his inherited apartments one by one, leaving himself in the end with only two maid's rooms, those were certainly the best years of his life, a quiet life in which short return trips to the capital were interspersed with long stays on his father-in-law's farm, in the middle of waterlogged meadows, in a low, well-lit house full of flowers and the smell of dubbin. It was there that Isabelle was born, in 1962, and her earliest memory has her riding with her father in a trap drawn by a little grey-dappled white horse.

On Christmas Eve, 1965, in a sudden fit of dementia, Arlette's father strangled his daughter and hanged himself. The next day Olivier came to settle in Paris with Isabelle. He didn't look for work, found ways of managing on his war-wounded pension, devoted himself to Isabelle, cooking her meals, mending her clothes, teaching her to read and do sums.

Today it is Isabelle's turn to care for her father, who is now often sick. She does the shopping, beats the eggs for the omelettes, scours the pots, keeps house. She is a thin little girl with a sad face and gloomy eyes who spends hours in front of her mirror whispering frightful stories to herself.

Olivier hardly moves any more. His leg hurts him now, and he can't afford to have its complex machinery adjusted. He spends most of his time sitting in his wing chair, dressed in pyjama trousers and an old check bed jacket, sipping little glasses of liqueur all day long, despite Dr Dinteville's formal prohibition. In an attempt to increase his meagre income ever so slightly he draws (atrocious) picture puzzles which he sends in to a sort of weekly magazine specialising in what is pompously called *mental gymnastics*; they pay him generously – when they take his pieces – at a rate of fifteen francs per item. The last one shows a river; on the prow of a boat is a seated woman lavishly clad and surrounded by sacks of gold and half-open chests spilling over with jewels; in place of her head is the letter "S"; standing at the stern, a male figure wearing a count's coronet is the ferryman; on his cape the letters "ENTEMENT" are embroidered. The solution: "Contentement passe richesse", a French proverb meaning "Happiness is worth more than money".

This fifty-five-year old widower and invalid, whose shabby fate has been forged by wars, is obsessed with two grandiose and illusory projects.

The first is of a fictional nature: Gratiolet would like to invent a proper hero, a true romantic hero; not some pot-bellied king of Poland absurdly obsessed with sausages and slaughter, but a true paladin, a doughty knight, a defender of women and orphans, a righter of wrongs, a parfit gentleman and a noble lord, a brilliant strategist, a man of elegance, courage, wealth, and wit; dozens of times has he thought up a face for him, with a determined chin, a broad forehead, teeth showing in a hearty smile, and a twinkle in the eyes; dozens of times has he clad him in impeccably tailored outfits with pale-yellow gloves, ruby cuff links, tiepins tipped with priceless pearls, a monocle, a gold-handled crop, but he still hasn't managed to find him fitting first and second names.

The second project is in the field of metaphysics: with the aim of showing that, in the words of Professor H. M. Tooten, "evolution is a hoax", Olivier Gratiolet has undertaken an exhaustive inventory of all the imperfections and inadequacies to which the human organism is heir: vertical posture, for example, gives man only a precarious balance: muscular tension alone keeps him upright, thus causing constant fatigue and discomfort in the spinal column, which, although sixteen times stronger than it would have been were it straight, does not allow man to carry a meaningful weight on his back; feet ought to be broader, more spread out, more specifically suited to locomotion, whereas what he has are only atrophied hands deprived of prehensile ability; legs are not sturdy enough to bear the body's weight, which makes them bend, and moreover they are a strain on the heart, which has to pump blood about three feet up, whence come swollen feet, varicose veins, etc.; hip joints are fragile and constantly prone to arthrosis or serious fractures; arms are atrophied and too slender; hands are frail, especially the little finger, which has no use, the stomach has no protection whatsoever, no more than the genitals do; the neck is rigid and limits rotation of the head, the teeth do not allow food to be grasped from the sides, the sense of smell is virtually nil, night vision is less than mediocre, hearing is very inadequate; man's hairless and unfurred body affords no protection against cold, and, in sum, of all the animals of creation, man, who is generally considered the ultimate fruit of evolution, is the most naked of all.

CHAPTER FIFTY-NINE

Hutting, 2

Hutting does not work in his large studio but in a little room off the gallery specially designed for the long sittings which he inflicts on his clients since he has become a portrait painter.

It is a bright and cosy room, kept spick-and-span, looking nothing like the conventionally messy artist's studio; no canvases face-down against the wall, no precarious piles of stretchers, no dented kettle on an antediluvian ring, but a black leather padded door, tall indoor plants spilling out of broad tripod stands and clambering up to the skylight, and white gloss walls, bare but for a long polished metal panel carrying three posters, attached to it by magnetised hemispheres masquerading as halved billiard balls: a colour reproduction of Roger van der Weyden's *Triptych of the Last Judgement* from the Hôtel-Dieu at Beaune, the poster advertising Yves Allégret's film, *The Proud Ones*, with Michèle Morgan, Gérard Philipe, and Victor Manuel Mendoza, and a photographic enlargement of a *fin-de-siècle* menu with flourishes reminiscent of Beardsley:

The client is Japanese, a man with a wrinkled face, wearing a gold-rimmed pince-nez and a formal black lounge suit, white shirt, and pearl-grey tie. He is sitting on a chair with his hands on his knees, legs together, back straight, turning his eyes not towards the painter but to a little card table inlaid with a backgammon board, and on which stand a white telephone, a silver-plated coffee pot, and a wicker basket full of exotic fruits.

Hutting is behind his easel with his palette in his hand, astride a stone lion, an inspiring sculpture whose Assyrian origin is doubted by none, but which nonetheless posed a problem for the experts, since the painter found it himself, buried at less than three feet under a field, at a time when as the standard-bearer of "Mineral Art" he was hunting for stones in the environs of Thuburbo Majus.

Hutting is bare-chested, and he is wearing printed cotton trousers, thick white wool socks, a fine cambric cravat around his neck, and a dozen multicoloured bangles on his left wrist. All his equipment – paint tubes, pots, brushes, knives, chalk, rags, vaporisers, scrapers, quills, sponges, etc. – is stored neatly in a long printer's case placed on his right.

The canvas on the easel is mounted in a trapezoidal stretcher, about six feet high, two feet wide at the top, and four feet wide at the bottom, as if the painting were intended to be hung very high up and were meant to exaggerate its own perspective by a kind of anamorphosis.

The painting is almost finished and shows three figures. Two are standing on either side of a tall dresser laden with books, small instruments, and diverse toys: astronomical kaleidoscopes exhibiting the twelve constellations of the zodiac from Aries to Pisces, miniature mechanical orreries, arithmetical gelatin lozenges, geometrical to correspond with zoological biscuits, globe-map playing balls, historically costumed dolls.

The figure on the left is a corpulent man whose facial features are entirely hidden by his costume, a bulky outfit for underwater fishing: a glossy black-and-white-striped rubber wetsuit, a black helmet, a facemask, an oxygen cylinder, a harpoon, a cork-handled dagger, a diver's watch, and flippers.

The right-hand figure, obviously the aged Japanese who is posing, is dressed in a long red-tinged black robe.

The third figure is in the foreground, kneeling, facing the other two, with his back to the viewer. He is wearing a lozenge-shaped headdress of the kind worn by staff and students at British universities at graduation ceremonies.

The tiled floor has been painted with great precision to reproduce the geometrical motifs of the marble mosaic brought by Italian artisans around 1268 to floor the chancel of Westminster Abbey, at the time of the abbot Robert Ware.

Ever since the heroic years of his "haze period" and of *mineral art* – the aesthetics of piles of stone, of which the most memorable manifestation was the "reclamation", then the "signing", and a little later the sale, to a town planner from Plant City, Fla, of one of the barricades put up in Rue Gay-Lussac in '68 – Hutting cherished the ambition of becoming a portrait painter, and many were his buyers who begged him to do theirs. His problem, as in all his previous pictorial enterprises, was to develop an individual procedure, to find a recipe, as he put it, which would allow him to "cook up" a proper dish of his own.

For some months Hutting used a method which, he said, had been revealed to him for three rounds of gin by a half-caste beggar he had met in a scruffy bar on Long Island but who wouldn't reveal its origin despite all Hutting's insistence. It involved selecting the colours for a portrait from an inalterable sequence of 11 hues by use of three key numbers, one provided by the date and time of the painting's "birth", "birth" meaning the first sitting for the painting, the second by the phase of the moon at the painting's "conception", "conception" meaning the circumstances which had initiated the portrait, for instance a telephone call asking for it to be done, and the third by the price.

The system's impersonality was the kind of thing to captivate Hutting. But perhaps because he applied it too rigidly, he obtained results more disconcerting than captivating. To be sure, his *Countess of Berlingue with Red Eyes* earned a deserved success, but several other portraits left critics and clients in the air, and above all Hutting had the confused and awkward feeling that he was using without any spark of genius a formula which someone else before him had obviously managed to bend to his own artistic requirements.

The relative failure of these trials did not discourage him overmuch, but led him to refine further what his appointed panegyrist, the art critic Elzéar Nahum, felicitously called his "personal equations": they allowed him to define a style lying somewhere between a genre painting, a genuine portrait, pure fantasy, and historical mythology, which he baptised "the imaginary portrait": he decided to do twenty-four of them at a rate of one a month, in a precise order, over the following two years:

1. Tom Dooley, polishing authentic *metal tractors*, meets three displaced persons.
2. Coppelia teaches Noah to crawl, as there are no amphibians on the Ark.
3. Septimius Severus, watching the Bey nab oodles of women, negotiates his sister Septimia Octavilla's hand.

4. Jean-Louis Girard explicates Isaac de Benserade's celebrated sestet.

5. Łukasiewicz's German disciple, der Graf von Bellerval, a friend of the eccentric Lord Bergerac, demonstrates in his teacher's presence that an island is an area surrounded by shores.

6. Jules Barnavaux, owner of a respectable aviary, regretting that he had not observed the twin signs in the Ministry toilets.

7. Nero Wolfe, wearing a bra for disguise, comes upon Captain Fierabras forcing the safe at the Chase Manhattan Bank.

8. The dachshund Optimus Maximus swimming to shore at Calvi, noting with pleasure that the mayor is waiting for him with a bone and some bitter local *vino*.

9. The "antipodee translator" wearing rich amber studs tells Orpheus he too can charm beasts.

10. Livingstone, realising Lord Ramsay's promised bounty has gone to another chap, manifests a fit of bad temper.

11. R. Mutt fails graduation for claiming at the oral that Champollion invented "Dew Shampoo".

12. Boriet-Tory drinks *Russkaya Dusha* tonic with his Château-Latour whilst watching the "Wolf Man" dance the foxtrot.

13. The young priest devising *concetti* in elucubrating on Lucca and T'ien Tsin.

14. Maximilian lands in Mexico and daintily scoffs four nelumbia and eleven tortillas.

15. The "poster of rhymes" demands that his farmer shear his wool and that his wife weave it in a hall at Issy-les-Moulineaux.

16. Narcisse Follaninio, a finalist at the Amsterdam Poetry Festival, puts a volume of Lely on a lectern and reads a rhyming dictionary in front of the jury.

17. Zeno of Didymus, a Caribbean Corsair, paid a handsome sum by William III, leaves defenceless Curaçao to the Dutch invaders.

18. The Recycled Razor Works' managing director's wife allows her daughter out on the streets of Paris alone

provided she wears her slummy "Schelm" attire and does not carry travellers' cheques in her bra.

19. The actor Archibald Moon dithers for his next show between the roles of Mata Hari, Methuselah, and Joseph of Arimathæa.
20. The painter Hutting tries to get a proper equation of tax and allowances from a trouble-shooting revenue inspector.
21. Dr LaJoie is struck off the medical register for having stated, in front of Ray Monk, Ken O'Leary, and others that, after seeing *Citizen Kane*, William Randolph Hearst had put a price on Orson Welles's head.
22. Before leaving on the Hamburg coach, Javert recalls Valjean's key value in saving his life.
23. The geographer Lecomte, descending the Hamilton River, is sheltered by Eskimos and to thank them helps their village accrue both fame and food supplies.
24. Listing from his album Irish *mitzvahs* and lively portraits of Vinteuil, Elstir, Bergotte and La Berma, the critic Molinet lectures at the Collège de France on the myths of impressionist art which readers of Proust and Joyce have by no means fully elucidated yet.

All paintings, and above all portraits, are, as Hutting explains, the confluence of a dream and of a reality. The very concept of the "imaginary portrait" grew out of this basic notion: the buyer, the person who wants a portrait of himself or of someone dear to him painted, constitutes only one element of the picture, and perhaps the least important one – who would still have heard of Monsieur Bertin without Ingres? – but that person is the initial element, and it seems right that he or she should play a determining, "founding" role in the picture: not as an aesthetic model, dictating shapes, colours, "verisimilitude", or indeed even the narrative content of the picture, but as a *structural* model: the commissioner or, more appropriately – as for medieval painting – the *donator*, would be the *initiator* of his or her portrait: the donator's identity, rather than his features, would nourish the artist's creative forces and slake his thirst for the imaginary.

One single portrait evades these laws, number twenty, the one depicting Hutting himself. A self-portrait was clearly called for within this unique series, but its eventual form was dictated, the painter asserts, by six years of continual battling with the income tax office, the outcome of which was a final victory for his point of view. His problem was this: Hutting sold three-quarters of his production in the United States, but he was obviously determined to pay tax in France, where he paid at much lower rates; in itself that was perfectly permissible, but in addition the painter wanted his income to count not as "income accruing overseas" – which is what the revenue office counted it as, with virtually no offsets or allowances – but as "income accruing from manufactures exported overseas" and thus eligible to benefit from the considerable allowances through which the State encourages exports. Now was there in the whole world a product more deserving of the term *manu*facture than a picture painted *manu*ally by the hand of an Artist? The Inspector of Taxes was forced to concede the etymological point, but took his revenge immediately by refusing to count as "*French* manufactures" paintings which, granted that they had been made manually, had been so made in a studio on the other side of the Atlantic, and it was only after brilliant exchanges of counsels' cases that it was established that Hutting's hand remained a French hand even when painting abroad and that, in consequence, even allowing for Hutting's dual nationality, since he had an American father and a French mother, it was right and proper to recognise the moral, intellectual, and artistic benefit which the world-wide exportation of Franz Hutting's *œuvre* brought to France, and therefore to apply the desired abatements to his income for tax purposes, a victory which Hutting celebrated by depicting himself as a Don Quixote with a long lance pursuing feeble and pallid black-clad functionaries scuttling out of the Treasury like rats leaving a sinking ship.

All the other paintings were based on the name, forename, and profession of the twenty-three *amateurs* who commissioned them and who committed themselves in writing to refraining from disputing either the title or the subject of the work, or the place they would be given in it. After being subjected to various linguistic and numerical procedures, the buyer's identity and profession determined, in order, the painting's dimensions, the number of represented figures, the dominant colours, the "semantic field" [mythology (2, 9), fiction (22), mathematics (5), diplomacy (3), show business

(19), travel (13), history (14, 17), detective investigation (7), etc.], the main narrative content, the secondary details (historical and geographical allusions, items of clothing, props, etc.) and finally the price. All the same, the system was subject to two overriding constraints: the buyer – or the person whose portrait the buyer wanted – had to be *explicitly* represented on the canvas; and one of the elements of narrative, in other respects determined rigorously without reference to the model's personality, had to coincide precisely with the buyer or his subject.

Putting the buyer's name in the painting's title was obviously thought too facile, and Hutting resigned himself to doing so on only three occasions: for No. 4, a portrait of the detective-novel writer Jean-Louis Girard, for No. 12, a portrait of the Swiss surgeon Boriet-Tory, director of the Department of Experimental Cryostatics at the World Health Organization, and for No. 19, a veritable virtuoso performance inspired by holography, in which the actor Archibald Moon is painted in such a way that as you move your eyes one way and then another across the painting you see him alternately as Joseph of Arimathæa, with a long white beard, grey wool burnous and pilgrim's staff, as Methuselah, and as a bare-breasted, red-headed Mata Hari, with studded leather bracelets on wrists and ankles. On the other hand, No. 8, though it does portray a dachshund – a dog belonging to the Venezuelan film producer Melchior Aristoteles, who sees it as the only true successor to Rin Tin Tin – the dachshund it portrays is not called Optimus Maximus at all but answers to the much more euphonious name of Freischütz.

Sometimes such overlapping of the imaginary and the biographical makes the portrait a striking *résumé* of its model's life: thus No. 13, a portrait of the aged cardinal Fringilli, who was abbot of Lucca before spending many years as a missionary in T'ien Tsin.

Sometimes, on the other hand, the work is related to its model by only a superficial element, the principle of which could even be easily disputed: thus a Venetian industrialist, whose young and ravishingly beautiful sister lives in constant fear of being kidnapped, provided the triple source for portrait No. 3, where he appears as Emperor Septimius Severus: first because his company regularly ranks seventh in the annual "top company" awards in the *Financial Times* and *Enterprise*, then because of his legendary severity, and finally because he has extensive links with the Shah of Iran (an imperial title if there ever was one), and it is not unimaginable for a kidnap of his sister to be used to influence this or that negotiation at an international level. And portrait No. 5 is connected to its commissioner by even more distant, diffuse, and arbitrary means: the model is Juan Maria Salinas-Lukasiewicz, the king of canned beer from Colombia to Cape Horn: the picture shows an episode – an entirely fictitious episode, moreover – in the life of Jan Łukasiewicz, the Polish logician and founder of the Warsaw school, entirely unrelated to the Argentinian brewer, who figures only as a little silhouette in the crowd.

Twenty of the twenty-four portraits are now completed. The twenty-first is at present on the easel: it portrays a Japanese industrialist, the quartz-watch tycoon Fujiwara Gomoku. It is destined to decorate his syndicate's boardroom.

The anecdote Hutting has chosen to depict was told him by its protagonist, François-Pierre LaJoie, of Laval University in Quebec. In nineteen forty, when he had just qualified as a doctor, François-Pierre LaJoie was visited by a man suffering heartburn and who said words to the effect: "It's that swine Hearst who's poisoned me, because I wouldn't do his filthy job for him"; asked to explain himself further, he is supposed to have declared that Hearst had promised him fifteen thousand dollars if he would dispose of Orson Welles. LaJoie couldn't stop himself repeating the story that very evening at his club. Next morning he was summoned urgently by the Medical Council, accused of breaking medical confidentiality by repeating in public a secret learnt in a professional consultation. He was found guilty and immediately struck off the register. A few days later he declared that he had made up the whole accusation in his head, but it was obviously too late, and he had to begin his career all over again in research, eventually becoming one of the leading specialists in the circulatory and respiratory problems of deep-sea divers. This last point alone explains the presence of Fujiwara Gomoku in the picture: in effect, LaJoie went on to research those coastal tribes in southern Japan called the Ama, and whose existence has been attested for over two thousand years, since one of the first references to these people can be found in the Gishi-Wajin-Den, presumed to date from the third century BC. Ama women are the best underwater divers in the world: for four or five months a year they are capable of diving up to one hundred and fifty times a day to depths of over eighty feet. They dive naked, protected only since the last century by goggles which two small lateral bubble chambers make pressurised, and they can stay under for two minutes on each dive, harvesting various algae, particularly agar-agar, sea slugs, sea urchins, sea cucumbers, shells, pearl oysters, and abalones, the shells of which were formerly highly prized. The Gomoku family, it so happens, is descended from one of these Ama villages, and moreover submarine watches are one of the firm's specialities.

The Altamonts hesitated for a long time before ordering their portrait, probably held back by Hutting's prices, pitched beyond the means of all but the chairmen and managing directors of very large companies, but they have finally decided to go ahead. They appear in picture No. 2, he as Noah, she as Coppelia, an allusion to the fact that she was once a ballerina.

Their German friend Fugger is also to be found amongst Hutting's customers. He is dealt with in the fourteenth portrait, since he is very distantly related on his mother's side to the Hapsburgs and once, having made a trip to Mexico, brought back eleven tortilla recipes!

CHAPTER SIXTY

Cinoc, 1

A kitchen. The floor is covered with a linoleum mosaic of jade and azure and cinnabar rhomboids. On the walls, paint that was once gloss. Against the rear wall, beside the sink, above a plastic-coated wire drainer, stuck one behind the other between the pipework and the wall, four post-office annual calendars with four-colour photographs:

1972: *Good Chums*: a jazz band composed of six-year-old kids playing toy instruments; the pianist, with his spectacles and deeply serious look, is vaguely reminiscent of Schroeder, the Beethovenish child prodigy in Schulz's *Peanuts*;

1973: *Summer Visions*: bees suck asters;

1974: *A Night on the Pampas*: three *gauchos* around a campfire strum guitars;

1975: *Pompon and Fifi*: a pair of monkeys play dominoes. The male wears a bowler hat and an acrobat's leotard with the number "32" inscribed in silver spangles on the back; the she-monkey smokes a cigar held between the thumb and index toe of her right foot, wears a feathered hat and crocheted gloves, and carries a handbag.

Higher up, on a sheet of almost identical dimensions, can be seen three daisies in a short-necked glass vase with a spherical base, whose caption simply states "PAINTED BY FEET AND MOUTH" and, in brackets, "original watercolour".

Cinoc is in his kitchen. He is a dry, thin old man dressed in a dingy-green flannel waistcoat. He is sitting on a Formica stool at a table with an oilcloth covering, beneath an adjustable metal ceiling light fixture enamelled white and equipped with a system of pulleys and a pear-shaped counterweight. He is eating pilchards in spice directly out of a badly opened tin. On the table in front of him are three shoe-boxes full of slips of card covered in meticulous handwriting.

Cinoc moved into Rue Simon-Crubellier in 1947, a few months after the death of Hélène Brodin-Gratiolet, whose flat he took over. He provided the inhabitants of the building, and especially Madame Claveau, with an immediate, difficult problem: how was his name to be pronounced? Obviously the concierge didn't dare address him as "Nutcase" by pronouncing the name "Sinok". She questioned Valène, who suggested "Cinosh", Winckler, who was for "Chinoch", Morellet, who inclined towards "Sinots", Mademoiselle Crespi, who proposed "Chinoss", François Gratiolet, who prescribed "Tsinoc", and finally Monsieur Echard, as a librarian well versed in recondite spellings and the appropriate ways of uttering them, demonstrated that, leaving aside any potential transformation of the intervocalic "n" into a "gn" or "nj" sound, and assuming once and for all, on principle, that the "i" was pronounced "i" and the "o", "o", there were then four ways of saying the initial "c": "s", "ts", "sh" and "ch", and five ways of pronouncing the final: "s", "k", "ch", "sh" and "ts", and that, as a result, depending on the presence or absence of one or another diacritic sign or accent and according to the phonetic particularities of one or another language or dialect, there was a case for choosing from amongst the following twenty pronunciations:

SINOS	SINOK	SINOCH	SINOSH	SINOTS
TSINOS	TSINOK	TSINOCH	TSINOSH	TSINOTS
SHINOS	SHINOK	SHINOCH	SHINOSH	SHINOTS
CHINOS	CHINOK	CHINOCH	CHINOSH	CHINOTS

As a result of which, a delegation went to ask the principal person concerned, who replied that he didn't know himself which was the most proper way of pronouncing his name. His family's original surname, the one which his great-grandfather, a saddler from Szczyrk, had purchased officially from the Registry Office of the County of Krakow, was Kleinhof: but from generation to generation, from passport renewal to passport renewal, either because the Austrian or German officials weren't bribed sufficiently, or because they were dealing with staff of Hungarian or Poldavian or Moravian or Polish origin who read "v" and wrote it as "ff" or who saw "c" and heard it as "tz", or because they came up against people who never needed to try very hard to become somewhat illiterate and hard of hearing when having to give identity papers to Jews, the name had retained nothing of its original pronunciation and spelling and Cinoc remembered his father telling him that his father had told him of having cousins called Klajnhoff, Keinhof, Klinov, Szinowcz, Linhaus, etc. How had Kleinhof become Cinoc? Cinoc really did not know; the only sure thing was that the final "f" had been replaced one day by that special letter (ß) with which Germans indicate double "s"; then, no doubt, the "l" had been dropped or had been replaced by an "h": so it got to Khinoss or Kheinhoss and, maybe, from there to Kinoch, Chinoc, Tsinoc, Cinoc, etc. Anyway it wasn't at all important whichever way you wanted to pronounce it.

Cinoc, who was then about fifty, pursued a curious profession. As he said himself, he was a "word-killer": he worked at keeping Larousse dictionaries up to date. But whilst other compilers sought out new words and meanings, his job was to make room for them by eliminating all the words and meanings that had fallen into disuse.

When he retired in nineteen sixty-five, after fifty-three years of scrupulous service, he had disposed of hundreds and thousands of tools, techniques, customs, beliefs, sayings, dishes, games, nick-names, weights and measures; he had wiped dozens of islands, hundreds of cities and rivers, and thousands of townships off the map; he had returned to taxonomic anonymity hundreds of varieties of cattle, species of birds, insects, and snakes, rather special sorts of fish, kinds of crustaceans, slightly dissimilar plants and particular breeds of vegetables and fruit; and cohorts of geographers, missionaries, entomologists, Church Fathers, men of letters, generals, Gods & Demons had been swept by his hand into eternal obscurity.

Who would know ever again what a *vigigraphe* was, "a type of telegraph consisting of watchtowers communicating with each other"? And who could henceforth imagine there had existed for perhaps many generations a "block of wood on the end of a stick for flattening watercress in flooded ditches" and that the block had been called a *schuèle* (shü-ell)? Who would recall the *vélocimane*?

> VELOCIMANE (masc. nn.)
> (from Lat. *velox*, *-ocis*, speedy, and *manus*, hand).
> Special locomotive device for children, resembling a horse, mounted on three or four wheels, also called *mechanical horse*.

Where had all the *abunas* gone, patriarchs of the Abyssinian Church, and the *palatines*, fur tippets worn by women in winter, so named after the Princess Palatine who introduced their use into France in the minority of Louis XIV, and the *chandernagors*, those gold-spangled NCOs who marched at the head of Second Empire processions? What had become of Léopold-Rudolph von Schwanzenbad-Hodenthaler, whose outstanding courage at Eisenühr allowed Zimmerwald to carry the day at Kisàszony? And Uz (Jean-Pierre), 1720–1796, German poet, author of *Lyrical Poems*, *The Art of Being Ever Joyful* (a didactic poem), *Odes and Songs*, etc.? And Albert de Routisie (Basel, 1834–White Sea, 1867). French poet and novelist. A great admirer of Lomonosov, he undertook a pilgrimage to his place of birth at Arkhangelsk, but the ship sank just before entering harbour. After his death his only daughter, Irena Ragon, published his unfinished novel, *Les Cent-Jours*, a selection of poetry, *Les Yeux de Mélusine*, and, under the title of *Leçons*, an admirable anthology of aphorisms which remains his finest work. Who would now ever know that François Albergati Capacelli was an Italian playwright born at Bologna in 1728, or that the master caster Rondeau (1493–1543) had been responsible for the bronze door of the funeral chapel at Carennac?

Cinoc began to dally on the banks of the Seine, rummaging through the open-air bookstalls, leafing through penny dreadfuls, out-of-date essays, obsolete traveller's guides, old textbooks on physiology, mechanics, or moral instruction, or superseded maps in which Italy still figured as a multicoloured patchwork of little kingdoms. Later on he went to borrow books from the municipal library of the XVIIth *arrondissement*, in Rue Jacques-Binjen, having them bring down from the attic dusty old folios, ancient users' manuals, volumes from the *Library of Miracles*, and old dictionaries: Lachâtre, Vicarius, Bescherelle aîné, Larrive, Fleury, the *Dictionary of Conversation* compiled by a Society of Men of Letters, Graves and d'Esbigné, Bouillet, Onions, Dezobry, and Bachelet. Finally, when he had exhausted the resources of his local library, he grew bolder and enrolled at Sainte-Geneviève, where he started to read the authors whose names he saw as he went in, carved on the stone façade.

He read Aristotle, Pliny, Aldrovandi, Sir Thomas Browne, Gesner, Ray, Linnaeus, Brisson, Cuvier, Bonneterre, Owen, Scoresby, Bennett, Aronnax, Olmstead, Pierre-Joseph Macquart, Sterne, Eugénie Guérin, Gastripheres, Phutatorius, Somnolentius, Triptolemy, Argalastes, Kysarchius, Egnatius, Sigonius, Bossius, Ticinenses, Baysius, Budoeus, Salmasius, Lipsius, Lazius, Isaac Casaubon, Joseph Scaliger, and even the *De re vestiaria veterum* by Rubenius (1665, quarto), which gave him a full & satisfactory account of the Toga, or loose gown, the Chlamys, the Ephod, the Tunica or jacket, the Synthesis, the Paenula, the Lacema with its Cucullus, the Paludamentum, the Praetexta, the Sagum or soldier's jerkin, and the Trabea: of which, according to Suetonius, there were three kinds.

Cinoc read slowly and copied down rare words; gradually his plan began to take shape, and he decided to compile a great dictionary of forgotten words, not in order to perpetuate the memory of the Akka, a black-skinned pygmy people of Central Africa, or of Jean Gigoux, a historical painter, or of Henri Romagnesi, a composer of romances, 1781–1851, nor to prolong the life of the scolecobrot, a tetramerous coleopter of the longicorn family, Cerambycid branch, but so as to rescue simple words which still appealed to him. In ten years he gathered more than eight thousand of them, which contain, obscurely, the trace of a story it has now become almost impossible to hand on:

RIVELETTE (fem. nn.)
Another name for myriophyllum, or water milfoil.

AREA (fem. nn.)
Med: A: Alopecia, fox-mange, a disease causing loss of body and head hair.

LOQUIS (masc. nn.)
Type of glass trinket used for trading with Negroes of the African coasts. Small cylinders made of coloured glass.

RONDELIN (masc. nn., from *rond*)
Vulgar word used by Chapelle to refer to a very fat man.

CADETTE (fem. nn.)
Ashlar suitable for paving.

LOSSE (fem. nn.)
Tchn: Iron hand-tool with a sharpened steel edge, shaped like a vertically sectioned semicone, hollowed out. Fits on a handle like a deck-scrubber's holystone, used for piercing barrel bungs.

BEAUCEANT (masc. nn.)
Name of the Knights Templars' standard.

BEAU-PARTIR (masc. nn.)
Showjumping. Fine departure of horse. Its straight-line speed up to a stopping point.

LOUISETTE (fem. nn.)
Name used for a time for the guillotine, whose invention was attributed to Dr Louis. "Louisette was the familiar name Marat gave to the guillotine" (Victor Hugo).

FRANCATU (masc. nn.)
Hort: Type of apple that keeps well.

RUISSON (masc. nn.)
Trench cut for draining a saltmarsh.

SPADILLE (fem. nn.)
(Span. *espada*, broadsword.) The ace of spades in the game of humber.

URSULINE (fem. nn.)
Small ladder leading to a narrow platform onto which fairground gypsies had their trained goats climb.

TIERÇON (masc. nn.)
A: *Meas*: Liquid measure containing a third part of a full measure. The volume of a *tierçon* was: 89.41 litres in Paris, 150.8 litres at Bordeaux, 53.27 litres in Champagne, 158.08 litres in London, and 151.71 litres at Warsaw.

LOVELY (masc. nn.)
(English *lovely*, pretty.) Indian bird resembling the European finch.

GIBRALTAR (masc. nn.)
A kind of cake.

PISTEUR (masc. nn.)
Hotel employee with the task of attracting customers.

MITELLE (fem. nn.)
(Lat. *mitella*, dim. of *mitra*, mitre.) *Ant: Rom*: Small mitre, type of headdress worn esp. by women, sometimes with lavish decorations.

Worn by men in the countryside. *Bot*: Genus of plant of the saxifrage family, thus called for the shape of its fruit, native of the cold regions of Asia and America. *Surg*: Sling for supporting the arm. *Moll*: Synonym of scalpella.

TERGAL, E (adj.)
(Lat. *tergum*, back.) Relating to an insect's back.

VIRGOULEUSE (fem. nn.)
Juicy winter pear.

HACHARD (masc. nn.)
Iron shears.

FEURRE (masc. nn.)
Straw from any kind of wheat. Long straw for rushing seats.

VEAU-LAQ (masc. nn.)
Very soft leather used for handbags, gloves, etc.

EPULIE (fem. nn.)
(From Grk. Eπι, on, and συλον, gum) *Surg*: Fleshy excrescence on or around the gum.

TASSIOT (masc. nn.)
Tchn: Cross made of two laths which basket-makers use to start certain items.

DOUVEBOUILLE (masc. nn.)
Mil: V: (deformation of *US: doughboy*, private, foot soldier) American soldier during First World War (1917–1918).

VIGNON (masc. nn.)
Prickly gorse.

ROQUELAURE (fem. nn.)
(From the name of its inventor, the Duc de Roquelaure.) Type of coat buttoned at the front from top to bottom.

LOUPIAT (masc. nn.)
Fam: Drunk. "She was bloody stuck with her *loupiat* of a husband" (E. Zola).

DODENAGE (masc. nn.)
Tchn: Way of polishing upholsterers' stud nails by putting them in a fine canvas or hide bag with emery or other abrasive matter.

CHAPTER SIXTY-ONE

Berger, 1

The Bergers' dining room. An almost square room, with a woodblock floor. In the centre, a round table on which two places have been set, alongside a metal lozenge-shaped dishstand, a soup pot, with the handle of a silver-plated ladle protruding from under its chipped lid, a white plate with a garlic sausage cut in two, garnished with mustard-flavoured sauce, and a Camembert with a label depicting a veteran of the Old Guard. Against the rear wall, a sideboard of indeterminate style bearing a lamp with a cube of opaline for a pedestal, and a bottle of Pastis 51, a single red apple on a pewter plate, and an evening paper with its banner headline clearly visible: PONIA CALLS FOR EXEMPLARY PUNISHMENT. Above the sideboard a painting has been hung, depicting an oriental landscape with weirdly twisted trees, a group of natives wearing tall conical hats, and junks on the horizon. It was supposed to have been painted by Charles Berger's great-grandfather, a professional NCO who was thought to have fought in the Tonkin campaign.

Lise Berger is alone in the dining room. She is a woman of about forty whose chubbiness verges quite distinctly on corpulence, not to say obesity. She is finishing laying the table for herself and her son – whom she'd sent down to empty the dustbin and buy the bread – and is putting a bottle of orange juice and a can of Munich Spatenbräu beer on the table.

Her husband, Charles, is a restaurant waiter. He is a jovial and rotund fellow, and the two of them make a plump pair of schmeckers with a taste for sausages, sauerkraut, a glass of white wine, and a nice cold can, the kind of couple you are more or less bound to come upon in your compartment whenever you catch a train.

For several years Charles worked in a nightclub portentously called *Igitur*, a kind of "poetic" restaurant where a performer, pretending to be some kind of spiritual son of Antonin Artaud, presented in a laborious drone a depressing anthology in which he included quite shamelessly all his own works, enlisting, in order to make them less unpalatable, the inadequate assistance of Guillaume Apollinaire, Charles Baudelaire, René Descartes, Marco Polo, Gérard de Nerval, François-René de Chateaubriand, and Jules Verne. But it didn't stop the restaurant from eventually going bankrupt.

Charles Berger is now at the *Villa d'Ouest*, a nightclub-restaurant near Porte Maillot on the west side of the city (whence its name), which presents a drag show and belongs to a man who formerly ran a team of door-to-door salesmen, going by the name of Désiré or, even more cosily, Didi. He's an ageless, unlined man who sports a toupee, has a fondness for beauty spots, chunky rings, bangles, and chain bracelets, and a penchant for spotless white flannel three-piece suits, with check breast-pocket handkerchiefs, crepe-de-Chine cravats, and suede shoes in mauve or violet hues.

Didi goes in for the "artistic" pose, that is to say he justifies his stinginess and pettiness with remarks of the sort: "You can't get anything done without bending the rules", or "If you want to be up to achieving your ambitions you have to be prepared to behave like a shit, expose yourself to risks, compromise yourself, go back on your word, behave like any artist taking the housekeeping money to buy paints".

Didi doesn't expose himself to risk that much, except on stage, and compromises himself as little as possible, but he is without doubt a shit, detested both by his performers and his staff. The waiters have nicknamed him "French veg" since the day, long past, when he ordered them, if a customer asked for an extra portion or serving of French fries – or any other garnish – to put it on the bill as a separate vegetable.

The food he serves is execrable. Under highfalutin names – Clear Vegetable Julienne with Vintage Sherry, Shrimp Pancake Rolls in Aspic, Chaud-froid of Bunting Souvaroff, Crayfish in Caraway Sigalas-Rabaud, Sweetbread Soufflé Excellence, Isard Vol-au-Vent in Amontillado, Prawns in Balaton Paprika, Exeter Ediles Dessert, Fresh Figs *Fregoli*, etc. – he serves pre-cooked, pre-cut portions delivered every morning by a wholesale delicatessen and which a pseudo-chef in a toque pretends to prepare, for instance heating in little copper pots gravy made of hot water, Oxo, and a dash of ketchup.

Fortunately customers don't flock to the *Villa d'Ouest* for its food. Meals are served at a gallop before the two shows at eleven and two in the morning, and people who can't get to sleep after it do not put their discomfort down to the suspicious, wobbling gelatin coating that they ingested but to the intense excitement experienced during the show. For the *Villa d'Ouest* is packed out from the first of January to the thirty-first of December, and diplomats, businessmen, political celebrities, and stars of stage and screen crush into the place to see shows of outstanding quality and in particular to see the two great stars who play with the company, "Domino" and "Belle de May": the unmatchable "Domino" who, in front of a set made of sparkling aluminium panels, does a stunning impression of Marilyn Monroe in that unforgettable sequence from *How to Marry a Millionaire* where her reflection is reflected in a thousand mirrors, itself in fact a remake of the most celebrated shot in *The Lady from*

Shanghai; and the fabulous "Belle de May", who metamorphoses in three flutters of her eyelids into Charles Trénet.

For Charles Berger, the work is much the same as what he did in his previous restaurant or what he would do in virtually any other establishment; it is probably rather easier, since all the meals are pretty well identical, all are served at the same time, and the job is markedly better paid. The only thing that is really different is that at the end of the second service, just before two a.m., after serving the coffee, the champagne, and the liqueurs, after moving tables and chairs so that as many people as possible can see, the four waiters, in their short waistcoats, their long aprons, carrying their white napkins and silver trays, have to get up on stage, line up in front of the red curtain, and, at a sign from the pianist, kick up their legs and sing as loud and as flat as possible, but all together:

Now you've had your di, di, di-dinner
You have to say thanks, yes you have-ter
To your friend and mine, to the mister
Who's gonna show, yes he is sir,
Oh yes sir! oh yes sir!
The best show in town, yes no less, sir!

upon which three showgirls spring from the tiny wings and open the show.

The waiters come on at seven p.m., when they dine together, then get the tables ready, put on the tablecloths and lay out the cutlery, get out the ice-buckets, arrange the glassware, the ashtrays, paper napkins, saltcellars, peppermills, toothpicks, and the samples of *Désiré* toilet water which are presented on the house as a welcome gift to customers. At four a.m., at the end of the second show, when the last of the audience is leaving after a final drink, they have supper with the performers, then clear and tidy the tables, fold the tablecloths, and leave, just as the cleaning lady arrives to empty the ashtrays, air the room, and do the Hoovering.

Charles gets home around six thirty. He makes coffee for Lise, wakes her by switching on the radio, and goes to bed as she gets up, gets washed and dressed, wakes Gilbert, smartens him up, and drives him to school on her way to work.

Charles, for his part, sleeps until two thirty, reheats a cup of coffee, lies in for a bit before shaving and dressing. Then he goes to fetch Gilbert from school. On his way back he shops at the market and buys a newspaper. He only just has time to skim through it. At six thirty he sets off on foot for the *Villa d'Ouest*, and on his way downstairs usually passes Lise on her way up.

Lise works in a health centre near Porte d'Orléans. She is a speech therapist and gives remedial help to children with stammers. She has Mondays off, and since the *Villa d'Ouest* is closed on Sunday nights, Lise and Charles manage to have some time together each week from Sunday morning to Monday evening.

CHAPTER SIXTY-TWO

Altamont, 3

Madame Altamont's boudoir. A dark and intimate room with oak woodwork, silk hangings, and heavy grey velvet curtains. Against the left-hand wall, between two doors, stands a tobacco-coloured divan on which a silky long-haired King Charles spaniel lies. Above the divan hangs a large hyperrealist canvas portraying a steaming plate of spaghetti and packet of Van Houten cocoa. In front of the divan is a low table on which are various silver trinkets, amongst them a little box of weights, of the sort that money-changers and assayers used to use, a circular box in which the cylindrical measures stack inside each other, in the manner of Russian dolls, and three piles of books, surmounted respectively by René Hardy's *Bitter Victory* (Livre de Poche), *Dialogues with 33 Variations by Ludwig van Beethoven on a Theme of Diabelli* by Michel Butor (Gallimard), and *Le Cheval d'Orgueil* by Pierre-Jakez Hélias (Plon, collection Terre humaine). Against the rear wall, beneath two prayermats decorated with black and ochre arabesques typical of Bantu esparto ware, is a Louis XIII chiffonier. On it stands a large, brass-rimmed oval mirror before which Madame Altamont sits, using a slender make-up stick to put kohl over her eyelashes and lids. She is a woman of about forty-five who has kept her beauty, with an impeccable bearing, a bony face, protruding cheekbones, and stern eyes. She is wearing only a brassiere and black lace panties. A narrow strip of black gauze is wrapped around her right hand.

Monsieur Altamont is also in the room. Wearing a broad check coat, he is standing by the window and reading a typewritten letter with a look of complete indifference. Beside him stands a metal sculpture probably representing a giant cup-and-ball: a V-shaped pedestal bearing a sphere on its top.

Cyrille Altamont completed his studies simultaneously at Polytechnique and the Ecole Nationale d'Administration, and at the age of thirty-one became permanent secretary and trustee of BIDREM (*Banque Internationale pour le Développement des Ressources Energétiques et Minières*), the International Development Bank for Energy and Mining Resources, an organisation sponsored by various public and private institutions, having its headquarters in Geneva, and responsible for funding all types of research and development touching on the exploitation of underground resources, including the awarding of grants to laboratories and of bursaries to researchers, the organisation of symposia, expert assessment, and, where appropriate, dissemination of new drilling methods, extraction devices, treatment processes, and transportation modes.

Cyrille Altamont is a long-legged man aged fifty-five, dressed in good English suiting and florid linen; with thinnish canary-yellow hair, blue eyes set close together, a close-clipped, straw-coloured moustache, and carefully manicured hands. In his own sphere he passes for a very energetic, cautious, and coldly practical man of business. But that didn't prevent him from behaving, on one occasion at least, with a lack of foresight which subsequently turned out to be disastrous for his bank.

In the early nineteen sixties, Altamont received a visit from a man with thin hair and poor teeth, Wehsal by name. Wehsal was at that time professor of organic chemistry at Green River University, Ohio, but during the Second World War he had been director of the mineral chemistry laboratory at the Chemische Akademie at Mannheim. In nineteen forty-five he was one of the men whom the Americans confronted with the following alternative: he could either agree to work for them, emigrate to the United States, and accept an interesting appointment, or be tried as an accessory to War Crimes and be sentenced to many years in prison. This operation, known as Operation Paperclip, hardly left much choice to men like Wehsal, and he was one of maybe two thousand scientists – the best known of them, even now, being Wernher von Braun – who set off en route to America together with several tons of scientific archives.

Wehsal was persuaded that, thanks to the war effort, German science and technology had made prodigious advances in many areas. Some techniques and methods had been made public since then: for instance, it was known that the fuel used to power V2s was potato alcohol; similarly, details had been released on the use of copper and tin in judicious proportion which had allowed the manufacture of field batteries found nearly twenty years later in perfect working order in the middle of the desert on tanks abandoned by Rommel.

But most of these discoveries had been kept secret; Wehsal hated the Americans, and he was sure that they were incapable of finding the answers for themselves and that they would not know how to use them effectively even if they were told. Whilst waiting for a rebirth of the Third Reich to give him the opportunity to apply such front-end research, Wehsal decided to rescue and preserve the scientific and technological heritage of Germany.

Wehsal's own specialism was in the field of carbon hydrogenation, that is to say petroleum synthesis; the principle was straightforward: theoretically, all that was needed was to combine a hydrogen ion and a molecule of carbon monoxide (CO) to produce petroleum molecules. The process could be performed using a carbon base, but it could be applied equally well to a lignite or peat base, and it was for that very reason that the German war industry had taken a formidable interest in the problem: Hitler's war machine effectively required supplies of petroleum which the country did not possess amongst its own subterranean resources, and it thus had to rely on synthetic fuels extracted from the huge deposits of lignite in Prussia and the no less colossal reserves of Polish peat.

Wehsal was perfectly familiar with the programme of experiments concerning this metamorphosis, for it was he who had devised the process at the theoretical level, but he knew almost nothing about the technology of some of the crucial intermediate stages, in particular, details of the quantities required and the duration of activity of the catalysts, the extraction of sulphuric deposits, and storage precautions.

So Wehsal set out to contact all his former colleagues, now dispersed all over North America. He steered clear of the sauerkraut clubs, the Sudeten Circles, the Sons of Aachen, and other set-ups fronting for organisations of old Nazis, which he knew were almost always infiltrated by informers, but, by using periods of leave and corridor conversations at congresses and conferences, he managed to find 72 of them. Many didn't want anything to do with his project: Professor Thaddeus, the magnetic-storm specialist, and Davidoff, the fragmentation specialist, would not say anything; and even less could be said by Dr Kolliker, the atomic scientist who had lost his arms and legs when his lab was bombed but who was considered to have the subtlest brain of his age, although he was, in addition, both deaf and dumb: permanently surrounded by four bodyguards and assisted by a specialist engineer who had been through intensive training for the sole purpose of lip-reading the invalid's equations, which he then wrote on a blackboard, Kolliker had developed a prototype of the strategic ballistic missile, the forerunner of Berman's classical Atlas rocket. Many others, at the Americans' instigation, had switched disciplines entirely, and had assimilated themselves to the American way of life to such an extent that they didn't want to remember what they had done for the Vaterland, or refused to talk about it. Some went so far as to denounce Wehsal to the FBI, which was quite pointless as the FBI had not ever ceased for a second its surveillance of all these recent immigrants, and two of its agents tailed Wehsal on each of his trips, wondering what he could be looking for; in the end they summoned him for questioning and, when he confessed that he was trying to recover the secret of turning lignite into petrol, they released him, since they really could not see anything basically anti-American about such an enterprise.

In time Wehsal nonetheless achieved his aim. In Washington he laid his hands on a bundle of archives which the federal government had had studied and had judged to be without interest: in it he found the description of the containers used for the transportation and storage of synthetic petrol. And three of his seventy-two former compatriots agreed to provide him with the answers he was after.

Wehsal wanted to return to Europe. He contacted BIDREM and, in exchange for appointment to the post of engineering consultant, he offered to reveal to Cyrille Altamont all the secrets relating to the hydrogenation of carbon and the industrial production of synthetic fuel. And, as an added bonus, he went on with a black-toothed grin, a method for making sugar from sawdust. By way of proof, he handed Altamont a few typescript sheets covered with formulae and figures: the overall equations of the transformation and – the only secret to be truly disclosed – the names, specifications, required quantities, and duration of activity of the mineral oxides to be used as catalysts.

The fantastic leap forward that the war was supposed to have fostered in science, and the secrets behind Germany's military superiority, did not interest Cyrille Altamont overmuch: he put that sort of thing in the same basket as the stories in the popular press about hidden SS treasure and the Loch Ness monster, but he was sufficiently conscientious at least to have a technical assessment made of the methods Wehsal was proposing. Most of his scientific advisers mocked the obsolete, burdensome, and clumsy techniques: in effect, you could have run rockets on vodka, just as the French had run their motor cars in wartime on charcoal gas; petrol could be made from lignite or from peat, and even from dead leaves, old rags, or potato peel: but it would be so expensive and would require such a monstrous plant that it was infinitely preferable to carry on using good old black gold from the ground. As for making sugar from sawdust, it was entirely devoid of interest, as the experts unanimously forecast that in the medium term sawdust would be a far more precious commodity than sugar.

Altamont filed Wehsal's documents and dropped the whole matter and for many years used the anecdote as a typical illustration of scientific stupidity.

Two years ago, towards the end of the first great oil crisis, BIDREM decided to sponsor research on synthetic fuels "based on graphites, anthracites, coal, lignite, peat, bitumen, resins, and organic salts": it has invested in such research more than a hundred times the amount Wehsal would have cost had the bank employed him. Altamont tried several times to get in touch with the chemist again; in the end he found out he had been arrested in November 1973, a few days after the OPEC meeting in Kuwait at which the decision was made to reduce deliveries of crude to most consumer countries by at least a quarter. Charged with attempting to pass "strategic" secrets to a foreign power – specifically, Rhodesia – Wehsal had hanged himself in his cell.

CHAPTER SIXTY-THREE

Service Entrance

A long corridor crisscrossed by pipes, with a tiled floor and walls partly hung with an old plastic-coated wallpaper vaguely representing clumps of palm trees. Milky glass globes, at each end, give it light, harshly.

Five delivery men are coming in, bringing various victuals for the Altamonts' party. The shortest leads the way, wilting under the weight of a fowl fatter than he is; the second one is carrying with extreme care a great beaten-brass tray laden with oriental sweetmeats – baklava, gazelles' horns, honey and date cakes – arranged as a set piece and surrounded with flowers; the third has in each hand three bottles of vintage Wachenheimer Oberstnest; the fourth bears on his head a metal plate covered in small meat pies, hot snacks, and canapés; and, lastly, the fifth man, closing the procession, carries a case of whisky on his right shoulder, a case on which is stencilled

THOMAS KYD'S
IMPERIAL MIXTURE
100% SCOTCH WHISKIES
blended and bottled in Scotland
by
BORRELLY, JOYCE & KAHANE
91, Montgomery Lane, Dundee, Scot.

In the foreground, partly occluding the last delivery man, a woman is leaving the building: a woman of about fifty, wearing a macintosh with a Dorothy bag – a green leather purse with a black leather string fastening – hanging on her belt, her head covered with a printed cotton scarf whose pattern is reminiscent of Calder's mobiles. She is carrying a grey she-cat in her arms and, between the index and middle fingers of her left hand, holds a postcard depicting Loudun, that town in Western France where someone called Marie Besnard was accused of poisoning all her family.

This lady does not live in this building, but in the one next door. Her cat, answering to the fond name of Lady Piccolo, spends hours on this staircase, dreaming perhaps of meeting a tom. A vain dream, alas, for all the male cats in the building – Madame Moreau's Pip, the Marquiseaux' Petit Pouce, and Poker Dice, who belongs to Gilbert Berger – have been doctored.

CHAPTER SIXTY-FOUR

In the Boiler Room, 2

In a tiny place with walls full of meters, manometers, and pipes of every calibre, adjacent to the room where the boiler itself is installed, a workman squats, poring over a plan on tracing paper placed on the bare concrete floor. He is wearing leather gloves and a jerkin and seems moderately angry, no doubt because he is obliged to carry out the stipulated terms of a maintenance contract, realises that this year cleaning the boiler is going to take longer than he had anticipated, and knows that therefore his profit will decline proportionately.

This was the hideout where Olivier Gratiolet set up his radio in the war, as well as the alcohol duplicator on which he printed his daily newssheet. It was a cellar in those days and belonged to François. Olivier knew he would have to spend long stretches down here and set it up appropriately, insulating all the exits with old doormats, rags, and bits of cork which Gaspard Winckler gave him. He used candlelight, kept out the cold by wrapping himself in Marthe's rabbit-fur coat and a bobbled balaclava, and for feeding himself brought down from Hélène Brodin's flat a little lattice-work larder in which he could keep for a few days a bottle of water, a bit of salami, some goat cheese his grandfather had managed to get to him from Oléron, and a few of those wrinkled acid-tasting cider apples which were just about the only fresh fruit you could get at all easily at the time.

He would settle into an ancient, oval-backed Louis XV-style armchair which had no armrests and only two and a half legs left, using a whole system of blocks to keep it stable. Its faded violet upholstery depicted a sort of Nativity scene: there was the Holy Virgin holding in her lap a newborn babe with an unnaturally large head, and, standing in for both the bearers of gifts and the Magi – and in the absence of the ass and ox – a bishop flanked by his two acolytes, all set in a surprising craggy landscape leading down to a sheltered harbour with marble palaces and hazy pinkish roofs.

To pass the long hours spent waiting during radio silence, he would read a bulky novel he had found in a chest. Whole pages were missing, and he had to try to find the links between the episodes he had. They concerned, amongst other things, a wicked Chinaman who snarled, a brave girl with hazel eyes, a big, quiet fellow whose knuckles turned white when someone really annoyed him, and someone called Davis who claimed to come from Natal, in South Africa, but had never set foot in the place.

Or he would rummage through the heaps of remnants that were piled up in burst wicker trunks. In them he found an old diary dating from 1926, full of obsolete phone numbers, a wasps' nest, a worn watercolour depicting ice-skaters on the Neva, and little Hachette editions of the French classics, which brought back painful memories of Corneille

Rome n'est plus dans Rome, elle est toute où je suis

and Racine

Oui, c'est Agamemnon, c'est ton roi qui t'éveille

and the celebrated muddle of

Prends un siège Cinna et assieds-toi par terre
Et si tu veux parler commence par te taire

and other gobbets of *Mithridate* and *Britannicus* which he had had to learn by heart and recite straight off without grasping a word. He also found some old toys which were certainly the ones François had played with: a clockwork spinning top and a little Negro of painted tin with a keyhole in his side and no breadth to speak of, just consisting of two more or less fused profiles, and his wheelbarrow now all bent and broken.

Olivier hid the wireless set in another toy: a chest whose slightly sloped top was pierced with holes that had originally been numbered – 03 was the only number still visible – into which you had to try to throw a metal quoit; the game was called barrel or frog, because the hardest hole to get was made to look like a frog with a huge gaping mouth. As for the duplicator – one of the small models used by restaurateurs to run off menus – it was hidden at the bottom of a trunk. After Paul Hébert's arrest, the Germans, led by the air-raid warden Berloux, came to search the cellars, but they scarcely glanced at Olivier's: it was the dustiest and most cluttered of all, the one where it was hardest of all to imagine a "terrorist" hiding.

During the Liberation of Paris, Olivier would have willingly fought on the barricades, but he wasn't given the chance to do so. The machine gun he had kept in reserve under his bed was set up, in the first hours of the Capital's insurrection, on the roof of a block at Place Clichy, and entrusted to a team of experienced marksmen. As for him, he was ordered to stay in his cellar to receive the instructions flooding in from London and all over the place. He stayed there for more than thirty-six hours on the trot, without sleeping or eating, with nothing to drink save some atrocious ersatz apricot juice, filling notepad after notepad with enigmatic messages like: "the presbytery has lost none of its charm nor the garden its splendour", "the archdeacon is a past master at Japanese billiards", or "all is well, Marchioness", which cohorts of helmeted couriers came to fetch at five-minute intervals. When he emerged next day in the evening, it was to hear the thunderous peal of the great tenor of Notre-Dame and of all the other church bells, celebrating the arrival of the armies of Liberation.

END OF PART THREE

PART FOUR

CHAPTER SIXTY-FIVE

Moreau, 3

At the beginning of the nineteen fifties, in the flat that Madame Moreau was to buy later on, there lived an enigmatic American woman whose beauty and blondeness as well as the mystery surrounding her, earned her the nickname of Lorelei. She claimed to be called Joy Slowburn and lived apparently alone in the vast space of her apartment, under the silent protection of a driver-cum-bodyguard answering to the name of Carlos, a short and swarthy Filipino always spotlessly dressed in white. People sometimes ran into him in luxury stores, purchasing candied fruits, chocolates, or sweets. She, for her part, was never seen in the street. Her shutters were always shut; she received no mail and her door only ever opened to caterers delivering cooked meals or to the florists who each morning delivered great heaps of lilies, arum, and tuberoses.

Joy Slowburn only ever went out after night had fallen, to be driven in a long black Pontiac by Carlos. The inhabitants of the building would watch her pass, a dazzling figure in a black, raw-silk ball gown with a long train which left almost all her back bare, with a mink stole on her arm, a large fan made of black feathers, and her hair of an unrivalled blondeness, skilfully plaited and crowned with a diamond-incrusted diadem; and on seeing her long, perfectly oval face, her narrow, almost cruel eyes, her almost bloodless lips (whereas the fashion then was for very red lips), neighbours felt a fascination such that they were unable to say whether it was delightful or frightening.

The most fantastical stories circulated about her. People said that on some nights she held sumptuous, silent parties, that men came to see her clandestinely, shortly before midnight, clumsily carrying bulky sacks; people said that a third, unseen person also lived in the flat but was not allowed to go out or be seen, and that ghostly and abominable noises sometimes rose through the cavities of the chimneys, making children sit bolt upright in bed out of fright.

* * *

One April morning in nineteen fifty-four, it was learnt that Lorelei and the Filipino had been murdered in the night. The murderer had given himself up to the police: he was the young woman's husband, that third tenant whose existence had been suspected by some, though none had ever seen him. He was called Blunt Stanley, and his revelations cleared up the mystery of the strange doings of Lorelei and her two companions.

Blunt Stanley was a tall man, as handsome as a Western hero, with dimples like Clark Gable's. He was an officer in the US Army when, one evening in 1948, he met Lorelei in a music hall in Jefferson, Missouri: born Ingeborg Skrifter, the daughter of a Danish pastor who had emigrated to the United States, she performed a clairvoyant act under the pseudonym of Florence Cook, a famous medium of the last quarter of the nineteenth century whose reincarnation Ingeborg claimed to be.

It was love at first sight for both of them, but their happiness was short-lived: in July nineteen fifty, Blunt Stanley left for Korea. His passion for Ingeborg was such that scarcely had he landed when, unable to live without her, he deserted so as to try to get back to her. The mistake he made was to desert not by going AWOL – it's true he wasn't granted any leave – but whilst leading a patrol not far from the thirty-eighth parallel: together with his Filipino guide – who was none other than Carlos, real name Aurelio Lopez – he abandoned the eleven men in his patrol, condemning them to certain death, and after a frightful peregrination arrived at Port Arthur, whence they managed to reach Formosa.

The Americans thought the patrol had been ambushed, that the eleven soldiers had died in it, and that Lieutenant Stanley and his Filipino guide had been taken prisoner. Years later, when the whole affair was about to reach its lamentable conclusion, the chancery division of Land Army general staff was still looking for Mrs Stanley, query widow, to give her the possibly posthumous Medal of Honor awarded to her absent husband.

Blunt Stanley was at the mercy of Aurelio Lopez, and it quickly became apparent that Aurelio Lopez intended to take full advantage of the fact: as soon as they were in safety, the Filipino told the officer that all the details of his desertion had been put in writing and deposited in sealed envelopes with lawyers having instructions to act on their contents if Lopez failed to give them signs of life at regular intervals. Then he asked for ten thousand dollars.

Blunt managed to get in touch with Ingeborg. On his instructions, she sold all that she could sell – their car, their trailer, her few jewels – and got to Hong Kong, where the two men joined her. When they had paid Lopez, the couple were together again, alone, with a fortune of some sixty dollars, which nonetheless got them to Ceylon, where they managed to land a paltry engagement in a show cinema: between the shorts and the feature film, a spangled curtain would descend over the screen, and a loudspeaker would announce Joy and Hieronymus, the famous seers from the New World.

Their first act was based on two classical tricks used by village-fair magicians: Blunt, dressed up as a fakir, would guess various things from numbers chosen apparently at random by Ingeborg; as for Ingeborg, dressed as a clairvoyant, she would take a steel nib and scratch the gelatin of a photographic plate representing Blunt, and a bleeding scar would appear on her partner's body at exactly the same place. The Singhalese public usually loves this sort of show, but it cold-shouldered this one: Ingeborg soon realised that, although her husband undeniably possessed stage presence, it was imperative that he keep his mouth shut, except to utter two or three inarticulate sounds.

The basic idea for their subsequent offerings grew out of this constraint and was soon perfected: after various divining exercises, Ingeborg would go into a trance and, communicating with the beyond, call forth the Illumined himself, Swedenborg, the "Buddha of the North", dressed in a long white tunic, his chest spangled with Rosicrucian emblems, a luminous, flickering, smoky, flashing, frightening apparition, accompanied by crackling, lightning, sparks, discharges, exhalations, and emanations of every kind. Swedenborg was content to utter a few indistinct grunts, or incantations such as "Acha Botacha Sab Acha", which Ingeborg would translate into sibylline sentences said in a screeching, strangulated voice:

"I have crossed the seas. I am in a central city, beneath a volcano. I see the man in his bedroom; he is writing, he is wearing a loose-fitting shirt, black with white and yellow trim; he puts the letter in a collection of Thomas Dekker's poetry. He stands; it is one o'clock by the clock on his mantelpiece, etc."

Their act, which relied on the usual sensorial and psychological preparations of this kind of attraction – mirror tricks, smoke tricks based on various combinations of carbon, sulphur, and saltpetre, optical illusions, sound effects – was a success from the start, and a few weeks later an impresario offered them a lucrative contract for Bombay, Iraq, and Turkey. It was there, during an evening at an Ankara nightclub called *The Gardens of Heian-Kyô*, that the meeting took place which would determine their careers: at the end of their show, a man called on Ingeborg in her dressing room and offered five thousand pounds sterling if she would agree to bring him into the presence of the Devil, and more precisely Mephistopheles, with whom he wished to make the usual pact: his eternal salvation against twenty years of omnipotence.

Ingeborg accepted. Making Mephistopheles appear was not intrinsically more complicated than making Swedenborg appear, even if this apparition had to happen in front of a single spectator rather than several dozen or several hundred indifferent, amused, or bemused onlookers who were all, in any case, seated much too far away from the thing to come and check any details if the whim so took them. For if this privileged spectator had believed in the appearance of the "Buddha of the North" to the extent of risking five thousand pounds to see the Devil, then there was no reason why his request should not be fulfilled.

Blunt and Ingeborg thus settled into a villa rented for the occasion and modified their act to fit the required apparition. On the appointed day, at the stated hour, the man turned up at the villa door. For three weeks, obeying Ingeborg's strict orders, he had tried never to go out before nightfall, to eat only boiled green vegetables and fruit peeled with non-metallic instruments, to drink only orange-flower water and fresh mint, basil, and oregano tea.

A native servant led the applicant into an almost unfurnished room, painted matt black throughout, barely lit by torches set in inverted conical holders giving off greenish-yellow flames. In the centre of the room hung a cut-glass globe, revolving slowly on its axis, whose thousand minute faces projected twinkling flashes in apparently unpredictable directions. Ingeborg sat beneath it, in a high-backed armchair painted dark red. About a yard away from her, a little to her right, a fire burned on flat stones set directly on the floor, giving off copious, acrid smoke.

According to custom, the man had brought a black hen in a brown canvas bag; he blindfolded it, then cut its throat over the fire whilst looking to the east. The hen's blood did not put out the fire; on the contrary, it seemed to make it burn more fiercely: tall blue flames shot up, and for a few moments the young woman observed them attentively, taking no notice of her client's presence. Finally she rose, took some cinders in a shovel, and spread them on the floor just in front of her chair, where, instantaneously, they formed a pentangle. Taking the man by his arm, she made him sit in the armchair, with his back straight, quite still, with his hands flat down on the armrests. For her part, she kneeled in the centre of the pentangle and began to declaim an incantation as long as it was incomprehensible, in an impossibly high-pitched screech:

> *Al barildim gotfano dech min brin alabo dordin falbroth ringuam albaras. Nin porth zadikim almucathin milko prin al elmin enthoth dal heben ensouim: kuthim al dum alkatim nim broth dechoth porth min michais im endoth, pruch dal maisoulum hol moth dansrilim lupaldas im voldemoth. Nin hur diavosth mnarbotim dal goush palfrapin duch im scoth pruch galeth dal chinon min foulchrich al conin butathen doth dal prim.*

In the course of this incantation the smoke grew more and more opaque. Soon there were reddish plumes of smoke accompanied by crackling and sparks. Suddenly the bluish flames grew unnaturally tall, then died away almost at once: just behind the fire, baring all his teeth in a broad grin, with his arms akimbo, stood Mephistopheles.

It was a fairly traditional Mephisto, almost a conventional one. He didn't have horns, or a long cloven tail, or goat's hooves, but a greenish face, dark eyes set deep in their sockets, bushy, very black eyebrows, a thin moustache, and a Napoleon III goatee. He was wearing a somewhat indeterminate costume: what could mainly be seen was an immaculate lace ruff and a dark-red waistcoat, the remainder being masked by a big black cape whose flame-red silk lining gleamed in the firelight.

Mephistopheles didn't say a word. All he did was bow his head very slowly whilst placing his right hand on his left shoulder. Then he put his hand out over the hearth, now burning with flames that seemed almost unearthly and giving off strongly scented smoke, and signalled the applicant to come forward. The man rose and went to stand next to Mephistopheles, on the other side of the fire. The Devil handed him a parchment folded in four, bearing a dozen or so incomprehensible signs; then he grasped the man's right hand and pricked his thumb with a steel needle, bringing forth a bead of blood which he placed onto the pact; on the opposite corner he swiftly signed his own mark with his left index finger, apparently covered with greasy soot, a signature resembling a large, three-fingered hand. Then he tore the sheet in two, put one half in his waistcoat pocket, and handed the other to the man with a low bow.

Ingeborg gave a strident scream. There was a noise of paper being crumpled, and the blinding glare of lightning flashed through the room, accompanied by a roll of thunder and an intense smell of sulphur. Thick, acrid smoke formed all around the fireplace. Mephistopheles had disappeared, and on turning round the man once again saw Ingeborg sitting in her armchair; in front of her there was no trace of the pentangle.

Despite the exaggerated precautions she took, and in spite of the rigid, somewhat overstylised aspect of the performance, it does indeed seem that this apparition matched what the man had expected, for not only did he pay up the promised sum without a grumble, but a month later, still without revealing his identity, he let Ingeborg know that one of his friends, living in France, had a keen wish to partake of a ceremony identical to the one he had been honoured to witness, and that the friend was disposed to give her five million French francs and in addition to meet her travelling costs and her expenses in Paris.

That is how Ingeborg and Blunt came to France. But unfortunately for them they did not come alone. Three days before they were to leave, Aurelio Lopez, whose affairs had taken a turn for the worse, joined them in Ankara and demanded to go with them. They were unable to refuse. All three settled in the big flat on the first floor. It had been agreed already that Blunt would never show himself. As for Aurelio, they decided that, rather than their taking on a maid and a butler, he would serve, under the name of Carlos, as chauffeur, bodyguard, and groom.

In the space of a little over two years, Ingeborg had the Devil appear 82 times for fees eventually rising to twenty, twenty-five, and once even thirty million (old) francs. The list of her customers included six members of parliament (of whom three in fact became ministers, and only one an Under-Secretary of State), seven top civil servants, eleven company directors, six officers of the rank of general or above, two professors at the Medical Faculty, various sportsmen, several top clothes designers, restaurant owners, a newspaper editor, and even a cardinal, the other applicants coming from the worlds of the arts, literature, and especially show business. All were men, with the exception of one black operatic singer whose ambition was to play the role of Desdemona: shortly after signing her pact with the Devil, she brought her dreams to reality thanks to a "negative" production which caused a scandal but ensured notoriety for the singer and the director: Otello's role was played by a white man, all the other parts were played by black artists (or whites in black make-up), with costumes and sets similarly "inverted", where everything light or white (the handkerchief and the pillow, for instance, to quote just those two indispensable props) became dark or black, and vice versa.

No one ever expressed a doubt about the "reality" of the apparition or the authenticity of the pact. Once only, one of their customers was amazed to have kept his shadow and to be able still to see his reflection in mirrors, and Ingeborg had to persuade him that this was a privilege Mephistopheles had granted to avoid his being "recognised and burnt alive *in foro publico*".

As far as Ingeborg and Blunt could tell, the effect of the pact was almost always beneficial: the certain belief in omnipotence was usually enough to make those who had sold their souls to the Devil accomplish what they expected of themselves. In any case, the couple had no problem in recruiting applicants. Barely three months after their arrival in Paris, Ingeborg had to start turning down the offers that were flooding in, charging applicants higher and higher rates, setting longer and longer waiting lists and more and more rigorous preparatory tasks. At her death, her "order book" was full for more than a year ahead, there were over thirty applicants on her waiting list, and four of them committed suicide when they learnt of her death.

The apparition scenario never differed very much from what it had been in Ankara, except that, from quite early on, the seances no longer started in darkness. The cone-shaped torches were replaced by heavy-looking floor-standing black cylinders surmounted by large spherical glass bulbs giving off a bright blue light which dimmed imperceptibly, allowing the applicant time to see for himself that the room was empty apart from the young woman and himself and that all exits were hermetically sealed. The couple brought their existing trick techniques to perfection – lighting adjustment and flame control, the sound-proofing required for thunder effects, remote ignition of the ferrocerium tablets which produced sparks, the manipulation of iron filings and magnets – and introduced some others, in particular the use of certain siphenapteroid insects endowed with a phospherescent power giving them a glowing green hue, and the use of special perfumes and incenses which, mixed with the smell of the lilies and tuberoses which permanently impregnated the place, created sensations favourable to manifestations of the supernatural. These ingredients would never have been adequate to persuade anyone ever so slightly sceptical, but people who had accepted Ingeborg's terms and endured the preliminary ordeals came, on the evening of their pact, ready to be convinced.

Unfortunately, their professional success did not free Ingeborg and Blunt from Carlos's continuing blackmail. Ingeborg was supposed to speak only Danish and some Upper Friesian dialect by means of which she conversed with Mephistopheles, and so it was the Filipino who negotiated with applicants, and he kept for himself the entirety of the colossal sums they paid him. His surveillance never ceased, and when he went out to buy things he forced the former officer and his wife to strip and put their clothes under lock and key, having no intention of letting go of this veritable goose with the golden eggs.

In 1953, the Armistice of Panmunjon raised their hopes of an imminent amnesty which would allow them to be free of this unbearable servitude. But a few weeks later, Carlos, with a triumphant smile on his face, handed them an already long-published issue of the *Louisville Courier and Journal* (Kentucky): the mother of one of the soldiers Lieutenant Stanley had had under his command had expressed surprise at the absence of Blunt Stanley's name from the list of prisoners released by the North Koreans. The Army had been alerted to this and had decided to reopen the case. Although not yet giving a final verdict, the investigators were at that point prepared to hint that they could no longer exclude the possibility that Lieutenant Stanley might have been a deserter and a traitor.

Several months later, Ingeborg succeeded in persuading her husband that he had to kill Carlos, so that they might flee. One evening in April 1954, Blunt managed to evade the Filipino's vigilance and throttled him with a pair of braces.

They searched the flat and found the hiding hole where Carlos kept more than seven million old francs, in banknotes of every denomination and in jewels. They hurriedly filled two suitcases and prepared to leave: they were planning to go to Hamburg, where several people had already suggested Ingeborg should set up her diabolical business. But, just before going out, Blunt automatically looked out of the window and through the shutters saw two men apparently watching the building; and he panicked. It was obviously not possible for Carlos's threats to have been carried out already, only a few seconds after his murder, but Blunt, who had not left the flat even once ever since he had moved in, imagined that the Filipino had been having them watched for ages and violently reproached his wife for not having noticed.

It was during this altercation, Stanley claimed, that Ingeborg, who was holding a small pistol in her hand, had been killed accidentally.

Blunt Stanley was tried in France on charges of premeditated murder, homicide by inadvertence, public exploitation of occult powers (articles 405 and 479 of the Penal Code), and fraud. He was then extradited, taken back to the United States, tried by court martial on a charge of high treason, and sentenced to death. But he was granted presidential clemency, and his sentence was commuted to life imprisonment.

The rumour spread rapidly that he possessed supernatural powers and that he was able to communicate – and to commune – with infernal forces. Almost all the warders and prisoners at Abigoz penitentiary (Iowa), as well as numerous policemen and several judges and politicians, asked him to intercede on their behalf with one devil or another on some particular problem or another. They had to install a special visiting booth so he could receive wealthy individuals from every corner of the United States who requested an audience with him. The less wealthy, instead of consulting him, and for a fee of fifty dollars, could touch his prison number, 1758064176, which is also the number of Devils in Hell, since there are 6 demoniacal legions each of 66 cohorts each of 666 companies each comprising 6,666 Devils. For a mere ten dollars, you could buy one of his fluidic needles (old steel pick-up needles). For numerous communities, congregations, and faiths, Blunt Stanley has become today the reincarnation of the Evil One, and several fanatics have come to Iowa to commit indictable offences with the sole purpose of being imprisoned at Abigoz so as to attempt to murder him; but, with the complicity of the warders, he has managed to set up a bodyguard consisting of other prisoners, who have, up to now, protected him effectively. According to the satirical journal *Nationwide Bilge*, he must be one of the ten richest lifers in the world.

It was only in May nineteen sixty, when the mystery of Chaumont-Porcien was clarified, that it was realised that the two men who were in fact watching the building were the two detectives Sven Ericsson had hired to tail Véra de Beaumont.

Madame Moreau decided to turn this room, where Lorelei made Mephisto appear and where the twin murder occurred, into her kitchen. The designer Henry Fleury devised an avant-garde outfit which he loudly proclaimed would be the prototype for the kitchens of the twenty-first century: a culinary laboratory a generation ahead of its time, equipped with the most sophisticated technology, fitted with microwave ovens, invisible automatic hotplates, remote-controlled domestic robots capable of carrying out complex food preparation and cooking programmes. All these ultramodern devices were cleverly integrated into antique-style cupboards, Second Empire ranges in enamelled cast iron, and curio cases. Behind brass-hinged polished oak doors hid electric slicers, electronic grinders, ultrasound chip-pans, infrared toasters, totally transistorised electro-mechanical blenders, regulators, mixers, and peelers; but on coming in all you could see were walls tiled in Old Delft style, unbleached cotton tea towels, old Roberval weighing scales, pitchers with little pink flowers on them, pharmacy jars, big check tablecloths, rustic dressers with Mayenne linen fringes, bearing little pastry moulds, pewter measuring cups, brass pots, and cast-iron *cocottes*, and, on the floor, a spectacular pattern of tiles, an alternation of white, grey, and ochre rectangles, some decorated with lozenge motifs, a faithful reproduction of the floor of the chapel in a monastery at Bethlehem.

Madame Moreau's cook, a sturdy Burgundian hailing from Paray-le-Monial and answering to the first name of Gertrude, was not going to be taken in by such gross trickery, and informed her mistress immediately that she would not ever cook anything in a kitchen like that, where nothing was in its proper place and nothing worked the way she knew. She insisted on having a window, a stone sink, a real gas cooker with rings, a deep frying pan, a chopping block, and especially a scullery to put her empty bottles in, for her cheese wickers, crates, potato bags, her buckets for washing vegetables, and her salad bowl.

Madame Moreau sided with her cook. Fleury, smarting, had to have his experimental equipment removed, break up the floor, dismantle the plumbing and electrical circuitry, and move the partitions.

Of the weathered old junk from French kitchens of times gone by, Gertrude has kept the pieces she might use – a rolling pin, the scales, the salt box, the kettles, *cocottes*, fish poachers, pot ladles, and butchering knives – and has had the rest put down in the cellar. She brought up from her homeland some of the utensils and accessories she could not have done without: her coffee grinder and her tea-egg, a flat strainer, a conical strainer, a potato masher, a *bain-marie*, and the box in which she has always kept her vanilla pods, her cinnamon sticks, her cloves, her saffron, her silver balls, and her angelica, an old biscuit box made of tin, square in shape, on the lid of which you can see a little girl munching the corner of her *petit-beurre*.

CHAPTER SIXTY-SIX

Marcia, 4

Just as she treats the furniture and objects which she trades as her own property, so Madame Marcia treats her customers as friends. Independently of the business she does with them (in which she often reveals herself to be particularly tough), she has succeeded in creating ties with most of her clients which go far beyond strictly business relations: they take each other out to tea, invite each other to dinner, play bridge together, go to the Opera, visit exhibitions, lend each other books, exchange recipes, and even go on cruises together in the Greek islands, or to summer schools at the Prado.

Her shop has no proper name. A plain inscription in small white cursive is fixed over the doorhandle.

C. Marcia Antiques

On the two small shop windows, there are several stickers announcing even more discreetly that this or that credit card is accepted, and that night surveillance is provided for the shop by a specialist service bureau.

The shop proper consists of two rooms communicating by a narrow passageway. The first room, the one you come into, is mainly devoted to small items, trinkets, curios, scientific instruments, lamps, jugs, boxes, porcelain, bisque ware, fashion plates, accessory furniture, etc., which, even if they are of high value, are all things which a customer can hasten off with once he has made a purchase. David Marcia, today twenty-nine years old, has been in charge of this part of the shop since 1971, when his accident in the 35th Gold Cup brought his days in motorcycle racing to an end.

Madame Marcia herself, whilst being in overall control of the store, is concerned more particularly with the second room, the one we are now in, the rear of the shopfront, which communicates directly with the back room and is devoted primarily to large pieces, to drawing-room suites, farm tables, refectory tables flanked by long benches, four-poster beds, and solicitors' filing cabinets. Madame Marcia usually spends her afternoons here, where she has installed her office – a small three-drawer walnut table, late eighteenth century, on which she has placed two grey metal card-index cases, one listing the regular customers whose tastes she knows and whom she regularly invites to come to see her latest acquisitions, the other containing the details of all the articles that have passed through her hands and of each of which she has tried to write the history, with its origin, its features, and its fate. A black telephone, a notepad, a tortoiseshell propelling pencil, a minute conical paperweight with a base less than an inch in diameter but whose small size does not prevent it from weighing three "troy ounces", that is to say 93 grammes, and a Gallé soliflor containing a purple moonflower, a variety of everlasting flower also called Star of the Nile, combine to clutter the table's narrow top.

Compared to the back room, or even to her bedroom, this room holds relatively few pieces of furniture; the season is certainly a poor one for business, but Madame Marcia, on principle, has never sold a lot of items simultaneously. Her back room, her cellar, and the rooms of her own flat give her plenty of opportunity to rotate her stock, without her being obliged to overload the room where she displays the pieces she wants to sell at a particular time and which she would rather show in a setting specifically designed for them. One of the reasons for the incessant circulation she inflicts on her furniture stems directly from her desire to show the pieces to their best advantage, which makes her change her displays more often than she would were she a window dresser in a department store.

Her latest acquisition, the centrepiece of the current arrangement of the room, is a late nineteenth-century lounge suite found in a family hotel in Davos where a Hungarian pupil of Nietzsche's is said to have spent some time: baroque easy chairs with little pads on the arms grouped about a small metal-bound table, behind which stands a sofa in the same style with velvet cushions. Around these rather heavy Austro-Hungarian, Ludwig-of-Bavarianish wedding-cake pieces, Madame Marcia has arranged items which either match their baroque contortions or provide a contrast of primitive or rustic strangeness, or of icy perfection: to the left of the table, a rosewood low table on which three finely chased antique clocks are placed, together with a very pretty leaf-shaped teaspoon, a few illuminated books with enamel-incrusted bindings and metal hasps, and a particularly fine skrimshanker, a trinket made by whalers to fill long hours of enforced idleness, representing a look-out perched in the rigging, carved from a sperm-whale tooth.

On the other side, to the right of the easy chairs, an austere metal music stand, equipped with two articulated extensions with ends designed to hold candles, displays a stunning print probably intended to accompany an ancient volume on natural history, depicting on the left-hand side a peacock in profile, a stiff and sharp-edged outline with the plumage bunched into an almost dull, blurred mass, with only a large, white-rimmed eye and an erect crest giving it a touch of life, and, on the right, the same beast seen in his pride, face-on, an exuberant mass of shimmering, sparkling, flashing, flaming colour beside which a Gothic stained-glass window looks like a pale imitation.

The rear wall is bare, setting off a light cherrywood wall panel and an embroidered silk hanging.

Finally, in the window, four objects, discreetly illuminated by unseen spotlights, appear to be attached to each other by a multitude of imperceptible threads.

The first one, leftmost from where we are looking, is a medieval *pietà*, a painted wood carving, almost life-size, mounted on a sandstone dais: a Madonna with gathered brows and a wry, wailing mouth, and a Man of Sorrows with crudely emphasised anatomy, great blobs of coagulated blood welling from the wound in his side and the nail-prints in hands and feet. It was thought to be of Rhenish origin, dating from the fourteenth century, and to illustrate the exaggerated realism of the period as well as its taste for the macabre.

The second object stands on a little lyre-shaped easel. It is a study by Carmontelle – a charcoal sketch touched up with pastels – for his portrait of Mozart as a child; it differs in several details from the finished portrait now in the Musée Carnavalet in Paris: Leopold Mozart is standing not behind his son's chair, but on this side of it, at three-quarters angle so as to be able to supervise the child whilst also reading the score; as for Maria-Anna, she is seen not in profile behind the harpsichord, but full-face, in front of the harpsichord, partly obscuring the score which the child prodigy is sight-reading; it is not difficult to imagine Leopold asking the artist to make the changes seen in the definitive version, as they do not impinge on the son's central position, but give the father a less secondary place.

The third object is a large sheet of parchment in an ebony frame, placed diagonally on a stand which cannot be seen. The upper half of the sheet bears a very fine copy of a Persian miniature; as day breaks, a young prince on his palace balcony gazes at the sleeping princess at whose feet he is kneeling. On the lower half of the sheet, six lines of verse from Ibn Zaydûn are written out in elegant copperplate:

And I should live in the anxiety of not knowing
Whether the Master of my Fate
Proving less indulgent than Sultan Shahriyar
In the morning when I broke off my tale
Would consent to a further reprieve of my sentence
And permit me to resume my story next evening

The last object is a fifteenth-century Spanish suit of armour, all of its pieces finally welded together by rust.

Madame Marcia's real specialism concerns that kind of clockwork automata called animated watches. Unlike other automata or musical boxes disguised as candy boxes, walking-stick handles, comfit boxes, perfume phials, etc., animated watches are not, generally speaking, miracles of craftsmanship. But their rarity is what gives them all their value. Whilst animated carriage clocks, such as Jack-o'-the-clocks, and animated case clocks, such as Swiss-chalet cuckoo clocks, have always been very common, it is extremely rare to come across an even moderately old watch – be it a fob watch, a turnip watch, or a hunter – in which the indication of the hours and minutes is the pretext for a clockwork picture.

The first to appear were in fact merely miniature Jack-o'-the-clocks in which one or two characters of minimal depth came out to strike the hours on virtually flat bells.

Then came lubricious watches, thus designated by watchmakers who, though they agreed to manufacture them, refused to sell them on site, that is to say in Geneva. Entrusted to the agents of the East India Company for trading in America or the Orient, they rarely got to their destinations: they were customarily traded in European ports, and this clandestine commerce quickly grew so intense that the watches became unobtainable. Barely a few hundred were made subsequently, and sixty or so at the most have survived. A single American watchmaker owns more than two-thirds of them. The sketchy specifications he has given of the contents of his collection – he has never given anyone permission to see or to photograph any one of his watches – suggest that the makers did not make much effort to display imagination: on thirty-nine of the forty-two watches that he possesses, the scene depicted is the same: heterosexual copulation between two members of the human species, both adult, belonging to the same race (white, or, as people also say, Caucasian); the male is prone on top of a supine woman (the so-called "missionary" position). Seconds are marked by a hip-movement of the male, whose pelvis moves back and forth once a second; the female marks the minutes with her left arm (visible shoulder) and the hours with her right arm (hidden shoulder). The fortieth watch is identical to the first thirty-nine, except that it was painted after manufacture, making the female a black woman. It belonged to a slave trader called Silas Buckley. The forty-first, of much more delicate construction, represents Leda and the Swan: the bird beats its wings every second to mark the rhythms of their amorous frolic. The forty-second, rumoured to have belonged to the nobleman Andréa de Nerciat, is supposed to illustrate a scene from his famous work *Lolotte, or My Noviciate*: a young man, disguised as a serving wench, is debagged and buggered by a man whose dress, as it opens, half-reveals an improbably oversized sexual organ; the two figures are standing, the man behind the maid, who leans on a doorpost. The specification given by the watchmaker unfortunately fails to state how the hours and seconds are marked.

Madame Marcia herself only owns eight watches of this kind, but that doesn't prevent her collection from being much more varied: apart from an antique Jack-o'-the-clocks representing two blacksmiths taking turns to hammer an anvil and a "lubricious" watch analogous to those in the American's collection, all her pieces are Victorian or Edwardian period toys whose clockwork mechanisms have miraculously remained in working order:

- a butcher chopping a leg of lamb on a block;
- two Spanish dancers: one marks the hours with her castanet-clacking arm, the other marks the seconds by lowering her fan;
- an athletic clown perched on a sort of vaulting horse, contorting himself so that his rigidly stretched legs mark the hours, whilst his head nods to the seconds;
- two soldiers, one making semaphore signals (hours), the other, at the ready, saluting each second;
- a man's head with a long, thin moustache serving as the hands of the watch; seconds are marked by his eyes moving right to left, left to right.

As for the oldest piece in this brief collection, it could have come straight out of *Le Bon Petit Diable*, that Victorian children's storybook by the Comtesse de Ségur: a horrible old hag, spanking a little boy.

Although he has always refused to have anything to do with this store, it was nonetheless Léon Marcia who gave his wife the idea of specialising to such a degree; although every major city in the world has experts on automata, toys, and watches, there was no one dealing with the specific field of animated watches. In fact it was by chance that Madame Marcia has come in time to own eight of them; she is not herself a collector in the slightest, and is quite willing to sell items she has lived with for years, never doubting she will find others of which she will grow just as fond. Her role is much more focused, and consists of finding such watches, tracing their histories, authenticating them, and putting their collectors in touch with each other. Ten years or so ago, whilst on a trip to Scotland, she stopped over at Newcastle-upon-Tyne and came across Forbes's painting *A Rat Behind the Arras*, in the City Gallery. She had a full-sized photograph made of it and on her return to France undertook an examination of it under a magnifying glass, so as to check whether Lady Forthright had any of this kind of watch in her collection. The result being negative, she gave the reproduction to Caroline Echard as a present on the occasion of her marriage to Philippe Marquiseaux.

The picture did not correspond to any of the desiderata the young marrieds had put on their wedding list. This hanged coachman and dumbfounded Lady gave the gift a rather morbid air, and it was hard to see how it could convey wishes for a happy future. But maybe that was exactly what Madame Marcia wished to convey to Caroline, who had broken off with David two years before.

Caroline was the same age as David, the two having been born within two months of each other; they had learnt to walk together, had made mud pies in the same park, and had sat side by side at nursery school, then at junior school. Madame Marcia adored and adulated Caroline as a little girl, then began to detest her as she grew out of plaits and gingham dresses. She began to call her a silly goose and to tease her son for letting her twist him round her little finger. She was relieved when they broke it off, but for David it was obviously more painful.

At that time he was an athletic lad, puffing with pride in his fully silk-lined red leather motorbike gear, with a golden beetle embroidered on the back. His bike was then a modest Suzuki 125, and one cannot entirely dismiss the theory that that little goose of a Caroline Echard went for someone else – not Philippe Marquiseaux, but someone called Bertrand Gourguechon, whom she dropped immediately – because he had a 250cc Norton.

Whatever the truth of the matter, the growth of David Marcia's emotional scar tissue can be gauged by the increasing cubic capacity of his machines: Yamaha 250, Kawasaki 350, Honda 450, Kawasaki Mach III 500, a four-cylinder Honda 750, Guzzi 750, a water-cooled Suzuki 750, BSA A75 750, Laverda SF 750, BMW 900, Kawasaki 1000.

He had turned professional several years before the day – 4 June 1971 – when, riding the last-named bike, he skidded on a slick of oil a few minutes before the start of the 35th Gold Cup at Montlhéry. He was lucky enough not to fall badly, and broke only his collarbone and his right wrist, but this accident sufficed to rule him out of competitive riding for good.

CHAPTER SIXTY-SEVEN

Basement, 2

Cellars. The Rorschachs' cellar.

Floorboards salvaged from the conversion of the duplex have been screwed to the wall, becoming makeshift shelving. On them are to be found remnants of wallpaper with vaguely fish-like semi-abstract patterns, paint pots of all sizes and shades, a few dozen grey boxfiles labelled ARCHIVES, the residue of some official function or other at TV Programme Control.

Indistinct objects – bags of plaster, jerry cans, burst trunks? – strew the floor. Some more identifiable objects can be made out: cartons of washing powder, a rusty stool.

A bottle rack, wire, plastic-coated, is placed to the left of the slatted door. The lower level of the rack holds five bottles of fruit brandies: kirsch, apricot, quetsch, plum, raspberry. On one of the middle rows there is the score – in Russian – of Rimsky-Korsakov's version of Pushkin's *Golden Cockerel*, and a probably popular novel entitled *Spice, or the Revenge of the Louvain Locksmith*, with a cover depicting a girl handing a bag of gold to a judge. On the top row, a lidless octagonal tin containing a few novelty chessmen made of plastic, crudely imitating Chinese ivory pieces: the knight is a kind of Dragon, the king a seated Buddha.

Cellars. Dinteville's cellar.

A remover's packing case spills over with piles of books which only left the cellar of the doctor's previous house at Lavaur (Department of Tarn) to be put in this one. Amongst them, *A History of the World War* by Captain Liddell Hart, with pages one to twenty-two missing, some pages from Béhier & Hardy's *Elementary Treatise on Internal Pathology*, a Greek grammar, an issue dating from 1905 of the *Annals of Ear and Larynx Diseases*, and an offprint of Meyer-Steineg's article on "Das medizinische System der Methodiker", *Jenaer med.-histor. Beiträge* fasc. 7/8, 1916.

On the old waiting-room sofa whose formerly green canvas upholstery is now split and rotting away, an imitation-marble plaque has been put: originally rectangular, now broken, it reads: CONSULTING R

Somewhere on a plank, beside cracked jars, dented bowls, unlabelled phials, lies Dr Dinteville's earliest medical souvenir: a square box full of small, rusty nails. He kept it in his consulting room for a long time and has never been able to decide to get rid of it.

When Dinteville settled in Lavaur, one of his first patients was a fairground juggler who a few weeks previously had swallowed one of his knives. Dinteville didn't know what to do, didn't dare operate, and gave him an emetic just in case: the patient brought up a heap of little nails. Dinteville was so bewildered that he wanted to write a paper on the case. But the few colleagues to whom he told the story advised him against it. Even if they themselves had sometimes heard tales of similar cases and stories of swallowed pins turning around in the œsophagus or the stomach of their own accord so as not to perforate the intestine, they were convinced that this case was a put-up job.

Near the cellar door a skeleton hangs dismally from a nail in the wall. Dinteville bought it when he was a student. It was nicknamed Horatio, in memory of Nelson, since its right arm was missing. He is still fitted out with a black blindfold over the right eye socket, a tattered waistcoat, and a paper bicorne.

When Dinteville got his practice, he made a bet that he would put

Horatio on a seat in his waiting room. But when the day arrived he preferred to lose his bet rather than his patients.

CHAPTER SIXTY-EIGHT

On the Stairs, 9

Draft inventory of some of the things found on the stairs over the years

Several photos, including one of a fifteen-year-old girl wearing a black swimsuit bottom and a white knitwear sweater, kneeling on a beach,

a radio alarm clock obviously destined for the mender's, in a plastic bag from the Nicolas company,

a black shoe decorated with jewels,

a slipper made of gilded goatskin,

a box of Géraudel cough pastilles,

a muzzle,

a Russian-leather cigarette case,

straps,

various notebooks and appointment books,

a cubic lampshade in bronze-coloured metallic paper, in a bag originating in a record shop in Rue Jacob,

a milk bottle in a bag from Bernard the butcher's,

a romantic engraving depicting Rastignac at the Père-Lachaise cemetery, in a bag from Weston's shoeshop,

a (humorous?) printed card announcing the engagement of Eleuthère de Grandair and the Marquis of Grandpré, a rectangular, 21cm x 27cm sheet of paper on which the genealogical tree of the Romanov family had been carefully drawn and framed with a frieze of broken lines,

Pride and Prejudice, a novel by Jane Austen, in the Tauschnitz edition, opened at page 86,

a cardboard box from the pastry shop "Aux Délices de Louis XV", now empty but having manifestly once contained blueberry tarts,

a copy of Bouvard and Ratinet's logarithmic tables, in poor condition, with the stamp: Lycée de Toulouse, and a name: P. Roucher, written in red ink, on the flyleaf,

a kitchen knife,

a little metal mouse, with a shoelace for a tail, on wheels, that could be wound up with a flat key,

a bobbin of sky-blue thread,

a novelty necklace,

a crumpled copy of *Jazz Review* containing an interview by Hubert Damisch with Jay Jay Johnson, the trombone-player, and an article by the drummer Al Levitt about his first stay in Paris in the mid-fifties,

a travelling chess set, in synthetic leather, with magnetic pieces,

a pair of tights, brand name "Mitoufle",

a carnival mask representing Mickey Mouse,

several paper flowers, paper hats, and some confetti,

a sheet of paper covered in childish drawings, in the gaps of which a laborious first draft of a second year Latin prose composition is fitted: *dicitur formicas offeri granas fromenti in buca Midae pueri in somno eius. Deinde suus pater arandum, aquila se posuit in iugum et araculum oraculus nuntiavit Midam futurus esse rex. Quidam scit Midam electum esse regum Phrygiae et* [illegible word] *latum reges suis leonis.*

CHAPTER SIXTY-NINE

Altamont, 4

Cyrille Altamont's study: a highly polished herringbone parquet floor, a wallpaper with a pattern of large red and gold vine leaves, and furniture constituting a very fine, heavy, cosy Regency suite: a nine-drawer kneehole desk, in mahogany, with the working surface covered in dark imitation leather, a rocking swivel chair in leather-padded ebony, horseshoe shaped, and a little reclining seat, something like a Recamier, in rosewood, with cast-iron claw feet. Against the right-hand wall, a large glass-fronted bookcase with a swan-neck pediment. Opposite, a large harbour chart on cloth-backed paper, framed in wooden beads, a slightly yellowing reproduction of

CARTE PARTICVLLIERE
·DE LAMER MEDITERRANEE·
FAICTE PAR MOY
FRANÇOÏS OLLIVE
·A·MARSEILLE·
EN LANNEE 1664

On the rear wall to the left of the door giving onto the entrance hall are three pictures of almost identical dimensions: the first is a portrait, by Morrell d'Hoaxville, an English painter of the last century, of the brothers Dunn, two Dorset parsons, experts in obscure subjects – palæopedology and æolian harps respectively. Herbert Dunn, the æolian harp specialist, is on the left: he is a man of tall stature, thin, wearing a black worsted suit, a red beard trimmed to frame his face, and rimless oval spectacles. Jeremy Dunn, the palæopedologist, is a rotund little man, portrayed in his working clothes, that is to say equipped for an expedition in the field, with a good military haversack, a surveyor's chain, a file, crowbars, a compass, and three hammers stuck in his belt, plus a staff taller than he is, with a long iron spike and a handle gripped with upstretched hand.

The second is a work by the American artist Organ Trapp, whom Hutting introduced to the Altamonts ten years or so ago on Corfu. It shows a gas station at Sheridan, Wyoming, in full detail: a green garbage can, very black, very whitewalled tyres for sale, bright cans of motor oil, a red icebox with assorted drinks.

The third work of art is a drawing signed Priou and entitled *The Joiner in Rue du Champ-de-Mars*: a young lad of twenty or so, wearing a secondhand sweater and trousers held up by string, warms himself at a brazier burning wood shavings.

Beneath Organ Trapp's picture is a little table with two levels: on the lower shelf lies a chessboard with the pieces set in the position following the eighteenth black move in the match played in Berlin in 1852 between Anderssen and Dufresne, just before Anderssen began his brilliant play for mate which gave the game the nickname "Ever Young":

19. QR–Q1!!	Q × N/KB3
20. R × N/K7+1!	N × R/K7
21. Q × P/Q7+1!	K × Q
22. B – KB5 + mate in 2	

On the upper shelf there is a white telephone and a vase with a trapezial profile overflowing with gladioli and chrysanthemums.

Cyrille Altamont now almost never uses the desk, for he has transferred all the books and all the things he needs or is fond of to the official flat that he is provided with in Geneva. There remain in this now almost always empty room only dead and frozen things, furniture with neat drawers and, in the locked bookcase, never-opened books: the *Grand Larousse Universel*, a nineteenth-century encyclopaedia bound in green morocco, the complete works of La Fontaine, Musset, minor poets, and Maupassant in the standard Pléiade editions; bound sets of reviews: *Preuves*, *Encounter*, *Merkur*, *La Nef*, *Icarus*, *Diogène*, *Le Mercure de France*, and some artbooks and collectors' editions, including a romantic *Midsummer Night's Dream* with etchings by Helena Richmond, *Venus in Furs* by Sacher Masoch in a mink presentation case on which the title characters seem to have been branded with a red-hot iron, and the manuscript score of *Incertum*, opus 74 by Pierre Block, for voice and percussion, bound in buffalo hide with bone and ivory encrustations.

They are just putting the last touches to the room for the reception. Two butlers all clad in black spread a big white tablecloth over the desk. Framed in the doorway, a waiter in shirtsleeves is waiting to come in, as soon as they have finished, to lay the contents of his two baskets on the table: bottles of fruit juice and two octahedral bowls in blue porcelain filled with rice salad garnished with olives, anchovies, hard-boiled eggs, shrimps, and tomatoes.

CHAPTER SEVENTY

Bartlebooth, 2

Bartlebooth's dining room is now virtually never used. It is an austere, rectangular room with a dark parquet floor, long raised-velvet curtains, and a large Brazilian rosewood table covered with a damask cloth. On the long sideboard standing at the back of the room there are eight round tins, each bearing an effigy of King Farouk.

*   *   *

Whilst staying in Cape São Vicente, in the south of Portugal, in late nineteen thirty-seven, shortly before beginning his long tour of Africa, Bartlebooth made the acquaintance of an importer from Lisbon who, on learning that the Englishman planned to travel to Alexandria in the near future, entrusted him with an electric heater which he asked him to be so kind as to deliver to his Egyptian agent, a certain Farîd Abu Talif. Bartlebooth carefully copied the trader's name and address into his diary; on arrival in Egypt towards the end of spring 1938, he enquired after this reputable businessman and had the gift from Portugal taken over to him. Though the temperature was already far too mild for anyone to really need an electric heater, Farîd Abu Talif was so happy with his present that he asked Bartlebooth to give his Portuguese friend, for trial and approval, eight tins of coffee which he had put through a process he called "ionisation", a treatment designed, so he explained, to make it retain its aroma virtually indefinitely. Though Bartlebooth made it absolutely clear that he would certainly not have occasion to see the importer again for some seventeen years, the Egyptian insisted, adding that the result of the trial would be all the more convincing if the coffee still kept some of its flavour after all that time.

In the years that followed, the tins caused endless trouble. At each border crossing Bartlebooth and Smautf had to open the tins and let suspicious customs officers sniff their contents, taste the grains on the tips of their tongues, and sometimes even brew up a cup of coffee with them to make sure they weren't some new kind of drug. By the end of nineteen forty-three, the tins were empty – and by then rather dented – but Smautf would not let Bartlebooth throw them away; he used them to keep various kinds of small change in, or for the rare seashells he happened to find on beaches, and on their return to France he put them, as a memento of their long voyage, on the dining-room sideboard, where Bartlebooth let them stay.

Each of Winckler's puzzles was a new, unique, and irreplaceable adventure for Bartlebooth. Each time, when he broke the seal that locked Madame Hourcade's black box and spread out on his tablecloth, under the shadowless light of his scialytic lamp, the seven hundred and fifty little pieces of wood that his watercolour had become, it seemed to him that all the experience he had accumulated over five or ten or fifteen years would be of no use, but this time, like every other time, he would have to deal with difficulties he could not even begin to guess at.

Each time he vowed to proceed methodically and with discipline, not to rush in headlong, not to try to recover straight away in his fragmented watercolour some detail or other which he thought he could still remember properly: this time he was not going to let his passion or his dreams or his impatience get the better of him, but would build up his puzzle with Cartesian rigour: divide up the problems the better to solve them, deal with them one by one, ruling out improbable combinations, placing the pieces as would a chess player constructing an unanswerable and ineluctable gambit: he was going to begin by turning all pieces face-up, then he would take out all those possessing a straight-line edge, and with them he was going to assemble the frame of the jigsaw. Then he would study all the other pieces, systematically, one by one, taking them in his hand, turning them round and round every possible way; he would extract the pieces which held some more apparent design or detail, and sort the remainder by colour and within each colour-group by shade, and so even before beginning to slot the centre pieces in he would have scored in advance three-quarters of his victory over the snares laid by Winckler. The rest would be just a matter of patience.

The main problem was to stay neutral, objective, and above all flexible, that is to say free of preconceptions. But that was exactly where Gaspard Winckler laid his traps. As Bartlebooth grew more familiar with these little slivers of wood, he began to see them in specific ways, giving prominence to a particular angle, as if the pieces were being polarised, or vectorised, or were solidifying into a perceptual model which, with irresistible seductiveness, assimilated them to familiar images, familiar shapes, familiar contours: a hat, a fish, an amazingly accurate bird with a long tail, a long curved beak with a swelling at the base, just like one he remembered seeing in Australia; or again, it would be the exact outline of Australia, or of Africa, or of England, or of the Iberian peninsula, the heel of Italy, etc. Gaspard Winckler enjoyed making lots of pieces like that, and Bartlebooth often found – as in children's solid-wood puzzles – that he had a whole menagerie, a python, a mountain cat, and two fully formed elephants, one of the African (long-eared) variety, the other Indian, or a Charlie Chaplin (bowler hat, stick, and bandy legs), a long-nosed profile of Cyrano de Bergerac, a gnome, a witch, a lady in a wimple, a saxophone, a coffee table, a roast chicken, a lobster, a champagne bottle, the dancing girl on the front of *Gitane* cigarette packs or the winged helmet of *Gauloises*, a hand, a tibia, a fleur-de-lys, various fruits, or an alphabet, almost entire, with pieces shaped like J, K, L, M, W, Z, X, Y, and T.

Sometimes three or four or five of the pieces would fit together with disconcerting ease; then everything would get stuck: the missing piece would look to Bartlebooth like a kind of black India with Ceylon undetached (it was precisely a little harbour on the Coromandel coast that this watercolour happened to depict). It wasn't until many hours – if not many days – later that Bartlebooth would notice that the matching piece was not black but more nearly light grey – a discontinuity of colour which ought to have been foreseeable had Bartlebooth not let himself get carried away, so to speak, by his excitement – and that it was shaped exactly like what he had persisted in calling "perfidious Albion" from the start, provided that the miniature Britain underwent a clockwise rotation of ninety degrees. Of course the empty space no more looked like India than the piece which fitted it exactly looked like Britain: what mattered, in this instance, was that for as long as he carried on seeing a bird, a bloke, a badge, a spiked helmet, an HMV dog, or a Winston Churchill in this or that piece, he was quite unable to discover how the piece would slot into the others without being, very precisely, reversed, revolved, decentred, desymbolised: in a word, de-*formed*.

Gaspard Winckler's illusions were essentially based on this principle: to oblige Bartlebooth to furnish the gaps with apparently anodine, obvious, easily named shapes – for instance, a gap for a piece with two sides necessarily forming a right angle, irrespective of the rest of its configuration – whilst at the same time pushing his perception of the pieces which would fit into the blanks in a completely different direction. As on the caricature by W. H. Hill which represents *simultaneously* a young and an old woman, the ear, cheek, and necklace of the young one being, respectively, an eye, the nose, and the mouth of the old one, the old woman being seen close-up in profile and the young one's bust being seen at three-quarters angle from the rear, Bartlebooth, in order to find that admittedly almost, but actually not quite, right angle, had to stop seeing it as the apex of a triangle, that is to say he had to switch his perception, see *otherwise* what the other had provided to mislead his eyes, and – for instance – work out that the yellow-tinged approximate Africa he had been fingering without knowing where to put it fitted precisely into the gap he thought would take that dull mauve four-leafed-clover shape which he couldn't find anywhere. The solution was obvious, as obvious as it had seemed insoluble for as long as he hadn't solved it, just as in a crossword-puzzle clue – like Robert Scipion's sublime "*du vieux avec du neuf*" in eleven letters – you hunt every other place for the answer that is very precisely stated in the clue itself, the whole labour consisting precisely in performing the *displacement* which gives the puzzle piece or the clue its *meaning* and thereby renders any explanation tiresome and unnecessary.

In Bartlebooth's particular case, the problem was complicated by the fact that he was the author of the original watercolours. He had taken care to destroy his drafts and sketches and had obviously not taken any photos or notes, but before beginning to paint he had stared at those seafront scenes with sufficiently close attention that twenty years later he had only to read the little legends that Gaspard Winckler stuck on the inside lids of the boxes – "Isle of Skye, Scotland, March 1936", or "Hammamet, Tunisia, February 1938" – and a memory would resurface of a sailor in a bright-yellow sweater and a tam o'shanter, or of the red-and-gold splodge of a Berber woman washing wool by the seashore, or of a cloud over a faraway hill, as airy as a bird: not a memory of the thing itself – for it was only too obvious that these memories had only existed to become, first, watercolours, then puzzles, then nothing again – but a memory of an image, of a touch with a pencil, of a line of erasure, of a stroke of his brush.

Bartlebooth sought such special signs almost every time. But it was illusory to put any trust in them: sometimes, Gaspard Winckler managed to make them disappear; that little red and yellow splodge, for instance, he had cut into a multitude of pieces from which the yellow and the red seemed inexplicably absent, drowned, dismembered into those minute overflows, those almost microscopic splashes, those little errors of the brush and rag which the eye absolutely could not see when the painting was looked at in its finished state, but which the puzzle-maker's patient saw-strokes had managed to exploit and exaggerate; more often, and much more cunningly, as if he had guessed that this exact shape was incrusted in Bartlebooth's memory, he would leave the detail just as it was, in a single piece, a cloud, a contour, a coloured spot which, deprived of any surround, became unusable, merely a monochrome, uniform cut-out, with no way of guessing what it might be surrounded by.

Winckler's tricks began with the edge-pieces, long before these advanced stages were reached. Like standard jigsaws, his puzzles had narrow white straight-edged borders, and custom and sense dictated that the puzzler should begin, as in go, with the edges.

It was equally true that one day Bartlebooth – exactly like that go-player who placed his first blot in the middle of the board and bewildered his opponent for long enough to win the game – seized by a sudden intuition, began one of his puzzles from the centre – a yellow sunset staining and reflected in the Pacific (not far from Avalon, Santa Catalina Island, California, November 1948) – and finished it off in three days instead of two weeks. But he wasted almost a whole month, later on, when he thought he could use the same stratagem a second time.

The blue glue Gaspard Winckler used sometimes spread a little, outside the edge of the intercalated white sheet which provided the border of the puzzle, making an almost imperceptible bluish fringe. For several years Bartlebooth used that fringe as a kind of guarantee: if two pieces which seemed to fit together perfectly had fringes which did not match, he held back from slotting them in; on the other hand, he was tempted, if their bluish fringes were perfectly continuous, to juxtapose pieces which at first sight should never have been associated with each other, and it often turned out a little later that they did in fact go well together.

It was only when this habit had been acquired and had grown sufficiently ingrained that it would be unpleasant to give it up that Bartlebooth realised that these "happy chances" could themselves perfectly well be booby traps, and that the puzzle-maker had allowed this tiny trace to serve as a clue – or rather, as a bait – on a hundred jigsaws or so only in order to mislead him the more later on.

For Gaspard Winckler, that was merely an elementary subterfuge, a limbering-up exercise. Two or three times it perplexed Bartlebooth for a few hours, but had no longer-lasting effects. But it was fairly typical of the spirit in which Gaspard Winckler designed his puzzles, and of how he aimed to arouse new confusion each time in Bartlebooth. The most rigorous methodology, an index of the seven hundred and fifty pieces, the use of computers or of any other scientific or objective system would not have had much point in this instance. Gaspard Winckler had clearly conceived of the manufacture of these five hundred puzzles as a single entity, as a gigantic five-hundred-piece puzzle of which each piece was a puzzle of seven hundred and fifty pieces, and it was evident that the solution of each of these puzzles called for a different approach, a different cast of mind, a different method, and a different system.

Sometimes Bartlebooth discovered the solution instinctively, like the time he began for no apparent reason in the centre, for instance; sometimes, too, he deduced the solution from the preceding puzzles; but most often he looked for the answer for three days on end, feeling acutely that he was a complete imbecile: he hadn't even finished the border, fifteen tiny Scandinavias put together at the outset formed only the dark silhouette of a cloaked man climbing three steps to a jetty, half turning to face the painter (Launceston, Tasmania, October 1952), and for several hours he hadn't fitted in a single further piece.

Bartlebooth found the very essence of his passion in this feeling of being stuck: a kind of torpor, a sort of repetitious boredom, a veiled befuddlement in search of a shapeless something whose outlines he could barely manage to mumble in his mind: a spout that would fit that little concave rent, a thing like that, a nasty yellow sticking-out thing, a bit with a slightly rounded indentation, some orange dots, that little chunk of Africa, the wee chip of an Adriatic coast: mere muddled muttering, background noises to a wretched madman's obsessive and sterile musings.

And then, after hours of such gloomy inertia, sometimes Bartlebooth would suddenly fly into frightful rages, which could be as terrible and as inexplicable as Gaspard Winckler's tempers at his games of backgammon with Morellet at Riri's. This man, who in the eyes of all the inhabitants of the building was the very symbol of

British phlegm, of discretion, courtesy, politeness, of exquisite urbanity, a man who had never been heard to raise his voice, would on these occasions let fly with such violence that it seemed he had been concentrating all of it inside himself for years. One evening he hit a marble-topped low table with his fist and split it in two with a single blow. Another time, when Smautf was unwise enough to come in, as he did every morning, with breakfast – two soft-boiled eggs, orange juice, three pieces of toast, tea with milk, some letters, and three dailies: *Le Monde*, *The Times*, and the *Herald* – Bartlebooth sent the tray flying with such force that the teapot, propelled more or less vertically at the speed of a tennis service, shattered the thick glass of the scialytic lamp before smashing into a thousand fragments which showered onto the puzzle (Okinawa, Japan, October 1951). It took Bartlebooth eight days to recover all seven hundred and fifty puzzle pieces, undamaged by the scalding tea thanks to Gaspard Winckler's protective glaze, but this burst of temper turned out to be far from useless, since, in the course of re-sorting the pieces, Bartlebooth finally found out how they fitted together.

Fortunately, it was more usual for Bartlebooth, at the end of such hours of waiting, having gone through every stage of controlled anxiety and exasperation, to reach a kind of ecstasy, a stasis, a sort of utterly oriental stupor, akin, perhaps, to the state archers strive to reach: profound oblivion of the body and the target, a mental void, a completely blank, receptive, and flexible mind, an attentiveness that remained total, but which was disengaged from the vicissitudes of being, from the contingent details of the puzzle and its maker's snares. In moments like that Bartlebooth could see without looking how the delicate outlines of the jigsawed wood slotted very precisely into each other, and taking two pieces he had ignored until then or which perhaps he had sworn could not possibly join, he was able to fit them together in one go.

This intimation of grace would sometimes last for several minutes, which made Bartlebooth feel as if he had second sight: he could perceive everything, understand everything, he could have seen grass grow, lightning strike a tree, erosion grind down a mountain like a pyramid very gradually worn away by the gentle brushing of a bird's wing: he would juxtapose the pieces at full speed, without error, espying, beneath all the details and subterfuges intended to obscure them, this minute claw or that imperceptible red thread or a black-edged notch, which all ought to have indicated the solution from the start, had he but had eyes to see: in a few instants, borne along by such exalted and heady self-assurance, a situation that hadn't shifted for hours or days, a situation that he could no longer even imagine untying, would be altered beyond recognition: whole areas would join up, sky and sea would recover their correct locations, tree trunks would turn back into branches, vague birds back into the shadows of seaweed.

These privileged instants were as rare as they were intoxicating, as fleeting as they were seemingly effective. Bartlebooth would soon revert to being a sandbag, a lifeless lump chained to his worktable, a blank-eyed subnormal, unable to see, waiting hours without knowing what he was waiting for.

He did not feel hunger or thirst, or heat or cold; he could stay awake for more than forty hours doing nothing apart from taking the remaining unassembled pieces one by one, staring at them, turning them around, and putting them back without even trying to fit them, as if any try whatsoever was destined to fail inexorably. One time he stayed up for 62 hours at a stretch – from eight a.m. on the Wednesday until ten p.m. on the Friday – in front of an uncompleted puzzle depicting the seashore at Elsinore: a grey fringe between a grey sea and a grey sky.

Another time, in nineteen sixty-six, he joined up in the first three hours more than three-quarters of that fortnight's puzzle: the little seaside resort of Rippleson, near Blawick, in Florida. Then, over the following fortnight, he tried in vain to complete it: he had before him a short stretch of almost empty beach, with a restaurant at the beginning of the promenade and granite rocks at the end; far to the left three fishermen were landing a rowing boat with kelp-brown nets, and directly under the pavement an elderly woman wearing a polka-dot dress and having for headgear a cocked newspaper sat knitting on the shingle; beside her a little girl wearing a seashell necklace was eating dried bananas, lying flat on her stomach on a sisal mat; far to the right a beachboy in old fatigues was collecting up parasols and deckchairs; in the distance, a trapeze-shaped sail and two black islets broke the horizon. Some rippling wavelets and a chunk of billowing sky were missing: two hundred pieces of identical blue with minute white variations, each one needing more than two hours' labour to find its place.

That was one of the few occasions when two weeks were not long enough to finish a puzzle. Customarily, the alternation of excitement and apathy, of exaltation and despair, of feverish expectancy and fleeting certainties, meant that the puzzle would be completed within the prescribed schedule, moving towards its ineluctable goal, where, when all the problems had been solved, there was in the end only a decent, somewhat pedantic watercolour depicting a seaport. Step by step, in frustration or with enthusiasm, he came to satisfy his urge, but by satisfying it caused it to expire, leaving himself with no recourse but to open a fresh black box.

CHAPTER SEVENTY-ONE

Moreau, 4

The old-style kitchen originally equipped with the ultramodern devices that Madame Moreau's cook soon had replaced was intended to contrast, in Henry Fleury's plan, with the great formal dining room, done in uncompromisingly avant-garde style, designed as a rigorously geometrical, impeccably formal model of icy sophistication where grand dinner parties would take on the aura of unique ceremonies.

To begin with, the dining room had been a heavy, cluttered, over-furnished place with a woodblock floor laid in a complicated pattern, a tall blue ceramic stove, walls with superabundant cornices and mouldings, skirting boards made to look like veined marble, a nine-branched counterpoise ceiling light equipped with 81 pendants, a rectangular oak table accompanied by twelve embroidered velvet chairs and at either end two light mahogany armchairs with X-shaped open-work backs, a bottom half of a Breton-style dresser which had always held a Second Empire liqueur-stand made of papier-mâché next to a smoker's set (with a cigarette box portraying Cézanne's *Card Players*, a petrol lighter looking quite like an oil lamp, and a few ashtrays depicting a club, a diamond, a heart, and a spade, respectively) and a silver fruit bowl full of oranges, over all of which hung a tapestry representing an imaginary landscape; between the windows, over a *coco weddelliana* (an indoor palm with decorative foliage), was a large, dark canvas, showing a man in judge's robes sitting on a high throne whose gilding dominated the whole painting.

Henry Fleury shared the widely held view that the tasting of food is conditioned not only by the specific colours of the foods tasted but also by the surroundings. Lengthy research and several experiments convinced him that the colour white, by virtue of its neutrality, "blankness", and luminosity, was the one which would best bring out the flavour of ingredients.

That was the basis on which he reorganised Madame Moreau's dining room from top to bottom: he eliminated the furniture, dismantled the chandelier, stripped off the skirting boards, and hid the mouldings and plaster roses behind a false ceiling made of sparkling white laminated panels, fitted in places with pristine spotlights, positioned so that their beams converged on the centre of the room. The walls were painted in brilliant white gloss, and a similarly white plastic covering was put on the crusty old parquet floor. All the doors were bricked up except the one giving onto the entrance hall – originally a double door with glass panes, replaced by two sliding panels controlled by a hidden photo-electric cell. As for the windows, they were concealed behind tall plywood panels sheathed in white synthetic leather.

Apart from table and chairs, no furniture and no accessories were allowed in the room, not even a switch or an electric cable. All crockery and tableware was to be kept in cupboards installed outside the room, in the entrance hall, where a serving table was also set for plate-warmers and carving boards.

In the centre of this spotless, shadowless, and perfectly smooth white space, Fleury placed his table: a monumental marble slab, absolutely white, cut to an octagon, with bevelled edges, standing on a cylindrical pedestal one yard in diameter. Eight moulded plastic chairs, also white, completed the furniture.

The white line stopped there. The china, designed by the Italian stylist Titorelli, was done in pastel shades – ivory, pale yellow, sea green, blushing pink, pale mauve, salmon, light grey, turquoise, etc. – which were selected according to the characteristics of the dishes to be served, themselves selected according to a basic colour which the table linen and waiters' attire would also match.

For the decade during which her health allowed her to carry on entertaining, Madame Moreau held a dinner party roughly once a month. The first one was a yellow dinner: Burgundy cheesecake, quenelles of pike in Dutch style, quails stewed in saffron, sweetcorn salad, lemon and guava sorbets, accompanied by sherry, Château-Chalon, Château-Carbonneux, and cold Sauternes punch. The last one she gave, in 1970, was a black meal served on plates of polished slate; it included caviar, obviously, and also squid Tarragon style, saddle of baby Cumberland boar, truffle salad, and blueberry cheesecake; it was more difficult to select the wines for this final repast: the caviar was served with vodka in basalt goblets, and the squid with a retsina wine which was a very dark red indeed, but for the saddle of boar the butler got away with two bottles of Château-Ducru-Beaucaillou 1955 decanted for the occasion into adequately black Bohemian crystal.

Madame Moreau herself hardly touched the dishes she had served to her guests. She was subject to an ever stricter diet which in the end allowed her only raw fish roes, chicken breasts, cooked Edam, and dried figs. Usually she had her meal before her guests, alone or in the company of Madame Trévins. That did not prevent her conducting her parties with the same energy that she showed in her daytime work, of which these dinners were in any case no more than a necessary extension: she planned the parties with minute care, drawing up her guest-list as one would draw up a battle plan; she invariably brought together seven people, amongst whom there would be: one individual with a more or less official function (ministerial private secretary, consultant to the public accounts committee, associate member of the *Conseil d'Etat*, official liquidator, etc.); an artist or writer; one or two members of her own team, but never Madame Trévins, who hated this kind of festivity and preferred to stay in her room, rereading her book on such evenings; and the French or foreign businessman she was dealing with at the time and in whose honour the dinner was being held. Two or three well-chosen wives made up the complement around the dinner table.

One of the most memorable of these dinners was given for someone who had been in this building many times on other accounts: Hermann Fugger, the German businessman who was a friend of the Altamonts and Hutting, and some of whose camping equipment Madame Moreau was to market in France: that evening, knowing of Fugger's repressed passion for cooking, she put on a pink meal – ham *au Vertus* in aspic, koulibiaca of salmon in aurora sauce, wild duck with vineyard peach, pink champagne, etc. – and she brought to her table, along with one of her closest colleagues, who ran the "hypermarket" division of her business, a good-food columnist, a flour-miller turned oven-ready foodpack manufacturer, and a Moselle wine-grower, the latter two guests flanked by wives as crazy about good food as their husbands. Leaving Flourens's piglet and the other pre-dinner talking points out of it for once, these guests concentrated all conversation on the joys of food, old recipes, bygone chefs, white-butter-sauce like mother used to make it, and suchlike taste bud topics.

Henry Fleury's dining room was of course only ever used for prestige dinners of this kind. The rest of the time, including when she was still in good health and enjoyed a sturdy appetite, Madame Moreau ate with Madame Trévins in one or the other's bedroom. It was their only moment of relaxation each day; they would chat interminably about Saint-Mouezy, bringing back memories they never tired of hearing.

In her mind's eye she could see the arrival of the old moonshiner, who came from Buzançais, with his red copper still drawn by a little black mare answering to the name of Belle; and the toothpuller with his red bonnet and his multicoloured leaflets; and the bagpipe-player who accompanied him, blowing his pipes as hard and as out of tune as he could so as to cover the cries of the unfortunate patients. She would relive the fear that had haunted her of not being allowed dessert and being put on bread and water for three days when the schoolma'am gave her a bad mark; she would retrieve the fright she had had on finding a big black spider underneath a pot her mother had asked her to scour; and her intense wonderment on seeing an aeroplane for the first time in her life, one morning in 1915, a biplane which emerged from the fog and landed in a field; out of it climbed a leather-jacketed young man as handsome as a Greek god, with big, pale eyes and long, slim hands in his thick sheepskin gloves. He was a Welsh airman who had got lost in the fog trying to get to the castle at Corbenic. In the plane there were several maps which he studied fruitlessly. She couldn't help him, any more than could the villagers to whom she led him.

Or from even further back, from as far back as she could remember, there rose the fascination she had felt as a little girl every time she saw her grandfather shaving: he would sit down, usually around seven in the morning, after a frugal breakfast, and with a serious air make up his lather with a very soft brush in a bowl of very hot water, a lather so thick and white and firm that even after more than seventy-five years it still made her mouth water.

CHAPTER SEVENTY-TWO

Basement, 3

Cellars. Bartlebooth's cellar.

In Bartlebooth's cellar there is some left-over coal on top of which still lies a black enamelled metal scuttle with a wooden grip fitted on its wire handle, a bicycle hanging on a butcher's hook, now unoccupied bottle racks, and his four travelling chests, four curved chests covered in tarred canvas, braced with wooden slats, with brass corners and hasps, and lined throughout with a sheet of zinc to ensure waterproofing.

Bartlebooth ordered them from Asprey's, in London, and had them filled with everything that might be needed or useful or reassuring or just nice to have throughout the duration of his long voyage around the world.

The first opens out into a spacious hanging cupboard, and

contained a complete wardrobe of clothes suited to every climatic condition and to the various circumstances of social life, just like those cut-out cardboard costume collections in which children dress fashion dolls: it went from fur boots to patent-leather shoes, from oilskins to tails, from balaclavas to bow ties, and from pith helmets to toppers.

The second trunk held all the various pieces of painting and drawing equipment required for the watercolours, the parcels made in advance to be sent to Gaspard Winckler, various guidebooks and maps, toiletries and maintenance supplies which could be thought occasionally difficult to obtain in the antipodes, a first-aid kit, the famous tins of "ionised coffee", and some instruments: a camera, binoculars, a portable typewriter.

The third still contains everything that might have been needed if a tempest or a typhoon or a tidal wave or a cyclone or a mutiny of the crew had shipwrecked Bartlebooth and Smautf and they had had to drift on a raft, land on a desert island, and survive. Its content simply repeats in modernised form those of the trunk which Captain Nemo attached to floats made of empty barrels and had washed up on shore for the good-hearted colonisers of Lincoln Island, the exact nomenclature of which was copied down on a page of Gédéon Spilett's notebook and which, together with two admittedly almost full-page illustrations, now occupies pages 223 to 226 of Jules Verne's *L'Ile mystérieuse* in the Hetzel edition.

The fourth, and last, which was intended for lesser disasters, contains – in a perfect state of preservation, and miraculously packed in such a small space – a six-place tent with all its accessories and equipment, from the standard canvas water-carrier down to a handy foot-pump (brand new at the time, since it had won a prize at the preceding Inventors' Exhibition), and including a ground-sheet, a roof liner, stainless steel pegs, spare ropes, duvets, inflatable mattresses, storm lanterns, pellet-burning camp cookers, Thermos flasks, stacking cutlery, a travelling iron, an alarm clock, a patent "anosmic" ashtray allowing the inveterate smoker to indulge his vice without disturbing his neighbour, and a fully folding table which would require approximately two hours, if two men got down to it, to be assembled – or dismantled – by means of tiny eight-sided box spanners.

The third and fourth trunks were virtually never used. Bartlebooth's natural taste for British comfort and the more or less unlimited resources at his disposal in those days allowed him to choose almost every time a suitably equipped residence – a grand hotel, an embassy, a house belonging to a wealthy individual – where his sherry would be served on a silver tray and the water for shaving would be eighty-six degrees Fahrenheit, and not eighty-four.

When he really couldn't find accommodation to suit him in the environs of the site chosen for that fortnight's watercolour, Bartlebooth would resign himself to camping. That happened a score of times in all, amongst other places in Angola, near Moçamedes, in Peru, near Lambayeque, on the southern tip of the Californian peninsula (that is to say in Mexico), and on various Pacific and Oceanian islands, where he could just as well have slept in the open without obliging Smautf to get out, to set up, and, above all, a few days later, to pack away all the equipment, in an immutable order in which every item had to be folded and placed in accordance with the instructions for use attached to the trunk, which otherwise could never have been made to shut again.

Bartlebooth never talked very much about his travels, and for some years now he hasn't spoken of them at all. Smautf, for his part, quite enjoys recounting them, but his memory lets him down with increasing frequency. During all those peripatetic years he kept a kind of notebook in which he noted his daily occupations (alongside prodigiously lengthy calculations calculating he no longer knew what). He had a rather curious hand, in which the strokes of his *t*'s appeared to be underlining the words in the preceding line and the dots on his *i*'s appeared to be punctuating the sentence above; and on the other hand the line below was interspersed with the tails and flourishes of the words above. The result of it is today far from always clear, particularly as Smautf was convinced that rereading a single word which had then summarised the whole scene perfectly would be enough to reawaken his integral memory of it, like those dreams that return all of a sudden as soon as you recall a single element: and so he noted down things in a far from explicit manner. For instance, the entry for 10 August 1939 – Takaungu, Kenya – reads as follows:

> Coach horses that go on order, without a driver
> Copper change given wrapped in paper
> Open rooms at the inn
> Do you want . . . me?
> It's calf's-foot jelly
> Way of carrying children
> Dinner at Mr Macklin's

Smautf no longer knows what he meant to remember by this. All he can recall – and he did not make a note of it – is that Mr Macklin was a botanist, aged over sixty, who had spent twenty years cataloguing butterflies and heathers in the basement of the British Museum before setting off into the field to make a systematic inventory of Kenyan flora. When Smautf arrived for dinner at the botanist's – Bartlebooth was at a reception that evening at the provincial governor's at Mombasa – he found the man kneeling in his drawing room sorting, into little rectangular tins, basil plants (*Ocumum basilicum*) and several samples of epiphyllum, one of which, with ivory-coloured flowers, was manifestly not an *Epiphyllum truncatum* but, he told him with trembling voice, might one day be named *Epiphyllum paucifolium* Macklin (he would rather have had *Epiphyllum macklineum*, but even then that was not done any more). Indeed, for more than twenty years, this old man had cherished a dream of leaving his name to one of these cacti or, failing that, to a local variety of squirrel, sending ever more detailed descriptions of it to his superiors, who persisted in replying that this variety was not sufficiently different from other African sciuridae (*Xerus getelus*, *Xerus capensis*, etc.) to merit a species name.

The most extraordinary part of this tale is that Smautf met another Mr Macklin twelve and a half years later, in the Solomon Islands, scarcely younger than the first, who was his uncle; his forename was Corbett: he was a narrow-faced missionary of ashen complexion who fed himself exclusively on milk and cream cheese; his wife was a bright, neat little woman, answering to the name of Bunny, who looked after the village girls; she made them do gym practice on the beach, and every Saturday morning they could be seen dressed in pleated slips, embroidered hairbands, and coral bracelets, swaying in time to the tinny sound of a Handel oratorio played on a clockwork phonograph, to the greater glee of some idle Tommies whom the good lady never let out of her lethal glare.

CHAPTER SEVENTY-THREE

Marcia, 5

The first room in Madame Marcia's store, the room her son David is in charge of, is full of small items of furniture: marble-topped coffee-tables, nesting tables, puffy poufs, trestle chairs, Early American stools from the old staging post at Woods Hole, Massachussetts, prayer stools, X-shaped canvas folding chairs with whorled feet, etc. Against the walls, hung with plain brown hessian, stand several bookcases of different depths and heights with shelves covered in green baize with red leather trim studded with large-headed brass nails, and on them a whole assortment of objects stands in meticulous order: a candy box with a crystal base and delicately chased gold feet and lid, antique rings displayed on narrow tubes of white card, a money-changer's weighing scales, some headless coins found by Engineer Andrussov whilst clearing the line of the Trans-Caspian railway, an illuminated book open at a miniature depicting a Virgin and Child, a print portraying the suicide at Bourg-Baudoin of Jean-Marie Roland de la Platière (the revolutionary politician, in mauve breeches and striped jacket, is kneeling to scrawl the brief note in which he explains his gesture. Through a half-open door can be seen a man in a Marseillaise waistcoat and a Phrygian bonnet, armed with a long pike, looking at him full of hatred); two of Bembo's tarot cards, one showing the devil, the other the House of God; a miniature fortress with four aluminium towers and seven spring-loaded drawbridges, equipped with little toy soldiers; other, bigger model soldiers, representing *Poilus* from the Great War: one officer looking through binoculars, another sitting on a powder keg and studying a map on his lap; a runner saluting as he hands a sealed dispatch to a general in a cape; a soldier fitting his bayonet; another, in fatigues, leading a horse by the reins; a third soldier unrolling a coil-dispenser supposedly containing Bickford fuse tape; an octagonal mirror in a tortoiseshell frame; several lamps, including two lamp brackets held out by human arms, similar to those which come alive, on some nights, in the film *Beauty and the Beast*; scale models of shoes, carved in wood, concealing pill boxes or snuff boxes; a young woman's head in painted wax, with red hairs stuck onto her head, one by one, for use by hairdressers in advertising displays; *Junior Gutenberg*, a child's printing set dating from the nineteen twenties, including not only a full case of rubber characters, a composing line, tweezers, and inking rollers, but also images in relief on lino blocks, allowing texts to be decorated with various colophons: flower garlands, bunches of grapes and vine leaves, a gondola, a large pyramid, a small Christmas tree, shrimps, a unicorn, a gaucho, etc.

On the little desk David Marcia sits at in the daytime can be found a numismatic book-collector's classic, the *Collection of the Coins of China, Japan, etc.* by Baron de Chaudoir, and an invitation card to the world premiere of *Suite sérielle 94* by Octave Coppel.

The Tale of the Saddler, his Sister and her Mate

The shop's original occupant was a glass-engraver who worked mostly for store outfitters and whose delicate flourishes could still be admired in the early nineteen fifties on the frosted-glass mirrors of Riri's Café, until Monsieur Riri, yielding to fashion, had them replaced with Formica and glued hessian panels. His successors who came and went were a seedsman, an old watchmaker found dead one day on the premises amongst his clocks which had all stopped, a locksmith, a lithographer, a deckchair maker, a fishing-tackle shop, and finally, around the end of the 1930s, a saddler by the name of Albert Massy.

The son of a Saint-Quentin fish farmer, Massy hadn't always been a saddler. At sixteen, whilst doing his apprenticeship at Levallois, he joined a racing club and immediately proved to be an exceptionally good cyclist: a good climber, a strong sprinter, a fantastic pacemaker, quick to pick up, instinctively knowing when and whom to attack, Massy had the makings of one of those giants of road-racing whose exploits spangle the golden age of cycling: at the age of twenty, scarcely having turned professional, he displayed his mettle to spectacular effect: in the penultimate stage (Ancona–Bologna) of the Giro d'Italia 1924, his first major trial, between Forli and Faenza, he broke away at such a rate of acceleration that only Alfredo Binda and Enrici could tuck in to his slipstream: this ensured Enrici his overall victory and got Massy a very honourable fifth place.

One month later, in his first and last Tour de France, Massy almost repeated his performance to even better effect, and in the very tough Alpine stage from Grenoble to Briançon he only just missed taking the yellow jersey from Bottecchia, who had worn it from day one. With Leduc and Magne, also doing their first Tour de France, he made a breakaway at the Aveynat bridge and had distanced the bunch by the time they reached the exit from Rochetaillé. Their lead grew progressively over the next fifty kilometres: thirty seconds at Bourg d'Oisans, one minute at Dauphin, two at Villar-d'Arène, before the long climb to the summit of the Col du Lautaret. Electrified by the crowds, who were delighted to see Frenchmen at last threatening the unbeatable Bottecchia, the three young racers breasted the Col with a lead of three minutes: all they now had to do was to let themselves go in a triumphant descent down to Briançon; in whatever order the others crossed the line, Massy, as long as he kept his three-minute lead over Bottecchia, would obligatorily become race leader: but twenty kilometres before the finishing post, just before Monêtier-les-Bains, he skidded on a turn and fell, doing no serious damage to himself but with a disastrous effect on his machine: the front forks snapped clean off. In those days the regulations forbade riders to change bicycles within stages, and the young roadster had to quit the race.

The end of his season was dismal. His team manager, who had almost unbounded faith in his star youngster's promise, managed to persuade him, as he went on saying he would give up racing for ever, that his bad luck in the Tour had left him with a real road-phobia, and succeeded in making him take up track-racing instead.

Massy thought first of all of doing Six-Day events and to this end got in touch with the veteran Austrian pursuit rider Peter Mond, whose usual team-mate, Hans Gottlieb, had just retired. But Mond had already signed with Arnold Augenlicht, so Massy decided – on the advice of Toto Grassin – to go in for motor-paced racing: of all the forms of cycle sport, it was at that time the most popular, and champions like Brunier, Georges Wambst, Sérès, Paillard, and the American Walthour were literally worshipped by the Sunday crowds which filled the Vélodrome d'Hiver, the Buffalo bowl, the covered track at Berny, and the stadium at Parc des Princes.

Massy's youth and enthusiasm worked miracles, and on the fifteenth of October 1925, less than a year after his debut in the event, the novice stayer beat the world one-hour record at Montlhéry by pedalling 118.75 kilometres behind his pacer Barrère's big motorcycle, fitted for the occasion with a primitive windshield. The Belgian Léon Vanderstuyft, motor-paced on the same circuit a fortnight earlier, using a rather bigger cowl, had only reached 115.098 kilometres.

In other circumstances this record might have been the start of a prodigious career in motor-paced championship riding; but it turned out to be no more than a sad apotheosis without a morrow. Massy was in fact at that time, and had so been for only six weeks, a private in the First Transport Regiment at Vincennes, and though he had obtained special leave for his championship challenge, he had not managed to get the leave postponed when one of the three judges required by International Cycling Federation rules cancelled two days before the date fixed.

His performance was thus not made official. Massy fought the decision as hard as he could, which wasn't easy from the back of his barracks despite the spontaneous support given not just by his hut comrades, for whom he was obviously an idol, but also by his superiors up to and including the colonel commanding the garrison, who even got a speech made in parliament by the War Minister, who was none other than Paul Painlevé.

The International Homologation Committee remained unmovable; all Massy could get was authorisation to make a second attempt in regulation conditions. He went back into training with determination and confidence, and in December, at his next attempt, impeccably motor-paced by Barrère, he beat his own record by covering 119.851 kilometres in the hour. But that didn't prevent him shaking his head in sadness as he dismounted: some two weeks previously, Jean Brunier, pedalling behind Lautier's motorcycle, had done 120.958 kilometres, and Massy knew he hadn't beaten him.

This injustice of fate which robbed him of ever seeing his name in the lists of champions, despite his having been, in actual fact, world champion in the professional one-hour motor-paced event from 15 October to 14 November 1925, so demoralised Massy that he resolved to give up cycling completely. But then he made a bad mistake: barely discharged from military service, instead of looking for a job far from the roaring crowds of the velodromes, he became a pacemaker, that is to say a motorcyclist, pacing a very young stayer, Lino Margay, a stubborn and inexhaustible chap from Picardy who had chosen motor-pacing out of admiration for Massy's exploits and had come at his own initiative to ride under his auspices.

The pacemaker's lot is not a happy one. He stands arched over his big motorbike with legs straight and elbows tucked in to the body to make the best windshield possible, he pulls along his stayer and directs him as he races in such a way that he minimises his energy output and at the same time puts himself in a favourable position for attacking one opponent or another. It is a terribly tiring posture; almost all the body's weight is carried on the tip of the left foot; the pose has to be held for an hour or ninety minutes without moving an arm or a leg, the pacemaker can barely see his stayer and is practically unable, given the noise of his machine, to hear any message from him: all he can do, at the most, is to communicate with him by brief nods of the head, with meanings agreed in advance, that he's about to accelerate, slow down, go up to the banked edge, dive off the banking, or overtake some opponent. All the rest, the rider's physical form, his aggressivity, his morale, has to be guessed. The racer and his pacer must thus be as one man, think and act as one man, make the same analysis of the progress of the race at the same time and draw the same consequences at the same instant: any delay, and the rider is lost: a pacer who allows an enemy motorcycle to get into a position that cuts his slipstream cannot then help losing his stayer; the stayer who fails to follow his pacer when the latter accelerates into a bend so as to attack a rival will burst his lungs when he tries to close up on the rollers again; in either case, in a few seconds, the rider loses any chance he might have had of winning.

From the start of their association, it was obvious to all that Massy and Margay would make a model tandem, one of those teams people still cite as examples of a perfect match, in the mould of those other celebrated two-man teams of the twenties and thirties, the great age of motor-paced racing, such as Lénart and Pasquier senior, De Wied and Bisserot, or the Swiss Stampfli and D'Entrebois.

For several years Massy led Margay to victory in all the great velodromes of Europe. And for many years, when he heard the audience in the stalls or on the stands cheer Lino on with a deafening roar and rise to their feet to chant his name as soon as he appeared on the track in his mauve-striped white jersey, when he saw him, the winner, step up to the podium to receive his medals and his bouquets of flowers, he felt only joy and pride.

But, as time passed, these acclamations that were not for him, these honours he should have known and which only an iniquitous fatality had deprived him of, aroused in him a resentment that grew ever sharper. He began to hate those howling crowds which ignored him and stupidly adored the hero of the day who owed his victories only to him, to his experience, to his willpower, to his technique, to his abnegation. And, as though he needed, in order to confirm him in his hatred and his contempt, to see his youngster heap up trophies, he came to demand greater and greater efforts of him, taking greater and greater risks, attacking from the start of the race, and leading from start to finish at an infernal average. Margay followed, doped by the inflexible energy of Massy, for whom no victory, no exploit, no record ever seemed enough. Until the day when, having incited the young champion to take his turn at challenging the one-hour event, at which he had once been the unacknowledged world champion, Massy forced him, on the wicked Vigorelli track at Milan, up to such a powerful pace and into such tight cornering that the inevitable finally happened: sucked along at over one hundred kilometres an hour, Margay missed a corner, got caught in a crosswind, lost his balance, and fell, coming to a halt more than fifty yards on.

He didn't die, but when he left hospital six months later he was horribly disfigured. The hardwood track had ripped off the whole right side of his face: he had but one eye, but one ear, no nose, no teeth, and no bottom jaw. All the lower part of his face was a horrible pinkish magma which quivered uncontrollably or alternatively froze into an unspeakable rictus.

After the accident, Massy finally gave up cycle sport for good and went back to the trade of saddler, which he had learnt and practised when he had still been only an amateur. He bought the premises in Rue Simon-Crubellier – his predecessor, the fishing-rod merchant, whose fortune had been made by the Popular Front government, was moving into a shop four times bigger in Rue Jouffroy – and shared the ground-floor flat with his young sister Josette. Every day at six he would go to see Lino Margay at Lariboisière Hospital, and when Margay was discharged he took him in. His feelings of guilt were inextinguishable, and when the former champion asked him a few months later for the hand of Josette in marriage, he worked at it so hard that he managed to persuade his sister to wed this larval monster.

The young couple moved to a little house by the lake at Enghien. Margay rented out deckchairs, rowing boats, and pedalos to holiday-makers and to people taking the waters. With his lower face permanently swaddled in a big white wool scarf, he more or less managed to hide his intolerable ugliness. Josette kept house, did the shopping and the cleaning, or did sewing for a lingerie shop which she had asked Margay never to set foot in.

This state of affairs lasted eighteen months. One evening in April nineteen thirty-one, Josette came home to her brother and begged him to free her of this slug-faced man who had become for her a nightmare of every minute.

Margay did not try to find Josette, to see her or to get her back. Some days later, a letter reached the saddler: Margay understood only too well what Josette had endured ever since she had sacrificed herself to him, and he implored her forgiveness; unable to ask her to return, but just as unable to get used to living without her, he preferred to go away, to leave the country, in the hope of finding the deliverance of death upon some foreign shore.

War came. Massy was conscripted into the Compulsory Labour Service and left for Germany to work in a shoe factory; Josette set up a tailoring business in the saddler's shop. In that time of penury, when almanacs recommended strengthening shoes with soles cut out of thicknesses of newsprint or old discarded felt and unpicking old pullovers so as to knit new ones, it was obligatory to have old clothes remade, so Josette was not short of work. She could be seen sitting by the window rescuing shoulderpads and linings, reversing an overcoat, cutting a loose jacket out of an old brocade offcut, or, kneeling at Madame de Beaumont's feet, chalking the hemline of her culotte-skirt contrived from a pair of tweed trousers that had belonged to her late husband.

Marguerite and Mademoiselle Crespi sometimes came to keep her company. The three women sat in silence around a little wood stove for which the only fuel was sawdust-and-paper pellets, drawing their needled threads for hours on end under the dim light of their blackout lamp.

Massy returned at the end of 1944. Brother and sister resumed their life together. They never uttered the name of the former stayer. But one evening, the saddler found his sister in tears, and in the end she confessed that she had not stopped thinking of Margay for a single day since she had left him: it was neither pity nor remorse that was torturing her, but love, a love a thousand times more powerful than the repulsion the face of her loved one inspired.

Next morning there was a ring at the bell, and a wonderfully handsome man stood in the doorway: it was Margay, returned from monstrosity.

Lino Margay had not only become handsome, he had grown rich. When he had resolved to leave the country, he had left it to fate to decide his final destination; he had opened an atlas and had stuck a pin in a map of the world without looking: fate, after falling a few times into the ocean waves, had in the end indicated South America, and Margay joined a Greek freighter, the *Stephanitos*, bound for Buenos Aires, as a cargo hand; during the long crossing he had befriended an old sailor of Italian extraction, Mario Ferri, known as Ferri the Eyetie.

Before the First World War, Ferri the Eyetie ran a small nightclub in Paris called *Le Chéops*, at 94 Rue des Acacias, which fronted for a clandestine gambling den known to habitués under the name of *The Octagon* because of the shape of the chips they used there. But Ferri's real business was of a different order: he was one of the ringleaders of the group of political agitators who went by the name of Panarchists, and the police, although they knew with certainty that *Le Chéops* concealed a gaming den known by the name of *The Octagon*, did not know that this same *Octagon* was only a cover for one of the Panarchists' headquarters. After the night of 21 January 1911 when the movement was beheaded and two hundred of its most active militants were gaoled, including its three historical leaders, Purkinje, Martinotti, and Barbenoire, Ferri the Eyetie was one of the few officials to escape the Police Chief's dragnet, but being denounced, then spotted, then hunted, all he could do, after going to ground in Beauce for a few months, was to lead a wandering life that took him without respite from one end of the planet to the other and obliged him, in order to survive, to ply the most various trades, from dog-clipper to election agent, from mountain guide to miller.

Margay had no precise plans. Ferri, though well over fifty, had ideas enough for two, and placed all his hope in a notorious gangster he knew in Buenos Aires, Rosendo Juarez, alias "The Thumper". Rosendo the Thumper was one of the men who walked tall in Villa Santa Rita. A guy with a real knack with a shiv, and what's more he was one of Don Nicolas Paredes's men, and *he* was one of Morel's men, and *he* sure was a real big guy. Scarcely had they landed than Ferri and Margay called on the Thumper and put themselves at his command. Which they had cause to regret, for the first job he gave them to do – a straightforward drug delivery – got them arrested, very probably on Thumper's own orders. Ferri the Eyetie was clobbered with a ten-year gaol sentence, and died a few months into it. Lino Margay, who had not been carrying any weapons, got off with three years.

Lino Margay – Lino the Dribbler, or Lino Knothead, as they called him at the time – realised in clink that his obscene ugliness inspired in everyone, cops and gangsters alike, feelings of pity and trust. On seeing him, people wanted to know his story, and when he'd told it, they told him theirs. Lino Margay discovered in this way that he had an astonishing memory: when he left prison, in June 1942, there was nothing he didn't know about the pedigrees of three-quarters of the South American underworld. Not only did he know their criminal records in detail, but he knew all the particulars of their tastes, their weaknesses, their favourite weapons, their specialities, their prices, their hide-outs, how to get in touch with them, etc. In a word, he was ideally equipped to become the impresario of the lower depths of Latin America.

He settled in Mexico in a former bookshop on the corner of Corrientes and Takahuano. Officially he was a pawnbroker, but, since he was convinced of the effectiveness of the double cover as formerly practised by Ferri the Eyetie, he let it be known that he was actually more of a fence. In fact, the gangsters who came to consult him from all over Latin America, including bigger and bigger bosses, rarely came to entrust valuable goods to him: henceforth he was known under the respectful nickname of "*El Fichero*" (The Index), for Lino Margay had become the New World's mobsters' who's who: he knew everything about everyone, he knew who was doing what, when, where, and for whom, he knew that this Cuban smuggler was looking for a bodyguard, that that Lima gang needed a good gunslinger, that Barrett had hired a killer called Razza to hit his rival Ramon, or that the safe of the Hotel Sierra Bella at Port-au-Prince contained a diamond rivière valued at five hundred thousand dollars and for which a Texan was ready to put three hundred thousand down in cash.

His discretion was exemplary, his efficiency was guaranteed, and his commission was reasonable: between two and five per cent of the final product of the operation.

Lino Margay made his fortune rapidly. By the end of 1944 he had accumulated enough money to go to the United States to try to get surgery: he had heard that a doctor in Pasadena, California, had just developed a proteolytic graft technique which allowed scar tissue to regrow without leaving any marks. The process, unfortunately, had only been tested satisfactorily on small animals and on fragments of human skin that were not innervated. It had never been applied to such a shattered expanse – or one of such long standing – as Margay's face, and a positive result seemed so remote and unlikely that the surgeon refused to undertake the experiment. But Margay had nothing to lose: the specialist was forced to operate on the former champion with the encouragement of four bruisers toting sub-machine guns.

The operation was a miraculous success. Lino Margay could finally return to France and find the woman he had always loved. A few days later, he took her off to a luxurious property he had had built near Coppet, by Lake Geneva, where there is every reason to suppose that he proceeded, on an even larger scale, with his lucrative activities.

Massy stayed a few more weeks in Paris, then sold his saddlery and retired to Saint-Quentin to finish his days in peace.

CHAPTER SEVENTY-FOUR

Lift Machinery, 2

Sometimes he imagined the building as an iceberg whose visible tip included the main floors and eaves and whose submerged mass began below the first level of cellars: stairs with resounding steps going down in spirals; long tiled corridors, their luminous globes encased in wire netting, their iron doors stencilled with warnings and skulls; goods lifts with riveted walls; air vents equipped with huge, motionless fans; metal-lined canvas fire hoses as thick as tree trunks, connected to yellow stopcocks a yard in diameter; cylindrical wells drilled into solid rock; concrete tunnels capped with regularly spaced skylights of frosted glass; recesses; storerooms; bunkers; strongrooms with armour-plated doors.

Lower down there would come a gasping of machinery, in depths momentarily glimmering with red light. Narrow conduits would debouch on vast enclosed spaces, on subterranean halls high as cathedrals, their vaults clustered with chains, pulleys, cables, pipes, conduits, joists, with movable platforms attached to jacks bright with grease, with frames of tubing and steel sections that formed gigantic scaffoldings, at whose summits men clad in asbestos, their faces shielded by trapezial visors, filled the air with the vivid flashes of arc lamps.

Lower still would come silos and sheds; cold-storage rooms; ripening rooms; mail-sorting offices; shunting stations with their switching posts; steam locomotives pulling railway trucks, flat wagons, sealed cars, container cars, tank cars; platforms stacked high with goods – cords of tropical wood, bales of tea, bags of rice, pyramids of brick and through-stone, rolls of barbed wire, extruded steel wire, angle irons, ingots, bags of cement, drums, hogsheads, cordage, jerry cans, tanks of butane.

And still further down: mountains of sand, gravel, coke, slag, and track ballast; concrete mixers; ash heaps; mine shafts glowing with orange light; reservoirs; gasworks; steam generators; derricks; pumps; high-tension pylons; transformers; vats; boilers bristling with nozzles, levers, and dials;

dockyards crowded with gangways, gantries, and cranes, with winches winding ropes taut as tendons, displacing stacks of veneer, aeroplane engines, concert grands, bags of fertiliser, bushels of feed, billiard tables, combine harvesters, ball bearings, cases of soap, tubs of asphalt, office furniture, typewriters, bicycles;

still lower: systems of locks and docking basins; canals lined with strings of barges loaded with wheat and cotton; highway terminals crisscrossed by trailer trucks; corrals full of black horses pawing the ground; pens of bleating sheep and fattened cattle; hills of crates overflowing with fruits and vegetables; columns of cheese wheels, hard and soft; perspectives of glassy-eyed animals split in two and slung from butcher hooks; piles of vases, pots, and wicker-covered flasks; cargoes of watermelons; cans of olive oil; tubs of fish in brine;

giant bakeries where bare-chested baker boys in white trousers withdraw from their ovens burning-hot trays lined with thousands of raisin buns; interminable kitchens where out of cauldrons as big as steam turbines hundreds of portions of greasy stew are ladled into giant rectangular pans;

and lower still, mine galleries with blind ageing horses drawing carts filled with ore and slow processions of helmeted miners; and oozing passageways, reinforced with waterlogged timbers, that lead down glistening steps to slapping blackish water; flint-bottomed boats, punts weighted with empty barrels sailing across a lightless lake, bestridden by phosphorescent creatures shuffling indefatigably from shore to shore with hampers of dirty laundry, complete sets of dishware, knapsacks, cardboard boxes fastened with bits of string; wherries filled with sickly indoor plants, alabaster bas-reliefs, plaster casts of Beethoven, Neo-Gothic armchairs, Chinese vases, tapestry cartoons depicting Henri III and his minions playing cup-and-ball, counterpoise lamps still trailing lengths of flypaper, garden furniture, baskets of oranges, empty birdcages, bedspreads, thermos flasks;

further down, another maze of ducts, pipes, and flues; drains winding among main and lateral sewers; narrow canals edged with black stone parapets; unrailinged stairs above precipitous voids; a whole inextricable geography of stalls, backyards, porches, pavements, blind alleys, and arcades, a whole subterranean city organised vertically into neighbourhoods, districts, and zones: the tanners' quarter with its unbearable stench, its faltering machines fitted with sagging drive belts, its stacks of pelts and leathers, its vats brimming with brownish substances; the scrapyards littered with mantelpieces of marble and stucco, with bidets, bathtubs, rusty radiators, statues of startled nymphs, standing lamps, and park benches; the quarter of those who deal in waste metal, the quarter of ragpickers and flea merchants, with its jumbles of old clothes, its stripped-down baby carriages, its bales of surplus fatigues, worn shirts, army belts and Ranger boots, its dentist's chairs, its provisions of old newspapers, lensless glasses, key rings, braces, musical table mats, light bulbs, laryngoscopes, retorts, flasks with lateral nozzles, and various types of glassware; the wine market and its mountains of demijohns and broken bottles, its staved-in tuns, its cisterns, vats, and racks; the streetcleaners' quarter full of overturned dustbins spilling out cheese rinds, wax paper, fish bones, dishwater, left-over spaghetti, used bandages, its heaps of refuse endlessly shoved from one place to the next by slimy bulldozers, its unhinged dishwashers, its hydraulic pumps, cathode-ray tubes, old radios, its sofas losing their stuffing; and the quarter of government offices, whose staff headquarters swarms with military personnel in impeccably ironed shirts moving little flags across maps of the world, its tiled morgues peopled with nostalgic hoods and the open-eyed bodies of the doomed, its record offices filled with bureaucrats in grey smocks who day after day look up birth, marriage, and death certificates, its telephone exchanges and their mile-long rows of polyglot operators, its machine room full of crackling telexes and computers that spew forth by the second reams of statistics, payrolls, inventories, balance sheets, receipts, and no-information statements, its paper-shredders and incinerators endlessly devouring quantities of out-of-date forms, brown folders stuffed with press clippings, account books bound in black linen with pages covered in delicate violet handwriting;

and at the very bottom, a world of caverns whose walls are black with soot, a world of cesspools and sloughs, a world of grubs and beasts, of eyeless beings who drag animal carcasses behind them, of demoniacal monsters with bodies of birds, swine, and fish, of dried-out corpses and yellow-skinned skeletons arrayed in attitudes of the living, of forges manned by dazed Cyclopses in black leather aprons, their single eyes shielded by metal-rimmed blue glass, hammering their brazen masses into dazzling shields.

CHAPTER SEVENTY-FIVE

Marcia, 6

David Marcia is in his bedroom. He is a man of about thirty, with a fattish face. He is lying fully dressed on his bed, having taken off only his shoes. He is wearing a tartan cashmere sweater, black socks, and a petrol-blue pair of gaberdine trousers. On his right wrist he wears a silver chain-like bracelet. He is thumbing through an issue of *Pariscop* which is marking the relaunch of *The Birds* at the *Ambassadeurs* cinema by carrying on its cover a photograph of Alfred Hitchcock, the director, looking through a barely open eye at a crow which is perched on his shoulder and seems to be laughing out loud.

The bedroom is small and summarily furnished: the bed, a bedside table, a wing chair. On the night table there is an English paperback edition of William Saroyan's *The Daring Young Man on a Flying Trapeze*, a bottle of fruit juice, and a lamp with a pedestal made from a cylinder of rough glass half-filled with multicoloured pebbles whence emerge a few tufts of aloe. Against the rear wall, on a china mantelpiece bearing a large mirror, stands a bronze statuette representing a little girl scything hay. The right-hand wall is covered with cork tiles, intended to sound-proof the room from next door, the bedroom of Léon Marcia, whose insomnia constrains him to interminable nocturnal comings and goings. The left-hand wall is hung with embossed paper and decorated with two framed prints: one is a large map of the town and citadel of Namur and its environs, with an indication of the fortifications carried out during the siege of 1746; the other is an illustration of *Twenty Years After*, depicting the escape of the Duke of Beaufort: the Duke has just taken two daggers, a rope ladder, and a choke-pear (which Grimaud is stuffing into La Ramée's mouth) from the pie they had been camouflaged in.

David Marcia came back to live with his parents not long ago. He had left home when he turned professional motorcyclist, and had gone to live at Vincennes in a rented villa possessing a large garage where he spent his days messing about with his machines. In those days he was an orderly, conscientious lad entirely consumed by his passion for motorcycle racing. But his accident turned him into a whimsical fellow, a daydreamer who poured into muddle-headed projects all the money he got from his insurance, totalling nearly one hundred million old francs.

First he tried to switch to car racing, and drove in several rallies; but one day, near Saint-Cyr, he killed two children who ran out of a level-crossing keeper's cottage, and he lost his licence for good.

* * *

He then became a record producer: during his stay in hospital he had met a self-taught musician, Marcel Gougenheim, alias Gougou, whose ambition it was to have a big jazz band like there used to be in France in the days of Ray Ventura, Alix Combelle, and Jacques Hélian. David Marcia realised it was vain to hope to earn a living from a big band: even the really small groups couldn't manage, and, more and more frequently, the Casino de Paris and the Folies-Bergères would engage just the soloists and provide them with backing on tape; but Marcia thought a record would do well, and he decided to finance the project. Gougou hired forty players or so, and rehearsals started in a suburban theatre. The band had an excellent sound which Gougou's Woody Herman-style arrangements brought out fantastically well. But Gougou had a terrible defect: he was a chronic perfectionist, and after every run-through of a piece he would always find a detail that wasn't good enough, something too slow here, a tiny muff there. Rehearsals, scheduled to take three weeks, went on for nine before David Marcia decided to cut his losses.

Then he got interested in a holiday village in Tunisia, in the Kerkennah islands. It was the only one of all these projects which might have come off: the Kerkennah islands were less overrun than Djerba but offered holiday-makers the same kind of facilities, and the village was well equipped: you could do horse-riding as well as sailing, and then water-skiing and underwater fishing, coarse fishing and camel rides, pottery sessions, spinning lessons and basket-weaving classes, body language and autogenous fitness training courses. The village was connected with a travel agency providing it with customers for almost eight months a year, and David Marcia became site manager; for the first few months it all went pretty well, until the day when he hired as drama-course director an actor by the name of Boris Kosciuszko.

Boris Kosciuszko was a man of about fifty, tall and spare, with an angular mien, protruding cheekbones, and smouldering eyes. His theory was that Racine, Corneille, Molière, and Shakespeare were second-rate playwrights who had been fraudulently elevated to the rank of genius by sheep-brained directors devoid of imagination. Real theatre, he decreed, was *Wenceslas*, by Rotrou, *Manlius Capitolinus*, by Lafosse, Maisonneuve's *Roxelane et Mustapha*, Longchamps' *Lovelorn Seducer*; the real playwrights were Colin d'Harleville, Dufresny, Picard, Lautier, Favart, Destouches; he knew dozens and dozens of that ilk, went into imperturbable ecstasies over the hidden beauties of *Iphigenia* by Guimond de la Touche, Népomucène Lemercier's *Agamemnon*, Alfieri's *Orestes*, Lefranc de Pompignan's *Dido*, and ponderously stressed the clumsy way such similar or related subjects had been handled by the so-called Great Classic Authors. The educated audiences of the Revolution and Empire periods – Stendhal being the leading light amongst them – put Voltaire's *Zaïre* on the same level as Shakespeare's *Othello*, or Crébillon's *Rhadamniste* on a par with *Le Cid*, and they hadn't been wrong; up to the middle of the nineteenth century, the two Corneilles were published together, and the works of the elder, Thomas, were appreciated quite as much as those of the younger, Pierre. But the introduction of compulsory non-Catholic schooling and bureaucratic centralism, from the Second Empire and Third Republic on, had smothered these energetic, fulsome writers and imposed the skimpy, feeble order which bore the pompous name of classicism.

Boris Kosciuszko's enthusiasm was apparently infectious, for a few weeks later David Marcia announced in the press the launching of the Kerkennah Festival, intended, the release specified, to "safeguard and promote the rescued treasures of the theatre". Four plays were programmed: *Jason*, by Alexandre Hardy, *Inès de Castro*, by Lamotte-Houdar, a one-act verse comedy by Boissy, entitled *The Chatterbox*, all directed by Boris Kosciuszko, and *The Laird of Polisy*, a tragedy by Malte d'Istillerie in which Talma had made her name, directed by Henri Agustoni, from Switzerland. Various other events were planned, including an international symposium, the subject of which – the myth of the classical unities – constituted a bold manifesto in itself.

David Marcia did not economise on resources, reckoning that the success of the Festival would rebound on the reputation of his holiday village. With support from various agencies and institutions, he put up an open-air, eight-hundred-seat auditorium and tripled the number of chalets so as to provide accommodation for all the actors and spectators.

Crowds of actors came – a score were required just to play *Jason* – and there was similarly a flood of designers, costumiers, lighting men, critics, and professors; on the other hand, there were few paying spectators, and several performances were cancelled or abandoned because of the violent storms which frequently break out in this area in midsummer: at the Festival's end, David Marcia worked out that total receipts were 98 dinars, whereas the whole operation had cost him nearly 30,000.

That was how David Marcia managed to get rid of his small fortune in three years. He then returned to live in Rue Simon-Crubellier. To begin with, it was to be a temporary solution, and he looked around unenthusiastically for a trade and a flat, until his mother, out of a soft heart, gave him one half of her shop, together with any profits he might make from it. The work is not too tiring for him, and the income he makes goes to support his latest craze – games of chance, and in particular roulette, at which, nearly every evening, he loses between three hundred and fifty and one thousand francs.

CHAPTER SEVENTY-SIX

Basement, 4

Cellars. Madame de Beaumont's cellar.

Old things: a lamp with a brass stand and a very chipped semicircular shade of pale-green opaline, formerly a desk lamp; the remains of a teapot; coat hangers. Souvenirs of voyages and holidays: a dried starfish, two tiny dolls dressed as a Serbian couple, a small vase decorated with a view of Etretat; then shoe-boxes brimful of postcards and love letters in elastic bands that have gone loose now; a pharmaceutical prospectus

ORABASE®

ORAL PROTECTIVE PASTE

---

what are the advantages?

- **strong adhesive properties hold the protective "bandage" at the site of application for up to two hours**
- **helps protect oral tissues against further irritation from chewing, swallowing, and other normal mouth activity**
- **easy to apply, convenient to use**
- **contains no antibiotic — harmless when swallowed**

how is it used?

Dab, do not rub, Orabase onto the affected area until the paste adheres well (rubbing this preparation on may result in a granular, gritty sensation). After application, a smooth, slippery film develops. Reapply as needed, particularly after eating; or as directed by your dentist or physician.

NOTE: Orabase is not intended for use in the presence of infection. If an infection is suspected, or if any mouth irritation does not heal within 7 days, consult your dentist or physician. If irritation is from dentures that do not fit properly, consult your dentist.

Available in 0.17 oz. (5 Gram) and ½ oz. (15 Gram) tubes.
Also available as ORABASE® with Benzocaine for protection and relief of pain associated with minor irritations of the mouth and gums.

children's books with pages missing and torn corners: *Tales of Grandma Goose*, *The History of France in Riddles*, open at a drawing of a kind of scalpel, a lettuce, and a rat: the riddle's solution (*Lancette, laitue, rat* = "L'An VII les tuera", Year VII will kill them), the book explains, is aimed at the *Directoire* government, despite the fact that the latter was overthrown on 18 Brumaire, Year VIII; school exercise books; diaries; photograph albums in raised leather, black baize, green silk, with on almost every page the glue-marks of triangular corners, unstuck long ago, plotting the shapes of now empty frames; photographs, dog-eared, yellowing, and crackled photographs: a photograph of Elizabeth at sixteen, at Lédignan, riding with her grandmother (who was already nearly ninety) in a little trap drawn by a very shaggy pony; a photograph of Elizabeth, small and badly focused, hugging François Breidel amidst a tableful of men in boilersuits; photographs of Anne and Béatrice: in one, Anne is eight, Béatrice seven; they are sitting in a meadow, beneath a little fir tree;

Béatrice is holding close to her chest a little black, curly-haired dog; Anne, beside her, with a serious, almost grave look, is wearing a man's hat: it belonged to their uncle Armand Breidel, at whose house they spent their holidays that year; in another snap from the same period, Anne is arranging wild flowers in a vase; Béatrice is lying in a hammock, reading *The Adventures of Babar*; the little dog is not visible; in a third photo, taken later, they are in fancy dress, with two other little girls, in Madame Altamont's beautifully oak-panelled boudoir, at a party given for the latter's daughter's birthday. Madame de Beaumont and Madame Altamont hated each other; Madame de Beaumont considered Cyrille Altamont a nincompoop and said that he reminded her of her husband Fernand and that Cyrille was one of those people who thought you only had to be ambitious to become bright. But Véronique Altamont and Béatrice, who were the same age, liked each other a lot, and Madame Altamont was obliged to invite the Breidel girls: Anne is dressed up as the Empress Eugénie and Béatrice as a shepherdess; the third little girl, the smallest, is Isabelle Gratiolet, dressed as a squaw; the fourth, Véronique, looks adorable in a nobleman's outfit: she has a powdered wig with her pigtail in a bow, a lace ruff, a short green cutaway jacket, mauve breeches, a sword at her side, and long white hide spats up to her thighs; photographs of the wedding of Fernand de Beaumont and Véra Orlova, on the twenty-sixth of November 1926, in the reception rooms at the Hôtel Crillon: the fashionable crowd, family, friends – Count Orfanik, Ivan Bunin, Florent Schmitt, Arthur Schnabel, etc. – the wedding cake, the happy couple, with him holding her outstretched hand in his, standing in front of heaps of roses strewn on the luxurious, fitted carpet with its blue pattern; photographs of the excavations at Oviedo: one of them, probably taken by Fernand de Beaumont himself, since he doesn't appear in it, shows the team at siesta time – a dozen slim, tanned students with sprouts of beards on their faces, wearing shorts down to their knees and greyish vests; they are under a big canvas awning which protects them from the sun's rays but not from its heat; four are playing bridge, three are asleep or drowsing, another one is writing a letter, yet another is using a tiny bit of pencil to solve a crossword puzzle, and another is diligently sewing a button back onto a much-patched pea jacket; another snapshot shows Fernand de Beaumont with

Bartlebooth, on the latter's visit to the archaeologist in January 1935. The two men pose standing side by side, smiling, screwing up their eyes against the sun. Bartlebooth is wearing knickerbockers, a check sweater, and a cravat. Beaumont, looking very short by comparison, is dressed in a fairly crumpled grey worsted suit, a black tie, and a double-breasted waistcoat decorated with a silver watch-chain. Smautf didn't take this snap since he is in it, in the background, washing the big two-tone Chenard & Walker, with Fawcett's help.

Despite the difference in their ages – Bartlebooth was then thirty-five, whilst the archaeologist was nearly sixty – the two men were great friends. They had been introduced at a reception at the British Embassy and had realised in talking to each other that they lived in the same building – though to tell the truth, Beaumont was hardly ever there, and Bartlebooth had only just moved in – and then, above all, that they shared a taste for early German music: Heinrich Finck, Breitengasser, Agricola. But what united them most, perhaps, beyond this shared taste, was the peremptory and confident way the archaeologist asserted a theory all his colleagues unanimously considered to be the least plausible, in which Bartlebooth found something of the sort that fascinated him, and which encouraged him also in his own project. In any event, it was Fernand de Beaumont's presence at Oviedo that made Bartlebooth choose the nearby port of Gijón to paint the first of his seascapes.

When Fernand de Beaumont took his own life, on the twelfth of November 1935, Bartlebooth was at sea in the Mediterranean and had just painted his twenty-first watercolour, in the little Corsican port of Propriano. He heard the news on the radio and managed to get back to the mainland in time to attend his poor friend's funeral, at Lédignan.

CHAPTER SEVENTY-SEVEN

Louvet, 2

The Louvets' bedroom: a sisal mat brought back from the Philippines, a 1930s dressing table entirely covered with tiny mirrors, a double bed covered with a printed spread of romantic inspiration, depicting a classical, pastoral scene: the nymph Io suckling her son Epaphos under the gentle protection of the god Mercury.

On the bedside table stands a so-called "pineapple" lamp (the body of the fruit is a blue marble – or, rather, imitation-marble – egg, the leaves and the remainder of the base are made of silvered metal); beside it, a grey phone fitted with an automatic answering device, and a photograph of Louvet, in a bamboo frame: he is seen barefoot, in grey denim trousers, with a bright-red nylon jacket open wide and revealing his hairy torso, strapped in the stern of a powerful outboard, very old-man-and-the-sea-like; he is leaning hard over, almost on his back, as he strives to pull from the water a sort of tuna of apparently remarkable size.

On the walls there are four pictures and a glass display case. The display case contains a collection of self-assembled scale models of antique military machines: battering-rams, the *vinea* which Alexander made use of at the siege of Tyre, the *catapulta* of the Syrians, which threw monstrous stones so many hundred feet, *balistae*, *pyroboli*, *scorpio* which cast thousands of javelins, and flaming mirrors – such as Archimedes' mirror, which ignited whole fleets in an instant – and columns armed with scythes carried on the backs of wild elephants.

The first picture is a facsimile of an advertising poster from the early 1900s: three figures are resting in a bower: a young man in white trousers and blue blazer, with a boater on his head and a silver-topped stick under his arm, holds a box of cigars in his hand, a pretty, painted box decorated with designs showing a globe, several medals, and an exhibition hall surrounded by unfurled, gold-bedecked flags.

Another young man similarly dressed sits on a wickerwork pouf: with his hands in his trouser pockets and his black-shod feet stretched out in front of him, he holds between his lips, where it droops slightly, a long dull-grey cigar still in the early stage of combustion, that is to say with ash still intact on the end; beside him, on a round table with a polka-dot cloth, are some folded newspapers, a phonograph with an enormous loudspeaker which he appears to be listening to attentively, and a liqueur case, open, fitted with five gilt-capped flasks. A young woman, a rather mysterious blonde, wearing a thin and loose-fitting dress, is pouring the sixth flask, full of a uniformly brown liquid, into three stem glasses. At the very bottom, on the right, in thick yellow sunk characters, in the face known as "Auriol Champlevé", much used in the last century, are written the words

POR LARRANAGA 89 cts

The second picture portrays a bouquet of wild clematis, also known as Old Man's Beard because beggars used to use it to treat minor facial sores.

The last two pictures are allegedly humorous caricatures of poor artistic quality representing very well-worn jokes. The first is entitled *No Money? No Swiss*: it depicts a mountaineer lost in the Alps, rescued by a Saint Bernard carrying what appears to be a little cask of life-saving rum, with a red cross painted on it. But the climber is amazed to find no rum in the cask: it is in fact a collecting box, with a caption beneath its coin-slot: *Give Generously to the Red Cross!*

The other cartoon is called *The Right Recipe*: in a grotesquely depicted restaurant an angry customer points to a hair in his soup. The head waiter, just as angry, has called out the chef to explain, but the latter puts his finger to his lips: "*Ssh*, or they'll all be wanting one now!"

CHAPTER SEVENTY-EIGHT

On the Stairs, 10

For forty years now the piano-tuner has been coming to Madame de Beaumont's twice a year, in June and December, and this is the fifth time he has brought along his grandson, who though he's not yet ten years old takes his role as guide very seriously. But the last time, the boy knocked over a jardinière of dieffenbachia, so this time Madame Lafuente won't let him in.

The piano-tuner's grandson is therefore sitting on the stairs waiting for his grandfather. He is wearing short navy-blue cotton trousers and a jerkin of "parachute material", that is to say sky-blue shiny nylon, with a complement of decorative badges: a pylon giving off four streaks of lightning and concentric circles, the symbol of radiotelegraphy; a pair of compasses, a magnetic compass, and a stopwatch, the supposed symbols respectively of geographers, surveyors, and explorers; the figure 77 written in red letters in a yellow triangle; the outline of a cobbler mending a heavy mountain boot; a hand refusing a glass of spirits with the legend beneath: *"No thanks, I'm driving"*.

The little boy is reading a biographical novel about Carel van Loorens entitled *The Emperor's Messenger* in *Le Journal de Tintin*.

Carel van Loorens was one of the oddest minds of his time. He was born in Holland but had himself naturalised French out of love for the *philosophes*; he lived in Persia, Arabia, China, and the two Americas; he spoke a dozen or more languages fluently. With his obviously outstanding but dissipated mind, which he seemed unable to devote to any single discipline for more than a couple of years, he undertook in the course of his life wildly different activities, practising as a surgeon just as happily and speedily as he did as a surveyor, setting up in Lahore a cannon foundry, founding in Shiraz a veterinary school, teaching physiology at Bologna, mathematics at Halle, and astronomy at Barcelona (where he dared to put forward the hypothesis that Méchain had made an error in calculating the length of the metre), smuggling guns for Wolfe Tone, or, as an organ-builder, imagining how to replace the coupler registers by lever-switches, as would in fact be done a century later. As a result of this systematic versatility, in the course of his life Carel van Loorens came to ask himself several interesting questions and got started several times on provisional answers which were lacking neither in elegance nor even, on occasions, in brilliance, but almost every time he failed to write up his results in a remotely comprehensible manner. After his death, mostly undecipherable notes were found in his study, dealing variously with archaeology, Egyptology, typography (plan for a universal alphabet), linguistics (letter to Humboldt on the language of the Ouarsenis: it was obviously only a draft; in any case, Humboldt doesn't mention it), medicine, politics (draft for a democratic regime taking account of the separation not only of the three powers of the legislature, the executive, and the judiciary but – with disquieting foresight – of a fourth power also which he dubbed publicitary [from *publicist*, journalist], in other words the power of information, numerical algebra (note on Goldbach's problem, proposing that any number n be the sum of K primes), physiology (hypotheses concerning the hibernation of marmots, the pneumatic body of birds, the voluntary breath-holding of hippopotami, etc.), optics, physics, chemistry (critique of Lavoisier's theories of acids, draft classification of the elements), together with several ideas for inventions, in most cases falling short of full development by very little: a steerable hobby-horse similar to the draisienne, but twenty years earlier; a material he baptised "pellette", a kind of artificial leather composed of a strong canvas base coated with a mixture of powdered cork, linseed oil, glues, and resins; or a "solar forge", made of an assembly of metal plates, polished like mirrors, focused convergently on a hearth-point.

In 1805, Carel van Loorens sought money to finance an expedition to find the source or sources of the Nile, a project many had thought of but which no one had been able to carry out before then. He turned to Napoleon I, whom he had already met a few years before when, as a general too popular by half for the taste of the Directoire, who sent him to Egypt in order to keep him well away, the future Emperor of the French had gathered around him some of the best scholars of his time to accompany him on the campaign.

Napoleon had set himself a difficult diplomatic problem: the largest part of the French navy had just been sunk at Trafalgar, and, anxious to find a means of stemming the formidable maritime hegemony of the British, the Emperor thought of hiring the services of the most famous of the Barbary corsairs, the one they called Hokab el-Ouakt, the Eagle of the Instant.

Hokab el-Ouakt commanded a veritable fleet of eleven galliots whose perfectly co-ordinated actions made him the master of a good portion of the Mediterranean. But though he had no reason to love the British, who had held Gibraltar for nearly a hundred years and Malta for five, and thus had increasingly threatened the activities of the Barbary corsairs, he had no reason to like the French any better, since they, like the Spaniards, the Dutch, the Genoese, and the Venetians, had never thought twice before shelling Algiers.

In any case, the first problem was to contact the Eagle, since, in his concern to protect himself from assassination, he had himself permanently escorted by eighteen deaf-mute bodyguards whose sole standing order was to kill anyone coming within three paces of their master.

So it was when he was wondering where to find the rare bird who could bring off such difficult negotiations, which looked so discouraging at the outset, that the Emperor gave an audience to Carel van Loorens; and on receiving him had to say to himself that fortune had once again smiled on him. Van Loorens, he knew, spoke perfect Arabic; and in Egypt he had had occasion to appreciate his intelligence, his quick mind and his decisiveness, his sense of diplomacy, and his courage. Without hesitation Napoleon agreed to fund the entire cost of an expedition to the sources of the Nile, in return for Loorens undertaking to get a message to Hokab el-Ouakt in Algiers.

A few weeks later, Carel van Loorens, metamorphosed into a prosperous merchant from the Persian Gulf answering to the respectable name of Haj Abdulaziz Abu Bakr, made his entry into Algiers at the head of a long procession of camels and an escort composed of twenty of the Imperial Guard's best Mamelukes. He was carrying carpets, guns, pearls, sponges, cloth, and spices, merchandise of the highest quality for which he quickly found takers even though Algiers was at the time a wealthy city where you could find produce in profusion from all over the world, diverted from its original destinations by the pirate raids of the Barbary corsairs. But Loorens kept to himself three big iron chests, and to all who asked what was in them he invariably replied: "None is worthy to see the treasures that these chests hold if he be not Hokab el-Ouakt!"

On the fourth day following his arrival, three of the Eagle's men came for Loorens at the door of his inn. They signalled him to follow. He acquiesced, and they made him get into a sedan chair hermetically sealed by thick leather curtains. They took him outside the city to an isolated bell tent where they locked him up after a thorough body-search. Several hours went by. At last, after nightfall, preceded by some of his bodyguards, Hokab appeared:

"I've had your chests opened," he said, "and they were empty."

"I have come to offer you four times as much gold as those chests could ever hold."

"What need do I have of your gold? The smallest Spanish galleon gives me seven times as much."

"When did you take your last galleon? The English sink them, and you daren't attack the English. Next to their three-masters, your galliots are bathtubs!"

"Who sent you?"

"You are an Eagle, and only another Eagle may address you! I come to you with a message from Napoleon I, Emperor of the French!"

Hokab el-Ouakt must have known who Napoleon was, and no doubt held him in high esteem, since without exactly answering in so many words the proposal he had received, he regarded Carel van Loorens from then on as an ambassador, and insisted on treating him with infinite consideration; he invited him to stay in his palace, an immense fortress overhanging the sea, with terraces of enchanted gardens resplendent with jujube and carob trees, oleanders and tame gazelles, and he gave sumptuous feasts in his honour where he made him sample rare dishes from America and Asia. In return for this, Loorens spent whole afternoons telling the Arab of his adventures and describing to him the fabulous cities where he had sojourned:

Diomira the city of sixty silver domes, Isaura the town of a thousand wells, Smeraldine the city of water, and Moriane with its alabaster gates transparent in the sunlight, its coral columns supporting pediments encrusted with serpentine, its villas all of glass, like aquariums where the shadows of dancing girls with silvery scales swim beneath medusa-shaped chandeliers.

Loorens had been the Eagle's guest for almost a week when, one evening, alone in the garden onto which his suite of rooms opened, as he was finishing a cup of exquisite mocha and puffing occasionally on the amber mouthpiece of a hookah perfumed with rose water, he heard a velvety voice sing out in the night. It was an ethereal and melancholy woman's voice, and the tune it sang sounded so familiar to Loorens that he lent his ear to the music and the words and was hardly surprised to recognise Chaucer's *Merciles Beaute*:

Sin I fro Love escapèd am so fat,
I never thenk to ben in his prison lene;
Sin I am free, I counte, him not a bene,

He may answere, and saye this or that,
I do no fors, I speke right as I mene.
Sin I am free, I counte him not a bene,
I never thenk to ben in his prison lene.

Loorens rose and went towards the voice, and on the yonder side of a recess in the fortress, vertically above the jagged shoreline rocks, about ten metres higher than his own apartments, he saw, on a balcony entirely enclosed by gilded mesh and lit up in the dark by the mellow light of tarry torches, a woman of such extraordinary beauty that he threw caution to the winds, jumped astride the balustrade of his balcony, made his way along a narrow ledge to the other side of the fortress, and, using the indentations of the rock face, hauled himself up with his bare hands to the level of the young woman. He called to her softly. She heard him, made as if to run away, then, returning, came closer to him, and in a few breathless whispers told him her baleful tale.

Her name was Ursula von Littau. Daughter of the Count of Littau, former aide-de-camp to Friedrich-Wilhelm II, she was to have been married at the age of fifteen to the son of the Spanish Ambassador to the Prussian court at Potsdam, Alvero Sanchez del Estero. The corvette taking her across the sea to her future husband in Malaga had been attacked by Barbary pirates. She owed it to her beauty alone that she had kept her life, and for ten years she had languished in the harem of the Eagle of the Instant, amongst his fifteen other wives.

Half-hanging in empty space, Carel van Loorens listened to Ursula von Littau with tears in his eyes, and when she had finished her story he swore to free her the very next day. As a token of his oath he slipped his signet ring onto her finger, a ring with an ovoid bezel within which was set an opaline corundum intagliated with an 8 lying on its side. "For the Ancients," he told her, "this stone was the symbol of memory, and there is a legend that whoever sees this ring once will never again be able to forget."

In less than twenty-four hours, abandoning entirely the mission the Emperor had entrusted him with, Loorens set up the escape of Ursula von Littau. Next day he obtained the necessary equipment, and in the evening returned to the foot of the harem balcony. Taking a heavy smoked-glass phial from one of his pockets, he poured a few drops of steaming liquid onto several parts of the wire mesh. Under the corrosive force of the acid the iron bars began to disintegrate, and Loorens was able to arrange the small opening which would allow the young Prussian woman to slip away.

She came towards midnight. It was a black night. Far away, outside the Eagle's suite of rooms, the guards paced nonchalantly up and down. Loorens unrolled a ladder of knotted silk which reached to the foot of the fortress, and which Ursula and then he used to descend ninety feet below to a sandy cove surrounded by rocks and reefs breaking the surface of the water.

Two Mamelukes from his escort awaited them on this strand, carrying shaded lanterns. Leading them between the rocks and across stony landslips beneath the cliff, they guided them to the mouth of a dried-up wadi that went far up into the interior. The rest of the escort awaited them there. Ursula von Littau was hoisted into an *atatich*, that kind of round tent carried by camels and in which the fairer sex ordinarily ride, and the caravan set off.

Loorens planned on getting to Oran, where Spanish influence still prevailed. But he didn't have the opportunity to do so. Before daybreak, when they were still only a few hours' ride from Algiers, the Eagle's men caught up with them and attacked. The battle was brief and from the Mamelukes' point of view a disaster. Loorens himself didn't see much of it, as a shaven-headed Hercules knocked him out at the start with a mere blow of his fist.

When Carel van Loorens awoke, aching all over, he found he was in a room that looked like a cell: flagstones, a bare, dark wall, with a built-in iron ring. Light came from a small round opening equipped with finely crafted wrought-iron bars. Loorens went up to it and saw that his prison was part of a tiny village of three or four shacks around a well, surrounded by a tiny palm grove. The Eagle's men were camping out, honing their scimitars, tipping their arrows, and practising feats of horsemanship.

Suddenly the door opened and three men appeared. They seized Loorens and took him to a place a few hundred yards from the village, beyond a few dunes, amidst dead palm trees which the desert had claimed back from the oasis; there they strung him to a wooden frame that was halfway between a camp bed and an operating table, with a long leather thong wound several times around his trunk and limbs. Then they went off at a gallop.

Night began to fall. Loorens knew that if he didn't die of cold in the night he would as certainly be burnt to death by the sun next day as if he had been in the middle of his "solar forge". He recalled describing this project to Hokab and the Arab nodding his head thoughtfully and mumbling that the desert sun needed no mirrors, and he reflected that in choosing to have him die by this means of torture the Eagle meant to teach him the meaning of his words.

Years later, when he was sure Napoleon could no longer have him arrested and that Roustan could no longer have him killed, as he had sworn to, to avenge the twenty comrades slaughtered in this escapade, Carel van Loorens wrote a short memorandum of his adventure and sent it to the King of Prussia in the secret hope that His Majesty would grant him a pension in reward for having tried to rescue the daughter of his late father's aide-de-camp. In it he told of how his life was saved by a mere stroke of chance, a chance that had the Eagle's men tie him up with a thong of plaited leather. Had they but used esparto or hemp rope, or a canvas strip, he would never have been able to get free. But leather, as everyone knows, stretches when saturated with sweat, and after hours of contorted straining, heavy panting, sudden excruciations followed by shudders verging on the throes of death, Loorens felt that the thong, which up till then had dug deeper into his flesh with every effort made, had begun, minutely, to yield. He was so exhausted that despite the throttling anguish he felt, he dropped into a feverish sleep broken by nightmares in which he saw armies of rats attacking him from all sides and tearing out lumps of living flesh with their long teeth. He woke up panting, bathed in sweat, and felt that he was at last able to move his swollen feet.

Within a few hours he had untied himself. The night was icy, and a violent wind whipped up swirls of sand which cut into his skin, badly bruised as it was. With the energy born of despair, Loorens dug a hole in the sand and hid himself as best he could, closing himself in with the heavy wooden frame to which he had been strapped.

He couldn't get back to sleep, and for a long time, struggling against the cold and the sand which got into his eyes and mouth and caked the open sores on his wrists and ankles, he tried to think out his position lucidly. It was not promising: to be sure, he could move his legs, and he would doubtless manage to survive this dreadful night, but he was critically weak, without food or water, and he didn't know where he was, apart from being a few hundred yards from an oasis where those who had left him for dead were camping.

If that was all so, then he had no chance of surviving. This certainty almost brought him some peace: it meant that his life no longer hung on his courage, intelligence, or strength, but on fate alone.

The day broke at last. Loorens extricated himself from his hole, stood up, and managed a few paces. Over the dunes in front of him the tips of the palm trees could be seen clearly. There did not seem to be any noise coming from the oasis. Loorens felt his hopes rise again: if the Eagle's men, their task done, had left their temporary lair and gone back to Algiers, that meant, first, that the coast was near, and, secondly, that he would find food and water at the oasis. This hope gave him the strength to haul himself as far as the palm trees.

His reasoning had been wrong, or, at the very least, purely hypothetical, but it proved correct on one point: the oasis was deserted. The shacks, more than half collapsed, seemed to have been abandoned years ago, the well was dried up and swarming with scorpions, the palm trees were living their last seasons.

Loorens rested for a few hours and dressed his wounds with palm fronds. Then he set off northwards. He walked for hours and hours, with mechanical and hallucinated step, across a landscape that was no longer a sandy desert but had become stony and grey, with sparse tufts of almost-yellow grass with sharp-edged blades and, now and again, a donkey's carcass, all white and powdery, or a crumbling pile of stones that had perhaps once been a shepherd's hut. Then, when the dusk was coming on once again, he thought he saw, far ahead, at the very end of a plateau bristling with crevices and lumpy protrusions, camels, goats, and tents.

It was a Berber camp. The night was dark when he finally reached it and slumped in front of the fire around which the men of the tribe were seated.

He stayed more than a week with them. They only knew a few words of Arabic and so could not communicate much, but they looked after him, repaired his clothes, and, when he left, gave him food, water, and a dagger whose handle was a polished stone girt with a strip of brass decorated with delicate arabesques. To protect his soles, unused to walking bare on stony ground, they made him a kind of wooden patten held onto his foot by a broad leather strap, and he took to it so well that afterwards he never went back to European shoes.

A few weeks later, Carel van Loorens was safely in Oran. He didn't know what had become of Ursula von Littau, and his attempts to organise a punitive expedition to free her were in vain. Only in 1816, after the Eagle of the Instant had been killed in the bombardment of Algiers on the twenty-seventh of August by an Anglo-Dutch flotilla, was it learnt from the women of his harem that the unfortunate Prussian girl had suffered the fate reserved for unfaithful wives: she had been sewn into a leather sack and thrown into the sea from the top of the fortress.

Carel van Loorens lived for almost forty years more. Under the borrowed name of John Ross he became the Governor of Ceuta's librarian and spent the rest of his days transcribing the Cordoban court poets and sticking on the flyleaves of the library's books an ex-libris depicting an ammonite fossil beneath the proud motto: *Non frustra vixi.*

CHAPTER SEVENTY-NINE

On the Stairs, 11

The Rorschachs' double door is wide open. Two trunks have been dragged onto the landing, two ship's trunks, reinforced with studded leather, garnished with many labels. A third must be in the hallway, a room with a dark woodblock floor, panelled to head-height, with "rustic enlightenment" hatstands resembling deer's antlers from a Ludwigshafen *Bierstube* and an *art-nouveau* chandelier, a hemispherical paste-glass bowl decorated with inlaid triangular motifs, giving a rather poor light.

Olivia Rorschach entrains at midnight tonight at the Saint-Lazare railway station for her 56th world tour. Her nephew, who will accompany her for the first time, has come to fetch her with no less than four commissionaires. He is a lad of sixteen, very tall, with very black curly hair down to his shoulders, dressed with a sophistication beyond his years: a white shirt opening wide at the neck, a check waistcoat, a leather jacket, a tangerine cravat, and brown denims tucked into wide-topped Texan boots. He is seated on one of the trunks and sucks thoughtlessly at a straw inserted into a bottle of Coke as he reads *The Frenchman's Companion in New York*, a small tourist-publicity fold-out published by a travel company.

Born in 1930 in Sydney, at the age of eight Olivia Norvell became the most adulated child in Australia when she acted in an adaptation of *Wee Willie Winkie* at the Royal Theatre, in which she played the role taken by Shirley Temple in the film of the same name. Her success was such that not only was the play a sell-out for two years, but also, when Olivia let it be known through cleverly released rumours that she had begun to rehearse a new part, that of Alice in *Alice's Dream*, a play vaguely based on Lewis Carroll and written especially for her by a professional playwright who had come over from Melbourne for that purpose, all the seats for the two hundred performances initially scheduled were bought out six months before the first night, and the theatre management opened a waiting list for possible subsequent performances.

Whilst she let her daughter pursue her fabulous career, Olivia's mother, Eleanor Norvell, an astute businesswoman, exploited the girl's popularity for all it was worth, and Olivia soon became the most sought-after model in the whole country. And the whole of Australia was soon flooded with small newssheets and coy posters showing Olivia stroking a teddy bear or, beneath the professionally sentimental gaze of her parents, reading an encyclopaedia twice her size (*Let Your Child Enter the Realm of Knowledge!*) or, dressed as an urchin in peaked cap and trousers with braces, sitting on a kerb playing fives with three twins of Pim, Pam, and Poum in an Australian forerunner of the *Mind That Child!* road-safety campaign.

Though her mother and her agent worried endlessly about the disastrous effect that adolescence and, even more, puberty would not fail to have on this living doll, Olivia reached the age of sixteen without having ceased for a moment to be an object of such adoration that in some places on the west coast riots broke out when the crypto-commercial weekly which held exclusive rights to her photographs failed to arrive with the expected mail delivery. And it was then, in a moment of supreme success, that she married Jeremy Bishop.

Like all pre-teen and teenage Australian girls of the period, Olivia had of course been a "war mother" to several serving soldiers between 1940 and 1945. In fact, for Olivia, it was a business of whole regiments, to which she sent her autographed photo; once a month, furthermore, she would write a brief letter to a private or NCO who had distinguished himself in some more or less heroic feat of arms.

Private Jeremy Bishop had joined up as a volunteer in the 28th Marine Infantry (under the famous Colonel Arnhem Palmerston, nicknamed "Old Lightning" because of the thin white scar running across his face, as if he'd been struck by lightning) and became one of the fortunate few: for having helped his lieutenant out of the water at the bloody battle of the Coral Sea in 1942, he got the Victoria Cross as well as a handwritten letter from Olivia Norvell, ending with "love and kisses with all my tiny heart", followed by a dozen little crosses each having the value of one kiss.

Carrying this letter on him like a talisman, Bishop swore to himself that he would get another, and to this end redoubled his spectacular efforts: from Guadalcanal to Okinawa, by way of Tarawa, the Gilberts, the Marshalls, Guam, Baatan, the Marianas, and Iwo Jima, he fought to such effect and purpose that by the end of the war he was the most decorated lance corporal in all Oceania.

Marriage between the two idols of the young was called for, and it was celebrated with all requisite pomp on 26 January 1946, Australia's National Day. Over forty-five thousand people attended the nuptial blessing in Melbourne's great stadium by Cardinal Fringilli, who was at the time the ecumenical vicar apostolic of Australasia and Antarctica. Then the public, paying ten Australian dollars per person (about five pounds sterling), was permitted to enter the young couple's new home and to process before the gifts sent in from all over the world: the President of the United States had given them the Complete Works of Nathaniel Hawthorne, bound in buffalo hide; Mrs Plattner, a Brisbane typist, had sent a picture of the happy couple made entirely out of typewriter characters; The Olivia Fan Club of Tasmania had sent seventy-one tame white mice trained to group themselves into the letters making up the name Olivia; and the Ministry of Defence had sent a narwhal's horn longer than the one Sir Martin Frobisher presented to Queen Elizabeth on his return from Labrador. For ten dollars more, you could even go into the nuptial chamber to admire the conjugal bed carved out of the trunk of a sequoia, a joint gift from the Wood and Allied Industries' Trades Association and the National Union of Foresters and Woodcutters. Finally, that evening, at a huge reception, Bing Crosby was brought by special plane from Hollywood to sing a version of the *Wedding March* composed in honour of the newly-weds by one of Ernst Krenek's best pupils.

That was her first marriage. It lasted twelve days. Rorschach was her fifth husband. In between, she married in succession a young actor whom she'd seen in the part of a moustached Austrian officer in a frogged dolman, who left her four months later for an Italian boy who'd sold them a rose in a restaurant in Bruges; an English lord who never left his dog, a small curly-haired spaniel named Scrambled Eggs; and a paralysed industrialist from Racine, Wisconsin (between Chicago and Milwaukee), who ran his foundries from the terrace of his villa, sitting in his wheelchair, his lap piled high with newspapers from all over the world that came in the morning post.

It was in Davos in February 1958, a few weeks after her fourth divorce, that she met Rémi Rorschach in circumstances worthy of a classical American comedy. She was in a bookshop looking for a book on the *Rich Hours of the Duc de Berry*, of which she had seen some reproductions the previous evening on a television programme. Of course the only available copy had just been bought, and the lucky customer, a man of mature years but obviously still sprightly, was just then paying for it at the cash desk. Olivia went up to him without hesitating, introduced herself, and offered to buy the book back. The man, who was none other than Rorschach, refused, but they agreed in the end to share it between them.

CHAPTER EIGHTY

Bartlebooth, 3

Two papers read at the IIIrd Congress of the International Union of Historical Sciences, held in October 1887 in Edinburgh, under the joint auspices of the Royal Historical Society and the British Association for the Advancement of Science, caused a sensation in international scholarly circles and, for a few weeks, aroused wide public interest.

The first of these papers was read in German by Professor Zapfenschuppe of Strasbourg University. It was entitled *Untersuchungen über die Taufe Amerikas*. Whilst studying archives retrieved from the cellar of the Bishop's Palace at Saint-Dié, the author had discovered a collection of old books which, beyond any possible doubt, came from the famous printing press founded in 1495 by Germain Lud. Amongst these books he found an atlas to which many sixteenth-century texts referred, but of which no single copy had previously been known to exist: namely, the famous *Cosmographiae introductio cum quibusdam geometriae ac astronomiae principiis ad eam rem necessariis, insuper quattuor Americii Vespucii navigationes* by Martin Waldseemüller, called Hylacomilus, the best known of the cartographers of the School of Saint-Dié. It was in this cordiform atlas that the new world discovered by Christopher Columbus, and which he himself called West India, first appeared under the designation TERRA AMERICI VEL AMERICA, and the date given on this copy – 1507 – finally put an end to three centuries of bitter controversy concerning Amerigo Vespucci: some held him to be a man of sincerity, a scrupulous and upright explorer who had never dreamt of having a continent named after him one day and never knew that it had been so named, or they believed that he only learnt of it on his deathbed (there are indeed many romantic prints – including one by Tony Johannot – showing the explorer as an old man passing away in Seville, in 1512, amidst his loved ones, with one hand on an open atlas held out to him by a man kneeling in tears at his bedside, for him to see once before he dies the word AMERICA unfurling across the new continent); but others viewed him as a buccaneer of the same breed as the Pinzón Brothers, trying, like them, at every turn to displace Columbus and to steal the glory of his discoveries. Thanks to Professor Zapfenschuppe, it was now proven that the custom of calling the new lands America had been established during Vespucci's lifetime. Vespucci had certainly been told this, even if he fails to allude to it in his letters and journals: the fact that he never disputed the appellation, and its persistent usage, suggest very strongly indeed that Vespucci must have been not at all displeased in the end to leave his name to a continent which he believed in good faith he had done more to "discover" than had the Genoese adventurer who, when all was said and done, did no more than explore a few offshore islands, taking cognisance of the mainland itself only much later on, on his third voyage, in 1498–1500, when he reached the mouth of the Orinoco and finally realised that the huge scale of such a hydrographic system was definitive proof of the existence of a vast, unknown hinterland.

* * *

But the second paper was even more sensational. It was called *New Insights into Early Denominations of America* and was read by a Spanish archivist, Juan Mariano de Zaccaria, who was working in Havana, at the Maestranza Donation, on a collection of almost two thousand maps, a number of which came from Santa Catalina after the fort there was dismantled; amongst these, he had come across a planisphere dated 1503 on which the new continent was explicitly designated by the name TERRA COLUMBIA!

When the aged Lord Lowager Colquhoun of Darroch, permanent Secretary of the Caledonian Society, whose imperturbable phlegm was never so valued as on this occasion when he was in the chair, had managed to quieten down the exclamations of amazement, excitement, disbelief, and delight which shook the austere dome of the Senate Room in Old College, and had brought the session back to a relative state of order more conducive to the dignity, impartiality, and objectivity which should always be the appanage of true scholarship, Zaccaria was able to proceed with his paper, and he passed around the electrified audience a photograph of the whole planisphere, as well as an enlargement of a (fairly damaged) fragment where the letters

TE RA COI B I A

were printed along a few inches of the edge of an approximate but undeniably recognisable representation of a large portion of the New World: Central America, the West Indies, and the coastline of Venezuela and Guyana.

Zaccaria was the hero of the day, and correspondents from *The Scotsman*, *The Scottish Daily Mail*, *The Scottish Daily Express* (Glasgow), the Aberdeen *Press and Journal*, and not forgetting *The Times* and the *Daily Mail*, of course, took it upon themselves to spread the news throughout the world. But a few weeks later, when Zaccaria was back in Havana putting the finishing touches to the article he had promised to give the *American Journal of Cartography*, in which a full reproduction of the precious document was to be inserted on a "special fold-out leaf", he received a letter emanating from a certain

Florentin Gilet-Burnachs, curator of the Municipal Museum at Dieppe: chance had it that he had opened an issue of *Le Moniteur Universel* and had read its detailed account of the Edinburgh congress and especially of Zaccaria's paper, including a description of the damaged fragment on which the Cuban archivist had based his claim that the New World was named COLUMBIA in 1503.

Florentin Gilet-Burnachs, who quoted in passing a sentence from someone called Monsieur de Cuverville ("enthusiasm is no state of mind for a historian"), and who of course fully appreciated the brilliance of Zaccaria's paper, wondered nonetheless whether the revelation – not to say revolution – it contained should not be subjected to a thoroughgoing critique. Obviously it was very tempting to read

COI B I A

as

COLUMB I A

and this reading gave voice to a widely shared feeling: unearthing a map where the West Indies were dubbed COLUMBIA, geographers and historians felt they were making amends for an historical error; for centuries, the West had resented Amerigo Vespucci's usurpation of the name which Christopher Columbus ought to have given to the lands he had been the first to explore: by applauding Zaccaria, the congress had meant to rehabilitate the Genoese seafarer and thus bring four centuries of injustice to an end.

However, the curator continued, in the last quarter of the fifteenth century, dozens of navigators, from the Cabots to the Cabrals, from Gomes to Verrezano, sought the westward route to the Indies and – he was coming to the point – there was a deep-rooted tradition in Dieppe, still flourishing in the late eighteenth century, which attributed the discovery of "America" to a local seaman, Jean Cousin, called Cousin the Bold, who was supposed to have reached the West Indies in 1487–1488, five years before the man from Genoa. The Municipal Museum at Dieppe, having inherited a selection of the maps made by order of the shipowner Jean Ango, which had given the Dieppe school of cartography (including mapmakers like Desceliers and Nicolas Desliens) its reputation as one of the best of the sixteenth century, possessed a map dated 1521 – markedly later, that is, than Zaccaria's map from the Maestranza Donation – on which the Gulf of Honduras – Christopher Columbus's "deep gulf" – was called MARE CONSO, clearly an abbreviation of MARE CONSOBRINIA, a Latin translation of "the sea of the cousin", Cousin's Sea (and not MARE CONSOLATRIX, as Lebrun-Brettil had stupidly claimed).

Therefore, Florentin Gilet-Burnachs went on mercilessly, the

COI B I A

which Zaccaria had read as

COLUMB I A

could be read much more plausibly, given the spacing of the three final letters, as

CONSOBRINIA

By way of conclusion, the curator suggested that Zaccaria should take pains to establish the provenance of the 1503 map. If it was of Portuguese, Spanish, Genoese, or Venetian origin, then the

COI B I A

could indeed be a designation of Columbus, despite the fact that he himself had imposed the usage INDIA. In any case it would not refer to Jean Cousin, whose fame went no further than Dieppe itself, and who had for rivals, even in the nearby ports of Le Tréport, Saint-Valéry-en-Caux, Fécamp, Etretat, and Honfleur, sailors just as bold as he was, and all busy at finding new routes. But if, on the other hand, the map was of the Dieppe school – that could be easily checked, all Dieppe maps having a monogram decorated with lower-case *d* at the centre of one of the mariner's cards – then it was TERRA CONSOBRINIA that was meant.

Finally, Gilet-Burnachs wrote in a postscript, if the monogram was two *Rs* intertwined, that would mean that the planisphere was the work of Renaud Régnier, one of the earliest cartographers of the Dieppe school, who was believed to have accompanied Cousin on one of his voyages. The selfsame Renaud Régnier had drawn a map of the coast of North America some years later, around 1520, and by an extraordinary coincidence had given the name of TERRA MARIA to the territory which, on account of Henriette-Marie, the daughter of Henri IV of France and wife of Charles I of England, would be baptised MARYLAND one hundred years later.

Zaccaria was an honest geographer. He could have ignored Gilet-Burnachs's letter, or he could have taken covert advantage of the generally poor condition of the planisphere to destroy any signs of its possible origin and then declare to the Dieppe curator that his was a Spanish map, and that therefore the latter's critique would not stand. But instead of doing that, he ascertained conscientiously that it was indeed a map by Renaud Régnier, informed his correspondent, and offered to co-author a correction with him which would close the debate on this thorny toponymic problem. The joint article appeared in 1888, in the journal *Onomastica*, but it caused infinitely less of a stir than his paper at the IIIrd Congress.

It remained the case nonetheless that the 1503 planisphere was the only map on which the continent now known as America was called Cousinia. This singular fact came to the ears of James Sherwood, who succeeded in purchasing this unique map a year later from the Rector of Havana University, for an undisclosed sum. And that is how the map is to be found today on one of the walls of Bartlebooth's bedroom.

It was not because it was unique that Bartlebooth, as a child, grew attached to this map, which he could look at in the great hall of the manor house where he grew up, but because it possessed another feature also: the map's north is not at the top, but at the bottom. This difference of orientation, much commoner in the period than is often realised, fascinated Bartlebooth to the highest degree:

representations rotated not always by one hundred and eighty degrees, but sometimes by ninety or forty-five, completely subvert habitual perceptions of space; the outline of Europe, for instance, a shape familiar to anyone who has been even only to junior school, when swung round ninety degrees to the right, with the west at the top, begins to look like Denmark. And in this minimal switch lay hidden the very image of his jigsaw-puzzle mind.

Bartlebooth was never a collector in the usual sense of the word, but nonetheless, in the early thirties, he looked out or had others look out for similar maps. He has two of that kind in his bedroom. One, which he got at an auction at Hôtel Drouot, is a fine impression of the *Imperium Japonicum . . . descriptum ab Hadriano Relando*, part of the Atlas published by Reinier Otten of Amsterdam; specialists rate the map very highly, not because north is to the right, but because the names of the sixty-six imperial provinces are given for the first time in Japanese ideograms with their transcriptions in Latin characters.

The other one is even more curious: it is a map of the Pacific of the kind used by the coastal tribes of the Gulf of Papua: it consists of an extremely dense network of bamboo sticks indicating the currents and prevailing winds of the sea; here and there, in seemingly random distribution, seashells (cowries) are set to represent islands and reefs. In terms of the universal standards of modern-day cartography, this "map" would seem to be an aberration: at first sight it provides neither an orientation, nor a scale, nor an identification of distances, nor a representation of relief; but, in fact, it appears that it serves its purpose incomparably well, just as, Bartlebooth explained one day, a diagram of the London Underground is quite impossible to match with a map of London but is sufficiently simple and obvious to be used without any trouble at all when you want to go from A to B by tube.

This map of the Pacific had been brought back by Captain Barton, who had studied the migrations of one of these New Guinea tribes at the end of the last century: he had looked at the Motu of Port Moresby, whose voyages bring to mind the *Kula* of the Trobriand Islanders. When he got back to London, Barton presented his trophy to the Bank of Australia, which had part-sponsored his expedition.

The bank exhibited it for a while in a reception room at its main office, then, in its turn, donated it to the National Foundation for the Development of the Southern Hemisphere, a semi-private agency aiming at recruiting emigrants for New Zealand and Australia. The Foundation went into liquidation at the end of the nineteen twenties, and the map, offered for sale by the official liquidator, was eventually brough to the attention of Bartlebooth, who bought it.

The rest of the room is almost devoid of furniture: it is a bright room, painted white, with thick cambric curtains and an ordinary bed: an English-made bedstead of brass, with a flowery printed cotton spread, and two Empire bedside tables. On the left-hand table stands a lamp with a base shaped like an artichoke and an octagonal pewter plate bearing two lumps of sugar, a glass, a spoon, a crystal water jug with a pine-cone stopper; on the right-hand table, a small rectangular pendulum clock whose mahogany case is inlaid with ebony and gilded metal, a monogrammed silver cup, and a photograph in an oval frame portraying three of Bartlebooth's grandparents – James's brother William Sherwood, his wife Emily, and James Aloysius Bartlebooth – all in formal dress, standing behind Priscilla and Jonathan, the newly-weds being seated at each other's side in the midst of a profusion of baskets of flowers and ribbon bows. On the lower shelf lies a large desk diary bound in black leather. On the cover the words DESK DIARY 1952 and ALLIANCE BUILDING SOCIETY in large gold-leaf upper-case lettering stand above a crest, of gules with chevrons, bees, and yellow bezant, adorned with a phylactery bearing the motto DOMUS ARX CERTISSIMA, the English translation of which is given immediately below: *The surest stronghold is the home*.

It would be tiresome to draw up a list of all the cracks and contradictions which appeared in Bartlebooth's plan. For if, in the end, as we shall now soon see, the programme the Englishman had set himself gave way under Beyssandre's resolute onslaught as well as Winckler's far more hidden and subtle attack, Bartlebooth's failure must be ascribed in the first place to his own inability to respond to those onslaughts at the appropriate time.

It is not a matter here of minor faults of the kind which never endangered the system Bartlebooth aimed to build, even if such blemishes did sometimes exacerbate the system's excessively rigid tyranny and the exasperation it caused. For instance, when Bartlebooth decided he would paint five hundred watercolours in twenty years, he chose the figures because they were round numbers; he would have done better to pick four hundred and eighty, which would have made two a month; or, at the limit, five hundred and twenty, that is to say one every fortnight. But to get to exactly five hundred, he was sometimes obliged to paint two a month except for one month when he would paint three, or alternatively to do one approximately every two and a quarter weeks. Added to the variability of his travels, this was a factor which compromised the temporal regularity of his plan, but only to a small degree: in general, Gaspard Winckler received a watercolour approximately every fortnight, for there were of course in practice minor variations of up to a few days and occasionally even a few weeks; but these, similarly, did not bring into question the overall organisation of the task Bartlebooth had set himself, any more than did the minor delays he got into when reassembling the puzzles and which meant that very often the watercolours, on being sent back to the places where they had been painted, were "erased" not precisely twenty years after, but roughly twenty years after, twenty years plus a few days after.

If we can speak of an overall failure, it is because Bartlebooth, in real terms, in concrete fact, did not manage to carry his challenge through to the end within the rules he had laid down: he wanted the whole project to come full circle without leaving a mark, like an oily sea closing over a drowning man; his aim was for nothing, nothing at all, to subsist, for nothing but the void to emerge from it, for only the immaculate whiteness of a blank to remain, only the gratuitous perfection of a project entirely devoid of utility; but though he did paint five hundred seascapes in twenty years, though Gaspard Winckler did saw the seascapes into puzzles each of seven hundred and fifty pieces, not all the puzzles were reassembled; and not all the reassembled puzzles were destroyed on the very site where the watercolours had been painted, roughly twenty years before.

It is hard to say whether the plan was feasible, or to know if it could have been completed without crumbling beneath the weight of its internal contradictions or falling to pieces as its constituent elements wore out. And even if Bartlebooth had kept his eyesight, perhaps, even then, he would not have managed to reach the end of the implacable adventure to which he had resolved to devote his life.

It was in the final months of nineteen seventy-two that he realised he was going blind. It had begun a few weeks before with headaches, a twisted neck, and disturbances of vision which gave him the sensation, at the end of a day spent working on a puzzle, that his eyes were clouding over, that the outlines of objects were acquiring a fuzzy halo. To begin with, he only needed to lie down in the dark to make it disappear, but soon the disorder grew worse, became more frequent and more intense, so that even in half-light it seemed that things were reduplicating themselves, as if he were constantly drunk.

The doctors he turned to diagnosed a double cataract, for which they operated on him, successfully. They fitted him with thick contact lenses and forbade him, obviously, to tire his eyes. In their mind that meant reading only the headlines in newspapers, not driving in the dark, not watching television for too long. It didn't even occur to them that Bartlebooth might ever envisage starting on another puzzle. But after only a month Bartlebooth sat down at his table and tried to catch up on lost time.

The trouble came back very quickly. This time Bartlebooth thought he could see a fly for ever flitting somewhere to the side of his left eye, and he caught himself constantly wanting to raise his hand to swat it. Then his field of vision began to shrink; in the end it was no more than a tiny crack which let in a dim fringe of light, like a door ajar in the dark.

The doctors he called to his bedside shook their heads. Some mentioned amaurosis, others said pigmentary retinitis. In neither case could anything be done, and the inexorable outcome was blindness.

Bartlebooth had been handling the little puzzle pieces for eighteen years, and the sense of touch played almost as great a role for him as sight. He realised with exhilaration that he could carry on working: henceforth it would be as if he had to strive to reassemble blank watercolours. In fact, in this period, he could still distinguish shapes. In early 1975, when he began to see nothing save immaterial spots of brightness quivering and shifting far away, he decided to find someone to help him sort the pieces of the current puzzle into their dominant colours, their shadings, and their shapes. Winckler was dead, and anyway he would have refused; Smautf and Valène were too old; and the trial runs he did with Kléber and Hélène did not prove satisfactory to him. Finally he turned to Véronique Altamont because he had learnt from Smautf, who had got it from Madame Nochère, that she was studying watercolours and enjoyed doing puzzles. Since then, almost every day, the chit of a girl comes to spend an hour or two with the old Englishman, putting the little wooden pieces into his hand one by one, as she describes in her still, small voice the imperceptible differences of colour between them.

CHAPTER EIGHTY-ONE

Rorschach, 4

Olivia Rorschach's bedroom is a bright, pleasant room hung with pale wallpaper patterned in Japanese style, and with furniture in agreeably light-coloured wood. The bed, covered with a patchwork-pattern cotton bedspread, stands on a broad woodblock platform which serves on each side as a bedside table: on the right-hand side, a tall alabaster vase filled with yellow roses; on the other side, a tiny night-light with a black metal cube for a base, a secondhand copy of *The Valley of the Moon* by Jack London, bought the day before for fifteen centimes at the flea market at Place d'Aligre, and a photograph of Olivia at the age of twenty: in a check shirt, fringed suede waistcoat, riding trousers, high-heeled boots, and cowboy hat, she is sitting astride a wooden fence with a bottle of Coca-Cola in her hand; behind her, a muscular streetseller waves a tray heavily laden with multicoloured fruit with a single strong sweep of his forearm: it is a rostrum photograph from her penultimate feature film – *Right On Lads!* – in which she starred in 1949, when she left Australia after her much-publicised separation from Jeremy Bishop and courageously attempted a new career in the United States. *Right On Lads!* didn't last long. Her following film, entitled by cruel coincidence *Don't Leave the Cast, Baby!*, in which she plays the part of a waitress (the fair Amandine) in love with a seventeen-year-old acrobat who juggles lighted torches, wasn't even edited, since the producers reckoned after seeing the rushes that they wouldn't be able to make anything out of them. After that Olivia became the star of a tourist serial, where she was the apple-pie American girl from a good home all full of good will off water-skiing in the Everglades, sunning herself in the Bahamas, the Caribbean, or the Canaries, having a ball at the Carnival in Rio, cheering the toreros in Barcelona, acquiring culture at the Escurial, spirituality at the Vatican, sipping champagne at the Moulin-Rouge, swigging beer at the *Oktoberfest* in Munich, etc., etc. From this she acquired a taste for travel, and she was doing her fifty-eighth short (*Unforgettable Vienna . . .*) when she met her second husband, whom she left on her fifty-ninth (*The Magic of Bruges*).

Olivia Rorschach is in her bedroom. She is a very short, rather podgy little woman with her hair in curls; she is wearing a beautifully tailored, severe, white linen two-piece, a raw-silk blouse, and a broad decorative neckscarf. She is seated next to her bed beside various things she will take with her – a handbag, a sponge bag, a light coat, a beret decorated with a medal bearing the old crest of the Order of Saint Michael, showing the Archangel slaying the Dragon, *Time* magazine, *Le Film Français*, *What's On in London* – and she is rereading the list of instructions she is leaving for Jane Sutton:

– *get in a delivery of Coca-Cola*

– *change the water for the flowers every other day, put in half an aspirin each time, throw them out when they wilt*

– *get the big crystal chandelier cleaned (call Salmon's)*

– *take back to the municipal library the books that should have been returned two weeks ago and especially* Love Letters of Clara Schumann, From Agony to Ecstasy, *by Pierre Janet, and* Bridge over the River Kwai *by Pierre Boulle*

- *buy cooked Edam for Polonius and don't forget to take him once a week to Monsieur Lefèvre for his domino lesson*[1]
- *check daily that the Pizzicagnolis have not broken the blown-glass grapes in the entrance hall.*

The pretext for this fifty-sixth world tour is an invitation to attend the world premiere, in Melbourne, of *The Olivia Norvell Story*, a film composed of old clips from most of her best performances, including film sequences made of her great stage hits; the voyage will begin with an ocean cruise from London to the West Indies, thence by air to Melbourne with stop-overs of a few days planned for New York, Mexico, Lima, Tahiti, and Nouméa.

CHAPTER EIGHTY-TWO

Gratiolet, 2

Isabelle Gratiolet's bedroom: a child's bedroom with orange-and-yellow-striped wallpaper, a narrow tubular bed with a Snoopy pillow, a tub chair with fringes and arms decked with tassels and bobbles, a small whitewood wardrobe with two doors decorated with a washable adhesive material imitating rustic tiles (*Delft style:* faintly crackled light-blue squares depicting alternately a windmill, a wine press, and a sundial), a school desk with a groove for pencils,

[1] Polonius is the 43rd descendant of a pair of tame hamsters which Rémi Rorschach gave Olivia as a present shortly after he met her: the two of them had seen an animal-trainer at a Stuttgart music hall and were so impressed by the athletic exploits of the hamster Ludovic – disporting himself with equal ease on the rings, the bar, the trapeze, and the parallel bars – that they asked if they could buy him. The trainer, Lefèvre, refused, but sold them instead a pair – Gertrude and Sigismond – which he had trained to play dominoes. The tradition was maintained from generation to generation, with each set of parents spontaneously teaching their offspring to play. Unfortunately, the previous winter an epidemic had almost wiped out the little colony: the sole survivor, Polonius, could not play solo, and, worse, was condemned to waste away if he was prevented from indulging in his favourite pastime. Thus he had to be taken once a week to Meudon to his trainer, who, though now retired, continued to raise little circus animals for his own amusement.

and three bookcases. On the table is a pencil-case decorated with stencilled designs representing rather stylised Scotsmen in national dress blowing into their bagpipes, a steel ruler, a slightly dented, enamelled tin on which the word SPICES is written, filled with ballpoints and felt-tips, as well as an orange; and several exercise books in sleeve covers made of that mottled paper bookbinders use, a bottle of Waterman ink, and four blotters belonging to the collection Isabelle is building up, though much less seriously than her competitor Rémi Plassaert:

- a baby in a romper pushing a hoop (presented by Fleuret Sons of Corvol L'Orgueilleux, Stationers);
- a bee (*Apis mellifica* L.) (presented by Juventia Laboratories);
- a fashion print depicting a man wearing scarlet shantung pyjamas, sealskin slippers, and a sky-blue cashmere dressing gown with silver piping (*NESQUIK: Another cup would be nice!*);
- and lastly, No. 24 of the series *Great Women of French History*, presented by the weekly magazine *La Semaine de Suzette*: Madame Récamier; a little room with Empire furniture, where a few men in black evening clothes are sitting about on sofas, listening, while beside a cheval glass supported by a figure of Minerva, a chaise longue, with a curved and cradle-like interior, discloses the figure of a young woman lying at full length, whose relaxed pose contrasts with the tropical sunset of her spectacular, thick satin gown.

Over the bed there hangs – surprisingly, in a teenager's bedroom – an oval-bellied theorbo, one of those double-necked lutes whose brief vogue began in the sixteenth century, reached its apogee in the reign of Louis XIV – Ninon de Lenclos, it seems, was an excellent player – and then declined as the bass guitar and 'cello came in. It is the only object Olivier Gratiolet took away with him from the horse farm after the murder of his wife and his father-in-law's suicide. It was supposed to have always been in the family, but no one knew where it came from, and in the end Olivier showed it to Léon Marcia, who was able to identify it without too much trouble: it was probably one of the last theorbos made; it had never been played, and came from Steiner's workshop in the Tyrol; it definitely did not date from the workshop's high period, when Jacques Steiner's violins were put on a par with Amati's, but from its late period, probably the very beginning of the second half of the eighteenth century, a time when lutes and theorbos were more collectors' curios than musical instruments.

At school no one likes Isabelle, and she does nothing, it seems, to be liked. Her classmates say she is completely bananas, and on several occasions parents have been to see Olivier Gratiolet to complain about his daughter, who, they say, tells scary tales to her classmates and sometimes, even, in the playground, to children much younger than she is. For instance, to get her own back on Louisette Guerné, who had spilt a bottle of Indian ink on her blouse during art, Isabelle told her there was a *pornographic* old man following her in the street whenever she went out of school and that he was going to attack her one day and take off all her clothes and make her do horrid things. Or again, that she convinced Dominique Krause, who is only ten years old, that ghosts really exist and that she had even seen her father appear one day dressed in armour like a medieval knight in the midst of terrified guards armed with halberds. Or yet again, that when given as a composition assignment: "Describe the best holiday you can remember", she wrote a long, convoluted love story in which, wearing gold brocade and pursuing a Masked Prince whose face she had sworn never to set eyes on, she marched through halls flagged with veined marble, escorted by armies of pages carrying tarry torches and dwarves who poured her heady wines in silver-gilt goblets.

Her French teacher was at a loss and showed the script to the headmistress, who first consulted a counsellor and then wrote to Olivier Gratiolet, urging him most strongly to have his daughter seen by a psychotherapist and suggesting next year he put her into a school for disturbed children where her intellectual and psychological development could be monitored more closely, to which Olivier replied, somewhat curtly, that just because schoolgirls of his daughter's age were almost without exception sheep-brained ninnies who could just about manage to parrot *the cat sat on the mat* and *the rain in Spain stays mainly on the plain*, there was no need to treat Isabelle as abnormal or even just sensitive on the mere pretext that she had some imagination.

CHAPTER EIGHTY-THREE

Hutting, 3

Hutting's bedroom, on the mezzanine, off the gallery he had put in when he converted his apartment, corresponds more or less to the old No. 12 maid's room which was occupied up until the end of 1949 by a very aged couple whom people called the Honorés; in fact Honoré was the man's forename, but no one, except perhaps Madame Claveau the concierge and the Gratiolets, knew their surname – Marcion – or used the woman's forename, Corinne, and so she went on being called Madame Honoré.

Up until nineteen twenty-six, the Honorés were in service with the Danglars. Honoré was the butler, and Madame Honoré was the cook, a cook of the old kind, wearing all year round a cotton scarf, a bonnet over her hair, grey stockings, a red skirt, and a pinafore with a bib on top of her blouse. The Danglar's staff included a third servant: Célia Crespi, taken on a few months before as a chambermaid.

On the third of January nineteen twenty-six, ten days or so after the fire that destroyed Madame Danglars's boudoir, Célia Crespi, when she came in around seven a.m. to start her day, found the flat empty. The Danglars had apparently flung a few vital necessities into three suitcases and gone, without telling anyone.

The disappearance of a deputy chairman of the Court of Appeal could obviously not be considered an insignificant event, and the very next day rumours began to fly about what was immediately called the Danglars Affair: was it true the judge had been threatened? Was it true that plain-clothes policemen had been trailing him for two months? Was it true that his office at the Law Courts had been searched despite the police chief being notified of a formal prohibition by the Lord Chief Justice himself? Such were the questions, asked by the satirical press in the first place, and then by the national dailies with their usual nose for scandals and sensations.

Answers came a week later: the Home Office stated in a press release that Berthe and Maximilien Danglars had been arrested on the fifth of January trying to jump the border into Switzerland. And it was revealed to general stupefaction that this high-ranking judge and his wife had carried out, since the end of the war, thirty or so burglaries or unparalleled audacity.

The Danglars didn't steal for gain, but rather, along the lines of the many cases described in abundant detail in the literature of psychopathology, because the risks they ran in carrying out these thefts gave them exceptionally intense feelings of exaltation and excitement of a basically sexual nature. This stiff, upper-class couple, who had always had relations *à la* Walter Shandy (once a week, after winding up the clock, Maximilien Danglars would perform his conjugal duty), had discovered that the act of purloining in public an object of great value released in each of them a kind of libidinal exhilaration which soon became their sole aim in life.

They had discovered their kink quite by chance; one day Madame Danglars took her husband to Cleray's to help him choose a cigarette case and was seized by an irresistible feeling of desire and fear: looking straight in the eye of the girl who was serving them, she lifted a tortoiseshell belt buckle. It was only a luxury larceny, but when she confessed it to her husband that evening – he hadn't noticed a thing – the narration of this illegal exploit unleashed a sexual frenzy normally lacking in their embraces.

They quickly developed rules for their game. As it turned out, the main thing was for one of them to commit some theft that had been set up in advance, and to do it within the other's sight. A whole system of forfeits, generally of an erotic kind, rewarded or punished the thief according to his or her success or failure.

The Danglars entertained a great deal and were invited out just as much, and they therefore selected their victims in the drawing rooms of embassies and at the great gatherings of Parisian high society. For example, Berthe challenged her husband to bring home the mink stole worn that evening by the Duchess of Beaufour, and Maximilien, picking up the challenge, demanded that his wife, in return, should get the Fernand Cormon cartoon (*The Auroch Hunt*) which hung on one of their host's walls. Depending on the ease or difficulty of access to the desired object, the candidate was granted extensions of time or, in some more complex instances, could even call on the complicity or protection of his or her partner.

Of the forty-four challenges they set each other, thirty-three were met. They stole amongst other things a large silver samovar from the Countess of Melan, a Perugino sketch from the Papal nuntio, the Hainault Bank's managing director's tiepin, and the almost complete manuscript of the *Mémoires sur la vie de Jean Racine* by his son Louis, which came from the home of a permanent secretary at the Ministry of Education.

Anybody else would have been spotted and arrested at once, but the Danglars, even when they happened to be caught in the act, were able to exculpate themselves with hardly any trouble at all: it seemed so impossible for a high-court official and his wife to be suspected of burglary that witnesses preferred to disbelieve their own eyes rather than accept the guilt of a judge.

So when he was caught on the staircase of the art dealer d'Olivet's town house carrying off three *lettres de cachet* signed by Louis XVI and dealing with the Marquis de Sade's sentences at Vincennes and the Bastille, Maximilien Danglars explained with all the calm in the world that he had just requested permission to borrow them for forty-eight hours from a man he had taken to be his host, a completely indefensible excuse which d'Olivet nonetheless accepted without a murmur.

Such virtual impunity made them crazily audacious, as witnessed in particular by the affair that resulted in their downfall. At a ball given by Timothy Clawbonny – of the merchant bankers Marcuart, Marcuart, Clawbonny, and Shandon – a precious, oily, aged English pederast, dressed up as a bespectacled Confucius in a long mandarin robe, Berthe Danglars filched a Scythian tiara. The theft was discovered in the course of the evening. The police were called immediately, and they searched all the guests, finding the jewel in the fake bagpipe of the judge's wife, who was disguised as a Highland chieftainness.

Berthe Danglars confessed with equanimity that she had forced open the display case in which the tiara was locked because her husband had told her to; with equal equanimity Maximilien confirmed the truth of this confession and produced on the spot a letter from the governor of the Santé prison begging him – in strictest confidence – not to let out of his sight a certain golden crown which one of his informers had told him was to be purloined during this fancy-dress ball by Boris the Baritone: that was the name given to a bold burglar who had committed his first felony at the Opera, during a performance of *Boris Godunov*; in fact, Boris the Baritone remained a mythical thief for ever; it was later realised that eighteen of the thirty-three swipes ascribed to him had been done by the Danglars.

On this occasion, yet again, the explanation, for all its apparent implausibility, was accepted by everyone, including the police. Nonetheless, as he walked back to headquarters on Quai des Orfèvres, deep in thought, a young inspector, Roland Blanchet, decided to have his men bring up the files on all the cases of theft that had taken place in Paris at society events and which remained unsolved; he felt a shiver go through him when he ascertained that the Danglars were on twenty-nine of the thirty-three guest lists. In his view, that constituted overwhelming proof; but the Police Chief, whom he told of his suspicions, and whom he asked to take on the case, viewed it as pure coincidence. And, after referring out of caution to the Ministry of Justice, which expressed indignation at a policeman doubting the word and the honour of a judge highly respected by all his colleagues, the chief forbade his inspector to concern himself with the investigation and, when the latter insisted on doing so, threatened to have him transferred to Algeria.

Mad with anger, Blanchet resigned, and swore he would find proof of the Danglars's guilt.

For weeks Blanchet followed the Danglars or had them followed, and broke into the office which Maximilien enjoyed the use of at the Law Courts, but to no avail. The proof he was after, if it existed, was definitely not at the office, and Blanchet's only chance was if the Danglars had kept some of the stolen articles in their flat. On Christmas Eve, 1925, knowing that the Danglars were dining out, that the Honorés were in bed, and that the young chambermaid was celebrating with three friends (Serge Valène, François Gratiolet, and Flora Champigny) at Fresnel's restaurant, Blanchet finally managed to slip into the flat on the third floor left. He did not find Fanny Mosca's sapphire-encrusted fan, nor the portrait of Ambroise Vollard by Félix Vallotton which had been spirited away form Lord Summerhill the day after he had finally purchased it, but he did find a pearl necklace which was maybe the one that had been stolen from Princess Rzewuska shortly after the armistice, and a Fabergé egg which fitted fairly well the description of one swiped from Madame de Guitaut. But Blanchet laid his hands on an exhibit for the prosecution which was far more dangerous for the Danglars than the other evidence whose authenticity his ex-masters could have gone on doubting: a foolscap notebook with ruled lines containing succinct but accurate descriptions of each of the thefts the Danglars had committed or attempted to commit, accompanied on the facing page by a list of the consequential forfeits the couple had inflicted on each other.

Blanchet was about to leave with the notebook of revelations when he heard the front door of the flat opening at the other end of the corridor: it was Célia Crespi, who had forgotten to light the fire in Madame's boudoir as Honoré had asked her to before he had gone up to bed, returning to fulfil her duty belatedly and to take advantage of so doing to offer her Christmas party companions a drop of liqueur and a taste of the marvellous candied sweet chestnuts Monsieur had been sent by a grateful offender. Hiding behind a curtain, Blanchet glanced at his watch and saw that it was nearly one in the morning. The Danglars were not expected back until late, no doubt, but every minute brought the risk of an awkward confrontation nearer, and Blanchet could not get out without passing the big glass door of the dining room where Célia was treating her guests to a feast. Catching sight of a bouquet of artificial flowers gave him the idea of setting off a fire before going to hide in the Danglars's bedroom. The fire spread with crazy speed, and Blanchet was beginning to wonder if he was going to be caught in his own trap, when Célia Crespi and the others finally noticed that the whole rear end of the flat was in flames. The alarm was given, and from then on it was easy for the ex-policeman to flee amongst the crowds of rescuers and neighbours.

Blanchet lay low for some days, cruelly prompting the Danglars to believe that the notebook which proved their guilt – and which they had searched for high and low on returning to their half-burnt-out flat – had been consumed by the fire which destroyed all the other objects in the boudoir. Then the former inspector rang Danglars: the triumph of justice and truth was no longer his sole motive; if his demands had been more reasonable, it is likely that the affair would never have become public and that the deputy chairman of the Court of Appeal and his wife would have gone on freely indulging their thieving libidos for many more years. But the amount Blanchet demanded – five hundred thousand francs – was beyond the Danglars's financial means. "Steal it," Blanchet retorted wryly before hanging up. The Danglars felt quite unable to steal for money, and, preferring to go for broke, they fled.

The Law does not look kindly on its supposed pillars when they mock it, and the jury dealt with them sternly: thirty years' penal servitude for Berthe Danglars, hard labour for life for Maximilien, who was deported to Saint-Laurent-du-Maroni, where he died shortly after.

A few years ago, Mademoiselle Crespi, out walking in Paris one day, recognised her former mistress: a toothless beggar sitting on a bench in Rue de la Folie-Régnault, dressed in a filthy brown dressing gown, pushing a pram full of odd belongings, who answered to the nickname of "The Baroness".

At the time the Honorés were both seventy. He was a pale-faced man from Lyons; he had travelled, had had his adventures, had been a puppeteer at Vuillermé and Laurent Josserand's, a fakir's mate, a waiter at the Bal Mabille, a barrel-organ grinder with a pointed bonnet and a monkey on his shoulder, before entering service in bourgeois households where his equanimity, which outdid the English at their own game, quickly made him irreplaceable. She was a sturdy Norman peasant who could do everything and would just as willingly have baked her own bread as stick a piglet had she been asked to. Engaged in Paris at the age of fifteen, in late 1871, she began as scullion in a pension, *The Vienna School and Family Hotel*, 22 Rue Darcet, near Place Clichy, an establishment ruled over with a rod of iron by a Greek, Madame Cissampelos, a short woman, as thin as a rake, who taught good manners to English girls sporting such fearsome incisors as to make people in those days think it witty to say you could use them for piano keys.

Thirty years later, Corinne was the cook there, but still only earned twenty-five sous a month. It was about this time that she made the acquaintance of Honoré. They met at the Universal Exhibition, at the *Bonshommes Guillaume* show, a toy theatre where dolls no more than eighteen inches high pranced and danced on a tiny stage, dressed in the latest fashions. On seeing her bewildered, he explained the technicalities, then took her to see the *Crazy House*, an old Gothic fortress turned upside-down on its chimneypots, with windows back-to-front and furniture on the ceiling, and the *Palace of Light*, a wonderland house in which everything, from furniture to wall hangings, from carpets to cut flowers, was made of glass, and whose maker, the master blower Ponsin, had died before seeing it finished; and the *Celestial Globe*, the *Palace of Dress*, the *Palace of Optics* with its big telescope through which you could see the MOON at a distance of ONE yard, the *Alpine Climbers' Diorama*, the *Transatlantic Panorama*, *Venice in Paris*, and a dozen other exhibition halls.

What struck them most of all was, for her, the artificial rainbow in the Bosnian pavilion and, for him, the Exhibition of Mining with its six hundred yards of tunnel which you went through on an electric train and then came out of into a goldmine with real Negroes working in it, and Monsieur Fruhinsoliz's gigantic hogshead, a veritable four-storey building containing no less than fifty-six kiosks serving every kind of drink in the world.

They dined at *The Fair Miller's Maid* beside the colonial pavilions, where they drank unbottled Châblis and ate cabbage soup and a leg of lamb that Corinne thought underdone.

Honoré had been hired on a one-year contract by Monsieur Danglars senior, a wine-grower with estates in the Gironde, who was president of the Bordeaux section of the Wine Committee, which had moved to Paris for the whole duration of the Exhibition, and who had rented a flat from Juste Gratiolet. On leaving Paris a few weeks later, Monsieur Danglars senior was so pleased with his butler that he made a present of him, and of the flat, to his son Maximilien, who was about to be married and had just been appointed assessor to a magistrate. Shortly after, on the advice of the butler, the young couple hired the cook.

After the Danglars Affair, the Honorés, too old to think of obtaining another post, got permission from Emile Gratiolet to stay on in their room. They eked out a living from their tiny savings, supplemented now and then by a few odd jobs, such as looking after Ghislain Fresnel when the nannies were busy, or collecting Paul Hébert from school, or making succulent little pies or chocolate-covered candied orange sticks for people in the building who were giving a dinner party. And so they lived on for twenty more years, keeping their attic in meticulous order, waxing the lozenge-tiled floor, measuring out the water they gave to their myrtle in its copper pot. They reached the age of ninety-three, with her ever more wrinkled, and him ever thinner and longer. Then one day in 1949 he fell over when getting up from the table, and died within the hour. She outlived him by only a few weeks.

As for Célia Crespi, who was in her first job, she was even more bewildered than they were by her employers' sudden disappearance. She was lucky enough to find another post almost straightaway in the same building, with a tenant who took over the Danglars's flat for a year, a Latin American businessman whom the concierge and others called the Conquistador, a jovial fat man with a waxed moustache who smoked long Havanas, cleaned his teeth with a gold toothpick, and wore a big diamond as a tiepin; then she was taken on by Madame de Beaumont when she married and moved into Rue Simon-Crubellier. Later, when almost straight after the birth of her daughter the singer left France for a long tour of the United States, Célia Crespi went onto Bartlebooth's staff as a seamstress, and stayed there until the Englishman went off on his lengthy circumnavigation of the globe. After that, she got a job as a salesgirl at *Aux Délices de Louis XV*, the most reputable cake- and tea-shop in the neighbourhood, where she stayed until she retired.

Although she has always been called Mademoiselle Crespi, Célia Crespi had a son. She delivered him discreetly in nineteen thirty-six. Almost no one had noticed she was pregnant. The whole house wondered who the father was, and the name of every member of the masculine sex living in the building aged between fifteen and seventy-five was put forward. The secret was never uncovered. The child, registered at birth as being of father unknown, was brought up out of Paris. No one in the building ever saw him.

Just a few years ago it was learnt that he had been killed during the battle for the Liberation of Paris whilst helping a German officer load a crate of champagne into his sidecar.

Mademoiselle Crespi was born in a village in the hills behind Ajaccio. She left Corsica at twelve and has never been back. Sometimes she closes her eyes and can see the landscape that lay beyond the window of the room in which everyone lived: the wall covered with bougainvillaea in flower, the slope on which tufts of spurge grew, the hedge of prickly pear, the caper espalier; but she cannot remember anything else.

Today Hutting's bedroom is rarely used. Over the divan-bed with its synthetic fur bedspread and its three dozen multicoloured cushions, a silk prayer mat from Samarkand has been pinned to the wall; it has a faded pink pattern and long black fringes. To the right, a tub chair covered in yellow silk serves as a bedside table: it has on it a brushed-steel alarm clock in the shape of a stubby oblique cylinder, a telephone whose dial has been replaced by a touch-sensitive device, and an issue of the avant-garde review *La Bête Noire*. There are no pictures on the walls, but, to the left of the bed, mounted on a steel frame on casters which make it a kind of monstrous windbreak, there is a work by the Italian Intellectualist Martiboni: a block of polystyrene, two yards high, one yard wide, five inches thick, in which the artist has submerged old corsets amidst piles of dance invitation cards, dried flowers, silk dresses worn to the thread, mite-infested strips of fur, chewed-up fans looking like ducks' feet minus the webbing, silver shoes missing soles and heels, party scraps, and two or three stuffed dogs.

END OF PART FOUR

PART FIVE

CHAPTER EIGHTY-FOUR

Cinoc, 2

Cinoc's bedroom: a rather dirty room, which feels musty, with stains on the woodblock floor and peeling paint on the walls. On the doorjamb is nailed a *mezuzah*, a domestic talisman adorned with the three letters

as well as bearing a few verses from the Torah. Against the rear wall, over the divan-bed draped in a printed material with a triangular leaf motif, books and pamphlets lean against each other on a little hanging shelf, and at the open window stands a high-legged, flimsy folding desk, with a small, thick felt mat on the floor beneath it, just large enough to afford standing room. To the right of the shelves, hanging on the wall, is a completely foxed engraving entitled *The Somersault*: it portrays five naked babes frolicking, over the following sestet:

A voir leurs soubresauts bouffons
Qui ne diroit que ces Poupons
Auroient bon besoin d'Ellebore;
Leur corps est pourtant bien dressé
Si, selon que dit Pythagore,
L'homme est un arbre renversé.

Beneath the engraving a low table with a green cloth cover holds a water-jug with a glass on top of it and various loose volumes amongst which some titles can be made out:

From Avvakum's Raskolniki *to the Insurrection of Stenka Razin. Bibliographic Notes to Studies of the Reign of Alexy I*, by Hubert Corneylius, Lille, Lime Press, 1954;

La storia dei Romani, by G. de Sanctis (vol. III);

Travels in Baltistan, by P.O. Box, Bombay, 1894;

When I Was a Little Ballerina. Memoirs of Childhood and Youth, by Maria Feodorovna Vyshiskava, Paris, 1948;

"The Miner" *and the Origins of the Labour Party*, by Irwin Wall (offprint from the journal *Annales*);

Beiträge zur feineren Anatomie des menschlichen Rückenmarks, by Goll, Ghent, 1860;

three issues of *Rustica* magazine;

Sur le clivage pyramidal des albâtres et des gypses, by Mr Otto Lidenbrock, Professor at the Hamburg Johanneum and Curator of the Mineralogical Museum of Mr Struve, Russian Ambassador, an offprint from the *Zeitschrift für Mineralogie und Kristallographie*, vol. XII, Suppl. 147;

and the *Souvenirs of a Numismatist* by M. Florent Baillerger, formerly Chief Clerk to the Department of Haute-Marne, Chalindrey, Le Sommelier Booksellers, n.d.

Hélène Brodin died in this room, in nineteen forty-seven. She had lived here, fearful and discreet, for nearly twelve years. After her death her nephew François Gratiolet found a letter in which she told how her stay in America had ended.

In the afternoon of 11 September 1935, the police came to fetch her and drove her to Jemima Creek to identify her husband's corpse. Antoine Brodin's skull was smashed, and he lay on his back with outstretched arms at the bottom of a muddy, waterlogged quarry. The police had put a green handkerchief over his face. His trousers and boots had been stolen but he was still wearing the grey pin-striped shirt Hélène had bought him a few days earlier at St Petersburg.

Hélène had never seen Antoine's murderers; she had only heard their voices, two days before, when they had calmly told her husband they would be back for his scalp. But she had no trouble identifying them: it was the two Ashby brothers, Jeremiah and Ruben, accompanied as ever by Nick Pertusano, a cruel and vicious dwarf who had an indelible ash-coloured mark in the shape of a cross on his forehead, who was their sidekick, butt, and scapegoat. Despite their gentle biblical forenames, the Ashbys were little bastards feared throughout the county who extorted protection money from saloons and from diners, those rail-cars equipped as restaurants where you could eat for a few nickels; and unfortunately for Hélène, the sheriff of the county was their uncle. Not only did this sheriff fail to arrest the murderers, he also had two of his men escort Hélène to Mobile and advised her against ever setting foot in the county again. Hélène managed to give her guards the slip, got to Tallahassee, the state capital, and filed a complaint with the Governor. That same evening a stone smashed one of the windowpanes of her hotel room. Tied to it was a message threatening death.

On the Governor's orders the sheriff was nonetheless obliged to conduct a phony investigation; he advised his nephews to keep clear of the place, for safety. The two hoodlums and the dwarf split up. Hélène learnt of this and realised she now had her only chance of revenge: she had to act fast and kill them one after the other before they even knew what was happening to them.

The first one she killed was the dwarf. He was the easiest. She learnt he had taken a job as kitchen lad on a steamboat travelling upriver on the Mississippi, a boat worked all year round by professional hucksters. One of them agreed to help Hélène: she disguised herself as a boy, and he got her on board as his groom.

During the night, when everyone not asleep was hellbent on endless games of craps and faro, Hélène had no trouble finding her way to the galley; the dwarf, half-drunk, was drowsing in a hammock beside a stove on which a huge mutton stew was simmering. She came up close and before he could react seized him by the neck and suspenders and dumped him into the gigantic cauldron.

She left the boat next morning, at Baton Rouge, before the crime had been discovered. Still dressed as a boy, she went back downriver, travelling this time on a floating timber raft, which was a veritable little town on water where several dozen men lived in comfort. To one of them, a gypsy of French extraction called Paul Marchal, she told her story, and he offered to help her. At New Orleans they rented a truck and began to crisscross Louisiana and Florida. They stopped at gas stations, railroad stations, roadside bars. They humped around a kind of one-man-band outfit, consisting of a sound box, a bandoneon, a harmonica, a triangle, cymbals, and bells; she dressed as a women from the East with a chador, did a vague belly dance before offering to tell fortunes by cutting cards: she would spread three rows out in front of her audience, cover two cards adding up to eleven as well as the three court cards: it was a type of patience she had learnt as a little girl, the only one she knew, and she used it to predict the most improbable things in an inextricable mixture of languages.

It took them only ten days to find a trail. A Seminole family living on a raft moored on the banks of Lake Apopka told them of a man who had been living for the last few days in a huge disused well, near a place called Stone's Hill, about fifteen miles from Tampa.

It was Ruben. They found him sitting on a wooden box trying to open a tin of food with his teeth. He was so desperate with hunger that he didn't even hear them coming. Before killing him with a bullet in the back of his neck, Hélène forced him to give away Jeremiah's hide-out. All Ruben knew was that before splitting up, the three of them had vaguely discussed the places they would go to: the dwarf said he wanted to travel around, Ruben wanted a cosy hole, and Jeremiah claimed there was no better place to lay up than in a big city.

Nick was a dwarf and Ruben an idiot, but Jeremiah frightened Hélène. She found him almost easily, two days later: standing at the bar of a boozer near Hialeah, the Miami racecourse, he was leafing through a racing paper whilst at the same time mechanically masticating a fifteen-cent portion of breaded veal cutlets.

She trailed him for three days. He lived off mean tricks, picking bookies' pockets and raising customers for the boss of a greasy gaming den proudly named *The Oriental Saloon and Gambling House*, after the famous joint which Wyatt Earp and Doc Holliday used to run at Tombstone, Arizona. It was a barn with walls made of planks literally nailed together from top to bottom with enamelled metal panels bearing electoral, advertising, or business announcements:

QUALITY ECONOMY AMOCO MOTOR OIL, GROVE'S BROMO-QUININE STOPS COLDS, ZENO CHEWING-GUM, ARMOUR'S CLOVERBLOOM BUTTER, RINSO SOAKS CLOTHES WHITER, THAL-CO PINE DEODORANT, CLABBERGIRL BAKING POWDER, TOWER'S FISH BRAND, ARCADIA, GOODYEAR TIRES, QUAKER STATE, PENNZOIL SAFE LUBRICATION, 100% PURE PENNSYLVANIA, BASEBALL TOURNAMENT, SELMA AMERICAN LEGION JRS vs.

MOBILE, PETER'S SHOE'S, CHEW MAIL POUCH TOBACCO, BROTHER-IN-LAW BARBER SHOP, HAIRCUT 25c, SILAS GREEN SHOW FROM NEW ORLEANS, DRINK COCA-COLA DELICIOUS REFRESHING, POSTAL TELEGRAPH HERE, DID YOU KNOW? J. W. McDONALD FURN'CO CAN FURNISH YOUR HOME COMPLETE, CONGOLEUM RUGS, GRUNO REFRIGERATORS, PETE JARMAN FOR CONGRESS, CAPUDINE LIQUID AND TABLETS, AMERICAN ETHYL GASOLINE, GRANGER ROUGH CUT MADE FOR PIPES, JOHN DEERE FARM IMPLEMENTS, FINDLAY'S, ETC.

On the morning of the fourth day, Hélène sent an envelope to Jeremiah. It contained a photograph of the two brothers – found in Ruben's billfold – and a brief note in which she informed him of what she had done to the dwarf and to Ruben and of the fate awaiting this son of a bitch if he had enough balls to find her in chalet 31 at Burbank's Motel.

Hélène hid all day in the shower of an adjacent chalet. She knew that Jeremiah had received her letter and that he would not be able to bear the idea of being outfaced by a woman. But that wouldn't be enough to make him respond to the provocation; he had to be sure, in addition, of being stronger than she was.

Around seven in the evening she knew her instinct had not deceived her: accompanied by four armed toughs, Jeremiah turned up in a steaming, dented, bucket-seated Model T. Taking all the customary precautions, they cased the joint and surrounded chalet 31.

The room was not well lit, just enough for Jeremiah to see through the crochet curtains his brother Ruben lying quietly on one of the twin beds with his arms folded and his eyes wide open. With a ferocious roar, Jeremiah Ashby stormed into the room, thereby setting off the bomb Hélène had planted in it.

The same evening Hélène embarked on a schooner sailing to Cuba, whence a regular packet took her back to France. Until her death she awaited the day when the police would come to arrest her, but the American Law never dared to imagine that this mere slip of a woman could have killed in cold blood three hoods, for whose murders they had no trouble in finding much more plausible culprits.

CHAPTER EIGHTY-FIVE

Berger, 2

The Berger parents' bedroom: an almost square, not very large room with a woodblock floor and walls hung with a light-blue paper with narrow yellow stripes; a map of the 1975 Tour de France, full size, presented by Vitamix, the tonic of sportsmen and champions, is pinned on the rear wall to the left of the door; beside each staging post there are black-lined boxes to be filled in by race followers as the Tour proceeds with the timings of the first six riders in each stage and of the three overall leaders in each of the classes (Yellow Jersey, Green Jersey, King of the Mountains).

The room is empty except for a fat alley cat – Poker Dice – curled up drowsing on the fluffy sky-blue quilt draped over a divan-bed flanked by two matching bedside tables. On the right-hand one stands an old valve-radio set (the one whose operation at what Madame Réol considers to be unreasonably early hours puts in jeopardy the otherwise friendly relations the two couples enjoy): its lid, which can be raised to reveal a primitive pickup, bears a bedside lamp with a conical shade decorated with the symbols of the four suits of playing cards, and a few 45 rpm record sleeves: the one on top illustrates Boyer and Valbonne's famous ditty, *Boire un petit coup c'est agréable*, sung by Viviane Malehaut with Luca Dracena on the accordion and tympani; it depicts a roughly sixteen-year-old girl clinking a glass with a group of fat, guffawing sausage-makers who, against a background of split pigs on butcher hooks, raise their glasses of sparkling wine in one hand and in the other proffer great white china trays spilling over with various pork delicacies: ham sprinkled with parsley, saveloy, muzzle, *andouille* sausages from Vire, red tongue, pigs' trotters, brawn, and sweetbreads.

On the left-hand bedside table, a lamp made from an Italian wine flask (Valpolicella) and a *Série noire* detective thriller, Raymond Chandler's *Lady in the Lake*.

* * *

It was in this flat that the lady with the little dog lived until 1965, with her son who aimed to take the cloth. Before her, for many years, the flat's tenant had been an old gentleman everyone called The Russian because he wore a fur cap all year round. The rest of his dress was markedly more Western: black trousers with a seat reaching up to his sternum held up both by braces and an underbelly belt, a white but rarely pristine shirt, a broad black tie, almost a cravat, and a walking stick with a top made from a billiard ball.

The Russian was actually called Abel Speiss. He was a soft-hearted man from Alsace, a former army veterinarian, who spent his spare time sending in solutions to all the little competitions published in newspapers. He solved riddles with disconcerting ease:

Three Russians have a brother. The brother dies leaving no brothers. How can this be?

history catch-questions

Who was John Leland's friend?

Who was threatened by a Railway share?

Who was Sheraton?

Who walked and talked after his head was cut off?

"word-chain" puzzles:

HIM	**LOVE**	**ONE**
HEM	**HOVE**	**ORE**
HER	**HAVE**	**ARE**
	HATE	**ALE**
		ALL

arithmetical puzzles:

Prudence is 24 years of age. She is twice as old as her husband was when she was as old as her husband is. How old is her husband?

Write the number "120" using four eights.

anagrams:

STREET = TESTER
ATHENS = HASTEN
ABSOLUTE = OUSTABLE

and logic problems:

> *What comes after* O T T F F S S E ?
>
> *Which is the odd item in the following list:*
> *French, short, polysyllabic, written, visible, printed, masculine, word, singular, American, odd?*

boxwords, crosswords, three-corner words, two-dimensional "ghosts" words (*a*, *at*, *ate*, *rate*, *grate*, *gyrate*), block-words, etc., and even "hidden questions", the nightmares of all puzzle-solvers.

His great specialism was cryptograms. But although he victoriously carried off the Grand National Contest, with a prize worth THREE THOUSAND FRANCS, run by the *Vienne and Romans Reveille*, by discovering that the message

aeeeil *ihnalz* *ruiopn*
toeedt *zaemen* *eeuart*
odxhnp *trvree* *noupvg*
eedgnc *estlev* *artuee*
arnuro *ennios* *ouitse*
spesdr *erssur* *mtqssl*

encrypted the first two lines of *La Marseillaise*, he never managed to decipher the puzzle set by *Dogs of France*:

t' cea uc tsel rs
n neo rt aluot
ia ouna s ilel-
-rc oal ei ntoi

and his only consolation was that no other contestant had managed it either, and the magazine decided to withhold the first prize.

Apart from riddles and logogriphs, The Russian had one other passion in life: he was madly in love with Madame Hardy, the wife of the olive-oil trader from Marseilles. She was a motherly, middle-aged woman with a sweet face and a faint moustache on her upper lip. He took advice from everyone in the building, but despite the encouragement he got from all, he never dared – in his own words – to "speak his flame".

CHAPTER EIGHTY-SIX

Rorschach, 5

In its heyday Rorschach's bathroom was a thing of luxury. Along the whole of the rear wall, connecting all the sanitary fixtures to each other, was a complex arrangement of lead and copper piping graced with lavishly convoluted bifurcations, as well as a probably superfluous plethora of manometers, temperature gauges, flow-meters, hygrometers, clappers, cocks, taps, control levers, handles, valves, and stoppers, providing a machine-room backdrop which made a striking contrast to the refinement of the remainder of the decor: a veined marble bath; a medieval font for a washbasin, a *fin-de-siècle* towel rail; bronze taps carved in the shapes of radiant suns, lions' heads, swans' necks; and a few curios and *objets d'art*: a crystal ball, of the kind you used to see in dance halls, was hung from the ceiling, refracting the light in its myriad cat's-eye mirrors; and there was also a Japanese ceremonial sabre, a screen made of two panes of glass trapping a host of dried hydrangea flowers, and a painted wooden Louis XV low table, holding three crudely moulded tall jars for bath salts, perfume, and bath oil which represented three maybe ancient statuettes: a very youthful Atlas carrying a scale world globe on his left shoulder, an ithyphallic Pan, and a frightened Syrinx already half-transformed into a reed.

There are four works of art which draw the eye especially. The first is a painting on wood, dating certainly from the first half of the nineteenth century. It is entitled *Robinson Making Himself as Comfortable as He Can on His Desert Island.* Above this title, written in two lines of white-on-black capital letters, can be seen a fairly naïve depiction of Robinson Crusoe in a pointed bonnet and a goatskin waistcoat, sitting on a stone; on the tree used to mark the passing of time he is making a notch for Sunday.

* * *

The second and third items are prints dealing differently with similar subjects: one, mysteriously called *The Purloined Letter*, portrays an elegant drawing room – herringbone woodblock floor, Jouy cretonne wallpaper – in which a young woman, seated by a window looking out onto a great park, is edging a piece of fine linen with bourdon lace; not far from her, an ageing, exaggeratedly English-looking man is playing the virginals. The second engraving, of surrealist inspiration, depicts a girl of maybe fourteen or fifteen wearing a short lace slip. The open-work clocks on her stockings end in arrowheads, and the little cross she wears on her neck has branches made of fingers, with slightly bleeding nails. She is sitting at a sewing machine, near an open window through which can be seen the mountainous boulders of a Rhineland landscape, and on the lingerie she is sewing can be seen this motto, embroidered in black-letter Gothic script.

Verſtörung
des hübſchen Schulmädchens

The fourth work of art is a cast standing on the rim of the bath. It is a full-length model of a woman walking, about one third life-size. She is a Roman virgin of twenty or so. Her body is long and supple, her hair is gently waved and almost entirely veiled. Her head is tipped slightly to one side, and in her left hand she holds a gather of the extraordinarily pleated robe which falls straight from her neck to her ankles, thus revealing her sandalled feet. She has her left foot forward, and her right foot, about to step on, touches the ground only by the tip of its toes, with its heel and sole almost vertical. This movement, expressing both the easy agility of a young woman and her self-confident calm, gives the statue its particular charm, a firm stride held steady, as it were, in mid-air.

A canny woman, Olivia Rorschach has rented out her flat for the months she will be away. The rental – which includes Jane Sutton's daily services – was arranged through a bureau specialising in temporary accommodation for very rich foreigners. This time the tenant is someone called Giovanni Pizzicagnoli, an international administrator normally resident in Geneva but spending six weeks in Paris to chair one of the budgetary commissions of the Unesco special assembly on the energy problem. This diplomat made his choice in a few minutes on the specifications provided by the bureau's Swiss agent. He won't arrive in France until the day after next, but his wife and young son are here already because, believing all Frenchmen to be thieves, he has given his wife – a sturdy Bernese of about forty – the job of checking, on the premises, that everything is as promised in the specification.

Olivia Rorschach thought her presence at this visitation pointless, and she withdrew at the start with a charming smile, using her imminent departure as an excuse; she did no more than to urge Madame Pizzicagnoli to watch that her little boy didn't break the decorated plates in the dining room or the blown-glass grapes in the entrance hall.

The girl from the bureau took her client over the rest of the flat, listing the fittings and fixtures and ticking them off on her list as they proceeded. But it quickly turned out that the visit, originally envisaged as a routine formality, was running into a serious difficulty: the Swissess, clearly obsessed to the highest degree by domestic safety problems, has demanded to have the workings of every household appliance explained to her, and to be shown the location of every circuit-breaker, fuse, and disjunctor. The inspection of the kitchen was manageable, but in the bathroom things quickly went critical: overwhelmed by events, the girl from the bureau called her boss to the rescue, and, given the size of the deal – the rental charge for the six weeks is twenty thousand francs – he could not but come over, but since he had obviously not had time to look up the file properly, he in turn had to call for help from various people: from Madame Rorschach, in the first place, but she declined, claiming it was her husband who had dealt with the installation; then from Olivier Gratiolet, the former landlord, who replied that it had ceased to be any business of his nearly fifteen years ago; from Romanet, the manager, who suggested asking the interior designer, who did no more than give the name of the plumber, who, given the time of day, could be materialised only in the form of a recorded message on his telephone answering service.

The final reckoning brings six people together in Madame Rorschach's bathroom:

Madame Pizzicagnoli, holding a pocket dictionary and exclaiming in a voice made tremulous and ear-shattering by anger, "Io non vi capisco! Una stanza ammobligliata! Ich versteh Sie nich! I am in a hurry! Moi, ne comprendre! Ho fretta! Je présée! My tailor is rich";

the girl from the agency, a young woman in a white alpaca two-piece, fanning herself with her ferret gloves;

the bureau's boss, frantically hunting for an ashtray in which to deposit his three-quarters chewed-up cigar;

the building manager, leafing through the co-ownership rule book, trying to remember whether there was anything in it anywhere about safety standards for bathroom water-heaters;

a plumber from a breakdown service called to an emergency, no one knows why or by whom, winding up his wristwatch whilst waiting to be told to go away;

and Madame Pizzicagnoli's little boy, a tot of four and a half in a sailor suit, quite unperturbed by the hubbub around him, kneeling on the marble flagstones, playing tirelessly with a clockwork rabbit which bangs a drum and blows a trumpet to the tune of *Colonel Bogey*.

CHAPTER EIGHTY-SEVEN

Bartlebooth, 4

The great drawing room of Bartlebooth's flat, a huge square room with pale-blue wallpaper, contains what is left of the furniture, objects, and knickknacks with which Priscilla had liked to surround herself in her town house at 65 Boulevard Malesherbes: a divan and four armchairs all in carved and gilded wood, upholstered with an old Gobelins tapestry depicting on a yellow latticed ground archways with flourishes laden with foliage, fruit, and flowers adorned with birds on the wing – doves, parrots, parakeets, etc.; a large four-leafed Beauvais tapestry screen, with arabesque designs and, lower down, costumed monkeys in the style of Gillot; a large seven-drawer chiffonier, a Louis XVI period piece, in mahogany with coloured-wood mouldings and piping; on its veined marble top stand two ten-branched candelabras, a silver trencher, a little shagreen writing case with two gold-stoppered inkpots, a golden penholder, a gold erasing knife and a gold spatula, a carved-crystal seal, and a tiny little rectangular fly-box of gold machined and enamelled in blue; on the big black stone mantelpiece, a pendulum clock of white marble and chased gold with a dial, marked *Hoguet, à Paris*, held up by two kneeling, bearded men; on each side of the clock, two porcelain pharmacy jars in Chantilly *pâte tendre*; the right-hand one bears the inscription *Ther. Vieille*, the left-hand one *Gomme Gutte*; finally, on a little oval rosewood table with a white marble top stand three Saxony porcelains: one represents Venus and a cupid seated in a flower-decked chariot drawn by swans; the other two are allegorical figures of Africa and America: *Africa* is personified by a Negro boy sitting on a lion; *America* is a plumed woman riding side-saddle on a crocodile and clutching a horn of plenty to her left breast; a parrot sits on her right hand.

Several pictures are hanging on the walls; the most awe-inspiring is to the right of the fireplace; it is a Groziano, a gloomy, harsh *Descent from the Cross*; to the left, a seascape by F. H. Mans, *Fishing Boats Coming in to a Dutch Beach*; on the rear wall, over the big divan, a cartoon study for Thomas Gainsborough's *Blue Boy*, two large engravings by Le Bas of Chardin's *L'Enfant au toton* and *Le Valet d'auberge*; a miniature of a priest with a face all puffed up with pride and contentment; a mythological scene by Eugène Lami depicting Bacchus, Pan, and Silenus accompanied by hordes of satyrs, aegipanes, agripanes, sylvans, fauns, lemurs, lares, elves, and hobgoblins; a landscape entitled *The Mysterious Island*, signed L. N. Montalescot: it portrays a seashore the left-hand half of which presents a pleasant prospect with a beach and a forest behind, the other half, all rocky walls broken up into towers and only a single entrance in them, suggesting an invulnerable fortress; and a watercolour by Wainewright, the painter, collector, and critic who was a friend of Sir Thomas Lawrence and one of the most famous "Bloods" of his day, and who, it was learnt after he died, had murdered eight people out of dilettantism; the watercolour is called *The Carter*: the carter is seated on a bench in front of a whitewashed wall. He is tall and broad, wears brown canvas trousers tucked into crackled boots, a grey open-neck shirt, and a gaily coloured neckerchief; on his right arm he wears a studded leather wristband; a tapestry bag hangs over his left shoulder; his plaited rope whip, with its tip separating out into several rough tails, lies to his right, alongside a jug and a round loaf.

The divans and armchairs are draped in transparent nylon dust covers. For ten years at least, this room has been used only as an exception. The last time Bartlebooth came into it was four months ago, when the developments that occurred in the Beyssandre affair forced him to have recourse to Rémi Rorschach.

In the early 1970s two major hotel chains – MARVEL HOUSES INCORPORATED and INTERNATIONAL HOSTELLERIE – decided to join forces so as to compete more effectively with the two rapidly expanding young giants of the hotel industry: Holiday Inn and Sheraton. Marvel Houses Inc. was a North American firm well-established in the Caribbean and in South America; as for International Hostellerie, it was a holding company registered in Zürich and managed funds originating in the Arab Emirates.

The top management of the two companies met for the first time at Nassau, in the Bahamas, in February 1970. Their joint analysis of the world situation convinced them that the only way to stem the rise of their two rivals was to invent a style of tourist hotel without any equivalent anywhere else in the world: "a conception of hotel management," declared the chairman of Marvel Houses, "based not on rabid exploitation of the kiddy cult [*clapping*], nor yet on management subservience to charge-account shysters [*more clapping*], but on respect for three fundamental values: leisure, relaxation, and culture [*continuous applause*]".

Several subsequent meetings at the head offices of the two companies over the following months filled in the outline which the chairman of Marvel Houses had sketched so brilliantly. When one of the directors of International Hostellerie made the witty point that the registered names of both firms had the same number of letters, 24, the publicity offices of both outfits seized on the idea and proposed a selection of twenty-four strategic sites in twenty-four countries where they could locate twenty-four hotel complexes of a totally new kind; with supreme sophistication, the list of the twenty-four selected sites displayed, from top to bottom and side by side, the registered names of the two parent companies (fig. 1).

In November 1970, the chairmen and managing directors assembled in Kuwait to sign a joint document which stipulated that Marvel Houses Incorporated and International Hostellerie would jointly establish twin subsidiary companies: a hotel investment company, to be called Marvel Houses International; and a hotel service banking company, dubbed Incorporated Hostellerie. These companies, duly endowed with capital by the two parent firms, would be responsible for designing, organising, and completing construction of the twenty-four hotel complexes in the places hereinafter specified. The chairman and managing director of International Hostellerie became chairman and managing director of Marvel Houses International, and deputy chairman of Incorporated Hostellerie; whilst the chairman and managing director of Marvel Houses Incorporated became chairman and managing director of Incorporated Hostellerie, and deputy chairman of Marvel Houses International. The registered office of Incorporated Hostellerie, with specific responsibility for the financial management of the operation, was set up in Kuwait itself; as for Marvel Houses International, destined to take on site preparation and supervision, it was registered, for tax purposes, in Puerto Rico.

The total budget of the operation was well over a billion dollars – more than five hundred thousand francs per hotel room. The aim was to create hotel centres with a degree of luxury unmatched by anything but the centres' own self-contained autonomy. In fact, the key idea of the promoters was that, whilst it is admissible for a hotel – that special *locus* of relaxation, leisure and culture – to be sited in a climatic zone suited to some specific demand (for warmth when it is cold elsewhere, for pure air, for snow, for iodine, etc.) and in proximity to a place with a particular avocation in tourist terms (sea bathing, skiing, spa waters, museums, cities, curiosities, natural features [reserves, etc.] or artificial attractions [Venice, Matmata, Disney World, etc.], etc.), it was by no means necessary that it should be so located. A good hotel, they believed, was one where a client can go out if he wants, and *not go out if going out is a burden for him.*

Consequently, the primary characteristic of the hotels Marvel Houses International planned to build was that they would include *intra muros* everything that a demanding, wealthy, and lazy clientele could wish to see or to do without having to go outside, which could not fail to be their wish in the case of the majority of North American, Arab, and Japanese visitors who feel obliged to do Europe and its cultural treasures from end to end but who do not for all that necessarily have any wish to foot-slog along miles of museum corridors or to be carted uncomfortably around the lung-damaging traffic jams of Saint-Sulpice or Place Saint-Gilles.

This idea had been fundamental to modern tourist-hotel management for many years: it had given rise to the creation of private beaches, to the increasing privatisation of seashores and ski slopes, and to the rapid development of entirely artificial clubs, villages, and holiday centres having no essential relationship with their physical and human environments. But in their plan, Marvel Houses took this idea to a spectacular degree of systematisation: clients of any one of the new Marvel Hostelleries would have at their disposal not only their beach, their tennis court, their heated pool, eighteen-hole golf course, riding stable, sauna, marina, casino, nightclub, boutiques, bars, newsstands, cigarette shop, travel agency, and bank, as in any run-of-the-mill four-star, but they would also have access to their very own ski slope, chairlift, skating rink, sea bed, surf waves, safari, giant aquarium, art gallery, Roman ruins, battlefield, pyramid, Romanesque church, Arab market, desert fort, cantina, Plaza de Toros, prehistoric cave, Bierstube, street party, Balinese dancers, etc., etc., etc., and so on and so forth.

To achieve such truly dizzying availability, which alone would justify the rates they envisaged charging, Marvel Houses International employed three concurrent stratagems: the first was to find isolated sites, or sites that could easily be made isolated, offering abundant tourist facilities that were not yet fully exploited; it is significant, in this connection, that five of the twenty-four sites selected – Alnwick, Ennis, Ottok, Soria, Vence – were in the immediate proximity of national parks; that five others were on islands: Aeroe, Anafi, Eimeo, Oland, and Pemba; and that the operation also called for the creation of two artificial islands, one off Osaka in the Osaka-Wan, the other facing Inhakea off the coast of

MIRAJ	India
ANAFI	Greece (Cyclades)
ARTIGAS	Uruguay
VENCE	France
ERBIL	Iraq
ALNWICK	England
HALLE	Belgium
OTTOK	Austria (Illyria)
HUIXTLA	Mexico
SORIA	Spain (Old Castile)
ENNIS	Eire
SAFAD	Israel
ILION	Turkey (Troy)
INHAKEA	Mozambique
COIRE	Switzerland (Chur)
OSAKA	Japan
ARTESIA	USA (New Mexico)
PEMBA	Tanzania
OLAND	Sweden
ORLANDO	USA (Disney World*)
AEROE	Denmark
TROUT	Canada
EIMEO	Tahiti archipelago
DELFT	Holland

Figure 1. Site locations of Marvel Houses International & Incorporated Hostellerie's 24 hotel complexes.

*The USA seems to have been selected twice – Artesia and Orlando – contrary to the decision to build the twenty-four centres in twenty-four different countries; but, as one of the directors of Marvel Houses pointed out very relevantly, Orlando is only superficially located in the United States, in the sense that Disney World is a world of its own, a world in which Marvel Houses and International Hostellerie had a duty to be represented.

Mozambique, as well as the conversion of an entire lake, Lake Trout, in Ontario, where it was planned to build a totally sub-aqua leisure centre.

The second stratagem was to offer local, regional, and national authorities, in the places where Marvel Houses International wished to build, the full cost of constructing "culture parks", against an eighty-year concession (the original forecasts showed that in most cases costs would be recouped in five years and three months, and become genuinely profitable for the remaining seventy-five years); such "culture parks" would either be built from scratch, or would encompass existing remains and buildings, as for example at Ennis, in Eire, a few miles from Shannon International Airport, where the ruins of a thirteenth-century abbey would be included within the hotel perimeter; or they would be integrated into existing structures, as at Delft, where Marvel Houses made the city an offer to save a whole neighbourhood of the old town and to revive *Old Delft* with potters, weavers, carvers, and blacksmiths living in, dressed in traditional costumes, working by candlelight.

Marvel Houses International's third stratagem was to plan to make their attractions profitable by developing – at least for the European sites, which comprised half of the total project – the possibilities for rotating features from one site to another; but this idea, initially designed only for staff (Balinese dancers, ragamuffins for the street parties, Tyrolean waitresses, bullfighters, ringside fans, sports instructors, snake-charmers, foot-jugglers, etc.), soon came to be applied to the equipment itself and resulted in what no doubt constituted the true originality of the entire project: the pure and simple negation of space.

Indeed, comparisons of fixed investments and running costs soon demonstrated that it would cost more to build sea beds, mountains, castles, canyons, rock-art caves, and the Pyramids twenty-four times over than to transport *gratis* any customer wishing to ski on the August bank holiday whilst in Halle, or to go tiger-hunting when in deepest Spain.

Thus the notion of a standard contract was born: for a minimum stay of four days of twenty-four hours, each night could be spent, at no extra charge, in any one of the hotels in the chain. Each new customer would be given on arrival a kind of calendar offering some seven hundred and fifty tourist and cultural events, each one having a specified weighting in hours, and the customer would be free to tick off as many as his envisaged length of stay at Marvel Houses entitled him to, the management guaranteeing to meet ninety per cent of the desiderata at no extra charge. To take a simplified example, if a client checking in at Safad ticks off in any old order events such as: skiing, taking the waters at a chalybeate spa, a tour of the Kasbah at Ouarzazate, a Swiss wine and cheese tasting, a canasta tournament, a tour of the Hermitage, a sauerkraut dinner, a tour of the château at Champs-sur-Marne, a concert given by the Des Moines Philharmonic conducted by Laszlo Birnbaum, a tour of the Bétharram caves (*You travel right through a mountain wonderland lit by 4,500 electric bulbs! Its huge wealth of stalactites and the wonderfully varied wall paintings are enhanced by a ride in a gondola that takes you back to Venice the Fair! Nature's most Unique creation!*), etc., the hotel management, after linking into the company's huge mainframe, will immediately plan transport to Coire (Switzerland) where glacier skiing, the Swiss wine and cheese tasting (Valteline wines), the chalybeate spring water, and the canasta tournament will be laid on, and then another transit from Coire to Vence, for the reconstruction of the Bétharram caves (*You travel right through a mountain wonderland, etc.*). The sauerkraut dinner could take place at Safad itself, as could the touring of the gallery and the château, provided by slide lectures which allow the traveller, comfortably seated in a club armchair, to discover, with the assistance of an intelligent commentary putting things in a proper perspective, the artistic marvels of every period and every land. On the other hand, the management would not provide transfer to Artesia, where a fabulous replica of the Ouarzazate Kasbah was located, nor to Orlando–Disney World, where the Des Moines Philharmonic had been hired for the season, unless the customer signed up for an extra week, and as a possible substitute would suggest a tour of genuine Safad synagogues (at Safad), an evening with the Bregenzer Kammerorchester conducted by Hal Montgomery, with the soloist Virginia Fredericksburg (Corelli, Vivaldi, Gabriel Pierné) (at Vence), or a lecture by Professor Strossi, of Clermont-Ferrand University, on *Marshall McLuhan and the Third Copernican Revolution* (at Coire).

It goes without saying that the directors of Marvel Houses would always do their best to equip each of their twenty-four culture parks with all the features promised. Where they ran into a major obstacle, they would restrict this or that feature to a single site and replace it everywhere else by a quality replica: so there would be, for instance, only one Bétharram cave, and the other caves elsewhere would be more like those found at Lascaux or Les Eyzies, maybe less spectacular but just as moving and intellectually stimulating. This flexible and well-thought-out policy was the key to unlimitedly ambitious projects, and by late 1971 architects and planners had achieved veritable miracles, on paper at least: Exeter College, Oxford, was to be dismantled, shipped over stone by stone, and rebuilt in Mozambique, the Château de Chambord to be reconstituted at Osaka, the Ouarzazate medina rebuilt at Artesia, the Seven Wonders of the World (1:15 scale model) at Pemba, London Bridge at Trout, and Darius' Palace in Persepolis replicated at Huixtla (Mexico), where the full glory of the Persian kings would be restored down to the smallest detail, including the authentic number of slaves, chariots, horses, and palaces, the beauty of their concubines, and their sumptuous concerts. It would have been a pity to consider reduplicating these masterpieces, given the degree to which the system's originality was based on the geographical uniqueness of such wonders, combined with the lucky customer's ability to have immediate enjoyment of them all.

Market research and attitudinal surveys banished backers' hesitations and doubts by showing irrefutably that there was a potential clientele of such size that it was perfectly reasonable to expect to recoup the investment not in five years and three months, as the preliminary estimates had suggested, but in a mere four years and eight months. Capital came flooding in; in early 1972 the project went operational, and construction work was started on two pilot complexes, Trout and Pemba.

According to Puerto Rican legislation, Marvel Houses International had to spend 1% of its total cash flow on the purchase of contemporary works of art; in most cases, compulsions of this kind in the hotel business usually result in each bedroom having an Indian-ink drawing touched up with watercolour depicting an Atlantic beach resort or a Mediterranean cliff, or else provide the main lobby with some sculptural mini-monument. But Marvel Houses International considered itself duty-bound to devise a more original solution, and after roughing out three or four ideas on paper – building an international museum of modern art in one of the hotel complexes, purchase or commission of twenty-four major works by the twenty-four greatest living artists, establishing a Marvel Houses Foundation giving grant aid to young creators – the directors of Marvel Houses got what was for them a minor problem off their plates by handing it over to an art critic.

Their choice alighted upon Charles-Albert Beyssandre, a Swiss critic of French mother-tongue, a regular columnist for the *Feuille d'Avis de Fribourg* and the *Gazette de Genève*, and Zürich correspondent for half a dozen French, Belgian, and Italian dailies and periodicals. The chairman and managing director of International Hostellerie – and thus of Marvel Houses International – was one of his faithful readers and had taken his advice several times on art investments.

Summoned by the Board of Marvel Houses and told of their problem, Charles-Albert Beyssandre had no difficulty in convincing the developers that the solution best fitted to their policy of prestige would be to collect a quite small number of major works: not a museum, nor a rag-bag, certainly not a litho over every bedhead, but a handful of masterpieces jealously secreted in a single spot, which art lovers the world over would dream of gazing at at least once in their lives. Excited at such a prospect, the directors of Marvel Houses entrusted Charles-Albert Beyssandre with the task of collecting these ultraselect items over the following five years.

Beyssandre thus found himself sitting on a budget that was theoretical – final settlements, including his own three per cent commission, were not due until 1976 – but, notwithstanding, colossal: more than five billion old francs, enough to buy the three most valuable paintings in the world, or, as he played around with figuring out in his first few days, enough to buy fifty Klees, almost every single Morandi, almost all of Bacon or practically every Magritte, maybe five hundred Dubuffets, a good score of the best Picassos, a hundred or so Staels, almost the entire output of Frank Stella, almost every Kline and every Klein, all the Rothkos in the Rockefeller collection with all the Huffings in the Fitchwinder and all the Huttings of the haze period (which Beyssandre did not appreciate overmuch anyway) thrown in on the side.

The somewhat puerile exaltation aroused by these calculations soon subsided, and Beyssandre quickly found that his task would be far harder than he had thought.

Beyssandre was a sincere man who loved painting and painters, an attentive, scrupulous, and open man who was happy when, at the end of a session of many hours in a studio or a gallery, he managed to let the unchanging presence of a painting invade his soul, to be filled by the work's calm and fragile existence, as its concentrated clarity imposed itself on him little by little, transforming the canvas into an almost living thing, a thing bodied forth, a thing *there*, both simple and complex, bearing the signs of a past history, of a labour, and of a craft finally brought into a shape transcending its difficult, tortuous, and maybe even tortured path of becoming. The task the directors of Marvel Houses had given Beyssandre was clearly mercantile; but at least it might allow him, as he reviewed the art of his time, to have many more of those "magic moments" – the phrase belonged to his Parisian colleague Esberi – and he thus undertook the task with a feeling not far short of enthusiasm.

But news travels fast in the art world, and often gets twisted; it was soon an open secret that Charles-Albert Beyssandre had become the agent of a formidable patron who had hired him to build up the richest private collection of living painters in the world.

After a few weeks Beyssandre realised he wielded power beyond even the size of his budget. The mere idea that the critic might, in certain circumstances, at some unspecified future date, consider purchasing some canvas or other for his super-rich client sent dealers crazy, and the least established talents shot up overnight to the rank of a Cézanne or a Murillo. Just as in the story of the man who had absolutely nothing apart from one hundred-thousand-pound banknote and managed to live on it for a month without touching a penny, so the presence or absence of the critic at an art-world event began to have sensational consequences. As soon as he came into an auction room the bids would begin to climb, and if he left after a quick look around, prices would soften, weaken, slump. As for his column, it became an event awaited with feverish impatience by investors. If he mentioned the first showing of some new painter's work, the artist would sell the lot in the day, and if he failed to mention an exhibition by a recognised master, collectors would suddenly turn away, resell at a loss, or take down the scorned canvases from their drawing-room walls to hide them in armourplated safes until the day their ranking moved up again.

Very quickly pressure began to be exerted on him. He was smothered in champagne and *foie gras*; liveried chauffeurs were sent to fetch him in black limousines; then dealers began to mention possible percentages; several reputable architects offered to build him houses, and several interior designers offered to decorate them for him.

For several weeks Beyssandre persevered with his column, believing that the scares and sensations it caused would necessarily subside. Then he tried using various pseudonyms – B. Drapier, Diedrich Knickerbocker, Fred Dannay, M. B. Lee, Sylvander, Ehrich Weiss, Guillaume Porter, etc. – but it was almost worse, because dealers now thought they could identify him behind any unfamiliar signature, and inexplicable turmoils continued to rock the art market long after Beyssandre had entirely given up writing and had announced the fact in full-page displays in all the papers he had ever worked for.

The following months were the hardest for him: he had to stop himself going into sale rooms and attending private views; he took elaborate precautions to visit galleries, but each time his incognito was blown it set off disastrous repercussions, and he ended up choosing to abandon all public appearances; henceforth he visited only artists' studios; he would ask the artist to show him what he reckoned to be his five best works and to leave him alone with them for at least an hour.

Two years later, he had visited more than two thousand studios dotted around ninety-one cities in twenty-three countries. His problem now was to reread his notes and to make his selection: one of the directors of International Hostellerie generously gave him free use of a chalet in the Grisons, and he went there to think over the strange task he had been given, and the curious side effects that had ensued from it. And it was at about this time, as he gazed on a landscape of glaciers with only cows ringing their low-pitched bells for company and reflected on the meaning of art, that he heard of Bartlebooth's adventure.

He learnt of it quite by chance as he was preparing to light a fire with a two-year old issue of the *St Moritz Latest News*, a local rag giving resort gossip twice a week during the winter season: Olivia and Rémi Rorschach had spent ten days at the *Engadiner* hotel, and each of them had been entitled to an interview:

– Rémi Rorschach, can you tell us what your current projects are?

– I've been told the story of a man who went round the world to paint pictures, and then had them scientifically destroyed. I think I'd quite like to make a film about it . . .

The résumé was thin and erroneous, but just the thing to arouse Beyssandre's interest. And when the art critic got wind of the thing in greater detail, the Englishman's project fired his enthusiasm. Then, very quickly, Beyssandre made his decision: those very works which their author absolutely wished to destroy would be the most precious jewels in the rarest collection in the world.

Bartlebooth received Beyssandre's first letter in early April 1974. By then all he could read were banner headlines, so Smautf read the letter to him. In it, the critic told his own story in detail, explaining how he had reached the view that those watercolours cut into so many jigsaws should be treated as works of art, a destiny which their begetter wished to deny them: whereas artists and their dealers the world over had been dreaming for months of getting one of their products into the fabulous Marvel Houses collection, he was offering the only man who wanted neither to show nor to keep his own work the sum of ten million dollars for the purchase of what he had left!

Bartlebooth asked Smautf to tear up the letter, to return any more that might come without opening them, and not to let the signatory enter if perchance he were to turn up.

For three months Beyssandre wrote, rang in, and rang on the doorbell to no avail. Then on 11 July he called on Smautf in his bedroom and instructed him to warn his master that he was making a declaration of war: Bartlebooth might think art consisted in destroying the works he had brought into being, but he, Beyssandre, considered that art consisted of saving one or more of these works at any price, and he defied the stubborn Englishman to stop him doing so.

Bartlebooth was sufficiently aware, if only from having experienced it himself, of the havoc that passion may wreak on the most sensible people, to know that the critic's words were no idle threat. The simplest precaution would have been to avoid any risk with the reconstituted watercolours by abandoning their systematic destruction on the very site where they had been painted long ago. But that would be to misjudge Bartlebooth: when challenged, he would face the challenge, and the watercolours would continue to be conveyed, as they always had been conveyed, to their place of origin to return to the blank whiteness of their original non-being.

This final phase of the great plan had always been carried out with much less rigidity than the prior stages. In the early years, Bartlebooth himself would deal with the operation when the sites were no more than a couple of plane or train rides away; a little later, Smautf took over, and then, when the places concerned became more and more distant, the custom arose of mailing the watercolours to the correspondents *in situ* whom Bartlebooth had contacted at the time, or to their successors; each watercolour was sent with a phial of special solvent, a detailed map showing exactly where the thing was to be done, an explanatory note, and a signed letter from Bartlebooth kindly requesting the said correspondent to be so good as to perform the destruction of the enclosed watercolour in accordance with the instructions contained in the explanatory note and, on completion of the operation, to send back to him the sheet of paper returned to its blank virginity. Up until then the procedure had worked as planned, and ten or fifteen days later Bartlebooth would receive his blank sheet, and it had never even occurred to him that anyone might have just pretended to destroy the watercolour and sent him back another sheet, which he checked up on nonetheless by making sure that all these sheets – especially made for him – did indeed bear his watermark and the tiny traces of Winckler's cutting lines.

Bartlebooth contemplated several answers to Beyssandre's attack. The most efficient would no doubt have been to entrust an associate with the task of destroying the watercolours and to give him a bodyguard escort. But where could he find such a trustworthy associate, now he was up against the almost unlimited power the critic had at his disposal? Bartlebooth trusted only Smautf completely, and Smautf was much too old; and what was more, the billionaire had neglected his inheritance for fifty years in favour of ensuring the success of his project and had left it more and more in the hands of his business advisers, and so he would not even have had the resources to provide his old servant with such costly protection.

After long hesitation, Bartlebooth asked to see Rorschach. No one knows how he got him to collaborate, but it was at all events through the producer's good offices that he was able to entrust television crews leaving on assignments in the Indian Ocean, the Red Sea, or the Persian Gulf with the task of destroying his watercolours in the customary way, and of filming the destruction.

For several months this system worked without too much trouble. On the eve of departure, the cameraman would receive the watercolour to be destroyed and a sealed box containing one hundred and twenty metres of reversible film, that is to say celluloid producing a positive image when developed without an intermediate negative stage. Smautf and Kléber would go to the airport to collect from the returning cameraman the now blank watercolour and the exposed celluloid which they would take directly to a laboratory. The same evening or, at the latest, next day Bartlebooth would view the film on a 16mm projector set up in the antechamber. Then he would have the film burnt.

Various incidents that could not easily be ascribed to chance proved nonetheless that Beyssandre had not given up. He was definitely responsible for the burglary that occurred in the flat of Robert Cravennat, the chemistry lab technician who had been dealing with the resolidification of the puzzles since Morellet's accident in 1960, and for the attempted arson which nearly caused a devastating fire in Guyomard's studio. Bartlebooth's sight had been getting worse and worse, and he was getting ever further behind in his schedule, so Cravennat had no puzzle in his flat that fortnight; as for Guyomard, he extinguished the petrol-soaked rags which were intended to start the fire, before whoever lit them could take advantage of the situation to steal the watercolour the restorer had just received.

But it would take much more than that to put Beyssandre off. Just over two months ago, on the twenty-fifth of April 1975, in the same week that Bartlebooth lost his eyesight for good, the inevitable finally happened: the documentary crew that had gone to Turkey, and whose cameraman was due to go to Trabzon to perform the destruction of Bartlebooth's four hundred and thirty-eighth watercolour (the Englishman was now sixteen months behind schedule), failed to return: two days later news came that the four crewmen had died in a mysterious car accident.

Bartlebooth decided to give up his ritual destructions; henceforth, completed puzzles would no longer be reglued, separated from their backing, and soaked in a solvent from which the sheet of paper would emerge entirely white, but simply put back in Madame Hourcade's black box and thrown into an incinerator. This decision came too late in the day to be of any use, for Bartlebooth would never complete the puzzle he began that week.

A few days later, Smautf read in a newspaper that Marvel Houses International, a subsidiary of Marvel Houses Incorporated and International Hostellerie, was being wound up. Fresh estimates had shown that in view of increased construction costs, amortisation of the twenty-four culture parks would take not four years and eight months, nor even five years and three months, but six years and two months; the major backers had taken fright and withdrawn their capital, to invest it in a gigantic scheme to tow icebergs. The Marvel Houses programme was suspended *sine die*. As for Beyssandre, he was never heard of again.

CHAPTER EIGHTY-EIGHT

Altamont, 5

In the main drawing room of the Altamonts' flat, two servants are putting the finishing touches to a reception they have laid out. One is a strapping Negro wearing his Louis XV livery with unconstrained ease – green pin-striped waistcoat and breeches, green cotton hose, and silver-buckled shoes – and lifting with no evident strain a three-seater sofa of dark-red varnished wood with foliate decorations and inlaid mother-of-pearl, adorned with chintz-covered cushions. The other, a sallow-skinned butler with a bulging Adam's apple, dressed in a slightly oversize black tuxedo, is laying out on a long marble-topped sideboard against the right-hand wall several large silver-plate dishes laden with small-cut sandwiches: red tongue, salmon roe, Swiss smoked beef, smoked eel, asparagus tips, etc.

On the wall above the sideboard hang two pictures signed by J. T. Maston, a genre painter of English origin who spent much of his life in Central America and became well known at the beginning of this century. The first picture, entitled *The Apothecary*, depicts a bald man in a greenish cloak, with eyeglasses perched on his nose and a huge wart afflicting his forehead, at the back of a gloomy store full of large cylindrical jars, apparently attempting with great difficulty to decipher a prescription. The second, entitled *The Naturalist*, shows an energetic-looking man, skinny and dry, with a beard cut in the American fashion, that is to say with bushy hair under the chin. Standing with arms akimbo, he is watching the torment of a small squirrel imprisoned in a close-knit web hung between two giant liriodendrons and woven by a hideous beast as big as a pigeon's egg and endowed with huge paws.

Against the left-hand wall, on the mantel of a veined marble fireplace, stand two lamps on pedestals made from brass shell-casings on either side of a tall glass cloche sitting over a bouquet of flowers of which each petal is a leaf of beaten gold.

Along almost the entire length of the back wall hangs a very worn tapestry whose colours have faded entirely. It probably depicts the three Magi, as there are three figures, one kneeling, the others standing, only one of which remains more or less intact, wearing a long robe with slit sleeves. A sword hangs at his waist, and in his left hand he holds a kind of gift box; he has black hair and a curious hat, somewhere between a beret, a tricorn, a crown, and a bonnet, decorated with a medallion.

In the foreground, a little to the right and sideways onto the window, Véronique Altamont is sitting at a leather-clad desk decorated with gilt arabesques on which several books are displayed: a novel by Georges Bernanos, *Joy; The Lilliputian Village*, a children's book on whose cover you can see some miniature houses, a fire station, a town hall with its clock, and wide-eyed, freckle-faced kids whom long-bearded dwarves serve with slices of bread and butter and big glasses of milk; Espingole's *Dictionary of Medieval French and Latin Abbreviations*, *Exercises in Medieval Diplomatic and Palaeography* by Toustain and Tassin, opened at facsimile pages of medieval texts. On the left-hand page, a model rental contract:

> *Connue chose soit à tous ceuz qui ces lettres varront et oiront que li ceuz de Menoalville doit a ceuz di Leglise Dauteri trois sols de tolois à randre chascun an a dict terme . . .*

On the right-hand page, an extract from *The True Story of Philemo and Bauci* by Garin de Garlande – a very free adaptation of Ovid's legend in which the author, a twelfth-century monk from Valenciennes, imagines that Zeus and Mercury were not content merely to provoke a flood to punish the Phrygians who had refused them hospitality, but also sent legions of fierce beasts which, on his return to his hut, now transformed into a temple, Philemon describes to Baucis:

> I saw three hundred and nine pelicans. Item, six thousand and sixteen Seleucid birds marching in battalia and picking up straggling grasshoppers in cornfields. Item, some cynamolgs, argatiles, caprimulgi, thynnunculi, onocrotals or bitterns, with their wide swallows, stymphalides, harpies, panthers,

dorcasses, or bucks, cemades, cynocephalises, marmosets, or monkeys, presteres, bugles, tarands, musimons, byturoses, ophyri, screech owls, goblins, fairies, and griffins.

In the midst of these books there is a stiff canvas folder, dark brown in colour, fastened by two elastic bands, with a rectangular self-adhesive label on which the following title has been carefully written in a copperplate hand:

Memoirs
towards the history of my own
Childhood
by Véronique Marceline Gilberte Altamont + Gardel

Véronique is an overgrown sixteen-year-old with very pale skin, extremely blonde hair, an unappealing face, and a rather sullen appearance. She is wearing a long white dress with lace cuffs, whose low-cut neck shows her shoulders and prominent breastbone. She is examining attentively a small, lined, cracked snapshot of two dancers, one of whom is none other than Madame Altamont, twenty-five years younger. The dancers are doing their barre exercises under the supervision of their teacher, a thin man with a birdlike head, bright eyes, a scraggy neck, and bony hands; he is barefoot and bare-chested, wearing only long underpants and a long knitted scarf over his shoulder, and in his left hand he carries a tall, silver-knobbed walking stick.

Madame Altamont, née Blanche Gardel, was at the age of nineteen a dancer with a company called Ballets Frère, founded and run not by two brothers, as you might have expected from the name, but by two cousins: Frère, who ran the business side, negotiated contracts, and organised tours, and Maximilien Riccetti (whose real name was Max Riquet), the artistic director, choreographer, and star dancer. The company stuck to the purest classical style – tutus, pointes, *entrechats*, *jetés-battus*, performing *Giselle*, *Swan Lake*, *pas de deux*, and *suites en blanc* – and did the rounds of the festivals in the Paris suburbs: the Musical Nights at Chatou, the Artistic Saturdays at La Hacquinière, Son et Lumière at Arpajon, the Festival of

Livry-Gargan, etc. Since the company was entitled to a minuscule subsidy from the Education Ministry, the Ballets Frère also performed in schools and introduced the top forms to the art of the ballet, giving demonstrations in the gym or refectory, where Jean-Jacques Frère would give an undemanding running commentary peppered with hoary puns and vulgar innuendos.

Jean-Jacques Frère was a paunchy little man, always game for a laugh, and would have been quite happy to settle for this second-rate existence in which he had all the opportunity he wanted for squeezing ballerinas' buttocks and ogling schoolgirls. But Riccetti had greater aspirations and ached to show the world just how exceptionally talented he was. And when that moment came, as he used to say to Blanche, whom he loved almost as passionately as himself, then his deserved fame would reflect on them both, and they would become the most beautiful dancing couple ever seen.

The long-hoped-for opportunity arose one day in November 1949. Count della Marsa, a wealthy Venetian patron of the ballet, decided to commission a certain René Becquerloux (rumour had it that the name served to mask the count himself) to write a *fantaisie-bouffe* in the manner of Lulli under the title of *The Dizzy Fits of Psyche* for the next international festival at Saint-Jean-de-Luz, and entrusted the production to the Ballets Frère, whom he had had occasion to appreciate the previous year at the Musical Hours of Moret-sur-Loing.

A few weeks later Blanche found that she was pregnant and that the due date would fall almost exactly on the opening night of the festival. The only solution was to have an abortion; but when she told Riccetti, the dancer flew into an indescribable rage and forbade her to sacrifice the irreplaceable being he was about to bring into the world for the mere sake of a night of fame.

Blanche hesitated. She was violently in love with Riccetti, and their love fed on their joint dreams of greatness; but between an unwanted child (and there would always be plenty of time to have another one) and the role she had always hankered after, the choice was obvious. She asked the opinion of Jean-Jacques Frère, for whom she felt genuine affection despite his vulgarity, and who, she knew, was also fond of her. Although he didn't come down on one side or the other, the company director made a few scabrous allusions to back-street angel-makers juggling with knitting needles and to parsley sprigs strewn on the chequered oilcloth of kitchen tables, and then advised her at least to go to Switzerland, Britain, or Denmark, where some clinics provided voluntary termination in less hair-raising surroundings. And that was how Blanche Gardel made up her mind to seek help and assistance from one of her childhood friends, who had moved to England. She turned to Cyrille Altamont, who had just graduated from the Ecole Nationale d'Administration and was doing a tour of duty at the French Embassy in London.

Cyrille was ten years older than Blanche. The parents of the two children had had country houses at Neauphle-le-Château, and in the years before the war Blanche and Cyrille had spent many a happy summer there amidst great swarms of cousins, boys and girls alike, all of them well-turned-out teacher's pets from Paris who had to learn afresh each year how to climb trees, suck raw eggs, and fetch the milk and the curds still dripping with whey from the local farm.

Blanche was one of the youngest and Cyrille one of the oldest of the bunch. When, at the end of September, on the eve of their dispersal for the new school year, the children gave the grown-ups a show that they had rehearsed in the deepest secrecy for a fortnight, Blanche would do a turn as a little ballerina and Cyrille would accompany her on the violin.

The war put an end to these high spots of childhood. Blanche and Cyrille didn't see each other again until she was a gorgeous girl of sixteen whose pigtails were no longer for pulling and he wore – if only briefly – the glorious halo of a lieutenant: he had seen action in the Ardennes and had just won places at Polytechnique and at the Ecole Nationale d'Administration at the same examination session. In the following three years, Cyrille took Blanche to dances several times and wooed her assiduously, but in vain, for she persisted in a silent passion for the three star dancers of the Ballets de Paris – Jean Babilée, Jean Guélis, and Roland Petit – until she fell into the arms of Maximilien Riccetti.

Cyrille Altamont agreed easily that Blanche was right to want an abortion and offered his help. Two days later, after a purely formal visit to a Harley Street doctor, for whose benefit Cyrille masqueraded as Blanche's husband, the young civil servant drove the ballerina to a clinic in the northern suburbs of London, housed in a cottage that looked identical to all the cottages around it. He picked her up, as agreed, the next morning, and accompanied her to Victoria Station, where Blanche boarded the Silver Arrow for Paris.

She telephoned him later that night, begging him to come to her rescue. On her return home, she had found Jean-Jacques Frère and two police inspectors sitting around her dining-room table finishing off a bottle of Calvados. They told her that Maximilien had hanged himself the night before. In the brief note he had left to account for his act, he had written only that he could never live with the idea that Blanche had killed his child.

Blanche Gardel married Cyrille Altamont eighteen months later, in April 1951. In May, they moved into the flat in Rue Simon-Crubellier. But Cyrille never really lived there, because a few weeks later he was appointed to a post in Geneva and settled there. Since then, he only comes to Paris for short periods, and even then he usually stays at a hotel.

Véronique was born in 1959, and it was in the first place to clarify the circumstances of her own birth that at the age of eight or nine she began her investigation into her parents. At an age when children enjoy telling themselves that they're foundlings, or the son or daughter of a king swapped over in the cradle, or a baby left by a back door and picked up by travelling players or gypsies, Véronique made up convoluted adventures to explain why her mother never took off her wrist and left hand a thin strip of black gauze, and also to account for the ever-absent man who called himself her father and whom she hated so much that for years she crossed out systematically the name of Altamont on her school identity card and on all her exercise books, writing in over it her mother's maiden name.

Then, with almost mesmerised fascination, painfully, painstakingly, obsessively, she tried to reconstruct the history of her own family. One day, when at last she answered Véronique's question, her mother said that she kept the cloth strip as a mark of mourning for a man who had meant a lot to her. Véronique thought that she must be that man's daughter and that Altamont was punishing her mother for having loved another before him. Later on, she found as a bookmark at page 73 of *The Age of Reason* the photograph of her mother practising at the barre with another ballerina under the direction of Maximilien, and she assumed that he was her real father. That day she took out a new folder and decided to confide secretly to it everything related to her history and to her parents' lives, and she began a systematic search of all her mother's cupboards and drawers. It was all too neatly kept, and there seemed to be no traces left of her life as a ballerina. One day, nonetheless, beneath a neat stack of bills and receipts, Véronique at last came across some old letters from schoolmates, cousins, long-lost friends, mentioning memories of past holidays, cycle rides, afternoon teas, seaside jaunts, fancy-dress balls, and plays at the Children's Theatre. Another time, she unearthed a programme of the Ballets Frère's performance at the Parents' Evening at the Lycée Hoche at Versailles, which listed an excerpt from *Coppelia* performed by Maximilien Riccetti and Blanche Gardel. On yet another occasion, whilst on holiday at her maternal grandmother's, who had long since sold Neauphle and moved to Grimaud on the Côte d'Azur, she laid her hands on a box labelled *The Little Dancer*: it contained sixty metres of film shot on a Pathé Baby. Véronique managed to get it screened and saw her mother as a tiny ballerina in a tutu, accompanied on the violin by a gawky, spotty scarecrow who was just recognisable as Cyrille. Then a few months ago, one day in November 1974, she found in her mother's wastepaper basket a letter from Cyrille, and on reading it grasped that Maximilien had died ten years before she was born and that the truth was the exact opposite of what she thought.

I was in London a few days ago and I couldn't help taking a ride to that distant suburb where I took you, twenty-five years ago almost to the day. The clinic is still there, at 130 Crescent Gardens, but now it's a three-storey block, quite modern. The rest of the scenery has hardly changed from what I remember. I relived the day I spent in those outskirts whilst you were being operated on. I never told you about the day I spent. I wanted to see you at the end of the afternoon, when you came round, so it wasn't worth going back into London, better to stay in the area even if it meant wasting a few hours in a pub or a cinema. It was barely ten a.m. when I left you. I wandered for more than half an hour in streets lined with semidetached cottages so similar to each other that you might have thought there was really only one, reflected in some huge system of mirrors – they all had the same doors painted dark green, with shiny brass knockers and boot-scrapers, the same manufactured lace curtains in their bay windows, the same pots of aspidistra in the landing window. In the end I managed to find what was presumably the shopping centre: a few apparently uninhabited shops, a Woolworth's, a cinema called *The Odeon*, obviously, and a pub proudly named *The Unicorn and Castle*, and unfortunately shut. I went and sat in the only place that gave any apparent sign of life, a kind of milk-bar housed in a long wooden caravan and run by three spinsters. I was served a cup of revolting tea and butterless toast (I wouldn't eat their margarine) with orange marmalade that tasted of tin.

Then I bought the newspapers and went to read them in a little park set beside a statue representing a gentleman sitting cross-legged, with an ironical expression on his face, and holding in his left hand a sheet of paper (of stone, of course) copiously furled in on itself at each end, and in his right hand a goose quill. Since he reminded me of Voltaire, I reckoned it must have been Pope; but it was in fact a certain William Warburton, 1698–1779, writer and priest, and the author, according to the inscription carved on the pedestal, of a *Divine Legation of Moses*.

Towards noon the pub finally opened its doors and I went in to drink a few beers whilst eating anchovy paste and Cheshire cheese sandwiches. I stayed there until two o'clock, sitting at the bar, hunched over my glass, beside two brothers-in-law who both worked for the Local Authority. One was an assistant accountant at the gasworks, the other an office manager in the retirement pensions department. They were ingurgitating a rather repulsive stew as they related to each other in an atrocious cockney accent some interminable family story involving a sister living in Canada, a niece who was a nurse in Egypt and another married in Nottingham, an enigmatic O'Brien whose first name was Bobby, and a Mrs Bridgett who ran a bed-and-breakfast at Margate, on the Thames Estuary.

At two, I left the pub to go to the cinema. I remember that the programme consisted of two full-length films and several shorts, newsreels, and cartoons. I've forgotten what the feature films were called; they were both equally bland. The first was the umpteenth story about RAF officers tunnelling their way out of a POW camp. The second was intended to be a comedy; it was set in the nineteenth century and began with a fat, gout-ridden rich man refusing his daughter's hand to a weedy young man since the latter weedy young man had no money and no prospects. I never learnt how the weedy young man managed to grow rich and prove to his future father-in-law that he was brighter than he looked, because I fell asleep after fifteen minutes. Two usherettes woke me quite roughly. The house-lights were up, I was the only audience left. Completely dazed, I couldn't understand a word of what the usherettes were shouting, and it was only when I got to the street that I realised I had forgotten my newspapers, my coat, my umbrella, and my gloves. Fortunately one of the usherettes caught me up and handed them back to me.

It was a dark night. It was half past five. It was drizzling. I returned to the clinic but they wouldn't let me see you. They only said that everything was all right, that you were asleep; and that I should call to collect you the next day at eleven a.m.

I caught the bus back into London, through vast and soulless suburbs, past thousand upon thousand home sweet homes, where thousand upon thousand men and women just back from their factories and offices were simultaneously raising the tea cosy from the teapot, pouring the tea into the cup, lacing it with a touch of milk, grasping with fingertips the slice of toast that had just popped out of the automatic toaster, and spreading it with Bovril. I had a feeling of total unreality, as if I were on another planet, in another world – a world of cottonwool, misty, wet, run through with yellow lights verging on orange. And suddenly I thought of you, of what was happening to you, of the cruel irony which meant that in order to help you suppress a child that was not mine we were pretending for a few hours to be husband and wife by saying not that you were Madame Altamont but that I was Monsieur Gardel.

It was half past seven when the bus got to its terminus at Charing Cross. I drank a whisky in a pub called *The Greens*, then went to the cinema again. This time I saw a film you had mentioned, *Red Shoes*, directed by Michael Powell, with Moira Shearer and choreography by Léonide Massine. I can't remember the story, but only one of the dances, in which a newspaper thrown away and blown by the wind turns disturbingly into a dancer. I came out of the cinema at about ten o'clock. Though I almost never drink spirits and feel ill on a single glass, I had an irresistible desire to get drunk.

I went into a pub called *The Donkey in Trousers*. Its sign showed a donkey whose four limbs were bound in a kind of white cloth legging with red polka dots. I thought such things only existed on the Ile de Ré, but there was obviously somewhere in England with the same custom. The donkey's tail was a plaited string, and the legend explained how this tail could function as a barometer:

If tail is dry	*Fine*
If tail is wet	*Rain*
If tail moves	*Windy*
If tail cannot be seen	*Fog*
If tail is frozen	*Cold*
If tail falls out	*Earthquake*

The pub was packed. In the end I found a seat at a table partly occupied by an amazing couple: an enormously corpulent man, getting on in years, with a high forehead and a geat mop of white hair hanging like a cloud over his powerful head, and a thirty-year-old woman with a look that was both Slav and Asiatic at the same time – broad cheekbones, narrow eyes, reddish fair hair plaited and wound around her head. She said nothing and frequently placed her hand on her companion's as if to stop him getting angry. He spoke incessantly with a slight accent I couldn't place; he didn't finish his sentences but broke them off all the time with "all in all", "well", "fine", "excellent", without ceasing for a moment to down huge quantities of food and drink, getting up every five minutes to make his way to the bar to fetch platefuls of sandwiches, packets of crisps, sausages, hot pies, pickles, apple pies, and pints and pints of brown ale which he drank in a single gulp.

He struck up a conversation with me quickly and we began to drink together, to chat about this and that, about the war, about death, London, Paris, beer, music, night trains, beauty, ballet, fog, and life. I think I also tried to tell him your story. His companion said nothing. From time to time she smiled at him. The rest of the time her eyes wandered around the smoke-filled bar whilst she sipped her pink gin and lit up gilt-tipped cigarettes which she snuffed out almost straight away in an ashtray provided by the makers of *The Antiquarian* whisky.

Obviously I soon lost my sense of time and place. Everything turned into a muddled buzzing punctuated by dull thuds, exclamations, laughter, and whispering. Then suddenly, opening my eyes, I saw I had been pulled upright, that my coat was over my shoulders, that my umbrella was in my hand. The pub had emptied almost entirely. The publican was smoking a cigar in his open doorway. A waitress was strewing sawdust on the floor. The woman had put her thick fur coat on again, and the man, helped by a waiter, was easing himself into a broad cloak with an otter-fur collar. And suddenly he swung his body round and turned towards me to proffer in an almost thunderous voice: "Life, young man, is a woman on her back, with swollen, close-set breasts, a smooth, soft, fat belly between protruding hips, with slender arms, plump thighs, and half-closed eyes, who in her grandiose and taunting provocation demands our most ardent fervour".

How did I manage to get back to my room, to undress, to get to bed? I can't remember anything about it. When I woke a few hours later to come to fetch you, I noticed that all the lights were on and that the shower had been running all night. But I remember very clearly that strange couple, and the last words spoken by the man, and in my memory I see the sparkle in his eyes as he spoke, and I think of all that happened a few hours after, and of the nightmare that our two lives turned into.

Thenceforth you built your whole life on hatred and on the stale illusion of the sacrifice of your happiness. You will punish me till the end of your days for having helped you to do what you wanted to do and what you would have done in any case, even without my help. To the end of your days you will reproach me for the failure of your love, for the failure of the life which your puffed-up ballet dancer would have squandered unpityingly in the sole name of his own despicable little stardom. To the end of your days you will put on for me your act of remorse, of the pure woman racked at night by the ghost of the man she brought to suicide, just as for yourself you will act out the pretty picture-book story of the suffering woman abandoned by a high-flying skirt-chaser, of the impeccable mother bringing her daughter up superbly by removing her from the noxious influence of her father. But you only gave me that child so as to be able to reproach me all the more for having assisted in killing the other child, and you brought her up in the hatred of me, forbidding me to see her, to speak to her, to love her.

I wanted you for my wife, and I wanted your child. I have neither the one nor the other, and that has been going on for so long now that I have stopped wondering whether it is hate or love which gives us the strength to continue this life of lies, which provides the formidable energy that allows us to go on suffering, and hoping.

CHAPTER EIGHTY-NINE

Moreau, 5

When Madame Moreau began to feel her body failing her, she asked Madame Trévins to come to live in with her, and gave her a room which Fleury had decorated as a rococo boudoir with flimsy draperies, violet silks screen-printed with great leaves, lace doilies, whorled candelabras, dwarf orange trees, and an alabaster figurine representing a child in a pastoral shepherd costume, holding a bird in his hands.

Of all these splendours, there remain: a still life depicting a lute on a table: the lute is placed face upwards, in full light, whilst underneath the table, almost drowned by the shadow, can be seen its black case, face down; a gilded wooden lectern, highly worked, bearing the controversial hallmark of Hugues Sambin, a sixteenth-century architect and woodcarver from Dijon; and three large hand-coloured photographs dating from the Russo-Japanese war: the first shows the battleship *Pobieda*, the pride of the Russian fleet, put out of action by a Japanese depth charge off Port Arthur on 13 April 1904; insets display four of Russia's military leaders: Admiral Makharov, commander-in-chief of the Russian fleet in the Far East, General Kuropatkin, generalissimo of the Russian army in the Far East, General Stoessel, military commander of Port Arthur, and General Pflug, chief of staff of the Russian army in the Far East; the second photograph, the other's twin, shows the Japanese battleship-cruiser *Asama*, built by Armstrong's, with insets of Admiral Yamamoto, navy minister, Admiral Togo, the "Japanese Nelson", commander-in-chief of the Japanese flotilla off Port Arthur, General Kodama, the

"Kitchener of Japan", commander-in-chief of the Japanese army, and General Viscount Tazo-Katzura, prime minister. The third photograph portrays a Russian military encampment near Mukden: it is evening; in front of each tent soldiers sit with their feet in bowls of tepid water; in the centre, in a taller tent with awnings in the form of a kiosk flanked by two Cossack guards, a most certainly high-ranking officer studies the plan of battles to come on charts heavily laden with pins.

The rest of the room is furnished in modern fashion: the bed is a foam mattress sheathed in black synthetic leather and placed on a podium; a low piece of furniture with drawers, made of dark wood and polished steel, serves as both a dressing table and a bedside table; on it stands a perfectly spherical bedside light, a wristwatch with digital display, a bottle of Vichy water with a special cap to stop it from going flat, a cyclostyled document 21cm x 27cm entitled *French National Standards for Watchmakers' and Jewellers' Items*, a pamphlet in the "Business" series with the title *Employers and Workers, The Dialogue is Still Open*, and a book of some four hundred pages covered in a flambé dust jacket: *The Lives of the Trévins Sisters*, by Célestine Durand-Taillefer [available from the author, Rue du Hennin, Liège (Belgium)].

These Trévins sisters are supposed to be Madame Trévins's five nieces, the daughters of her brother Daniel. The reader who wonders what in the lives of these five women made them deserve such a lengthy biography has his mind put at rest on page one: the five sisters were in fact quintuplets, all born in the space of eighteen minutes on 14 July 1943, at Abidjan, kept in an incubator for four months, and since then never ill.

But the fate of these quins goes a mile higher than the mere miracle of their birth: Adelaïde, after beating the French record for the sixty-metre sprint (juniors) at the age of ten, was seized, from the age of twelve, by a passion for the circus, and dragged her sisters into an acrobatic act which was soon famous throughout Europe: *The Fire Girls* jumped through flaming hoops, switched trapezes in mid-air whilst juggling lighted torches, or did the hula-hoop on a wire twelve feet above ground. The fire at the Hamburg *Fairyland* ruined these precocious careers: the insurers claimed that *The Fire Girls* were the cause of the disaster and refused henceforth to give cover to any theatres where they performed, even after the five girls had proved in court that they used perfectly harmless artificial fire sold by Ruggieri's under the name of "jam" and specifically designed for circus artists and cinema stunt men.

Marie-Thérèse and Odile then became nightclub dancers; their impeccable shapeliness and their identical appearances ensured almost immediate and stunning success: the *Crazy Sisters* could be seen at the Paris *Lido*, at *Cavalier's* in Stockholm, at *Naughties* in Milan, at the Las Vegas *B and A*, and at *Pension Macadam* in Tangiers, the Beirut *Star*, the *Ambassadors* in London, the *Bros d'Or* in Acapulco, the Berlin *Nirvana*, at *Monkey Jungle* in Miami, at *Twelve Tones* in Newport and *Caribbean's* in Barbados, where they met two men of substance who took sufficient fancy to them to marry them on the spot: Marie-Thérèse wedded the Canadian shipowner Michel Wilker, the great-great-grandson of one of Dumont d'Urville's unlucky competitors, and Odile married an American industrialist, Faber McCork, the king of the diet delicatessens.

Both divorced the next year; Marie-Thérèse, who had become Canadian, threw herself into business and politics, founding and running a huge Consumer Defence Movement, of ecological and autarchic tendencies, simultaneously manufacturing and distributing on a massive scale a whole range of products suited to the return to Nature and to the true macrobiotic life style of primitive communities: canvas water bottles, yoghurt-makers, tent canvas, Pan pipes (kit form), bread ovens, etc. Odile, for her part, came back to France; taken on as a typist by the Institute for the History of Texts, she found that, although entirely self-taught, she had a taste for Late Latin, and for the next ten years did four hours' unpaid overtime every evening at the Institute in order to establish a definitive edition of the *Danorum Regum Heroumque Historia* by Saxo Grammaticus, which is still considered the authoritative edition; later, she married an English judge and undertook a revision of Jerome Wolf and Portus's Latin edition of the so-called *Lexicon* of Suidas, which she was still working on at the time the story of her life was written.

The three other sisters had destinies no less impressive: Noëlle became the right hand of Werner Angst, the German steel magnate; Roseline was the first woman to circumnavigate the globe solo, on board her thirty-six-foot yacht, the *C'est si beau*; as for Adelaïde, she became a chemist and discovered a method for splitting enzymes, allowing "delayed" catalyses to be obtained; this discovery led to a whole series of patents, now widely used in industry for making detergents, varnishes, and paints; since then Adelaïde has become an extremely wealthy woman and devotes her time to her two hobbies, the piano and the handicapped.

The exemplary biographies of the five Trévins sisters, unfortunately, do not stand up to closer scrutiny, and the reader who smells a rat in these quasi-fabulous exploits will soon have his suspicions confirmed. For Madame Trévins (who, unlike Mademoiselle Crespi, is called Madame despite being a spinster) has no brother, and consequently no nieces bearing her surname; and Célestine Durand-Taillefer cannot live in Rue Hennin in Liège because in Liège there is no Rue Hennin; on the other hand, Madame Trévins did have a sister, Arlette, who was married to a Mr Louis Commine and bore him a daughter, Lucette, who married someone called Robert Hennin, who sells postcards (collectors' items only) in Rue de Liège, in Paris (VIIIth *arrondissement*).

A closer reading of these imaginary lives would no doubt lead to discovering the key and seeing how some of the events that have influenced the history of the building, some of the legends and semi-legends that go round about one or another of its inhabitants, some of the threads that connect them to each other, have been buried in the narrative and have given it its skeleton. Thus it is more than probable that Marie-Thérèse, the exceptionally successful businesswoman, represents Madame Moreau, who moreover bears the same forename; that Werner Angst is Hermann Fugger, the German industrialist friend of the Altamonts', and a client of Hutting's and a colleague of Madame Moreau; and that Noëlle, Angst's right hand, as the result of a very significant sideways shift, could be a figure for Madame Trévins herself; and though it is less easy to see what hides behind the other three sisters, it is by no means impossible to surmise that underneath Adelaïde, the chemist well disposed towards the handicapped, lies Morellet, who lost three fingers in an unfortunate experiment; that behind Odile, the autodidact, lies Léon Marcia; and that behind the solitary yachtswoman loom the very different profiles of Bartlebooth and Olivia Norvell.

Madame Trévins took many years to write this story, in the infrequent moments of respite that Madame Moreau allowed her. She took particular pains over her choice of pseudonym: a first name very faintly suggestive of something cultural, and a double-barrelled surname composed of a first part as banal and ordinary as Jones, and a second part alluding to a famous fictional character. That did not suffice to convince publishers, who didn't want anything to do with a first novel written by an 85-year-old spinster. In fact Madame Trévins was only eighty-two, but that didn't cut much ice with the publishers, and in the end Madame Trévins lost heart and had a single copy printed, which she dedicated to herself.

CHAPTER NINETY

Entrance Hall, 2

The right-hand section of the building's entrance hall. In the background, the first flight of the staircase; in the foreground, to the right, the door to the Marcias' flat. In the middle distance, below a large mirror in a surround of gilded mouldings which imperfectly reflects the silhouette of Ursula Sobieski's back as she stands in front of the concierge's office, is a large wooden chest with a padded lid upholstered in yellow velvet, serving as a bench. Three women are seated on it: Mademoiselle Lafuente, Madame Albin, and Gertrude, Madame Moreau's former cook.

The first, that is to say the one on the extreme right from our point of view, is Mademoiselle Lafuente: though it is nearly eight in the evening, Madame de Beaumont's domestic help has not yet finished her day's work. She was about to leave when the piano-tuner turned up: Mademoiselle Anne was at gym, Mademoiselle Béatrice was upstairs, and Madame was having a rest before dinner. So Mademoiselle Lafuente had to show the tuner in herself, and also send his grandson out onto the landing with his comic to prevent any repetition of the stupid way he had behaved last time. Then Mademoiselle Lafuente had opened the fridge and realised that all that was left for dinner were three Bulgarian-flavour low-calorie yoghurts, since Mademoiselle Anne had raided the fruit and the roast beef and chicken leftovers that were intended to be the main ingredients of the meal; despite the lateness of the hour, and even though most of the local shops were closed on Mondays, in particular all the stores she prefers to give her custom to, she hurried down to get in some eggs, sliced ham, and two pounds of cherries at the *Parisienne* in Rue de Chazelles. On returning with the shopping in her net, she found Madame Albin, on her way home from her daily visit to her late husband's grave, deep in conversation with Gertrude in the entrance hall, and since she hadn't seen Gertrude for several months, she stopped to say hello. For Gertrude, who for ten years was Madame Moreau's awesome cook, the one who cooked her monochrome meals and whom all Paris envied her, had ended up yielding to the offer she had been made, and Madame Moreau, who had given up her grand dinner parties for good, let her go. Gertrude now has a position in England. Her employer, Lord Ashtray, made his fortune in recycling non-ferrous metal and nowadays spends his great wealth by leading the lavish life of a great lord on his enormous estate, Hammer Hall, near London.

Gossip writers and visitors gape before his Regency rosewood furniture, his leather settees which shine with a patina made by eight generations of authentically aristocratic backsides, his cloisonné floors, his 97 lackeys in canary-yellow liveries, and his sectioned ceilings repeating in profusion the emblem which he has associated with his activities all his life: a red cordiform apple pierced right through by a long worm, and surrounded by little flames.

The most disturbing statistics are given about this character. People say he has forty-three full-time gardeners, that he has so many windows, glazed doors, and mirrors in his property that he employs four servants solely for their maintenance, and that since he couldn't get enough replacement glass to keep up with repairs he solved the problem by simply buying the nearest glassworks.

According to some people he owns eleven thousand ties and eight hundred and thirteen walking sticks, subscribes to every English-language newspaper in the world, not to read them – his eight archivists look after that – but to do the crosswords, a pastime of which he is so inordinately fond that his bedroom is entirely repapered once a week with grids designed especially for him by his favourite cruciverbist, Barton O'Brien, of the *Auckland Gazette and Hemisphere*. He is also a keen rugby fan and has built up a private team that he has had in training for months in the hope of seeing it successfully challenge the next victor of the Five Nations tournament.

According to others, the collections and crazes are just camouflage, designed to hide the three true passions of Lord Ashtray: boxing (Melzack Wall, the contender for the world flyweight title, is supposed to be in training at Hammer Hall); three-dimensional geometry: he is said to have been funding for the last twenty years a professor researching polyhedrons, who still has twenty-five volumes to write; and, especially, Indian horsecloths: he is alleged to have collected two hundred and eighteen of them, all belonging to the best warriors from the best tribes: White-Man-Runs-Him and Rain-in-the-Face, of the Crows; Hooker Jim, of the Mohawks; Looking-Glass, Yason, and Alikut, of the Nez Percé Indians; Chief Winnemucca and Ouray-the-Arrow, of the Payute; Black Beaver and White Horse, of the Kiowas; Cochise, the great Apache chief; Geronimo and Ka-e-ten-a, of the Chiricachuas; Sleeping Rabbit, Left Hand, and Dull Knife, of the Cheyennes; Restroom Bomber, of the Saratogas; Big Mike, of the Kachinas; Crazy Turnpike, of the Fudges; Satch Mouth, of the Grooves; and several dozen Sioux cloths, including ones owned by Sitting Bull and his two wives, Seen-by-Her-Nation and Four Times, and those of Old-Man-Afraid-of-His-Horse, Young-Man-Afraid-of-His-Horse, Crazy Horse, American Horse, Iron Horse, Big Mouth, Long Hair, Roman Nose, Lone Horn, and Packs-His-Drum.

* * *

One might have expected such a character to impress Gertrude. But Madame Moreau's robust cook had seen plenty before and didn't have Burgundian blood in her veins for nothing. After three days in service, and in spite of the very strict regulations Lord Ashtray's head secretary had handed her on arrival, she went to see her new employer. He was in the music room, listening to one of the final rehearsals of the opera he intended to have performed for the next week's guests, a lost work by Monpou (Hippolyte) entitled *Ahasverus*. Esther and five choristers, inexplicably dressed as mountain climbers, were just starting on the chorus which closes Act II

When Israel went out of Egypt

when Gertrude burst in. Without noticing the disturbance she had caused, she threw her apron in Lord Ashtray's face and told him the ingredients she was supplied with were revolting, and there was no question of her doing the cooking with them.

Lord Ashtray was especially keen to keep his cook as he had almost not tasted her cooking. To retain her, he accepted without demur that she should do her buying herself, wherever she wanted to.

That is why Gertrude now comes once a week, on Wednesdays, to Rue Legendre and fills a small truck with butter, fresh-laid eggs, milk, fresh cream, green vegetables, fowl, and various spices; she takes the opportunity, if she has any spare time, to visit her former mistress and to have a cup of tea with Madame Trévins.

She has come to France today not for shopping – in any case she would not have been able to do it on a Monday – but to go to Bordeaux for her granddaughter's wedding; she is to marry an assistant inspector of weights and measures.

Gertrude is seated between her two former neighbours. She is a woman of about fifty, plump, red-faced, with chubby hands; she wears a black moiré silk top and a matching green tweed jacket and skirt which don't suit her at all. On her left lapel she has pinned a cameo representing a virginal young lady with a delicate profile. It was a present from the Soviet vice-minister for foreign trade, in thanks for a red meal invented especially for him:

Salmon Roes
Cold Borshch
Crayfish Cocktail
Fillet of Beef Carpaccio
Verona Salad
Steamed Edam
Salad of Three Red Fruits
Blackcurrant Charlotte

Pepper Vodka
Bouzy Rouge

CHAPTER NINETY-ONE

Basement, 5

Cellars. The Marquiseaux' cellar.

In the foreground can be seen a sectioned stack made of metal angle pieces containing cases of champagne with coloured stick-on labels depicting an old man holding out a narrow *flûte* to a nobleman in seventeenth-century dress followed by a large retinue: a tiny caption specifies that he is Dom Pérignon, cellarer at the abbey of Hautvillers, near Epernay, who, having discovered a way of making the wine of the Champagne region effervescent, is giving the result of his invention to Colbert to taste. Above these are cases of *Stanley's Delight* whisky: the label shows an explorer of white race, wearing a pith helmet but dressed in Scottish national dress: a predominantly yellow and red kilt, a broad tartan over his shoulder, a studded leather belt supporting a fringed sporran, and a small dirk slipped into his sock-top; he strides at the head of a column of 9 blacks each carrying on his head a case of *Stanley's Delight* with a label depicting the same scene.

In the background, to the rear, various objects and pieces of furniture that had belonged to the Echard parents: a rusty birdcage, a collapsible bidet, an old handbag with a chased clip incrusted with a topaz, a low table, and a jute sack spilling over with school exercise books, homework on squared paper, filing cards, file paper, spiral notebooks, kraft-paper dustcovers, press cuttings stuck on loose sheets, postcards (one showing the German Consulate at Melbourne), letters, and sixty-odd copies of a slim cyclostyled brochure entitled

CRITICAL BIBLIOGRAPHY
OF SOURCES RELATING TO THE
DEATH OF ADOLF HITLER
IN HIS BUNKER
ON APRIL 30, 1945

★★

first part: France

★

by
Marcelin ECHARD
sometime Head of Stack
at the Central Library, XVIIIth arrdt., Paris

Of all Marcelin Echard's monumental labours over the last fifteen years of his life, only this brochure was ever published. In it, the author subjects to harsh scrutiny every press announcement, statement, communiqué, book, etc. in the French language referring to Hitler's suicide, and demonstrates that they all derive from an implicit belief based on dispatches of unknown origin. The following six brochures, which got no further than card-index form, were to comb in the same critical spirit all the English, American, Russian, German, Italian, and other sources. After thus proving that it was not proven that Adolf Hitler (and Eva Braun) had died in their bunker on the thirtieth of April 1945, the author would have compiled a subsequent bibliography, as exhaustive as the first one, listing all the documentary evidence suggesting that Hitler had survived. Then, in a final work to be called *Hitler's Punishment. A Philosophical, Political, and Ideological Analysis*, Echard, shedding the strict objectivity of the Bibliographer to ride the faster steed of the Historian, would have got down to a study of the decisive impact of this survival on world history from 1945 to the present, in which he would have demonstrated how the infiltration of the highest echelons of national and supranational governmental spheres by individuals attached to Nazi ideals and manipulated by Hitler (John Foster Dulles, Cabot Lodge, Gromyko, Trygve Lie, Singhman Rhee, Attlee, Tito, Beria, Sir Stafford Cripps, Bao Daï, MacArthur, Coude du Foresto, Schuman, Bernadotte, Evita Perón, Gary Davis, Einstein, Humphrey, and Maurice Thorez, to mention only a few) had allowed the conciliatory and pacifist spirit laid out of the Yalta Conference to be sabotaged and had fomented an international crisis, a run-up to the Third World War which only the sang-froid of the Four Powers had managed to avert in February 1951.

Cellars. Madame Marcia's cellar.

An unbelievable tangle of furniture, objects, and trinkets, a jumble even more inextricable, it would appear, than the muddle reigning in the back room of her store.

Here and there a few more identifiable objects can be made out amongst the bric-a-brac: a goniometer, a type of articulated wooden protractor, said to have belonged to the astronomer Nicolas Kratzer; a *marinette* (the mariner's mate), a magnetised needle pointing to the north and supported by two straws floating on water in a half-full phial, a primitive instrument from which the compass proper, equipped with dial, did not emerge until three centuries later; a ship's desk, of English make, fully collapsible, presenting a whole assortment of drawers and flaps; a page from an old herbarium with several specimens of hawkweed (lobed hawkweed, *Hieracium pilosella*,

Hieracium aurantiacium, etc.) under a glass plate; an old peanut dispenser, still half-full, with a glass case inscribed with "EXTRA DELICIOUS GOURMET BRAND"; several coffee grinders; seventeen small gold fish with Sanskrit inscriptions; a whole stock of walking sticks and umbrellas; siphons; a weathervane topped by a pretty rusty rooster, a metal washhouse sign, an old tobacconist's carrot-shaped sign; several rectangular, painted biscuit tins: one has an imitation of Gérard's *Cupid and Psyche*; on another, a Venetian *fiesta*: masked figures dressed as marquises and marchionesses standing on a floodlit palazzo terrace cheer a brilliantly decorated gondola; in the foreground, perched on one of those painted wooden posts at which watercraft tie up, a little monkey looks on; on a third tin, entitled *Rêverie*, you can see a young couple sitting on a stone bench in a landscape of great trees and lawns; the young woman wears a white dress and a large pink hat and leans her head on the shoulder of her companion, a melancholy young man dressed in a fieldmouse–grey tuxedo and a frilly shirt; finally, on the shelving, there is a whole stack of old toys: children's musical instruments, saxophone, vibraphone, a tympani set consisting of a tom-tom drum and high-hat cymbals; building blocks, ludo, Pope Joan, petits-chevaux, and a dolls' bakery with a tin counter and cast-iron display cases with minuscule ring, round, and stick loaves. The baker's wife stands behind the counter, giving change to a lady with a little girl munching a croissant. To the left you can see the baker and his lad shovelling kneaded dough into the mouth of an oven whence painted flames emerge.

CHAPTER NINETY-TWO

Louvet, 3

The Louvets' kitchen. On the floor is a greenish mottled linoleum; on the walls, a washable flowery wallpaper. Along the whole right-hand wall stand "space-saving" devices on either side of a worktop: a waste-grinder sink, hotplates, a rotisserie, a fridge-freezer, a washing machine, and a dishwasher. A range of pots and pans, shelves and cupboards complete this model fitted kitchen. In the centre of the room stands a small oval table in Spanish rustic style with metal trim, surrounded by four rush-seated chairs. On the table there is a porcelain plate-warmer decorated with a picture of the three-master *Henriette*, under the command of Captain Louis Guion, entering Marseilles harbour (after an original watercolour by Antoine Roux senior, 1818), and two photographs in a twin leather mount: one depicts an old bishop giving his ring to be kissed by a very beautiful woman, dressed as a Greuze peasant, kneeling at his feet; the other, a small sepia print, portrays a young captain in the uniform of the Spanish–American war, with earnest candid eyes beneath a high, fine brow, and a full-lipped, sensitive mouth beneath the dark silky moustache.

Some years ago the Louvets had a big party in their flat and made such a racket that around three in the morning Madame Trévins, Madame Altamont, Madame de Beaumont, and even Madame Marcia, who after all does not usually bother about such things, having knocked at the revellers' door to no avail, ended up phoning the police. Two officers were dispatched to the scene, soon to be joined by an official locksmith, who let them in.

The kitchen was where they found the bulk of the guests, a dozen or so of them, improvising a concert of contemporary music conducted by the master of the house. He was dressed in a green-and-grey-striped dressing gown, with leather babouches on his feet and a conical lampshade for a hat, and sat astride a straw-seated chair, beating time with his left arm raised and his erect right index finger close to his lips, as he repeated, roughly every second and a half, trying to stop himself laughing: "softly softly catchee monkey, softee softee catchly monkly, softly softly catchee monkly", etc.

The musicians, slumped on a sofa which had no reason to be where it was or wallowing on cushions, performed to the conductor's gesticulations either by banging forks, ladles, and knives on diverse kitchen utensils, or by mimicking more or less successfully the sound of some instrument with their mouths. The most infuriating noises were those emitted by Madame Louvet, who sat in a veritable puddle banging two bottles of bubbly cider together until one or the other of the corks popped. Two guests seemed to be ignoring Louvet's instructions and were making their own contribution to the concert: one was playing continually with one of those toys known as "Jack-in-the-box", a golliwog head mounted on a powerful spring, which jumps out of the wooden cube in which it is loaded whenever opened; the other was slurping as noisily as he could a soup plate full of the kind of cottage cheese known in France as "silk-worker's brains".

The rest of the flat was virtually empty. There was no one in the living room, where a Françoise Hardy record (*C'est à l'amour auquel je pense*) carried on turning on the gramophone turntable. In the entrance hall, snuggled into a heap of coats and macintoshes, a ten-year-old child was fast asleep, still holding in his hands Contat and Rybalka's bulky essay on *Les Ecrits de Sartre*, open at page 88, concerning the original performance of *The Flies* at the Sarah Bernhardt Theatre, then called *Théâtre de la Cité*, on 3 June 1943. In the bathroom, two men indulged in the game known to American schoolkids as tick-tack-toe and to the Japanese as go-moku: they were playing without paper or pencil, directly on the floor tiles, respectively using as playing tokens the remains of some Hungarian-brand cigarettes from an overflowing ashtray and wilted petals torn from a bouquet of red tulips.

Apart from causing this nocturnal disturbance, the Louvets have not been very noticeable. He works in some bauxite (or maybe wolfram) business, and they are often away.

END OF PART FIVE

PART SIX

CHAPTER NINETY-THREE

Third Floor Right, 3

The third room in this ghost flat is empty. The walls, the floor, the ceiling, the skirting boards, and the doors are painted in black gloss. There is no furniture.

On the back wall hang twenty-one engraved steel plates of identical dimensions and uniformly rimmed with matt black metal beads. The steel plates are arranged in three rows of seven, one above the other; the leftmost on the top row depicts ants carrying a large crumb of gingerbread; the rightmost on the bottom row portrays a young woman squatting on a shingle beach, studying a stone bearing a fossil imprint; the nineteen intermediate etchings depict respectively:

a girl stringing cork stoppers to make a curtain;

a carpet-layer kneeling on a floor, taking measurements with a folding yardstick;

a starving composer in a garret feverishly scribbling an opera the title of which, *The White Wave*, is legible;

a prostitute with an ash-blonde kiss curl facing a gentleman wearing an Inverness cape;

three Peruvian Indians sitting on their heels, their bodies almost entirely hidden by their grey rough-cloth ponchos and with old felt hats pulled over their eyes, chewing coca;

a man in a nightcap, straight out of Labiche's *Italian Straw Hat*, taking a mustard foot-bath whilst leafing through the annual accounts for 1969 of the Upper Dogon Railway Company;

three women in a courtroom, at the witness box; one wears a low-corsaged opal dress, and elbow-length ivory gloves, a sable-trimmed brick-quilted dolman, a comb of brilliants and a panache of osprey in her hair; the second: a cap and coat of seal coney, wrapped up to the nose, scanning the scene through tortoiseshell quizzing glasses; the third in amazon costume, hard hat, jackboots cockspur-red, waistcoat, musketeer gauntlets with braided drums, long train held up, and hunting crop;

a portrait of Etienne Cabet, who founded a newspaper entitled *Le Populaire*, wrote the *Voyage en Icarie*, and attempted unsuccessfully to set up a communist colony in Iowa before his death in 1856;

two men in tuxedos sitting at a flimsy table playing cards; close scrutiny would show that the cards depict the same scenes as those depicted on the etchings;

a kind of long-tailed devil hauling a big round tray covered in mortar to the top of a ladder;

an Albanian brigand at the feet of a vamp draped in a white kimono with black polka dots;

a worker perched on the top of a scaffold, cleaning a great crystal chandelier;

an astrologer in a pointed hat and a long black robe spangled with silver-foil stars, pretending to look up through an obviously hollow tube;

a corps de ballet curtseying before a lord in the uniform of a colonel in the Hussars – silver-braided with dolman and boars'-hair sabretache;

pupils giving a gold watch to Claude Bernard, the physiologist, on his forty-seventh birthday;

a besmocked porter with his leather straps and regulation numberplate carrying two cabin trunks;

an old lady dressed in the fashions of the 1880s – lace coif, mittens on her hands – proffering fine grey apples on a large oval wicker tray;

a watercolourist with his easel on a little bridge over a narrow channel lined with oystermen's huts;

a handicapped beggar offering a cheap horoscope to the sole customer on a café terrace: it is a printed sheet bearing under the title *The Lilac* a branch of lilac as a background to two rings encircling respectively a ram and a crescent moon pointing to the right.

CHAPTER NINETY-FOUR

On the Stairs, 12

Draft Inventory of some of the things found on the stairs over the years

(second and final instalment)

25 A set of "Fact Sheets" on dairy farming in the Poitou-Charentes region,

a macintosh bearing the brand name "Caliban" made in London by Hemmings & Condell,

six varnished cork glass-mats portraying the sights of Paris: the Elysée palace, Parliament House, the Senate Building, Notre-Dame, the Law Courts, and the Invalides,

a necklace made from the spine of an alosa,

a photograph taken by a second-rate professional of a naked baby lying prone on a sky-blue tasselled nylon cushion,

a rectangular piece of card, about the size of a visiting card, printed on one side: *Have you ever seen the Devil with a nightcap on?* and on the other side: *No! I've never seen the Devil with a nightcap on!*

a programme for the *Caméra* cinema, 70 Rue de l'Assomption, Paris 16, for the month of February 1960:

3 – 9: *The Criminal Life of Archibaldo de la Cruz,* BY LUIS BUÑUEL

10 –16: JACQUES DEMY FESTIVAL: *Le Bel Indifférent,* ADAPTED FROM COCTEAU, AND *Lola,* WITH ANOUK AIMÉE.

17 –23: *Don't Give Up the Ship,* BY GORDON DOUGLAS, WITH JERRY LEWIS.

24 – March 1 : CONTEMPORARY HUNGARIAN CINEMA: A FILM A DAY; ON 26 FEBRUARY, THE WORLD PREMIERE ATTENDED BY THE DIRECTOR OF *Nem szükséges, hogy kilépj a házból*, BY GABOR PELOS.

a packet of nappy pins,

a well-worn copy of *If You're So Funny Why Don't You Laugh?*, a collection of three thousand puns by Jean-Paul Grousset, opened at the chapter entitled 'At the Printer's';

> See Naples and Didot
> There's nothing a printer can't justify
> Good morning, serif!
> Inset information is worth its weight in bold

a goldfish in a plastic bag half-full of water, hung on Madame de Beaumont's doorhandle,

a weekly season ticket for the inner circle (PC) rail line,

a small, square, black Bakelite powder box with white dots, with an undamaged mirror but missing powder and puff,

an educational postcard in the *Great American Writers* series, N° 57: Mark Twain

Mark Twain, whose real name was Samuel Langhorne Clemens, was born in 1835 at Florida, Missouri. He lost his father at the age of twelve. He was apprenticed to a printer and became a pilot on the Mississippi where he gained the nickname Mark Twain (an expression meaning literally "mark twice", calling on the sailor to measure the draught of water with a plumbline). He was subsequently a soldier, a miner in Nevada, a gold digger, and a journalist. He travelled to Polynesia, Europe, and the Mediterranean, visited the Holy Land, and, disguised as an Afghani, went on pilgrimage to the holy cities of Arabia. He died at Reading (Connecticut) in 1910, and his death coincided with the reappearance of Halley's Comet, which had also marked his birth. A few years before, he read in a newspaper that he had died and cabled the editor straightaway with the message: NEWS OF MY DEATH HIGHLY EXAGGERATED! *Nonetheless, money worries, the death of his wife and of one of his daughters, and the mental illness of his other daughter, darkened the last years of this humorist and gave his later works an unaccustomed gravity. Principal works:* The Celebrated Jumping Frog of Calaveras County *(1867)*, The Innocents Abroad *(1869)*, Roughing It *(1872)*, The Gilded Age *(1873)*, The Adventures of Tom Sawyer *(1875)*, The Prince and the Pauper *(1882)*, Life on the Mississippi *(1883)*, The Adventures of Huckleberry Finn *(1885)*, A Yankee at the Court of King Arthur *(1889)*, Personal Recollections of Joan of Arc *(1896)*, What is Man? *(1906)*, The Mysterious Stranger *(1916)*.

seven marble lozenges, four black and three white, laid out on the third-floor landing so as to make the position called *Ko* or *Eternity* in the game of go:

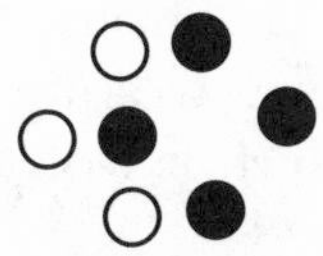

a cylindrical box, wrapped in paper from *The Gay Musketeers* toy and games shop, 95[a] Avenue de Friedland, Paris; the packaging depicted, as was only right and proper, Aramis, d'Artagnan, Athos, and Porthos crossing their brandished swords ("All for one and one for all!"). The packet carried no indication of an addressee when Madame Nochère found it on the doormat of the then empty flat occupied later by Geneviève Foulerot. After checking that the anonymous packet did not make any suspicious ticking noises, Madame Nochère opened it and found it contained several hundred little bits of gilded wood and imitation tortoiseshell plastic which, when appropriately assembled, were supposed to constitute a faithful reproduction at one-third life-size of the water clock presented to Charlemagne by Haroun al-Rashid. None of the inhabitants of the building claimed the object. Madame Nochère took it back to the shop. The sales ladies recalled that they had sold this rare and expensive scale model to a ten-year-old child; they had been very surprised to see him pay for it with one-hundred-franc notes. The enquiry was carried no further, and the puzzle was never solved.

CHAPTER NINETY-FIVE

Rorschach, 6

On the bedside table in Rémi Rorschach's bedroom there is an antique lamp with a base made of a silvered-metal candle-trimmer; a cylindrical cigarette lighter; a tiny polished-steel alarm clock; and, in an over-elaborate wooden frame, four photographs of Olivia Norvell.

In the first image, taken at the time of her first marriage, Olivia makes her appearance dressed in pirate's trousers and a no doubt blue and white horizontally striped jersey, wearing a middy's cap and holding a deck-swab in her hand which it would have been pointless, no doubt, to ask her to use.

In the second she is wallowing on a lawn, flat on her front, beside another young woman; Olivia is wearing a flowery dress and rice-straw hat, her companion is in Bermudas and big sunglasses with frames made to look like Michaelmas daisies; at the bottom of the snap, the words *Greetings from the Appalachians* are written above the signature: *Bea*.

The third photograph shows Olivia dressed up as a Renaissance princess: a brocade robe, a big cloak with fleur-de-lys motifs, a diadem; Olivia is posing in front of flats on which technicians are using jumbo staplers to fix up shiny panels decorated with heraldic emblems; the photograph dates from the period when Olivia Norvell had given up all filming, even semi-advertising shorts, and was hoping to go back to stage acting: she decided to use the alimony paid her by her second husband to back a show in which she would be the star, and her choice alighted upon *Love's Labour's Lost*; reserving the role of the daughter of the King of France for herself, she handed the production over to a young man with romantic airs, a man bubbling with ideas and inventions, by the name of Vivian Belt, whom she had met a few days before in London. Critics turned up their noses; a snide and witless diary-columnist wondered if the noise of the seats hitting the backrests was part of the sound effects. The production ran for only three nights, but Olivia consoled herself by marrying Vivian, whom she had meantime discovered to be wealthy and a Lord, and about whom she had not yet discovered that he went to bed and took his bath with his curly-haired spaniel.

The fourth photograph was taken in Rome, in full noonday sun at the height of the summer, in front of *Stazione Termini*: Rémi Rorschach and Olivia are going by on a Vespa scooter; he is driving, wearing a light short-sleeved shirt and white trousers, shod in white rope-soled espadrilles, his eyes shaded by black spectacles in circular gold frames like those American army officers used to wear; she is in shorts, an embroidered blouse, and slave sandals, and hangs on to him with her right arm round his waist whilst waving to invisible admirers with a grand gesture of her left hand.

Rémi Rorschach's bedroom is impeccably tidy, made up as if its occupant were coming to sleep there that very night. But it will stay empty. No one will enter it again, ever, leaving aside Jane Sutton who will come, every morning, for a few minutes, to air the room and throw onto the large Moroccan beaten-brass tray the producer's mail, all those professional publications he subscribed to – *French Cinematography*, *Film Technician*, *Film and Sound*, *TV News*, *Le Nouveau Film Français*, *Film Daily*, *Image et Son*, etc. – all those papers he liked nothing better than to flick through while muttering curses as he ate his breakfast, and which henceforth will heap up with uncut wrappers, amassing their out-of-date box-office listings to the end. The bedroom is already a dead man's room, and furniture, objects, and knickknacks already seem to be awaiting this coming death with polished indifference, standing in their proper places, properly clean, fixed for all time in impersonal silence: the bedspread turned down perfectly; the little Empire-style claw-foot low table; the olivewood bowl still holding a few foreign coins, pfennigs, pennies, groschen; and a packet of matches presented by Fribourg and Treyer, Tobacconists & Cigar Merchants, 34, Haymarket, London SW1; the very fine cut-glass tumbler; the burnt-coffee dressing gown, hanging on a turned-wood coatstand; and, to the right of the bed, the copper and mahogany clothes horse with its curved jacket hanger, its patent trouser press giving a permanent crease, its belt strap, its fold-away tie-rack and honeycomb tidy tray into which every evening Rémi Rorschach conscientiously emptied his key-pouch and his small change from his jacket pocket and tidied away his cuff links, his handkerchief, his wallet, his pocket diary, his chronometer watch, and his pen.

This now dead room was the lounge-dining room of almost four generations of Gratiolets: Juste, Emile, François, and Olivier lived here from the end of the eighteen eighties to the early nineteen fifties.

The concessions for Rue Simon-Crubellier were first allocated after 1875 on land belonging, for one part, to a timber merchant named Samuel Simon and, for the other part, to a Norbert Crubellier, a hirer of hansom cabs. Their immediate neighbours – Guyot Roussel, the animal-painter Godefroy Jadin, and De Chazelles, the nephew and heir of Madame de Rumford, who was none other than Lavoisier's widow – had begun to build long before, taking advantage of the construction permits allocated to the area surrounding the Monceau Gardens, which were to make the neighbourhood an area favoured by the artists and painters of the period. But Simon and Crubellier did not believe in the residential future of a suburb still largely given over to small trades, full of washhouses, dye works, workshops, warehouses, storerooms of all kinds, factories and small plant, such as Monduit and Béchet's Foundry at 25 Rue de Chazelles, where the restoration work on the Vendôme column was carried out and where, from 1883, Bartholdi's gigantic Liberty would rise, section by section, with a head and arms reaching higher than the roofs of the surrounding buildings for over a year. So Simon was content to fence his land and claimed there would always be time to parcel it out for building when there was a demand for it, and on his land Crubellier put up a few clapboard huts where he had his worst cabs botched up; the neighbourhood was almost completely built up before the two landowners finally grasped where their true interests lay and decided to cut the road which has borne their name ever since.

Juste Gratiolet had been doing business with Simon for some time already, and he immediately put himself down for a parcel of land.

The same architect, Lubin Auzère, sometime winner of the celebrated Prix de Rome, built all the blocks on the odd-numbered side, the even side being entrusted to his son, Noël: they were both decent architects, but without imagination, who built virtually identical blocks: ashlar façades, the rear side having wooden facing panels, with balconies on the second and fifth floors and two floors of attics, one under the eaves.

Juste Gratiolet himself lived in the building very little. He preferred his farm in Berry and, for stays in Paris, a bungalow he rented at Levallois. Nonetheless, he reserved some of the apartments for himself and for his children. He fitted out his own dwelling with extreme simplicity: a bedroom with an alcove, a dining room with a fireplace – these two rooms floorboarded in the English style, thanks to the grooving machine he had just patented – and a big kitchen floored with hexagonal tiles which created an illusion of cubes that could be looked at from two different angles. There was piped water in the kitchen; gas and electricity were not put in until much later.

No one in the building ever knew Juste Gratiolet, but several tenants – Mademoiselle Crespi, Madame Albin, Valène – remember his son Emile very clearly. He was a man with a harsh look and a worried face, which is hardly surprising if you think of the troubles he had as the eldest of the four Gratiolet children. He was only known to have two pleasures in life: playing the pipes – he had been a member of the city pipe and drum band at Levallois, but all he could remember how to play was *Le Gai Laboureur*, which tended to get on his audience's nerves – and listening to the radio: the only luxury he ever allowed himself in all his life was the purchase of an ultramodern wireless set: beside the dial bearing the exotic and mysterious names of broadcasting stations – Hilversum, Sottens, Allouis, Vatican, Kerguélen, Monte Ceneri, Bergen, Tromsö, Bari, Tangiers, Falun, Horby, Beromünster, Puzzoli, Muscat, Amara – a disc lit up, and four orthogonal beams coming from a luminous centre point shrank as the set tuned in progressively to the required wavelength, until they were nothing more than an ultrathin cross.

François, the son of Emile and Jeanne, was not a very jovial man either; a long-limbed creature with a thin nose and short sight, who suffered premature balding and gave off an impression of sometimes almost poignant melancholy. Unable to live solely on the income the building produced, he took a job as an accountant with a wholesale tripe dealer. He sat in a glass-walled office overlooking the shop and entered his columns of figures with no distraction other than watching butchers in bloody aprons doling out heaps of calves' heads, lungs, spleens, ruffles, tongues, and necks. He, for his part, hated offal, and found its smell so fetid that he almost fainted every morning when he had to cross the main hall to get to his office. These daily trials certainly did nothing to improve his humour, but for some years allowed those in the building who liked kidneys, livers, and sweetbreads to obtain top-class supplies at rock-bottom prices.

None of the Gratiolet furniture remains in the two-roomed flat Olivier has converted for himself and his daughter on the seventh floor. For lack of space in the first place, and then for need of money, he disposed of the furniture piece by piece, as well as the carpets, the tableware, and the trinkets. The four things he sold last were four large drawings which Marthe, François's wife, had inherited from a distant cousin, an enterprising Swiss who had made a fortune during the First World War by buying carloads of garlic and bargefuls of condensed milk and reselling trainloads of onions and holds full of Gruyère cream cheese, orange concentrate, and pharmaceutical products.

The first drawing, signed Perpignani, was called *The Dancer with Gold Coins*: the dancer, a Berber girl wearing brightly coloured clothing, with a snake tattooed on her right forearm, dances amongst the gold coins thrown by the crowd around her;

the second was a meticulous copy of *The Crusaders' Entry at Constantinople*, signed by someone called Florentin Dufay, who is known to have been a regular visitor to Delacroix's studio for a while, but who left very few works;

the third was a large landscape after the taste of Hubert Robert: in the background, Roman ruins; in the foreground, to the right, young girls, one of whom carries on her head a large, almost flat basket full of Agen plums;

the fourth and last was a study in pastels by Joseph Ducreux for his portrait of the violinist Beppo. This virtuoso, who was extremely popular throughout the Revolutionary period ("I shalla playa violina", he replied when he was asked, during the Terror, how he intended to serve the Nation), had come to France at the beginning of the reign of Louis XVI. His ambition then was to be appointed King's Violinist, but Louis Guéné was the one chosen. Racked by jealousy, Beppo dreamt of outshining his rival in everything: on learning that François Dumont had just painted a miniature on ivory portraying Guéné, Beppo rushed to Joseph Ducreux and commissioned his own portrait. The painter accepted, but it soon turned out that this fiery instrumentalist was incapable of holding a pose for more than a few seconds; the miniaturist tried to work in the presence of this voluble and excitable model who kept interrupting him every minute, but soon decided he would rather quit, and there remains from the commission only this preparatory sketch in which the unkempt Beppo, with his eyes upturned, holding his violin firmly and with his bow at the ready, is apparently striving to look even more inspired than his enemy.

CHAPTER NINETY-SIX

Dinteville, 3

The bathroom adjacent to Dr Dinteville's bedroom. At the rear, through a half-open door, you can see a bed with a tartan cover, a black, varnished wooden chest of drawers, and an upright piano with an open score on its music stand: a transcription of Hans Neusiedler's *Dances*. At the foot of the bed lies a pair of clogs; on the chest of drawers, a bulky work in a white leather binding, Alexandre Dumas's *Great Dictionary of Cooking*, and, in a glass bowl, crystallography models, minutely sculpted pieces of wood representing some of the holohedral and hemihedral shapes of crystalline systems: the straight prism on a hexagonal base; the oblique prism on a rhombus base; the pointed cube; the cubo-octahedron; the cubo-dodecahedron; the rhomboid dodecahedron; the pyramidal hexagonal prism. Above the bed hangs a picture signed D. Bidou: it portrays a very young girl, lying in a meadow, flat on her front, shelling peas; beside her, a little dog – a long-eared, long-nosed Artois beagle – sits panting, with the look of a good dog.

The bathroom floor has hexagonal tiles; the walls have rectangular white tiles up to shoulder height, the remainder being hung with a light yellow washable wallpaper with sea-green stripes. Beside the bath, which is half hidden by a rather dirty white nylon shower curtain, stands a wrought-iron jardinière containing a few sickly sprouts of a green plant with delicately yellow-veined leaves. On the washbasin splashback various accessories and toiletries can be seen: a razor of the cut-throat variety, in a shark-skin sheath, a nailbrush, a pumice stone, and a bottle of hair-restorer on the label of which a hirsute, guffawing, and big-bellied Falstaff character displays advantageously an exaggeratedly bushy red beard beneath the gaze, more astounded than amused, of two merry wives whose bosoms spill out of slack-laced corsages. On the towel rail beside the sink a dark-blue pyjama trouser has been carelessly thrown.

Dr Dinteville received an absolutely standard upbringing and education: a boring, properly looked-after childhood with a touch of something sinister as well as something shameful, medical school at Caen, medics' pranks, military service at the Navy Hospital at Toulon, a thesis written up at top speed by ill-paid hack students on *Dyspneic Frequencies in Fallot's Tetralogy. Etiological Considerations on Seven Observations*, a few locum jobs until, in the late nineteen fifties, he took over a general practice which his predecessor had served for forty-seven years without a break.

Dinteville was not an ambitious man, and he was quite content with the notion of becoming just a good small-town doctor, a man everyone in the little place would call Good Old Dr Dinteville just as they had called his predecessor Good Old Dr Raffin, and whose patients would be relieved just to hear him say "Say Aah". But about two years after he moved to Lavaur, a chance discovery altered the tranquil course of his life. One day, as he was taking up to the loft some old volumes of *La Presse Médicale* which good old Dr Raffin had judged desirable to keep and which he himself couldn't allow to be thrown away – as if there were still things to be learned from these volumes with their collapsed bindings, going back to the twenties and thirties – Dinteville found in a trunk of old family papers a nicely bound booklet in 16° format entitled *De structura renum*, and whose author was one of his ancestors, Rigaud de Dinteville, surgeon ordinary to the Princess Palatine, a man famous for his skill in operations on gallstones, which he did with a little blunt-pointed knife of his own invention. Summoning the remnants of his school Latin, Dinteville skimmed through the work and found sufficiently interesting things in it to bring it down to his office, together with an old edition of Gaffiot's Latin dictionary.

De structura renum was an anatomico-physiological description of the kidneys based on dissections using colouring techniques which were completely new for the period: by injecting a black liquid – wine spirits mixed with Indian ink – into the *arteria emulgens* (renal artery), Rigaud de Dinteville had observed the whole ramified system changing colour, from the canaliculi, which he called *ductae renum*, to what he called the *glandulae renales*. These discoveries, made independently of the work being done in the same period by Lorenzo Bellini in Florence, Marcello Malpighi in Bologna, and Frederyk Ruysch at Leiden, but similarly prefiguring the theory of glomerulus as the basis of renal function, were accompanied by an explanation of the secreting mechanisms based on the presence of humours attracted or repelled by the organs according to the organism's need for assimilation or elimination. A sharp and sometimes even violent dispute set this Galenist theory of "vital forces" against the harmful doctrines of "atomist" and "materialist" inspiration as propounded by someone called Bombastinus, a pseudonym under which the present-day Dinteville eventually identified a Burgundian doctor of more or less alchemical persuasion who was also a supporter of Paracelsius, by the name of Lazare Meyssonier. The reasons for these polemics were far from clear to this twentieth-century reader, who could imagine only very roughly what Galen's theories had stood for, and to whom terms like "atomist" and "materialist" certainly did not mean what they had meant to his distant ancestor. Nonetheless Dinteville was excited by his discovery, which aroused his imagination and awoke his dormant, secret vocation for research. And so he decided to compile a critical edition of this text which, even if it contained nothing of truly major importance, provided an excellent example of medical thought as it was at the dawn of modern times.

On the advice of one of his former teachers, Dinteville submitted his project to Professor LeBran-Chastel, a consultant at the Hôtel-Dieu hospital, Member of the Academy of Medicine, Member of the Medical Association Board, and a member of the editorial boards of several internationally known reviews. Alongside his activities as a clinician and as a teacher, Professor LeBran-Chastel was keenly interested in the history of science, but he received Dinteville with friendliness mixed with scepticism: he did not know the *De structura renum*, but he doubted whether its resuscitation held any real interest: everything from Galen to Vesalius, from Barthélemy Eustache to Bowman had been published, translated, and annotated at length, and in 1901, Paolo Ceneri, a librarian at the Medical Faculty at Bologna, where Malpighi's manuscripts were kept, had even published a four-hundred-page bibliography dealing solely with the theoretical problems of uropoïesis and uroscopy. Of course, it was still possible, as Dinteville's experience showed, to come across previously unpublished texts, and of course one could imagine making advances in our understanding of ancient medical theories, correcting the often rather rigid assertions of nineteenth-century epistemologists who, with the supreme confidence born of scientific positivism, had seen value in experimental approaches alone and had swept aside everything else which seemed, to them, irrational. But a project of that sort was a long-term undertaking, a thankless, difficult job fraught with traps, and the professor wondered whether the young practitioner, unfamiliar as he was with the archaising jargon of the older medical writers or with the strange aberrations their commentators had occasionally ascribed to them, would be able to deal with it successfully. Nonetheless, he promised to give him his help, provided a few letters of introduction to foreign colleagues, and offered to read his results before supporting their publication, if appropriate.

* * *

Dinteville was encouraged by this initial interview and set to work, spending evenings, Saturdays, and Sundays on research and using even the shortest breaks he could take without neglecting his patients too much for trips to one foreign library or another, not just to Bologna, where he quickly discovered that more than half the entries in Paolo Ceneri's bibliography were erroneous, but also to Bodley at Oxford, to Aarhus, to Salamanca, to Prague, Dresden, Basel, etc. He kept Professor LeBran-Chastel informed of the progress of his investigations at regular intervals, and, at much longer intervals, the professor responded with laconic notes which seemed to express continuing doubts about the interest of what he called Dinteville's "little finds". But the young doctor was not to be discouraged for all that: over and above the groping complexity of his research, each one of his minute discoveries – an implausible vestige here, a doubtful reference there, ambiguous evidence everywhere – seemed to him to be destined to fit into a project that was unique, global, and almost grandiose; and his enthusiasm was renewed every time he started on unearthings, as he hunted at random through shelves collapsing under vellum bindings, following the alphabetical order of vanished alphabets, up and down halls, stairs, bridges cluttered with newspapers tied up in string, archive boxes, and bundles of documents almost completely eaten away by worms.

It took him four years to complete his work: a manuscript of over three hundred sides, of which the edition and translation of the *De structura renum* proper took up only sixty; the rest of the work consisted of critical material, including 33 pages of notes and variants, sixty pages of bibliography, one-third of which listed errata to the Ceneri, and an introduction of nearly one hundred and fifty pages in which Dinteville recounted, at an almost spanking pace, the story of the long struggle between Galen and Asclepiades, showing how the doctor of Pergamos had misrepresented, in order to ridicule them, the atomist theories which Asclepiades had brought to Rome three centuries before and which his followers, the ones called "Methodists", had followed perhaps too pedantically; but in stigmatising the mechanistic and sophist underpinning of this school of thought, in the name of experimentation and the sacrosanct principle of "natural forces", Galen had in fact inaugurated a causalistic, diachronic, and homogenist tradition, all the faults of which reared their heads again in the classical age of physiology and medicine, and which had ended up functioning, in a way exactly analogous to Freudian repression, as a censorship device. Using a framework of formal oppositions such as organic/organistic, sympathetic/empathetic, humours/fluids, hierarchy/structure, etc., Dinteville illuminated the subtlety and pertinence of Asclepiades' notions, and of Eresistrates' and Lycos of Macedon's before him, showed their relationship to the main trends of Indo-Arabic medical thought, stressed their connections with Jewish mysticism, hermeticism, and alchemy, and finally demonstrated how official medicine had systematically repressed diffusion of these ideas until men like Goldstein, Grodeck, and King Dri had managed to get a hearing and, by bringing to light the subterranean current which had continuously flowed through the world of science from Paracelsius to Fourier, had raised far-reaching doubts about the very foundations of medical physiology and semiology.

Barely had the typist (brought over specially from Toulouse) finished typing this difficult text sprouting with cross-references, footnotes, and Greek characters, than Dinteville mailed a copy to LeBran-Chastel; the professor sent it back one month after: he had studied the doctor's work with care, without partiality and without malice, and his conclusion was firmly negative: to be sure, the editing of Rigaud de Dinteville's text had been done with a thoroughness which honoured his descendant, but the treatise of the surgeon ordinary of the Princess Palatine added nothing very new in comparison to Eustache's *Tractatio de renibus*, Lorenzo Bellini's *De structura et usu renum*, Etienne Blancard's *De natura renum*, and Malpighi's *De renibus*, and did not seem to merit separate publication; the critical material bore witness to the young researcher's immaturity: he had tried too hard, and had succeeded only in overloading his text to an excessive degree; the errata on Ceneri were quite irrelevant to the issue, and the author would have done better to check his own notes and references (followed by a list of fifteen errors or omissions which LeBran-Chastel had had the kindness to note down: for instance,

Dinteville had written *J. Clin. Invest.* instead of *J. clin. Invest.* in reference No. 10 [Möller, McIntosh & van Slyke], and had cited the article by H. Wirz in *Mod. Prob. Pädiat. 6*, 86, 1960, without referring to the prior study by Wirz, Hargitay & Kuhn published in *Helv. physiol. pharmacol. Acta 9*, 196, 1951); as for the historico-philosophical introduction, the professor preferred to leave it to Dinteville's sole responsibility, and for his own part refused to take any action whatsoever which might lead to its publication.

Dinteville was ready for anything except a reaction of this kind. Though convinced of the pertinence of his own research, he did not dare question the intellectual honesty or the competence of Professor LeBran-Chastel. After several weeks of dithering, he decided he ought not to give way to the hostile views of a man who, after all, was not his boss, and that he should try to have his manuscript published by his own efforts; he corrected the trivial errors in it and sent it to several specialist journals. They all turned him down, and Dinteville was obliged to give up trying to publish his work, abandoning by the same token all his research ambitions.

The excessive interest he had taken in his investigation, to the detriment of his daily work as a medical practitioner, had done him considerable harm. Two family doctors had set up in Lavaur after him and, over the months and years, had filched nearly all his patients. With no support, abandoned, disgusted, Dinteville finally gave up his practice and came to settle in Paris, determined to be only a local doctor whose harmless dreams would no more offend the prestigious but fearsome world of scholarship and learning, but would be confined instead to the domestic pleasures of making music and good food.

Over the following years, Professor LeBran-Chastel, Member of the Academy of Medicine, published in succession:

- an article on the life and work of Rigaud de Dinteville (*A French Urologist at the Court of Louis XIV: Rigaud de Dinteville, Arch. Intern. Hist. Sci.* 11, 343, 1962);

– a critical edition of the *De structura renum*, with a facsimile reproduction, translation, notes, and glossary (S. Karger, Basel, 1963);
– a critical supplement to Ceneri's *Bibliografica urologica (Int. Z. f. Urol. Suppl. 9*, 1964); and lastly
– an epistemological article entitled "A sketch history of renal theories from Asclepiades to William Bowman", published in *Aktuelle Probleme aus der Geschichte der Medizin* (Basel, 1966), a revised version of his opening report to the XIXth International Congress on the History of Medicine (Basel, 1964), which raised a considerable stir.

The critical edition of the *De structura* and the supplement to the Ceneri bibliography were purely and simply copied down to the last comma from Dinteville's manuscript. The other two pieces, which were also lifted directly and watered down by various rhetorical and precautionary insertions, cited the good doctor only once, in the very small print of a footnote where Professor LeBran-Chastel thanked "Dr Bernard Dinteville for having been so kind as to communicate his ancestor's work to [him]".

CHAPTER NINETY-SEVEN

Hutting, 4

Hutting has not used his great studio for a long time now, as he prefers the intimacy of the smaller room he had converted on the gallery level for painting his portraits and has acquired the habit of working at his other pieces, according to their genre, in one or another of his other studios: large-scale canvases at Gattières, in the hills behind Nice, monumental sculptures in the Dordogne, drawings and prints in New York.

All the same, his Paris *salon* was for many years a hub of intense artistic activity. That is where Hutting's famous "Tuesday Group" gathered between '55 and '60, where artists and artistes as diverse as the poster-designer Félicien Kohn, the Belgian baritone Léo van Derckx, the Italian Martiboni, the Spanish "verbalist" Tortosa, the photographer Arpad Sarafian, and the saxophonist Estelle Thierarch' first made their names, and whose influence on some of the major trends in contemporary art has by no means run its full course yet.

It was not Hutting who first had the idea of the Tuesdays, but his Canadian friend Grillner, who had successfully organised similar events at Winnipeg directly after the end of the Second World War. The principle of such gatherings was to bring creators together in free confrontation and see how they would influence each other. Thus on the first of these "Tuesdays" Grillner and Hutting took turns every three minutes at painting the same canvas, as if they were playing each other at chess, before an audience of fifteen or so attentive onlookers. But the recipe for the sessions soon became much more sophisticated, and artists working in quite different fields were brought in: a painter painted whilst a jazz musician improvised, or a poet, a musician, and a dancer would each give his own interpretation in his own idiom of a work presented to them by a sculptor or a dress-designer.

The first sessions were well-behaved, conscientious, and very slightly boring. Then, with the arrival of Vladislav the painter, they took a much livelier turn.

Vladislav was a painter who had had his hour of glory at the end of the nineteen thirties. The first time he came to one of Hutting's "Tuesdays" he was dressed as a muzhik. On his head he wore a kind of scarlet bonnet made of very fine cloth, with a fur rim all around, except in the front, where a small gap of a few inches revealed a lightly embroidered sky-blue background; and he was smoking Turkish tobacco-pipes with a flexible tube of morocco leather and gold wire, mounted at its end with black ebony tipp'd with silver. He began by telling how on a stormy day in Brittany he had practised necrophilia and how he could only paint if his feet were bare and if he had a handkerchief soaked in absinthe to sniff and how after summer rain in the country he would sit in tepid mud to get back in touch with Mother Nature and how he ate raw meat macerated in the Magyar manner which gave it incomparable savour. Then he spread a great roll of blank canvas on the floor, hurriedly put in a score of nails to hold it flat, and invited the gathering to trample on it all together. The result, whose indeterminate shades of grey were somewhat reminiscent of the "diffuse greys" of Laurence Hapi's last period, was immediately baptised *Man with Sole Out*. Bedazzled, all present decided Vladislav would be henceforth the gatherings' appointed master of ceremonies, and all left with the certain feeling that they had helped to give birth to a masterpiece.

The following Tuesday it did indeed seem that Vladislav had done things properly. He had rounded up everyone who was anyone in Paris, and there were more than one hundred and fifty of them cramming the studio. A huge canvas had been stapled to the three walls of the big room (the fourth wall was formed by a tall glass screen), and several dozen buckets, with decorators' paint brushes soaking in them, were arranged in the centre of the room. At Vladislav's command, the guests lined up along the glass screen and, at a signal he gave, rushed to the paint pots, grabbed the brushes, and hurried to daub their contents as fast as they could onto the canvas. The resulting work was considered interesting, but it did not really capture the unanimous support of its scratch creators, and despite his continuous efforts, week after week, to demonstrate his inventiveness, Vladislav's vogue was short-lived.

In the ensuing months his place was taken by a child prodigy, a lad of twelve or so, who looked like a fashion plate, with curly hair, big lace ruffs, and black velvet waistcoats with mother-of-pearl buttons. He improvised "metaphysical poems" whose titles alone took his listeners' breath away:

Evaluation of the situation
Enumeration of things and beings lost on the way
Sort of summing up
Clip clop horses unsaddled grazing in the dark
Red glow of campfire under the starry sky

But alas one day it was realised that it was his mother who composed – or, more often, copied – these poems, which she forced her son to learn by heart.

Then came a mystical labourer; a striptease star; a tie-seller; a sculptor describing himself as neo-renascent who took several months to extract a work entitled *Chimaera* from a lump of marble (a few weeks later a worrying crack appeared in the ceiling of the flat below, and Hutting had to have it repaired and to replace his own woodblock floor); the director of an art review, a follower of Christo who wrapped small live animals in nylon sachets; a popular café singer who called everyone "Handsome"; a chap who ran a talent-spotting show on radio, a thickset lad with a houndstooth waistcoat, kiss curls, chunky rings, and novelty charms, who did impressions, using his voice and his body and with intonations and movements worthy of a wrestling commentator, of the dancers and musicians on his show; an advertising executive into yoga who tried in vain for three weeks to initiate the other guests into his art by making them do the lotus position in the centre of the great studio; the proprietress of a pizzeria, a silky-voiced Italian, who sang Verdi arias with absolute poise whilst improvising sublimely scrumptious spaghetti dishes; and the ex-director of a minor zoo who had trained fox terriers to jump through hoops backwards and ducks to run rings, and who set up in the studio with a juggling walrus which ate horrifying quantities of fish.

The fashion for happenings which began to invade Paris towards the end of that period gradually robbed these society events of their principal interest. The journalists and photographers who had been assiduous attenders at the start came to find them just a bit old hat and to prefer wilder sprees at which Mr X would have a ball munching light bulbs whilst A. N. Other systematically dismantled the central heating system and Muggins slashed his wrists so as to write poetry in his own blood. Moreover Hutting made no effort to keep them: he had eventually seen that he was largely bored at his parties and that they had never done anything for him. In 1961, on his return from a stay in New York that he had prolonged more than was his custom, he informed his friends that he was giving up the weekly gatherings whose predictability had made them wearisome, and that it was time to invent something else.

Since then, the great studio has almost always been empty. But, maybe out of superstition, Hutting has left plenty of equipment in it and, on a steel easel lit by four ceiling spots, a large canvas, entitled *Eurydice*, which he likes to say is and always will be unfinished.

The canvas portrays an empty room, painted grey, virtually empty of furniture. In the centre, a metallic grey desk on which lie a handbag, a bottle of milk, a diary, and a book open at the twin portraits of Racine and Shakespeare[1]. On the rear wall there hangs a picture of a landscape with a setting sun. To the side, a door ajar, through which, one surmises, Eurydice, just a few seconds before, has disappeared for ever.

CHAPTER NINETY-EIGHT

Réol, 2

Shortly after moving into Rue Simon-Crubellier, the Réols set their hearts on a modern bedroom suite which they had seen in the department store where Louise Réol worked as an invoice clerk. The bed alone cost 3,234 francs. With its bedspread, bedside tables, dressing table, matching pouf, and mirrored wardrobe, the suite came to over eleven thousand francs. The store management gave its employee a preferential credit arrangement with no deposit and twenty-four months to pay; interest on the loan was charged at a rate of 13.65%, but taking account of the arrangement fee, the life-insurance premium, and the capital repayments, the Réols found they had a monthly outgoing of nine hundred and forty-one francs and thirty-two centimes, deducted at source from Louise Réol's pay

[1] It may be useful to mention in connection with this that Franz Hutting's maternal great-grandfather, Johannes Martenssen, professor of French literature at the University of Copenhagen, was the Danish translator of Stendhal's *Racine et Shakespeare* (København, Gjoerup Publishers, 1860).

cheque. That represented nigh on one-third of the couple's income, and it soon became clear they could not survive decently on those terms. Maurice Réol, who was a junior executive officer at MATRASCO (Maritime Transportation Assurance Company) thus resolved to ask his head of department for a raise.

MATRASCO was a company suffering from elephantiasis whose acronym no longer corresponded more than marginally to its activities, which had become ever more numerous and polymorphous. For his part, Réol was responsible for producing a comparative report each month on the number of policies and the amount of the premiums written for public bodies in the Northern area of France. These reports, like those which Réol's colleagues of equivalent rank produced on different geographical or economic areas (insurances written for farmers, for traders, for the professions, etc., in West-Central France, the Rhône-alps region, Brittany, etc.) were fed into the quarterly reports of the "Statistics and Forecasts" section which Réol's head of department, a certain Armand Faucillon, submitted to the managing directors on the second Thursday of March, June, September, and December.

In principle Réol saw his head of department every day between eleven and eleven thirty during what was called the Executive Conference, but that, obviously, was not a setting in which he could hope to approach him to talk over his particular problem. Anyway the head of department usually got his deputy head of department to deputise for him and only chaired the Executive Conference in person when the drafting of the quarterly reports began to be an urgent business, that is to say from the second Monday in March, June, September, and December.

So one morning when, quite exceptionally, Armand Faucillon was present at the Executive Conference, Maurice Réol made up his mind to ask for an appointment to see him. "Sort it out with Miss Yolande", was the head of department's cheery reply. Miss Yolande was the keeper of the head of department's two appointment books, one being a diary of small size, for his personal appointments, and the other an office desk diary; and one of Miss Yolande's trickiest tasks was of course to avoid mistaking one diary for the other, and not to put down two appointments for the same time.

Armand Faucillon was undoubtedly a very busy man, for Miss Yolande could not give Réol an appointment with him for six weeks: in that period the head of department had to go to Marly-le-Roi for the annual meeting of heads of department of the Northern Zone, and on his return would have to deal with corrections and revisions to the March quarterly report. Then, as every year, on the day after the directors' meeting on the second Thursday in March, he would be off for a ten-day skiing holiday. An appointment was fixed therefore for 30 March at eleven thirty, after the Executive Conference. It was a good day and a good time, for everyone in the department knew that Faucillon had his on days and his off times: on Mondays, like everyone else, he was in a bad mood; on Fridays, like everyone else's, his mind wandered; and on Thursdays, he had to attend a seminar run by one of the Computer Centre engineers on "Computing and Business Management", and he needed the whole day to reread the notes he had tried to take at the previous week's seminar. And in addition, of course, there was no talking to him about anything at all before ten in the morning or after four in the afternoon.

Unfortunately for Réol, his head of department broke his leg on his winter sports vacation and did not return to the office until the eighth of April. Meanwhile the Board had appointed him to the Joint Committee which was to visit North Africa to study the unresolved dispute between the Company and its former Algerian partners. On his return on the twenty-eighth of April, the head of department cancelled all the appointments he could get away with cancelling and locked himself up for three days with Miss Yolande to draft the talk to go with a show of the slides he had brought back ("Many-splendoured Mzab: Ouargla, Touggourt, Ghardaïa"). Then he went off for the weekend, a weekend that stretched since May Day fell on a Saturday and as was customary in cases of this kind managerial staff in the company could take either the Friday or the Monday as an extra day off. The head of department thus returned on Tuesday, the fourth of May and made a brief appearance at the Executive Conference to invite members of his staff and their spouses to a slide talk he had organised for the following evening at eight p.m. in Rm. 42. He had a kind word for Réol and reminded him they were due to meet. Réol went straight to see Miss Yolande and obtained an appointment for Thursday the day after next (as the Computer Centre engineer was on a course in Manchester, the compulsory seminar was in temporary abeyance).

The slide show was not a great success. The audience was sparse, and the noise of the projector rendered the lecturer's voice inaudible; and he kept on losing the thread of his long sentences. Then, when the head of department, after showing a palm grove, had said the next slide would be of sand dunes and camels, the screen lit up with a shot of Robert Lamoureux playing in Sacha Guitry's *Let's Have a Dream*, followed by a slide of Héléna Bossis in the premiere of Sartre's *The Respectable P . . .*, then Jules Berry, Yves Deniaud, and Saturnin Fabre wearing the full ceremonial garb of members of the French Academy, in a mid-twenties light comedy entitled *The Immortals*, pretty much based on *The Men Who Wear Green*. The head of department lost his temper and put the houselights back on, at which point it was realised that the projectionist who had sorted out the slide cartridges had been dealing both with Faucillon's talk and with one to be given the next day by a famous theatre critic on "The French Stage High and Low". The incident was quickly put right, but the only company bigwig who had consented to come out for the talk, the director of the "Overseas" department, took advantage of it to slip away, using a business dinner as an excuse. In any case, the head of department was somewhat out of sorts next day, and when Réol went to see him and laid out his problem, he reminded him almost curtly that proposals for salary increases were looked at in November by Personnel Management, and it was out of the question to consider any such request any earlier.

After going over his problem in his head from every possible angle, Réol reached the conclusion that he had committed a huge blunder: instead of requesting a pay raise straight on, he should have asked to be included in the Young Couples' Assistance Scheme which the company's welfare department ran to help households become owner-occupiers, rehabilitate or modernise their principal dwelling, or acquire capital equipment. The welfare officer, whom Réol was able to see as early as the twelfth of May, told him that such assistance would be perfectly possible in his case, provided the Réols were indeed married. But in fact, although they had been living together for over four years by then, they had never bothered to get officially conjugated, as they say, and had never had any intention of so doing, even after the birth of their son.

So they got married, in early June, as simply as possible, since, meanwhile, their material circumstances had gone steadily downhill: their wedding feast, with their two witnesses as their only guests, took place in the setting of a city centre self-service eatery, and their wedding rings were made of tin.

Preparation work for the directors' meeting on the second Thursday in June kept Réol too busy to get all the papers together that were needed for his submission for assistance from the welfare scheme. It was not finally ready until Wednesday, 7 July. And from noon on Friday, 16 July, until 8:45 a.m. on Monday, 16 August, MATRASCO shut down for the summer break without anything having been yet decided on Réol's case.

There was no question of the Réols going on holiday; whilst their little boy spent the whole summer at Laval at his maternal grandparents' house, the Réols, thanks to their neighbour Berger, who put in a word for them with one of his colleagues, were hired for a month, respectively as a dishwasher and as cigarette and novelty salesgirl (ashtrays, cravats depicting the Eiffel Tower and Moulin-Rouge, Ooh-là-là dolls, streetlamp cigarette lighters marked "Rue de la Paix", glass hemispheres with the Sacré-Cœur in a snowstorm, etc.) in an establishment which called itself *La Renaissance*: it was a restaurant serving Bulgarian-style Chinese food, located between Pigalle and Montmartre, where thrice a night there landed a coach-load of Paris-by-Nighters who, for seventy-five francs no extras, got a tour of floodlit Paris, a dinner at *La Renaissance* ("its Bohemian charm, its exotic menu") and a massed charge through four cabarets, *The Two Hemispheres* ("Striptease and Folk; the essence of naughty Paris"), *The Tangerine Dream* (serviced by a pair of belly dancers, Zazoua and Aziza), *King Wenceslas* ("with its vaulted cellars, its medieval ambience, its minstrels, and its ancient ribald folksongs") and finally the *Villa d'Ouest* ("a showplace of elegant depravity – Spanish nobles, Russian tycoons, and fancy sports of every land crossed the world to ride in"), before being dumped back at their hotels, bespattered with sweetened champagne, dubious spirits, and greyish zakuski.

*   *   *

On returning to MATRASCO Réol found a nasty surprise awaiting him: the welfare department, finding itself overburdened with submissions, had just decided that henceforth it would consider only those requests coming to it through the proper channels and countersigned by the director of the department to which the applicant was attached. Réol dropped his submission onto Miss Yolande's desk and begged her to do all in her power to get the head of department to scrawl three lines of balanced appreciation on it over his initials.

But the head of department never signed things without due consideration, and moreover, he would say as a joke on himself, he often had cramp in his writing finger. For the moment, the priority was to get the September quarterly report ready, a report to which, for reasons he alone knew, he seemed to attach especial importance. And he made Réol do his report three times over, reproving him each time for taking the figures too pessimistically instead of highlighting the progress that had been made.

Repressing his fury, Réol resigned himself to another two or three weeks' wait; their situation was more and more precarious, they were six months in arrears with the rent, and owed the grocer four hundred francs. A stroke of luck at least enabled them to enroll their son at the municipal nursery, relieving them of the thirty or fifty francs' daily expenditure which the nanny had cost them up to then.

The head of department was away all of October: he was on a study tour of West Germany, Sweden, Denmark, and Holland. In November, a viral ear infection obliged him to stop work for three weeks.

In despair, Réol gave up hoping he would ever get his request through. Between the first of March and the thirtieth of November, the head of department had managed to absent himself for four full months, and Réol worked out that what with long weekends, convenience days, inconvenience days, deputised days, business trips and travel recovery leave, courses, seminars, and other days out, he had been to his office less than one hundred times in nine months. Not to mention his three-hour lunch breaks or his dashing away at five forty so as not to miss the train at six-o-three. There was no reason for that to change. But on Monday the sixth of December the head of department was appointed Deputy Director of the Overseas Dept and in the joy of his promotion finally returned Réol's submission with his approval. Fifteen days later the welfare aid was granted.

It was then that the Company's accounts department noticed that the level of repayments made by the Réol couple for the purchase of their bedroom suite exceeded the official ceiling for home-improvement loans: twenty-five per cent of net income after deduction of outgoings arising from the principal dwelling. The credit the Réols had been given was therefore illegal, and the Company had no right to guarantee it!

By the end of year one, therefore, Réol had obtained no raise and no welfare assistance, and he had to begin all over again with a new head of department.

The new man, who came straight from graduation at a top college with bees in his bonnet about computers and market research, held a meeting of all staff on his first day and informed them that the work of the "Statistics and Forecasts" department was based on obsolete, not to say medieval, methods, that it was not feasible to think you could have a reliable middle- or long-term strategy on information assembled only every quarter, and that henceforth, under his leadership, they would proceed to make daily estimates using specified socio-economic sampling techniques so as to have at all times an ongoing model of the firm's activities on which to ground any forecasts. Two programmers from the Computer Centre did the necessary, and after a few weeks Réol and his colleagues found themselves swamped by rolls of print-out from which it emerged more or less evidently that eighteen per cent of Normandy farmers opted for Formula A whilst forty-eight point four of the shopkeepers in the South Coast–Pyrenees region claimed to be happy with Formula B. The "Statistics and Forecasts" department, accustomed as it was to a more classical methodology whereby policies subscribed and cancelled were marked by making little five-barred gates (down strokes for one, two, three, four, and the fifth diagonally across the others), quickly grasped that if it did not wish to be completely sunk it had to take steps, and began a work-to-rule which consisted of bombarding the new head of department, the two computer persons, and the computer itself with questions of greater and lesser degrees of relevance. The computers coped, the two computer persons managed, but the new head of department eventually snapped and seven weeks later asked for a transfer.

This episode, which has gone down in the Company's annals as the Quarrel of the Ancients and Moderns, did nothing to improve Réol's affairs. He had managed to borrow two thousand francs from his in-laws to pay off his rent arrears, but debts were piling up on all sides, and he was more and more at a loss for a solution. It was no use for him and Louise to build up overtime, to do Sunday and Bank Holiday duties, to take on work at home (addressing envelopes, copying out commercial address lists, knitting, etc.); the gap between their resources and their needs kept on getting wider. In February and March they began to take things to the pawnshop: their wristwatches; Louise's jewels; their television set; and Maurice's camera, a Konica automatic reflex with zoom lens and electronic flash, which was the apple of Maurice's eye. In April, the manager again threatened to evict them, and they were forced to seek another private loan. Relatives and friends declined, and they were saved at the last minute by Mademoiselle Crespi, who withdrew three thousand francs which she had been saving at the Savings Bank for her funeral expenses.

With no right of appeal against the decision made by the welfare department, with no head of department to support a fresh request for a raise, since the former deputy head was now acting head and was far too frightened of losing his job to take the slightest initiative, Réol had no prospect whatsoever. On 15 July, Louise and he decided that they had had enough, that they would not cough up another penny, that creditors could recover whatever they liked, that they would not do anything to stop that happening. And they set off for a holiday in Yugoslavia.

When they got back, summonses and final demands were heaped on the doormat. Gas and electricity were cut off, and then, on the building manager's application, valuers came to prepare the bankruptcy auction of their furniture.

That was when the incredible happened: at the very moment they were pasting a yellow notice on the main door of the building announcing that a roup sale of furniture formerly the property of Réol, M and L (fine modern bedroom suite, large case clock, Louis XIII–style dresser, etc.) would be held on the fourth day following,

Réol, on going in to work, discovered that he had been appointed deputy head of department and that his salary would rise from one thousand nine hundred to two thousand seven hundred francs a month. At a stroke, the Réol couple's total monthly repayments became to all intents and purposes smaller than one quarter of their net income, and the MATRASCO accounts office could legally unfreeze the very same day a special grant-in-aid totalling five thousand francs. Although in order to stave off the confiscation Réol was obliged to pay hefty bailiffs' and valuers' fees, he was in a position to put himself on the right side of the gas and electricity companies and of the building manager within forty-eight hours.

Three months later they paid off the last instalment on the bedroom suite and had almost no trouble at all, the following year, in paying back Louise's parents and Mademoiselle Crespi and redeeming their watches, jewels, television, and camera.

Today, three years on, Réol is head of department, and the hard-won bedroom suite has lost none of its splendour. Standing on the violet nylon carpet, the bed, set against the middle of the rear wall, is an extra-low carcass sheathed in a material just like suede, amber in colour, with a "master saddler" finish of a strap with a bronze buckle, and a white acrylic fur bedspread. It stands flanked on both sides by a pair of matching bedside tables with brushed-steel surfaces and built-in adjustable spotlights and SW-LW radio alarm. Against the right-hand wall there is a chest of drawers-cum-dressing table, standing on a semi-elliptical metal pedestal, trimmed in hide-style suedette, with two drawers and a special tray for storing bottles, a large seventy-eight-centimetre mirror, and a matching pouf. Against the left-hand wall stands a large four-door mirror-fronted wardrobe on a matt anodised aluminium plinth with a strip-light under the pelmet and a frieze upholstered, like the side panels, in a material matching the rest of the suite.

Four objects more recently acquired have been incorporated into the original furniture. The first is a white telephone, on one of the bedside tables. The second, hanging over the bed, is a large rectangular print in a bottle-green leather frame: it portrays a small seaside square: two boys are sitting on the harbour wall playing dice. On the steps of a monument a man is reading a newspaper in the shadow of a sword-wielding hero. A girl is filling her tub at the fountain. A fruit-seller is lying beside his scales. Through the empty window and door openings of a tavern, two men can be seen drinking their wine in the depths.

The third object, between the bedroom door and the dressing table, is a crib in which a newborn babe sleeps on his stomach, clenching his fists;

and the fourth is a photographic enlargement, fixed to the wooden door with four drawing pins: it portrays the four Réols: Louise, in a flowery dress, holds their elder son by the hand, and Maurice, with his white shirtsleeves rolled above his elbows, holds in arms outstretched towards the camera a naked baby, as though he wants to demonstrate that it is a perfect model, without a blemish.

CHAPTER NINETY-NINE

Bartlebooth, 5

Je cherche en même temps l'éternel et l'éphémère

Bartlebooth's study is a rectangular room whose walls are lined with dark wooden bookshelves; most of them are now empty, but 61 black boxes still remain, all identically tied with grey ribbon sealed with wax, stacked together on the last three shelves on the rear wall, to the right of the padded door giving on to the entrance hall, on whose lintel has hung for many, many years an Indian puppet with a big wooden head which seems to be watching over this austere and neutral space through its big, slit eyes like an enigmatic and almost disturbing guardian.

In the centre of the room, a scialytic lamp, held up by a whole system of cords and pulleys distributing its huge weight over the whole area, illumines with its unfaltering light a large square table draped with a black cloth in the middle of which an almost completed puzzle is laid out. It depicts a little port in the Dardanelles at the mouth of the river which the Ancient Greeks called Maiandros, the Meander.

* * *

The shore is a chalky, arid strip of sand, sparsely dotted with gorse and dwarf trees; in the left foreground, the shoreline widens into a creek cluttered with dozens and dozens of black-hulled fishing boats whose flimsy rigging merges into an inextricable tangle of vertical and diagonal lines. In the middle distance, a mass of coloured spots picks out vines, seedbeds, yellow fields of mustard, black gardens of magnolia trees, red stone quarries on the shoulders of gentle slopes. Further behind, over the whole right-hand side of the watercolour, far inland, the ruins of an ancient city loom with surprising sharpness: preserved by a miracle for centuries and centuries beneath layers of silt deposited by the sinuous stream, the marble and ashlar flags of the recently excavated thoroughfares, dwellings, and temples trace out the city's ground plan quite perfectly: it is a crisscross of extremely narrow streets, a life-size model of an exemplary labyrinth made of blind alleys, backyards, crossroads, side streets, which girdle the remains of a huge and sumptuous acropolis surrounded by the remnants of pillars, crumbling arcades, gaping stairways opening onto collapsed balconies, just as if, in the heart of this now almost fossilised maze, this unforeseeable vista had been purposely concealed, in the manner of those palaces in oriental tales whither mysterious agents convey by night a person who, brought back home before daybreak, can never find his way back to the magic dwelling which he ends up believing he visited only in a dream. A stormy, crepuscular sky, full of dark-red scudding clouds, dominates this immobile and leaden landscape from which all trace of life seems to have been banished.

Bartlebooth is seated at his table, in his great-uncle Sherwood's armchair, a swivelling and rocking Napoleon III armchair in mahogany and *lie-de-vin* leather. To his right, on the top of a little drawer-desk, stands a dark-green lacquered tray bearing a crackled porcelain teapot, a cup and a saucer, a jug of milk, a silver egg-cup with its egg untouched, and a white napkin rolled in a whorled napkin ring, said to have been designed by Gaudi for the refectory of the College of Saint Theresa of Jesus; to his left, in the revolving bookcase beside which James Sherwood had his photograph taken long ago, lies an unsorted pile of miscellaneous books and objects:

Berghaus's World Atlas; the *Dictionary of Geography* by Meissas and Michelot; a photograph portraying Bartlebooth at the age of thirty or so mountaineering in Switzerland, wearing ventilated snow-goggles, with alpenstock, mittens, and a wool cap pulled over his ears; a detective novel called *Dog Days*; an octagonal mirror with a frame inlaid with mother-of-pearl; a wooden Chinese puzzle in the shape of a star-faced dodecahedron; a French translation of Thomas Mann's *Zauberberg* in a two-volume edition bound in fine grey cloth with gold-leaf titles on black labels; a walking stick with a secret compartment in the top concealing a diamond-studded watch; a tiny full-length portrait of a long-faced Renaissance man wearing a broad-brimmed hat and a long fur coat; an ivory billiard ball; an incomplete set of the works of Walter Scott in English, in magnificent bindings embossed with the arms of the Chisholm clan; and two Epinal woodcuts, one of Napoleon I inspecting the Oberkampf manufactory in 1806 and unpinning his own Legion of Honour cross to attach it to the spinner's lapel, the other a very free version of *The Ems Telegram* in which the artist, flaunting all verisimilitude, has brought together in the same scene all the main actors in the affair, showing Bismarck, with his mastiffs lying at his feet, using a pair of scissors to edit the message which Councillor Abeken has handed him, whilst at the other end of the room Kaiser Wilhelm I indicates with an insolent smile to Ambassador Benedetti, who bows his head at the affront, that the audience granted him is now closed.

Bartlebooth is seated at his puzzle. He is a thin, old man, almost fleshless, with a bald head, a waxy complexion, blank eyes, dressed in a washy blue wool dressing gown tied at the waist with a grey cord. His feet, in goat-kid moccasins, rest on a fringe-edged silk rug; his head is very slightly tipped back, his mouth is half open, and his right hand grips the armrest of his chair whilst his left hand, lying on the table in a not very natural way, in not far short of a contorted position, holds between thumb and index finger the very last piece of the puzzle.

It is the twenty-third of June nineteen seventy-five, and it will soon be eight o'clock in the evening. Madame Berger is back from her surgery and is making a meal, and Poker Dice slumbers on a fluffy sky-blue bedspread; Madame Altamont is putting on her make-up in front of her husband, who has just come in from Geneva; the Réols have just finished dinner, and Olivia Norvell is about to leave on her fifty-sixth world tour; Kléber is playing patience, and Hélène is mending the right sleeve of Smautf's jacket, and Véronique Altamont is looking at an old photograph of her mother, and Madame Trévins is showing Madame Moreau a postcard coming from the village where they were born.

It is the twenty-third of June nineteen seventy-five, and it will soon be eight o'clock in the evening. Cinoc, in his kitchen, opens a tin of pilchards in spice whilst looking up an index of obsolete words; Dr Dinteville finishes examining an old woman; on Cyrille Altamont's deserted desk two butlers spread a white tablecloth; in the service-entrance corridor five delivery men pass a lady who has come to search for her cat; Isabelle Gratiolet builds a precarious house of cards beside her father as he reads a treatise on anatomy.

It is the twenty-third of June nineteen seventy-five, and it will soon be eight o'clock in the evening. Joseph Nieto and Ethel Rogers are about to go down to the Altamonts'; on the stairs, porters have come for Olivia Norvell's trunks, and a woman from an estate agency is coming to have a late look at the flat Gaspard Winckler used to occupy, and a displeased Hermann Fugger comes back out of the Altamonts', and two similarly dressed doorstep salesmen pass by on the fourth-floor landing, and the blind tuner's grandson waits for his grandfather, sitting on the stairs reading of the adventures of Carel van Loorens, and Gilbert Berger takes down the dustbins as he wonders how to solve the complicated puzzle of his serial novel; in the entrance hall Ursula Sobieski looks for Bartlebooth's name on the list of occupants, and Gertrude, who has returned to drop in on her former mistress, stops for a minute to say good day to Madame Albin and Madame de Beaumont's home help; right at the top the Plassaerts do their accounts, and their son sorts out once more his collection of illustrated blotters, and Geneviève Foulerot takes a bath before collecting her baby from the concierge, who looks after him, and "Hortense" listens to music on headphones whilst waiting for the Marquiseaux, and Madame Marcia in her bedroom opens a jar of malosol cucumbers, and Béatrice Breidel has her classmates in, and her sister Anne tries out another way of slimming.

It is the twenty-third of June nineteen seventy-five, and in a moment it will be eight o'clock in the evening; the workers converting Morellet's old room are knocking off; Madame de Beaumont is resting on her bed before dinner; Léon Marcia remembers the lecture Jean Richepin came to give at his sanatorium; in Madame de Beaumont's drawing room two sated kittens sleep deeply.

It is the twenty-third of June nineteen seventy-five, and it is eight o'clock in the evening. Seated at his jigsaw puzzle, Bartlebooth has just died. On the tablecloth, somewhere in the crepuscular sky of the four hundred and thirty-ninth puzzle, the black hole of the sole piece not yet filled in has the almost perfect shape of an X. But the ironical thing, which could have been foreseen long ago, is that the piece the dead man holds between his fingers is shaped like a W.

END OF THE SIXTH AND LAST PART

Epilogue

Serge Valène died a few weeks later, during the mid-August bank holiday. It was nearly a month since he had left his room. The death of his old pupil and the disappearance of Smautf, who had left the building the very next day, had dealt him a terrible blow. He hardly took any food any more, lost his words, left sentences hanging. Madame Nochère, Elzbieta Orlowska, and Mademoiselle Crespi took turns caring for him, went up to see him two or three times a day, made him a bowl of clear soup, tidied up his bedclothes and pillows, did his laundry, helped him wash and change, and took him to the lavatory at the end of the corridor.

The building was virtually empty. Several of the people who usually didn't go on holiday, or had stopped going on holidays, were away that year: Madame de Beaumont had been invited to be honorary president at the Alban Berg Festival held in Berlin to commemorate the 90th anniversary of the composer's birth, the 40th anniversary of his death (and of the *Concerto in Memory of an Angel*) and the 50th anniversary of the world première of *Wozzeck*; Cinoc, overcoming his fear of flying and of US Immigration, which he thought still happened on Ellis Island, had finally responded to the invitations he had been getting for years from two distant cousins, a Nick Linhaus who owned a nightclub (*The Nemo Club*) at Dempledorf (Nebraska), and a Bobby Hallowell, a police doctor at Santa Monica (California); Léon Marcia had let his wife and son drag him off to a rented villa near Divonne-les-Bains; and Olivier Gratiolet, despite the very poor state of his leg, had insisted on spending three weeks with his daughter on the Isle of Oléron. Even those who had stayed on at Rue Simon-Crubellier for the month of August took advantage of the long weekend of the fifteenth to get away from Paris for three days: the Pizzicagnolis went to Deauville and took Jane Sutton with them; Elzbieta Orlowska went to see her son at Nivillers, and Madame Nochère left to go to her daughter's wedding at Amiens.

On Friday the fourteenth of August, the only people left in the building were Madame Moreau, attended day and night by her nurse and Madame Trévins, Mademoiselle Crespi, Madame Albin, and Valène. And when Mademoiselle Crespi went up towards the end of the morning to take the aged artist two boiled eggs and a cup of tea, she found him dead.

He was resting on his bed, fully dressed, peaceful and puffy, with his arms crossed on his chest. A large square canvas with sides over six feet long stood by the window, halving the small area of the maid's room in which he had spent the largest part of his life. The canvas was practically blank: a few charcoal lines had been carefully drawn, dividing it up into regular square boxes, the sketch of a cross-section of a block of flats which no figure, now, would ever come to inhabit.

END

Paris, 1969–78

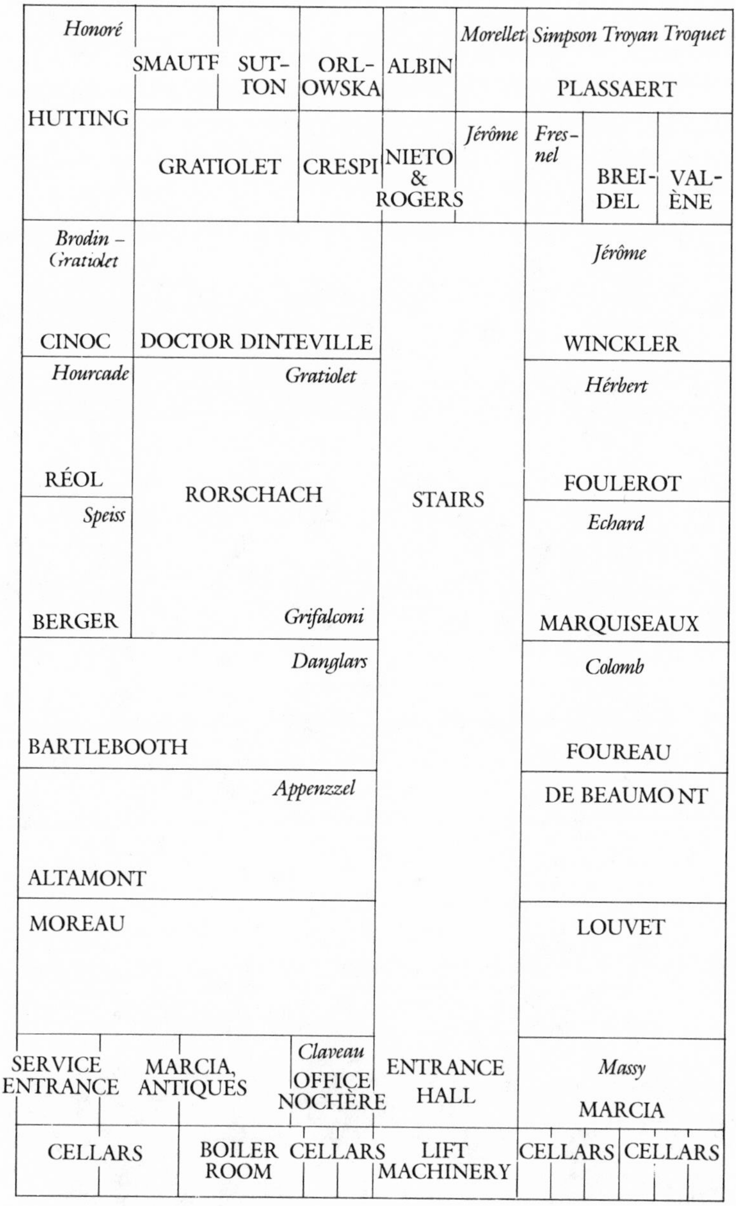

Honoré HUTTING | SMAUTF | SUTTON | ORLOWSKA | ALBIN | *Morellet* | *Simpson Troyan Troquet* PLASSAERT

GRATIOLET | CRESPI | NIETO & ROGERS | *Jérôme* | *Fresnel* | BREIDEL | VALÈNE

Brodin – Gratiolet CINOC | DOCTOR DINTEVILLE | *Jérôme* WINCKLER

Hourcade RÉOL | *Gratiolet* RORSCHACH *Grifalconi* | STAIRS | *Hérbert* FOULEROT

Speiss BERGER | *Echard* MARQUISEAUX

Danglars BARTLEBOOTH | *Colomb* FOUREAU

Appenzzel ALTAMONT | DE BEAUMONT

MOREAU | LOUVET

SERVICE ENTRANCE | MARCIA, ANTIQUES | *Claveau* OFFICE NOCHÈRE | ENTRANCE HALL | *Massy* MARCIA

CELLARS | BOILER ROOM | CELLARS | LIFT MACHINERY | CELLARS | CELLARS

11 RUE SIMON-CRUBELLIER

Names of previous occupants are given in italics.

APPENDICES

Index

Annals of Ear and Larynx Diseases, 326.
Annecy (Haute-Savoie), 199.
Antarctica, 382.
Anthology of Neo-Creative Painting, An, edited by S. Gogolak, 35.
Antigvarisk Tidsskrift, 90.
Antiquarian, The, brand of Scotch whisky, 445.
ANTON, Parisian tailor, 186, 188.
Apache, Indian tribe, 453.
Apis mellifica L., 396.
APOLLINAIRE (Guillaume), pen-name of Wilhelm Apollinaris de Kostrowitsky, French poet, Rome 1880 – Paris 1918, 292.
Apopka, lake, 412.
Apothecary, The, painting by J. T. Maston, 436.
Appalachians, 468.
APPENZZELL (Marcel), Austrian ethnologist, 59, 106, **107–112.**
APPENZZELL (Madame), his mother, 108, 112, 214.
Arab Emirates, see UAE.
Arabia, 45, 371, 466.
Arabian Knights, The, by Charles Nunnely, 264.
ARAMIS, character in novels by A. Dumas, 467.
ARAÑA (Madame), first concierge at 11 Rue Simon-Crubellier, 59, 168, 217.
ARCHIMEDES, Greek scholar, Syracuse, c.287–c.212 BC, 369.
Archives internationales d'Histoire des Sciences, 479.
ARCONATI (Julio), Italian composer, 1828–1905, 19, 229.
Arctic Circle, 54.
Ardennes, Department of, 20, 143, 149, 230, 440.
Ares Resting, sculpture by Scopas, 132.
ARGALASTES, 289.
Argentina, 78, 95.
Argonne, forest, 33.
ARISTOTELES (Melchior), Venezuelan film producer, 283.
ARISTOTLE, Greek philosopher, C.384–c.322 BC, 289.
Arizona, 412.
Arkhangelsk (USSR), 228, 289.
Arles (Bouches-du-Rhône), 137, 144, 199.
Arlon (Belgium), 138, 139.
Armentières (Nord), 43.
ARMINIUS, figure in German mythology, 34.
ARMSTRONG'S, shipbuilders, 447.
Army Historical Review, 48.
ARNAUD DE CHEMILLE, French historian and hagiographer, 1407?–1448?, 84.
ARON (Raymond), French ideologist, 241.
ARONNAX (Pierre), French naturalist, 1828–1905, 289.
Arpajon (Essonne), 438.
Arras (Pas-de-Calais), 156, 273.
Ars vanitatis, 137.
ARTAGNAN, D', character in novels by Alexandre Dumas père, 159, 256, 467.
ARTAUD (Antonin), French writer, 1896–1948, 292.
Arte brutta, 39.
Artesia (New Mexico), 425, 427, 428.
Art et Architecture Aujourd'hui, review, 48.
Artifoni, House of, Flower arrangers, 151.
Artigas (Uruguay), 425.
Artistic and Scientific Society (Utrecht), 89.
Art of Being Ever Joyful, The, didactic poem by J.-P. Uz, 288.
Asama, Japanese battleship-cruiser, 447.
ASCLEPIADES, Greek doctor, c.124–c.40 BC, 233, 478, 480.
Ascona (Switzerland), 172.
ASHBY (Jeremiah), 410, 411, 412, 413.
ASHBY (Ruben), 410, 411, 412, 413.

Ashtray (Anthony Corktip, Lord), 452, 453, 454.
Asia, 54, 250, 291, 374.
Asprey's, London leather-goods shop, 344.
Asquith (Sarah), 581.
Astrat (Henri), 234–236.
Asturias, 9.
Athos, character in novels by A. Dumas, 467.
Atlantic Ocean, 91, 234, 282.
Atlantic Ocean, South, 178.
Atlas, figure of Greek mythology, 417.
Atri (Italy), 173.
Attila, King of the Huns, c.395–453, 85.
Attlee (Clement Richard), English politician, 1883–1967, 457.
Auber (Daniel-François-Esprit), French composer, 1782–1871, 198.
Aubervilliers (Seine-Saint-Denis), 249.
Auckland Gazette and Hemisphere, New Zealand daily, 453.
Augenlicht (Arnold), Austrian racing cyclist, 351.
Au Pilori, French anti-Semitic newspaper of the 1940s, 112.
Auroch Hunt, The, by Fernand Cormon, 399.
Aurore, L', French daily, 30.
Austen (Jane), English novelist, 1775–1817, 328.
Australasia, 382.
Australia, 333, 381, 382, 389, 394.
Austria, 87, 151, 425.
Austro-Hungarian Empire, 88.
Autery, 437.
Auvergne, 178, 199.
Auvergne Messenger, The, 30.
Aux Délices de Louis XV, cake- and teashop, 27, 328, 405.
Auzere (Lubin) and Auzere (Noel), architects, 471.
Avalon (California), 336.
Aveynat, bridge, 350.
Avignon (Vaucluse), 144.
Avvakum, 409.
Axminster (England), 99.
Ayrshire (Scotland), for the best bacon, 85.
Ayrton, character in Jules Verne's novels, 25.
Azincourt (Pas-de-Calais), 52.
Aziza, 488.

Baatan (Philippines), 382.
Babar, character invented by Laurent and Jean de Brunhoff, 367.
Bab-Fetouh (Morocco), 245.
Babilee (Jean), pseudonym of Jean Gutmann, French ballet-dancer, 440.
Bacchus, 421.
Bach (Johann-Sebastien), German composer, 1685–1750, 100.
Bachelet (Th.), lexicographer, 289.
Bachelier (Henri), 263.
Bacon (Francis), Irish painter, 429.
Bad Joke, A, decorated plate, 249.
Bagnols-sur-Cèze (Gard), 139, 140.
Bahamas, 394, 422.
Baignol & Farjon, brand of pencils, 243.
Baillerge (Florent), 410.
Balaton (Hungary), 293.
Baldick (R), 581.
Ballard (Florence), 103.
Ballets de Paris, 440.
Ballets Frère, 438, 439, 442.
Bal Mabille, a popular dance café, 403.
Baltard (Victor), French architect, 1805–1874, 169.
Baltistan, 409.
Bamako (Mali), 222.
Bamberg (Germany), 206.
Banania, brand of breakfast cereals, 61.
B and A, Las Vegas nightclub, 449.
Bank of Australia, 389.
Bao Daï, 457.
Barbados, 449.
Barbenoire, political agitator, 356.

BARBOSA-MACHADO (Diego), Portuguese man of letters, 1682–1770, 172.
Barcelona (Spain), 371, 394.
Barents Sea, 55.
Bari (Italy), 471.
Bar-le-Duc (Meuse), 125.
BARNAVAUX (Jules), 280.
Baroness, The, Berthe Danglars's nickname, 403.
BARRERE, cyclist, 351, 352.
BARRETT, American gangster, 357.
BARRETT (Henry), 183.
BART (Jean), French sailor 1650–1702, 198
BARTHOLDI (Frédéric-Auguste), French sculptor, 1834–1904, 470.
BARTLEBOOTH (James Aloysius), 390.
BARTLEBOOTH (Jonathan), 94, 390.
BARTLEBOOTH (Percival), 4, 5, 10, 17, 20–23, 26–28, 33–35, 40, **51–58**, 60, 65, 66, 94, 95, **113–119**, 125–127, 158, 169, 191–193, 214, 219, 227, 228, 242, 245, 246, 269, **331–340**, 344–347, 368, **388–393**, 405, 420, 422, **432–435**, 451, **494–497.**
BARTLEBOOTH (Priscilla, née Sherwood), 94, 115, 390, 420.
BARTON (F.), English explorer, 389.
Basel (Switzerland), 288, 477, 480.
Bastille, prison, 199, 256, 400.
Baton Rouge (Louisiana), 411.
BAUCIS (See PHILEMON),12, 437.
BAUCIS, glassworks, 51.
BAUDELAIRE (Charles), French poet, 1821–1867, 292.
Baugé (Maine-et-Loire), 84.
BAUMGARTEN (C. F.), German musician, 100.
BAYARD (Pierre du Terrail, seigneur de), 1475–1524, 198.
Bay of Bengal, 54.
Bay of Biscay, 52.
Bayonne, 85, 154.
BAYSIUS, 289.
Bazooka affair, 139.
BBC, 64, 273.
BEARDSLEY (Aubrey Vincent), English artist and writer, 1872–1898, 277.
Beasts of the Night, monumental sculpture by Franz Hutting, 34.
Beauce, French plain, 356.
BEAUFORT (François de Bourbon-Vendôme, Duke of), 1616–1669, 362.
BEAUFOUR (Duchess of), 399.
Beaugency, 85, 160.
BEAUMONT (Countess Adelaïde de), mother of Fernand, 19, 146, 147, 366.
BEAUMONT (Elizabeth Natasha Victorine Marie de, later married name Breidel), 19, 142, 143, **145–151**, 366.
BEAUMONT (Fernand de), French archaeologist, 1876–1935, **8–10**, 19, 52, 145, 151, 367.
BEAUMONT (Véra de, née Orlova), 4, 6, 17, 127, **137–139**, 143, **175**, 218, 316, 355, 365, 367, 371, 405, 459, 496, 497, 499.
Beaune (Côte d'Or), 277.
Beauty and the Beast, film by René Clément and Jean Cocteau (1946), 349.
Beauvais (Oise), 270, 420.
BECAUD (Gilbert), pseudonym of François Silly, French folk singer, 158, 228.
BECCARIA (Cesare Bonesana, marquis of), Italian jurist, 1738–1794, 88, 91, 94.
BECQUERLOUX (René), 439.
BEDE (The Venerable, Saint), Anglo-Saxon scholar and historian, 673–735, 85.
BEETHOVEN (Ludwig van), German composer, 1770–1827, 184, 295, 360.
BEHIER (Louis-Jules), French doctor, 1813–1876, 326.
Beirut (Lebanon), 38, 156, 449.

Bête Noire, La, avant-garde review, 406.
Bétharram caves (Pyrénées-Orientales), 427, 428.
Bethlehem (Israel), 255, 317.
BEYSSANDRE (Charles-Albert), art critic, 39, 66, 390, 422, **429–435**.
Bibliografica urologica, by Paolo Ceneri, 480.
Bibliotheca Lusitana, 172.
Bibliothèque de l'Opéra, 234–236.
Bibliothèque Nationale (Paris), 140.
BIDOU (D.), painter, 474.
BIDREM (International Development Bank for Energy and Mining Resources), 296, 299.
BIENENFELD (Ela), 581.
BIG MIKE, Indian chief, 453.
BIG MOUTH, Sioux chief, 453.
BINDA (Alfredo), Italian racing cyclist, 350.
Birds, The, film by Alfred Hitchcock, 362.
Birmingham (England), 84.
BIRNBAUM (Laszlo), conductor, 427.
BISHOP (Jeremy), 381–382, 394.
BISMARCK, 495.
BISSEROT (Pierre), pacemaker, 353.
Bitter Victory, by René Hardy, 295.
BLACK BEAVER, Indian chief, 453.
Black Sea, 54.
BLANCARD (Etienne), 478.
BLANCARD (Jacques-Emile), French caricaturist, 105.
BLANCHET (Roland), 401–403.
Blawick (Florida), 339.
BLOCK (Pierre), French musician, 331.
BLONDINE, character in Mozart's opera *Die Entführung aus dem Serail*, 175.
Blue Boy, The, by Thomas Gainsborough, 421.
Bohème, La, opera by Puccini, 234.
BÖHM (Karl), conductor, 235.
Boire un petit coup c'est agréable, 414.
BOISSY (Louis de), French playwright, 1694–1758, 364.
Boka-Kotorska (Yugoslavia), 246.
BOLIVAR (Simon-José-Antonio), South American general, 1783–1830, 34.
Bolivia, 151.
Bologna (Italy), 289, 350, 371, 475, 476, 477.
BOMBASTINUS, nickname of Lazare Meysonnier, 475.
Bombay (India), 54, 310, 409.
BONACIEUX (Constance), character in *The Three Musketeers* by A. Dumas, 158.
BONAPARTE (Napoleon), see Napoleon I, 39.
BONIFACE, a donkey, 246.
BONNAT (Léon), French painter, 1833–1922, 16.
BONNER (A.), 581.
BONNETERRE (François-Marie), Canadian seaman, c.1787–?1830, 289.
Bon Petit Diable, Le, 323.
Bonshommes Guillaume, mechanical doll display, 404.
Booz endormi, poem by Victor Hugo, 271.
BORBEILLE, a doctor, character in G. Berger's story, 160.
BORBEILLE (Isabella), his daughter, character in G. Berger's story, 160.
Bordeaux (Gironde), 154, 198, 199, 290, 404, 454.
BORGES (Jorge Luis), 579.
BORIET-TORY (J.), a Swiss surgeon, 280, 283.
Boris Godunov, opera by Mussorgsky, 401.
BORIS THE BARITONE, a mythical thief, 401.
Borneo, 54, 212.
BOROTRA (Jean), tennis champion, 196.
Borrelly, Joyce and Kahane, whisky distillers, 300.
BOSCH (Hieronymus van Aeken), Flemish painter, 1450–1516, 18.
BOSSEUR (J.), art critic, 34.

Bossis (Héléna), French actress, 487.
Bossius, 289.
Bossuet (Jacques-Bénigne), French writer, 1626–1704, 198.
Boston (Massachusetts), 82, 86, 87, 94.
Bottecchia (Ottavio), Italian cycling champion, 1894–1927, 350.
Botticelli (Sandro di Mariano Felipepi), Italian painter, 1445–1510, 152.
Boubaker, **266–269.**
Bougret (Inspector), a character in works by Marcel Gotlib, 160.
Bouillet (Marie-Nicolas), French lexicographer, 1798–1864, 289.
Bouise (Jean), French actor, 64.
Bou-Jeloud (Morocco), 245.
Boulanger (Georges), French general, 1837–1891, 105.
Boulez (Pierre), French conductor, 156.
Boulle (Pierre), French writer, 394.
Bounty Islands, 179.
Bourg-Baudoin, 348.
Bourg d'Oisans (Isère), 350.
Bourges (Cher), 198.
Bourgueil (Indre-et-Loire), 154.
Bourvil, pseudonym of André Raimbourg, French comedian, 1917–1970, 64.
Bouvard, see Ratinet.
Bovril, 444.
Bowman (William), English anatomist, 476, 480.
Box (Patrick Oliver), English explorer, 409.
Boxers, 67.
Boyer, songwriter, 414.
Bradshaw's Continental Railway Steam Transit and General Guide, 199.
Braun (Eva), 456.
Braun (Wernher von), 297.
Brazil, 258.
Bregenzer Kammerorchester, 427.
Breidel (Anne), 18, 20, 28, 149, 150, 175, **176–179**, 227, 366, 367, 452, 497.
Breidel (Armand), 367.
Breidel (Béatrice), 18, 20, 28, 150, 175, 176, 227, 366, 367, 452, 497.
Breidel (Elizabeth, née de Beaumont), see Beaumont, 20, 138, **139–150**.
Breidel (François), 20, 138, 139, 148, 149, 366.
Breidel (parents), 138.
Breidel's Tower, 179.
Breitengasser, sixteenth-century German Composer, 368.
Bretzlee (George), American novelist, 114.
Briançon (Hautes-Alpes), 350.
Brice (Vera), 581.
Bridge over the River Kwaï, The, by Pierre Boulle, 221, 394.
Bridgett (Mrs), English hotelkeeper, 443.
Brief History of the Origins and Progress of Engraving, Woodcuts and Intaglio, by Humbert (1752), 171.
Brinon (Fernand de), French politician, 1885–1947, 273.
Brisbane (Australia), 382.
Brisson (Mathieu-Jacques), French naturalist, 1723–1806, 289.
Britannicus, tragedy by Jean Racine, 303.
British Association for the Advancement of Science, 383.
British Museum, 144, 347.
Brittany, 481, 485.
Brive (Corrèze), 149.
Brod (M.), 581.
Brodin (Antoine), 75, 77, 410.
Brodin (Hélène, née Gratiolet), 128, **410–413**.
Brøndal (Viggo), Danish linguist, 110.
Bros d'Or, Acapulco nightclub, 449.
Brouwershaven (Holland), 52, 55.
Brown (Jim), see Guido Mandetta, 91.

Jacques L'Aumône, pop singer, 137.
Charlemagne, 742–814, 467.
Charles i, King of England, 1600–1649, 69, 388, 415?
Charles ii, King of Spain, 1661–1700, 204.
Charlotte, Henri Fresnel's acting partner, 255–257.
Charny (Meuse), 33, 244.
Charolles, a character in works by Marcel Gotlib, 160.
Chartres (Eure-et-Loir), 198, 237.
Chase Manhattan Bank, 280.
Chateaubriand (François-René de, viscount), French writer, 1768–1848, 292.
Château de la Muette (Paris), 120–123.
Château d'Oex (Switzerland), 140.
Châteaudun (Eure-et-Loir), 199.
Châteaumeillant (Cher), 85.
Chateauneuf (Count of), character in G. Berger's story, 158, 160.
Chateauneuf (Eudes de), an aristocratic ancestor, character in G. Berger's story, 160.
Châtiments, Les, collection of satirical poetry by V. Hugo (1853), 59.
Chatou (Yvelines), 438.
Chatterbox, The (Le Babillard), by Boissy, 364.
Chaucer (Geoffrey), English poet, 1340–1400, 375.
Chaudoir (Baron de), French numismatist, 349.
Chaumont-Porcien (Ardennes), 20, 138, 142, 143, 149, 316.
Chavignolles (Calvados), 13.
Chazelles (De), landowner, 470.
Chemische Akademie (Mannheim), 297.
Chenany (Jeanne de), seventeenth-century French engraver, 171.
Chenard & Walker, makers of motorcars, 115, 368.
Chéops, Le, Paris nightclub, 356
Chéri, see Ribibi, 231.
Cheshire (England), 443.
Cheval d'Orgueil, Le, by Pierre-Jakez Hélias, 295.
Chevalier (Maurice), French singer, 1888–1972, 234, 258.
Chevreuse valley, 116.
Cheyenne, Indian tribe, 453.
Chicago (Illinois), 73, 383.
Children of Captain Grant, The, novel by Jules Verne, 25.
Children's Corner, by Claude Debussy (1908), 165.
Chimaera, a sculpture, 483.
China, 371.
Chinoc, see Cinoc.
Chinon (Indre-et-Loire), 154.
Chiricachua, Indian tribe, 453.
Chisholm, clan, 495.
Cholet (Maine-et-Loire), 148.
Chopin (Frédéric), French composer, 1810–1849, 50, 231.
Christie (Agatha), pseudonym of Agatha Mary Clarissa Miller, English novelist, 1891–1976, 160, 579.
Christina, Queen of Sweden, 1626–1689, 89.
Christo, painter, 483.
Chur (Switzerland), see Coire, 425.
Churchill (Sir Winston Leonard Spencer), statesman, 1874–1965, 334.
Cicero (Marcus Tullius Cicero), Latin orator, c.106–c.43 BC, 249.
Cid, Le, tragi-comedy by Pierre Corneille, 160, 364.
Cincinatti (Ohio), 175.
Cinna, character in Corneille, 302.
Cinoc (Albert), 197, 216, 227, **285–289**, 409, 496, 499.
Cissampelos (Madame), manageress of a family hotel, 403.
Citizen Kane, film by Orson Welles, 281.
Civil Engineering College (Paris), 185.

CLAIR (René), pseudonym of René Chomette, French film-maker, 164.
Clairvaux (Aube), 84.
CLAVEAU (Madame), formerly concierge at 11 Rue Simon-Crubellier, 17, 55, 60,128, **161–162**, 168, 211, 217, 286, 398.
CLAVEAU (Michel), her son, 17, 55, 162.
CLAWBONNY (Timothy), banker, 400.
CLÉRAY, Parisian leather-goods trader, 399.
Clermont (Meuse), 33.
Clermont-Ferrand (Puy-de-Dôme), 199, 427.
CLIFFORD (Augustus Brian), US colonel, 156.
CLIFFORD (Haig Douglas), English baritone, 235.
Clocks and Clouds, detective novel, 151.
CLOVIS, King of the Franks, 85.
CNRS (National Centre for Scientific Research), 205, 215, 269.
COCHET (Henri), French tennis star, 196.
Cochinchina, 198.
COCHISE, Apache chief, 453.
Coco weddelliana, 341.
COCTEAU (Jean), 465.
COEUR (Jacques), 198.
COHEN (J. M.), 581.
Coin-Collector's Almanach, The, 214.
Coire (Switzerland), 425, 427.
COLBERT (Jean-Baptiste), French politician, 1619–1683, 231, 455.
COLERIDGE (Samuel Taylor), English poet, 1772–1834, 172.
COLIN (Paul), French poster designer, 98.
COLIN D'HARLEVILLE (Jean-François), French playwright, 1735–1806, 364.
Collection of the Coins of China, Japan, etc., by Baron de Chaudoir, 349.
Collège Chaptal, 120, 125.
Collège de France, 205, 281.
COLLOT (Henri, called "Monsieur Riri"), café owner, 124, 206, 232, 337, 349.
COLLOT (Isabelle and Martine, called "les petites Riri"), 124.
COLLOT (Lucienne, called "Madame Riri"), **28–31**, 124.
COLLOT (Valentin, known as "Young Riri"), 124.
Colmar (Bas-Rhin), 85.
Cologne (Germany), 155.
COLOMB (M.), almanach publisher, 170, 214.
Colombia, 284.
Colonel Bogey, English soldiers' song, 420.
COLQUHOUN OF DARROCH (Lord Lowager), 385.
COLUMBINE, character in the *commedia dell'arte*, 136.
COLUMBUS (Christopher), seafarer, 1451–1506, 384, 386, 387.
COMBELLE (Alix), tenor saxophonist, 363.
Come in, Little Nemo, song by Sam Horton, 181.
Commercy (Meuse), 61.
COMMINE (Arlette, née Trévins), 450.
COMMINE (Louis), 450.
COMMINE (Lucette), see Hennin, 450.
Comoedia, theatre magazine, 156.
Comoro Islands, 46, 126.
Compaña Mexicana de Aviación, 31.
Compiègne (Oise), 134, 135.
Complete Table of Energy Values of Customary Foods, 176.
Concerto in Memory of an Angel, by Alban Berg, 499.
CONCINI (Concino Concini, called the Marshal of Ancre), 1575–1617, 49.
CONFUCIUS (K'ung Tzu), Chinese philosopher, 555–479 BC, 400.

Crécy (battle of), 9.
CRECY- COUVÉ (Duke of), 51.
CRECY-COUVÉ (Marshal), 51.
CRESPI (Célia), 41, 58, 60, 127, 212, 217, 218, 227, 261, 286, 355, 398, 401, 402, **405–406**, 450, 471, 491, 499, 500.
CRESSIDA, heroine of *Troilus and Cressida* by W. Shakespeare, 172.
Crete, 127.
Crimea (USSR), 151.
Crimén piramidal, El, detective novel, 168.
Criminal Life of Archibaldo de la Cruz, The, by Luis Buñel, 465.
CRIPPS (Sir Richard Stafford), statesmen, 1889–1952, 457.
Critical Bibliography . . . Relating to the Death of Adolf Hitler, by M. Echard, 456.
CROCKETT (Davy), American hero, 249.
CROSBY (Bing), American singer, 1904–1977, 382.
Crossed Words, musical work by Sven Grundtvig, 181.
Crows, Indian tribe, 453.
Crozet Islands, 179.
CROZIER, officer commanding *The Terror*, 192.
CRUBELLIER (Norbert), landowner, 470.
Crusader's Entry at Constantinople, The, by F. Dufay, after Delacroix, 472.
CRUSOE (Robinson), character in novel of same name by Daniel Defoe, 229, 417.
Cuba, 413.
CUMBERLAND (William Augustus, Duke of), 1721–1765, 100.
Cumberland (England), 342.
Cupid and Psyche, by Gérard, 458.
Curaçao, 280.
CURIE (Pierre) and CURIE (Marie), French physicists, 83.
Curiously Strong Altoids Peppermint Oil, 243.
Cusenier, brand of bleach, 60.
CUVELIER (Marcel), French actor, 64.
CUVERVILLE (de), French moralist, 386.
CUVIER (Georges, Baron), French zoologist, 1769–1832, 289.
Cyclades, 127, 425.
Cyclops (project), 187.
Cypraea caput serpentis, 46.
Cypraea moneta, 45–46.
Cypraea turdus, 45–46.
Cyprus, 55.
CYRANO DE BERGERAC (Savinien de), 334.

D. (Emile), 140, 141.
DADDI (Romeo), character in Pirandello, 17, 189, 232.
DAGUERRE (Jacques), French inventor, 1787–1851, 199.
Daily Mail, London daily, 385.
Damascus (Syria), 210, 211.
DAMISCH (Hubert), 328.
Dancer with Gold Coins, The, by Perpignani, 472.
Dances, by Hans Neusiedler, 473.
DANGLARS (Berthe), 128, 219, **398–403**.
DANGLARS (Maximilien), 59, 128, 161, 219, **398–403**.
DANGLARS (Senior), 404.
Danish Cultural Centre (London), 142.
DANNAY (Fred), pen-name of C.-A. Beyssandre, 431.
Danorum regumque . . ., by Saxo Grammaticus, 449.
Dante Alighieri Foundation (London), 142.
DANTON (Georges Jacques), French politician, 1759–1794, 83.
Dardanelles, 493.
Dar-es-Salaam (Tanzania), 46.
Daring Young Man on a Flying Trapeze, The, by William Saroyan, 362.
DARIUS, King of Persia, 428.

DUFRESNY (Charles-Rivière), French playwright, 1684–1724, 364.
DUKAS (Paul), French composer, 1865–1935, 165.
DULLES (John Foster), US polotician, 1888–1959, 457.
DULL KNIFE, Indian chief, 453.
DUMAS (Alexandre, père), 473.
DUMONT (François), French miniaturist, eighteenth century, 473.
DUMONT D'URVILLE (Jules-Sébastian-César), French seafarer, 1790–1841, 449.
Dumyât (Egypt), 113.
Dundee (Scotland), 300.
Dunkirk (Nord), 187, 198.
DUNN (Herbert), 329.
DUNN (Jeremy), 329.
DURAND-TAILLEFER (Célestine), pen-name of Mme Trévins, 448.
Dyspneic Frequencies in Fallot's Tetralogy, by Dr B. Dinteville, 474.

Eagle of the Instant, The, see Hokab el-Ouakt, 233.
EARP (Wyatt), semi-legendary Western hero, 412.
East India Company, 322.
East Knoyle, an airport, 259.
East Lancing (Michigan), 208.
ECHARD (grandfather), 171, 214.
ECHARD (Caroline), see Caroline Marquiseaux, 28, 324.
ECHARD (Marcelin), library stack manager, **134–136**, 179, 286, 456–457.
ECHARD (Mme), **134–136**, 179, 456.
Ecole Centrale, 178.
Ecole Nationale d'Administration, see Civil Service College, 296, 440.
Ecole Normale Supérieure (Rue d'Ulm) 203, 206.
Ecole Normale Supérieure (Sèvres). 18.
Ecole Polytechnique, 21, 22, 23, 50, 296, 440.
Ecole Pratique des Hautes Etudes, 6th section, 205.
Ecole Pyrotechnique (sic), 23.
Ecole Supérieure de chimie, 185.
Ecrits de Sartre, Les, by Contat & Rybalka, 460.
Edinburgh (Scotland), 383, 385.
EDISON (Thomas Alva), American inventor, 1847–1931, 95.
EDITIONS DU TONNEAU, French publishing house, 47, 48.
Eger (Hungary), 154.
EGER (Meglepett), Hungarian sculptor, 174.
EGNATIUS, 289.
Egypt, 93, 166, 194, 242, 248, 332, 372, 373, 443, 454.
EHRENFELS (Christian, Baron von), Austrian philosopher, 1858–1932, 173.
Eiffel Tower, 488.
Eighteen Lectures on Industrial Society, by Raymond Aron, 241.
Eimeo (Tahiti), 424, 425.
EINSTEIN (Albert), American physicist, 1879–1955, 83, 457.
Eisenühr (Austro-Hungary), 288.
Elementary Treatise on Internal Pathology, by Béhier & Hardy, 326.
ELIZABETH I, Queen of England, 1533–1603, 382.
ELLIOTT (Harvey), see A. Flexner, 175.
Elsinore (Denmark), 339.
ELSTIR, a character in Proust, 281.
Emperor's Messenger, The, 371.
Employers and Workers, 448.
Ems (Germany), 83, 495.
Ems Telegram, The, popular print, 495.
Encounter, London literary and political weekly, 331.
Encyclopædia Britannica, 99.
Enfant au Toton, L', by Chardin, 421.
Enfant et les Sortilèges, L', by Maurice Ravel (1925), 170.
Engadiner, St Moritz hotel, 432.

48, 58, 60, 74, 77, 120, 124, 156, 197, 215, 216, 227, **271–276**, **301–303**, 396, 397, 419, 470, 472, 496, 499.
GRAVES (Ernest), French lexicographer, 1832–1891, 289.
Graz (Austria), 108.
Great Battles of the Past, television series, 66.
Great Britain, 87, 142, 144, 334, 440.
Great Dictionary of Cooking, by A. Dumas, 473.
Great Parade of the Military Tattoo, engraving by Israël Silvestre, 26.
Great Women of French History, 396.
Great Works at Risk, television series, 66.
Greece, 425.
GREEN (Silas), music hall show producer, 413.
GREENFIELD (Albert), pseudonym of Rémi Rorschach, 43.
Greenhill, school in England, 35.
Green Pastures, film by Marc Connelly, 30.
Green River University (Ohio), 296.
GREGORY IX (Ugolino de Segni), pope, 1145–1251, 36.
Grenoble (Isère), 198, 350.
GRESSIN, 187.
GREUZE (Jean-Baptiste), French painter, 1725–1805, 459.
GRIFALCONI (Alberto), 120, 121, 122, 123.
GRIFALCONI (Emilio), Italian craftsman, 59, **120–123**, 128, 273.
GRIFALCONI (Laetizia), his wife, 59, **120–123**, 124, 128, 273.
GRIFALCONI (Vittorio), 120, 121, 122, 123.
GRILLNER, Canadian artist, 35, 481.
GRIMAUD, Athos's valet in A. Dumas's *Twenty Years After*, 362.
Grimaud (Var), 442.
GRISI (Carlotta), known as La Grisi, Italian dancer, 1810–1899, 103.
Grisons (Switzerland), 120, 431.
GRODECK (Georg), Austrian psychosomatician, 1866–1934, 478.
GROMECK, an art dealer, character in G. Berger's story, 159, 160.
GROMECK (Lisa), his wife, 159, 160.
GROMYKO (Andrey Andreevich), Soviet diplomat, 457.
GRONCZ, mayor of New York, 259.
Groove, Indian tribe, 453.
GROUSSET (Jean-Paul), 466.
GROZIANO (Vecello), 421.
GRUNDTVIG (Svend), Swedish musician, 181.
Guadalcanal, 382.
Guadaloupe, 198.
Guam, 382.
Guatemala, 55.
GUELIS (Jean), French ballet dancer, 440.
GUEMENOLE-LONGTGERMAIN (Astolphe de), Duke, 259.
GUENE (Louis), king's violinist to Louis XVI, 473.
GUERIN (Eugénie de), French writer, 1805–1848, 289.
GUERNE (Louisette), 397.
Guimet Museum, 204.
GUIMOND DE LA TOUCHE (Claude), French playwright, 1723–1760, 364.
Guinness, type of Irish beer, 52.
GUION (Captain Louis), 459.
GUITAUT (Madame de), 402.
GUITRY (Sacha), 487.
Gulf of Honduras, 387.
Gulf of Papua, 389.
Gustav Line, 5.
GUSTIN (Dr), inventor of 'lithium tablets', 61.
GUTENBERG (Johannes Gensfleisch), German printer, 1400–1468, 349.
Guyana, 385.
GUYOMARD (Gérard), painter and restorer, 23, 231, 434.
GUYOT, landowner.
GYP, pseudonym of Sybille Gabrielle Marie-Antoinette de Riquetti de Mirabeau, comtesse de Martel de

MALLEVILLE (Mickey), a singer, character in *The Murder of the Goldfish*, 222–225.
Malmaison, 242.
MALPIGHI (Marcello), Italian anatomist, 1628–1694, 475, 476, 478.
MALRAUX (André), French Minister of Culture, 1901–1976, 74.
Malta, 373.
MALTE D'ISTILLERIE (Alexandre-Amand-Olivier), 1697–1774, 364.
Mamers (Sarthe), 156.
Manchester (England), 487, 581.
MANDETTA (Guido), alias Theo Van Schallaert, alias Jim Brown, alias ?, 83–4, 87, 90, 91.
Manifeste du Mineral Art, book by F. Hutting, 34.
Manila (Philippines), 11.
Manlius Capitolinus, by Lafosse, 364.
MANN (Thomas), 1875–1955, 495, 579.
Mannheim (Germany), 297.
MANS (F. H.), Dutch landscape painter, 421.
MANSA (J. H.), Danish cartographer, 186.
Man with Sole Out, collective work by Vladislav, 482.
Many-Splendoured Mzab, talk by A. Faucillon, 486.
Map of the Town and Citadel of Namur, by T. Shandy, 227, 362.
MARAT (Jean-Paul), French revolutionary, 1743–1794, 290.
MARCEAU (François-Séverin Marceau-Desgraviers), French general, 1769–1796, 198.
MARCHAL (Paul), 411.
Marches and Fanfares of the 2nd Armoured Division, The, recording, 132–133.
MARCIA (Clara, née Lichtenfeld), antique dealer, 28, 60, **101–102**, 151, 152, 173, 227, **318–324**, 348, 457, 459, 497, 499.
MARCIA (David), 101, 173, 217, 227, 318, 324, 348, 349, **361–365**.
MARCIA (Léon), art historian, 60, 101, 127, **171–174**, 218, 323, 362, 396, 451, 497, 499.
MARCION (Corinne), see Honoré, 398.
MARCION (Honoré), see Honoré, 398.
MARCO POLO, Italian traveller, 1254–1324, 292.
Marcoule (Gard), reactor site, 140.
MARCUART, banker, 400.
MARECHAL (Maurice), French actor, 64.
Margate (England), 443.
MARGAY (Lino), alias Lino the Dribbler, alias Lino Knot-head, **352–358.**
Mariana Islands, 382.
MARIE-ANTOINETTE, 232.
MARKHAM AND COOLIDGE, publishers, 35.
Marly-le-Roi, 486.
Marne (river), 272.
Marolles-les-Braults (Sarthe), 157.
MARQUEZ (Gabriel Garcia), 579.
MARQUISEAUX (Caroline, née Echard), 60, 128, **134–136**, 179, 215, 216, 227, 234, 301, 324, 455, 497.
MARQUISEAUX (father), 137.
MARQUISEAUX (Philippe), **134–137**, 179–182, 215, 227, 234, 324, 455, 497.
MARR (Robin), 263.
Marseillaise, La, French patriotic song, 416.
Marseilles (Bouches-du-Rhône), 43, 108, 139, 198, 199, 214, 244, 261, 329, 416, 459.
    Saint-Charles barracks, 244.
    Rue Bleue, 244.
Marshall Islands, 382.
Marshall McLuhan and the Third Copernican Revolution, lecture by Prof. Strossi, 427.
MARTENSSEN (Johannes), Danish man of letters, 484n.

MEYER-STEINEG, medical historian, 326.
MEYSONNIER (Lazare), doctor and alchemist from Mâcon, 1602–1672, 475.
Miami (Florida), 261, 412.
Burbank's Motel, 413
Hialeah, 412
Monkey Jungle, nightclub, 449.
Michael Strogoff, novel by Jules Verne, xiii.
MICHARD (Félicien), a floor scrubber, character in G. Berger's story, 158–161.
MICHELOT, 495.
Michigan, 208.
Mickey Mouse, 328.
MIDAS, King of Phrygia, 328.
Middle East, 44, 45.
Midsummer Night's Dream, play by William Shakespeare, 331.
Milan (Italy), 353, 449.
Milo (Cyclades), 127.
Milwaukee (Wisconsin), 383.
Mimizan (Landes), 140.
Mindanao (Philippines), 54.
Minerva, 396.
MIRABEAU (Honoré Gabriel Riqueti, count of), 1749–1791, 132.
Miraj (India), 425.
MIRBEAU (Octave), 1848–1917, 103.
Miscellany, by E. Renan, 50.
Misérables, Les, novel by Victor Hugo (1861), 257.
Mississippi (river), 411, 466, 467.
Mississippi Sunset, song by Sam Horton, 181.
MISTER MEPHISTO, stage name of Henri Fresnel, 257–258.
MISTINGUETT, pseudonym of Jeanne Bourgeois, singer, 1875–1956, 258.
Mithridate, tragedy by Jean Racine (1673), 303.
Mobile (Alabama), 411.
Moçamedes (Angola), 346.
Moderne Probleme der Pädiatrie, 479.
Mohawks, Indian tribe, 453.
Moka (North Yemen), 126.
MOLIERE, pseudonym of Jean-Baptiste Poquelin, French playwright, 1622–1673, 255, 364.
MOLINET, professor at the Collège de France, 281.
MÖLLER, urologist, 479.
Mombasa (Kenya), 347.
Monachus tropicalis, 83.
MONACO (Mario del), Italian tenor, 234.
Mona Lisa, portrait by Leonardo da Vinci, 39.
MOND (Peter), six-dayer, 351.
Monde, Le, French daily newspaper, 136, 237, 338.
MONDINO DI LUZZI, Milanese anatomist, died in 1326, 271.
MONDUIT & BECHET, foundrymen, 470.
Monêtier-les-Bains (Hautes-Alpes), 350.
Moniteur Universel, Le, Paris news digest, 386.
MONK (Ray), 281.
MONPOU (Hippolyte), French composer, 1804–1851, 454.
MONROE (Marilyn), stage name of Norma Jean Baker, American actress, 1926–1962, 293.
MONSIEUR JOURDAIN, character in Molière's *Le Bourgeois gentilhomme*, 257.
MONSIEUR LULU, pseudonym of Lucien Campen, 141.
MONTALESCOT (L. N.), French painter, 1877–1933, 421.
Montargis (Loiret), 41, 66, 127.
Montauban (Tarn-et-Garonne), 85.
Monte Carlo, 146.
Monte Ceneri (Italy), 471.
Montenegro (Yugoslavia), 246.
Montenotte (Italy), Battle of (1796), 50.
MONTESQUIEU (Charles de Secondat, seigneur de la Brède et

Naples (Italy), 84, 269, 466.
NAPOLEON I, French Emperor, see also Bonaparte, 39, 83, 152, 174, 198, 242, 372, 373, 374, 376, 377, 495.
NAPOLEON II, François-Charles-Joseph-Napoléon Bonaparte), Duke of Reichstadt, known as "L'Aiglon", Paris, 1811–Schönbrunn, 1832, 156.
NAPOLEON III, 207, 312, 494.
Nassau (Bahamas), 422.
Nassau Bay (Cape Horn), 178.
Natal (South Africa), 302.
National Foundation for the Development of the Southern Hemisphere, 390.
National Union of Foresters and Woodcutters (Australia), 382.
Nationwide Bilge, American satirical journal, 316.
Natural History Museum, 83.
Naturalist, The, 436.
Naughties, Milan nightclub, 449.
Naxos (Cyclades), 127.
Neauphle-le-Château, 440, 442.
NEBEL, German officer, 120.
Nef, La, literary review, 331.
NELSON (Horatio, Viscount), British Admiral, 1758–1805, 227, 326, 447.
NEMO (Prince Dakkar, called Captain), character in Jules Verne, 25, 181, 345.
Nemo Club (Dempledorf), 499.
Nem szükséges, hogy kilépj a házból, film by Gabor Pelos, 466.
NERCIAT (André-Robert Andréa, chevalier de), French writer, 1739–1806, 322.
NERO (Claudius Dominicus Claudius), Roman Emperor, 37–68 AD, 38, 64.
NERVAL (Gérard de), pseudonym of Gérard Labrunie, French writer, 1808–1855, 270, 292.
Neuilly-sur-Seine (Hauts-de-Seine), 204.
NEUSIEDLER (Hans), German musician, 473.
Neuweiler (Germany), 140.
Neva (river), 302.
Nevada, 466.
New Art Review, 35.
New bedford (Massachusetts), 91, 92, 94.
    Hotel Xiphias, 91.
New Brass Ensemble of Michigan State University at East Lansing, 208.
New Caledonia, 127, 198.
Newcastle (NSW), 16.
Newcastle-upon-Tyne (Tyne and Wear), 15, 16, 324.
New Century Dictionary, 99.
Newfoundland (Canada), 55.
New Guinea, 389.
New Insights into Early Denominations of America, paper given by J. M. de Zaccaria at the 3rd Congress of the International Union of Historical Sciences (Edinburgh, 1887), 385.
New Key to your Dreams, attributed to Henry Barrett, 183.
New Mexico, 425.
New Orleans (Louisiana), 92, 411, 413.
Newport (R. I.), 449.
New South Wales (Australia), 16.
New York (NY), 31, 39, 40, 86, 87, 91, 114, 173, 181, 258, 395, 480, 483, 581.
    Broadway, 259.
    Carson College, 175.
    Columbia University, 85.
    Ellis Island, 499.
    Frick Collection, 173.
    Manhattan, 32.
    Rockefeller Collection, 429.
    St Marks-in-the Bowery, 258.
    Statue of Liberty, 258, 470.
    Wall Street, 47.
New York Herald Tribune, 338.
New Zealand, 390.
NEZ PERCÉS, Indian tribe, 453.
Nicaragua, 258.
Nice (Var), 40, 113, 165, 480.

PFLUG, chief of staff of the Russian army in the Far East, 447.
PHILEMON and BAUCIS, legendary characters, 437.
PHILIP III, King of Spain, 1598–1621, 204.
PHILIP IV, King of Spain, 1621–1665, 204.
PHILIPPE (Gérard), French actor, 1922–1959, 164, 277.
Philippines, 369.
PHILIPS (Sunny), pseudonym of Felipe Solario, Portuguese actor, 262.
Phrygia, 328.
PHUTATORIUS (Fredryk), Danish astronomer, 1547–1602, 289.
PICARD, 364.
Picardy, 352.
PICASSO (Pablo Ruiz y Picasso, known as Pablo), Spanish painter, 1881–1973, 258, 429.
PIERNE (Gabriel), French composer, 1863–1937, 427.
PIM, PAM, POUM, cartoon characters, 381.
PINCHART, maker of folding stools, 116.
Pinocchio, by Collodi, 257.
Pin-Up, nude magazine, 199.
PINZON brothers (Martin Alonso, Francisco Martin, & Vincente Yanez), Spanish seafarers, late fifteenth century, 384.
PIP, Mme Moreau's tomcat, 101, 301.
PIRANDELLO (Luigi), Italian writer, 1867–1936, 17, 188, 231.
Pirano (Yugoslavia), 246.
PISANELLO (Antonio di Puccio di Cerreto), Italian painter, 1395–1455, 113.
PISSARRO (Camille), French painter, 1830–1903, xvi, 190.
Pithiviers (Loiret), 254.
PITISCUS (Samuel), Dutch philologist, 1637–1717, 88, 89, 91.
PIZZICAGNOLI, 419–420, 499.
Plant City (Florida), 278.
PLASSAERT (couple), cotton-goods traders, 164, 195, 196, 216, 217, 227, 234, **247–252**, 496.
PLASSAERT (Rémi), 195, 196, 396, 496.
PLATTNER (Mrs), a Brisbane typist, 382.
PLAUTUS (Titus Maccius Plautus), Latin writer, 254–184 BC, 263.
PLENGE, Danish pastor, 56.
PLINY (Caius Plinius Secundus, the Elder), Roman naturalist, 23–79 AD, 248, 289.
PLON, Parisian publisher, 295.
Ploughman and his Children, The, fable in Parisian slang by Pierre Devaux, 133.
Ploughman Killer, The, detective novel, 206.
Pobieda, Russian battleship, 447.
Point de Vue, French magazine, 156.
POIS, hairdresser, 57.
Poitou, 465.
POKER DICE, Gilbert Berger's cat, 301, 414, 496.
Poland, 173, 267, 270, 275.
POLISHOVSKY, a chemist, 185.
POLLOCK (Paul Jackson), American painter, 1912–1956, xvi, 190.
POLONIUS, hamster, 394 & n.
Polynesia, 466.
Pompeii (Italy), 38, 106.
Pompon and Fifi, calendar, 286.
PONIATOWSKI (Michel), known as Ponia, French politician, 292.
PONSIN, master blower, builder of *The Palace of Light,* 404.
Pontarlier (Switzerland), 34.
Pont-Audemer (Eure), 259.
Pontcarral, Colonel d'Empire, film by J. Delannoy, 185.
Pontiac, make of motorcar, 307.
POPE (Alexander), English poet, 1688–1744, 443.
Populaire, Le, newspaper founded by Etienne Cabet, 464.
Port Arthur (Lû-Shun, China), 308, 447.

RICCETTI (Maximilien), pseudonym of Max Riquet, dancer and choreographer, **438–441**, 442, 446.
RICHARDSON (Sylvia), 581.
RICHARDT & SECHER, boiler manufacturers, 74.
RICHELIEU (Armand Jean du Plessis, cardinal, Duke of), 1585–1642, 256.
RICHEPIN (Jean), French writer, 1849–1926, 174, 497.
Rich Hours of the Duke de Berry, television programme, 383.
RICHMOND (Helena), romantic engraver, 331.
Richmond (Virginia), 25.
RICHTHOFEN, the "Red Baron", German First-World-War air ace, 156.
Ricqlès, brand of chewing gum, 196.
Right On Lads!, starring Olivia Norvell, 393.
Right Recipe, The, cartoon, 370.
RIMSKY-KORSAKOV (Nikolai Andreevich), Russian composer, 1844–1908, 325.
Ring des Nibelungen, Der, tetralogy by R. Wagner, 234.
RIN TIN TIN, a dog, 283.
Rio de Janeiro, 394.
Rippleson (Florida), 339.
RIQUET (Max), see Riccetti, 438.
RIRI (Henri Collot, called Monsieur), café owner, see Collot (Henri), 25, 30, 124.
ROBERT (Hubert), French painter, 1733–1808, 472.
Robinson Making Himself as Comfortable as He Can on His Desert Island, painting on wood, 417.
Rochefort (Charente-Maritime), 199, 273.
ROCHEFORT, character in works by Dumas, 158, 256.
Rochetaillé, 350.
RODOLFO, character in *La Bohème*, 234.
RODOLPHE, a trapeze artist, 214.
RODRIGUEZ, King of Spain, 9.
ROGERS (Ethel), Franz Hutting's maid, 33–34, 496.
Roissy-en-France, 129.
ROLAND DE LA PLATIERE (Jean-Marie), French politician, 1734–1793, 348.
ROLANDI, London bookseller, 144.
Roll over Clover, novel by Paul Winther, 68.
Rolypoly, Mme Nochère's dog, 164.
ROMAGNESI (Henri), composer of romances, 1781–1851, 290.
Romainville (Seine-Saint-Denis), 96.
ROMANET, manager of 11 Rue Simon-Crubellier, 24, 124, 164, 203, 216–217, 419, 420, 491.
Romania, 151.
ROMAN NOSE, Indian chief, 453.
ROMANOV, Russian Imperial family (1613–1917), 328.
Romans (Drôme), 416.
Rome (Italy), 36, 84, 85, 248, 302, 477.
  Campus Martius, 64.
  S Giovanni in Laterano, 84, 85.
  S Maria-di-Trastevero, 85.
  S Maria Maggiora, 85.
  St Mark's, 84.
  S Paolo fuori le Mura, 84.
  St Peter's, 84, 248.
  S Silvestro-in-capite, 85.
  Stazione Termini, 469.
ROMMEL (Erwin), German Field Marshal, 1891–1944, 297.
RONDEAU, master caster, 1493–1543, 289.
ROOSEVELT (Franklin Delano), 32nd president of the USA, 1882–1945, 260.
ROQUELAURE (Antoine-Gaston, Duke of), *maréchal de France*, 1656–1738, 291.
RORSCHACH (Olivia, née Norvell), see Olivia Norvell, 35, 228, 380–383, **393–395**, 418–420, 432.

Salamanca (Spain), 477.
SALAMMBO, eponymous heroine of a novel by Gustave Flaubert (1862), 267.
SALINAS-LUKASIEWICZ (Juan Maria), 284.
SALINI (Léon), Mme de Beaumont's lawyer, 139, 142, 143.
Salle Erard, 19.
SALMASIUS, 289.
SALMON, cleaning firm, 394.
Salzburg (Austria), 40.
Samarkand (Uzbekistan), 406.
SAMBIN (Hugues), sixteenth-century architect, 447.
Sampang, type of perfume, 144, 145.
SAMUEL (Henri), Belgian publisher, 59.
SANCHEZ DEL ESTERO (Alvero), 376.
SANCHO PANZA, character in Cervantes, 52.
SANCTIS (G. de), Italian historian, 409.
San Diego (California), 581.
San Francisco (California), 167.
Santa Catalina Island (California), 336, 385.
Santa Monica (California), 499.
Santé, prison, 400.
São Paolo Island, 179.
Saponite, brand of washing powder, 61.
SARAFIAN (Arpad), photographer, 481.
Saratoga, Indian tribe, 453.
Saratoga (NY), 175.
SAROYAN (William), American writer, 362.
SARTRE (Jean-Paul), French writer, 1905–1980, 460, 487.
SATCH MOUTH, Indian, 453.
Saumur (Maine-et-Loire), 154.
Savings Bank, 491.
SAXE (Maurice, comte de), *maréchal de France,* 1696–1750, 88, 94.
SAXO GRAMMATICUS, Danish historian, c.1150–c.1206, 449.
Saxony, 421.
SCALIGER (Joseph), humanist teacher, 1540–1609, 289.
Scandinavia, 337.
SCARECROW PUBLISHING CO., 73.
SCHAPSKA (Philoxanthe), composer, 271.
SCHARF-HAINISCH (Oskar), philologist, 263.
Scheldt (river), 52.
SCHLENDRIAN, French general, 47, 48.
SCHLENDRIAN, cowrie smuggler, 46, 47.
SCHLIEMANN (Heinrich), German archaeologist, 1822–1890, 8.
SCHMETTERLING (Morris), American composer, 208.
SCHMITT (Florent), French composer, 1870–1958, 367.
SCHNABEL (Arthur), Austrian pianist, 1882–1951, 367.
SCHOENER (Johannes), sixteenth-century German astronomer, 206.
SCHÖNBERG (Arnold), Austrian composer, 1874–1951, 19, 228.
SCHRODER, character in Schulz's *Peanuts*, 286.
SCHULZ (Charles M.), American cartoonist, 286.
SCHUMAN (Robert), European politician, 1886–1953, 457.
SCHUMANN (Clara, née Wieck), 394.
SCHUMANN (Robert), German composer, 1810–1856, 19.
SCHWANN (Madame), 23.
SCHWANZENBAD-HODENTHALER (Léopold-Rudolph von), Austrian general, 288.
Science et Vie, popular science magazine, 160.
Scipio Africanus, opera by J. S. Kusser, 21.
SCIPION (Robert), cruciverbist, 229, 335.
SCOPAS, Greek sculptor, late 5th century BC, 132.
SCORESBY (William), English seafarer, 1760–1829, 289.

SIGIMER, figure of German mythology, 34.
SIGISMOND, a hamster, 395n.
SIGONIUS, 289.
Silbermann, by J. de Lacretelle, 172.
SILBERSELBER, American painter, 151.
SILENUS, 421.
Silver Arrow, rail/air cross-Channel service, 441.
Silver Glen of Alva, a Panamanian tanker, 178.
SILVESTRE (Israël), French artist, 1621–1691, 26.
SIMON (Samuel), woodseller and developer, 470.
SIMONE, Bartlebooth's former kitchen maid, 114.
SIMPSON (Grégoire), 59, **234–241**.
Sioux, 453.
SITTING BULL, Indian chief, 453.
Sixteenth Edge of this Cube, The, television programme, 13, 63, 64.
Sketch History of Renal Theories, A, by LeBran-Chastel, 480.
SKRIFTER (Ingeborg), see Ingeborg Stanley, 148, 308.
Skye (Scotland), 335.
SLAUGHTER (Grace), see Grace Twinker, 259.
SLEEPING RABBIT, Cheyenne chief, 453.
SLOWBURN (Joy), see Ingeborg Stanley, 307.
Slumbering Wabash, song by Sam Horton, 181.
SMAUTF (Mortimer), Bartlebooth's servant, 13, 16, 17, 21–23, 27, 31, **51–58**, 65, 113, 114, 117, **126–127**, 162, 193, 212, 214, 227, 332, 338, 345, 346, 347, 368, 393, 432–435, 496, 499.
Smeraldine, 375.
Smith (Cyrus), character in Jules Verne's *Mysterious Island,* 25.
SNARK, THE, character (?) in Lewis Carroll's *The Hunting of the Snark,* 415.
SNOOPY, the dog in Schulz's *Peanuts,* 395.
SOBIESKI (Ursula), American novelist, 81, 95, 451, 496.
Société Générale, a French bank, 194.
Socotra, 126.
SOELLI, Malay guide, 107.
Sofia (Bulgaria), 85.
Soft Drink Echo, The, trade journal, 30.
Soissons (Aisne), 85.
Solomon Islands, 347.
Somersault, The, print, 409.
Somme (river), 70.
SOMNOLENTIUS, Bavarian theologian, fourteenth century, 289.
SONNET (L.), map-maker, 198.
Sorbonne, 134, 205.
Soria (Spain), 424.
Sottens, 471.
SOUVAROFF, a chef, 293.
Souvenir de Saint-Mouezy-sur-Eon, postcard, 69.
Souvenirs of a Numismatist, by Florent Baillerger, 410.
Soviet Union, see Union of Soviet Socialist Republics.
SPADE (Cat), pseudonym of Jeffrey Ornette, American boxer, 175.
Spain, 8, 10, 47, 52, 55, 98, 193, 208, 257, 258, 397, 425, 426.
Spalato (Split) (Yugoslavia), 246.
SPANIARDEL, a chemist, 185.
SPEISS (Abel), known as "The Russian", a retired vet, 415–416.
SPENCER (Herbert), English philosopher, 1820–1903, 35.
SPENGLER (Oswald), German thinker, 1880–1936, 173.
Spice, or The Revenge of the Louvain Locksmith, 325.
Spice Road, The, doctoral thesis by Adrien Jérôme, 204.
Spilett (Gédéon), character in Jules Verne's *Mysterious Island,* 25, 233, 345.
Spinning Top, The, waltz by E. de Dinteville, 50.

Szczyrk (County of Krakow, Poland), 287.
Szinowcz, see Cinoc.

Tabarka (Tunisia), 181.
Tableau des riches inventions couvertes du voile des feintes amoureuses . . ., by Béroalde de Verville, 271.
Tahiti, 395, 425.
Taiwan (Formosa), 54, 308.
Takaungu (Kenya), 347.
Tales of Grandma Goose, by Charles-Robert Dumas, 366.
Tallahassee (Florida), 411.
Talma (François-Joseph), actor, 1763–1826, 364.
Tampa (Florida), 412.
Tanganyika, 46.
Tangerine Dream, The, Paris nightclub, 488.
Tangiers, 449, 471.
Tanzania, 425.
Tarawa, 382.
Tarbes (Hautes-Pyrénées), 45.
Tarragon (Spain), 342.
Tarzan, character in works by E. R. Burroughs, 83.
Taskerson (Hambo), Swedish philologist, 110.
Tasmania, 337, 382.
Tassin (René-Prosper), Benedictine monk and scholar, 1697–1777, 437.
Tauschnitz, German publisher of English books, 328.
Tavernier (Jean-Baptiste), French traveller, 1605–1689, 175.
Tazo-Katzura, Japanese prime minister, 448.
Tebaldi (Renata), singer, 234.
Tempesta di mare, La, concerto in E^{b} major, opus 8, No. 5, by Vivaldi, 133.
Temple (Helen), 581.
Temple (Shirley), American actress and politician, 380.
Terror, The, ship, 192.
Thaddeus (Ludwig), American physicist of German origin, 298.
Thames (river), 443.
Théâtre de la Cité, see *Théâtre Sarah Bernhardt.*
Théâtre Sarah Bernhardt, 460.
The Beast, pseudonym of Julien Etcheverry, pop singer, 137.
The Donkey in Trousers, London pub, 445.
The Empire, Paris concert Hall, 158.
The Famous Bouillabaisse, restaurant, 214.
The Gay Musketeers, toyshop, 467.
The Greens, London pub, 444.
"The Miner" and the Origins of the Labour Party, by Irwin Wall, 410.
The Star, Beirut nightclub, 38, 449.
The Two Hemispheres, cabaret at Montmartre, 488.
Thierarch' (Estelle), saxophonist, 481.
Thiers (Louis-Adolphe), French politician, 1797–1877, 198, 204.
This Golden Serp in the Field of Stars, chamber opera by Philoxanthe Shapska, after V. Hugo's *Booz endormi*, 271.
Thomas, Bartlebooth's former footman, 114.
Thomas di Giovanni (N.), 581.
Thomas Kyd's Imperial Mixture, brand of whisky, 300.
Thonon-les-Bains (Haute-Savoie), 241.
Thorez (Maurice), French politician, 1900–1964, 457.
Thorn, see Toruń.
Thorwaldsson, Norwegian painter, 133.
Those Ladies in Green Hats, by Germaine Acremant, 211.
Three Free Men, The, sect, 11, 13, 230.
Three Magi, The, tapestry, 302, 437.
Three Sergeants' Syndrome, The, 162.
Three sisters, 415.
Thuburbo Majus (Tunisia), 228, 277.

Trout (Canada), 425, 426, 428.
TROYAN, bookseller, 59, 196, 199, 234, 240.
TROYAT (Henri), French novelist, 144.
True Story of Philemo and Bauci, 437.
TSINOC, see Cinoc.
TS'UI PEN, Chinese philosopher, 263.
Tunis, 267.
Rue de Turquie, 268.
Tunisia, 94, 232, 266, 267, 269, 335, 363.
TUNNEY (James Joseph, alias Gene), American boxer, 175.
Turin (Italy), 15, 85.
Turkey, 28, 54, 310, 425, 435.
Turkish Bath, The, painting by Ingres, 40, 228.
Turkish March, The, by W. A. Mozart, 165.
TURNER (Joseph Mallard William), English painter, 1775–1851, 40.
TV News, American specialist journal, 461.
TWAIN (Mark), pseudonym of Samuel Langhorn Clemens, American writer, 1835–1910, 232, 466–467.
Twelve Tones, Newport nightclub, 449.
Twenty Thousand Leagues Under The Sea, novel by Jules Verne, 25.
Twenty Years After, sequel to *The Three Musketeers,* by A. Dumas, 362.
TWINKER (Grace), **258–260.**
TWINKIE, see Grace Twinker, 258, 259, 260.

U (Caroline Islands), 52.
UAE, 422.
Ulan Bator Hoto (Mongolia), 249.
Ulverston (Lancashire, UK), 82.
Umetnost, Yugoslav art review, 174.
Uncle Tom's Cabin, novel by Harriet Beecher Stowe (1852), 30.
Underwood, make of typewriter, 155.
UNDERWOOD (J. A.), 581.
UNESCO, 419.
Unfinished Symphony, The, novel, 14.
Unforgettable Vienna, tourist film, with Olivia Norvell, 394.
Unicorn and Castle, The, London pub, 443.
Union of Soviet Socialist Republics, 54, 128.
United States of America, 75, 92, 141, 173, 175, 182, 187, 233, 258, 260, 282, 297, 308, 315, 316, 357, 382, 394, 405, 425 & n.
Universal Exhibition (1900), 404.
Untersuchungen über die Taufe Amerikas, lecture by Zapfenschuppe, 383.
Upper Boubandjida (Cameroon), 76.
UPPER BOUBANDJIDA MINING CO., 74, 75–76.
Upper Dogon (Mali), 463.
UPPER DOGON RAILWAY COMPANY, 463.
Urbana (Illinois), 34.
Urbino (Italy), 235.
URQUHART (Sir Thomas), 581.
Uruguay, 425.
USHIDA, Japanese engineer, 187.
UTHERPANDRAGON, King, 36.
Utrecht (Holland), 88, 89, 91, 94.
College of St Jerome, 88, 89, 91.
Hoogeland Park, 90.
Museum van Oudheden, 89, 90, 94.
UTSUSEMI, character in the *Genji-Monogatari,* 103.
Uz (Jean-Pierre), German poet, 1720–1796, 288.

VALBONNE, songwriter, 414.
Valdrada, 222.
Valence (Drôme), 148.
Valencia (Spain), 253.
Valenciennes (Nord), 437.

Chronology

1833 Birth of James Sherwood.

1856 Birth of the Countess of Beaumont.
Birth of Corinne Marcion.

1870 Birth of Grace Twinker.
Sherwoods Cough Pastilles boom.

1871 Corinne Marcion enters service in Paris

1875 Rue Simon-Crubellier parcelled out for building.

1876 Birth of Fernand de Beaumont.

1885 Lubin Auzère completes the construction of the apartment house at No. 11.

1887 IIIrd Congress of the International Union of Historical Sciences.

1891 Theft of the "Vase of the Passion" from the Museum of Antiquities at Utrecht.

1892 Birth of Marie-Thérèse Moreau.

1896 James Sherwood buys the "Vase of the Passion".

1898 Arrest of a ring of counterfeiters in Argentina.

1900 Corinne and Honoré Marcion meet at the Universal Exhibition.
Death of James Sherwood.
Birth of Véra Orlova.
Birth of Cinoc.
Birth of Percival Bartlebooth.

1902 Birth of Léon Marcia.

1903 Caruso makes his debut at the Metropolitan.

1904 June 16: Bloom's Day.
Birth of Albert Massy.

1909 Birth of Marcel Appenzzell.

1910 Birth of Gaspard Winckler.

1911 Birth of Marguerite.
21 January: arrest of Panarchist leaders.

1914 26 September: Death of Olivier Gratiolet at Perthès-lez-Hurlus.

1916 Birth of Hervé Nochère.

1917 Birth of Clara Lichtenfeld.
Death of Juste Gratiolet.
19 May: Augustus B. Clifford and Bernard Lehameau lose their right arms when their HQ is shelled.

1918 Summary execution of all the males of the Orlov family; Véra Orlova and her mother flee to Crimea and then to Vienna.

1919 Under various names, Rémi Rorschach attempts to make a career in music hall.
Monsieur Hardy opens a restaurant in Paris and takes on Henri Fresnel as chef.
October: Serge Valène moves into Rue Simon-Crubellier.

1920 Birth of Olivier Gratiolet.
Birth of Cyrille Altamont.
Work starts on the Upper Boubandjida mines.

1922 Gaspard Winckler begins his apprenticeship with Monsieur Gouttman.

1923 8 May: Ferdinand Gratiolet reaches Garoua.
Léon Marcia falls ill.

1924 Henri Fresnel marries Alice.
Albert Massy rides in the Giro d'Italia, then in the Tour de France.
July: Adrien Jérôme sits the *agrégation* examination in history; in October, he is appointed to the Lycée Pasteur at Neuilly and moves into Rue Simon-Crubellier.

1925 Birth of Paul Hébert.
Lift installed.
Bartlebooth begins taking watercolour lessons.
15 October: Massy beats the world record for the one-hour motor-paced time trial, but his performance is not officially recognised; on 14 November, his second attempt fails.
24 December: fire in the Danglars's flat.

1926 3 January: sudden disappearance of the Danglars. One week later, they are arrested at the Swiss border.

Ferdinand Gratiolet returns from Africa and founds an exotic-hides business.
Jean Richepin lectures at the Pfisterhof.
26 November: Fernand de Beaumont marries Véra Orlova.

1927 The Pfisterhof patients subscribe to a scholarship to allow Léon Marcia to pursue his studies.

1928 Rémi Rorschach begins his African adventure.

1929 Death of Gouttman.
Birth of Blanche Gardel.
Birth of Elizabeth de Beaumont; Véra Orlova tours North America.
Cat Spade wins the Combined Forces' boxing tournament.
Bartlebooth buys a flat at 11 Rue Simon-Crubellier.
March: Gaspard Winckler arrives in Paris; in October, he enlists and leaves for Morocco.
October: Henri Fresnel abandons his restaurant.

1930 Fernand de Beaumont begins excavating at Oviedo.
Léon Marcia begins to publish.
January: birth of Ghislain Fresnel.
Birth of Madame Nochère.
Birth of Olivia Norvell.
November: Gaspard Winckler, discharged from military service, meets Marguerite at Marseilles.

1931 April: fire at Ferdinand Gratiolet's exotic-hides warehouse.
May: Marc Gratiolet passes the *agrégation* in philosophy.

1932 Marcel Appenzzell leaves for Sumatra.
Rémi Rorschach's novel, *African Gold*, is published.
Death of Ferdinand Gratiolet in Argentina.
Gaspard and Marguerite Winckler move into 11 Rue Simon-Crubellier.
Henri Fresnel's troupe breaks up.

1934 Mme Hourcade makes 500 black boxes for Bartlebooth's future jigsaw puzzles.
Birth of Joseph Nieto.
March: Death of Emile Gratiolet.
3 September: Death of Gérard Gratiolet.

1935 Death of Madame Hébert.
January: Bartlebooth paints his first watercolour at Gijón.

August: end of excavations at Oviedo.
11 September: murder of Antoine Brodin in Florida; in the following weeks, Hélène Brodin tracks down and executes his three murderers.
12 November: suicide of Fernand de Beaumont; he is buried on 16 Nov. at Lédignan, in the presence of Bartlebooth, who returns specially from Corsica.

1936 Bartlebooth in Europe; in March, Scotland (Isle of Skye).
Birth of Michel Claveau.
Birth of Célia Crespi's son.

1937 Bartlebooth in Europe; in July, on board his yacht *The Halcyon*, he follows the Yugoslav coast from Trieste to Dubrovnik, with Serge Valène, Marguerite and Gaspard Winckler as his guests; in December, he is at Cap São Vicente (Portugal).
April: Henri Fresnel sets off for Brazil.
Lino Margay marries Josette Massy.

1938 Bartlebooth in Africa; in February, Hammamet; in June, Alexandria.
15 March: Anschluss.
Death of Henri Gratiolet.
Marcel Appenzzell arrives in Paris.

1939 January: Smautf buys a tricephalous crucifix in the Agadir *souk*.
March: Marcel Appenzzell returns to Sumatra.
April: Josette Margay returns to live with her brother; Lino Margay meets Ferri the Eyetie en route to South America.
August: Bartlebooth reaches Kenya; on the 10th, Smautf dines at Mr Macklin's.

1940 Bartlebooth in Africa.
François-Pierre LaJoie struck off the medical register.
April: Henri Fresnel reaches New York, where he is taken on as cook by Grace Twinker.
20 May: Olivier Gratiolet taken prisoner.
6 June: Death of Marie-Thérèse Moreau's husband.

1941 Bartlebooth in Africa.
7 December: Pearl Harbor attacked.

1942 Bartlebooth in Africa.
Operation "Cyclops" in Normandy.
Battle of the Coral Sea.
Death of Anne Voltimand, Gaspard Winckler's sister.

18 April: Marc Gratiolet appointed to the staff of Fernand de Brinon; in May, takes steps to have Olivier released.
June: Lino Margay leaves prison.

1943 Bartlebooth in South America.
Death of Louis Gratiolet.
23 June: assassination of Ordnance General Pferdleichter.
14 July: imaginary birth of the five Trévins sisters.
7 October: arrest of Paul Hébert.
November: death of Marguerite Winckler.

1944 Bartlebooth in South America.
May: death of Grégoire Voltimand on the Garigliano.
June: Mme Appenzzell killed near Vassieux-en-Vercors.
June: Marc Gratiolet murdered in Lyons.
July: Albert Massy returns from Compulsory Labour Service.
August: Liberation of Paris; death of Célia Crespi's son.
September: Troyan returns to Paris.

1945 Bartlebooth in Central America.
Elizabeth de Beaumont runs away from her mother.
Birth of Elzbieta Orlowska.
Paul Hébert liberated.
Anti-French riots in Damascus; death of René Albin.
The chemist Wehsal turned around by the US as part of Operation Paperclip.
Lino Margay, transfigured, comes back for Josette.
Léon and Clara Marcia move into Rue Simon-Crubellier; Clara buys Massy's saddlery and turns it into a curio shop.

1946 Bartlebooth in North America.
Birth of David Marcia.
Birth of Caroline Echard.
Flora Albin repatriated.
26 January: Olivia Norvell marries Jeremy Bishop; on 7 February, she leaves him, and Australia, for the US.

1947 Death of Hélène Brodin.
Cinoc moves into Rue Simon-Crubellier.

1948 Bartlebooth in North America; November, Santa Catalina Island (California).
Fire at the Rueil Palace cinema: François and Marthe Gratiolet amongst those killed.
Ingeborg Skrifter and Blunt Stanley meet.

1949 Bartlebooth in Asia.
Birth of Ethel Rogers.
November: death of the Honorés.
November: Count Della Marsa commissions the Ballets Frère; in December, Blanche Gardel goes to London to have an abortion; suicide of Maximilien Riccetti.

1950 Bartlebooth in Asia.
Birth of Valentin Collot, called Young Riri.
Olivia Norvell makes her last two feature films.
July: Blunt Stanley leaves for Korea; a few weeks later, he deserts.

1951 Bartlebooth in Asia; October, Okinawa.
Death of Grace Twinker.
April: marriage of Cyrille Altamont and Blanche Gardel; in May, they move into 11 Rue Simon-Crubellier; almost simultaneously, Cyrille Altamont joins BIDREM and leaves for Geneva.

1952 Bartlebooth in Oceania; February, Solomon Islands; October, Tasmania.
Ingeborg, Blunt, and Carlos arrive in Paris.
Paul Hébert returns to Rue Simon-Crubellier after treatment in a sanatorium and meets Laetizia Grifalconi.

1953 Bartlebooth in the Indian Ocean; in the Seychelles, Smautf swaps his crucifix for a statue of the tricephalous Mother-Goddess.
11 June: accidental (or intentional) death of Erik Ericsson; flight of Elizabeth de Beaumont; suicide of Ewa Ericsson; on 13 June, Sven Ericsson finds the two corpses; at the same period, François Breidel leaves Arlon.

1954 Bartlebooth and Smautf cross Turkey, the Black Sea, the USSR up as far as the Arctic Circle, then follow the Norwegian coast; on 21 December, Bartlebooth paints his last seascape at Brouwershaven; on the 24th, he is back in Paris.
Sven Ericsson identifies Elizabeth de Beaumont.
April: Ingeborg Stanley and Aurelio Lopez murdered.

1955 Bartlebooth begins to assemble the puzzles made by Gaspard Winckler.
Death of Michel Claveau.
Kléber enters service with Bartlebooth.
Elizabeth de Beaumont hides in the Cévennes.
Hervé Nochère dies in Algeria.
October: Paul Hébert transferred to Mazamet.

1956 The Claveaus leave the concierge's office, which is taken over by Mme Nochère.
Lise and Charles Berger meet at a recital by Gilbert Bécaud.
Olivier Gratiolet is recalled to Algeria and is blown up by a land mine.
July: publication of Pirandello's *In the Abyss* in No. 40 of *Les Lettres nouvelles*.
July: Elzbieta Orlowska meets Boubaker at a summer camp at Parçay-les-Pins.

1957 February: Countess of Beaumont dies at the age of 101.
June: Elizabeth de Beaumont meets François Breidel; they marry in August, at Valence.

1958 Olivia Norvell and Rémi Rorschach meet at Davos.
Bernard Dinteville begins his research.
27 July: birth of Anne Breidel; 8 August: first letter from Elizabeth Breidel to Sven Ericsson.

1959 7 September: birth of Béatrice Breidel; second letter from Elizabeth to Sven Ericsson; 14 September, murder of Elizabeth and François Breidel; 17 September, suicide of Sven Ericsson.
October: birth of Véronique Altamont.

1960 Foundation of the sect of The Three Free Men.
Rémi Rorschach buys from Olivier the last two flats still owned by the Gratiolet family at 11 Rue Simon-Crubellier.
Birth of Gilbert Berger.
Olivier Gratiolet marries his nurse, Arlette Criolat.
February: Morellet loses three fingers from his left hand.
May: Grégoire Simpson loses his job at the Bibliothèque de l'Opéra.
May: Private view of Hutting's "Hazes" at Gallery 22.
7 May: Léon Salini concludes his investigation of the death of the Breidel couple.
19 December: première of Schmetterling's *Malakhitès*.

1961 Disappearance of Grégoire Simpson.
The Bergers move into 11 Rue Simon-Crubellier.
Dinteville ends his research.

1962 The Plassaerts move into 11 Rue Simon-Crubellier.
Birth of Isabelle Gratiolet.
First of Professor LeBran-Chastel's "stolen" publications.

1963 Birth of Rémi Plassaert.

1964 Caroline Echard breaks with David Marcia.

1965 Winckler begins to make Witches' Mirrors.
24 December: Arlette Criolat's father strangles her, then commits suicide.

1966 Caroline Echard marries Philippe Marquiseaux.
Elzbieta Orlowska gets to Tunis at last.

1967 *The Silver Glen of Alva* goes down.
Birth of Mahmoud Orlowski.

1968 Death of Mme Echard.
Death of M. Marquiseaux.
May: Elzbieta Orlowska flees from Tunisia and reaches Paris; Bartlebooth's seamstress, Gervaise, retires; Elzbieta moves into her room.

1969 Hutting sells a "Barricade" from Rue Gay-Lussac to an American collector.

1970 "Young Riri" bumps into Paul Hébert at Bar-le-Duc.
Mme Hourcade retires; the Réols move into the flat vacated by her; an imprudent purchase of a luxurious bedroom suite forces them to marry a few months later. Henri Fresnel comes back to see Alice, who then leaves almost straight away to stay with her son in New Caledonia.
February: first joint meeting of Marvel Houses Incorporated and International Hostellerie; in November, foundation of Marvel Houses International and Incorporated Hostellerie.

1971 Alice Fresnel writes to Mlle Crespi.
4 June: David Marcia's motorcycle accident in the 35th Gold Cup.
December: the Rorschachs stay at St Moritz.

1972 Beyssandre hired by Marvel Houses International.
Mme Adèle retires.
Death of Emilio Grifalconi.
Serge Valène sees Bartlebooth for the last time.

1973 Bartlebooth has an operation for a double cataract.
Sam Horton changes sex.
Beyssandre discovers Bartlebooth's project.
29 October: death of Gaspard Winckler.

1974 Publication of *Memories of a Struggler*, by Rémi Rorschach.
April: Beyssandre's first letter to Bartlebooth; 11 July: Beyssandre

calls on Smautf and challenges Bartlebooth.
August: ruined by the Kerkennah Festival, David Marcia returns to live at 11 Rue Simon-Crubellier.
November: Morellet is put away.

1975 25 April: Bartlebooth learns of the death of the cameramen entrusted with the destruction of the 438th jigsaw.
May: Marvel Houses abandon their plans.
23 June: death of Percival Bartlebooth.
15 August: death of Serge Valène.

Alphabetical Checklist of Some of the Stories Narrated in this Manual

(Numbers refer to the chapter in which the story occurs, generally for the first time, but not necessarily in full)

Postscript

This book contains quotations, some of them slightly adapted, from works by: René Belletto, Hans Bellmer, Jorge Luis Borgès, Michel Butor, Italo Calvino, Agatha Christie, Gustave Flaubert, Sigmund Freud, Alfred Jarry, James Joyce, Franz Kafka, Michel Leiris, Malcolm Lowry, Thomas Mann, Gabriel García Marquez, Harry Mathews, Herman Melville, Vladimir Nabokov, Georges Perec, Roger Price, Marcel Proust, Raymond Queneau, François Rabelais, Jacques Roubaud, Raymond Roussel, Stendhal, Laurence Sterne, Theodore Sturgeon, Jules Verne, Unica Zürn.

Translator's Note

This translation contains quotations, occasionally somewhat modified, from published translations done by Robert Baldick, Anthony Bonner, Max Brod, J. M. Cohen, Ernest Jones, Anthony Kerrigan, Terence Kilmartin, Alban Krailsheimer, H. T. Lowe-Porter, Dmitri Nabokov, Vladimir Nabokov, Sir Malcolm Pasley, Alastair Reid, Francis Steegmuller, Helen Temple, Norman Thomas di Giovanni, Ruthven Todd, J. A. Underwood, Sir Thomas Urquhart, William Weaver, Barbara Wright.

Chapters 27 and 74 of *Life A User's Manual* have appeared previously, in *Grand Street* (New York), Autumn 1983, and in *Fiction International* (San Diego), 1985, in translations by Harry Mathews, which are reused here, with minor modifications, with the kind permission of the translator.

This translation is greatly indebted to Ela Bienenfeld, Eugen Helmle, Bianca Lamblin, and Harry Mathews: without their help and encouragement I would have made many more errors than I have done.

My thanks go also to all those who have answered queries, solved puzzles, and helped with the material production of this translation: Alexander Bellos, Philip Bennett, Vera Brice, Julian Kinderlerer, Una Kelly, Andy Leak, Susan Lendrum, Terry Lewis, Sylvia Richardson and especially Sarah Asquith, Ruth Sharman and Dorothy Straight.

DB
Sheffield, 1986–
Manchester, 1987.

LIFE is an unclassifiable masterpiece, a sprawling compendium as encyclopedic as Dante's *Commedia* and Chaucer's *Canterbury Tales* and, in its break with tradition, as inspiring as Joyce's *Ulysses*. Structured around a single moment in time—towards 8:00 p.m. on June 23, 1975—Perec's spellbinding puzzle begins in an apartment block in the XVIIth *arrondissement* of Paris where, chapter by chapter, room by room, like an onion being peeled, an extraordinarily rich cast of characters is revealed in a series of tales that are bizarre, unlikely, moving, funny, or (sometimes) quite ordinary. From the confessions of a racing cyclist to the plans of an avenging murderer, from a young ethnographer obsessed with a Sumatran tribe to the death of a trapeze artist, from the fears of an ex-croupier to the dreams of a sex-change pop star to an eccentric English millionaire who has devised the ultimate pasttime, LIFE is a manual of human irony, portraying the mixed marriages and fortunes, passions and despairs, betrayals and bereavements, of hundreds of lives in Paris and around the world.

But the novel is more than an extraordinary range of fictions; it is a closely observed account of life and experience. The apartment block's one hundred rooms are arranged in a magic square, and the book as a whole is peppered with a staggering range of literary puzzles and allusions, acrostics, problems of chess and logic, crosswords, and mathematical formulae. All are there for the reader to solve in the best tradition of the detective novel.

In what is a spellbinding exploration of the relationship between imagination and reality, possibility and actuality, Perec revealed not only his acute grasp of the human condition but also formidable powers of observation and a rare comic talent. This utterly original work, as compulsively readable as it is complex, will be recognized as a milestone of the postwar European experience.